DARK GAMBIT TRILOGY

THE CHILDREN OF THE GODS BOOKS 65-67

I. T. LUCAS

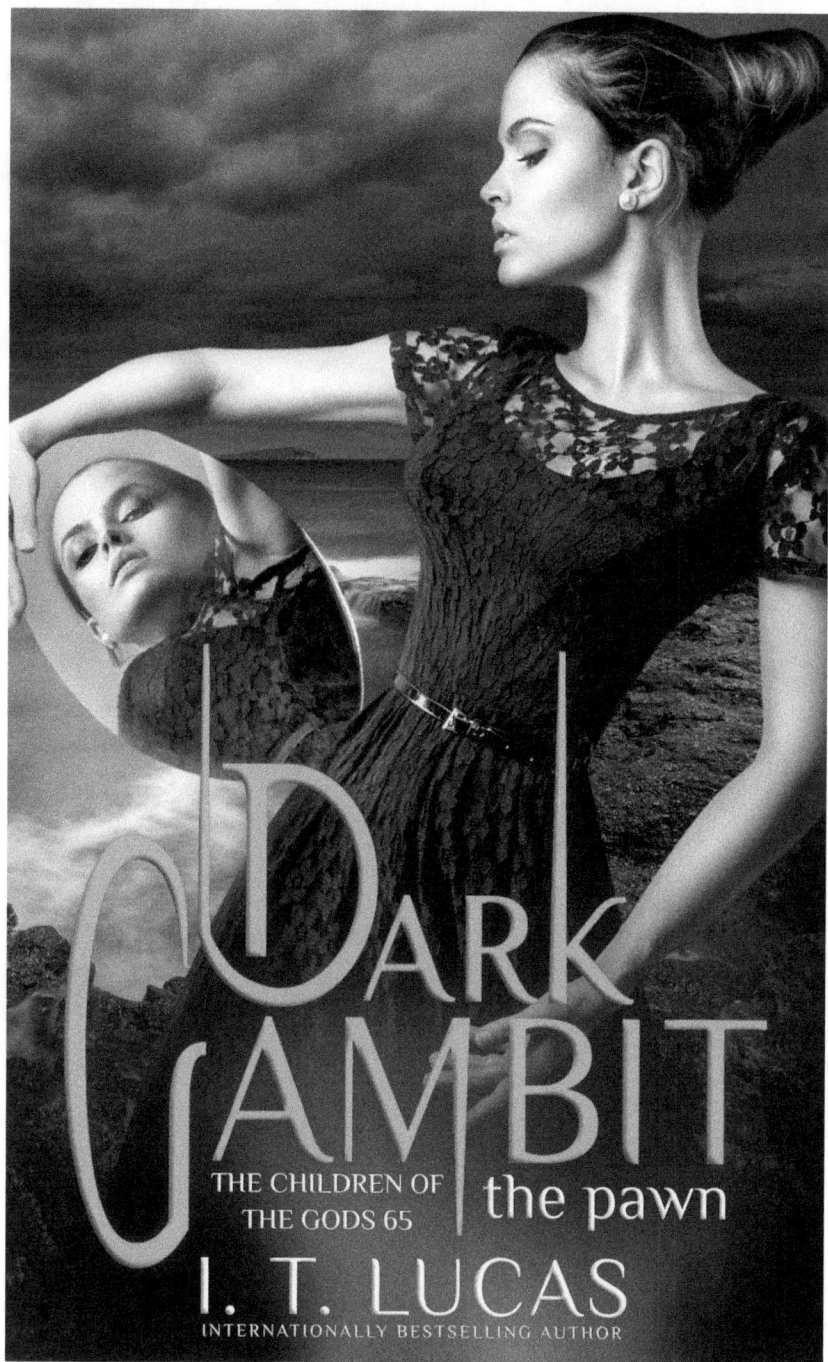

DARK GAMBIT

the pawn

THE CHILDREN OF
THE GODS 65

I. T. LUCAS

INTERNATIONALLY BESTSELLING AUTHOR

1

SOFIA

"You know who I am." Sofia handed the guard her identification card. "Why do you stop me every time I come home?"

"It's the protocol." Pioter smiled apologetically as he scanned her card and handed it back to her. "Are you here just for the weekend? Or are you going to stay longer this time?"

"I don't know. It's up to Igor."

Everything was up to Igor, but she shouldn't complain. At least she was allowed to leave the compound and attend university. Most of his subjects weren't as fortunate.

The founding group of purebllooded Kra-ell males were the elite of the compound and had more freedom and privileges than anyone else, but they couldn't come and go as they pleased either. Igor was a control freak who kept even his nearest and dearest on a tight leash.

Not that anyone was dear to him.

The male was cold and calculating, and if he were human, he probably would be classified as a sociopath. The Kra-ell might have a similar opinion of him, but no one was stupid enough to voice it.

He was ruthless and cruel to the purebloods and the hybrids, but surprisingly, he wasn't a monster to the human inhabitants of his compound. Perhaps he thought of them as pets, or maybe he pitied them for their short lifespans.

Supposedly, the pureblooded Kra-ell could live for a thousand years, but no one knew how long the hybrids would live. The oldest one was in his eighties, and he looked like he was in his twenties, so they might live just as long as the purebloods.

It was frustrating how little she knew.

Igor and his cohort of close pureblooded males didn't share what they knew with anyone. Not even their children and grandchildren.

One would think that being related to Igor's second-in-command would allow Sofia access to more information or get her preferential treatment, but it didn't. It might have elevated her status just a little over the humans with no Kra-ell blood in them, but most importantly, it provided her with a little more protection from unwanted advances.

Valstar might barely acknowledge her existence, but she was thankful for whatever advantage having him as a grandfather provided her.

Her relation to a high-ranking Kra-ell was most likely the reason she'd been selected to pursue higher education in the human world. Like the other fortunate young humans who'd been granted the opportunity, Sofia was under Igor's heavy-handed compulsion to keep the compound and the existence of the Kra-ell people on Earth a secret. She had to call once a week and report her progress to him, and she also had to make the long drive from the university to the compound for a monthly face-to-face meeting with her dear leader to reinforce the compulsion. But all of that was a small price to pay for her slice of freedom.

What was Igor afraid of, though? That she or one of the other students would reveal that they were the human descendants of aliens who drank blood? Or that their leader was most likely conspiring to take over the human world?

First of all, no one would believe them, and they would be subjected to a mental health evaluation. Secondly, none of them would do that willingly and endanger their families.

Well, she wouldn't, but in truth, she couldn't speak for the others.

Her mother was a piece-of-work Kra-ell hybrid who resented her human daughter, but she wasn't horrible enough for Sofia to want her dead, and her human father was great. Sofia loved him and her two aunts. She also had friends who were dear to her. Most were human, but there were a couple of Kra-ell hybrids who she considered friends as well.

Both were males who were interested in her as more than a friend, but Sofia had no intentions of hooking up with anyone from the compound, human, hybrid, or pureblooded Kra-ell.

She might never escape Igor's rule and live a normal life in the human world, but she could stretch out her studies for many more years and enjoy her freedom. He wanted her to learn foreign languages and master them, and that took time. Thankfully, the linguistics department of the University of Helsinki offered enough variety to keep her studying for many years to come.

After parking her ten-year-old Honda in the underground garage of the administrative building, Sofia climbed the stairs to the first floor, where she was stopped by a guard and her backpack was searched, and when she reached the second floor, she was stopped again by one of Igor's personal guards.

"Good evening, Gordi." She handed him her backpack for inspection. "Do you need to search me?"

She was wearing leggings and a form-fitting long-sleeved shirt that clung to her slim frame like a second skin. She couldn't hide a pin under that outfit, which was why she'd chosen to put it on. She'd hoped it would spare her a pat down.

"You know that I do." He motioned for her to lift her arms.

"Where do you think I can hide anything?" She did as he asked.

4

"Your hair." He motioned for her to release her tresses from the bun she had it gathered in. "You could hide a small firearm in that thing."

She rolled her eyes. "As if I would do something as stupid as that." She pulled out the pins holding the bun up, shook her long hair out, and let it cascade down her back. "Better?" She handed him the pins for inspection.

Gordi's eyes lit up with arousal. "You have such beautiful hair. Why do you always put it on top of your head like that?" He returned the pins to her.

It wasn't a style any of the Kra-ell pureblooded or hybrid females would ever adopt, which was precisely why she had.

It pissed her mother off.

"That's how I like it." She pretended not to notice the gleam in his eyes as she gathered her hair, twisted it on top of her head, and secured it with the pins. "Can I go now?"

Regrettably, the hybrids found her attractive for some reason.

Her dark hair, her height, and her slimness were traits she'd inherited from her Kra-ell grandfather, and her blue eyes and her gentle nature came from her Finn father. She was too thin to be considered attractive by human standards, and wasn't exotic enough to be attractive to the pureblood, but the hybrids found her features pleasing.

"Wait here." Gordi returned the backpack to her. "I'll check if Igor is ready to see you."

Slinging a strap over her shoulder, Sofia let out a silent breath and thanked the Mother that she was Valstar's granddaughter. If she were any other female, human or hybrid, Gordi could have commanded her into his bed, and there would have been very little she could have done to refuse him without courting severe retaliation.

Technically, it wasn't regarded as a command but as an invitation, and technically she could refuse, but in reality, no one dared to. To refuse a hybrid or pureblooded Kra-ell was to offend him, and since they held all the power in the compound, they could and would make her life and the lives of her family hell.

Gordi came out of Igor's office. "You can go in now."

"Thank you." She ducked into the room and immediately bowed her head. "Good evening, sir."

"Good evening, Sofia." Igor regarded her with his cold, calculating eyes. "How are your studies progressing?"

"Very well, sir. I receive top grades in all my classes."

It was the same exchange they had every month, and she often wondered whether Igor checked her grades by having them emailed to him.

Perhaps he had done it in the beginning, when he hadn't been sure she was up to the task, but after eight years of proven success, it would have been a waste of his time to keep checking on her.

Sofia was fluent in six languages and could converse in seven more, and she had no intentions of stopping unless Igor commanded her to quit.

He nodded. "I am satisfied with your progress. Keep up the good work."

She bowed again. "Yes, sir."

"Let's take care of your compliance with the compound's security rules, shall we?"

Sofia swallowed. Despite having gone through that once-a-month process for years, she still hated how it felt to have her will re-squashed with a ten-ton anvil.

"Yes, sir."

2

EMMETT

"*H*ere are all the contest entries." Riley dropped a pile of printed papers on Emmett's desk. "I'm surprised that we only got forty-two." She glanced at the stack. "Are you sure you don't want me to read through them first? I can rate them and save you some time."

"Thank you for the offer." He smiled at her. "But I will enjoy reading them myself. I'm curious to find out what we caught in our net."

It wasn't a writing competition, and Emmett didn't care how well or how badly the essays were written. All he cared about was whether they hinted at the author's paranormal talent.

The contest had been Eleanor's idea. Those who couldn't afford to participate in a paranormal retreat could submit an essay to win a free subscription to Safe Haven's newsletter. They would also get unlimited access to its extensive library of self-improvement seminars and motivational materials. It was a good way to collect the names and email addresses of potential paranormal talents. Later, they could invite those who showed promise to participate for free and continue testing their abilities.

"As you wish." Riley cast another disapproving look at the stack. "It's such a waste of paper to have them printed. You could've read the emails on your computer screen."

"You know that I'm old-fashioned." Emmett lifted the first page. "I don't like staring at screens."

Shrugging, his office manager turned on her short, sensible heel and walked out the door.

Riley, who had taken over the management of the community and the retreats in his absence, was still adjusting to his return and her perceived demotion. She didn't like it, but she needed to get over it, or he would have to replace her with someone with a more subservient attitude.

Safe Haven was Emmett's baby, his creation, and even though he was sharing it now with Kian and the clan, he had close to full autonomy to do with it as he pleased.

Eleanor was running the paranormal enclave with the government talents that she'd recruited in her former job. Marcel had replaced William at the lab the clan had built on the premises and was temporarily supervising a team of scientists. Leon was in charge of security for the entire complex, and Anastasia was helping create content for the new paranormal retreats. That left Emmett to do what he did best, which was promoting the spiritual and paranormal retreats with his guru persona and giving the place its spiritual spin.

Leaning back in his chair, he got comfortable and started reading the first essay. He found nothing of interest and put it in the *no* pile. The next five landed on top of it, and the next two formed the *maybe* pile.

The tenth one was titled: *How the Lions and the Rats became allies. A fable.*

That should be interesting.

Emmett leaned back in his executive chair, lifted his feet onto the desk, and began reading.

A long time ago, in a far, faraway land, there lived a ferocious lioness named Viva who led a very large pride. Many different animals lived in that land, some big, some small, but the lions ruled over them all.

Viva was a proud female, and she paid little regard to the animals living in her territory who were too small for a lioness to eat. But there was one rat named Crafty, whose shenanigans were so outrageous that they had reached even Viva's ears. As his name implied, Crafty was cunning and smart, and he got away with mischief that other animals would never dare to try.

Emmett's heart thundered in his chest.

His father had named him Veskar after an animal from their home world that was similar to a rat and was known for being crafty. Only members of Jade's tribe knew him as Veskar, and Emmett knew of only two who were still alive and free, both residing in the immortals' village. The rest of their tribe had been either murdered or captured, so if this was written by one of them, it must have been submitted from captivity. Given that the first part of the fable was written from the pride leader's perspective, Jade must be the author.

The next part was written from the rat's perspective.

Crafty had a healthy respect for the lions, and he stayed away from them whenever he could. Those big cats normally didn't eat rats, but they might eat a rat who was prone to mischief.

Wishing to find a place where there were no lions and where rats were treated with respect, Crafty left the lions' territory and never looked back.

He traveled across the lake to where the humans lived, and he found a community of village rats who were all very well fed.

With his cunning and his smarts, it didn't take Crafty long to take over as the

leader of the pack. Those spoiled village rats who never had to work hard for their
scraps were now his to command.
He was the king of the rats.
Happy and contented, Crafty basked in his success, and the only thing missing from
his perfect life was the satisfaction of showing his fellow wilderness rats how well he
had done for himself. From time to time, he thought about swimming back across
the lake to tell his family and friends about his wonderful new life in the human
village, but it was too risky.
What if, while he was gone, another rat took over as the leader of the pack?
What if, on the way, Crafty encountered one of those ferocious cats and got eaten?
He stayed where he was and forgot all about those he had left behind.

This part did not give Emmett any new clues, and he was starting to doubt that the email had been sent by Jade. There were probably many fables featuring rats and other animals. If he searched the internet, he would probably find many more that had nothing to do with him.

The next part reverted to the lioness.

One day, when the big cats were all asleep, a massive earthquake shook the ground,
collapsing the pride's home, killing some, and trapping the rest under a pile of stone.
Not just the lions suffered. Many of the small cave dwellers were squashed under
the avalanche of rocks. Those who survived fled through passages and openings that
were too small for the big cats to fit through. The lions' size, the foundation of their
superiority, was now a hindrance.
They were doomed.
"How many survived?" Viva asked once the count was done.
"Thirty adults and sixty cubs," answered the lion who had counted the live ones.
Viva's heart sank. "How many died?"
"One adult female and her four cubs," the one who'd counted the dead said mourn-
fully. "And if we don't find a way out of the collapsed caves soon, we will all die
here as well."
"Who could save us?" a lioness cried out. "Does anyone even know that we are
trapped?"
"Maybe the little critters who escaped through the nooks and crannies will tell
someone who will be willing to help us," another lion said.
The only ones who could help were the humans, and they didn't understand animal
language.
Despondent, Viva did not say a thing. She lay down and put her head on her paws.

Emmett was done with only the first one out of the three printed pages when he straightened in his chair, snatched the phone off his desk, and called Eleanor. "Come to my office right away. It's urgent."

"On my way." She ended the call.

3

MARCEL

*M*arcel didn't appreciate being called mid-morning by Eleanor and asked to come immediately to Emmett's office. If it were anyone else, he would have demanded explanations before rushing over, but Eleanor wasn't the type to get worked up over nothing.

The door to Emmett's office opened before he had a chance to knock. "Thanks for coming." Eleanor smiled apologetically. "I would have come to you, but I'm not allowed in the lab."

Normally, she would have been correct, but he would have allowed her in if she'd called and explained her problem. As long as he was there with her and made sure that she didn't see what he and the team were working on, it would have been okay.

"What's the emergency?" Marcel closed the door behind him.

"This." Emmett waved a stack of papers. "The email arrived two days ago, but I only read it today." He handed him a three-page document. "I need Kian to see it, but I don't want to send it from here in case it's encoded, and someone can follow the email to the village. I don't know the protocol for sending secure emails, but I assume that you have a safe channel of communication in your lab, and I need you to send it to him along with a note from me explaining what's going on."

Marcel read the title. "How the Lions and the Rats become allies. A fable." He lifted a brow. "It's a children's tale. Why does it need encryption, and what does it have to do with Kian?"

"It's from Jade," Eleanor said, cutting straight to the chase. "She wrote it in such a way that only Emmett would know it's from her. It's a call for help."

"Did you read it?"

Emmett might have seen in the story what wasn't there, but Eleanor was not prone to flights of fancy.

"I did. Without Emmett's explanation, I would have thought nothing of it, but with his input, the fable becomes a coded cry for help."

"How do you know it's from her?" Marcel asked Emmett.

The guy grimaced. "My Kra-ell name is Veskar. My father wasn't happy about the birth of a hybrid son who looked too human for his taste, so he gave me an insulting name. Veskar can be loosely translated as a crafty rat." Emmett pointed to the pages in Marcel's hands. "The fable's hero is called Crafty, and he's a rat."

"I see."

Marcel sat down and read the first page. "Do those numbers mean anything to you?"

Emmett shook his head. "They don't, but I'm sure that they are not random. I just don't know what she's trying to communicate."

"How many members did her tribe have?"

"None of those numbers add up to anything that makes sense," Eleanor said. "Emmett and I already tried to figure it out, but the numbers don't match the total number of the tribe's population, not the number of males or females, and not the number of humans. Not during Emmett's time in the tribe, and not right before the attack."

Marcel nodded. "That's what I thought. The sixty-four and thirty-one or the sixty and thirty could be latitude and longitude coordinates." He read the passage. "Thirty adults and sixty cubs lived. One female and her four cubs died." He lifted his head and looked at Emmet. "Longitude is also called meridian, and the synonyms for meridian are the greatest, the uppermost, and so on. Therefore, the number of adults could represent longitude. Latitude lines are also called parallels, and some of the synonyms for parallels are secondary and kin, which means that the number of cubs could represent the number for latitude."

"Oh, that's so clever of her." Eleanor crossed her arms over her chest. "And it's even cleverer of you to figure it out."

Marcel wasn't sure that it was. If Jade was trying to communicate a secret message in an email that she knew was monitored, that wasn't clever at all. He wasn't the only one who could figure out that those numbers were coordinates. Not that he was convinced that they were. It was just a hypothesis.

"Let's check those coordinates." Marcel pulled out his phone, opened the map application, and typed in the numbers. "Sixty longitude and thirty latitude point to St. Petersburg. Let's check sixty-four and thirty-one." His brows lifted. "Interesting. It's probably a coincidence, but this set of coordinates is smack in the middle of a place called Karelia, which sounds a lot like Kra-ell. The area straddles northwest Russia and the eastern portion of Finland. The coordinates fall on the Russian side."

Eleanor turned to Emmett. "Mey said that the enemy Kra-ell male's echo she'd heard had a Russian accent."

They could be reading into the fable things that weren't there, and combining mismatched pieces of a puzzle, but Marcel was willing to suspend disbelief.

"Let's see if there are any more clues hiding in the story." He continued reading.

One day as Crafty was sitting on his throne and conducting pack business, a rabbit

11

he had known from the wilderness hopped over. "Crafty, how good it is to see you. Did you hear what happened to the lions' pride?"

"I did not."

After the rabbit told Crafty about the earthquake that had trapped all the big cats underground, he sighed. "Even the cubs are too big to fit through the crevices that my family and I used to escape. They will all die in there." The rabbit shook his head. "I wish I could help, but I'm just a small rabbit, and all I can do is run."

Crafty might have disliked the lions' haughty attitudes, but they had never been his enemy, and he did not wish to see them all dead. He wouldn't leave the cubs to die of starvation.

The rabbit might be helpless, but a smart rat with a large pack could do what even the powerful lions could not.

He could dig an escape tunnel and prove the real value of rats. They weren't just parasites who lived off human scraps. They could be powerful and respected allies. Crafty summoned his followers and told them his plan. "The pride will forever be in our debt, and we will never hunger for meat again." He stretched to his full height and lifted his paws. "We will prove to everyone that rats are not at the bottom of the food chain and that we deserve as much respect as the lions. With our smarts, determination, and cooperation, we can do what none of the other animals can."

One of the bigger rats lifted his paw. "How do we know that they won't eat us once we get to them? Lions don't usually eat rats, but they will be hungry, and they have cubs that they will be desperate to feed."

"I will tunnel through the last couple of feet alone and talk to their leader. If she swears not to let anyone of her subjects eat us, I will come back, and we will enlarge the tunnel so they will be able to get out."

"She might promise you that and then eat us after we free her," a female said. "Or she might just eat you before giving you a chance to explain."

Crafty laughed. "I would not be much of a meal, and the pride's leader is too smart to eat her only hope of survival. She's a mother, and she'll do anything to save the cubs, even if it means making an alliance with rats. She's also proud, and if she gives me her word, she will stand by it."

"What about the other cats?" the big male asked. "They will eat us for sure."

It was possible. The leader might have lost her hold on the pride, or she might be injured and weakened, and they might not listen to her, but Crafty couldn't just do nothing and let them all die.

"She won't let them. Let's go!" He singsonged that special tune that would ensure the pack's compliance. "We will prove to the world that rats are not to be sneered at."

It took the pack three days to swim through the lake and then another seven days to burrow underground, and when Crafty smelled the lions, the live ones and the dead, he made the signal for his pack to stop. "I shall continue alone from here."

As he dug through the last three feet, he didn't bother to make the tunnel more than two inches wide, compressing his body and squeezing through.

When he emerged from the tunnel the lions were asleep, and as he scurried as fast as his paws could carry him to the largest lioness, the others lifted their massive heads and bared their teeth.

He slid between her outstretched paws. "Don't eat me! I came to save you!"

Her big feline eyes widened. "How?"

He stood up and stretched to his full height of seven and a half inches. "My name is Crafty, and I am the leader of a big rat pack. I promised my subjects that you and yours would forever be in our debt if we dug a tunnel and got you out. But you and your subjects must swear alliance to me and mine. You also need to swear that you will not eat any members of my pack and that once you are free, you will share your kills with us."

Hope surging in her heart, the leader nodded her massive head.

To save her family, she would kiss the rat on his little whiskers if that was what he demanded in payment, but all he was asking for was assurance for the safety of his pack and future scraps. It was a very small price to pay to save the weakening cubs. They wouldn't last much longer.

"I have heard of you, Crafty, and I know that you are a very smart rat. I swear it on my life and the lives of everyone in my pride that if you and your pack save us, you will never go hungry for meat for as long as we live. My pride and I will share our kills with you and yours, and we will never eat any of your subjects or any other rats." She grimaced. "Rats were never a food source for us and never will be." Weakened from hunger, she lifted herself with effort and turned to the others. "Swear it, and let's get out of here."

After the lions repeated the vow that their leader had made, Crafty returned through the tiny tunnel he had dug for himself and told the others what was promised.

When the rats had finished digging the rest of the tunnel and freed all the lions, the leader of the pride and her subjects kept their promise. From that day on, the pride of lions and the pack of rats lived in harmony and mutual respect, and no one in that part of the world dared to look down their noses or whiskers at Crafty or any other rat.

Marcel shifted his gaze to Emmett. "Does seven or three mean anything to you or seven and a half inches?"

Emmett shook his head. "They don't. The only thing I got from the fable was that Jade and the other females were trapped, that they had children with them, and that they needed me to save them in a stealthy manner, maybe literally by digging a tunnel. Without your input, I would have never suspected that the numbers of the adults and cubs could represent coordinates."

4

KIAN

*A*fter Kian had read the fable, Emmett's explanations, and Marcel's interpretation of the numbers, he read it again and groaned.

The last thing he needed to add to the long list of things he had to worry about was damned Jade. He didn't want to get involved, and he hated getting dragged into a conflict that didn't concern him. Not directly anyway.

Then again, perhaps Jade and the Kra-ell were part of the complicated tapestry the Fates were weaving, and the clan had to get involved.

He needed to talk to someone about it, and that someone was Syssi.

Turner was a great strategist, and Kian planned on consulting him next, but the guy lacked vision. He was excellent at analyzing what was but not as good at imagining what could be.

Syssi, on the other hand, was excellent at it without allowing herself to get carried away, and he needed his wife's level-headed perspective before getting back to Emmett.

He picked up the phone and called her.

"Hello, my love," she answered with a smile in her voice. "Did you miss me since we talked this morning?"

"Terribly. Are you on your way back?"

It wasn't even noon yet, but on Fridays, Syssi and Amanda ended their day early to avoid the weekend traffic, and sometimes they cut it even shorter and headed home before lunch.

"We are. Do you want to meet for lunch at the café?"

"I'd love to. But first, I need your opinion on something. Amanda's too."

"Of course."

"Emmett got an email that he thinks is from Jade. It was written as a fable and contained a hidden message that only Emmett would get. It was submitted to a contest Safe Haven was running. I would like to read it to you."

"I'm curious to hear it," Amanda said. "I remember Vrog and Aliyah talking about Jade's storytelling skills."

After Kian had read the fable to them and then Emmett and Marcel's take on it, Amanda asked, "Did Jade have children before getting captured? I don't remember Emmett or Vrog mentioning it."

"I don't know, but I assume that she did. Like us, the Kra-ell welcomed children and did everything they could to have more, especially purebooded ones. I doubt that Jade would have failed to conceive during the time since her arrival on Earth."

"Then if she had sons, they were murdered along with the other males." Amanda sighed. "I can't imagine the horror of being the captive of the murderers of her children, and then having more kids with them. From all we've learned about her, she's a powerful and ruthless female who's also a strong compeller. If she could, she would have killed them and escaped. Given that she didn't, her captor or captors must either be keeping her locked up in a dungeon and chained to a wall, or they are more powerful compellers than her."

"The other possibility is that they took her children and threatened to harm them if she didn't cooperate," Syssi said. "In the fable, she said that a mother would do anything to save her family. It might have been a clue."

As Kian had expected, Syssi and Amanda were looking at the fable from a completely different angle. Marcel had focused on the coordinates, Emmett had focused on what Jade was expecting of him, and Eleanor, well, she was probably focused on the threat that Jade posed to her personally and to the clan.

"Fables are usually full of clues," Syssi said. "And we know that Jade is smart. She might have hidden more information in there than is apparent at first glance."

Kian groaned. "Did either of you deduce how many enemy warriors we would be facing and what safeguards they employ? That would be very helpful."

For a moment, neither one said anything, and he could imagine Syssi and Amanda exchanging looks and shrugging.

"We probably need to read it again," Amanda said. "The only thing that comes to mind is the caves where the pride lived. Can you check in the satellite footage if there are any caves in the area of those coordinates?"

"The resolution is not that good, and in a heavily wooded terrain like Karelia, the visibility will be minimal. That's probably the main reason they chose it for their base."

"I wonder if the name Karelia has any significance," Syssi said. "It's phonetically almost the same as Kra-ellia. If you switch the third and second letter around, you get the land of the Kra-ell."

"It's probably a coincidence."

"I'll research it later," Amanda said. "If it's older than the estimated year of the Kra-ell's arrival, then it has nothing to do with them."

"Not necessarily," Syssi said. "Remember what Aliyah said about the scouting team? Kra-ell scouts might have arrived many centuries before Jade and her cohorts."

As Syssi and Amanda continued discussing the name, Kian leaned back in his chair and closed his eyes. There were too many variables to the story, and he wasn't ready to risk his people to rescue Kra-ell, who could potentially become his clan's enemies.

On the other hand, the three who had joined his clan seemed fairly loyal, but that was because it was in their best interest. They were alone among an ocean of humans, with no tribe to call their own, and the clan offered them protection and a community that accepted them.

Things might change when they got reunited with the other survivors of their tribe.

But that was a secondary worry. First, he needed to figure out whether attacking Jade's captors or finding a way to smuggle Jade and the others out would benefit the clan in the long run or harm it.

Opening his eyes, Kian leaned forward. "Can you both stop by my office when you get here? I will get lunch delivered and arrange for a conference call with Emmett, Eleanor, and Leon. Maybe Marcel as well. We can all brainstorm it together."

"I would love to brainstorm with you." Amanda sighed. "We used to do it all the time, and then you fell in love with Syssi and forgot all about your baby sister."

"You introduced us."

"True. So, it's my fault." She laughed. "Oh well. I can't say that I'm sorry. Anyhoo, we will need to drop the girls at Mother's first. We promised to visit her after lunch, but she won't mind if we leave. She's more interested in spending time with her granddaughters than with Syssi and me."

"That's not true." Syssi chuckled, probably because Amanda was making a face. "Okay. It's somewhat true. But even so, we need to explain why we can't stay and apologize. It would be rude to just drop the girls at her place and leave."

5

MARCEL

*M*arcel had hoped that sending the email and notes to Kian would be the end of his part in the Jade saga, but the call he'd just gotten from the boss dispelled his illusions.

Kian wanted him, Emmett, and Eleanor to assemble in Leon's office and participate in a video conference meeting with him, Syssi, and Amanda.

Did Kian hope Syssi would get a vision about Jade? And why did he need Amanda?

Hell, what did Kian need him for?

Marcel was a computer engineer, talented, but nowhere near William's caliber, and he wasn't a Guardian or a strategist either. He'd been a Guardian back in the day, but that was a long time ago, and his military career had been short.

He hadn't been well suited for the role.

It required a certain level of emotional detachment that he'd struggled to achieve. Some of the things he'd seen and experienced still haunted him. Ironically, what had finally helped him achieve detachment had happened after he'd left the force, but he refused to let his mind go to that dark time in his life.

He'd left it all behind and had chosen a very different path.

Marcel had realized that using his brain appealed to him much more than using his brawn, and dealing with numbers was much less stressful and gut-wrenching than dealing with death and misery.

He'd chosen the field of engineering, mechanical at first, then electrical, and recently computer science, but even though he'd left active duty, Marcel had never regretted the long years of training and the time he'd served. The skills he'd learned were useful, and he was part of the reserve force, training a couple weekends a year to maintain his skills.

If the clan needed him, he was ready and able to defend his people, but the Kra-ell were a different story. Jade and her plight tugged at his heartstrings, but so did many other misfortunes.

The world had many maladies that needed fixing, but even the gods had failed at that task, and that was when the world had been a much smaller and simpler place.

As a male ruled by logic, Marcel didn't dwell on the impossible. Jade was not his problem, and he didn't think she was the clan's problem either. In fact, he regretted deciphering the fable and figuring out that the numbers of adults and cubs could potentially represent coordinates.

Without that piece of knowledge, Kian wouldn't have even considered a rescue attempt that could cost the lives of Guardians.

As Marcel entered Leon's office, Emmett and Eleanor were already there, and the big screen behind Leon's desk was on, displaying an aerial video of downtown Los Angeles.

"I brought us coffee." Eleanor motioned to the lone paper cup on the round conference table.

The others held theirs in their hands.

"Thank you." He took the lid off and sat down. "Were you waiting just for me?"

"We are waiting for Kian," Eleanor said. "He will call as soon as Syssi and Amanda get to his office."

Marcel leaned back with the cup in hand. "Did Kian say why he wants Syssi and Amanda to attend the meeting?"

"He didn't." Emmett crossed his arms over his chest. "He should have included Vrog and Aliyah instead." He cast a glare at Leon and then shifted his dark gaze back to Marcel. "I wanted to call them to let them know about Jade, but your buddy Leon said that I needed to ask Kian's permission first. I would have ignored him and called them anyway, but I didn't want to antagonize Kian. I can't rescue Jade and the other members of my tribe with only two other hybrids to help me. I need the clan's Guardians, and I need Turner to come up with a plan."

It was on the tip of Marcel's tongue to say that Emmett might have to make do with his two former tribe members and perhaps advice from Turner. The clan shouldn't get involved in the Kra-ell mess, and Turner would no doubt advise Kian to stay out of it. Marcel was still trying to come up with a diplomatic way to say it without quashing the guy's hope, when Leon's phone rang.

"Yes, boss," Leon said. "Everyone is here. I'm switching to video."

As they all faced the camera mounted on top of Leon's laptop, half of the screen behind the desk showed the four of them crowding the small round table in Leon's office, while the other half showed Kian, Syssi, and Amanda in a similar setup, only larger.

"Hello, everyone." Syssi waved. "This is such exciting news. Kian read the fable to me and Amanda, and we are both sure that there are many more hints hidden between its words. We will make copies and take them home with us."

Amanda waved as well. "I have a question for Emmett. Did Jade have children while you were still a member of her tribe?"

Emmett nodded. "She had a son, and Vrog told me that she had another one after I left. They were both massacred along with the other males."

18

6

KIAN

Syssi sucked in a breath. "That's horrible. I can't imagine the suffering, the rage, the need for revenge."

Surprised by her vehemence, Kian looked at Syssi with new eyes. She was usually so gentle, so mellow, but perhaps becoming immortal had changed her, or maybe it was motherhood.

Her eyes blazed, and if she had fangs, he suspected that they would have been fully elongated by now.

"If she hasn't killed them all, it means she can't," Emmett said. "Jade is a force to be reckoned with. She's a powerful compeller, and she has no qualms about killing. Whoever is holding her must be even more powerful than her."

"That's what Amanda and I figured," Syssi said. "She has access to the internet, so she's not rotting in some dungeon, but they must have something that they are holding over her. Maybe she had more children in captivity, and she's not striking against her captors because she is protecting her kids."

Amanda shook her head. "They must have kept her in a dungeon until they got her pregnant and then used the child or children to control her. Otherwise, she would have retaliated before getting with child. They probably used drugs as well. That's what the traffickers do, and it works." She shivered. "I know that Jade is not a clan member, and we don't owe her anything, but she and the other females are basically sex trafficking victims, and rescuing them is what we do."

"It's not the same." Kian let out a breath. "The local dens that we raid to free the victims are not fortified compounds with super-strong Kra-ell guarding them."

Leon nodded. "I bet Jade's tribe wasn't the only one those Kra-ell have raided, killed the males, and abducted the females. Their goal is obviously to breed more pureblooded Kra-ell, so by now, they might have a large number of warriors."

"Jade didn't know that other Kra-ell survived the crash, but her captors did," Kian said. "They also knew how to locate them."

"Maybe they managed to save some of their advanced technological gear," Leon said. "The original Kra-ell settlers could have been implanted with locator devices that only their technology could detect. We know that Navuh tried to implant his warriors with trackers, so it's not such a far-fetched scenario."

It was possible, but thankfully, the Kra-ell who had been born on Earth and the hybrids didn't have them. If they had, Jade's captors would have found Emmett a long time ago, and since he'd spent months in the village, that would have been a catastrophe. The same went for Vrog and Aliyah.

Just to be safe, though, he would ask Julian to run scans on them again.

"We still don't know how they got scattered in the first place." Kian crossed his arms over his chest. "We assume that their arrival had something to do with the Tunguska event, and the assumption that their ship was sabotaged is based on what Aliyah overheard as a small girl. The explanation might be completely different. Jade and her original group of purebloods might be the bad guys, and her captors might be law enforcers who brought them to justice. Maybe there was a mutiny, and the commanders executed the deserters but spared the females because of their value as breeders. Or maybe tribal wars are part of their culture, and maybe executing the males and capturing the females is a common tactic."

Syssi gaped at him. "Including their young children? The Kra-ell are ruthless, but they value children. They wouldn't do that."

Amanda winced. "The Japanese used to do that. If someone was deemed a traitor, their entire family was killed. They weren't the only ones either. I can start listing all the known offenders, but the list is long and depressing."

Shaking her head, Syssi slumped in her chair. "I have no words. Is there no limit to cruelty?"

Not knowing how to comfort her, Kian put a hand on her shoulder. "Let's focus on Jade's fable. If it even came from her."

"It did," Emmett said. "I recognize her style of storytelling. If I show Vrog and Aliyah the fable, they'll probably confirm my assessment."

Kian could understand Emmett's eagerness to share the news with his fellow tribe members, but it was premature.

"I don't want them to know yet. We need to figure out what to do about it first."

"Jade needs help," Emmett said. "She wouldn't have reached out to me if she could find a way out of captivity herself. She and the other females must be suffering terribly." He rubbed a hand over his long beard. "I'm surprised that she recognized me from my picture, and I'm also curious about how she stumbled upon Safe Haven's advertising. We ran ads on Facebook, but mainly in the US. We did very little international advertising and then only in the English-speaking markets."

The same had occurred to Kian, and the answers he'd come up with were worrisome. The least bothersome and the most likely was that Jade had been searching for something that had led her to Safe Haven's website. She'd recognized Emmett, and if she could see the male behind the long hair and beard, so could others from her tribe, and someone might have alerted their captors to the Kra-ell male disguising himself as a human spiritual leader.

"Maybe she searched for something related to self-improvement or free love,"

Syssi offered. "The system Emmett implemented and the rules of conduct mimic traditional Kra-ell sexual exchanges. The men must wait for an invitation from the women, and they are not allowed to initiate. That might have caught her interest, and she dug deeper. She could've also searched for information about paranormal talents. Did she know that you could compel?" she asked Emmett.

"I thought that she didn't, but given what she wrote in that fable, she did. Crafty had a special sing-song voice that ensured his pack's cooperation. That's a good way to hint at my ability to compel."

"I agree." Syssi turned to Kian. "She probably wanted to butter Emmett up. She described Crafty in a very flattering light."

Emmett chuckled. "Jade is incapable of buttering anyone up. It's not part of her makeup."

"Twenty-some years in captivity can change a person," Eleanor said. "She has children, and so do the other females. Viva the proud lioness was willing to do anything to save the cubs, and so is Jade."

Both Syssi and Amanda nodded their heads.

"So, what do we do next?" Emmett looked at Kian. "Do I answer her fable with one of my own?"

"A fable is a good idea, but not as an answer email," Marcel said. "The contest winners will have access to the Safe Haven library. You can hide your fable somewhere among the other stuff."

"Don't do anything yet." Kian pushed his chair back. "I'll collect satellite footage from the area those coordinates point to, but given how densely wooded Karelia is, I don't expect to glean much information from that. I also need to discuss the situation with Turner. He's an expert on hostage retrieval, which is what we are dealing with. If anyone can get Jade out of there without a war, it's him."

"I think war is inevitable." Eleanor put a hand on Emmett's shoulder. "It's not just about getting Jade out. They have many Kra-ell females and their children trapped there as well. Besides, they pose a threat to the clan that needs to be eliminated."

"That's the part I'm not sure about," Kian said. "They don't know about our clan's existence, and I want to keep it that way. If they ever find out that our females can provide them with long-lived offspring, they will do everything in their power to hunt us down."

"They can try," Leon said. "Navuh has been trying to find us for centuries, and he has thousands of warriors at his disposal. One small group of Kra-ell is irrelevant to us."

Kian took a deep breath. "I think that if Navuh really wanted to find us, he would have by now. We are good at hiding, but we are not that good. He needs an enemy to keep his people united and motivated, and humans are deemed irrelevant. They are the sheep, and we are the lions protecting them. We are the real threat. The moment we are out of the picture, he will lose the glue that holds the Brotherhood together, and he knows that."

7

SYSSI

*S*o that was why Kian had been less paranoid about security lately.

Syssi had been wondering about that. A couple of years ago, he wouldn't have allowed prospective Dormants to come and go as they pleased, and he'd been much more careful about who he allowed into the village and when.

She'd heard Kalugal voice the same argument about Navuh and his lack of effort to locate the clan, and it seemed that Kian had bought it.

Was it smart, though?

It sounded logical, and maybe it was even true, but despots did not always act logically, especially when their followers became restless. When that happened, the dictators became desperate to distract them from whatever they were unhappy about, which was a lot given that they served a ruler who didn't give a hoot about them.

The easiest way to distract people and unite them behind a cause was to stir up trouble and rile them up. The violent emotion of hate overshadowed the grievances they had with their leaders, and suddenly the vilified enemy became the focus, and not their crappy living conditions and lack of freedom.

Navuh's warriors hadn't seen a battlefield in several years, and Syssi had no doubt that they were getting restless. They couldn't be satisfied with the Brotherhood's weapons, drugs, and prostitution activities. They were trained to fight, and lately, Navuh had trouble finding hot spots he deemed relevant for them where they could spread their particular brand of terror.

Then again, the world was changing, and the most vicious battles took place in the political arena. Perhaps Navuh had decided to limit his efforts to influence policies, and since that required a lot of money, he utilized his warriors to make it.

The days of well-paid mercenary armies were apparently over, or maybe he'd just realized that there was more money in the business of war than in the war itself.

"I will have to announce the contest winners by next Friday," Emmett said. "But I want to do it earlier and open a channel of communication with Jade. I like the idea of hiding my response among the seminars and motivational material, but I need a couple of days to figure out how to do it so only Jade will find it and not her captors."

He was such a vain male. Jade was an experienced storyteller, and it still had probably taken her weeks to come up with the fable that would convey all she wanted to tell Emmett. It would take him just as long.

"I won't have an answer for you that quickly," Kian said. "I also want you to show Turner and me what you've written before you post it on the website. This is a new enemy we are facing, and I don't know what their capabilities are and what kind of risk they pose. I refuse to be rushed." He gave Emmett a hard look. "Jade has waited for twenty-some years. She can wait a couple more weeks."

Emmett shook his head. "I need to announce the winners no later than next Friday, and she will have to be one of them. That's the limiting factor."

"I might decide that not answering her is the best option," Kian said. "If her captors suspect something, they will be monitoring her web browsing activity, and if there is nothing for her to find, they won't either, and they will let it go."

"Turner will tell you to do just that," Leon said. "The compound is located on the Russian side of Karelia, and Turner doesn't like working on their turf. The best he can offer you is hiring a local operator."

Kian nodded. "That might be good enough to assess the situation. As I mentioned before, satellite footage is likely to give us very little information, and flying drones in a remote area where no one else does it will raise the captors' suspicions. We need boots on the ground, and it's better if they are locals who know the language and customs and can play the part of innocent passers-by."

"Jade might be out of time." Emmett's eyes turned pleading. "The Mother only knows what she's being subjected to. The least I can do is acknowledge her."

"I know that you're impatient," Kian said softly. "But Safe Haven is a strategic location for us, and if your message is discovered, you will lead Jade's captors straight there. Even if we could manage to evacuate our people in time, we would lose our new base and the investment that went into it, and you would lose Safe Haven. Are you willing to sacrifice it for Jade and the other females? I was under the impression that you didn't care for them much."

"I didn't, and I still don't. They were stuck-up elitists who looked down their noses at me because I was a hybrid. It didn't matter that I was smarter and craftier than all the pureblooded males put together. I still didn't get to breed with one of the pureblooded females. But I have a feeling that the years in captivity have taught Jade a valuable lesson." He smiled. "She now appreciates Crafty, the smart rat."

From the corner of her eye, Syssi could see Eleanor bristling.

"If you hope to breed with a pureblooded female, tell me now." Eleanor pushed to her feet. "I will have no problem finding immortal males to breed with me."

Smiling, Emmett pulled on her hand. "I love it when you get jealous, but you have nothing to fear. I was talking about the past before I knew you even existed.

23

You are the only female for me, and I will never look upon another with desire in my eyes. Only you stir my heart, my love."

8

SOFIA

*S*ofia's heart was racing as she made her way to Igor's office. What could he possibly want with her this late in the evening?

He wasn't interested in humans for his sexual needs, so that wasn't it, and she hadn't broken any rules. She'd been an obedient little human, doing everything by the book.

Was he going to inform her that her days at the university were over?

As usual, she was searched as she entered the administrative building and then again when she got to his floor.

"What did you do?" Gordi asked, adding fuel to the fear gnawing a hole through her stomach.

"Nothing. I don't know why he wants to see me. Is he angry?"

Gordi chuckled. "Igor doesn't show emotions. He looks the same when he's happy and when he's mad."

She knew that. Igor never raised his voice, never sighed or groaned, and he never smiled or scowled, either. If not for his alien looks, the male could have been a world champion poker player.

"Wait here." Gordi left her standing by his station and knocked on Igor's door. "Sofia is here," he told the boss.

"Let her in," Igor said in an even, unhurried tone.

With a pitying look, Gordi motioned for her to go in.

She crossed the threshold with her eyes cast down and bowed. "Good evening, sir."

"Good evening, Sofia. Please take a seat."

That was surprising.

Igor hardly ever told her to sit down during their once-a-month meetings. Usually, she would remain standing for the entire ten-minute or less ordeal, with her legs shaking and her knees about to give out.

"Thank you, sir." She lowered herself to the edge of the chair and lifted her eyes to her ruler.

"You are going on a trip." He pushed a brown envelope toward her. "All the information is inside, including your passport."

She reached for the envelope with shaking hands. "Where am I going?"

"The United States. I enrolled you in a paranormal talent retreat. It starts in a week and will last two weeks. I want you to snoop around and collect information for me."

Her head snapped up. "What kind of information?"

"Anything that's noteworthy. A member of my staff showed a great interest in that place, and I'm curious whether there was more to it than she claims."

Igor didn't have females on his staff. The only one he could be referring to was Jade, the prime female and the mother of his only daughter. She wasn't officially part of his staff, but she held an elevated position.

Ugh. Why me?

The last thing Sofia needed was to make an enemy out of Jade. The female might be under Igor's compulsion, but she could still do a lot of damage to a human and call it an accident. Igor might punish her, but he wouldn't execute her. She was the most powerful female in the compound, and she produced the most powerful offspring for him.

"Fall semester starts in two weeks," Sofia tried feebly.

"You can lose a week or two of language studies. It's not rocket science."

Desperate for another excuse, she tried to play on Igor's patriarchal philosophy. Perhaps it would work in her favor for once.

"Maybe someone else is better suited for a spying job? A male perhaps?"

"Females are better for undercover work. Humans don't expect trouble from their women, and the only attention you will attract will be carnal in nature, which you can use to your advantage. Human males are easily manipulated when they are sexually interested in a good-looking female like you."

Sofia's hands became clammy.

Igor expected her to have sex with men to get information out of them, and if she refused, even her grandfather couldn't protect her.

Not that he would try.

She was a dispensable human, and he would demand of her to be a good little soldier and do exactly what she was told.

"Human males don't find me attractive," she tried, not expecting it to work. "I'm too skinny and too tall."

Igor regarded her with his expressionless eyes. "You are a pretty girl, and you're soft and submissive, which is what they prefer. You'll do just fine."

He was wrong about that. She might be considered soft and submissive by Kraell standards, but she was just an average human female who enjoyed sex that didn't involve a fight for dominance and was a natural extension of a loving and respectful relationship, or at least friendship. She had nothing against others enjoying casual hookups, but it wasn't for her.

During her years in the university, Sofia had dated many guys, and she'd had two serious boyfriends. One relationship had lasted for over a year, and the other

26

four months, and both had been about more than sex, but they hadn't been the all-consuming love she'd read about and yearned for. It had been difficult to get close to a guy when she couldn't tell him anything about herself or bring him home to meet her parents.

Her preferences didn't matter to Igor, though, and she couldn't afford to keep arguing. He'd been patient with her so far, but she knew that she'd reached the limit of what he was willing to allow.

Bowing her head, she said, "I will do my best not to disappoint you."

"Make sure that you don't," he said without changing his tone, but the threat was palpable.

"What should I tell them when they ask me personal questions? I mean, what's my cover?"

"When lying, it is always best to stay as close to the truth as possible. You are a linguistics student from Finland who has a paranormal talent that she wants to explore. Valstar will explain the rest." Igor motioned for her to get up. "Wait outside by the guard station. He will see you when he's ready."

Pushing to her feet, Sofia bowed. "Thank you, sir. Goodnight."

9

KIAN

*S*aturday mornings were usually reserved for playtime with Allegra, but it wasn't unusual for emergencies to eat into that special time. The best way to handle it was to combine business with pleasure, which was what Kian had done by inviting his mother to share breakfast with him, Syssi, and Allegra and inviting Turner and Bridget to join them a little later for cappuccinos and Okidu's latest baking masterpiece—a chocolate cake with raspberry topping.

He needed to give his mother an update about the latest developments with Jade, and he needed to get Turner's advice.

Sitting on the couch and sipping on a cup of tea, Annani regarded him from under her long, red eyelashes. "You are not inclined to assist Jade, are you?"

"I'm not." He handed Allegra another piece to try to fit into the cube. "I don't want to poke that sleeping bear."

"So why did you invite Turner? Are you worried that at some point Jade's captors might pose a threat to the clan?"

Kian nodded. "She might have led them to Safe Haven with that email. I've told Leon to raise the alert level, and I'm considering taking the paranormals out of there and dismissing the bioinformaticians. If Jade's captors come to investigate, they will find nothing of interest."

Annani cradled the teacup between her palms. "Except for an underground lab with the latest innovations in computing."

"After Marcel locks it up, they won't be able to get in, and if they do, it's not what they are looking for."

"What will they be looking for?"

"Emmett or other Kra-ell."

Syssi walked into the living room and sat on the floor next to Kian. "You need to get Emmett out of there as well."

"I do. But he will not leave willingly."

28

As the doorbell rang, Okidu opened the door and then escorted Bridget and Turner into the living room.

Turner bowed to Annani. "Good morning, Clan Mother."

"Good morning to you too, Victor, and please, call me Annani."

He smiled. "As you wish."

She'd asked him to call her by her given name several times in the past, and he did, but then he'd reverted to calling her Clan Mother.

"Good morning." Bridget walked over to her and leaned to kiss her cheek.

"Cappuccinos, anyone?" Syssi asked. "They are a must with Okidu's chocolate raspberry cake."

"I will have one." Bridget sat next to Annani. "I stopped by the clinic to check up on Eric. He's doing exceptionally well for someone who has been unconscious for so long. I really don't understand why he hasn't woken up already."

Annani's lips twitched with a suppressed smile. "He must be dreaming very pleasant dreams and does not wish to wake up."

So far, Eric had received transfusions only from Toven and none from Annani. Toven's blood seemed to be working just as well. Annani and Toven had decided not to risk mixing their blood donations unless Eric took a turn for the worse.

"Is Hildegard watching Eric?" Syssi walked over to her cappuccino station.

"She is." Bridget sighed. "I wish we had one more nurse. With Gertrude setting up shop in Safe Haven, Hildegard has to do double shifts. She's not happy about it."

"What about Julian?" Annani asked. "What is he doing with his time?"

"He has his hands full with the halfway house and the sanctuary, but we are considering hiring a human doctor for that and having Julian work more hours in the clinic. Until now, we haven't needed a doctor full-time in the village, and I was able to make do with Hildegard and Gertrude shouldering most of the care. But now that we are expecting several Dormants to attempt transition at the same time, and with Gertrude gone, we need him here."

"You could ask Merlin to fill in temporarily," Kian suggested.

"Julian has been apprenticing with me for a while, and he knows how to handle transitioning Dormants. Merlin doesn't have the same experience."

Annani sighed. "I wish for your clinic to be so busy that you, Julian, and Merlin have your hands full with transitioning Dormants."

Bridget smiled. "I wish it too, but then someone will need to take over managing the rescue missions."

"About that." Kian rose to his feet and sat on one of the armchairs. "I think you should train someone to take your place, or at least take over the day-to-day management. I know that this project is your baby, but your medical expertise is wasted on administrative tasks that a less qualified person can do. Now that we have a gifted bioinformatician in the village, you should go back to research and find out what makes us immortal."

Bridget let out a long breath. "I've been thinking a lot about that lately, and the truth is that I'm afraid to discover the secret. What will we do with it? Can we share it with humanity? The consequences could be disastrous."

Syssi walked over with a tray loaded with five cappuccino cups. "That won't be that bad if their immortality comes with reduced fertility like it does for us."

Bridget took one of the cups. "It's not something I want to be responsible for." She shuddered. "I would feel like the inventor of the atomic bomb. Was he aware of what he was unleashing upon the world?"

"He was," Turner said. "But his team wasn't the only one developing a nuclear weapon. The Nazis were also developing their own bomb, and so were the Japanese. It was a macabre race with the highest of stakes. The champion got to win the war and protect their own people, but at a terrible cost. In a later interview, the head of the American team of scientists quoted a line from the *Bhagavad Gita*; 'Now I am become Death, the destroyer of worlds.'"

ANNANI

A loaded moment of silence followed Turner's historical reference.

Annani doubted that Turner or Syssi were aware of the clan's part in helping the United States win that race. Bridget knew, and so did Kian, but they chose not to mention it.

It was a sad reality that a technology that could provide clean, inexpensive energy to the world could also be used for such mass destruction. And it was an even sadder reality that sometimes the only choice was to either become the destroyer or be destroyed.

Kian was the one to break the silence. "Let's move to the subject of Jade and what to do about her."

As he read aloud Jade's fable and then added Emmett and Marcel's explanations, Annani's heart went out to the female. How terrible it was for her to be captured and used for breeding by the murderers of her children and her mates.

Annani did not believe that the Kra-ell did not feel love for their mates and their offspring. Their society might be rigid and militant, but they came from the same stock as the gods and the humans, and therefore must feel love.

Hopefully, Turner would convince Kian that it was essential to the clan's security to eliminate the threat Jade's captors posed and rescue her and the other females.

However, Annani was not going to pressure Kian into going to war with those Kra-ell. If he and Turner decided that the risks of an attack outweighed the future risks of not addressing the problem now, she was not going to intervene.

"Can you send me a copy of the fable?" Turner asked. "I would like to read it again and pay attention to the details. Maybe I will discover more clues."

"I'll do it right now." Kian pulled out his phone and searched for the document. "I'll send you a copy as well," he told Bridget.

"I want to take another look at it, too," Annani said. "Maybe I will notice something that no one else did."

"Of course." Kian typed on his phone, and a moment later, Annani's device pinged with an incoming message.

Knowing that it was from him, she did not bother retrieving it from the hidden pocket in her gown.

Turner did not look at his phone either. "If you want my opinion, I can tell you right now that I don't think you should get involved. There is a slight risk of those Kra-ell coming to sniff around Safe Haven, and you should make sure that there is nothing for them to find. The paranormals can stay, but Eleanor and Emmett and all the other immortals should either make themselves scarce or return to the village. Safe Haven managed without them for many months, and it can do it for many more."

"That was my gut instinct as well, but it's not as simple as that. The first ever paranormal retreat is about to begin, and I need Emmett and Eleanor to monitor the incoming talents. You know how robust the security in Safe Haven is. It should be fine."

Turner's expression was smug. "The place is a fortress, and it could easily withstand a Doomer attack, but we don't know what kinds of weapons and tricks the Kra-ell have."

"That's my next point," Kian said. "I want to collect intel on the potential threat these Kra-ell represent. I want to know how many of them there are and what kind of weapons and technology they have."

Turner nodded. "I agree. Start with collecting satellite footage, and we will take it from there."

"What about people on the ground?" Kian asked. "Do you have a local contact you can employ?"

"I do, but only for collecting intel. If you decide to launch a rescue mission, I wouldn't use humans for that. Unless I can assemble an army, which I can't do in Russia, a team of humans doesn't stand a chance against the Kra-ell." He rubbed his chin. "Maybe they do if we equip them with earpieces and your exoskeleton battle suits."

Kian shook his head. "The suits are built with immortals in mind. Humans won't be able to move fast enough in them. They are too heavy."

"That's what I thought," Turner said. "But the earpieces will be necessary for the human recon team as well as for the immortal assault team. My hunch is that the leader of Jade's captors is a powerful compeller. We know that Jade is one, and yet she didn't manage to get free in over two decades. Also, since he's going against Kra-ell tradition and committing what is no doubt considered sacrilege for them, he must have a way to exert his will over them."

"Maybe the leader is a she?" Syssi suggested. "Since they are murdering Kra-ell males and taking the females captive, it makes more sense to us that the leader is a male, but as the saying goes, assumption is the mother of all failures. Kian speculated that Jade's tribe might have been considered rogue. If so, the female in charge of their expedition might have punished them for their act of treason. Males are expendable in their society, so they were executed, but females are rare and precious, so they were taken prisoner."

Turner's pale blue eyes did not reveal any emotion, but in their depths, Annani could see the wheels of his brain spinning.

"It's possible," he said after a long moment of contemplation. "If that's the case, she would not be breaking away from tradition, and she would have her people's loyalty. It would also explain why the humans and their children were allowed to leave unharmed. Females are more merciful. Still, my hunch is that the leader is a male who got tired of the matriarchal world order of the Kra-ell and decided to make a change. A powerful compeller can make his people do whatever he or she pleases." His lips twisted in a grimace. "History is full of such examples, which I don't wish to repeat. You all know what I'm talking about."

"You are assuming that the leader is a he who got tired of the matriarchal rule based on human history," Bridget said. "That's why it makes more sense to you. It doesn't mean that it is so. The Kra-ell have a different tradition, a different belief system, and a different morality."

"Well said." Turner smiled at his mate. "We won't know until we get more information."

Kian let out a breath. "I don't have any Guardians who are compellers, Emmett has no military training, and Kalugal, who is our strongest compeller, hasn't seen combat since WWII. He's also a new father who is obsessed with keeping his son away from exposure to germs. He would not want to go out on a rescue mission."

Annani knew better than to offer herself. Kian would never agree to risk her, and although she had confidence in her ability and was willing to go, even she knew it would not be a smart move.

"I need to talk to him," Bridget said. "The child needs to be exposed to human germs so he can develop immunity. Kalugal can't keep him in a bubble until he's thirteen and ready to transition."

Syssi chuckled. "I think that's what he plans."

Kian took a sip from his cappuccino and put the cup down on the coffee table. "I like having Kalugal staying in the village. It adds another layer of security that I've grown accustomed to, even depended on. So much so that I didn't like it when he left for more than a day until Toven arrived. And before anyone suggests Toven, there is no way the guy would agree to go on a mission, and I wouldn't risk him either. He's too valuable."

"Is that why you relaxed the security?" Syssi asked. "Because we have powerful compellers in the village now? Or is it because you believe Navuh is not really making an effort to find us?"

He arched a brow. "The only thing I allow now that I didn't before is letting more people into the village, and that's definitely because I have powerful compellers to keep them from telling anyone about us. Navuh is a threat that I would be a fool to take lightly, but having Lokan watching his father's moves enables me to sleep better at night."

Turner leaned back against the couch cushions and crossed his legs. "That only works as long as the other side doesn't have an even stronger compeller. If any of these people fall into Navuh's grasp, he can get them to talk. And if Jade's captor is of the same caliber as Navuh, he can get anything he wants out of them, including from immortals. But that's only a problem if either of those compellers captures a head Guardian or a council member. No one else knows how to get into the village."

"You do," Kian smiled at him. "But even if a civilian is caught and questioned, he or she knows enough to point our enemies in the right direction. We can withstand most attacks, including from above, but I don't want us to be in a position where we have to defend ourselves. That being said, I need to balance the two critical components necessary for the clan's survival. One is security, and the other is new blood. The lack of either one would have the same end result, just in different time frames. If we isolate ourselves, we will be safer, but we will eventually die out."

SOFIA

*T*he wait next to Gordi's station was even worse than the meeting with Igor.

There was no extra chair, which meant that Sofia was forced to stand and suffer the covetous looks from the guard. She could've opened the envelope and read the instructions, but maybe Gordi hadn't been informed about her new mission, and she was supposed to keep it a secret?

Igor hadn't compelled her to keep it quiet. Was it an oversight? Or was it just temporary so she could discuss it with her grandfather, and she would have to see Igor again after the briefing?

It was her first mission, so she didn't know what to expect.

Damn. It was also her first trip abroad, outside of Russia and Finland, and she should be excited. Instead of focusing on the negatives and what Igor expected her to do, she should focus on the positives.

She was about to fly on an airplane for the first time, and she was about to visit the great United States. Would she get a budget to buy new clothes?

"I found one of your pins." Gordi held it out to her. "You must have dropped it when you were fixing your hair."

"Thanks." She took it from him and stuck it in her bun.

How come Gordi was always there when she was summoned?

Was he Igor's only guard?

Would he answer her if she asked?

"It's always you when I come here. Doesn't Igor have any other guards?"

He crossed his arms over his chest. "Why do you ask? Do you want to come visit me?"

"I was just curious. I never see anyone else outside Igor's door."

"I'm his daytime guard. When he retires for the night, someone else takes over."

Leaning against the wall, she mirrored Gordi's pose and crossed her arms over her chest. "I don't know why he bothers with guards. The entire compound is under his complete control, and no one from the outside can get to him." She chuckled. "Even a helpless human like me is under compulsion to defend Igor if he's attacked."

Gordi gave her a once-over that had goosebumps rise on her arms, and not the good kind. He gave her the creeps.

"A pretty female like you has other weapons at her disposal."

Sofia rolled her eyes. So, he was in on Igor's plans for her and her mighty vagina.

Males were so stupid. How the hell did they get to be in charge? Brawn was no longer a prerequisite for leadership. In the twenty-first century, brains ruled.

Besides, if what her cousin Helmi had told her was true then the Kra-ell were supposed to be ruled by females.

Helmi had learned that from her hybrid boyfriend, who'd learned it from one of the fables Jade taught the kids. According to the fable, the Kra-ell society was supposed to be ruled by females. They were like a pride of lions, but instead of one male lion and four lionesses, it was the other way around, and a Kra-ell female had a harem of several males. It was such an absurd notion that Sofia would have dismissed it completely if not for the fear in Helmi's eyes when she'd told her what she'd learned.

Her cousin feared for her boyfriend's life and what would be done to him if Igor realized that he had figured it out. Helmi believed that the Kra-ell who knew about the traditional ways were compelled to never mention it. Jade was powerful, so it was possible that she'd somehow managed to circumvent the compulsion with her stories, and only a smart hybrid like Tomos could uncover the hidden message.

It was true that the pureblooded females were as vicious and ruthless as the males, but the males were obviously stronger. Also, many more boys were born to them than girls, but somehow, the number of adult pureblooded males and females was more or less even. She had her suspicions about how that was achieved, but they were too terrible to even think about.

What if they did what the Chinese had done when the one child per family policy had been in effect? They had supposedly killed newborn baby girls because the parents wanted a boy to inherit the family's name and assets. Did the Kra-ell dispose of the boys?

As a door down the hallway opened, and her grandfather stepped out, Sofia pushed away from the wall and dipped her head. "Good evening, sir."

He would have beaten her up if she called him Grandfather.

"Come." He ducked back into his office, leaving the door open for her.

Sofia followed him inside and closed the door behind her.

"Sit down." He pointed to the chair across from his desk.

"Thank you, sir."

"Do you have any questions about your mission?"

"I have many." She lifted the envelope and put it on his desk. "I didn't have a chance to read through it yet, and I don't want to ask questions that are already answered."

He waved a hand in dismissal. "We will meet every day until it's time for you to leave, so you'll have many more opportunities to ask questions. The more prepared you are, the better. Ask away."

Letting out a breath, Sofia allowed her shoulders to slump a little.

Valstar might be gruffer and less polite than Igor, but he was easier to deal with. There was emotion in his dark eyes, and he was less terrifying.

"I asked Igor about my backstory, and he said to stay close to the truth. I'm supposed to be a linguistics student who is interested in exploring her paranormal talent. First of all, what paranormal talent? And secondly, what do I tell people when they ask me where I'm from?"

He regarded her with puzzlement in his eyes. "Your mother told me that you have an eerie ability to tell whether a person is telling the truth when you look at their reflection in a mirror while they talk. That's a good enough paranormal ability to get you into the retreat."

She chuckled. "It's a parlor trick. I entertain my friends with it."

Sometimes the image in the mirror twisted, showing her an expression that the person looking in the mirror didn't wear. But it was probably just in her mind, and even if it wasn't, it didn't tell her whether they were telling the truth or lying. All the mirror revealed was what they were really feeling at the moment.

"It doesn't matter if it's real or bogus as long as you have something you can talk about at the retreat."

Valstar opened one of his desk drawers and pulled out a small box. "You are not there to actually explore your talent. You are there to snoop around and report back home." He opened the box, pulled out a pendant, and let it dangle on its chain from his fingers.

"What is that?"

"It's a communication device. At the retreat, they ask the guests to leave their phones in the office. We need you to be able to communicate with us at all times." He opened the locket and showed her the small picture they had put inside.

It was of her, her father, and one of her aunts.

"This is your family. You are an only child, and your aunt is your mother." He chuckled. "You can explain the familial resemblance by saying that your parents are second cousins."

She took the locket from him. "Or I can say that my mother died when I was little, and I was raised by my aunt. Igor said to stay close to the truth."

Valstar looked at her with appraising eyes. "You don't look like your father or your aunt, so a dead mother could explain that. But on the other hand, you don't want people to remember your story too clearly, so it needs to be as mundane as possible. A dead mother will stick in their memory."

"You are right, sir."

"I'm always right."

12

JADE

"What's wrong with you?" Drova offered Jade a hand up. "Are you feeling okay?"

"I'm not in my best form today." Jade took her daughter's hand and let her pull her up. "I should go hunting."

"Yeah, you should. You look pale."

The concern in her daughter's tone was surprising. Drova was usually too self-centered and full of herself to notice, and even when she did, she didn't care.

"Do you want to come with me?" Jade offered.

Drova arched a brow. "Don't you prefer your trusty sidekick to hunt with? You always say that I'm too slow and cramp your style."

Jade offered her a tight smile. "You bested me today and proved yourself. Maybe you will manage to keep up."

Drova grinned. "Let's go. Just you and me."

Her excitement over a simple thing like going on a hunt with her mother made Jade pause.

Perhaps she'd been too hard on the girl. Maybe if she had pretended to lose before and complimented Drova on her win, the girl would have grown more confident in her ability and would have strived to do better to impress her.

They stopped by the security office, got their badges, and headed out the gate.

"What's been going on with you lately?" Drova asked once they were away from earshot. "Are you going into your fertile cycle?"

"Yeah. That must be it. I hate it."

That wasn't it at all. Jade's nerves had been frayed since she'd sent the email to Veskar three days ago.

So far, Igor hadn't said a thing or indicated in any other way that he was onto her, but that didn't mean much. The guy had the best poker face in the known universe.

Drova nodded. "I get it. I would hate it too."

Would she?

Igor's compulsion prevented Jade, and the other captured females, from telling those who were born in the compound about how they'd gotten there and what happened to the males of their tribes.

There hadn't been any new captures in over a decade, and when the last group of females had arrived, Drova had been too young to question where they had come from.

Had Igor found all the remaining survivors? Or had he just exhausted those he could find?

There had been many more people on the ship, and if they'd survived, they would have had children, and there would have been many more females for him to capture.

She hoped the others weren't dead and that they were just better at hiding than she had been.

"I'm not looking forward to my first fertile cycle," Drova said quietly. "Going into heat is a bitch."

"It's not that bad when you have a choice of partners." That was the most Jade could say on the subject, and even that had been difficult to get out.

"I have a choice." Drova regarded her with puzzlement. "Don't you?"

How little she knew.

"It's considered a great affront to refuse a summons. I wouldn't dare say no to your father."

When things were the way they should be, and females controlled reproduction, refusing an invitation had been considered an insult to the female who'd issued it, but no male had been raped or whipped for refusing.

He just hadn't been invited again.

It was very different in Igor's camp, and especially for her. Igor was worse than most of his lieutenants. He felt entitled to all the females in the compound, including the mothers whose sons he'd slaughtered.

But of course, she couldn't tell Drova any of that.

"I know that you can't stand him," Drova said quietly. "You don't even try to hide it. And I also know that you can't refuse him. Perhaps if you weren't as ferocious, he would choose someone else. He wants the strongest female in the compound, and that's you."

Drova seemed to be more astute than Jade had given her credit for. She was right about that, of course, but she didn't understand Jade's motives. Being the prime female allowed her access to things that the other captured pureblooded and hybrid females didn't get.

The humans in the compound had the most freedom, but Igor made sure they couldn't be used to get information in or out of the compound.

The guy was evil incarnate and just as smart as the humans' devil. He was very precise in phrasing his compulsion. He didn't leave any wiggle room.

"What can I say? I'm a proud female, and I like the position of Prime too much to give it up."

It was a total lie, but that was what she let everyone believe. No one was under the illusion that she enjoyed Igor's company. They all knew that she despised him, but they also knew her to be vain and power-hungry, and that was explanation enough for them as to why she was willing to tolerate him.

No one other than Kagra knew that she was doing it in the service of her fellow captured females, tirelessly looking for a way out and risking her life. It wasn't a selfless quest. Jade wanted revenge, and if she got to avenge her family, she would gladly die for it.

Her daughter smiled smugly. "I'm the daughter of the two most powerful purebloods in the compound. It was only a matter of time before I overpowered you."

Jade clapped Drova on her back. "Only because I was distracted and malnourished. It won't happen again."

"We shall see about that." The girl sprinted ahead.

13

DARLENE

"Five days." Darlene sighed. "And still no change."

Geraldine put her hand on her arm. "Bridget says Eric is doing great, and five days is not that long."

"I know. That's what everyone keeps telling me, but he's unconscious, and I can't just shake it off and think it's fine because his vitals are strong, and his fever has gone down."

The truth was that it was becoming her new routine, and that worried her as well.

Darlene slept on a cot in Eric's room, showered in his bathroom, and ate breakfast, lunch, and dinner at the café, usually accompanied by members of her family or Max.

Shai, Cassandra, and Onegus didn't work on Saturdays, so they'd joined her and Geraldine for breakfast today, and William and Kaia had promised to stop by later.

Those two were a match made in heaven. They loved their work nearly as much as they loved each other and didn't take breaks even on the weekend. Heck, they were so enamored with the secret project they were working on that it was like their honeymoon.

Nevertheless, they made time to keep her company nearly every day.

It wasn't only her family and Max, though.

People stopped by their table and asked about Eric, offering their support and promising to pray for him, which was really nice.

The sense of community in the village was amazing, and even though she was worried and stressed, or maybe because of that, she appreciated it greatly.

How had she lived without it for so many years?

Living with Leo hadn't been a life. They'd traveled, and they'd gone out to nice restaurants, but they had been mostly alone, and given that they hadn't gotten along, it had been miserable.

"Hello." Cassandra waved and smiled, pulling Darlene out of her reverie.

When she turned around to see who her sister was waving at, she saw Mia, Toven, and Mia's grandparents heading their way.

"Good morning." Mia's grandmother smiled. "How is Eric doing?"

"As well as can be expected," Cassandra answered for Darlene. "Come join us."

"We are heading out to Arcadia," Mia's grandfather said. "But we can stay for a few minutes."

Shai and Onegus got up and brought another table and more chairs to make room for everyone.

"Can I get you something to drink?" Onegus asked.

"No, thank you." Mia smiled up at him. "We are meeting Margo and Frankie for brunch."

"When are they moving into the village?" Cassandra asked.

Mia had been talking nonstop about her friends moving to the village and about matching them up with immortals. Darlene had never met them, but she felt as if she already knew them.

"The additional Perfect Match machines are not ready yet," Toven said. "I don't want them to quit their jobs before I can provide them with new ones in the village."

"Are they not ready yet because William is busy with other things?" Geraldine asked.

Darlene shook her head. "Some of the components are delayed. I'm sure you heard about the chip shortage. Those machines need thousands of them."

Geraldine turned to her father. "Can't you do anything about it? Money talks and your compulsion ability talks even louder."

"I wanted to, but William said that it's not a good idea. We don't want to draw attention, and it's better to let things progress at their natural pace. They will get here when they get here. There is no rush."

Geraldine scrunched her nose. "I don't like it. We have two potential Dormants that could make two clan males very happy. Why waste time? When you go back to your home in Arcadia, you should invite some of the eligible bachelors to come over and meet your friends. Maybe they can find their truelove matches even before they get here."

"That's a wonderful idea." Mia's grandmother said. "I had my eyes on a couple of gentlemen. The next time I see them, I'll invite them to dinner in our house to meet Margo and Frankie."

"We should go." Toven rose to his feet. "I don't want us to be late."

"Of course, dear." Mia's grandmother followed him up and so did her husband.

As the four headed toward the pavilion, Darlene smiled and waved, but her mind wandered back to Eric. All that talk about matchmaking and truelove mates made her restless. She should go back and sit by his side, but as she shifted her gaze to the clinic door, she saw William and Kaia walking out.

"Eric is fine." William pulled out a chair for Kaia. "I took a peek while Bridget tested Kaia's healing progress."

"How is it going?" Geraldine asked.

Kaia sighed. "The healing time shortens by a few seconds every day. It's frustrating how slow the progress is."

"I can imagine." Geraldine patted her arm. "Your family must be very far from the source."

"Yeah. That's what Bridget suspects. I'm young, so my transition was easy but slow. Syssi and Andrew are also far from the source, but they are older, so their transition was more difficult and longer than mine, but once they woke up, their healing time was much faster than mine. Bridget is worried that future generations of Dormants will have their immortal genes so diluted that transition will no longer be possible."

14

PARKER

"*What's* taking that girl so long?" Lisa gave the swing a mighty push. "She was supposed to meet us here more than half an hour ago."

Parker swung slowly, patting Scarlett's head on every downswing. "Are you in a hurry to go somewhere?"

Lisa huffed. "I'm not, but I don't like being stood up. My mother told us to be here at ten to meet Cheryl, and we were here right on time."

Parker had seen the girl only once when he'd passed by the café and she was entering the clinic, but other than her long dark hair, he hadn't seen much of her because she'd had her nose glued to her phone.

"Oh boy," Lisa exclaimed. "I take it all back." She jumped off the swing and rushed toward a girl who was pushing a double stroller with two crying babies inside and a little girl with an angry face stomping beside her. "What happened?"

The babies were covered in snot, and their puffy cheeks were streaked with tears, the little girl was glaring daggers at them, and Cheryl was pretty.

She was short and a little chubby, but in a cute way, and she had smart eyes.

"They are stupid." The little girl clutched a doll to her chest. "They want Sylvia, but she isn't theirs." She stuck her chin up and headed toward the swing Lisa had vacated.

Realizing that it was too tall for her to reach, she looked at Parker. "Can you help me get on the swing?"

"Sure." He hopped down and lifted her into the seat. "Do you need me to hold you?"

"No. I'm a big girl. Just give me a push. Not too hard."

"Yes, ma'am."

Cheryl rolled her eyes. "I'm never going to have kids."

"Can I take one of them out of the stroller?" Lisa waited as Cheryl wiped their noses and faces with a bunch of tissues.

"Yeah." Cheryl crumpled the tissues and put them on the shelf under the double stroller. "Let's put them in the sandbox. I brought toys for them to play with."

As soon as Cheryl dumped the plastic buckets and shovels in front of the twins, the babies forgot all about the doll they'd wanted so badly and got busy digging.

"I'm sorry for getting here late." Cheryl sat down on the edge of the sandbox. "I wasn't supposed to babysit today, but my mom looked exhausted, and I saw an opportunity to make a quick buck, so I offered to take the little ones to the playground with me. Usually, they are not that difficult. I don't know why the boys got so upset over the stupid doll. They never wanted to play with it before."

"Maybe something else is bothering them." Parker sat down next to her. "It's all new to them."

"Or they might be coming down with something." Lisa sat on Cheryl's other side. "By the way, I'm Lisa, and I'm still human." She offered Cheryl her hand. "Welcome to the village. I'm so glad to have another human girl here." She smiled at Parker. "No offense, but you are no good at applying nail polish."

She'd never asked him to do that, so how would she know that he was no good at it?

Maybe he was a natural?

"Thanks." Cheryl shook Lisa's hand and then shifted her eyes to Parker. "What about you? Are you still human?"

He puffed out his chest. "I'm immortal."

"Awesome." She smiled tightly. "My mother wanted me to talk to you about your school."

"What do you want to know?" Lisa asked.

Cheryl shrugged. "The usual stuff. Is Instatock popular here?"

So that's why she'd had her nose glued to her phone.

Lisa nodded. "It's the new craze, but Parker and I decided to stay away from it. It's way too addictive."

"For a good reason." Cheryl pulled out her phone. "Most kids might watch the funny videos and take part in the challenges, but did you know that you can make tons of money from it?"

Parker's interest got piqued. "How?"

"Becoming an influencer. Brands will pay you to put up videos wearing their clothes or shoes or applying their makeup. I didn't know that until I started getting offers. I'll show you."

Her videos were very subtle, and if he hadn't known that she'd been paid to promote the product, he wouldn't have noticed anything promotional about the video. Cheryl explained that was what the people paying her wanted. They didn't want it to look like an advertisement.

An hour later, Parker's head was spinning with the possibilities. How come he hadn't known about the money that could be made on Instatock?

"I don't get it," Lisa said. "If you make so much money from the app, why do you need to babysit?"

Cheryl narrowed her eyes at her. "I don't make a lot of money yet. My channel is not big enough. But when I get more followers, I'll get paid more. It's a lot of work, but it's worth it."

"I don't know about that." Parker helped one of the twins retrieve a lost shovel. "It sounds like too much work for too little money to me. How long have you been putting videos on the platform?"

"Almost a year, but I'm still building an audience, and the potential is there. It just takes time."

"When you actually start making money, I will consider giving it a try, but I don't think I can come up with enough things to talk about."

"When I started, I didn't know what to do either, and my first videos sucked, so no one watched them. You learn as you go, and you build a following. It all takes time." Cheryl smiled conspiratorially. "It's a golden opportunity. The app is new, and not many people know how to produce the kind of content that attracts an audience. By the time the big influencers figure it out, I will be way ahead of the crowd."

Parker liked the girl's entrepreneurial spirit. Lisa was great, and she was smart, but it was book smarts. One day she would probably become a doctor like her brother. He was also a good student, but he wanted to be a businessman and make a lot of money, and apparently, he and Cheryl had that in common.

15

SYSSI

*S*yssi hurried after Amanda, trying to catch up to her leggy sister-in-law. Even in four-inch heels and pushing a double stroller Amanda walked faster than her.

"Slow down." Syssi jogged through the ten-foot gap Amanda had created. "Do you need to pee, is that why you're rushing?"

Amanda huffed out a laugh. "That only happened when I was pregnant. I'm just excited about our good news."

"I still think we should let her know that we are coming. What if the house is a mess?"

"So? I don't mind a messy house, and I want to surprise her."

Spoken like a woman who'd had a butler clean after her, her entire life.

"If she looks embarrassed, we stay on the front porch and don't go inside. I'll tell her that we are in a hurry to get home."

"Da-da," Allegra said in a demanding tone.

"We are going to see Daddy in a little bit, sweetheart."

"Da-da." Allegra's tone changed, indicating frustration.

"I don't think she means Kian." Amanda leaned down and smiled at Allegra. "What are you trying to say, sweetie?"

"Da-da. Da-da."

Syssi shook her head. "She wants to talk so badly, and she gets annoyed when we don't understand what she wants to say with her da-das and her ni-nis and all the other sounds she makes."

Allegra's bottom lip quivered, and a moment later, a tear slid down her little cheek, tugging on Syssi's heartstrings.

"Come to Mommy, baby girl." She unbuckled the straps and lifted Allegra from the stroller.

Her daughter heaved a sigh and put her head on her shoulder.

"Maybe she's tired," Amanda suggested.

"She napped in the car on the way to the village, and she was fine until I couldn't decipher her meaning."

On her shoulder, Allegra heaved another dramatic sigh and sniffled.

Syssi had a feeling that her daughter had inherited her auntie's and grandmother's penchant for drama. Given that she also seemed to have Kian's temper and assertiveness, they would have their hands full with her.

As they reached Amanda and Dalhu's former home, Amanda lifted the double stroller over the three steps and walked up to the front door.

"It feels strange to knock on my own door." She looked at Syssi over her shoulder.

"It's no longer your home. It's now Karen and Gilbert's."

Given the cooking smells, Karen was home, but she must have not heard the knock. Amanda knocked again, louder this time.

When the door opened a moment later, Karen looked surprised but not put off by the unexpected visit.

"Hello, ladies. What a nice surprise." She pulled the door open all the way. "Please, come in."

Syssi smiled apologetically. "I wanted to call ahead, but Amanda wanted to surprise you. I hope we are not inconveniencing you."

"Not at all. I've gotten used to visitors dropping by throughout the day. It's actually quite nice." She led them to the living room, where the twins were playing on a mat on the floor. "My only interaction with my neighbors back in the Bay Area was the occasional hello."

"Da-da!" Allegra chirped happily.

Syssi laughed. "This time I have no problem understanding what she wants." She put her down on the mat next to the boys.

Evie was sleeping in the stroller, so Amanda left her there but kept an eye on her.

"Can I get you something to drink?" Karen asked. "I can't offer you cappuccinos, but I can make Turkish coffee."

"That sounds lovely," Syssi said. "But we are not going to stay long. I just wanted to deliver the good news. The university will need a new system administrator in a couple of months. The current sysadmin is pregnant, and she's taking maternity leave in seven weeks. She wants to stay home with her baby for a year and come back to work part-time after that. She was very happy to hear that you are looking for a position and wouldn't mind switching to part-time when she returns. Not that I think she will. I think she will decide to stay home for longer than that."

Karen sat down on one of the armchairs. "That's very serendipitous. Are you sure you didn't use mind tricks to make the current sysadmin take such a long maternity leave?"

Syssi put her hand over her heart. "I would never do that even if I could, but I can't thrall. Amanda can, of course, but she wouldn't do it either. We spoke to

Nikki together. She said that the job is yours, but you still need to come in for an interview and fill out all the necessary paperwork."

"That's not a problem. Thank you for arranging the job for me."

She didn't ask about the pay, but Syssi doubted it mattered. Gilbert was making more than enough to support the family, and Karen didn't need to work if she didn't want to.

"How is Gilbert doing with managing his projects remotely?" Syssi asked.

"It's a learning process, and he will have to go back from time to time until he has all the systems in place." Karen pulled up her almost black hair and twisted it into a bun on top of her head. "The transition can't happen overnight even with Kian's tutoring." She chuckled. "I've never used the word transition so many times in a day. I need to find some synonyms."

"Change, transformation, evolution," Amanda offered. "Progression."

"When is Gilbert going to do it?" Syssi asked.

"He's waiting for Eric to wake up. He's not going to do it until Eric is back on his feet." Karen swallowed. "Gilbert wants to make sure that his brother is there for us in case he doesn't make it."

Gilbert was several years older than Eric, and he was slightly overweight, but he seemed to be in decent shape and didn't have any medical problems. "Gilbert is going to be just fine," Syssi said with conviction in her voice.

"I hope so," Karen said with much less conviction.

"Do you think your boss will give you a letter of recommendation?" Amanda asked, probably just to change the subject.

"I know she will. Surprisingly, she was very accommodating. When I told her that I need to be here for my daughter, and I don't know when I'll be able to go back, she said that she understood. She's also a mother. I told her that I would make an effort to be available to train the new person over the phone and through video calls."

"Excellent." Amanda clapped her hands. "Now she has the motivation to give you a stellar recommendation letter. Not that I think you'll need it for this job, but it's always good to have."

"Certainly. I told a similar story to Cheryl's principal. She wants to finish this year online and join Parker and Lisa at the school next year, but I hope to change her mind about that. The year has just started, and there is no reason for her to be cooped up at home the entire time. She needs the company of other kids her age."

"You should take her to visit the school," Amanda said. "It's a beautiful campus, and she can hitch a ride with Lisa and Parker."

Karen winced. "Is Lisa driving?"

"She is, but you don't need to worry." Amanda pushed to her feet and walked over to Evie, who was starting to wake up. "The car can practically drive itself, and it's very safe. It won't let her get into an accident."

"I heard. Shai ordered cars for us and explained the features. The clan should market and sell them. I think they will make a lot of money."

"Speaking of money," Syssi said. "The pay is probably less than what you were making at your previous job, but the position comes with benefits." She smiled.

"Daycare is included, and your babies will be a five-minute walk away. For a mother, it doesn't get any better than that."

"I agree." Karen smiled at the children playing on the carpet. "That alone is worth the move here." She winked. "The immortality is just an added bonus."

16

SOFIA

"This is for you." Helmi handed Sofia a package wrapped in brown paper. It was soft, so it was probably a shirt or a dress. "You didn't have to get me anything. I will be back in two weeks."

Helmi didn't get to leave the compound, and her ability to purchase clothing and other small luxuries was limited to mail orders that arrived twice a month, together with the other supplies.

A lot could be said about Igor's ruthless hold over his people, but he wasn't stingy, and in some ways, he treated the humans living on his compound better than the purebloods and the hybrids.

They earned wages that corresponded to the jobs they held and how well they performed them, their living quarters were adequate, and once a woman delivered at least one hybrid child or reached the ripe age of thirty-five without conceiving, she was allowed to get married and have human children with one of the human males living in the compound. They were also free to choose a hybrid, but hybrids didn't usually commit to one woman. Tomos was the exception rather than the norm, but there was no future for him and Helmi. To survive among the other hybrids, he had to pretend that he only used her for sex and had no feelings for her.

Hybrids were supposed to emulate the purebloods and be all about honor and duty. To the Kra-ell, feelings were considered a weakness.

Still, Igor knew that duty and honor as well as fear and compulsion were not enough to motivate people to do a good job. He was never going to be loved or admired, but it was much easier to control humans as well as hybrids and purebloods when they had something to lose other than their lives and the lives of their loved ones.

"I got you a nice dress." Helmi smiled sheepishly. "Well, I got it for me, but it's way too small, and returning it is too much hassle."

That made more sense.

Except Sofia didn't wear dresses or skirts. She was too tall and too skinny to look good in them.

"Try it on." Helmi waved a hand at the package. "I want to see how you look in it."

Checking the time, Sofia shook her head. "Igor expects me in fifteen minutes, and it's a ten-minute walk to his office."

Helmi shuddered. "You are so brave. I feel like peeing myself every time I see him. Thankfully, as far as he's concerned, I don't exist, so I just dip my head and wait until he goes away."

Since Helmi didn't leave the compound, she didn't need private meetings with Igor to reinforce her compulsion. The once-a-week speeches he delivered were good enough to keep her and the other humans under control. The purebloods and hybrids were a much smaller group, and they were treated to separate sessions.

Sofia had no idea what went on in those, but she suspected it was more or less the same sermon-like lectures, just more of them.

"I felt like peeing myself as well the first few times." She chuckled. "He still scares me, but I can handle it better now."

She tore open the wrapping paper and unfurled the black dress. "It's beautiful."

The bodice was made from a stretchy fabric and looked slim. The double skirt was wide and long enough to cover her knees, the outer lace layer a little longer than the slip underneath. It also had a narrow patent-leather belt to cinch the waist.

"I'll try it on when I get back."

"Knock on my door when you return. I want to see it on you." Helmi rose to her feet and kissed Sofia's cheek. "Good luck with Igor."

She flinched. "Thanks. I need it."

Sofia hadn't seen Igor since he'd assigned her to the mission last Saturday. During the week, Valstar had trained her on using the communication device discreetly, and he coached her on the cover story they had prepared together.

Igor probably wanted to see her to reinforce his compulsion. He would ensure that she did what she was supposed to and kept her mouth shut about the Kra-ell and the compound and everything that was even remotely connected to it. He was very precise in his wording, ensuring that he didn't leave any loopholes.

After she'd passed both inspection points, Gordi announced her, and a moment later, he let her into Igor's office.

She bowed. "Good evening, sir."

"Please, sit down." He motioned to the chair.

For some reason, his politeness made him even more terrifying. Sofia would have preferred to remain standing and be done with the meeting faster.

"Thank you, sir." She sat on the edge of the chair and put her clammy palms on her leggings.

"Valstar tells me that you are ready," Igor said.

"I hope I am. I'm still not sure what I'm looking for."

"Report to Valstar anything that catches your attention, and he will tell you what to do next." His voice was imbued with compulsion.

"Yes, sir."

He pinned her with his intense, dark eyes. "You will keep the existence of Kraell and anything that pertains to us a secret. You will not tell anyone about us in any form—oral, written, mimed, or implied."

The oily sensation his compulsion always evoked in her slithered over her skin, coating her in a filthy film that felt suffocating.

"Yes, sir."

"You will keep the location of this compound a secret."

Wasn't that part of the previous prohibition?

"Yes, sir."

"You will not tell anyone who you really are, and you will stick to the story Valstar composed for you."

"Yes, sir."

When he was done with his list of compulsive orders, Sofia thought that they were done and started to push to her feet.

"Sit down."

"Yes, sir."

"I want you to be clear on your duties. As long as you report once a day to Valstar, tell him everything you found out, and follow his instructions, I'll consider it a job well done."

"Yes, sir." She closed her hand over the pendant.

His eyes followed her hand. "That pendant stays on you at all times. You don't take it off for any reason other than to shower or to swim in the ocean. If anything happens to it, find a phone and call the emergency number Valstar made you memorize."

"Yes, sir."

His eyes bored into hers. "If you fail to do any of those things, your family and friends will pay. Am I clear?"

She was under such a heavy compulsion to obey his every word that the threat was redundant, but it still filled her with dread and made her gut clench painfully.

"Yes, sir."

17

MARCEL

$\mathcal{K}$ ylie Baldwin poked her head into Marcel's office. "I'm making myself a coffee. Would you like some?"

There wasn't a drop left in his mug, and he would have loved a fresh one, but letting Kylie make it for him would mean her planting her butt in his office and flirting with him, which he preferred to avoid.

"Thank you, but I'm good."

She eyed his empty mug. "I'll put it in the sink." She snatched it off his desk before he had a chance to refuse.

He let out a resigned sigh.

She would be back with the coffee. She'd done that before.

He hated manipulative people, and he was especially wary of manipulative females. It was a mistake to underestimate them just because they were less aggressive and more subtle in their dealings. What they lacked in brawn, they compensated for with brains and an innate ability to make men do stupid things to gain their favor.

He'd been a victim of female manipulation once, but he was a quick study, and it wasn't going to happen again.

The surest way to avoid it was to disengage when a female was showing too much interest in him.

He knew that Kylie's interest wasn't because he was such a charming fellow or a good conversationalist, and he wasn't handsome enough to justify her persistence either. He was good-looking in the same way that most immortals who were not too far removed from the source were, and it was usually sufficient to get hookups but not enough to incite such intense pursuit.

Even if he allowed a woman to remember him after the sex, chances were that she wouldn't want a relationship with a guy who barely talked, rarely smiled, and was more interested in machines than people.

As he'd expected, Kylie returned with two mugs of coffee and put one on his desk. "You're not being a chauvinistic boss if you accept my offer to get you coffee." She sat across from his desk. "It only counts if you expect me to get it for you."

"Thank you." He took the mug. "It didn't occur to me even for a moment that accepting your offer might be misconstrued as chauvinism. I just wasn't in the mood for coffee five minutes ago." He lifted the mug to his lips and took a sip.

"Right." She eyed him from under lowered lashes. "How are William and Kaia doing? Is her mother getting better?"

Despite his opposition, Kaia's mother's health had been the excuse they had ended up telling the crew. Evidently, Kaia and her family were not superstitious. Besides, it was true to some extent.

Kaia's step-uncle was still unconscious, and her stepfather was just waiting for his brother to wake up from the coma to attempt transition himself. Kaia's mother would probably wait for her partner to grow fangs and develop venom to activate her dormant genes, but her life would be in peril at some point.

"Her mother's condition is stable but not improved." That wasn't a lie, either. Karen's health had not changed in any way since her arrival at the village. "Kaia and William will most likely not be back by the time the project is done." He forced half a smile. "You are stuck with old, boring me."

"You're not boring. Compared to William, you are fascinating." She looked at him from under lowered lashes, her lips curving in a suggestive smile.

Marcel stifled a groan. Kylie was getting bolder with her flirtation attempts.

She was pretty and smart, and if Marcel had met her in a bar, he probably would have hooked up with her. But she was too pushy for his taste, and there was something unpleasant about her that he couldn't put his finger on. She wasn't a bad person, but she wasn't kind either. He wasn't attracted to her, and on top of that, she was his employee.

"I assure you that there is nothing fascinating about me. What you see is what you get." He waved a hand over his outfit. "Every single day."

To save time in the mornings, he didn't bother with a variety of clothing. Instead, he had several identical sets of turtlenecks and slacks. It was casual yet elegant and suitable both for work and for club hunting.

Boring but efficient.

Her eyes sparkled. "What I see is a handsome, well-dressed, well-spoken, and well-educated man. You found what looks best on you and stuck with it. There is nothing wrong with that."

Should he be blunt and just tell her to back off?

The contract the bioinformaticians had been hired for would reach its term in several weeks, and he wouldn't have to see Kylie or the other two ever again. The problem was that the project was not nearly finished, and if Kaia and William decided that they wanted to keep the team until they were done deciphering the journals, the contracts would have to be renewed for at least another year.

Smiling tightly, he picked up his mug and took a sip.

It was time for a white lie. "You are a fine woman, Kylie, and if you weren't my employee and I was single, I would have very much liked to get to know you better. Regrettably, it's not in the cards."

Kylie's face fell. "Are you married?"

"I am not, but I am involved with someone."

"Then why isn't she here?"

"What makes you think it's a she?"

He wasn't gay, but Kylie deserved some payback.

"You are not into men, Marcel. Don't insult my intelligence."

Busted.

"How can you tell?"

She rolled her eyes. "I watch you in the dining room. Your eyes follow the pretty ladies, not the pretty lads."

"I'm an aficionado of female beauty. But you are right. My significant other is a lady, and she's currently working on a project abroad."

"That's a shame." She rose to her feet. "If things don't work out between you and your lady, or you get tired of waiting for her to return, you know where to find me." She walked out the door and slammed it behind her.

Marcel let out a breath.

Kylie wasn't stupid, and she'd figured out he'd been lying, but so be it. At least she wouldn't bother him again.

Or so he hoped.

18

SOFIA

*S*ofia boarded the bus with a fake smile on her face, nervous butterflies in her belly, and a new friend.

Roxana, or Roxie as she preferred to be called, had started talking to her as soon as she'd walked into the Safe Haven designated meeting place at the train station, and she hadn't stopped chattering since.

The woman was the perfect companion, exactly the type Valstar had told her to befriend.

Roxie was in her late thirties or early forties, she wasn't too smart or too pretty, but she was bubbly, kind, and funny. Everyone liked her, but people quickly tired of her never-ending prattle and drifted away.

Sofia smiled and nodded and kept close to her. As Valstar had coached her, a talkative person attracted attention at first, but then they became invisible because people wanted to avoid her, and being inside that invisibility bubble with Roxie was great for a wannabe spy.

If only Sofia knew what she was supposed to spy on.

Clutching the pendant, she walked to the back of the bus with Roxie trailing behind her and introducing herself and Sofia to every person they passed.

"That knockout is my new friend Sofia. She's a ballet dancer from Finland, but she didn't get a spot in the Finnish national ballet because she was too tall."

Sofia rolled her eyes but didn't comment. Roxie had asked her if she was a ballet dancer, probably because she was so slim and flat-chested, but Sofia had told her that she'd never been to a ballet class in her life.

Evidently, Roxie thought that she'd been lying and was inventing a whole backstory for her.

Sofia didn't mind.

On the contrary, she was going to encourage Roxie's stories. The more outrageous they were, the more unlikely it was that anyone would dig deeper to find out the truth.

"Can you imagine that?" Roxie stood with her hand on her hip next to two women sitting a couple of rows over. "They are so discriminatory in those ballet troupes. Someone should do something about it. I want to see fat girls and tall girls and every body type in between getting equal time on the stage."

"You are absolutely right," one of the women said. "Who said that all ballerinas need to be skinny and flat like boys? I hate those outdated standards."

"I agree with you completely," the other woman said. "I'm so happy to see Victoria's Secret finally showcasing full-bodied models wearing their lingerie. Those are their real customers, not some starved, stick-insect with legs." She turned to look at Sofia. "No offense, but you would fit right in with those emaciated models."

Right, no offense. Did they think that only overweight people had issues with their body image? Sofia would have loved to have cleavage and hips.

"That's the way I am, and it's not because I'm starving. I can eat cheesecake all day long and not gain any weight."

"Poor baby," the woman said in a mocking tone. "If I even look at a cheesecake, I immediately gain five pounds."

As Roxie and the other women laughed and commiserated, Sofia pulled out the book she'd gotten at the airport and started reading.

When everyone was on board, Roxie sat down next to her. "Lydia and Felicity are so nice. I'll ask if we can be put in adjacent rooms so we can party together." She winked.

What kind of partying did she have in mind?

Sofia had read everything she could find about the Safe Haven resort. They offered spiritual retreats and had only recently added a paranormal one to their portfolio. They promoted free love, but thankfully they left all the power in the females' hands. The males were not allowed to even issue an invitation, but they were allowed to try to impress the ladies.

Hopefully, they wouldn't pester her. If she had to hook up with someone to get information for Igor, she would reluctantly do it, but not for any other reason.

After the bus driver checked everyone's names, verifying that all the guests were accounted for and no one who wasn't supposed to be there had boarded the bus, they were on their way.

As the two guys sitting in the row in front of them started discussing their paranormal talents, Roxie gasped. "I can't believe that I didn't ask you what's your paranormal talent yet." She tilted her head. "Or did I forget, and you told me already?"

"You didn't forget." Roxie had been too busy telling Sofia about her dream interpretations. "My talent is catoptromancy."

Roxie made a face. "What's that?"

"It's also called enoptromancy, and it is divination using a mirror."

Sofia had never heard those terms either. She'd looked them up so she could talk about her so-called talent as if it was a real thing.

"What's divination?" asked the guy sitting across from them. "Is it like fortune-telling?"

"It is, but mine has a twist. I can see a person's true nature when I see their reflection in the mirror. If they are pretending to be nice but are evil, they will look ugly to me. And if they are not very attractive but have a pure soul, they will look beautiful to me."

No one was purely good or bad, not even Igor, so that was a bogus claim, but it was a simple way to explain it.

"Does any mirror work?" Lydia or Felicity asked. Sofia didn't know which name belonged to which lady.

"It has to be either round or oval."

It was another fake claim, but that was the mirror she'd brought with her, and she intended to keep it in her room so no one could ask her to actually demonstrate her ability.

Lydia or Felicity nodded. "When you get settled in and get your mirror unpacked, I want to take a look. Maybe your mirror will show me that I'm an angel." She batted her eyelashes.

"You will just see your own reflection. I'm the only one who might see something else."

19

MARCEL

*M*arcel chose a seat in the back of the dining hall. It wasn't the best spot if he wanted to sneak out before Emmett's performance ended, but it was good for observing the crop harvested for the first paranormal retreat.

Emmett was excited to welcome his guests, and according to Eleanor, he'd been rehearsing his speech in front of the mirror in his full prophet regalia, but with how preoccupied he was with Jade's communication attempt, his performance might not be one of his best.

The guy was bristling with impatience as he waited for Kian to get back to him about a response to Jade's email.

Marcel could understand Emmett's frustration. But unlike Emmett, he believed that Kian would tell him to forget that he'd ever received the email.

If left alone, those militant Kra-ell posed a remote risk to the clan. If provoked, they would pose an immediate threat. Besides, Jade and her people were not the clan's problem.

The dining hall was filling up slowly, and as several people sat at his table, Marcel nodded in greeting and then pretended to read on his phone so they would leave him alone.

He was there as a spectator, not a participant.

"Why are you sitting all the way back here?" Eleanor loomed over him. "Come sit with me at the front."

"I prefer it back here if you don't mind. I'm tall, and people always complain about me blocking their view."

Eleanor put a hand on her hip and struck a pose. "You're not that tall. What are you? Six two? Six three?"

"Six feet and three inches."

Eleanor huffed out a breath. "I'll tell Emmett that you are all the way in the back. He's upset enough as it is, and he doesn't need the added aggravation of thinking that you didn't come." She turned around and strode purposefully to the front of the room.

The two people sitting across the table from him avoided his eyes, probably thinking that he'd been offended by Eleanor's harsh tone.

He wasn't. In fact, he admired how protective she was of her mate. Some found Eleanor abrasive and unpleasant, but he liked her. She was direct, assertive, and devoted to those she cared about. He'd heard that it hadn't always been the case, but he didn't hold her past against her. Fates knew that his own past was far from perfect and that he had changed significantly, perhaps not for the better.

He'd turned disillusioned and mistrustful.

If he ever found his truelove mate, which he probably wouldn't, she would hopefully be an honest, strong woman like Eleanor, but perhaps a little softer around the edges.

The problem was that he was attracted to the exact opposite. Fragile damsels in distress were his Achilles' heel and the type he had to fight the hardest to resist. As his experience had taught him, in most cases it was just an act.

Luckily, Kylie Baldwin hadn't figured out his weakness yet, and she was pretending to be tough and assertive like Kaia, thinking that she could snag her own happily ever after with William's replacement.

He couldn't fault the woman for wanting that, but he could fault her for being obtuse and not giving up when he had done everything he could do to discourage her. Even after the lie he'd told her about his supposed lady friend, Kylie was still making him coffee and giving him suggestive looks.

"Do you know Emmett Haderech?" the woman sitting across from him asked. "I couldn't help overhearing your conversation with the lady, and it sounded like you were friends with him." She sounded like a teenager talking about her celebrity crush.

Marcel nodded. "I know him." He shifted his eyes away from her, indicating that the conversation was over.

He and Emmett were not pals, and Marcel had nothing to do with the paranormal program and shouldn't have been invited to the opening luncheon. But ever since he'd found the coordinates hidden in Jade's fable, Emmett had regarded him as a confidant, and he'd insisted on Marcel watching him deliver his speech to the attendees of the first paranormal retreat.

As a new group entered the dining hall, a willowy young woman caught Marcel's eye. She looked like a ballerina, very slim and seemingly fragile, but her posture and the way she walked indicated otherwise.

There was coiled strength in her, and her gait was fluid, like a dancer's.

Her shoulders were squared, her head held high, and her dark hair was gathered in a neat bun. Not even a wisp escaped the carefully done coif.

She was too tall to be a ballet dancer, but she looked the part.

Perhaps she was a yoga enthusiast, but she lacked the calm that yoga was supposed to provide its practitioners. Even from across the room, Marcel could see that she was tense and uncomfortable, which made his protective instincts flare.

He forcefully doused the flames as soon as they had ignited.

The woman wasn't in any danger at Safe Haven. After the village, it was probably the best guarded civilian complex.

Perhaps she wasn't used to being among so many people, or maybe she wasn't used to talking about her paranormal talent. Some flaunted their abilities, real or imagined, while others tried to hide them, afraid of being ridiculed or called freaks.

As she scanned the room looking for a place to sit, her eyes met his for a brief moment, and her lips parted as if she was surprised.

Marcel tried to smile, but he was too slow. By the time he commanded his lips to curve up, she had shifted her eyes away, and the connection was lost.

Still, even though the entire thing hadn't lasted more than a second, her face remained etched in his memory. The blue eyes, so big and intense, the incredibly smooth olive-toned skin, the pronounced cheekbones, and the lush, red lips.

Was she wearing lipstick? Or was it the natural color of her lips?

For some reason, Marcel felt compelled to find out.

20

SOFIA

*T*he blond man in the back was gorgeous, and shifting her gaze away from him had required effort.

He looked about her age, maybe a year or two older, but his bearing was of someone who was in charge, someone who shouldered a lot of responsibility.

Sofia was willing to bet that he wasn't one of the retreat's attendees. He just didn't look the part of someone with a paranormal talent.

He dressed like an executive, with slacks, not jeans, and a black turtleneck, Steve Jobs style. His hair was perfectly groomed, he wore a severe expression on his handsome face, and he was too good-looking.

What was he doing in the retreat?

Maybe he was a news reporter?

Or maybe a biographer?

Emmett Haderech was a colorful character, and the free-love community he'd built was fascinating. Without a doubt, there was plenty to write about, but when she'd researched Safe Haven, she hadn't found any books about it, and what she'd found on the internet wasn't much either.

Apparently, Emmett Haderech enjoyed being steeped in mystery. It added to his mystical and spiritual guru appeal.

After she and Roxie found a place to sit, she dared to peek at him again. His eyes were still on her, and she quickly looked away, pretending that she was looking for someone or something else.

Roxana elbowed her. "Sofia darling, you are not paying attention." She leaned closer to whisper in her ear. "If you keep looking at the young man in the back of the room, he will expect an invitation. I'm sure that you've read about the free-love philosophy of Safe Haven."

"I've read about it," Sofia whispered back. "But I'm here to explore my paranormal talent. Not to hook up with anyone."

Roxie giggled. "Yeah, I can see that you are so uninterested that you keep gazing at the back wall," she said loudly.

"Please, keep it down," Sofia murmured. "You're embarrassing me."

"Oh, sweetheart." Roxie patted her arm. "You need to loosen up. We are here to have fun." She made a suggestive gesture that didn't leave room for misinterpretation.

As several of the people at their table started chuckling and laughing, Sofia wanted to slide down her chair and hide under the tablecloth, but thankfully, Safe Haven's spiritual leader chose that moment to walk into the dining hall.

All eyes turned to him, and the laughter stopped, replaced by clapping.

Emmett Haderech cut an impressive figure in his flowing white robe, his rich dark beard, and shoulder-length hair. Based on a simple calculation of how many years the resort had been operating under his leadership, he had to be at least in his mid-fifties, but he didn't have a single white hair.

Maybe he was coloring it or wearing a wig?

That made more sense. His hair was way too thick and shiny to belong to a middle-aged human.

"Good afternoon." Emmett Haderech lifted his arms, the sleeves of his white robe flowing down his sides like two sails, or maybe wings. "I'm overjoyed to have so many paranormally talented people attend this first-of-its-kind retreat. Before I begin, I would like to reward you all for being the pioneering group. Since the paranormal program is a perfect complement to our regular personal growth and spiritual offerings, and the benefit of participating in both is astounding, I invite everyone who completes this retreat to enroll in an additional one at a fifty percent discount. Also, everyone who enrolls today will be entered into a lottery for three free spots on our upcoming retreat." He smiled. "From past experience, I can assure you that you will experience such monumental personal growth that you will want to extend your stay at Safe Haven."

He was an excellent salesman, but it was too soon to make a sales pitch. He should have made the offer at the end of the retreat, and not before he even delivered his welcome speech.

Then again, what did she know about sales? Maybe now was the best time, before the actual classes began and people got disappointed.

After the clapping subsided, Emmett Haderech continued. "I would like to welcome you all to explore your paranormal talents and share your experiences with each other. I know that it is not easy to be different in a world of conformity. It's difficult enough to think critically and independently and express your opinions in this harsh and judgmental world, let alone have abilities that others do not understand. Leave that world outside of Safe Haven's walls. You are safe within them."

As clapping and cheers erupted, Emmett Haderech smiled, his very white teeth gleaming against his olive-toned skin and dark beard.

He let the audience clap and cheer, only lifting his arms when the cheers started to taper off.

After a long moment, everyone hushed, and he lowered his arms, "I want you to know that within these walls, you are all precious, you are all appreciated for who you are, and you are free to be the best version of yourselves, whatever that might be. In the first few days, most of you will still carry the weight of that oppressive outside world on your shoulders, and many will fear to open up their minds and hearts, but when you realize that you are safe, that you are loved for who you are, and that you are not judged, you will start to thrive. Hopefully, the seed planted in this safe haven will continue to grow and blossom long after you go home, and if we've done our job right, you will spread the light to those you care about and who care about you." He paused and lifted his arms again. "Welcome to the rest of your lives."

As the clapping resumed with even more enthusiasm than before, Sofia wiped tears from her eyes, and she wasn't the only one. Next to her, Roxie was crying unabashedly, and Lydia was blowing her nose into a napkin.

During the speech, Sofia had felt as if Emmett Haderech had been talking directly to her, but everyone else in the audience had probably felt the same. Except, their oppression was all in their minds, while hers was very real. His words didn't apply to them as directly as they applied to her.

These people didn't know what real oppression was like. They could speak their minds, and the worst that could happen to them was a heated argument with those who didn't agree with them. She lived in a place where dissent was impossible because Igor ruled them with his power of compulsion. Those who had strong minds and could somewhat resist knew that they would be severely punished, and their disobedience would result in pain or even death, not just to them but to their loved ones.

"Oh, my God." Roxie sniffled. "I want to move in here. I never felt like I belonged anywhere before. I was always the odd bird that didn't fit in. It would be so nice to just be me and not worry about what anyone thinks of me. I'm so tired of subduing my spirit to appease others."

"I hear you, sister," the woman sitting next to her said.

Sofia stifled a chuckle.

If that was Roxie subdued, she didn't want to be around the woman when she wasn't.

MARCEL

$\mathcal{M}$arcel hadn't intended to stay for the luncheon, but he couldn't leave without at least learning his mystery lady's name.

He'd watched her during Emmett's speech, which had been surprisingly shorter than he'd expected and quite good. It had been somewhat moving, but not enough to be a tear-jerker, and yet many in the audience were shedding tears, including his mystery woman.

He hadn't seen the tears, but he'd seen her wiping them off with her thumbs.

Perhaps paranormals were more emotional or just more open with their emotions, or maybe Emmett had imbued his voice with a little compulsion to amplify the effect of his words.

Marcel hadn't felt it, but if the compulsion had been subtle enough, he wouldn't have.

As people lined up for the buffet, he rose to his feet and walked over but didn't join the line until his dancer arrived with her friend.

Standing right behind them, he waited for the other woman to stop talking so he could introduce himself, but as she kept going on and on, he was reduced to discreetly sniffing his mystery lady's hair.

It wasn't a scent that he recognized. She didn't wear a commercially made perfume, and it wasn't a soap fragrance he was familiar with either. To him, she smelled like pine trees and sunshine.

Poetic much?

Marcel shook his head. It had been many years since a woman had captured his interest so strongly and even longer since he'd felt poetic.

Finally, the talkative one noticed him and turned around. "Well, hello, handsome fellow. I'm Roxana." She offered him her hand. "And you are?"

"Marcel." He brought her pudgy hand to his lips and feathered them over her skin.

"Oh, my." She fanned herself with her other hand. "Are you French?"

"I'm originally from Scotland." He let go of Roxana's hand and shifted his gaze to the object of his fascination, offering her his. "Hello."

"Nice to meet you." Hesitantly, she put her long-fingered hand in his palm but didn't give him her name.

"I detect a slight accent." He forced a small smile. "Where are you from?"

"Sofia is from Finland," Roxana said. "She's a ballerina."

Finally, he knew her name, and his suspicion as to her occupation had been confirmed.

"Then I guessed correctly. When I first saw you enter the dining hall, I thought that you were a dancer."

"I'm not." Sofia found her voice. "I can dance as well as the next person, but I've never studied ballet or received any other formal dance lessons."

"You didn't?" Roxana tilted her head. "So why did you tell me that you were a ballerina?"

"I didn't. You said I was, and I didn't want to correct you in front of your friends and cause you embarrassment."

Roxana rubbed a hand over her forehead. "Maybe one day you will be a dancer. Sometimes my precognition plays tricks on me, and I confuse the future with the present." She smiled brightly. "I'm a dream interpreter and a seer."

"That's lovely." Marcel was still looking at Sofia.

She smiled. "I'm twenty-seven years old, so it's probably too late for me to pursue a career in ballet."

"If you're not a dancer, then what do you do?" Marcel asked.

"I'm a linguist."

He'd expected her to say that she was a yoga instructor or maybe even a self-defense teacher, but he hadn't expected something as mundane as a linguist.

"Do you teach languages?"

She nodded. "I assist several of my professors with undergrad classes while I keep expanding my repertoire."

So, she was a perpetual student like Sylvia. Some people enjoyed the lifestyle of academia, and if they could afford it, why not. Perhaps Sofia came from a wealthy family who didn't mind supporting her academic endeavors.

As their turn at the buffet arrived, they loaded their plates, and when they were done, Roxana turned to him. "Join us at our table."

He would have preferred for Sofia to extend the invitation, but she seemed remote. If not for the look they had exchanged when she'd entered the dining hall, he would have thought that she was uninterested, but that one unguarded moment gave him hope.

"Is there room for one more?" he asked.

"Of course." Roxana gripped his forearm as if she was afraid he would run off if she didn't hold on to him. "People are mingling. I'm sure some of our companions have moved to other tables."

Sofia still didn't look enthused about him joining them, but she didn't object either.

In contrast, Roxana's exuberant friendliness was endearing, and he was grateful to her for inviting him to join them. She didn't seem to be interested in him for herself, probably assuming that he was too young for her, so she must be doing it for Sofia.

That was sweet.

Some might think her pushy and loud, but Marcel saw the good heart underneath. Not that he was such a good judge of character, but as long as she had nothing to gain from being friendly toward him, he had no reason to suspect her of not being genuine.

As they sat down, he prepared to ask Sofia a thousand questions, but since she looked tense, he switched to Roxana. "Did you know Sofia from before, or did you two meet here?"

"We met at the train station," Roxana said. "Did you arrive at one of the other collection points?"

"I'm not a retreat attendee. I work here."

"Oh, how fascinating." Roxana's eyes sparkled with mischief while Sofia lowered hers to her plate. "I'm so excited to meet a member of the free-love community. I have so many questions about how the community works and the rules of engagement, so to speak." She waggled her brows.

"I'm not a member. I'm here temporarily to work on a project. I'm a computer engineer." He shifted his gaze to Sofia. "Where are you from?"

She paused with her fork midway to her mouth. "Roxie already told you that I'm from Finland."

"Originally. I meant, where are you from in the United States?"

"I don't live here. I live in Helsinki." She hesitated. "I came for the retreat, and then I'm going to tour the country for several months and absorb the language. I'm fluent in English, but there are so many idioms and phrases that I still need to learn. I figured that the best way to do that was to travel and talk to people, so I took a semester off to learn firsthand."

Something was off about that speech.

Sofia didn't seem like the talkative type, and yet she'd just given him a long explanation that had been delivered so fast that it seemed rehearsed.

"Your English is flawless, and you have only a very slight accent. What other languages do you speak?"

"I'm fluent in German, French, Russian, Swedish, Norwegian..." She was much more relaxed when she spoke about the various languages she'd studied and her level of proficiency in each. It also seemed less rehearsed.

Sofia was hiding something, but it was probably as mundane as her visa status. She'd probably entered the United States on an ESTA, which was valid for only ninety days, and she planned on staying longer or maybe even finding a job.

Lunch went by with Roxana monopolizing the conversation, which seemed to suit Sofia just fine, and Marcel wasn't complaining either. He wasn't a great conversationalist, and with Roxana doing all the talking, he could relax and focus on watching Sofia.

When lunch was over, and the retreat attendees were summoned to proceed to their next activity, Sofia gave him a shy smile. "It was nice meeting you."

"The pleasure was all mine. I would like to see you again."

Grinning, Roxana gave him a discreet thumbs up and then turned to join the throng of people leaving the dining hall. She'd deliberately left them alone.

He made a mental note to thank her later.

Clutching her pendant, Sofia gave him a tight smile. "I'm sure we will bump into each other again. Safe Haven is not a big place."

Nice try, but he wasn't as easily deterred. "How about coffee later today after your activities are over?"

"I don't know when that will be, and I still need to unpack. Perhaps we could meet tomorrow?"

"Tomorrow it is. I'll meet you in the dining hall after lunch."

"I might have a class right after."

"Then we will make plans for the evening. I know that you had to surrender your phone when you came here, so I have no way of contacting you." He took her hand. "It's like in the old days when people had no phones. If a gentleman wanted to pursue a lady, he had to show up in person. I think it was better that way." He kissed the back of her hand. "Until we meet again, Sofia." He dipped his head. "Farewell."

22

SOFIA

"Let's try it again." The instructor, a chubby woman called Barbara, held up a pen. "Close your eyes, imagine an object as vividly as you can, including how the light is reflected off it, its smell, if it has any, its shadow, and hold the image in your mind. Partners, do your best to guess what the object is."

"Shoes," Roxie said. "Elegant men's dress shoes."

Sofia shook her head. "Wrong again."

"Damn it." Roxie let out a breath. "I was so sure that you were thinking about Marcel, and he did wear very nice dress shoes. I remember thinking that he could check his hair in their reflection because they were so clean and shiny. That man knows how to dress, and he is meticulous about his appearance, which can be a warning sign. It's never good to get involved with a perfectionist. It's not good to get involved with a schlump either, but someone that's in between is a good choice."

As Roxie kept going on about the qualities of the perfect man, Sofia tuned her out.

It was the last introductory class of the day, and after that, all she had to do was find a secluded spot so she could report what she'd observed so far to Valstar and be done with her duties for the day.

A shower, a comfortable bed, and the Spanish romance she'd gotten at the airport seemed like the perfect ending to a stressful day. And since the novel was meant to help her with Spanish reading comprehension, it wouldn't be a frivolous activity either.

The introductory classes had been interesting, especially Dr. Eleanor Takala's presentation, but it had been difficult to concentrate, with Roxie's constant blabbering and muttering. She never ended a comment with just one sentence. One idea flowed into the next in a never-ending stream of consciousness. But that wasn't the only thing distracting her. Her thoughts kept wandering back to Marcel, his handsome face and his shy smile popping into her mind's eye.

When she finally managed to banish him from her thoughts, Roxie would make a comment about him, and he would once again occupy her mind.

There was something about Marcel that called to her, and it wasn't just his good looks or his smooth, cultured voice. She wasn't a young girl anymore, and she wasn't foolish enough to get infatuated with a guy only because he was handsome, well-dressed, soft-spoken, eloquent, and intelligent.

Oh, well. Those qualities were plenty enough to deserve infatuation, but she wasn't attending the retreat to find a boyfriend.

She was on a mission, and so far, she hadn't observed anything important enough to report unless Igor was interested in learning about paranormal abilities.

Most of the purebloods could compel humans, and some could compel hybrids, but none of them were as powerful as Igor. Maybe he wanted to find out why?

Dr. Takala explained the various paranormal abilities and the scale she used to evaluate their strength. It was a simple one-to-ten scale, with one being intuition and ten being able to read thoughts or affect objects with one's mind, which none of the attendees could do. But she hadn't explained why some people's abilities were stronger than the abilities of others.

It was probably genetic.

That was why Igor tolerated Jade's disdain for him and kept her as his main breeder. He wanted his children to be powerful compellers like him, and none of the other pureblooded females were as strong as her.

Unsurprisingly, Dr. Takala had never heard of mirror divining, and she'd been rightfully skeptical of Sofia's supposed talent, but she hadn't seemed suspicious. Many of the other purported talents seemed just as bogus as Sofia's.

Some people claimed to be able to retrieve memories stored in objects or remote view what was happening in a specific location without ever visiting it before, just from seeing a photograph. There were telepaths, seers, fortune tellers of different kinds, and a host of other paranormal terms that Sofia didn't remember offhand but had written down in her notebook.

She could recite what she'd written to Valstar, but she doubted Igor would find it useful. Most of that stuff could be found on the internet, and Igor didn't need her to attend a retreat thousands of miles away from the compound to learn the terms of various paranormal abilities.

"Earth calling Sofia." Roxie waved a hand in front of her eyes. "The class is over." She put her hands on her hips. "Were you daydreaming about tall, blond, and handsome?"

"I was not." Sofia collected her things and put them in her backpack.

As they followed the string of people leaving the class, Roxie fell in step with her. "Do you want to grab a coffee before dinner?" she asked. "Or are you meeting *Marrrcel...*" she rolled the r's. "Even his name is sexy."

"I'm not meeting him today."

"Oh, yeah?" Mirth danced in Roxie's eyes. "Are you meeting him tomorrow?" She threaded her arm through Sofia's.

"Maybe. He said that he would wait for me outside the dining hall after lunch, but I'm not sure it's a good idea."

Roxie regarded her with incredulous eyes. "Why the hell not?"

"I don't enjoy casual sex, and I don't want to lead him on. The retreat ends in two weeks. It's better not to get involved with anyone while I'm here."

Perhaps it was a mistake to say that. If Valstar commanded her to seduce some guy, she would have to explain to Roxie why she'd changed her mind.

Roxie shrugged. "Suit yourself, but I'm going to partake in the free-love community, and since we share a room, you might have to make yourself scarce for a couple of hours each night." Roxie winked. "So maybe going out with Marcel could fill in the time pleasantly."

Roxie hadn't left her side since they'd met earlier that morning, so she couldn't have met anyone yet. Maybe she'd seen someone she liked?

Was it possible that she was asking to find out whether Sofia was interested in Marcel because she was interested in him herself?

He was way too young for her, but Roxie didn't seem like the type who would be bothered by a thing like that. The woman was unconventional in every way, wearing outrageously colorful clothes and a wild multi-colored hairdo, so there was no reason to think she would follow convention regarding the appropriate age of her lovers.

"Did you see someone you liked?" Sofia asked

"Not yet, but I'm going to during tonight's social."

"What social?"

Roxie rolled her eyes. "Didn't you look at the schedule?"

"I didn't," she admitted. "I planned to go over it later."

"Well, there is some kind of social activity each night." She grinned. "Maybe you can invite Marcel to join. The community members are going to be there."

"He's not a community member. He's here temporarily."

"So? I'm sure he can attend the social."

"Maybe tomorrow." Sofia pulled her arm free. "I'm going to drop my backpack in our room and then go for a run on the beach. I'll meet you in the dining hall for dinner."

Roxie didn't look like she engaged in athletic activities, so hopefully, she wouldn't offer to join her. Sofia needed to find a secluded spot and report to Valstar.

"Isn't it too late for running on the beach?"

"I love running at night. The moon is out, and it's so peaceful."

Roxie shrugged. "Have fun. I'm going to find Lydia and Felicity. See you later, alligator."

Sofia smiled and waved.

Should she tell Valstar about Marcel?

The only thing interesting about him was that he worked at Safe Haven, so if Igor wanted to find out things about the people who lived and worked there, Marcel could be a good source. But then Valstar might tell her to get close to him.

It wouldn't be a hardship.

Marcel wasn't a charmer, but there was a quality about him that Sofia found attractive. He was reserved and refined, like a gentleman in one of the historical romances she liked or a prince from a fairytale. But most importantly, he liked her, and seducing him would be easy.

DARLENE

"Good morning, sunshine." Max walked into Eric's room with two cups of cappuccino and two wrapped pastries.

"Thank you." Darlene took the cup from him and patted the spot next to her on the cot. "Come sit with me and tell me about your mission last night."

They'd gotten into a routine during the two weeks since Eric had lost consciousness. Early each morning, Max showed up with coffee and pastries or sandwiches from the vending machines. They sat on her cot and used the chair as their table. He told her about his missions, and she listened, hoping that Eric was listening too.

Bridget had said that it was important to talk around him, and maybe that was why she pretended not to notice that Max was with her in the room. As long as they stayed out of the waiting area, it seemed to be fine with her.

The thing Darlene loved the most about Max was that he wasn't treating her as the poor woman who was anxiously waiting for her mate to wake up. He was treating her like a fellow soldier who was keeping a vigil over an injured comrade.

His visits cheered her up.

The question was why he was doing that. Was it just out of friendship? Was he doing it for Eric's sake or for hers?

Max glanced at the monitors instead of asking her whether there was any change, which was another thing she appreciated about him. He knew that if there was anything to report, she would tell him without being asked.

"We freed four girls and one boy, and we left two of the scumbags for the police to find. The other two didn't make it." He smiled evilly. "Oops."

"I'm glad." She took the lid off the cappuccino and took a sip. "It would have been even better if all four were an oops."

He shook his head. "We need to leave some behind to feed the authorities a story about a rival trafficking gang. Otherwise, the police will start looking for the missing victims and the vigilantes who are cleaning up the scum for them."

"It's sad and shameful." Darlene unwrapped the Danish. "The authorities don't do anything when they think the victims were taken by other traffickers, but they would have if they thought someone saved them."

Max nodded. "It was easier in the old days when there was a sheriff in town with a deputy or two. Most of the time, he didn't mind getting help from citizens ridding his community of filth."

She eyed him with a frown. "Have you been watching Westerns lately? When have you ever lived in a frontier town? From what I was told, the clan always resided in the city."

"Not back in Scotland. I'm talking about the old, old days. But you are right. They weren't called sheriffs. I just thought that the term would be more familiar to you."

"Oh." She shook her head. "I can't wrap my mind around how old you and the others are."

He grinned. "But we don't look it."

"No, you don't." She gave him an appreciative look. "Can I ask you something?"

"Anything."

"Why are you being so nice to Eric and me? I appreciate it, but it also makes me uncomfortable not knowing what your expectations are."

Eric hadn't had a chance to tell Max about his outrageous threesome idea, so it couldn't be about that.

Max looked away and then sighed. "Eric reminds me of someone I cared a lot about."

Oh, boy. So, Eric had been right, and Max was gay. Had he been in love with a human who resembled Eric? But if that was the case, why had he flirted with her? Had it been for show?

Maybe his macho Guardian friends weren't as tolerant of his sexual preferences? After all, they'd been born and raised in a different era, and they might have retained those awful attitudes toward gay people.

"Who was it? Was he a human?"

He shook his head. "Din is an immortal, and thankfully very much alive."

Perhaps the taboo on mating within the clan didn't apply to same-sex couples? They wouldn't produce a child together, so it made sense that the rules were laxer for them. Still, it had probably been frowned upon.

"Do you want to talk about it?"

"It's not a story I'm proud of. I was a bastard to my best friend. Din was like a brother to me, and I ruined our friendship over a girl." He sighed. "I'm still a bastard, but at least now I'm aware of it and strive to do better. I'm competitive and aggressive, and my empathic ability is almost nonexistent. I often don't realize that I'm being a jerk until it is too late. Like I didn't realize that Din had fallen in love with the girl and was taking it slow because he cared for her. I thought that he was just failing to seduce her, and since I always had to win, I seduced her instead and bragged to him about it."

Darlene grimaced. "Ouch. That's really douchey. I hope he beat you up."

"I wish he had. I would have taken the beating and pretended to lose so we could still be friends. But all he did was give me a look that said he was never going to forgive me and walked away. It happened nearly fifty years ago, and he still doesn't talk to me. It was one of the reasons I answered Bridget's call and moved here. The castle wasn't big enough for the two of us not to bump into each other, and the hatred in his eyes slew me each time anew."

"Did you try to talk to him?"

Max chuckled sadly. "Numerous times. I even asked Sari to intervene. He's never going to forgive me, and I can't really blame him. I deserve his eternal contempt."

Darlene shook her head. "Fifty years is a long time to hold a grudge. He should have gotten over it by now."

"First of all, fifty years is not long for an immortal. Your perspective on time will change once you transition. And secondly, he probably decided that I'm too rotten to deserve his friendship, and he's not wrong."

Putting herself in Din's shoes, she might have thought the same thing. Max had considered the guy his best friend, and yet he'd failed to realize that Din's feelings for the girl had run deeper than usual and that he hadn't thought of her as a hookup. On the other hand, Max had saved Din a lot of heartache down the line. The girl was human, so there had been no future for them anyway, and secondly, if she'd let Max seduce her while she was seeing Din, she hadn't deserved those deep feelings.

"Is she still alive?"

"I didn't keep tabs on her, but I hope she is. She would be in her seventies now."

"I bet she's been married a couple of times. In the long run, you did Din a favor."

"Maybe. But it was still a rotten thing to do, and I'm ashamed of myself."

"You've learned from your mistake, and you're striving to become a better man. You should forgive yourself."

"I thought that I did and that I moved on, but then I met Eric, and he reminded me of the friend I lost."

"Does Din look like Eric?"

"It's not so much the looks that are similar as it is the temperament and the attitude." Max sighed again. "Din and I used to have so much fun together, swapping silly banter and pretending to be more than friends to confuse the girls. Eric exudes a similar vibe. He embraces life and doesn't take himself too seriously. Din used to be like that until I betrayed him. After that, he became bitter." He sighed. "I have a confession to make."

Guessing where he was going with that, Darlene tensed. "You felt the same urge to compete with Eric. That's why you pursued me. And now you are trying to compensate for it."

"It's not as straightforward as that. I liked Eric from the moment I met him, but I didn't think of him as competition because he was human, and I knew that you would have to move on and find an immortal male to induce your transition. I stayed close to you so when you realized that you needed to let him go and choose an immortal, I would be the obvious choice. I offered to induce Eric because I was impatient to find out whether he was going to turn immortal or not."

Suddenly feeling suspicious again, she narrowed her eyes at him. "Did you botch his induction on purpose?"

His brows dipped low. "I'm not that rotten, and even if I were, I'm not stupid. I knew that if I failed to induce him, someone else would step in and give him another shot. I did my best and left the rest to the Fates."

She believed him about that but was still mad as hell. "Did you hang around hoping that Eric wouldn't make it?"

He put his hand over his chest. "Fates forbid. I hung around because I realized that you and Eric were truelove mates, and there was no room for me in your life as a lover or a mate. But I still want to be part of your and Eric's life as a friend."

She was still not convinced that he didn't have ulterior motives. "What about your attraction to me? Did it just disappear?"

He chuckled. "Not at all. I still think you are sexy as sin. But once Eric's fangs come online and he starts pumping you with his venom, the attraction will go away." He lifted his hand to his chest. "Just so there is no confusion, I didn't hang around to try to seduce you. I wasn't going to repeat that mistake and lose your and Eric's friendship. I promise you. I've learned my lesson."

24

SOFIA

*S*ofia must have jogged three miles along the rocky shore before she felt that she was far enough from the resort to stop and initiate the communication with Valstar.

The last person she'd met was so far away by now that even if he were a pure-blooded Kra-ell he couldn't hear her, but she was worried about him nonetheless, checking every couple of minutes if he was following her.

He'd stopped her, asked her a few friendly questions, warned her to not get too far away, and even given her a once-over, but it hadn't been sexual. If it were, she would have been much less worried. There was nothing unusual about a guy talking to a girl he found attractive, but his interest had been more professional in nature and indicated that despite his civilian clothes, he was a guard.

Why would the resort's security wear civilian clothing? Were they working undercover?

After that encounter, Sofia had decided to put even more distance between herself and Safe Haven than she'd originally planned.

A rock formation that stretched from the shore inland looked like a good place to hide. She didn't need much space, and even a crevice would do.

She found one that was shallow, not deep enough to shield her completely, but enough for her to press her back against and blend into the rock. With the dwindling light and her dark coloring, she would be nearly invisible from afar, so even if someone decided to venture as far as she did, she would see them long before they saw her.

Pulling the miniature earpiece out of the locket, she put it in her ear and pressed on the picture side of the pendant to activate the device.

"Sofia." Her grandfather came online right away.

He was also wearing a device like hers. Only his was stored inside a pocket watch. It wasn't necessary for him to hide the communication device, but he'd explained that the spy gear was sold in pairs of either two pendants, two pocket watches, or a pendant and a watch.

It was most likely manufactured in China, like everything else.

"I'm ready to submit my daily report," she said.

"First, tell me, how are you fitting in with the paranormal crowd?"

Since when had Valstar become chatty or cared about how she was doing? Their interactions had never been personal. Preparing for the mission was the most time she'd ever spent with her grandfather, and it had been as impersonal as if they weren't related.

"I followed your instructions and found a talkative friend. She is a great cover for me. As I was afraid, my supposed mirror divining was so unusual that I was the only one the instructors had ever encountered, and it raised a few eyebrows, but there were others with all kinds of strange talents that I'd never heard about, so I didn't stand out. Do you want me to tell you about what the others claimed they could do?"

"Igor is not interested in humans with paranormal abilities."

For a moment there, she'd thought that was why Valstar had asked how she fitted in, but apparently, he was inquiring whether anyone suspected that she was a spy.

"If someone could tell me what Igor is interested in, I would know what to look for. As it is, I'm flying blind."

"Find out more about the organization and the people who run it. I've researched the founder on the internet, but there isn't much about him. See if you can get an audience with him."

Why was Igor interested in Emmett Haderech?

The guy could deliver good speeches, but his theatrics were ridiculous. Was anyone impressed by his white robe and shiny wigs?

"I'll try. I need to settle in first. It will be suspicious if I ask for an audience right away."

Valstar growled. "You have all of two weeks to find out everything there is about those people. Don't waste time. You know what's at stake."

Sofia swallowed.

Valstar would most likely suffer for her incompetence, but that didn't bother her as much as what Igor might do to other members of her family who were not as important.

Should she mention Marcel?

She didn't have anything else to report, and she needed to buy herself and her family time. Marcel knew Emmett Haderech, so maybe he could help her get an audience.

"I might have an in," she said quietly. "One of the guys working here showed interest in me. I thought that getting involved with him would waste precious time, but he might know things about Emmett Haderech and the other people working here. What do you think I should do?"

"Take advantage of him, of course. Pump him for information."

Sofia stifled a groan. "He said that he's here only temporarily and that he's working on some project, but he didn't say what that project was. What if he doesn't know anything? Given what's at stake, I really don't want to waste time."

"It's not going to be a waste," Valstar said. "In fact, that's great news. I'll report to Igor that you've already found a source. That will dispose him more favorably toward you, and he might grant you an extension to complete your mission. Seduce the guy and make him fall for you, so he will invite you to stay with him after the retreat is over. It will give you access to the management and more time to collect information."

Right. She could seduce Marcel easily, but to make him fall in love with her? How was she supposed to do that?

It either happened, or it didn't.

She had very limited experience with men, and neither of her two boyfriends had fallen head-over-heels in love with her.

She wasn't the type to evoke extreme emotions in a guy.

Sofia closed her eyes and let her head drop against the rock behind her. "I'm meeting him tomorrow for coffee. He seems interested, and I'm going to encourage him, but I'm afraid of botching it. I'm not a great seductress."

"You'd better be."

"I know." She let out a breath. "I'll try to contact you tomorrow, but if I'm successful and I end up in his bed, I might not be able to."

"Find the time. Igor wants to hear from you daily."

"Yes, sir."

As Valstar ended the communication on his end, Sofia slid down the monolithic stone and sat on the rocky sand, oblivious to the discomfort. What was a little physical pain when her soul was shriveling from what she was forced to do?

She wasn't a spy. Her heart wasn't in it, and yet she had no choice but to manipulate and deceive an innocent man. The worst part was that she didn't even know to what end.

What was Igor going to do with the information? Attack Safe Haven? He hadn't asked her to find out about its defenses, so it didn't seem like that was his plan.

He was right to suspect Jade's interest in the place, though.

The only reason Sofia could think of for Jade to show interest in Safe Haven and its paranormal program was to find a way to circumvent Igor's compulsion.

Heck, everyone living under Igor's thumb, including her grandfather, would have loved to find a way to do that. But if that was what Igor suspected, he should be interested in the various paranormal abilities, especially anything that had to do with nullifying compulsion. Except, that was not what he wanted her to investigate.

How the hell did he expect her to succeed when he wasn't telling her enough to point her in the right direction?

Sofia wanted to scream her frustration, to cry and sob for the injustice of the predicament he'd put her in, and most of all, the threat to her family and friends.

Love was a liability, she realized.

Maybe that was why the Kra-ell tried to eradicate it from their vocabulary. Honor and duty were their mantras, but deep inside, they were not all that different from humans. They were very good at hiding their softer feelings, but they had them.

Except for Igor.

He was the poster child for what the pureblooded Kra-ell strived to be, but what they didn't realize was that if more of them became like him, their society would be doomed.

25

KIAN

$\mathcal{K}$ ian spread the satellite photos over the conference table. The coordinates in Jade's fable were not accurate enough to pinpoint a specific location, which made the task of finding where she was being held difficult.

Each degree of latitude equaled about sixty-nine miles, and each degree of longitude equaled about fifty-five miles. That meant searching an area of about 3,800 miles. It was nearly as big as Connecticut.

It wasn't as densely populated, but it was still a lot of ground to cover. Karelia was densely wooded, and the few villages that fell within the area he'd delineated were small and situated near a lake. Any of them could be where Jade was being held.

When the knock sounded on the door, he walked over and opened the way for Turner. "Good morning." He offered the guy his hand.

"Good morning." Turner shook it and walked over to the conference table. "I've been looking at these satellite photos all week." He pushed them aside. "I need more time and more money. I thought my Russian subcontractor would have something for me by now, but he says he needs to hire more men and bribe more officials."

The investigation was already costing a small fortune, which Kian wouldn't have minded spending if he thought that it was crucial to find Jade or her captors, but neither he nor Turner thought that it was.

After the initial excitement over the email had subsided, Kian had decided not to evacuate the immortals from Safe Haven. Eleanor had to stay because she was the director of the paranormal program, and she couldn't just get up and leave, and Marcel couldn't leave the team of bioinformaticians to idle while he returned to the village either.

Leon and his team of Guardians had the complex on high alert, but no visitors had arrived during the week following the email.

The attendees of the new paranormal retreat had been carefully screened, with Roni hacking into their medical histories and finding out whether they had been vaccinated and treated for diseases.

If the captors wanted to infiltrate Safe Haven, they would send a hybrid who could pass for a human, but since hybrid Kra-ell didn't get sick and didn't require vaccinations, they wouldn't have a medical record at all. Even Turner doubted that Jade's captors would have thought to fabricate that.

In fact, Kian had made a mental note to include a fake medical record for immortals who needed a human cover, starting with Onegus and the Guardians.

"What did your contractor do so far?"

Turner sat down and crossed his arms. "He covered most of the villages, but he still has a few that he needs to investigate, and then he needs to comb the area. Drones are useless there, and there are many trails aside from the few paved roads. It will take him weeks to cover the entire area. Are you sure that you want to continue spending money on that?"

Kian groaned. "I've already started, so I'd better finish. Tell your contractor that he has until the end of the week. I promised Emmett to give him an answer before Friday."

"About that." Turner uncrossed his arms. "You should tell him to go ahead and notify the winners, including Jade. I hope he used the time to come up with a clever way to hide a message for her inside the Safe Haven's virtual library. Maybe she will respond with more clues and save us the trouble of continuing the search."

"She might not have the exact coordinates." Kian pulled one of the photos closer to him. "Think about it. If you were held captive and no one told you your exact location, you might be able to figure out approximately where you were, but not the precise coordinates. I doubt Jade's captors gave her a cellular phone with location services."

"She must have access to the internet to stumble upon Emmett's promotional videos. By the way, did the Clan Mother or Syssi find more clues in the fable?"

Kian let out a breath. "Nothing concrete. There is a strong emphasis on children and their importance to the lioness, which they interpret as Jade warning us not to bomb the place when we find it. Syssi thinks that Jade wants Emmett to sneak her out by digging out an escape tunnel, but I doubt that part of the fable should be taken literally. My mother thinks that the rabbit's part was significant, and that Jade wants someone to know that she's still alive and trapped."

"That makes sense." Turner rubbed a hand over his jaw. "As far as she knows, Emmett is a solo operator who can't do anything to help her. She also probably assumes that Vrog is alive, but two hybrids don't make an army or even a rescue team. Her goal was to let someone know that she and the other females are still alive."

"To what end?" Kian asked. "She took a great risk by sending that email."

Turner pushed to his feet. "If I were in her situation, I would want someone to know. Besides, she probably suspects that there are more survivors out there and that Emmett might someday find them. The Kra-ell are long-lived, so that day could be a year from now or a hundred. If nothing else, it gives her hope."

26

EMMETT

*W*hen Emmett's phone rang and Kian's number flashed on the screen, his heartbeat accelerated, and his robe suddenly felt too stifling.

"Good morning, Kian," he managed with a nonchalant tone. "How are things back in the village?"

He couldn't care less, but it was important not to sound anxious. Kian was a damn good negotiator, and he would pounce on the opportunity to get Emmett to make even more concessions in exchange for allowing him to communicate with Jade.

Hell, after ten days of waiting for a response, he was more than willing to give Kian anything he might ask for to get the green light to announce her as one of the winners.

"Everything is fine, but regrettably, the same cannot be said about our investigation in Karelia. Turner's guy is barely done with questioning people in the villages, and he will only start combing the wooded areas tomorrow. I told Turner to pull him out if he doesn't find anything by Friday."

Emmett's heart sank. "What am I supposed to do with the contest winners? I need to announce them the latest by Friday."

"Go ahead and announce them. I assume that you came up with a way to hide a message for Jade in Safe Haven's virtual library?"

"I wrote my own fable, and I asked the community members to each write one so mine wouldn't be the only one. So far, I collected twenty-seven of them, and more are coming in."

"Excellent. When you announce the winners, treat Jade exactly like the other two. Put the three names up and send her a template email congratulating her on the win. If you can, try to hint in your fable that we need more precise coordinates. Nearly 4,000 square miles is a lot of ground to cover. When you're done, send it to me. I want to read it and give it to Turner to read as well."

84

"What about the satellite photos?" Emmett asked.

"Useless. Our satellite is not equipped with thermal imaging, and even if it was, I doubt it would have done us any good. Thermal imaging is usually of much lower quality compared to visual wavelengths because of thermal noise being an issue. Drones are better for that, but deploying them in that area would alert Jade's captors. There are no military bases in the area, and no tourists with camera drones. It's hard to believe that places like Karelia still exist."

"Sounds like the perfect place for you to hide your clan in."

Kian chuckled. "No, thank you. I like to be close to civilization. I'm not a farmer."

"What about your sister's people? Isn't the castle located in a remote area?"

"I thought that it was, but compared to Karelia, it's not."

"St. Petersburg is nearby." Emmett swiveled his office chair around.

"The distance from St. Petersburg to the edge of the quadrant is four and a half hours by car. To get to the middle of it would take ten hours. Do you still think it's not a big deal?"

"It doesn't sound that bad. Driving from Los Angeles to San Francisco along the coast takes eight hours."

"Trust me, it is. Especially since it's so wooded. Turner's contractor operates a team of six men. They go in twos and try not to attract too much attention. It's going slow."

"I hope Jade can tell us more." Emmett leaned back in his chair. "When I send the reply email, I will word it the same to all three, but I'll do it in a way that will point her in the right direction."

"Don't be too obvious."

"I won't. I know how to play the game."

"I'm sure you do, but you are also anxious to establish a line of communication with her, and you might not be as cautious as you should be. Let Eleanor and Leon read the email before you send it."

"I'll do that. Can I tell Vrog and Aliyah now?"

"It's your prerogative. Just remember that the more people who know about it, the riskier it becomes for Jade. Tell them just the highlights and use the clan phone. I don't want Vrog rushing to Karelia and playing the hero. He's waited for Jade's return for over two decades. If he has to choose between her and the clan, I'm not sure who he will choose."

"The clan. He might feel loyalty to Jade, but he has a son who is a member of your clan. He will not betray him. Or you."

"I hope you're right."

27

VROG

"Vrog, my man." Anandur clapped him on the back before pulling a chair out and sitting down with his sandwich and his coffee. "When did you come back?"

"Last night. I thought that as a Guardian you would know that."

"Nah." Anandur unwrapped his sandwich. "You are a trusted honorary clan member now. We track you only for your own safety, and since you are not important, I don't follow your comings and goings." He took an enormous bite of the sandwich.

"I don't know whether I should be flattered or offended."

Anandur finished chewing the huge chunk he'd taken and followed it with a sip from his coffee. "How did the trip go?"

"I sold the school, but I agreed to remain available as an advisor for the next twelve months, so I'm not completely done with it."

On the one hand, his continued involvement with the school made the sale easier, but on the other hand, it wasn't a clean break, which could have been better.

"You are a rich man now. What are you going to do with all that money?"

Vrog shrugged. "I don't know. The clan is providing the funds for the school I'm planning to open here, so I don't need to use any of mine. I might invest it in the stock market."

Anandur nodded. "Ask Kian for help. The market is crap right now, but some stocks are still doing well."

"Which ones?"

The Guardian laughed. "No clue. I transfer most of my pay to Shai, and he invests my money in the stocks Kian tells him to get. I don't even know how much I've made. I might have lost money and not know it."

"If you put such trust in Kian and Shai, I might as well do it too and save myself the headache of figuring out what to do with the money."

Taking a look around, Anandur leaned closer and whispered conspiratorially. "You should also ask Kalugal's advice. His dealings might be a little shadier than Kian's, but he makes more money on them."

Vrog lifted his hands. "I'm not a big risk taker. I prefer the safer, aboveboard investments."

"Yeah, I'm with you on that. But I heard people talking about the killing they've made with Kalugal's help, so I thought I would mention it." Anandur turned and looked at Aliyah, who was delivering a tray to the next table over. "Hello, pretty lady. Are you happy to have your man back?"

"I'm very happy." She leaned over Vrog's shoulder and kissed his cheek. "I thought that the five days he was gone would not be a big deal, but it was difficult." She pulled out a chair and sat down. "Next time, I'm going with you."

"I offered." He took her hand and brought their joined hands to his lap. "You said that you couldn't leave Wonder alone in the café."

"I couldn't. With Callie gone and Wendy working only part-time, most of the time, it's just the two of us, and one person can't handle everything. We put an ad on the clan's virtual bulletin board, but so far there have been no takers. Vivian said that she was willing to help out from time to time, but just as a volunteer. She doesn't want to commit."

"That's a shame." Anandur put his paw on Aliyah's shoulder. "But I can't say that I'm sorry. Callie's semi-official opening night is this Saturday. I'm crossing my fingers for her restaurant to succeed. She's an awesome cook, but she doesn't have enough help either."

Leaning back, Aliyah pulled her hand out of Vrog's. "I wish we had more Odus. That would solve everyone's problems."

"Yeah, well." Anandur finished his coffee in one sip. "It is what it is." He pushed to his feet. "I need to get back. Have a great rest of your day, you two."

He turned around and strode toward the pavilion.

"What did I say to sour his mood?" Aliyah asked quietly. "Does he have something against the Odus?"

"Why would he? I think he just needed to get back to work."

"Speaking of work, did Vlad tell you that he quit his job at the bakery?"

Vrog nodded. "His graphic design business has taken off faster than he expected, and he can no longer juggle both jobs."

"I'm happy for him." Aliyah sighed. "He's doing what he loves, while I didn't even figure out what I want to do with the rest of my life yet."

"There is no rush. You are working at the café and taking online classes. Wait until something catches your interest."

She grimaced. "The classes I'm taking are just stopgaps for the holes in my general education, and they are boring. I need something I can get passionate about." She pushed to her feet. "I'd better get back." She leaned and kissed him on the lips. "I have plans for you tonight."

"Oh, yeah?"

"Yeah. We are going hunting."

28

DARLENE

*D*arlene flipped a page, read a few more paragraphs without actually absorbing the story, and closed the book with a groan.

It was a sweet romance, the kind she usually devoured in one go, but lately the overly flowery language and the instant love had been annoying her. Reading about romance while her partner was in a coma felt like a betrayal, but what else was there for her to do?

If she were a Catholic, she could have clutched a rosary and prayed, but she'd been an atheist before joining the clan, and now she was a pagan who believed in multiple gods and the Fates.

Darlene chuckled.

The gods were real, so it was not a question of believing in them or not. Only yesterday, Toven had given Eric one of his blessings, and Annani was scheduled to give him one at the end of the day.

No one knew what the gods were doing when they were alone in Eric's room, and the monitoring camera was always turned off for these visits. For some reason, they were both very secretive about the ritual they were performing.

She imagined them laying their hands on him while their glow intensified, encompassing Eric with their healing energy. Or maybe they were breathing into his mouth. Wasn't there something in the Bible about God's breath of life granting immortality? Or was it something in Egyptian mythology?

Whatever they were doing, it was helping, and she was grateful to them. Eric was stable, he wasn't dying, and that was all that mattered.

It would have been better if he'd woken up already, but she was counting her blessings—literally. He'd gotten eight so far, five from Toven and three from Annani.

Letting out a breath, Darlene put the book down on the cot, pushed to her feet, and walked over to the bed.

Maybe she should read to Eric?

Not the romance, but maybe the one that Max had been reading to him. It was so gruesome that she left the room whenever he was reading it. Men loved those kinds of stories and considered sweet romances beneath them.

Silly gooses.

Real life was difficult enough. Why make themselves even more miserable by reading about torture and murder?

"You know what?" She brushed her fingers over Eric's forehead. "I'm going to read to you my romance novel, and if you think it's silly, you can make fun of it after you wake up."

Darlene turned back, picked up the book from her cot, and returned to his bed.

Before Max had brought her a stepping stool, she'd had to hoist herself up to the bed, but now she could climb easily and prop her feet on the step while sitting.

"Here it goes." Darlene cleared her throat. "As Veronica's legs encircled Marco's hips, he started pounding into her in earnest. Her eyes fluttered closed, but he would have none of that. Look at me, he commanded, and she snapped her eyes open. He kissed her then, his tongue thrusting into her mouth as brutally as his shaft was thrusting below."

She was about to flip the page when she noticed that Eric's lips had curled up slightly, and when she turned around to watch him closer, his eyelids fluttered.

Her heart racing, she put her hand on his cheek. "Eric? Are you awake?"

His lips curved up a little more, and then his beautiful eyes opened, but when he tried to open his mouth, he only managed a weak groan.

"Hold on. I'll get Hildegard. I can't believe the romance novel did it. I should have read it to you every day."

The door opened, and the nurse came in. "I called Bridget. She's on her way." Hildegard walked over to the cabinet, pulled out a paper cup, and filled it with water.

"You can wet his lips, and if he's up to it, he can drink a little."

Darlene's hands shook so badly that the nurse ended up doing it for her, and then Bridget walked in and took over.

"Welcome back, Eric." She raised the back of the bed, so he was reclined, and held up the straw to his lips. "Take very small sips. You were unconscious for two weeks. If you drink too much at once, it will all come back up."

29

MARCEL

$\mathcal{M}$arcel debated whether he should eat at the lodge or at the small dining room in the paranormal enclave he and his team were sharing.

He was eager to see Sofia again, but he'd told her that he would meet her outside the dining hall, not inside.

Why was he making such a big deal out of such a small decision?

He should get her a phone or just ask Eleanor to allow her to use hers. Emmett's excuse for not allowing the retreat attendees to have phones was that it forced them to socialize. If they wanted to spend the night with someone or just meet people, they had to get out of their rooms and find the person they were looking for at the common area of the lodge.

It made sense, but Marcel knew that in the past, Emmett hadn't allowed phones because he'd enjoyed the complete control he'd had over the community members and the retreat attendees.

Now the community members had personal phones, but they had agreed to limit their use so they would keep some of their former way of life, which was all about the community and togetherness.

To Marcel, it sounded like a description of hell. He never could have survived in a place like that and would have blown his brains out.

Those who claimed that hell was a custom-tailored experience were correct. What was a safe haven to some was hell to others and vice versa.

"Aren't you joining us for lunch?" Kylie asked when he passed the dining hall and kept walking.

"Not today. I need to discuss a few things with Emmett."

"I see." She gave him a smile. "Then I'll see you at the lab after lunch." She opened the door to the dining hall and walked inside.

Why had he felt the need to lie to her?

Well, firstly, because he'd told her that he had a girlfriend, so telling her about Sofia would have confirmed her suspicion that he'd lied before. And secondly, deep down, he was a nice guy, and he didn't want to hurt her feelings. But that was a mistake. If things went well with Sofia, Kylie would find out anyway, and her feelings would be doubly hurt when she figured out that he'd lied to her not just once but twice.

In the lodge, he walked into the packed dining hall and scanned it for Sofia. He found her sitting with Roxana and two other ladies and headed toward them.

Her hair was once again gathered in a large bun on top of her head, and he wondered how it looked when it was loose. It had to be very long to create such a large thing.

She wasn't wearing any makeup, not even the lipstick she'd had on the day before. She looked lovely, fresh, and delicate. A natural, effortless beauty. Still, he had enough experience with women to realize that the lack of effort meant that she didn't consider him worthy of it.

She'd known he would come, and she hadn't bothered to make herself pretty for him. But wasn't that ironic?

He didn't like that Kylie was working so hard to tempt him, and now he was upset that Sofia hadn't.

"Good afternoon, ladies. May I join you?"

"Of course," Roxana said. "But we are done." She looked at the two other women. "Aren't we, ladies?"

Their plates were still half full, and they didn't look happy to abandon them.

"Please." Sofia rose to her feet. "Don't leave because Roxie wants to give Marcel and me space. We will move to another table." She gave him a tight smile. "Have you eaten?"

"Not yet." He gave her a discreet once-over.

She wore slim jeans, a white T-shirt, and a pair of flat, black shoes. It was such a simple outfit, and yet she made it look stunning with her poise and her grace. Small earrings adorned her ears, and the same gaudy pendant she'd worn yesterday hung around her neck. He assumed it held sentimental value because it looked like a cheap trinket.

Sofia nodded as if she'd expected that to be his answer. "I'll accompany you to the buffet." She surprised him by threading her arm through his. "The chicken dish I chose was dry. I want to try something else."

As he turned to wave goodbye at Roxie, she winked and gave him the thumbs-up.

Had she convinced Sofia to give him a chance?

Sofia was definitely acting friendlier toward him today than she had the day before.

"How was your first day at the retreat?" he asked, to start a conversation.

"Interesting." She took a fresh plate and put a tiny portion of fish on it. "I'm fascinated by all the paranormal talents."

He loaded his plate with the fish as well, but a much bigger portion of it, and added a scoop of rice and another scoop of grilled vegetables.

Sofia didn't add anything else.

"Is that all you're eating?"

"I'm saving room for coffee and dessert. We were supposed to meet for coffee, right?" She turned to look at him. "I thought that you would wait for me outside the dining hall."

"I couldn't wait," he admitted.

She lowered her eyes, but her lips curved up in a small, shy smile.

Damn, that demure expression made his shaft harden in an instant, and as he sucked in a breath, she looked at him with surprise in her blue eyes. "Are you okay?" she asked.

"Perfect. I saw a vacant table. Let's grab it before someone else takes it."

She laughed. "If you want us to dine alone, you'll have to eliminate six of the eight chairs. Otherwise, we will have company."

30

SOFIA

S ofia was nervous, but so was Marcel, which made it a little easier for her to flirt with him.

Despite his good looks and his sophistication, he was awkward around her, as if he hadn't dated in a while and didn't know what to do.

Maybe he was recently divorced, and she was the first woman he was flirting with in years?

If only that was true, it would make her job so much easier. He wouldn't notice how inexperienced she was.

As she sat down, he put his plate on the table and then started tilting the other six chairs, so their backs were resting against the table.

"If anyone asks, we are saving these seats for our six imaginary friends." He lifted the one remaining chair and brought it closer to hers. "It is a paranormal retreat, right? Imaginary friends or ghosts shouldn't surprise anyone."

She couldn't help the giggle rising up in her throat. "It shouldn't. What're their names?"

He pointed at the first chair. "That's Albert. Next to him is his wife Josephine, and the other four are their children. Susie, Sarah, Stephan, and Sirius."

"Are they ghosts or imaginary friends?"

"They not ghosts because that would make you sad. They are our friends."

He was right. It would have made her sad to think of a family that had died together.

"How did you know that it would make me sad?"

He shrugged. "It would make anyone sad, and especially a sensitive paranormal. I saw the tears you wiped from your eyes after Emmett's speech, and before you feel embarrassed about it, I can tell you that you weren't the only one. The guy has a knack for tugging on people's heartstrings."

How had he seen her tearing up? He'd sat all the way on the other side of the dining hall, which was at least fifty feet away from where she'd been sitting.

He either had very good eyesight, or he had a phone on him and had used the zoom feature on his camera to spy on her.

That would have been an ironic role reversal.

"I'm not embarrassed. Roxie was sobbing openly, and Lydia and Felicity were tearing up as well. We all feel oppressed in some way, even if it's only in our heads."

Her oppression was real, but everyone else listening to Emmett's speech could probably think of how and why they were oppressed as well.

Marcel tilted his head. "We are all prisoners of our own belief systems. We live in a democratic country, and as long as we don't break the law, we can say and do whatever we please. If we don't, it's because of fear. There is fear of ridicule, fear of rejection, fear of not fitting in with the crowd, and so on."

As Marcel cut a piece of his fish, Sofia did the same. "Fear is a powerful motivator or rather an inhibitor. It's a prison for the soul."

For the next few moments, they ate in silence, or rather Marcel ate, and she nibbled. She wasn't hungry, and even if she were, she was too nervous to eat.

Besides, watching Marcel eat was a treat.

He had such perfect table manners. She'd never seen anyone eat with such precision, and especially not any males. Usually, they shoved food into their mouths as if they were afraid someone was going to take it away from them.

When he was done, he patted his lips dry with a napkin and then glanced at her plate. "You haven't eaten your fish."

"I was already full." She pushed the plate away.

"Then I guess it is time for coffee and dessert." Marcel rose to his feet.

"Definitely." She followed him up and took the plate and the silverware.

After dropping the dishes in the wash bin, they headed to the other side of the dining hall, got their coffees and cakes, and returned to their table.

By now, most of the lunch crowd had dispersed, and only a few had stayed behind to sip on coffee or tea and chat with newfound friends.

It was only her second day in the retreat, and she'd already gained three new friends and one potential boyfriend. That was unprecedented for her, and she could only surmise that paranormals were special not just because of their abilities, real or imagined, but they were also nice people who were more open and inclusive than most.

"The coffee is not bad." Marcel put his mug down. "I hear that it's a big improvement over what they used to serve here, which was some sort of imitation coffee that was caffeine-free."

"That sounds nasty. Why would they serve such a thing?"

"The management hired a gourmet chef and tasked her with creating a healthy menu for the guests. You know, the healthy mind in a healthy body philosophy. But people complained about the food and the coffee and tea, and changes were made."

Perhaps that was her opening. "By management, do you mean Emmett Haderech?"

He shook his head. "This place is Emmett's baby, but he made some mistakes and had to take on a partner who was more business savvy. The partner was the one who hired the chef."

"Interesting. Who's the partner? Is it anyone famous?"

"Not at all. In fact, the partner is an organization. Not just one person."

Sofia took a tiny bite of the cake and washed it down with the coffee. "Do they run other resorts like this one?"

"They run hotels and vacation resorts. This is a new type of venture for them."

That didn't sound like anything Igor would be interested in, and she decided to drop that line of questioning. "How well do you know Emmett Haderech?" she asked.

Marcel leaned back in his chair. "Emmett is an acquaintance, not a friend. I know him, but not that well."

31

MARCEL

*M*arcel was starting to get suspicious.

Sofia was asking a lot of questions, and she was anxious. Could she be an undercover reporter?

If she was, her cover story was perfect. As a Finnish citizen on a tourist visa, she was an unknown, and he doubted that Roni could find out much about her. But then, it didn't make much sense for anyone to go to such lengths for a story.

Maybe she was just fascinated with Emmett, as most of the retreat guests were, and she was curious about the enigmatic former cult leader. Not that Emmett had ever called himself that. He claimed to be just a spiritual leader, a shepherd, but even after the changes Kian had made, the community members still worshiped Emmett with blind devotion. At least he couldn't take advantage of them anymore.

Perhaps his past had made Marcel more suspicious and less trusting than most, but he wouldn't feel comfortable with Sofia until he found out more about her and laid his suspicions to rest.

Leaning back, he smiled. "We've been talking about this and that, but you didn't tell me about your paranormal talent yet. Why are you here, Sofia? What do you hope to gain from participating in the retreat?"

She let out a breath. "My talent is very strange. It started as a party trick and grew into more." She seemed embarrassed to tell him about it.

"Come on, you can tell me. I promise not to make light of it."

She eyed him from under lowered lashes. "You are a computer engineer, the most pragmatic of professions. Do you even believe in paranormal abilities?"

"I've seen enough proof to make me a firm believer in paranormal phenomena." Marcel had no paranormal talent, but he was surrounded by people with a variety of them.

"My talent is catoptromancy. It's also called enoptromancy, and it is basically divination using a mirror."

He'd never heard of a talent like that. "Fascinating. What kind of fortunes do you see?"

"I don't see fortunes. I see people's true nature. You're a handsome man, but if you are rotten on the inside, your reflection will show the monster you are on the inside. It also works in reverse. An ugly or deformed person with a pure soul would appear beautiful in my mirror."

The mirror was probably just a focusing tool, and the real ability was inside of her, with or without it.

"What about you?" Marcel leaned closer to Sofia. "What do you see when you look in the mirror?"

She winced. "I just see my reflection. It only works on others."

For some reason, he had a feeling that she wasn't telling him the truth.

"Does your divination require a special kind of mirror, or will any mirror do?"

"It needs to be rounded. A mirror with corners doesn't work."

He crossed his arms over his chest. "That's a shame. I wanted to stop by the lobby and have you look at my reflection in the mirror there, but it's not round."

She chuckled. "I know what I will see. You are the same on the inside as you are on the outside."

If her talent was real, she would be able to tell him things that he kept hidden, but if she thought that she needed the mirror for that, she would block the knowledge even from herself.

Marcel arched a brow. "And what am I like on the outside?"

"You are meticulous about your appearance, but you are not vain, which makes me think that you are a perfectionist. It means that you are never satisfied with what you do, and you always think that you can do better. You have a good heart, but you are afraid of getting hurt, so you keep it protected, and you are very careful about who you call a friend. How did I do so far?"

"Pretty good. You are very astute."

She shrugged. "It's a survival skill."

That was an odd answer. "What did you have to survive?"

She swallowed, suddenly looking even more anxious. Strangely, though, she emitted no emotional scents. Before, he'd thought that the scents of other humans were masking hers, but now that they were sitting alone and there wasn't anyone near them in a twenty-foot radius, he still couldn't scent anything other than pine and sunshine.

"My mother and I don't get along," she said after a long moment of silence. "She's very demanding, and I'm never good enough. I've learned to observe her moods."

"Did she abuse you?"

Marcel's fangs itched, but he forced them to stay dormant. Even if Sofia's mother abused her, she wasn't his enemy, and he would never use his fangs against a woman.

"No, she didn't. She just ignored me. She still does."

"What about your father?"

That brought a smile to her lips. "He's a good man, but he's powerless."

That was another odd thing to say. "Do you mean that he's powerless in the relationship?"

She tilted her head as if she didn't understand his question. "They are not together. Not anymore. He's just not very strong."

"Physically, mentally?" Marcel pressed, needing to get to the bottom of what she'd meant by powerless.

"He's not impaired in any way if that's what you're asking. He just could never stand up to her." Sofia chuckled nervously. "My meaning must have been lost in translation. As good as my English is, I still translate phrases and idioms from Finnish and get it wrong."

She was lying, and he didn't need to smell the lie to detect it.

But why? What was it about her parents that she was trying to hide?

Looking into her eyes, he sent a small thrall into her mind, but under the most recent memories of her interactions with Roxana and with him, he encountered a wall. It was as if her mind was locked up, or rather her memories were.

If Marcel hoped to get Sofia in his bed, he needed to find out whether she could be thralled to forget things, and he'd better do it now before she got to know him better.

"It's okay." He reached for her hand. "Men like to think that they are in charge, that they are strong, but most of us are putty in the hands of a strong woman. Your father is not the only one who ended up with the short end of the stick. I also allowed myself to get manipulated by a woman I cared about."

"Did she betray you?"

He nodded. "It was worse than that. She manipulated me into doing things for her that I shouldn't."

"Like what?"

Even though he was about to thrall it out of her memory, he wouldn't tell her the truth. He couldn't stand to even voice what he had done and why.

Instead, he told her the least of it. "She asked me to buy her a diamond necklace that cost me my entire savings. I could have bought a house with that money, but instead, I spent it on diamonds, and she walked away with them."

"That's terrible. She's a thief."

She'd been worse than a thief, but he pushed the ugly memories from his mind and reached into Sofia's, making her forget about the diamond necklace he'd given his evil paramour all those centuries ago.

32

SOFIA

S ofia couldn't imagine a woman being so manipulative and conniving unless it was revenge for serious wrongdoing on Marcel's part, like a betrayal of some sort.

The Kra-ell didn't believe in exclusivity, so the concept of cheating on one's partner was nonexistent. They practiced something that was very similar to Safe Haven's free-love attitude, but instead of calling it love, they called it survival of the fittest.

Heck, even Igor didn't demand exclusivity from Jade. If someone else could get her pregnant, that was fine with him. Since the male Kra-ell knew right away if their seed had implanted, there was no doubt about paternity.

Humans were different, and if Marcel had had sex with another woman, and his girlfriend or wife had found out, then she was entitled to revenge. The extravagant gift she'd demanded might have been her way of punishing him.

What had she asked for, though?

Why couldn't she remember what it was?

He'd just told her about it, but all she remembered was that it had been a very expensive gift.

Damn. Igor's repeated compulsion sessions must have messed with her brain, and she was starting to lose her short-term memory.

"What's the matter?" Marcel asked. "You seem troubled."

"I'm having issues with my memory. For some reason, I can't remember what you've just told me about that expensive thing that you got for your ex."

"I didn't tell you what it was. I only said that I spent a lot of money on it."

"Oh." She let out a breath. "That's a relief. Still, I should have remembered that you didn't specify what the gift was. I was panicking, thinking that I was starting to lose my memory at twenty-seven. That's too early for dementia."

"I'm sorry." He reached for her hand. "I didn't intend to cause you to panic."

"It's not your fault." She pulled her hand out of his grasp and looked at her wristwatch. "The lunch break is over, and I need to get going."

He rose to his feet. "I should get back as well. My team is waiting for me to open the lab for them."

She wanted to ask what they were working on, but she was out of time.

"Can I see you later in the evening? We can have dinner together and then go for a walk on the beach. Or, if you want, we can hang out in the common area of the lodge. There is some kind of social activity happening every night."

He shook his head. "I'm sorry, but I have plans. Maybe we can meet tomorrow."

It felt like a kick to the gut, and only sheer willpower prevented Sofia from wincing and clutching her middle.

He had plans? With whom?

And tomorrow was just a maybe?

What had she done to turn him off?

It didn't matter. She couldn't allow him to distance himself. She needed him.

"Tomorrow then." Sofia forced a smile. "Lunchtime?"

He nodded. "I'll try to make it."

That sounded like a no, and she felt like crying. Instead, she gave him a small wave and an even smaller smile and turned around.

The moment Sofia was out of the dining hall, she ran into the ladies' bathroom and locked herself in a stall.

Hyperventilating, she put her head between her knees and tried to regain control.

It wasn't about her stupid infatuation with Marcel. She would get over that. It was about losing her only thread and disappointing Igor. If she failed at her mission of collecting information, he would take it out on her family, probably her father and her aunts and cousins, and there was nothing she could do about it.

Perhaps she could lie?

She could make up stories about things that Marcel had supposedly told her. Valstar and Igor had no way of knowing. Not until she returned to the compound and Igor compelled her to tell him the truth. But then she would be there, and she could beg him to punish her and not her family.

Yeah, as if begging would help.

He would make an example out of her to put fear in the hearts of others.

But maybe she could lie and then kill herself so he wouldn't know that she'd lied. She could make it look as if she was murdered, and then her family would be rewarded instead of punished.

Sofia didn't want to die. But she would give her life to save the lives of those she loved.

33

MARCEL

$\mathcal{A}$ s Marcel headed toward the lab, he analyzed his interaction with Sofia and the oddities he'd noticed.

She had a block on her memories, but she hadn't been difficult to thrall. He'd erased the diamond necklace story with ease and precision and hadn't encountered any problems except her distress over forgetting what he'd told her.

So why were her other memories locked up tight?

If she'd been abused as a child, she could have suffered a trauma that had caused her to lock down the painful memories to shield herself from them.

Marcel didn't know much about human psychology, and no abuse took place in Annani's clan, but the Doomers were honed by it, and they were notoriously difficult to get information out of. But that was also because of Navuh's compulsion. Besides, abuse by a parent was much more emotionally damaging than the physical abuse Doomers went through in the training camp. There was no shame involved and no need to hide. All the boys were tormented the same way, even Navuh's own sons.

Perhaps if he pushed harder, he could've broken through Sophia's mental block, but could he justify the invasion?

The little test he'd conducted was allowed as a precaution to ensure that she could be thralled after they had sex. But to subject her to an intrusive thrall just to satisfy his curiosity was wrong, even if it was allowed, and it wasn't.

On the other hand, Safe Haven had become a strategic location for the clan, and anything suspicious happening there should be investigated, even if it was just a gut feeling or a hunch.

He couldn't just do it, though. He needed to call Onegus, explain about Sofia's peculiarities, and ask his permission to thrall her more intrusively.

Except, he didn't feel right about sharing what she'd told him with others. He had a feeling that she didn't give her trust easily and that not many knew about her family situation.

It was a conundrum, but when in doubt, the clan's security always came first.

He also wanted Roni to check her background and see if there were any shady holes in it. Until he sorted all of that out, he preferred not to engage with Sofia.

"It's about time." Corinne huffed when he reached the entrance to the building. "We've been waiting for you for nearly half an hour."

"I'm sorry. I lost track of time." He opened the door and led them inside.

"We don't have phones with us," Kylie said. "We can't even call you to remind you that you left us waiting for you in the heat. This whole thing sucks, and I want to go home. I'm so sick of seeing the same faces every day, eating the same food, and not getting laid. There, I said it. I'm not shy about it." She stomped after him into the lab.

"I'm sorry I kept you waiting," he repeated. "It's not going to happen again."

"Right." Kylie dropped into her chair. "This project is boring."

When he walked into his office, Corinne followed him inside. "When are Kaia and William coming back? They were supposed to be gone for a couple of weeks, but it has been much longer than that. Are they coming back at all?"

"I don't know. It depends on Kaia's mother and her health."

"How is she doing?" Corinne's tone softened.

"She's stable, but she's not out of the woods yet."

He hated to lie, but it was a necessity for immortals. Their survival depended on their ability to hide.

"If you speak with either of them, tell them that I wish Kaia's mother a full recovery."

"I will. I'm sure Kaia will appreciate it."

After Corinne left, he closed the door and called Roni.

"What's up, Marcel? Did you miss me?"

"Not really. Can you do me a favor, though? And by me, I mean the clan. I want you to do a thorough background check on one of the retreat attendees. You should have her on file. Her first name is Sofia, and she's a tourist from Finland. I didn't get her last name."

"I know who you're referring to. Did she do anything suspicious?"

"I befriended her and discovered that she has a block on her long-term memories. I thought it would be prudent to go over her file again and see if you could find more about her."

"No problem, but it might take me a day or two. I'm swamped."

That was regrettable, but he couldn't justify calling a hunch an urgent matter, and he knew that Roni wasn't exaggerating.

"Do it as soon as you can. It's not top priority as far as the clan security goes, but it's important to me."

34

ERIC

*A*fter showering, Eric felt like a new man.

He'd been in a coma for two weeks, and yet he didn't feel as feeble as he should have after such a long time without moving his muscles.

In fact, he felt pretty great, considering he'd woken up only a couple of hours ago.

The worst part had been when Hildegard removed the catheter, but other than that, he felt no pain. Wasn't he supposed to start growing fangs and venom glands?

Everyone had warned him that would be the worst part of the transition, but it seemed like it hadn't started yet.

Darlene had helped him get into the shower, and he'd only needed to lean on her lightly, and seated on a stool, he could have managed the rest on his own, but she'd refused to leave and had insisted on shampooing his hair.

Eric had been tempted to cut himself while shaving to test how quickly the wound would heal, but Darlene had taken the razor from him and shaved him so gently and lovingly that he didn't have the heart to take the disposable shaver from her.

"Look at you," she breathed. "You look ten years younger."

He grinned at her through the mirror. "Youth is in the eyes of the beholder. I still have wrinkles on my forehead and around my eyes."

"They are much less pronounced." She wrapped her arm around his middle and helped him back into the room. "Now I really look like your mother."

"Bullshit." He stopped and turned to her. "You are beautiful." He leaned and kissed her lips.

When he let go, she smiled. "Beauty is in the eyes of the beholder. I look my age, and you don't. Those are the facts."

"Screw the facts." He cupped her cheek. "You don't look a day over thirty-five."

"Right." She laughed. "Sit on the bed before you fall down on your handsome face."

He glanced at the cot that was tucked against the wall. "Did you sleep on that the entire time?"

"Most of it. I usually lay next to you until I was about to fall asleep, and then I moved to the cot."

"Thank you." He put his hand on her shoulder as he lowered himself to the bed. "I know that I couldn't have done it without you."

"I wish I could take credit for helping you through your transition, but that credit goes to Toven and Annani. They took turns giving you their blessings."

He hadn't known that. "I'm grateful."

Darlene nodded. "So am I." She pulled a duffle bag from under the bed and unzipped it. "You can get dressed if you want. I brought you a pair of track pants and a T-shirt."

It seemed like too much effort, and he was tempted to lie down with just the towel wrapped around his hips, but he didn't want Darlene to worry about him running out of steam all of a sudden.

She frowned. "What's the matter?"

"Nothing." He smiled. "I'm just not as strong as I thought I was. Do you mind if I lay down for a little bit?"

"Not at all." She dropped the duffel bag on the floor. "I'll help you." She lifted his legs up to the bed and pulled the sheet over him. "Rest for as long as you need to."

"My gums don't hurt." He patted them with his finger. "I was supposed to start growing fangs."

Suddenly, he was worried that he wasn't transitioning or that his transition was going to be a slow process like Kaia's. But they weren't related by blood, so why would they have similar experiences?

"Can you call Bridget? I want her to perform the test."

Darlene smiled knowingly. "Did you look at your face? I don't think there is any doubt that you are transitioning."

"I don't know. Maybe the long rest did that. Or maybe the gods' blessings had something to do with it."

She shook her head. "Don't be silly. If you weren't transitioning, you wouldn't have been in a coma after Toven bit you."

He couldn't argue with that, but he needed to know for sure. Except, his eyelids felt as if they weighed a ton, and he had to close his eyes. "Maybe I'll rest a little first."

35

VROG

The American Chinese couple who had bought Vrog's school had endless questions that he was more than happy to answer, but he would have preferred it if they made a list and sent them all at once instead of bombarding him with emails about every little thing.

Dr. Wang was more than capable of answering most of them, but for some reason, they preferred directing them to the former owner.

He was reading over his latest answer when his phone rang. Answering it without checking who the caller was, he was surprised to hear Emmett's voice.

"Good afternoon, Emmett. It is so nice to hear from you. How are things going in Safe Haven? I heard that the first paranormal retreat has started. Congratulations."

"Thank you. I have news that will make you very happy. Are you sitting down?"

The first thing that popped into his mind was that Eleanor and Emmett were expecting a child. That would indeed be good news.

Aliyah didn't want to have children yet, and the clan's doctor had given her medication that prevented pregnancies in humans. Vrog wasn't sure it would work on a Kra-ell hybrid, and secretly he hoped that it wouldn't.

"I am sitting down. What's the good news?"

"Jade contacted me."

Vrog felt the blood drain from his face, and dizziness assailed him. "When? How?"

"A little less than two weeks ago and very cleverly. She might have recognized me from the advertisements we ran, or maybe she stumbled upon Safe Haven's website. She sent in a fable for the competition we were running. She wrote it in a way that only I would know it was from her. I'll read it to you."

When Emmett was done reading it, Vrog had no doubt that the author was Jade. He still remembered the fables and stories she'd told him and the other children all those years ago, and the one she'd sent Emmett had been written in the same style.

"How did you know the fable was written by her? Did you hear her telling stories as a child?"

"Back then, she didn't spend time with the children, but she used my name." Emmett sighed. "My father wasn't happy about having a hybrid son, and he called me Veskar. Need I say more?"

Vrog frowned. "I don't understand."

"Maybe you are too young to know what it means, and no one mentioned it to you. Veskar is a small animal on the home planet that is very similar to a rat and is known for its craftiness and survival ability."

"I know what Veskar means. I just don't think it was meant as an insult. Your father must have seen in you the man you would become one day and gave you a fitting name. You are very crafty, and you have not just survived, you have thrived."

"It is nice of you to say so, but my father was not a good male, and his intention was to belittle me. The name he gave me made me the laughingstock of the pure-blooded kids and the hybrids. I was bullied mercilessly."

That was regrettable, but at the moment, Vrog didn't care about Emmett's childhood torment. "Why did you wait so long to tell me?"

"Orders from Kian. He wants to keep it hush-hush, and he's right. Jade took a great risk by sending this email to me, and the fewer people who know about it, the less dangerous it is to her. Unknowingly, though, she also put the clan in danger. If her captors realize that her fable is more than a children's story entered into a competition, they might come to investigate. If it were only me, it wouldn't be so terrible, but there are many immortals at Safe Haven right now."

Worry churned in Vrog's stomach. "Then they should leave."

"It's not that simple, and so far, no one has come to investigate. Leon and his Guardians are on high alert."

"Hopefully, they have a good escape plan. I just don't understand what Jade thought to achieve by sending you this fable. How can we help her if we don't know where she is?"

"She opened a channel of communication. I will announce her as one of the three winners, which will give her access to Safe Haven's virtual library, and I will hide a message for her among a collection of fables written by the community members. I will also instruct her how to encode a message so only I will understand it."

"Do you need help writing it?"

"Thank you for the offer, but I've already figured it out." Emmett chuckled. "As my name suggests, I am crafty. After we hang up, I will send it to you. I'm curious to see whether you'll be able to decipher it."

"I'll gladly help in any way I can." Vrog closed his eyes for a moment. "If she sends you enough clues for us to be able to find her, do you think the clan will help us liberate her and the other females?"

"Frankly, I don't know, but I hope so. The three of us alone can't take on a group that overpowered the females and killed all the males of our tribe who were at the compound at the time."

"Maybe we can. The three of us can't launch an attack, but maybe we can help her and some of the others escape. Jade is pragmatic, and she wouldn't have risked communicating with you if she thought you couldn't help her. She must have a plan."

"Perhaps she does. I'll keep you informed."

"Can I tell Aliyah?"

"Of course. She's your mate. Just tell her not to mention it to anyone. You can also show her my email and see if she can decipher the hidden message. I'll give both of you access to the library so you can look for the clues."

"Sounds exciting. I'm looking forward to the challenge."

36

DARLENE

"Hi," Eric murmured as he turned toward her. "Did I take a nap?"

"You slept for over twelve hours. I was afraid that you had slipped away again."

Darlene had kept a vigil all night, lying next to him and making sure that he hadn't slipped into a coma again. She was exhausted but also elated. Eric was alive, he was transitioning, and he was with her.

He smirked. "If I did, all you'd have to do would be to read me that smutty romance again." He lifted his head. "Where is it?" He glanced at the cot.

"I hid it when your family arrived at the clinic yesterday to congratulate you and witness the test. You couldn't keep your eyes open, so it was postponed to today."

He looked at her with a frown. "Was I awake anytime during their visit?"

"Don't you remember? They came in here, and you told Gilbert that it was his turn now."

"I must have been talking in my sleep."

"Maybe you were." She cupped his cheek. "How are you feeling? Are your gums hurting?"

"No. Maybe I should go back to sleep."

She frowned. "Do you still feel sleepy?"

"I'm fine." He leaned closer and pressed a soft kiss to her lips. "I dreamt that you were reading that steamy romance novel to me."

"So that's what woke you up this morning?" She laughed. "When it brought you out of your coma, I half expected your first reaction to be a hard-on, but I guess your blood flow was still so-so."

"My blood flow is just fine now." He pressed closer to her, his unmistakable length hard against her thigh.

"So it would seem." She reached with her hand and stroked him over the sheet. "Should I lock the door?"

He chuckled. "Right now, it's just bluster, but tonight I intend to compensate you for the two weeks you've had to do without."

With Leo, going for two weeks without sex had been nothing. Sometimes a month had gone by without him touching her, and she hadn't missed it. Darlene had had much more fun with a smutty book and her own fingers than she'd ever had with him. But she hadn't touched herself since Eric had lost consciousness. She had been too anxious to let herself enjoy anything. Besides, it would have felt wrong to pleasure herself while he was fighting for his life.

Now that he was awake, though, and the dark clouds of anxiety had lifted, she couldn't wait to reaffirm life with him.

As molten heat gathered at her core, she wrapped her arms around him and kissed him for all he was worth, which was everything. It took her a few seconds to realize that his arms were not as tight around her as they used to be, and it wasn't because of a lack of passion.

Eric was still recovering, and she shouldn't allow him to exert himself until Bridget gave them the green light.

With a sigh, she let go of his mouth. "I need to use the bathroom." She really needed to pee, but it was also an excuse to stop what they were doing. It was robbing Eric of the little energy he'd managed to regain. "Do you need me to help you get there?"

"You go first."

"Are you sure? I can wait."

"Go."

"Okay." She slid off the bed and ran into the bathroom, barely making it on time.

When she was done, she opened the door to find Eric standing there naked, with his erection at full mast.

"Is that for me? Or do you need to use the bathroom?"

"Let's see what happens after I use it." He winked at her and swaggered inside.

For a moment, she watched his ass as he leaned over the toilet and braced his hand against the wall, but even though she'd helped him use the toilet yesterday, she figured he would prefer to have some privacy and ducked back into the room.

A few minutes later, she heard the shower going and went back inside.

Leaning against the vanity, she watched Eric soap up his muscular body. He hadn't been very hairy before the start of his transition, but she had a feeling that he'd lost some of his body hair when he'd showered yesterday, and as she lowered her eyes to the shower floor, her suspicion was confirmed. Small hairs were floating in the soapy water, and more were falling as Eric washed his legs.

"You are shedding hair." She pointed.

He lifted a hand to his head. "I am?"

"Not from your head. From your body. I guess immortal males have less body hair."

"Huh, interesting." He ran a hand over his chest and then lifted it to look at the hairs sticking to it. "I'll be damned. You're right." He smiled at her. "Do you like the hairless look?"

"I like everything I'm looking at."

37

ERIC

"Who wants to hold the timer?" Bridget asked.

As Eric had expected, Gilbert raised his hand. "I'd be honored."

There was no doubt in anyone's mind that Eric was transitioning, but given that Kaia was still having her healing speed timed every couple of days, the cut test was more than ceremonial.

Making a one-time exception, Bridget allowed his and Darlene's family to gather around his bed, crowding the small room. Toven and Mia stayed outside together with Max and watched through the open door.

"Ready?" Bridget lifted her scalpel.

"I'm scared." He pretended to pout and held on to Darlene's hand.

Gilbert chuckled. "If you are a good boy and let the doctor cut you, I'll get you a lollipop."

"Okay." Eric extended his arm. "I'm ready."

Moving quickly, Bridget grabbed his hand, turned it palm side up, and made the cut.

Gilbert started the stopwatch at the same time.

It didn't even hurt, but a split second later, blood welled over the cut and it started to burn.

Still holding up his hand, Bridget reached for a square of gauze. "I'm going to wipe the blood off so we can watch the wound close."

As the cut was exposed, Eric watched it with bated breath, and it seemed to him that everyone else was holding their breath as well.

The bleeding stopped, which happened faster than it would have taken if he were still human, and then slowly, the skin started knitting itself back together.

When the wound disappeared, Gilbert stopped the timer. "One minute and nine seconds. That's not bad."

"Welcome to immortality, Eric." Bridget grinned. "I never get tired of saying that." She collected her tools. "You have ten minutes to be done with the congratulations, and then I want everyone out. I need to take measurements and blood samples."

Eric wanted to make a joke about losing too much blood already, but Darlene stopped him with a kiss.

He wrapped his arms around her. "I love you."

"I love you too." She smiled and backed away to let others come closer.

"You healed much faster than me," Kaia said as she hugged him lightly. "Congratulations."

Eric waited for Gilbert to approach the bed. "Now it's your turn, big brother. You have no more excuses for waiting."

"I know." Gilbert hugged him tightly. "For now, I'm just glad to have you back. Bridget kept reassuring us that you were doing fine, but you know me. Always the skeptic. I was worried."

Eric clapped him on the back. "Did you forget that my paranormal talent is staying alive? There was no way I wouldn't make it."

"I'm just happy that talent will no longer be tested."

Eric didn't want to correct Gilbert, but even immortals couldn't survive a plane crash, and he was a pilot. He had no doubt that his talent would be tested again, but it was good to know that he was more resilient now.

When everyone was done hugging and congratulating him, he cleared his throat. "Thank you all for praying for my successful transition. I'm sure your prayers, along with Toven and Annani's blessings, saved my life."

Karen wiped tears from her eyes. "When are you going home?"

"After Bridget is done with her testing."

"Do you need help getting there?" Gilbert asked.

"I can do that." Max walked into the room. "I'll get the golf cart. But if you want to take your brother home, it's fine with me. I don't want to butt in where I don't belong."

Eric hoped that Gilbert would accept Max's offer because he needed to talk to him. Darlene had told him about how supportive he had been over the past two weeks and also about his confession.

Evidently, friendship was important to the guy, and it was also important to Eric. Now that his move to the village had become permanent, he needed to start making friends.

Still, he didn't buy the story that Max's actions had been purely in the name of friendship. The guy had had his eye on Darlene, and he might have guessed Eric's intentions. Getting Darlene to like him and gaining her trust would go a long way toward making Eric's threesome plan work.

"You can help Eric." Gilbert clapped Max on the back and turned to Darlene. "Just let me know when you are heading home. I'll bring you dinner." He winked at Darlene.

Knowing his brother, Gilbert was planning some sort of celebration, and as usual he wanted it to be a surprise, but he was as subtle with hints as a bull in a china shop.

When everyone other than Darlene had cleared the room, the doctor returned. "Let's start with measuring you to see if you've grown."

When Eric's eyes drifted down to his groin, Bridget and Darlene laughed.

"Men." Bridget shook her head. "That's the first thing they all check."

"What do women check?" Eric asked.

"Their faces to see if their skin looks better."

Eric lifted a brow. "Not the boobs?"

The doctor smiled. "Some check that as well."

"I knew that. What about my fangs? Why are they not starting to grow yet?"

Frowning, she pulled out a penlight. "Open wide and say ahh."

"Ahh."

She looked down his throat. "Your throat is a little swollen where the venom glands will eventually grow." She flicked the pen closed, put it in her pocket, and pulled out a pair of latex gloves. "You might be just going slow." She motioned for him to open his mouth and patted his gums. "Nothing here yet." She snapped the gloves off and threw them into the disposal container. "When they start growing, you will know, and you will want medication for the pain. It's not pleasant."

He didn't mind the pain. He would have gladly welcomed it to have everything progressing at the proper pace.

DARLENE

*A*s Bridget took Eric's measurements, Darlene read the message that Gilbert had sent her earlier.

Karen and I are organizing a Welcome to Immortality party for Eric at your place, and we need time to put up tables, chairs, and decorations and to prepare food. If you can ask Bridget to keep Eric in the clinic for a few hours, preferably until after five in the afternoon, that would give us enough time to get everything done without a mad rush to the finish line.

She typed up an answer. *I'll talk to her after she's done with Eric and let you know.*

She waited patiently as the doctor measured Eric's weight and checked his eyesight, his hearing, and his muscle strength.

He'd gained only a quarter of an inch in height, had lost nearly twenty pounds, and his eyesight and hearing had improved dramatically.

"So what's next?" Eric asked when the doctor pulled a tablet out of her pocket.

"The blood samples you've been dreading." She noted the last measurement on her tablet. "I'll send Hildegard to take your blood." She turned toward the door.

"I'll look for a lollipop." Darlene hurried after her. "I've seen some in your office."

When Bridget lifted a brow, Darlene put her finger over her lips, winked, and tilted her head in the direction of Bridget's office.

When they got inside, she closed the door behind them. "I'm sorry about that, but with Eric's improved hearing, I didn't know if it was safe to talk in the waiting room. Gilbert and Karen are preparing a party for him at our place, and they need as much time as you can give them. Can you come up with an excuse to keep Eric here until after five?"

Bridget glanced at the clock hanging on the wall. It was ten minutes to twelve. "I don't need to keep him here for five hours." When Darlene steepled her fingers and gave her a pleading look, Bridget relented. "Fine. I can tell him that I need the results from the blood test before I can release him, but since I didn't keep any of the other transitioning Dormants here until I got the results, including Kaia, he might get suspicious."

Darlene lifted a hand. "I'll handle it. You can go home, so he won't be able to ask you anything, and Hildegard will make herself scarce as well. I can tell him that you are concerned about his fangs not starting to grow, and that's why you are waiting for the test results."

Bridget shook her head. "Make some other excuse. I don't want to be in the position of having to lie."

"Please?"

Bridget rolled her eyes. "I was debating whether to put him through an MRI scan to check whether his fangs have started growing, and you've just helped me decide to do it. The technician who operates it works in the city, and she won't be back until after five, so that works out perfectly."

"Why MRI?"

"It provides a better image."

"Gotcha." Darlene gave her the thumbs up.

She waited until Hildegard was done taking blood samples before telling Eric about the MRI.

"First of all, where is my lollipop?"

She'd forgotten about it. "Bridget didn't have any."

Mirth dancing in his eyes, he pulled her into his arms. "I can return for the MRI later. I want to go home and get you in bed."

"You're not allowed strenuous activities. When Bridget tested your muscle strength, you got dizzy from lifting a kettlebell."

"Bummer." He pursed his lips. "Then again, I can think of a few activities that are not strenuous and yet very pleasurable."

"So can I." She pulled out of his arms. "But we can explore those activities after you are done here. It's better to complete the battery of tests and know that you don't have to come back to the clinic for anything other than pain meds."

"True." He sat on the bed. "Perhaps you can read that naughty romance to me."

If that would keep him in the clinic, she would, but after they'd had lunch.

"First order of business is to get you fed. I'll get us lunch from the café, and after we are done, I can read to you."

He lay back and pulled up his legs on the bed. "Can I read it while you are getting us food?"

"Sure." She pulled the book out of her purse and handed it to him. "Have fun."

39

ERIC

$\mathcal{E}$ric's face was stuck in a smile as he read Darlene's romance. He could understand the allure now. No one died, the bad guy was not scary, and there was plenty of humor mixed in with the steam. It was pure enjoyment.

"Can I come in?" Max asked from the doorway.

"Sure." Eric put the book down open on his chest and raised the back of the hospital bed with the remote.

"What are you reading?" Max eyed the cover. "That's not the book I was reading to you."

"You were reading to me?"

"Bridget said that it was good for you. Some people are aware of their environment when they are in a coma, and keeping them engaged helps bring them back." He lifted the chair, brought it closer to the bed, and sat down.

"Thanks for reading to me, but I had no idea that you did that. Darlene didn't tell me."

"You're welcome. Where is she?"

"She went to the café to get us lunch." Eric glanced at the door and then at the camera mounted near the ceiling.

Could Bridget hear what was being said in the room?

Darlene had said that the doctor had gone to her office next door, so only Hildegard was left to look over him, and she was chill. He would have preferred if she didn't hear the conversation he was about to have with Max, but if she did, it wasn't a big deal.

If Max agreed to his proposition to help activate Darlene's dormant genes, they wouldn't be able to keep it a secret anyway. Everyone knew that Eric's fangs and venom glands were not active yet, so he could not activate his mate.

"I need to talk to you," he said quietly. "And I'd appreciate it if you keep what I'm about to ask you confidential."

"Of course." Max put a hand on his chest. "No one will get it out of me. Not even with torture."

Eric smiled. "Dramatic much? If you are ever tortured to reveal my secret, you have my permission to spill the beans."

"Noted."

Eric scooted aside and patted the spot next to him on the bed. "Come closer. I don't want anyone to overhear me."

"There is no one out there." Max pushed to his feet and sat on the bed. "Bridget is gone, and Hildegard told me that she'd be in the back, filling up the supply cabinet, but if you needed her, you could press the button, and she'd come running."

"That's good to know." Eric took a deep breath. "So, you know that my venom glands and fangs won't come online until six months from now."

Max nodded.

"And it might take even longer than that because they didn't start growing yet. Bridget saw some swelling in the area where the glands are supposed to grow, but I can't feel anything, and since my transition started two weeks ago, they should have been well on their way by now."

"They'll come. Everyone experiences transition differently."

"Yeah, you're probably right. The problem is that Darlene doesn't have six or eight months."

"I know. But what can be done about it? She's your truelove mate. She can't choose another male to activate her genes."

Eric swallowed the bile that had risen up his throat at the mere thought of what he was about to suggest. He couldn't allow his possessiveness to stop him, though. Darlene's very life was on the line.

"I love Darlene, and I want to spend the rest of my very long life with her, but to do that, she needs to transition, and she's not getting any younger. It's extremely difficult for me to suggest what I'm about to, but I have to do it for Darlene." He swallowed again. "Have you ever taken part in a threesome?"

As understanding dawned, Max's eyes widened. "Was that what you wanted to ask me? If I was willing to be the salami in your sandwich?"

Eric winced. "Technically, Darlene will be the salami, but yes. I can't think of anyone else I can tolerate touching her."

Max shook his head. "If you can tolerate the thought of me touching her, you are not her truelove mate. Fated mates are incapable of sharing their partners."

That was a surprise. Eric had been sure that Max had been hanging around Darlene because he'd guessed Eric's intentions. He'd told Darlene the sappy story about the best friend whose girl he'd seduced, and it might have even been true, but that was not why he'd been bringing her coffee and pastries each morning. Men were not that altruistic when it came to the women they desired.

It was also a huge relief.

If Max refused to do the deed, the threesome was not going to happen because Eric hadn't been lying when he'd said that there was no one else he could tolerate the thought of touching his mate.

Letting out a breath, he draped an arm over his eyes. "I'm such a jerk. I shouldn't feel so relieved. Darlene can't wait six months, and I need to beat my inner caveman into submission. Her life is more important than anything else."

Max rubbed a hand over the back of his neck. "Maybe we can do it in a way that I won't need to touch Darlene or even see her nude."

"How?"

"All I need to do is bite her, right? You can make love to her while I'm jerking off in the next room over, and when you are about to climax, I rush in, bite her, and leave as soon as I pump her with enough of my venom."

"Will that work? Don't the sperm and the venom have to come from the same male?"

Max shrugged. "That's a question for Bridget, but I doubt she would know the answer. I don't think anyone has ever attempted anything like that."

"There is a first time for everything," Eric murmured. "I need to run it by her. I mean Bridget. Darlene too."

Max shook his head. "First, let me explain how we will have to go about it. You will have to be shackled to the bed, or you'll attack me as soon as I enter the room. Darlene will have to ride you."

"Why would I attack you when I asked you to do that?"

Max smiled indulgently. "Your immortal hormones are not fully online yet. Wait a few days for them to kick in, and you'll know what I mean. You will become possessive and aggressive, and in the beginning, you won't be able to tamp down your urges. You will want to tear apart any male who even looks the wrong way at your mate."

"If that's so, time is of the essence. We need to do it before my immortal hormones kick in."

Max shook his head. "I won't do it unless you are shackled to the bed. I don't want to fight you. I'm a Guardian. It would look bad for me if I injure a civilian."

"Then shackled I shall be. I'll ask Bridget what she thinks when she comes in."

"Talk with Darlene first. There is no point in involving Bridget unless you get Darlene's consent."

"Good idea."

He'd already talked it over with Darlene, but that had been before he'd spent two weeks in a coma. She might have changed her mind.

40

DARLENE

*W*hen Darlene returned from the café, Max was there, looking as if he'd gotten some disturbing news. She didn't want to ask and spoil the elated mood she was in.

It was probably Guardian business, and she needed to take care of Eric, who looked so exhausted that she offered to feed him the soup she'd gotten him.

"I can manage." He took the spoon from her. "You can have my sandwich." He handed it to Max.

"Thanks, buddy. I'll eat it on the way. I'm needed at the office."

Darlene cast him a smile. "Are you still taking Eric home when he's done with the MRI?"

"Yeah. Call me when he's ready to go."

"Thanks." She turned to Eric.

The poor guy had fallen asleep while still sitting and holding the spoon.

Sighing, she took the spoon from his hand, wiped his mouth with a napkin, and lowered the bed so he could sleep comfortably.

The funny thing was that she shouldn't have bothered Bridget with an excuse to keep Eric in the clinic. He'd supplied the excuse himself by falling asleep.

Nevertheless, she was glad that he was getting the fangs situation checked. It worried him, and hopefully the MRI would show that they'd started to grow.

A little after five, a knock sounded on the door and Hildegard rolled a wheel-chair into Eric's room. "The MRI operator is here." She winked at Darlene. "Let's go, big boy." She patted the seat.

"I can walk," Eric murmured as he got off the bed and pushed his feet into a pair of flip-flops.

"I know you can, but this is the procedure. I don't want you swaying on your feet and bumping your head into something."

"You don't have to deal with lawsuits here," he grumbled as he sat down in the chair. "So, you don't have to follow silly hospital procedures."

"They are not silly." Hildegard motioned for him to lift his feet and put them on the footrests.

"Can I come?" Darlene asked.

"No, sweetheart." Hildegard winked again. "You'll have to wait here. It will only take a few minutes."

"Okay." Darlene leaned and kissed Eric's cheek. "I'll let Max know that you are ready to go. Do you want him to bring the golf cart, or do you want to take a ride in the wheelchair?"

"The wheelchair. I need fresh air."

"No problem. I'll let him know."

She was surprised that Eric didn't insist on walking home. It meant that despite his bluster, he still felt weak as a kitten.

When the door closed behind the nurse, Darlene whipped out her phone and dialed Karen. "Our ETA is about half an hour. Is everything ready?"

"We are almost done. We will be ready by the time you arrive."

"Don't hide and jump out from behind furniture. I know that he's supposed to be immortal now, but he's still very weak, and I don't want him getting a fright. He fell asleep after eating one small cup of soup."

"Don't worry," Karen said. "He'll be back on his feet in no time. Eric was resilient as a human, and he's an immortal now."

"I know, but I still don't want him to get scared."

Karen chuckled. "We can't hide even if we wanted to. Idina is waiting for Eric on the front porch with a bunch of balloons in her hand that say congratulations and you are number one. She refuses to come in until her favorite uncle arrives."

"Does she have any other uncles?"

"Nope. That's why Eric is her favorite."

Darlene smiled. "Now she has many honorary uncles. Eric will have to work hard to keep his favorite status."

"I'm not worried," Karen said. "He has a way with kids."

Darlene had a feeling that Karen wanted to add something about her and Eric having children in the future, but it was premature. Unless she transitioned and her biological clock was reversed, children were not an option.

"I'll let you go back to the preparations. I'll see you in a bit."

After ending the call, Darlene made another one to Max. "Eric will be ready to head out in about fifteen minutes. Can you come? You don't have to. I can push him myself."

"I'll be there. We are just finishing a briefing. Onegus is heading out to the surprise party."

"Awesome. Remember not to say anything to Eric."

"I won't."

When ten minutes later the door opened, and Hildegard pushed the wheelchair through, the smile on Eric's face was enough for Darlene to guess the results. "Did the MRI show your fangs?"

He nodded. "They are tiny, but they are there. I just need to wait patiently for them to push my canines out." He took her hand and pulled her onto his lap. "Where is Max? He said that he was going to wheel me home."

"He's on his way." Darlene pushed out of his hold. "I need to collect our things." She turned to Hildegard. "Should I take the bedding down?"

The nurse waved her hand. "That's my job, sweetie, but thanks for offering. I think you are the first one who's done that. All the others just assume that the cleaning happens by magic."

"I know that you don't have anyone to help you do the cleaning here." She pulled the nurse into a quick hug. "Thank you for taking care of Eric."

"It was my pleasure. I'll see you guys later." Her eyes widened when she realized her slip-up. "I mean, I'll see you when you come back for the pain meds."

Bridget was probably already at their house, and Hildegard would follow a few minutes behind them. The party was supposed to be just for the family, but how could they celebrate Eric's successful transition without inviting the people who'd taken care of him?

41

ERIC

$\mathcal{E}$ ric hadn't missed Hildegard's winks and Darlene's excitement, which he guessed had to do with the surprise his brother was planning for him.

In fact, he could feel Darlene's emotions in a way that he couldn't before or rather smell them.

The scent was lovely.

There was a purity to Darlene that he'd sensed before, but he'd thought that he was seeing her through the rose-tinted lenses of a man in love. She had a core of goodness inside her that had been stifled for far too long and was just now beginning to blossom.

Was it because of him?

He wanted to believe that it was. She was loved by him and by her family, and she was safe, and in that cocoon, she was finally free to be herself.

"I see balloons," he said as Max turned the wheelchair around the corner. "Is it someone's birthday?" He pretended not to know that they were for him.

Only the tops were visible above the shrubs blocking his view, but there was a big bunch of them swaying in the breeze.

"Yeah, it is." Darlene put a hand on his shoulder. "Yours. Yesterday, you were reborn, and today, we are celebrating."

Max made another turn, and as their house was in full view, he saw who was holding the balloons, and a grin stretched his face.

"Uncle Eric!" Idina jumped up and down. "You're back."

"I am." He motioned for Max to stop pushing the wheelchair and got up. "I can walk from here."

He rushed toward his niece and lifted her into his arms. "I missed you, munchkin." He kissed her soft cheeks, two kisses on each side. "Are these balloons for me?"

"Yes." She handed him the bouquet. "They say you are number one, and congratulations. I can read the number one," she said proudly.

Congratulations was printed on a banner that had been hung from the porch railing, and more balloons were tied to the posts.

Eric climbed the steps with Idina in his arms but lowered her to her feet before entering through the open door.

"Oh, wow." He pretended surprise. "Thank you for throwing a party for me." He walked over to where the two gods sat and bowed. "Thank you for saving my life."

He hadn't seen the Clan Mother before, but there was no mistaking who she was, and it wasn't only the glow that gave her away.

"You are welcome," Toven said before rising to his feet. "You should sit down before you fall over and waste all those blessings I worked so hard on." He motioned for Eric to sit in the armchair he'd vacated.

"I can't take your seat." He glanced at Gilbert. "Can you get me a chair?"

"Coming up." His brother swung one of the dining room chairs around and shoved it behind Eric's butt.

"Congratulations, Eric." As the goddess smiled, her otherworldly beauty turned blinding. "Welcome to my clan."

"Thank you." He dipped his head again. "I promise that I will earn my keep."

"I can't thank you enough," Darlene said. "Thank you."

"You are most welcome," the goddess said.

Toven nodded.

Eric glanced at Kian, who was sitting with Syssi on the couch. "Do you need another pilot?"

"Always. I also need a ship's captain. Do you know one?"

"I know a few navy captains, but I doubt they can pilot a cruise ship." He'd heard about the ship Kian was renovating for Alena's wedding.

Kian grimaced. "That's what I thought. I have a ship, a crew, servers, cooks, maids and security people, all except for a captain. I didn't know they were in such short supply."

"Dinner is served in the backyard," Karen said.

Eric sniffed the air. "I smell steak."

"Roni barbecued a mountain of them," Darlene said. "That's how he shows love. He came over a few times and read to you."

"I wish I were aware of what was going on around me, but I was out. I didn't even dream. When I woke up, I had no idea that two weeks had gone by."

"Shall we?" Toven offered Annani a hand up. "The smell is making me hungry."

"Indeed." The goddess took his hand, but it didn't look as if he was pulling her. It looked more like she was floating up.

"Where is Mia?" Eric asked his brother as Toven and Annani walked outside.

"She's back there with Kaia, William, and the twins." Gilbert offered him a hand up. "Do you need the wheelchair?"

Eric shook his head. "Not anymore. This was the last time." He was still a little weak, but he could walk.

He waved a hand at Max. "Come on. Let's eat some steak. I need to start building back the muscle I've lost."

Max grinned. "As soon as you are up to it, I'll start you on a muscle-building routine in the gym."

42

ANNANI

"To Eric." Kian lifted his beer bottle. "And to the successful transition of the other members of his family."

Annani lifted her wine glass. "To Eric, Gilbert, Karen, Idina, and in a few years, Cheryl, and a few more, Evan and Ryan." She smiled at the little girl. "She is still young enough to benefit from spending time with me." She turned to look at the twins. "The boys will have to wait a little longer."

As she shifted her gaze to Eric, she noticed how pale and tired he looked, but he also looked happy, and he was having a good time. "How are you faring, Eric? Do you need to lie down?"

"Thank you for your concern, Clan Mother, but I'm fine. I'm a happy man."

She nodded. "Do not overdo it on your first day out of the sick bed. As joyous as the occasion is, I think we should end the festivities soon and let you rest."

"I can last a little longer." Eric wrapped his arm around Darlene's shoulders and turned to his brother. "Let's make plans for your induction ceremony."

"Not yet." Gilbert shifted in his chair. "I have many loose ends I need to tie up, and now that you are out of the woods, I need to attend to them. It will have to wait until I return."

"I'll induce you," Toven said. "It worked well for Eric, so it should work well for you."

Toven's offer created a moment of stunned silence around the table, but it did not surprise Annani. He had assured Karen and Gilbert that they had nothing to fear, and he intended to do his best to provide them with the outcome he had promised.

Toven had told her that he felt responsible for the family, and he wanted to give Gilbert the same help he had given his younger brother.

"Thank you. That is very generous of you." He shook his head. "Wow. I did not expect that." He took Karen's hand. "Now you have less reason to fret."

"I still do." She smiled at Toven. "I can't help it. But I'm so grateful to you for doing this for us."

Toven lifted his wine glass and saluted her. "Eric was the first male I've induced, and it was much easier than I expected. It was really no trouble at all."

Poor Eric looked like he had swallowed a lemon, but he wisely did not say anything. He was no match for a god, and there was no shame in his swift defeat.

"It's not fair that Idina gets to be immortal first," Cheryl grumbled. "I should be next."

"About that." Karen turned to Annani. "How does it work? How much time does Idina need to spend with you to transition? And is it dangerous?"

"It is not dangerous at all. Idina will not even feel the change until she notices that her hearing, eyesight, and strength have improved. She will also need less sleep. As for how much time, it varies, but daily visits for a couple of weeks should do it. I will ask Alena to contact you and arrange playdates at my house with Phoenix. The girls can play while I watch over them."

Annani was looking forward to spending time with the girls. It had been a long time since she had more than one toddler girl at the sanctuary, and she missed the lively sounds of children playing.

"Thank you, Clan Mother."

"You are most welcome." Annani smiled at Idina. "She reminds me of Amanda when she was a little girl. Smart, willful, and full of mischief."

She caught Kaia frowning at her from the corner of her eye. The girl was smart and suspicious of the blessings and about the way the Dormant girls transitioned. It was time to do something about that before she figured it out.

Kaia was under strong compulsion not to reveal any of the clan secrets, but as Kian had pointed out, if Kalugal could overpower Emmett and Eleanor's compulsion, so could someone else. It was not likely, but it was possible, and the secret of what a god's blood could do was too great to risk.

"I was not willful," Amanda said. "You always said that I was a sweet girl."

"You were a pleasure." Annani patted her hand. "You still are, and there is never a dull moment with you around."

As always, Amanda was easy to placate with a compliment.

She smiled. "Evie is also such a good baby. She eats well, she sleeps well, and she's not fussy at all. Allegra is also an easy child, but with the twins joining our little daycare, we will need to hire another nanny. Four babies are too much for one person to handle."

"Did you tell Eric the good news?" Syssi asked Karen.

"Not yet. I didn't get the chance." She turned to Eric. "I got a job at the university, and I'm starting in two months. Their sysadmin is going on maternity leave."

"Congratulations." Eric lifted his glass of water. "The Fates are smiling upon us."

"Indeed." Annani lifted her wine glass. "Let us make a toast to our good fortune."

43

KAIA

"*I* need a hug." Kaia wrapped her arms around Eric. "I'm so happy to have you back." As she held him to her tightly, her eyes misted with tears.

She'd kept her stress and her worry hidden inside, in part because Gilbert and Karen had been worried enough without her adding to their anxiety and in part because she'd been afraid to let go of the tight leash on her emotions.

So much was resting on her shoulders that she couldn't afford to fall apart.

William had gone back to managing the lab, so she was in charge of the deciphering project with only minimal help from him. They worked in the same room, which meant that they could consult with each other at all times, but mostly, they worked on different things.

The truth was that she hadn't made any breakthroughs during the two weeks Eric had been in a coma.

At the rate she was going, Marcel would need to sign the team of bioinformaticians up for another three-month term. They weren't good for any breakthroughs, but they were helping her chip away at the manuscripts one sentence at a time, and that was better than nothing.

To solve the puzzle of Okidu's journals, Kaia needed a calm mind and a positive attitude, and she hadn't managed either since Eric had started his transition. But her worry about him hadn't been the only reason for the turmoil in her head and her crappy mood. She was still dealing with Edgar.

Kaia had met with Annani twice since the first time the goddess had entered her mind and had done her version of psychoanalysis on Edgar. Even though the Clan Mother was a masterful thraller, and she was very gentle, frequent thralling was not recommended, and Annani refused to endanger Kaia's mind.

Edgar was still taking up a big chunk of her soul, and she was impatient to banish him and her memories of her life as a man completely.

Well, except for the mathematical knowledge and analytical ability she'd gotten to keep. Losing that would mean losing her edge and her so-called genius.

Perhaps that was the nature of gifts. They came with strings attached, and she needed to figure out if the one she'd been given was worth the baggage it had come with.

Without Edgar, Kaia was a nothing special, somewhat intelligent girl, but with him, she was a deviant. Was it worth it?

If she got to decipher Okidu's journals because of Edgar's contribution, then the answer was yes. They might hold the secret to immortality for everyone, and not just those who carried the godly genes.

The thing was, Kaia had a feeling that until Gilbert and her mother also transitioned successfully, she wouldn't be able to get into the zone needed for solving this most important puzzle.

"I'm happy to be back." Eric kissed her forehead. "You shouldn't have worried about your old uncle. I'm a survivor."

"I don't have an old uncle." Letting go of him, she clapped his back. "I have a young, handsome, awesome uncle." She wiped her eyes with the back of her hands.

"That's right." Eric grinned.

"Who wants to join me for cigars?" Kian asked.

"I do." Eric turned around. "I'm immortal now. I can smoke as many as I want."

Darlene shook her head. "You are still as weak as a baby. You shouldn't smoke."

"Then come with me." He took her hand. "We can sit on the swing and smooch while Kian and Gilbert puff on cigars."

Darlene smiled. "That sounds like a much better idea."

"I am going inside," Annani announced.

"So am I." Syssi rose to her feet. "Whoever wants a cappuccino, follow me."

Kaia walked over to William. "Are you going to stay outside with the smokers?"

"If you don't mind." He cupped her cheek and kissed her lips lightly. "You can stay, you know. You are an immortal as well."

William didn't smoke, and he wasn't overly fond of alcohol either, but he enjoyed chatting with Kian and the other guys, and Kaia didn't want him to miss the fun because he didn't want her to feel left out.

The truth was that they both needed some time apart. It wasn't healthy for a couple to spend every minute of every day together.

"I'll join the Clan Mother and Syssi for cappuccinos." She gave him a peck on the lips. "Have fun with the guys."

44

ANNANI

"$\mathcal{I}$'m scared for Gilbert," Karen said. "But not as much as I was before Toven said he was going to induce him. He's done exactly as he promised with Eric." She smiled at Annani. "I want to thank you again for helping Eric with your blessings."

"You are most welcome. I am glad that I was able to help."

The truth was that she had not. Annani had only pretended to *bless* Eric, spending twenty minutes or so in his room and telling him stories. But she had not given him her blood because Toven's had been sufficient. She and Toven had decided that it was better not to experiment on Eric.

Even Toven had not known whether any gods had attempted providing a human with a mixture of their blood or taking turns with their transfusions. The blood of two gods might be even more beneficial than the blood of one, but it could also be harmful.

Perhaps if Eric's situation had deteriorated to a critical point, Annani would have given him her blood as a last resort.

"I'm so curious about how it works," Kaia said. "I wonder if the energy gods emit can be studied or measured. There must be something therapeutic in it."

"Some humans have healing energy as well." Syssi handed Annani a cappuccino cup with a heart shape, artfully created from the foam. "It makes sense that gods would have that ability in order of magnitude. After all, we came from them, even those of us who don't carry the immortal genes."

That was a very astute assumption, and Annani wished it was true, but it was not. Hopefully, though, it would be good enough to steer Kaia's curious mind in that direction and away from the truth.

The girl was smart, and she loved solving puzzles. As long as the *blessings* remained a mystery, she would keep trying to figure out how they worked.

Perhaps it would be better if Annani nipped it in the bud, as the saying went.

Thanks to Kaia's past life memories and her wish to banish them, Annani had free access to the girl's mind. She could take a detour and plant a suggestion to stop her from thinking about the blessings and how they worked.

"Kian and Toven seem unconcerned about Gilbert's and my mother's transition," Kaia said. "They must have great faith in the blessings." She put her cappuccino cup down. "Maybe it's a male macho thing. The ladies, and especially Bridget, seem much more concerned."

"It's the motherly instinct," Amanda said. "Generally, women are more empathic and tend to worry more. Men are less so. Maybe that's why they make better soldiers."

Syssi shook her head. "That's because they are physically stronger, and until recently, it was a deciding factor. With modern weaponry, physical strength became less and less important, and that's why we see more and more women in the military."

"Brawn is not the only factor. Generally speaking, men are more ruthless and less emotional." Amanda lifted her hands in the air. "Don't shoot me for not being politically correct. Some women are ruthless too and they make exceptional soldiers, but generally speaking, men are better at warfare."

"We are still apes," Mia murmured. "Aggressive for no reason."

"The gods were not peaceful creatures either," Annani said. "They only pretended to be." She sighed. "I wish we were as benevolent as we wanted humans to believe we were. I am doing my best to uphold that ideal, but I am not an angel even though I glow." She smiled at Kaia. "We should have another meeting soon. Perhaps tomorrow?"

The sooner she dealt with the girl's suspicions, the better. She also needed to talk with Kian and Toven about keeping up better charades. They needed to pretend to be more concerned than they actually were for the transitioning Dormants.

Kaia perked up. "I would love to. What time is convenient for you?"

"Can you come to my house at noon? We can have lunch together."

"Thank you." Kaia dipped her head. "I'll be there at twelve."

45

ERIC

*B*y the time the last of their guests had departed, Eric could barely keep his eyes open, but he'd been waiting the entire afternoon to tell Darlene about his conversation with Max, and he didn't want to postpone it until tomorrow.

Besides, he was horny as hell and wanted to play.

He might not be good for much, but he at least needed to hold Darlene in his arms with nothing between them. He'd been craving the feel of her skin on his, her lips, the look in her eyes that was full of love and lust for him.

Sitting like a useless sack of potatoes on the couch, he watched her cleaning up after the party and felt like shit for not offering to help. If he didn't fear falling on his face the moment he tried to get off the damn couch, he would have helped, but if he fell, he would just be adding more work for her.

"I know you are busy, and I wish I could help clean, but I'm exhausted. Can I bother you for a cup of strong coffee?"

She stopped wiping the dining room table and turned to him. "You should be in bed. Do you need help getting undressed?"

"I don't want to go to bed yet. Well, I do, but I want to sit with you on the couch and talk for a little bit. We haven't had any alone time in hours, and I miss being with you."

Her lips curved up in a smile. "That's an invitation I can't refuse." She looked at the mostly clean table and shrugged. "It can wait for tomorrow. I'll make us coffee." She headed toward the kitchen.

He gave her a grateful smile. "You're the best."

A few minutes later, Darlene returned with two cups of coffee and two pieces of leftover cake. "Karen is a surprisingly good baker for a career woman. This cake is delicious."

She set the tray on the coffee table and sat next to him. "This is nice. Just the two of us." She handed him a cup, took one for herself, and leaned into him. "I missed cuddling on the couch with you."

Eric ran his hand over Darlene's bare arm. "I was asleep for the entire time, so I didn't get to miss you, but since I woke up, I missed us being home together."

She leaned her head on his shoulder. "How is it possible that we've known each other for such a short time, and I can't imagine life without you in it? I'm not immortal yet, and you are a baby immortal, so it can't be the truelove mates' bond."

"We were meant to be together." He kissed the top of her head. "The Fates planned our union even before we were born."

She lifted her eyes to him. "You really think so?"

"I know so. I can feel it in here." He patted his chest. "That being said, I still think that you should transition as soon as possible. The Fates brought us together, but they expect us to put in some work as well and not leave everything to them. That's not how it works."

Darlene grimaced. "Can we talk about that some other time? I don't want to ruin the moment with talk about threesomes."

"We have to talk about it, and we have to do it now. I told Max about my idea."

Her muscles stiffening, she pulled out of his arms. "When?"

"While you were getting us lunch. He had an interesting idea that I think you will like."

Darlene shook her head and put the coffee cup down on the table. "No wonder he was looking at me funny. What's his brilliant idea?"

"He thinks that it might work with him only biting you and doing nothing else. While we get going, he will work himself up in the next room, and when I'm about to climax, he will come in, bite you, and leave."

Pursing her lips, Darlene tilted her head. "That doesn't sound too awful. I can even stay partially dressed. But will it work with the venom and sperm not coming from the same male?"

"I don't know, and neither does Max, but it's worth a try. If it works, great, and if it doesn't, we try something else. I can ask Bridget's opinion, but I want to know your thoughts on the subject first."

"I can't have sex with Max. If that doesn't work, we will wait until your fangs and venom are functional."

On the one hand, he was glad to hear that, but on the other hand her declaration made him anxious. If Max's idea didn't work, Darlene would have no choice but to have sex with the guy. The problem was that Eric no longer believed that he could take part in it.

He would have to ask Bridget to knock him out.

He let out a breath. "Max said that I wouldn't be able to tolerate another male touching you and that I would probably attack him when he comes to bite you. He wants me to be tied down to the bed."

Darlene shook her head. "It gets kinkier and kinkier. What's next? Brundar's club?"

Eric lifted a brow. "Brundar has a club?"

46

DARLENE

"*Y*ou didn't know?"

Eric chuckled. "I don't know a lot of things about the clan. I might have been here for a couple of weeks, but I wasn't conscious for it. Brundar is the last person I would have ever suspected of owning a club. What kind of a club is it?"

"The kind that caters to various kinks."

Eric nodded. "That I can imagine. When does he have time for it, though? Isn't he Kian's personal bodyguard?"

"He is, but since Kian hardly ever leaves the village, Brundar has plenty of time on his hands. Anandur takes part in the rescue missions when Kian doesn't need him, but not Brundar."

"I can imagine why. They don't want to traumatize the victims even more. The dude scares me, and I'm a veteran."

"Brundar obviously has issues, but Callie seems happy with him, and from what I hear, she helps him run the club, so she must be into some kink herself."

"Now you've made me curious. Can we go there?"

Darlene swallowed. "You might be sexually adventurous, but I'm not, and I'm certainly not into exhibitionism, which I hear is a big part of it. I heard Callie talking about a bondage class and other live presentations. I blush just thinking about it."

Brundar and Callie were both beautiful and had perfect bodies. They might be comfortable performing in front of other people, but she wasn't. Heck, even if following her transition she had a bombshell figure, she would never strip in front of strangers, and definitely not have sex while people were watching.

Eric frowned. "How can Brundar and Callie tolerate other people seeing them having sex? According to Max, they should be so possessive of each other that they would attack anyone who touches their mate or looks at her with desire. Or him. Max said that immortal females are just as bad as the males."

"Or good." Darlene leaned against his arm. "I like exclusivity, and I don't get excited thinking about performing for strangers. That's not my thing."

Hooking a finger under her chin, he turned her to look at him. "What is your kink?"

She felt her cheeks heating up. "I used to read a lot of ménage romances, and then I switched to reverse harem romances, which is basically the same thing. But fantasy is not reality, and in reality, I'm a one-man woman."

He dipped his head. "And I'm a one-woman man. I'm Darlene's man." He kissed her softly.

When they came up for air, Darlene was panting. "Let's go to bed."

"What's wrong with the couch?" He snaked his hand under her shirt and cupped her breast over her bra.

"There is too much light in here, and I'm still not comfortable making love with the lights on." She pushed to her feet and offered him a hand up. "Besides, I haven't slept in a proper bed for two weeks. I want to be comfortable tonight."

"Yes, ma'am." He let her pull him up.

In their bedroom, she led him to the bed and gave him a light push. "Sit down."

When he tried to plop back and pull her on top of him, she shook her head. "Tonight, I'm going to take care of you, and you are going to lay back and enjoy. Is that clear?"

"Yes, ma'am." Eric smiled.

Dropping down to her knees, she lifted one of his feet and took the flip-flop off, then repeated with the other.

"You have very nice feet." She threaded her hands under his pants and massaged his calves. "Nice legs too."

"Keep going," Eric smirked.

She tugged on his pants. "You will need to help me a little."

"Of course." He lifted his butt and pushed his pants and underwear down, exposing his erect shaft.

"You have a very nice arousal too." She wrapped her palm around his smooth length and dipped her head to give it a kiss.

Eric groaned. "More. Take it into your mouth."

"Yes, sir." She licked around the head for a moment and then sucked it in without warning, taking it as deep as she could.

He groaned. "Fuck, Darlene. That's so good."

If she could smile around the length filling her throat, she would have. That was the idea. She was going to fuck him with her mouth.

When her gag reflex kicked in, she backed off and rolled her tongue around the tip while pumping the length with her hand. His shaft was slick from her saliva, and her palm glided over it with ease.

Should she tighten her hold on him?

She wasn't great at oral, as Leo had told her countless times, and she was still too embarrassed to ask Eric for directions.

Given his reaction, though, she was doing something right.

Breathing heavily, he threaded his fingers into her hair and pulled, holding her at his mercy, and thrust up.

When he hit the back of her throat, tears came to her eyes, but she wasn't going to back off, and she pushed past the gagging sensation to take him even deeper.

The loss of control was an illusion because she knew he would let go the moment she signaled any kind of distress, but it excited her nonetheless.

Forcing her throat muscles to relax, she took him as deep as she could and then backed off, only to slam down once more.

"That's it." Eric fisted her hair, pulling on the roots and causing pinpricks of pain that only added to her excitement. "Take it all!" He thrust up into her throat.

His encouraging words made her work harder, her head bobbing fast over his length, her hand pumping in tandem, and then he jerked, and a split second later, his seed filled her mouth.

After she swallowed it all and licked him clean, he cupped her cheeks, pulled her up, and kissed her deeply, passionately.

Letting go of her mouth, he didn't release her cheeks and looked into her eyes. "I love you so damn much."

She smiled. "Because I give great blowjobs?"

Say yes, she pleaded with him silently, needing the reassurance.

Eric chuckled. "You blew my mind, but you know what I love even more than your fabulous blowjobs?"

"What?"

"Returning the favor." In a move that was too fast to follow, he flipped her on her back and pulled down her pants. "My turn." He dove between her spread legs.

Evidently, he wasn't as weak as she'd thought.

4 7

JADE

$\mathcal{T}$wo weeks had passed since Jade had submitted her fable to the contest. She didn't dare check the email account often because that would have made her seem eager, which would have made Igor suspicious. Instead, she acted blasé and checked no more than twice a week.

If confronted, her story would be that she'd entered the contest to get free access to the Safe Haven library, which was supposed to contain a lot of material she could use to teach the children.

She'd found two other contests which she'd entered as well, so her original submission to Veskar's contest would not look out of place, and she'd also subscribed to several others that offered a free trial. Her desk was stacked with printouts from those sites, and her notebook was filled with ideas that those articles and stories had inspired.

She left the notebook on her desk during lunch breaks and bathroom visits so Igor could take a look and see that she was utilizing the material he'd allowed her to collect.

So far it seemed to be working, and he hadn't confronted her about any of it, but if he did, she had plenty of material to defend herself. The only way he could guess what she was up to was if he went on the Safe Haven site and recognized Emmett Haderech as a hybrid Kra-ell.

That wasn't likely.

Veskar had done a great job disguising himself and his inhumanly youthful appearance for someone his age. His long beard and hair looked like he was wearing a wig or extensions and coloring his hair, and the robes he favored hid his body shape. Only someone who knew him as well as Jade could recognize him in that disguise.

As she knocked on the door and entered Igor's office, he lifted his head and pinned her with a dark look. "You've got an email from one of those contests you entered. You won free access to their library."

Her heart threatened to break through her ribs and flop on the floor, but she forced herself to calm down and nodded. "Which one?"

Schooling her features, she sauntered over to her seat in the corner of his office and flipped the old laptop open.

"The one with all the free-love spiritual nonsense. I don't know what you hope to gain from winning it."

"They have a big library with many motivational stories," she said as nonchalantly as she could. "The contest winners get lifetime access, so anything they add over the years will be at my disposal. Not a bad deal for a silly little story that took me ten minutes to write."

She hoped he hadn't read it, and if he had, that he hadn't figured out the coordinates that she'd so cleverly weaved into the story.

The question was whether Veskar had guessed what those numbers were. She didn't have the precise coordinates, and the ones she'd found were from a globe she used to teach the children about Earth's geography. Karelia was not enormous, and she didn't know the exact location of the compound, so it was just a guesstimate.

Some of the young humans were allowed to study either in Helsinki or St. Petersburg, and since they drove to and from their universities, they could tell her the exact coordinates, but asking them was out of the question.

They would have reported her to Igor even if they didn't want to. The compulsion would have forced them to do that.

Angling her screen so she could see Igor's reflection in it, she checked whether he was watching her, but he had gone back to what he'd been doing when she'd entered.

Jade stifled a relieved breath, turned the laptop on, and opened the email from Safe Haven.

Dear Ms. Solveika,

Congratulations.

You are one of the three contest finalists. You should be proud of yourself. Out of a hundred and thirteen submissions, yours and two others were chosen to enter the final round.
Only one entry will win a free ticket to one of our world-renowned retreats, and we wish you the best of luck in winning it.
As one of the three finalists, you've won lifetime access to our extended library of motivational and spiritual material. We encourage you to read through the other contest submissions, which you can find under http://Safe.Haven.org/contest.
Your access code is Winners-Circle-3.
The winner of the final round will be announced at the end of the month.

Best of luck,

Riley Montgomery.
Executive Director, Safe Haven.

Leaning back, Jade folded her arms over her chest and turned to look at Igor. "I'm one of three finalists. After the final round, only one of us will be selected, winning a free ticket to one of their retreats. What if I win?"

She knew he'd read the email, but she had to keep up the pretense of no big deal.

He didn't even lift his head. "You will give it to the runner-up."

"I know that you won't let me attend one of those retreats, but maybe you can send someone else in my place. It would be a shame to waste the prize. Those retreats are costly."

"So is a plane ticket to Oregon, United States."

Jade's heart thundered in her chest. Igor had obviously checked out Safe Haven and its location, but hopefully, his disinterest was genuine and not faked.

Just to be safe, though, she didn't immediately log into the website and use her access code. She would do that in a day or two. In the meantime, she would check the other websites and download more material to throw Igor off.

48

SOFIA

"Why are you scowling at me?" Roxie put her plate down. "I'm not the one who stood you up."

Sofia let out a breath. "First of all, I wasn't scowling at you. I was just gazing into the distance. And secondly, he hasn't stood me up because we didn't make any plans. He just disengaged, which is his prerogative."

That was only partially true, but it sounded less humiliating. Marcel had told her that he would try to make it after lunch yesterday, but it had sounded like a brush-off. Sofia had hoped that she'd misinterpreted it and that he would be there, but when he hadn't shown up yesterday or today, that hope had been squashed.

"Maybe he had a work emergency." Roxie patted her shoulder. "You don't have a phone with you, so he couldn't let you know."

"Maybe you are right." Sofia cast her a smile and pretended to dig into her meal.

Roxie was wrong.

Even if Marcel had to leave on short notice, he could have left her a note, or he could've stopped by the dining hall and told her that he was leaving.

The fact that he'd just disengaged meant that he wasn't interested and that he had no respect for her. Otherwise, he wouldn't have just ghosted her. As much as it hurt to accept it, that was the reality, and she had to move on.

Time was of the essence, and Sofia needed to find a different source of information.

Last night, she had lied to Valstar and said that she was meeting Marcel later, but she'd been smart enough not to mention his name, so Valstar didn't know who she was seeing, and she could find a substitute.

Maybe one of the instructors, or maybe she could pursue Emmett Haderech himself and tell Valstar that her previous source had turned out to be a dud.

Was Emmett Haderech married? He seemed very cozy with Dr. Takala, but since he'd created a community based on the philosophy of free love, he most likely practiced it himself.

Sofia's skin crawled just thinking about seducing someone other than Marcel, but what choice did she have? She had to get over it.

Maybe if she got drunk enough, she could tolerate some other male's hands on her.

Right.

To get invited to stay, she needed to make the guy fall in love with her, or at least in lust, and she wasn't going to achieve that objective by just faking it. She needed to put on the best performance of her life and convince him that he was a superb lover and she couldn't live without him and his amazing, magical wand.

Ugh.

She would have had no problem with any of it if Marcel was that guy. But if he walked into the dining hall right now, she would punch him in the face for ruining her plans and endangering her family. He didn't know what was at stake, but he'd been rude and heartless, and she was mad as hell at him.

She was the spy who was supposed to feign interest to lure him, but her interest had been genuine while his had been fake. Why had he put on such a great show of being interested in her if he wasn't?

He couldn't have possibly known why she was there, so he had no excuse for the way he behaved.

But what if he knew?

Marcel hadn't mentioned having a paranormal talent, but he might have lied by omission. What if he could read her thoughts?

Nah, that wasn't likely.

Dr. Eleanor Takala had said that it was one of the rarest talents and that she'd only met one person who could do that. Most telepaths could sense emotions, intentions, and the strong ones could see the visuals in someone's thoughts.

If Marcel was a level nine telepath or below, he couldn't have guessed her purpose from sensing her emotions or intentions. Sofia's emotions were all over the place because she was attracted to him, and it confused her, because she was scared for her family and because she was scared for herself. And as for her intentions, they weren't nefarious because she had no idea what Igor intended to do with the information she was supposed to gather.

Mother above, the guy was confusing and infuriating. She was usually a mellow person, agreeable and nonconfrontational, but Marcel evoked extreme emotions in her.

She didn't know what she wanted to do more, punch him in the face or jump his bones and have furious hate sex with him.

She'd never done either, but there was a first time for everything. Sex sounded better than hitting, but it looked like she wouldn't get to do either because the damn male was a rude jerk who didn't have the guts to tell her to her face that he was no longer interested.

49

MARCEL

*M*arcel glanced at his phone, picked it up, and checked the incoming calls. Sometimes he didn't hear it ringing, not because there was anything wrong with his ears but because he was so immersed in solving a problem that he didn't pay attention to anything else.

As Roni used to say, when Marcel was on a mission, the sky could be falling, and he wouldn't notice. His ability to hyper-focus was useful for a scientist, but it had been a hindrance when he was a Guardian. A soldier had to be aware of his surroundings.

There had been no missed phone calls, but there was a message from Roni asking him to give him a call.

Good.

Marcel had been avoiding Sofia until Roni found out more about her background and whether there was anything suspicious in her past, and he felt bad about that.

Frankly, he needed to put some distance between them because she was threatening to ruin the calm and unemotional persona he'd worked so hard to build.

Marcel didn't want to go back to the way he'd been before.

He'd been too trusting, too quick to fall in love and too easily hurt. That guy was dead, and Marcel had no intentions of resurrecting him. Not for Sofia and not for anyone else.

That guy had been a liability. A Guardian with no teeth had no business on the force, and that was one of the reasons why he had never felt as if he belonged and had eventually left.

He wasn't an empath, just slightly on the sensitive side, and he couldn't understand how a powerful empath like Arwel had the strength to endure a bombardment of emotions without closing his heart and his mind to the suffering of others.

Marcel's only option had been to turn that part of himself off, and he preferred it to stay in the off position.

Leaning back in his chair, he placed the call to Roni. "Good afternoon. How are you doing?"

"Busy as usual. So here is what I found out about your lady. I confirmed that she's been a student at the University of Helsinki for the last seven years, just as she claimed. I checked her records, including her grades, teachers' comments, her employment record, the hours she logged teaching, and a lot of other information. There is too much of it to be fake. Even I wouldn't have gone to such lengths to create a fake identity, and I'm pretty thorough. She doesn't have social media, which is odd for a person her age but not odd enough to be suspicious. A lot of people shun social media. More so lately. It's too politicized and too intrusive."

"What about before she joined the university? Did you find any high-school records?"

"I did. But there wasn't much in there. Just the basics. I checked the medical records of everyone attending the retreat, and she's gotten all of her immunization shots. Other than that, she had one case of strep throat when she was thirteen, and that was it. She sees a dentist every six months and gets her teeth cleaned. Anything else?"

"What about her family? Does she have a birth record?"

"Yep. I can email you the details. Her parents have different last names, so they either weren't married, or her mother chose to retain her maiden name. Do you want me to run a background check on them as well?"

Roni sounded like that was the last thing he wanted to do, and Marcel couldn't blame him. Roni's time was too valuable to waste on a wild goose chase for something that wasn't there.

"Since everything she said checks out, I see no reason to keep digging."

"What made you suspicious of her in the first place?"

"Her mind is like a vault, but she's not immune. It's as if parts of her are locked down, and others are not. I was able to thrall her to forget a little snippet of information, but I wasn't able to see anything deeper."

"You are not supposed to."

"I know." Marcel sighed. "I asked Onegus for permission to use a stronger thrall to get into her mind, but he said that I needed probable cause to dig deeper. Since you didn't find any inconsistencies in her story, I don't have probable cause." He chuckled. "Aside from my gut feeling, that is."

"Then go for it. Onegus is a lawman, and he must follow the law. You are a civilian, and the rules are laxer for us."

"I used to be a Guardian."

"I didn't know that. Does it mean that you are still bound by the same rules as active Guardians?"

"No, but civilians are supposed to follow the same rules, and I'm not a lawbreaker."

"Suit yourself. If I were you, and I suspected something, I would have dug deeper, but then I can't thrall for crap, so it's a moot point."

50

KIAN

*K*ian was about to turn into the pathway leading to his front door when he saw Kaia leaving Annani's house.

"Good evening, Kian." She waved at him and turned toward William's place, or rather her and William's home.

He waved back. "Good evening, Kaia."

It seemed like she'd arrived at the village only a few days ago, which wasn't that far off, and already she was another permanent resident, adding to the rich tapestry of the village population.

Kaia was a valuable addition.

Wondering what she'd been doing at his mother's, he decided to pay her a visit. If his mother was agreeable, he could call Syssi and ask her to join them with Allegra.

Kian knocked on the door, and a moment later, Oridu opened up. "Good evening, master." He bowed.

"Hello." Kian walked in.

"What a lovely surprise." His mother opened her arms. "Come and give me a hug."

Sitting next to her on the couch, he wrapped his arm around her slim shoulders and kissed her cheek. "I saw Kaia leaving here a moment ago. What was she doing here?"

Annani arched a brow. "She needed my help with a personal matter. It does not concern the clan or its security, so I am not going to share it with you." She sighed. "But while I was helping Kaia with what was bothering her, I also took care of a problem that did have to do with my security, so I should share that with you."

Kian's hackles rose. "Your security? What do you mean?"

His mother signaled Oridu to come over. "Could you please bring a cup of tea for my son?"

"Of course, Clan Mother." He bowed.

"Kaia is very smart, and she loves to solve puzzles." Annani took a sip of her tea. "She wondered why you and Toven seem less worried about transitioning Dormants than other members of the clan are, including Bridget, and she came to the conclusion that you two must know something that the others do not. Then she wondered about the so-called blessings, and she set out to find the truth."

That was a troubling development.

"How do you know that?"

"I stumbled upon those thoughts while I was helping her with her private issue. Anyway, I thralled her to stop thinking about it. From now on, every time she starts wondering about Toven and my blessings, she will not be able to hold on to the thought, and her mind will wander to a different topic."

Kian let out a breath. "I'm glad you nipped it in the bud."

"Here is your tea, master." Oridu put the teacup in front of Kian.

"Thank you." He took a couple of sips before putting it down.

"Kaia is not the only one with good observational skills," his mother said. "I have already spoken to Toven and advised him to act more concerned about transitioning Dormants. You should put up a better act as well."

"You are right. I've become overly complacent lately. Maybe it's because of Navuh's lack of interest in us over the last year or so. What's going on with him? Did you talk with Areana about him?"

"Of course." Annani smiled. "I love my sister, and I enjoy talking with her, but I also do it to keep tabs on her mate and his plans. He does not tell her much about his day-to-day activities, but he does tell her about his grand plans. Areana says that Navuh is becoming more and more obsessed with China. He realizes that he has been ignoring the rising star to the detriment of the Brotherhood's future, and he is adamant about rectifying his neglect. The West is no longer his main focus. His new mantra is that to take over the world, he has to gain control over China."

Kian snorted. "At this point, no one can control China. It is on its way to becoming the next superpower, and it is not open to foreign influence like the West was. He has no chance."

Annani tilted her head. "I would not be so sure about that. Navuh might be unhinged, but he is very smart. Lokan says that he started bringing smart Chinese male students to breed with his Dormants. Once he breeds a new crop of Dormant girls with Asian features, he will breed them again until he gets warriors who look fully Chinese, are smart, and can blend in. It might take him several decades, but Navuh is not in a hurry. He makes very long-term plans."

"I'm not worried. This time around, Navuh's plans are not going to succeed. He's too late to the game. But I'm glad that's where his focus is. As long as he's obsessing about China, he's not bothering us."

5 1

SOFIA

*W*hen the last class ended, Sofia pretended to organize her backpack as she waited for the other attendees to leave. Naturally, Roxie stayed behind, tapping her foot impatiently. "Are you coming?"

Sofia cast her a smile. "Go ahead. I'll catch up with you." She kept an eye on the instructor, hoping he wouldn't leave.

He was an average-looking guy, but he seemed kind, and he'd been smiling at her throughout the class. Not only that, but he was also fascinated by her mirror divination and wanted to see a demonstration.

It was a great excuse to get him alone so she could put the moves on him.

"I'll wait." Roxie pulled out a chair.

"Please, don't." Sofia signaled with her eyes, hoping Roxie would get the hint that she wanted to have a word with the teacher.

A grin spread over Roxie's face. "I'll save a seat for you." She was out of the chair in an instant and practically ran out of the classroom.

Sofia turned to the instructor and rolled her eyes. "I thought she would never leave." She sauntered toward him and affected a suggestive smile. "I thought that maybe we could meet up later tonight at the social. If you want me to demonstrate my mirror divination, you can come to my room. I brought my special mirror with me."

"I would be delighted."

"Wonderful." She let out a breath. "I was afraid that there were rules about instructors and attendees fraternizing."

"Not in Safe Haven, and not as long as the lady initiates."

"Awesome." She slung her backpack over her shoulder. "I'll look for you at the social." She gave him another smile and waved goodbye.

Her smile vanished as soon as she was out of the classroom.

She hated it, absolutely detested having to seduce a guy she felt nothing for.

Igor and Valstar would pay for forcing her to do that. She didn't know how or when, but one day, she would have her revenge.

Walking down the hallway, she debated whether she should go on a run and report to Valstar before having dinner or do it after. On the one hand, getting it out of the way would be a relief, but on the other hand, she shouldn't talk to Valstar while consumed by rage.

Not that she had high hope for feeling any calmer about what she had to do after dinner, but she might.

As she neared the dining hall, a tall, elegant figure leaning against the wall made her heartbeat accelerate, but she commanded it and herself to remain unaffected.

If Marcel expected her to fall into his arms, grateful that he had finally shown up, he was gravely mistaken. She was tempted to ignore him and just walk past him into the dining room.

But that was a coward's move.

She was a coward at heart, but she refused to bow to her cowardice.

In the end, she gave him a slight nod as she passed and continued walking.

"Sofia, wait." He rushed after her. "I'm sorry for not being here yesterday."

"No biggie." She gave him a tight smile. "I didn't wait for you." She scanned the room for Roxie and waved at her. "See you around." She lengthened her stride.

Luckily, there was only one vacant chair at Roxie's table, so Marcel couldn't join them.

Nevertheless, he followed her and just looked at her as she sat down. "Can I get you a plate?"

"I don't need help." She ignored him and turned to Roxie. "I'm meeting Edward later today at the social. I told him that I would give him a demonstration of my divination. I hope it's okay with you if I invite him to our room."

"Sure." Roxie cooperated. "I'm not planning to make use of my bed tonight." Smiling suggestively, she shimmied on her chair.

That should have been enough to make Marcel leave, but the guy was more stubborn than she'd given him credit for and not as mellow as he appeared.

With a growl that sounded a lot like male Kra-ell on a hunt, he pulled a chair from a nearby table and put it behind hers. "I'm not going to move from here until you let me explain."

"I'm not interested in your explanation."

Everyone sitting at the table was watching the spectacle they were making, and even though Marcel deserved to be embarrassed, Sofia didn't enjoy performing for a crowd.

"The facts speak for themselves." She rose to her feet. "I'm getting food."

She knew he would follow, but that was okay. She would say her piece, get rid of him, and that would be it.

Except, a small voice at the back of her head was calling her a fool.

So what if he was a jerk?

She wasn't looking for a boyfriend, and he was a means to an end. In addition, she was still attracted to him despite his jerkiness, and hate-sex with him would be a million times better than pretending to enjoy Edward's touch.

On the other hand, Edward would be easier to manipulate. He wasn't as smart and as guarded as Marcel, and she knew he would be putty in her hands.

Succeeding in the mission was more important than any other consideration, and since Edward would be much easier to ply for information, he was the obvious choice. But what if he didn't know as much as Marcel did?

Maybe Marcel was the better choice after all?

52

MARCEL

*S*ofia was pissed, and she had every right to be. Marcel had some groveling to do, and he was happy to do it if it helped him win her back.

He liked it that she didn't forgive him right away and was trying her best to get rid of him. It was a good sign that she wasn't planning on manipulating him. It also indicated that she'd liked him enough to be upset with him for not showing up.

He took a plate and stood behind her in line for the buffet.

"I said that I would try to make it yesterday at lunch. I didn't promise that I'd be there. It didn't work out."

"You could've sent a note or stopped by for a moment to say that you had something that needed to be done." She looked at him over her shoulder. "Not showing up was a clear sign that you were uninterested, and it was also rude. It was disrespectful."

"You are right, and I apologize. I didn't realize how it would seem to you. Can I make it up to you?"

She shrugged. "I don't see how. The damage was done, and I moved on. There are plenty of nice single men here for me to choose from." She put a piece of chicken on her plate and added rice pilaf.

"I'm not ready to give up on you." He put the same things on his plate. "It has been years since I've felt so strongly about a woman." He got close behind her so he could whisper in her ear. "Frankly, it scared me, and I needed to get some distance to make sure that I wasn't making a mistake."

She turned a pair of incredulous eyes on him. "Seriously? We were supposed to meet for lunch, not at the altar. It wasn't a monumental decision that you needed to examine with care."

How the hell was he going to get through to her?

Should he thrall her to forgive him?

No, that wouldn't be right.

Maybe humor was the key. His social skills sucked, but he was a good observer and a quick study. As a last resort, he could channel Anandur, and, if that didn't work, Onegus.

The chief was in a league of his own in the diplomatic and charm departments, so he would be more difficult to emulate, but Anandur was easy.

"Let's sit down and talk like the adults we are and sort it out. If by the end of dinner you still feel like punching me in the face, I will stand still and take it."

That got half a smile out of Sofia. "How did you know that was what I wanted to do?"

"The talk or the punch to the face?"

"Obviously, the punch to the face. I've already told you that I'm not interested in hearing your excuses."

"You looked like that was what you wanted to do. You were radiating aggression. It's not good for you to carry such anger, and because I'm the cause of it, it is fitting that you use me to give your rage an outlet." He scanned the room for a vacant table and found one next to the back wall. "Is over there okay?" He pointed, hoping she wouldn't just walk back to her table.

Sofia shrugged. "It's fine." She strode toward the table he'd pointed to.

Marcel felt like pumping his fist in the air.

Despite her tough talk, she was going to listen to him.

He'd better make it quick and to the point, because she was angry and impatient.

Catching on to the vibe she was emitting, people got out of her way. For a willowy dancer type with a delicate face, she cut an imposing figure when riled. There was coiled energy in her, like in a tigress, and apparently he wasn't the only one who sensed it.

When they reached the table, he pulled out a chair for her, and as she sat down, a guy who'd been heading their way with a plate changed his mind at the last minute and turned to search for a spot at a different table.

It hadn't been Marcel who'd scared him away. It was the stormy cloud hovering over Sofia's lovely head.

When he sat down, she waved a hand. "I'm willing to listen to what you have to say, but I can already tell you that it probably will not make a difference. The only excuse I can accept is that you had a death in the family and were too overtaken with grief to remember that you made plans with me."

"Thankfully, no one has died, so I can't use that as an excuse. I can only use my ineptitude in courtship. As I said, it has been a very long time since I courted a lady, and I'm not very good at social interactions in general." He rubbed his hand over his beard. "I should have gotten you a phone or at least a walkie-talkie. I didn't think any of this through, and I apologize."

53

SOFIA

*S*ofia's resolve to stay angry was weakening, and she didn't like it. She wanted to be strong, to stay angry and adamant, but Marcel looked so apologetic, and his excuses were so pathetic that she knew he wasn't making them up.

He was an intelligent man, so if he wished to lie, he could've come up with a much more compelling story.

Besides, he looked so damn good and smelled divine, which couldn't be said for Edward. The guy hadn't stunk, but he hadn't emitted a pleasant odor either, and he couldn't hold a candle to Marcel in any department, looks, smarts, or even charm.

Given that Marcel wasn't particularly charming, that was saying a lot.

The question was how to make the transition from wanting to punch him in the face to jumping his bones.

"Your excuses are not good enough." She looked at his plate and the food he had barely touched. "I think that by the end of dinner, I will still feel like punching you in the face, and you will have to stand still and take it."

"Would that earn me your forgiveness?"

Her lips twitched with a suppressed smile. "It might."

"Then you're on. Tell me where and when."

Resting her chin on the knuckles of her left hand, she pretended to think it over. "I don't want to embarrass you, and I don't want security to come running to arrest me for assault, so it will have to be either my room or yours. Do you have a roommate?"

"I have my own bungalow, but guests are not allowed in there. It's a fenced-off area reserved for the project I'm working on."

Maybe Marcel's project was what Igor was interested in? It sounded like he was working on something top secret, and he'd mentioned working in a lab. Could he be developing a drug to enhance paranormal abilities?

Otherwise, why work on it at Safe Haven?

But he was a computer engineer, not a doctor or a scientist, so maybe his project was related to artificial intelligence.

Both of those subjects could interest Igor.

Leaning forward, she gave him a seductive smile, and this time, she didn't have to pretend. "I share a room with Roxie. I can ask her to stay away for a couple of hours, but the walls are thin, and I can hear our neighbors talking, which means they can hear everything that's going on in our room, and if I punch you, and you groan, they might come in to see if you need help. You'll have to sneak me into your bungalow."

The gleam in his eyes looked like they were glowing from the inside, but that couldn't be. Marcel wasn't Kra-ell. He was human. It must be a trick of the light.

Smiling, he leaned closer to her. "Are you planning on hitting me for two hours straight?"

Oops. She'd let her real plans slip.

"It depends. If you sneak me into your bungalow, I might consider going easy on you and punch you only a couple of times."

"I'm sorry, but I can't." He seemed genuinely upset about it, but then his eyes gleamed again. "There is somewhere I can take you where no one will hear me scream when you punch me."

"And where is that?"

"I can't tell you. It's a secret, and you will have to wear a blindfold. But don't worry. I'll carry you so you won't stumble."

Was he taking her to his secret lab?

That would be perfect for what she needed from him, and it also sounded sexy as hell. The image of being carried by Marcel while blindfolded had her nipples harden in anticipation.

Mother of All Life, it had been so long since she'd last had sex, and she was overdue for some carnal fun. But did she trust Marcel enough to let him take her to a place where no one could hear her scream?

She could tell Roxie that she was going with him and if she didn't return in the morning, to alert security.

"Fine. But I'm going to tell Roxie, and if I'm not back in two hours, she'll call security."

He laughed. "That's fine with me, but I happen to be friends with everyone on the security detail. I don't think you'll get much help from them." His expression turning serious, he reached for her hand. "Nevertheless, you have nothing to fear from me. Even though I'm not officially affiliated with Safe Haven, the resort's rules apply to me too. Everything is your call, and I have to abide by your wishes, no objections and no questions asked."

"I like these rules," she whispered, her voice sounding husky to her own ears. "Wait here." She rose to her feet. "I need to find Roxie."

"Hurry back."

She still intended to punish him for making her miserable for two days straight, and the blindfold he insisted she wore would come in handy.

Roxie grinned like a fiend when Sofia got back to their table. "Did you kiss and make up?"

"Not yet, but we are working on it. I need you to do me a favor."

"Anything."

"I'm going on a date with Marcel, but I promised Edward to meet him at the social tonight. Can you find him and apologize for me? Tell him that I couldn't make it, but don't tell him why. I'll bring the mirror to class tomorrow and give him a demonstration then."

Roxie tilted her head. "He doesn't care about your divination. He was hoping to hook up with you."

"I know, and I feel bad about doing to him what Marcel did to me, but I didn't promise him a hookup, only implied it, and I can pretend that the mirror was the only reason I invited him."

"Don't worry about it." Roxie rose to her feet. "I'll fill in for you."

Sofia's eyes widened. "That's going above and beyond. I can't expect you to do that."

Roxie shrugged. "I like Edward, and I have no problem being his consolation prize." She winked and fluffed her crazy hair.

54

MARCEL

$\mathcal{W}$hen Sofia had gone to talk to Roxana, Marcel pulled out his phone and called Leon.

"What's up, Marcel?"

"I have a favor to ask. Can I take a lady to Emmett's old bunker? I can't take her to my bungalow, and she shares a room with another lady."

"Marcel, you scoundrel. Since when did you become a player?"

"Since I met a lady who tugged at my heartstrings. Can I use the bunker or not?"

"Go ahead. I'll text you the code for the keypad. Who's the lady?"

"A retreat attendee from Finland. I asked Roni to check her background before going deeper into the relationship."

"What's her paranormal talent?"

"Mirror divining. Have you ever heard of that?"

"Nope. Sounds fake to me."

"It might be, but she's special regardless of her talent."

"What's her name?"

"Sofia."

There was a moment of silence and then a whistle. "She's beautiful. A little too skinny for my taste, but she looks graceful and refined."

"She is. She's a linguist." Marcel couldn't help but boast a little. "She's fluent in several European languages, knows many others, and is a professor's assistant at the University of Helsinki."

"Quality lady. Enjoy your time with her."

"I intend to."

"I'll text you the code as soon as we hang up."

"Thank you."

When he ended the call, Sofia was already walking back toward him, her narrow hips swaying from side to side in an alluring way. She was so graceful it was hard to believe she wasn't a professional dancer.

She should have been, but then people's choice of path often wasn't solely based on their aptitudes and preferences.

He was a classic example of that.

He'd chosen to become a Guardian because two of his best buddies had joined the force, but it had never been a passion for him like it had been for them.

He'd found his passion centuries later when he'd discovered that he loved engineering. The occupation wasn't emotionally laden, but it was creative and useful and benefited others. He could do much more to improve the lives of immortals and humans alike as an engineer than as a Guardian.

"I'm ready." Sofia stood next to him. "Are you?"

"I am." He glanced at his phone. "I got the code for the door."

"How about the blindfold?"

He didn't have that, but a cloth napkin would do. He took a clean one from the table, folded it several times over, and tucked it in his pocket.

Sofia tsked. "I never would have suspected you of being capable of stealing. You are so straitlaced."

"Appearances can be misleading." He rose to his feet and wrapped his arm around her shockingly narrow waist. "I'm not as dorky as I look."

"Dorky? You don't look dorky at all."

He led her toward the door. "What do I look like to you?"

"An executive. Someone who has an important job. I bet you are in charge of that special project you are working on."

"I am, but only because my boss, who was running the project, had to leave and asked me to take over."

She eyed him from under lowered lashes. "Don't sell yourself short, Marcel. I'm sure you are a big shot in the organization you work for."

He stopped at the edge of the back courtyard and pulled out the napkin he'd pilfered from the dining hall. "This is where I need to blindfold you."

She looked at his hands as he folded the napkin into the proper shape for a blindfold. "Are you sure you want to carry me? My skinny looks are deceiving. I'm heavy."

He snorted. "How much do you weigh? A hundred pounds?"

For some reason, she looked offended. Had he overestimated her weight?

Women were touchy about those things.

"I weigh sixty kilos, and I worked hard on getting to that weight."

Sixty kilos was a little over one hundred and thirty pounds, which was adequate for her height and slim build, but she didn't look it.

"My apologies." He dipped his head. "I meant no offense."

"None taken."

He snapped the folded napkin between his hands. "Turn around."

"Yes, sir." She pivoted on her heel.

"You will need to let your hair down. The napkin is not long enough to tie around your hairdo."

"Okay." She took out several pins and then shook her hair out.

It was magnificent, long, thick, and glossy, with a small curl at the bottom. She looked absolutely stunning with it tumbling down her back and tickling the tops of her butt cheeks.

Sucking in a breath, he got behind her and tied the blindfold around her eyes. "Okay? Or is it too snug?"

"It's okay," she breathed. "You smell so good."

Unable to stop himself, he brushed her hair aside and kissed her silky soft neck. "So do you."

5 5

SOFIA

*M*arcel's arms came around Sofia's back and legs, and he lifted her with ease, not even huffing out a breath, and carried her as if she weighed no more than a pillow.

How was he so strong?

He walked with her for a few minutes, but even though it was still early in the evening and the retreat guests were milling around, she couldn't hear anyone. Marcel must have taken her to a secluded part of the resort where the guests were not allowed.

Maybe she could learn something that she could report to Valstar?

As they entered a structure, she asked, "Where are you taking me?"

He chuckled. "Now you're asking?"

"Yes." She tried to wiggle out of his arms when he loosened his hold to type in the code. "There is no one around."

It must be the lab. What other structure had a door with a key code?

"That was the idea, wasn't it? You needed a place where you could hit me in the face, and no one would hear me scream."

"Yeah, but that means that no one would hear me scream either."

Suddenly, she felt nervous, and it wasn't only the excited butterflies about getting intimate with a new man. After Marcel's comment about the security team being his friends, Sofia hadn't asked Roxie to get them if she didn't return by morning.

Roxie would probably do that even without being asked, but if they were Marcel's buddies, would they help her?

As the door closed behind them, his arms tightened around her. "This used to be Emmett's old place before he met Eleanor. She wanted a fresh start with him, so they moved into one of the bungalows, and this place was turned into guest quarters but not for the retreat attendees. Emmett's partner and his wife sometimes stay down here."

Marcel started down a flight of stairs. He was incredibly strong for a human, and his arms felt like bands of steel around her.

"Did Emmett used to live in a basement?"

"Sort of. It's a very nice basement." Marcel sat down with her still in his arms and removed the blindfold. "Take a look."

It was indeed a very nicely appointed underground apartment. She slid off his lap and sat down beside him. "Don't think that you are getting off with just a scolding. I intend to punish you."

He didn't look scared. In fact, he looked excited. "I hoped that you had changed your mind about punching me in the face and decided to torture me sexually instead."

They hadn't even kissed yet, hadn't touched each other intimately, and hadn't even talked dirty to each other.

How was she going to do this?

Sofia was out of her element, and since the entire encounter had been unplanned, she hadn't come up with a strategy.

"That's actually not a bad idea." She affected a grin that she hoped looked wicked. "Maybe I should put the blindfold on you, tie you down to the bed, and then pleasure you for hours, holding you on the brink but not letting you climax."

Marcel's eyes blazed with an inner light. "That sounds like the best kind of torture possible." He cupped the back of her neck. "But before I submit to your ministrations, I need a kiss."

She needed it too.

As he captured her lips, she moaned and wound her arms around his neck.

With a groan, he cupped her face and licked into her mouth, sweeping his tongue inside and sucking on her lower lip.

An electric current rushed through her body, igniting all those forgotten feminine parts of her that had been yearning for such a moment, but she wasn't going to succumb to her need or his.

Not yet.

Marcel expected a punishment, and she had to deliver what she'd promised or lose credibility.

Besides, delaying gratification heightened the pleasure.

Pushing on his chest, she leaned away and took the folded napkin that he'd dropped on the couch. "What should I do first? Blindfold you or tie you to a bed?"

He chuckled nervously. "Let's see what kinds of beds they have down here. Not every bed lends itself to bondage."

She lifted a brow. "How much experience do you have with that?"

"None, but I have a vivid imagination."

56

MARCEL

$\mathcal{M}$arcel had never engaged in bondage, not as the one doing the tying or the one being tied up. He'd never been curious enough about kink to even visit Brundar's club.

But for some reason, being at Sofia's mercy excited him. Maybe it was just the scent of her arousal and the pheromones she was emitting, and he would have gotten excited by any kind of scene she suggested.

Well, except doing it in public. He was too reserved to enjoy exhibitionism.

Then again, he'd also thought that he was too traditional and naturally dominant to enjoy being at a female's mercy.

Not that he would really be helpless. Unless she used titanium alloy handcuffs, he could get free from any restraints, so fear was not part of the equation.

Pain wasn't either.

He wasn't a masochist.

It was the power exchange, and also the atonement. He wanted her to forgive him, and he was willing to go to great lengths to clean the slate between them.

Why?

Because Sofia had forced him to feel again, to desire and yearn for more than physical gratification, and he hadn't allowed himself to have those feelings for so long that he had believed he'd lost the ability.

At the time, toughening up seemed like the right thing to do, but he hadn't foreseen the cost. To protect himself from emotional pain, he'd given up on the exhilaration of falling in love, or even just in lust, and on forming meaningful connections not just with females but also with males.

Since anyone he cared about could potentially hurt him, he closed himself off and didn't allow anyone to get close enough for him to care for.

Basically, he'd given up on everything that had given him joy, trading it for professional satisfaction in the lab and a humdrum existence outside of it.

"How many bedrooms does this place have?" Sofia opened the first door in the hallway.

"I believe there are four bedrooms. Emmett used to host orgies down here, so I bet we can find some rope or handcuffs."

She looked at him over her shoulder. "Orgies? Are you serious?" She waved at the bedroom's decor. "This doesn't look like a setup for anything kinky. It's just a regular bedroom."

It was nicely furnished, but Sofia was right about it looking mundane.

"That's what I heard. Perhaps the decor got updated under the new management."

Talking about decor helped deflate his raging erection, not completely but enough for him to walk comfortably. He opened a door on the other side of the hallway. "This one is almost identical to the other one."

The third bedroom had a four-poster bed.

"This is the one." Sofia walked over to one of the nightstands and opened the top drawer. "Nothing in here." She opened the bottom one. "And nothing in here either." She looked at him over her shoulder and smiled. "I guess we will have to make do with pillowcases. I can twist them into ropes."

"Hmm." He ran his hand over the footboard that was at least a foot thick. "This looks like it has a hidden compartment." Marcel tried to flip the top open, but it didn't budge. "It's either stuck or locked."

"If it's locked, the key could be hidden somewhere in this room." Sofia walked over to the other nightstand, opened the top drawer, and then lay on the floor to look under it. "No key glued to the underside."

Marcel could've forced the top of the footboard open, but that would have betrayed his super-strength. Instead, he ran his fingers over the underside. "Bingo. There is a hidden latch."

To release it required some strength, probably because it hadn't been used in a while, but when he flipped the top open, he was glad that it hadn't been easy. Syssi had stayed down here, and if she found what he was looking at, she would have been shocked.

Kian's mate was such a pure, gentle soul. She had probably never heard about such kinks let alone seen any of the paraphernalia.

"What's in there?" Sofia walked over to join him in front of the footboard.

"Take a look." He took a step back, curious to see her reaction.

57

SOFIA

*A*s Marcel took a step back, Sofia leaned over the footboard and looked inside the compartment.

At first, she couldn't see a thing in the dark cavity, but as her eyes adjusted to the dim interior, she saw a slim handle and pulled it out.

It was a riding crop, with a small leather flap at the end. She held it up to show to Marcel. "What do you think?"

"Doesn't look too scary. Check what else is in there."

Sofia hesitated.

When she'd conceived the game, she hadn't had instruments of torture in mind. The crop looked like it could be used lightly, and she was going to test it on herself before using it on Marcel, but if the next thing she pulled out was a whip, she would have a panic attack.

To her, it wasn't a theoretical thing that she'd read about in a book. She'd seen whipping and flogging, and it was horrendous.

Thankfully, it was never used on humans, or at least not since she was old enough to be aware of it, but purebloods and hybrids who displeased Igor were severely punished.

What would he do to her if she failed to deliver what he was looking for?

Did he kill humans who displeased him?

She jerked as Marcel put his hand on her shoulder. "What's the matter? Are you having second thoughts about our game?"

She forced a smile. "I didn't plan on using torture implements. That's too much."

He chuckled. "Those are just toys." He pulled out a pink flogger. "See? The strands are soft suede, and it's pink." He handed it to her. "Check it out."

The strands were indeed soft, and as she flicked it over her thigh, she could barely feel anything through her jeans.

"I'm sure it stings more on bare skin." She flicked it on her arm, and it stung a little, but it wasn't painful.

Feeling better about the game, she put the flogger on the bed and pulled out the next item, which was a set of leather restraints.

That was what she needed, and all the rest was superfluous. She wasn't going to flog Marcel or hit him with a crop. All she was going to do was keep him on the edge until he could take it no more.

Turning around she held out the restraints. "Are you ready for your torment?"

His expression was hard to read, but she was sure he wasn't afraid, not for himself, anyway. He must have sensed her surge of anxiety and wondered what had caused it.

Hopefully, he thought it was her inexperience. He couldn't possibly guess that she'd witnessed whipping and knew how horrific it really was.

"I am, but are you? You seem out of your element." He gave her a crooked smile. "We can go back to the punch in the face idea, and after you punish me, I can take over and show you why it was a smart move to give me another chance."

It was tempting, but she didn't want to punch him either.

"Are you stalling, Marcel?" She ran the leather restraints over her hand. "What are you afraid of?"

"Nothing." He toed off his shoes and pulled his turtleneck over his head. "Nothing that you can do to me with those implements. But I'm terrified of what you can do to my heart."

Sofia swallowed.

Marcel had been hurt before. He'd told her about the girlfriend who'd demanded expensive gifts and then left him. He must have loved her very much to fall victim to her manipulation, or maybe it had happened a long time ago when he was still very young and naive and hadn't known better.

As he turned his back to her and pulled his turtleneck off, Sofia's eyes roamed over his surprisingly defined back muscles. The guy must be spending serious time in the gym to have a body like that. His socks and pants were next, exposing nearly hairless smooth skin and powerful leg muscles, and when he hooked his thumbs in the elastic of his boxer shorts, Sofia held her breath.

He deprived her of the sight of his manhood, climbing on the bed and lying down on his stomach.

The view was magnificent, and she couldn't wait to have her hands all over those beautiful muscles, but what she planned to do required him to lie on his back.

The flogger and the crop were still on the bed where she'd left them. Marcel probably thought that she was going to use them on him, which was why he'd left them there.

She wasn't going to cause him physical pain, but regrettably, hurting his feelings was inevitable. He might not realize that she'd seduced him for information, but at some point she would have to leave, and she would need to make a clean break, ensuring that he didn't even think to follow her.

It was going to be painful for both of them, and she cursed Igor and her fate for forcing her to hurt a good man, a man she would have loved to keep for longer than a few weeks and see where the relationship took them. But she wasn't free to choose her guy, and her days of freedom were numbered. Igor might send her on missions where her linguistic skills were needed, but he would demand that she return to the compound.

So far, she hadn't been asked to breed with any of the purebloods to produce a hybrid, and in a few years, she would be deemed too old to serve in that capacity, and then she would be free to choose a human partner to father her children.

But he would have to be from the compound.

Her future was not with Marcel even if they turned out to be perfect for each other.

He was right. The pain she could inflict with the flogger or the crop would be nothing compared to the pain of betrayal.

58

MARCEL

*M*arcel lay face down on the bed and waited for Sofia to make her move.

He could hear her breathing, and he could sense her nervousness. The arousal he'd scented before had diminished when she examined the sex toys, but when he'd gotten naked, it was back, but not to the same level it was when he'd kissed her.

Didn't his body look pleasing to her?

He was in good shape, but he wasn't as muscled as he used to be during his Guardian days. Still, he knew that females found him attractive, so that wasn't it.

She was way over her head with that idea of hers.

"If you want to stop, just say the word. I don't want you to do anything you're uncomfortable with."

"For what I have in mind, you need to turn around," she said quietly.

"Yes, ma'am. You're running the show." He turned to lie on his back.

As Sofia's eyes roamed over his nude body and stopped at his manhood, her cheeks flushed. "You are even better-looking naked," she murmured.

When she licked her lips, his shaft twitched. He fisted it, running his hand up and down lazily. "You can come closer and get a better look."

She smirked as she sauntered over to the side of the bed. "Enjoy it while you can. I'm going to restrain the other hand first."

He flopped his arm to the side, offering it to her. "What are you going to do when you have me at your mercy?"

"You'll find out." She attached one end of the strap to the left post of the head-board, put the wide leather cuff over his wrist, and threaded the end of the tongue through the buckle. "Is it okay?" She tugged on it lightly. "Or is it too tight?"

The scent of her arousal was intensifying by the moment, and his body was reacting predictably. It was good that he had such incredible control over his fangs, or he would be flashing them at her by now.

"It's fine." Marcel gave the strap a perfunctory yank. "Good job." If he yanked any harder, he would either snap the leather or tear down the post.

She smiled as she moved to his left ankle and anchored it the same way. "Too tight? Not tight enough?"

He pretended to yank again. "It's a bit loose, but that's okay. I'm not going anywhere. There is nowhere I'd rather be."

Sofia turned to look at his swelling shaft. "So it would seem. Or is your manhood reacting to your skillful hand?"

"It's all for you, Sofia. Please hurry up and punish me already so we can get to the fun part."

"Patience, big boy." She moved to his right ankle. "We are going to have a lot of fun but not in the way you imagine."

Should he be worried?

What did Sofia intend to do to him?

The crop and the ridiculous pink flogger were still on the bed next to his feet, but so far, she'd ignored them.

The question was what she would do after she had him all tied up.

After securing his right ankle, she walked to the right side of the bed. "Play time is over, lover boy. I need that hand."

As he let go of his shaft and plopped his arm sideways, she didn't grip it immediately. Instead, she seemed mesmerized by his bobbing erection.

He chuckled. "Like what you see?"

"Very much so." She gripped his wrist lightly and secured it to the right bedpost.

Spreadeagled, he looked at her with hooded eyes, waiting for her next move.

He'd expected her to lift one of the implements and strike him with it, but he didn't expect her to start stripping.

"Is that your idea of torture? Are you hoping to taunt me with your nude body and not let me touch you?"

"That's the general idea."

When she pulled her T-shirt over her head and tossed it aside, Marcel sucked in a breath. She was wearing one of those pushup bras that he usually found ridiculous, but it looked damn good on her.

She was very delicately built, so he knew she wouldn't be well-endowed, not naturally anyway, but that was okay. Size didn't matter, and he preferred her breasts to be tiny but natural and not surgically enlarged.

Holding his gaze with her blue eyes, she reached behind her, unhooked the bra, and let it fall down her arms.

She was exactly like he'd expected. With only a slight swell, she was nearly as flat-chested as a boy, but there was nothing boyish about her nipples. They were dark, turgid, and begging to be sucked.

"I want to put my mouth on those berries so badly that I'm salivating."

59

SOFIA

*M*arcel's eyes were glowing, Sofia was sure about that, but since he was obviously human, she glanced up at the light fixture hanging over the bed.

It was probably a reflection. With his blond hair and fair skin, he couldn't be a hybrid. The Kra-ell dark coloring was a dominant trait, and even hybrids who had blond human mothers were dark-haired and olive-skinned.

It didn't matter.

All that mattered was the way he was looking at her as if she was a goddess of feminine sexuality, and he couldn't wait to have her.

But he would have to because she was about to teach him a lesson about leaving a woman hanging.

After pulling down her jeans and panties, she sauntered naked over to the bed, climbed on top, and leaned over him. "Do you want to suck on my nipples?"

"Yes." He hissed.

She kissed him lightly on the lips and then brought a nipple to hover several inches over his mouth, almost within reach.

He arched up, pulling the restraints taut, and caught it between his lips, sucking on it greedily.

Her eyes rolling back in her head and moisture pooling between her legs, Sofia moaned. When it became too much, she pulled back and offered him her other nipple.

His neck must be killing him, but Marcel was oblivious to his discomfort as he sucked, nibbled, and nipped, eroding her resolve to keep him on the edge.

She was so turned on that prolonging his suffering meant suffering alongside him, but it was a sweet kind of torment, and she was adamant about stretching it out for as long as she could.

"That's enough," she commanded.

With a groan, he obeyed and let his head drop back on the pillow. "That wasn't nearly enough."

Smiling, she turned around and fisted his erection. He jerked up, thrusting it into her palm, and when she dipped her head and kissed the tip, he groaned.

"Straddle my face and let me taste you."

She wanted to reply that he wasn't in charge and that she would do what she pleased, but her needy core had other ideas, and apparently, she was the boss because Sofia did as he'd asked.

When he licked into her, she closed her eyes and took a third of his erection into her mouth. It was as much as she could comfortably fit, but then it swelled even more, and her mouth got stretched further.

Pushing back to get more of his tongue and lips on her, she tried to keep a steady rhythm, her hand and mouth working in tandem, but with the sensations bombarding her on the other end, it was becoming more and more difficult to concentrate.

In mere moments, they were both right on the edge of orgasming, and Sofia was so damn tempted to let it happen that she teared up as she pulled her bottom away from Marcel's mouth and squeezed his erection tight to prevent him from coming.

Marcel groaned. "You're evil."

She turned her head to look at him over her shoulder. "That's your punishment. I'm going to keep you on the edge until you scream in frustration."

"Can't you just flog me instead?"

"That wouldn't be as satisfying." She loosened her hold on his erection and licked off the drop of pre cum that had accumulated there. "Hmm. You taste good."

"Not as good as you. Give me back that sweet pussy of yours."

"Gladly."

He attacked it with such fervor that Sofia orgasmed in less than thirty seconds, but she didn't let him finish, repeating what she'd done before.

The leathers straps securing his restraints to the bedposts groaned as he pulled on them, and she had a feeling that he could have snapped them if he really wished to get free, but he was either enjoying the torment she was inflicting on him or determined to let her get her revenge.

When he brought her to her third orgasm, she turned around and straddled his hips. "I'm going to fuck you now."

It had been a while for her, and he was a fairly large male, but she was so slick from climaxing three times that she didn't hesitate. Gripping his aroused member, she lowered her soaking core onto him and pushed down until he was fully seated inside her.

The feeling of being filled by him was so incredible that if not for the slight discomfort of her sheath stretching to accommodate him, she would have orgasmed again.

Marcel's eyes rolled back in their sockets, and the animalistic growl he emitted pulled a new gush of wetness from her that eliminated the discomfort, leaving only intense pleasure behind.

For a long moment, she didn't move, absorbing the feeling of being connected to Marcel in such a primal way. But then he arched up, getting impossibly deeper inside her, and his arm muscles contracted pulling the restraints taut.

They were about to give, and when they did, she had no doubt that he would flip her under him and take over.

Rising on her knees, she looked into his glowing eyes as she slammed down on his arousal, and when she pulled up and slammed down again, a loud crack sounded and then Marcel's arms closed around her.

"My turn." He hissed as he flipped her under him.

60

MARCEL

$\mathcal{A}$s Marcel got Sofia under him, his fangs were already elongated. Reaching into her mind, he thralled her to keep her eyes closed, and as he licked the spot on her neck, he sent another thrall to make her ignore his bite, and bit down.

She cried out, her body tensing under him, and as the venom did its thing, she cried out again, this time in ecstasy, and climaxed along with him.

She'd kept him on the edge for so long that his self-control had eventually snapped, and he was going at her full power, pumping her with copious quantities of his essence.

Long moments passed before the crazed haze of sexual frenzy subsided and his mind came back online, and when it did, he retracted his fangs, licked the puncture wounds closed, and prayed to the Fates that she was on birth control.

Immortal males were nearly infertile, so usually he didn't worry about getting a woman pregnant, but there had been nothing usual about Sofia, and not just because she'd tormented him and hadn't allowed him to climax until she'd been good and ready.

He felt it in his bones, in his veins, in his entire being, but he didn't know what it was.

He wasn't in love with her. He barely knew her. The attraction was there, and it was strong, but that couldn't explain the way she'd made him lose himself in her.

Perhaps she was a Dormant?

He hadn't allowed himself to entertain that thought, but it had been lurking in the back of his mind.

Sofia's paranormal talent was strange and unheard of, but so were Mey's and Jin's, so there was that. There was also the immediate connection he felt with her, and given her response, she'd felt it too.

Sofia didn't strike him as the kind of woman who routinely hooked up with men she'd just met, and he had enough experience with women who did that to know that she wasn't like them. And yet she'd been the driving force of their encounter.

She had been in full control of it, so he hadn't stopped to think it was odd that she hadn't asked him to procure a condom or brought one herself. She must be on birth control, but still. Pregnancy wasn't the only thing a human female needed to worry about.

Lifting his head, he looked at her blissed-out face, soaking up her beauty for a long moment before dipping down and stealing a kiss from her parted lips.

When she sighed contentedly, he thought she would wake up, but when she didn't open her eyes, he remembered that he'd thralled her to keep them closed.

She shouldn't be awake so soon after a venom bite, especially given the quantity he'd pumped into her. If she were a male, she would be dead by now. Thankfully, the venom produced in response to sexual desire was not deadly. It didn't slow the heart, and the euphoric effect only lasted a few hours.

Naturally, he would stay awake and watch over her to make sure she was okay.

But first, he needed to get them both cleaned up and throw the ruined restraints into the trash. He should probably get new ones and put them in the hidden compartment.

Pulling out gently, he kissed Sofia's puffy lips again, and then padded to the bathroom to clean himself and bring washcloths for her.

When he returned, he found her on her side, which was not how he'd left her.

Normally women didn't move a muscle until the venom's effect was spent, but as he'd already realized, there was nothing usual about Sofia.

She'd blown his mind.

After cleaning her up, he dropped the washcloths on the nightstand, pulled the covers over them both, and wrapped her in his arms.

She was so slight, seemingly so fragile, but he knew it was an illusion. He'd felt how strong she was, which was why he'd unleashed on her the beast hidden inside of every immortal without fearing that she would break. It hadn't been a conscious decision, but his beast had known she could take it.

61

SOFIA

*S*ofia opened her eyes with effort. She'd had the most wonderful dreams of soaring above the clouds and looking at beautiful landscapes. She felt at peace, happy like she'd never been before, but an insistent buzzing in the back of her mind intruded on those contented feelings of wonderment, reminding her that there was something urgent she had to do.

Something unpleasant, by the feel of it. Something that would shatter the beautiful bubble she was floating in.

Her mind was still too scattered to focus on what that thing was, the strong arms wrapped around her and the warm chest she was pressed against making it even more difficult to concentrate on anything other than the happiness she felt.

It was naive and a little ridiculous to think that fabulous sex could have a healing effect on her, but that was how she felt.

The truth was that she hadn't thought of herself as sick, injured, or impaired before, but with how wonderful she felt now, it was obvious that she hadn't been well.

She'd lived in constant fear.

Oh, yeah. Now she remembered. She needed to contact Valstar.

"Hello, beautiful." Marcel dipped his head and kissed her lightly. "Did you have pleasant dreams?"

Had he fallen asleep too and had woken up at the same time as she had? Or had he been waiting for her to open her eyes?

"The best." She smiled up at him. "Did we both fall asleep?"

"Only you did." His hand smoothed over the curve of her ass. "I enjoyed lying awake and watching you." His hand traveled back up. "You looked so peaceful."

"Yeah. I had such beautiful dreams."

"Was I in them?"

"No, but I'm sure you inspired them." She shifted in his arms, getting more comfortable in his embrace. "How long did I sleep?"

"Nearly nine hours."

Alarm bells rang in her head. "It can't be. What time is it?"

"It's a little after five in the morning."

"I have to go." She pushed on his chest.

Damn, she'd fallen asleep without telling Valstar that she'd report later this morning. He was going to be furious.

Marcel's arms tightened around her. "Breakfast starts at seven. You have plenty of time."

"I didn't go jogging after dinner last night, so I have to do it before breakfast. I never miss a day."

"I'll come with you."

Damn. What was she going to do now? She couldn't let him accompany her, but after the night they'd spent together, Marcel would expect her to want to spend more time with him, and since she needed him to fall for her, she couldn't rudely refuse.

Smiling up at him, she ran her hands over his nearly hairless chest. "Don't take it the wrong way, but I jog to gather my thoughts, and if you come with me, I won't be able to think about anything other than how wonderful last night was. In fact, I will probably think about it even if you don't come with me." She lowered her eyes demurely. "It was the best sex I've ever had." She chuckled. "By a wide margin."

Hooking a finger under her chin, he lifted her head so she had to look into his eyes. "It was the best for me as well." His lips lifted on one side only, giving him a roguish expression. "I've never let anyone tie me up and torment me with pleasure before. If I'd known how turned on it would make me, I might have tried it. Although I doubt it would have been that explosive with anyone but you. You are special, Sofia."

His words shouldn't have meant so much to her, but they did. She'd never been told that she was special, or that she was anyone's best.

"Thank you." She lifted her hand and cupped his cheek. "I've never done anything like that before, and I don't even know where the idea came from."

"That's easy to guess. You probably saw that movie everyone was talking about or read the books."

Sofia shook her head. "I know what movie and books you're talking about, but I didn't see or read any of them. Causing or receiving pain does not appeal to me." She shivered as memories of whipping flitted through her mind. "That's why I punished you with pleasure."

"I think it's called funishment, and you are welcome to funish me anytime you want." He pulled her on top of him. "Maybe instead of a morning run, you can have a morning ride." He moved his hips, rubbing his erection against her stomach.

"I can have both." She reached between their bodies and gripped his rigid length.

62

MARCEL

This time, their lovemaking was sweet and unhurried, and when they both reached their climax, Marcel didn't have to work hard to force his fangs to retract without biting Sofia.

He'd pumped her with so much venom last night that it would take a long time before the urge to bite would become overwhelming again.

For a long moment, they lay entangled in each other, enjoying the feeling of connection, until Sofia sighed. "I hate to go, but I have to."

"Stay." He cupped her cheeks and kissed her. "I'll call in sick."

She laughed and pushed on his chest. "I need to go to the bathroom."

Reluctantly, he released her and turned on his back. He felt too good to ruin it by going back to the lab. Hell, he didn't feel like doing any work at all. Not today, and not tomorrow, and not for the next couple of months. He imagined spending long days walking on the beach with Sofia, taking her out to restaurants, going shopping, to movies, plays, even musicals.

He didn't like them, but it didn't matter. Everything would be pleasurable with Sofia by his side.

Somewhere in the back of his mind a voice of reason whispered that he was falling down the rabbit hole again, and that his tendency to fall fast and hard for a woman had nearly destroyed him before. But he'd been listening to that voice for so long that he was tired of hearing it.

A life full of feeling was too good to squander on fear.

Sofia opened the bathroom door and frowned at him. "Why are you still in bed? We need to go." She collected her clothes off the floor and started putting them on. "Unless you can let me out of here without blindfolding me again, you can't stay in bed."

She pulled her pendant out of the pocket of her jeans and draped it around her neck.

"I don't need to blindfold you." No guests were supposed to know about the bunker, but it wasn't a clan secret that he needed to protect. "You just have to promise not to tell anyone about Emmett's bunker." He got out of bed and reached for his pants. "The orgies I told you about were not public knowledge, and he would like to keep it that way. It would be embarrassing for him and hurt the resort if rumors of it leaked out."

Marcel didn't want to thrall Sofia again to make her forget where the bunker was, but he intended to do that before the retreat was over and she left.

When imagining her gone felt like a kick to the gut, he pushed those thoughts aside. There was time, and many things could happen between now and the end of the retreat.

Maybe he would find out that Sofia was a Dormant and they would live happily ever after.

Yeah, right.

Even a dreamer like him didn't believe that would happen. He wasn't that lucky, and the Fates had never been kind to him.

In fact, they'd been quite bitchy.

"I won't tell anyone." Sofia looked around, and when she didn't find what she was looking for, she opened the bedroom door and walked into the living room. He followed, tucking his turtleneck into his pants.

"Here it is." She lifted her backpack. "I had a moment of panic when I thought I'd lost it." She pulled out a comb and ran it through her magnificent hair. "Why did you blindfold me last night if it wasn't necessary?"

"I thought it was. But I realized that if I trusted you enough to let you tie me up, I can trust you to keep a secret." He pulled her into his arms and kissed her.

"You knew that you could get free, so I don't know how much trust was really involved." She untangled herself from his arms. "Let's get going. I need to change into exercise clothes, and there isn't much time left before breakfast."

He led her up the stairs, punched in the code to the door at the top, and walked her through the cottage to Emmett's small garden.

"How long is your usual run?" he asked as they entered the lodge.

"Half an hour to forty-five minutes."

He wrapped his arm around her tiny waist. "Can you make it to breakfast at seven-thirty?"

Sofia smiled. "I definitely can. Will you meet me for lunch and dinner as well?"

"I would love to, but I need to have at least one meal a day with my team. They are cranky enough as it is because I've been neglecting them."

She tilted her head. "Why can't we all eat at the same table? You can introduce me to your coworkers."

"We have our own dining room, and I'm supposed to be eating over there."

"I didn't know that there was another dining room in the lodge."

"It's not in the lodge." He could tell her about the government leasing part of Safe Haven. That wasn't a secret. Only what they were doing there was. "The government rents the area north of the resort, and they are running a secret project there. That's why guests are not allowed inside the enclave."

Sofia's back muscles tensed under his arm. "Do you work for the government?"

"I don't. My team and I work on our own project, but since we also require enhanced security, we share space with them."

When they reached her door, Sofia put her hand on his shoulder and kissed him on the lips. "I guess you can't talk about either of those projects, right?"

He nodded.

"Then I'm not going to ask." She smiled, kissed him again, and opened the door. "See you at breakfast," she whispered and ducked inside, closing the door quietly behind her.

For a long moment, he stood in front of that door, staring at it with a goofy smile on his face and feeling like a lovesick teenager.

Reminding himself that he still needed to go back to the bunker and launder the sheets and towels they had used, he shook his head and forced his feet to start walking.

He was well aware that he was setting himself up for heartache, but it was too late to stop now.

He was already falling in love with Sofia.

63

SOFIA

*S*ofia waved at the guard as she jogged past him. "Good morning."
    It was the same guy she'd seen there when she jogged in the evenings.
Did he work around the clock like Igor's guards?

He smiled at her. "You're early today."

"I missed my run yesterday."

"Busy night?" he called after her.

"Very." She cast him a smile over her shoulder.

Laughing, he waved her off.

It was good that he'd grown to expect her jogging along the coastline. Routine was the best antidote to suspicion.

When Sofia reached her usual spot, she took a few moments to even out her breathing before reaching under her shirt and pulling out the pendant.

Valstar would be furious, but he would calm down when she told him the good news that she'd seduced the man she'd said she would. She'd done it mostly for herself, but he didn't need to know that.

If not for the axe hanging over her loved ones' necks, she would have taken her time and gotten to know Marcel better before tying him to a bed and having her way with him.

At the memory, a smile curved her lips and a blush crept up her cheeks. He'd brought her to orgasm so many times that she'd lost track, and he'd exhausted her so thoroughly that she'd fallen asleep before he'd even pulled out of her.

That had never happened to her before, and it was a little embarrassing, but Marcel had thought nothing of it. This morning, he'd made love to her so gently and sweetly that she felt like tearing up from how emotional it made her.

He was such an amazing man. What a shame that building a life with him couldn't even be a fantasy.

Sighing, she pulled out the tiny earpiece from the pendant, stuck it in her ear, and pressed on the picture.

"Are you okay?" her grandfather barked.

That hadn't been the question she'd expected from him. Did Valstar actually care about her?

"I'm fine. I didn't get a chance to contact you last night because I was busy working on my objective. I seduced the guy."

He let out a breath. "Good job, Sofia. Did you get more information out of him?"

"I did, but I don't know how relevant it is to Igor. Turns out that the American government is using a portion of Safe Haven for a secret project they are running. The guy I seduced also runs a secret project, but it's not connected to what the government is doing, or so he says. I find it odd that his lab is located within their secure area, but he doesn't work for them."

"That's interesting. Did he just volunteer the information, or did you get it out of him?"

"A combination of the two." Sofia leaned against the rock and looked at the shoreline to make sure no one was coming. "I try not to ask direct questions, so he doesn't get suspicious, but I steer the conversation in the right direction for him to tell me more about what he does here."

"That's good. Make him trust you."

Marcel had let her tie him up, so he must trust her. But then he'd somehow gotten free without her help, so he'd probably known all along that he wasn't really at her mercy.

"I'm doing my best."

"I'm going to tell Igor what you've just told me and get further instructions. Stay where you are."

"Yes, sir."

Several minutes passed before Valstar came back to her. "Igor wants to talk to your guy. What's his name?"

She would have preferred to keep it ambiguous, but at this point in the game, she doubted that Marcel would ghost her again.

"Marcel. Why does Igor want to talk to him and how?"

"Instead of you wasting days on getting small tidbits of information out of him, Igor can just compel him to talk and get it done. And as for how you're going to achieve that, I have a plan. You'll go to the office and say that you need to call home because your father wasn't feeling well when you left, and you worry about him. When you call the number I'll give you, make sure that you are heard. I'll pretend to be your father and ask you if you've met any nice young men. You will tell me about Marcel, and I will demand to speak to him to make sure that he's not taking advantage of my daughter. After I disconnect, you'll make a fuss about your unreasonable father and ask if you can keep the phone so your boyfriend could call him."

A shiver ran down Sofia's spine.

Marcel would know that he'd been compelled, and he would have her kicked out of the retreat, or worse, arrested. If what he was working on was for the government, or even if not, her part in getting him to reveal the project's secrets would be considered espionage.

"Marcel is not attending the retreat, and he has his own phone, but I don't think that's a good idea."

"Why not?"

She'd better do a fantastic job of explaining, or contradicting Valstar and Igor would cost her dearly.

"Marcel is a computer engineer, so what he's working on has to do with computers, and it's not affiliated with Safe Haven and its management. Even if Igor is curious about Marcel's project, I doubt it's worth blowing my cover for. Marcel will know that he was compelled, and he will get me kicked out at best or arrested for espionage at worst. In either case, I will lose access to any further information."

"Igor can compel him to tell no one about the compulsion and to keep pretending that he's your boyfriend."

That could solve that problem, but it would cost her Marcel and still not help Igor achieve his objectives. Even though it would be his doing, he would blame her and punish her for a failure that wasn't her fault.

"That's an option, but I still won't be any closer to achieving the objectives of this mission, whatever they are."

"I'll talk it over with Igor and contact you in a few minutes. Stay where you are."

"Yes, sir."

64

DARLENE

$\mathcal{A}$s Darlene entered the lab, she was greeted with cheers and claps from her coworkers as if she'd been the one who had transitioned.

"Thank you, but I didn't do anything to deserve your cheers." She headed toward William's office.

The door was open, and as usual, William and Kaia were sharing William's enormous desk, which was also less cluttered than usual thanks to Kaia, and also as usual, the two stopped talking the moment she crossed the threshold.

Darlene knew that they were working on a secret project, but that was ridiculous. Her so-called office was inside William's, and she had no choice but to go through his to get to hers.

"What are you doing here?" William asked. "You should be home with your mate."

She waved a dismissive hand. "Eric is doing great, and I have work to do. I can just imagine the mess waiting for me to sort out."

"I organized it in stacks," Kaia said. "I hope that helps."

"You're an angel." Darlene blew her a kiss. "By the way, I was thinking. Maybe Kaia can have my office and you can find me somewhere else to work? I hate coming in here and the two of you stopping your conversation mid-sentence."

William shook his head. "We are maxed out on space. Kian has left a lot of room for home expansion, but he didn't expect us to be doing so much work in the lab."

"Maybe we can use one of the homes," Kaia suggested. "Toven is already turning two houses into a studio and a test lab for the Perfect Match machines."

William let out a sigh. "He's working with the completed product, so he can do it in a residential environment. We are building things here, and we need a lot of space to do that. It's also messy and noisy and no one wants it near their homes."

"I can work from home," Kaia said. "Maybe we both can."

"I can't. I need to be here. You see how many times a day people come to me with questions and I go to help them. We will just have to manage." He gave Darlene an apologetic look. "I'm sorry, but you are stuck with your tiny office and with us as your roommates."

"That's no biggie. I like my tiny office." She opened the door, walked in, and hung her purse on the back of the chair.

"Do you need me to close the door?" she asked.

It was stuffy in there, and the air circulation wasn't good, but Kaia and William needed privacy for their super-secretive project, and she didn't want to force them to whisper.

"Leave it open," William said. "We will talk quietly."

"Thanks." She turned on the desk fan and sat down to work.

There were orders to file and track, inventory lists to update, and expenses to enter into the ledger.

Fun stuff, and Darlene didn't mean it sarcastically. She was good at organizing things, and a job well done provided her with the calm and satisfaction that she desperately needed.

Her life was better than ever, but it was also more complicated and full of turmoil than it had ever been before.

Eric's transition and subsequent coma had taken a toll on her, making her feel older and more exhausted than she'd felt when she'd first moved into the village. Then there was the scandalous threesome idea that Eric was pushing her into, and that was stressing her out even in its modified and less scandalous version.

Ever since Eric had told her about Max's idea, she'd been thinking about the logistics of it a lot.

During Eric's coma, she and Max had gotten closer as friends, which made the threesome idea even more complicated. She didn't want Max to see her naked, let alone climaxing while Eric was inside of her.

Maybe she could buy one of those burka things in size extra-large and wear it like a tent to hide her body while she rode Eric. She could position them in such a way that Max would only see her back when he came in to deliver the bite.

Could he bite her through the fabric, though? Or would she have to expose her neck and shoulder?

Ugh. Why couldn't Bridget milk Max's fangs like a snake's and put his venom in a syringe.

That would have made things so much easier.

65

SOFIA

Sofia's heart was racing. Contradicting Valstar and Igor had been such a gutsy move that it bordered on suicidal, and she was still reeling from it.

Her primary instinct had been to protect Marcel and their relationship, but the more she thought about it, the more she realized that she'd been right. It all depended on what Igor was after, and since the whole thing had started because of Jade's interest in Safe Haven and its paranormal retreats, it couldn't be about Marcel's project.

She didn't know much about computers, but she knew enough that they were not the answer to Igor's compulsion. Machines were not susceptible to it, but they probably couldn't protect biological beings from it.

Even animals fell under the power of compulsion.

But what if Marcel's project was about some innovative brain implant that could shield people from mind manipulation?

Hopefully, that wouldn't occur to Igor, and in the meantime, she had to come up with an alternative to Marcel. Emmett Haderech would be the best source of information about everything that had to do with Safe Haven, but how could she pull it off with him? He wasn't her boyfriend, and he was taken, so Igor couldn't tell her to seduce him. It wasn't because he was concerned with morality, but because she wasn't likely to succeed.

What excuse could she give Emmett Haderech to convince him to call her so-called father?

Maybe something about the rumors of Safe Haven being a cult and Emmett Haderech swindling money out of people?

"I'm back," Valstar said in her earpiece. "Igor agrees with your assessment of the situation. But since your boyfriend is useless as a source of information, he wants you to shift your focus to someone in Safe Haven's management."

That was what she'd expected.

"While waiting, I was thinking, and I came to a similar conclusion. Who knows better about what's going on in Safe Haven than its founder? I can ask for an audience with Emmett Haderech, and when I'm alone with him, I can beg him to call my father."

"Why would he oblige you if you are not fucking him?"

Sofia flinched at the crude language. "Emmett Haderech likes attention and flattery, and he likes to talk about how great he is. I can butter him up, telling him how much I admire him and the wonderful community he built, and that he's nothing like what my father warned me about. I can say that my father read the rumors about Safe Haven being a cult and Emmett Haderech swindling money out of people, and he thinks that Emmett is a crook. My father tried to convince me not to attend the retreat and we had a huge fight over it. If the benevolent and charismatic leader could do me a big favor and talk to my father, he would vindicate me. I would love to prove my father wrong."

Valstar chuckled. "That's not bad, and since Emmett Haderech is most likely not harboring government secrets, you won't be accused of espionage. Depending on what Igor gets out of him, he might not even realize that he was under compulsion to talk. Good thinking on your feet, Sofia."

The relief that washed over her had her knees buckle, and she slid down the rock to sit on sand. She still needed an argument to keep Marcel. "Marcel knows Emmett Haderech. He can help me get an audience with Emmett sooner rather than later."

"Good. You don't have much time left, and if Emmett doesn't have the information Igor is seeking, you will need to keep digging."

Sofia closed her eyes. "It would be really helpful if I knew what he was looking for."

"I agree, but that's how Igor wants to play it, and what Igor wants, Igor gets. Do you catch my drift?"

She grimaced. "Loud and clear."

"Good day, Sofia. May the Mother keep you safe."

"Thanks."

Was it her imagination, or was her grandfather being nicer than usual to her? He sounded proud of her, and that just didn't happen between pureblooded Kraell and their half-human children or completely human grandchildren.

The purebloods only valued their pureblooded offspring, and they sneered at hybrids and humans. Heck, they barely acknowledged being their progenitors.

66

MARCEL

---

*M*arcel had gone back to the bunker with the intention of removing the sheets and towels he and Sofia had used, but then he thought that maybe they would spend another night there, so why bother. Maybe he should wait to see whether Sofia wanted a repeat of last night and this morning?

Nah. He should launder the bedding regardless so they would be fresh for tonight, and if Sofia changed her mind about him for some reason and refused to see him, he would at least leave the place as he'd found it.

The community cleaning crews who worked at the resort probably didn't bother with the bunker while no one was supposed to be staying there.

After loading the washing machine, Marcel checked the time. He should go back to his bungalow and change, but it wasn't urgent. One of the advantages of wearing a nearly identical outfit day in and day out was that no one would notice that he hadn't changed clothes this morning.

He could stay in the bunker until the washing cycle was done and load the bedding and towels into the dryer before heading to the dining hall.

In the kitchen he loaded the coffeemaker, and as he waited for the coffee to brew, he opened the refrigerator to check whether there was anything inside. Unsurprisingly, it was empty, and so was the freezer.

Still, the kitchen was fully equipped to handle meal preparation, and it occurred to him that he could prepare dinner in the bunker and treat Sofia to a proper romantic evening.

Fates knew that his courtship had been deplorable. She deserved so much more. One problem was getting groceries, and the other was his limited culinary abilities.

Perhaps he could pay the chef to prepare the meal? It would need to be reheated, but it would most likely taste better than anything he could make.

A quick search through the cabinets produced a white tablecloth, two candleholders, and several candles. The living room was well stocked with plenty of good wines to choose from.

He had everything needed for a wonderfully romantic evening.

He could meet Sofia at the dining hall, ask her to put on the blindfold, carry her to the bunker again, and surprise her with a beautifully set table for two.

After the washing cycle was done and the bedding transferred to the dryer, Marcel headed out.

When he got to the dining hall, he scanned the room for Sofia, and saw that she hadn't returned from her morning jog yet. However, he found her friend.

Roxana waved him over. "Sofia will be here in a few minutes. Come sit with us."

He smiled at her and the other two ladies, then leaned to whisper. "If you don't mind, I'd rather have Sofia all to myself this morning."

Roxana pouted. "I do mind. You stole my friend from me, but who am I to stand in the way of love?"

"Thank you, and I promise not to steal her at lunch. She'll be all yours."

"Yeah, yeah." Roxana waved him away. "Off you go, you scoundrel."

When he found a vacant table, Marcel repeated the trick of leaning the chairs against the table to make it seem as if he was saving them for his companions, sat down, and waited for Sofia to appear.

He saw her enter the dining hall and scan the breakfast crowd, her face brightening when she found him.

She was still wearing her exercise clothes, and she looked good enough to eat in the tight leggings and cropped top. She was very slim, but she wasn't bony, and her body was toned. Her long hair was gathered into a ponytail instead of her customary bun, the dark tresses glossy and thick.

The girl was the picture of health and vitality, and despite her delicate build, there was nothing fragile about her. And yet Marcel felt an overwhelming need to protect her.

From what or who? He had no idea.

It was instinctive—an immortal male's need to protect his mate.

But since immortals could only bond with other immortals or Dormants, did it mean that Sofia was a Dormant?

Hope surging in his chest, he pushed to his feet and waited for her to reach him. "Good morning, beautiful." He pulled her into his arms and kissed her cheek.

"I'm sweaty." She pushed on his chest. "I didn't have time to shower and change."

"You look and smell amazing." He inhaled. "Morning sunshine and pine. Two of my favorite scents."

67

SOFIA

$\mathcal{M}$arcel's compliment was so sweet, so sincere, that if Sofia weren't so stressed, she would have turned into a pile of goo.

"Thank you. That's such a nice thing to say." She smiled at him. "I didn't want to keep you waiting."

He glanced at the buffet. "There is no line. Let's grab something to eat before it gets busy again."

"Let's. I'm famished."

"No wonder. You've been very active." Marcel wrapped his arm around her middle, his hand resting possessively over her thigh. "You need to replenish your energy stores."

"I certainly do." She leaned against him. "Especially since I plan on being very active later tonight again."

She liked that he was flaunting their relationship. After he'd stood her up, she'd thought that he didn't want to be seen with her, but apparently his explanation had been sincere, and he wasn't very adept at courtship, which she liked as well. It meant that he wasn't a player.

Not that it mattered. Their relationship couldn't last, but she was going to enjoy it to the fullest as long as it did.

As they took their loaded plates and coffee mugs back to the table, she cast him a sidelong glance. "It just dawned on me that you didn't sleep at all last night. How are you so peppy?"

"Peppy?" He chuckled. "I haven't heard that expression in years."

"Oh." Her face fell. "That's why it is important to live in a country to learn its language properly. My English professors at the university must have not updated the textbooks they were using."

"Your English is perfect." He put his plate down and pulled out a chair for her. "It's easy to forget that you are not a native speaker."

"Thank you." She sat down. "I try my best. Being here and speaking only English helps. I pay attention to how people talk and the idioms they use."

"You said that you plan on touring the country after the retreat is over. Do you have any concrete plans? Do you have friends you can stay with?"

She shook her head. "Other than the people I've met here, I don't know anyone. Roxie is from Washington DC, and she invited me to stay with her for a few days. I heard that it's a very interesting city."

She held her breath, waiting for him to suggest that she stay with him after the retreat was over.

Regrettably, she couldn't just enjoy Marcel's company. She had a mission to accomplish, and the timer was ticking.

He took her hand. "I wish you could stay longer. How about staying for the next retreat? I heard Emmett offering a fifty percent discount, and I might be able to convince him to allow you to attend for free."

That wasn't the same as Marcel asking her to stay with him, but it was a move in the right direction. It also opened the way for what she needed to ask of him.

"Speaking of Emmett Haderech, on the way here, I stopped by the office, and I've put in a request for a private audience with him." She scooped up scrambled eggs with her fork.

Marcel grinned. "You were going to ask him for a discount on the next retreat?"

"Frankly, it didn't occur to me to ask." She cast him a shy smile. "I didn't know that you wanted me to stay."

"Isn't it obvious?"

She shook her head.

"Then why did you ask for an audience with him?"

She shrugged. "While I was jogging, I remembered Roxie telling me about Lydia requesting an audience with Emmett, and I thought to myself, why not? He's a fascinating character, and I didn't think that I was going to attend another retreat. I'm still not sure that I will. But if I want to meet him face to face and get some words of wisdom from him, I'd better do it now."

Marcel regarded her with suspicion in his eyes. "Why was it urgent to put in the request this morning when you were pressed for time?"

She shrugged, pretending indifference. "He might take his time to answer, and I thought there might be a long list of requests ahead of mine. I wanted to make sure that I get to see him before the retreat ends." She took a sip from her coffee and put the mug down. "If you were serious about asking Emmett to give me an additional discount on the next retreat, maybe you could also ask him to meet me sooner rather than later?"

68

MARCEL

*M*arcel's suspicion kicked in.

Sofia's sudden interest in Emmett coincided too closely with their night of passion. Had she used him to get closer to Emmett?

Groupies did all kinds of crazy things to get to their idols, including hooking up with those surrounding the star.

She didn't look like the type, but he had a proven record of being a bad judge of character when it came to women.

It was still too easy to get him to fall head over heels and make him believe that the object of his desire was the epitome of goodness and perfection.

"You haven't expressed a desire to meet Emmett before. What has changed your mind?"

"I wasn't aware that he was granting private audiences until Roxie told me about it. He's a fascinating character, who has been the spiritual leader of a free-love community for over two decades. It would be an honor to meet him face to face."

She talked too fast, sounding nervous, even breathless. Where was the confident woman who had rocked his world last night? Had it been an act?

He narrowed his eyes at her. "Are you attracted to him? Is that what this is all about? He's taken, you know. He and Eleanor are together."

Unexpectedly, Sofia laughed. "Are you jealous? That's so cute."

"I am not." He crossed his arms over his chest. "It's just that none of this computes. You haven't breathed a word about him until this morning, and suddenly, right after we spent the night together, he's all you can talk about. I find it odd."

"Okay." She let out a breath. "I'll fess up. The truth is that I'm doing it because of my father. He read about Emmett Haderech and his cult of free love, and the rumors of him swindling his followers out of their money. My father didn't want me to attend the retreat, and we had a huge fight over it. He said that I was being naive and that I was spending my hard-earned money on a scam. Now that I'm here and I see how thriving the community is, and I'm learning so much about paranormal abilities, I know that Emmett Haderech is not a crook. He might have a penchant for theatrics, and he looks ridiculous with those wigs and robes he wears, but when he speaks, all of that is forgotten. His message is valuable, and he is very charismatic. I think that if Emmett spoke to my father, he could convince him that he was wrong." She sighed. "I don't want this argument to hang over my father and me. I want it settled so when I return home, he will treat me with respect and not look down his nose at me."

She sounded sincere, but he doubted a call from Emmett could convince her father one way or another. The truth was that Emmett was a crook, and the only reason he was no longer swindling his community was that Kian had taken over and was forcing him to pay them decent wages and share the retreat's profits with them.

"I can get Emmett to see you, but I don't know whether he'll be willing to talk to your father. Does your dad even speak English?"

Her whole body language perked up. "He does, and that would be awesome. I can't thank you enough." She leaned to kiss him on the lips. "But I'll think of ways to express my gratitude later tonight."

Marcel leaned away. "I think you're deluding yourself that a talk with Emmett will change your father's mind about him. The guy can sell ice to Eskimos, and he might charm your father during their talk, but if your dad is a smart guy, and he has to be to have such a smart daughter, he won't be fooled by Emmett's gift of gab."

"Maybe he will, and maybe he won't, but it's worth a try. My father thinks that I'm naive and easy to manipulate, so he won't take anything I say seriously."

"Do you want me to talk to him?"

Her eyes widened in alarm. "No. He's also very strict and thinks that I'm still a virgin. I never brought any of my boyfriends home because of that."

"How many boyfriends have you had?"

She smiled and lifted her hand to look at her watch. "Oh, look at the time. My first class of the day is about to begin."

"Nice try. How many?"

"Including you?"

"Yes."

"Three." She leaned and kissed his cheek. "See you at dinner."

69

ERIC

"Good morning." Gilbert walked in with two cups of coffee and a food container. "Karen made lunch for you and Darlene, and she's inviting you two to dinner."

"That's nice of her." Eric put the book he was reading on the coffee table. "I should learn how to cook. I'm out of a job for now, and Darlene went back to work, and Karen has enough on her plate without cooking for us as well."

Gilbert put the glass container on the kitchen counter and walked over to the couch with a paper cup in each hand. "She's just cooking larger quantities. It's not like she's cooking separately for you and Darlene." He handed Eric one of the cups and sat next to him. "How are you feeling?"

"Not bad given that I'm toothless." Eric smiled and pointed to his mouth where both his canines were missing. "The pain meds are a lifesaver, but they also make me drowsy, so there is that." He removed the lid and took a sip. "I'm not complaining, though. I was so happy to wake up two days ago with both canines wiggling. The sooner my fangs show up, the sooner I can pleasure my mate properly."

Gilbert arched a brow. "I thought that the pain meds were making you drowsy."

"Not that drowsy." Eric chuckled. "I thought that I was a horny bastard before, but that was nothing compared to now, and Max says that my immortal hormones didn't kick in full force yet. Once they do, I'll turn into a rabbit." He leaned back, taking the cup with him. "Thankfully, Darlene is not complaining even though she's not immortal yet and doesn't have the stamina to match." He took another sip. "So, Gilbert, when are you taking the plunge?"

"Soon, but not yet. Now that you are okay, I can finally leave and take care of business. We left our house in the Bay Area as if we were just going for the weekend. I need to pack everyone's things and ship them to the clan's warehouse downtown, I need to put the house up for rent, and I need to visit my job sites and make sure that everything is running as it should. Once I'm back, I'll take Toven up on his offer."

"How long will all that take?"

Gilbert winced. "Too long. I don't want to be away from Karen and the kids for longer than I have to. I will have to hire someone to prep the house so it's presentable for rental."

"A week then?"

"Maybe two. Trust me, I won't stay a minute longer than I have to. I want to get going on the immortality thing before I lose my nerve again." He smiled. "Thanks for taking the plunge first and proving to me that it can be done."

"I was in a coma for two weeks, but Bridget said that I was never in danger and that I remained stable the entire time." Eric leaned back with the cup in his hand. "I want Darlene to start her transition as soon as possible too. She's about your age, and she shouldn't wait any longer."

Gilbert's brows dipped low. "Are you suggesting that she sleep with another male?"

"No. I don't think I can handle that. But I can handle another male biting her." He grimaced. "I hope. I asked Max if he was willing to help us out, and he said that he wasn't going to do it unless I was chained to the bed. He says that even though I want it done, I will attack him if I'm not restrained."

Gilbert put his cup down and leaned forward. "I can't even think of another man in the room with me and Karen when we are making love. I don't want another man's eyes on her. How the hell am I going to manage that?"

Eric chuckled. "You are already talking like an immortal, all possessive alpha-hole."

"Alpha-hole?"

"Yeah, the macho guy who needs to be in charge and beats his chest like a gorilla to scare other males away."

Gilbert pursed his lips. "Yep, I guess that's me. Don't forget that Karen and I have been together for many years, and we have children together. She's every-thing to me, and it's going to kill me to let another male bite her. I know for sure that I would need to be restrained to allow that to happen. But even if I could force myself to do that, I don't think Karen would agree."

"I was afraid of that, and I've spent the last two days thinking about a solution, and I think I've found it. What if the male's arousal is not directed at Karen but at you? Would you be able to tolerate a gay guy biting her while the two of you were getting it on?"

The face Gilbert made was comical. "Why would he agree to do that? And where am I going to find a gay immortal male?"

"I'm sure the clan has a similar percentage of gays as humans do, and since Dormants are so important to the clan, it shouldn't be too difficult to find a volun-teer or two."

"I don't know about that." Gilbert rubbed the back of his neck. "It would sure make it easier for Karen and me, but I doubt any gay man would find my hairy ass and the tire I carry around the middle attractive." He slapped his rounded belly.

Eric laughed. "Don't sell yourself short. You are still an attractive dude. I see how women look at you."

"Women are much more forgiving than men, especially when the object of their attention has money or at least a decent job. Men are visual creatures, and I'm not a young stud anymore."

"If you are attractive to women, you are attractive to gay men as well. I don't think there is a difference. Not all gay men look like they stepped off the cover of GQ. Most are just ordinary dudes with hairy asses and pudgy middles and all that crap that you are worried about."

"Yeah, maybe for humans it's true, but did you look at these immortals? They all look like they could be on the cover of a men's fashion magazine."

Eric regarded his brother with a frown. "Since when did you develop confidence issues? You've always been the most confident guy I've known."

"Since I got here and saw all these perfect people."

"They are not all perfect. Did you know that William used to be fat?"

Gilbert waved a dismissive hand. "The guy is a little padded, but he's tall, so it's not a big deal. He looks good."

"He does now. Darlene told me that he used to be really fat, and that he lost a lot of weight by changing his eating habits and engaging in physical activity. That means that these immortals have to work at looking good, and they are not perfect by design."

Gilbert let out a breath. "First, let's see if it works for you and Darlene. Perhaps both venom and semen have to come from the same male to work, and I would hate to go to all that trouble for nothing."

70

MARCEL

"*N*ice of you to grace us with your presence." Kylie gave Marcel a withering look. "I thought that you forgot about us."

"I'm sorry, I'm late." He lifted his eye to the scanner and waited for the door to open.

Breakfast with Sofia had taken a little longer than it should have, and his team had been waiting for him outside the lab when he'd gotten there. But the reason Kylie was making a stink out of it was that she was angry at him for not eating dinner with them last night or breakfast this morning.

Safe Haven was like the village, and rumors spread fast. She must have heard about his involvement with Sofia, or maybe had just guessed the reason for his absence from meals as of late.

Good. Maybe now she would leave him alone.

After going over their assignments for the day, Marcel left the three bioinformaticians in the main lab, walked into his office, and closed the door.

Sitting at his desk, he pulled out his phone and called Emmett.

"Marcel, my friend. How can I help you?" Emmett sounded more cheerful than usual.

The guy thrived on attention and adoration from the retreat attendees.

"Did you give a presentation today?" Marcel asked.

"How did you know?"

"You sound energized. Extroverts like you absorb energy from others. Introverts like me expend energy when they interact with people."

"True. I love interacting with my fans, and the paranormals are even more fun than the spiritualists. They are so open and accepting that it's a joy to teach them."

"I'm glad you're enjoying yourself. I have two favors to ask of you, and both are for the same person."

"Let me guess. It's for the Finnish linguist you took to my bunker."

Talk about rumors spreading fast. Had Leon told him?

"I hope you don't mind."

"Not at all. I'm glad someone is making use of my former pad. So, what can I do for Miss Sofia Heikkinen?"

"I would like her to stay for the next retreat. I heard you offer everyone a half off, but is there a way you can let her participate for free?"

"For you, of course. I owe you for deciphering the coordinates in Jade's fable."

"You don't owe me a thing, but thanks. The other favor I want to ask is if you can grant her a private audience. She put in a request, but she asked me if I can expedite things for her. She's quite taken with you."

He debated whether to tell Emmett about what Sofia wanted him to do, but decided not to. His task was to get her the audience. She could take it from there.

"I've seen the request." Emmett sighed. "I used to love granting those audiences, especially to beautiful ladies, but Eleanor is the jealous type, and she gets upset when I do them, so I try to limit the number of audiences I grant, and when it is with a lady, I make sure to have Eleanor there. But that's neither here nor there. I can see Sofia after lunch today."

That was a surprise. "Thank you. She will be over the moon."

"Naturally. Tell me a little bit about her, and by that, I mean things that were not included in the file Roni prepared on each of the attendees."

"She's who she claims to be. When I started seeing her, I sensed that she was hiding things about her past, and since I needed to check whether she can be thralled, I peeked into her mind and encountered a wall. I later thralled her to forget a detail I told her, so I knew she could be thralled, but that wall she'd erected about her past bothered me, so I asked Roni to double-check her information. Everything checked out. She's a student and a teacher at the University of Helsinki, and she'd been doing that for the past seven years. Her medical record is legit as well."

"Have you gotten her to tell you more about herself?"

"She doesn't get along with her mother, and she argues with her father, who is very strict. That's all I got so far."

"You should have brought her to me sooner. I would have gotten her to tell you any information you wanted." Emmett chuckled. "It's advantageous to have a strong compeller as a friend."

"I could have also pushed harder and gotten deeper into her mind with a thrall, but that's against the rules, and the same rules apply to compulsion. Unless clan security or lives are at risk, thralling and compelling is not allowed."

Emmett huffed. "Those rules are more like guidelines, and as such they are meant to be bent."

"Not for a former Guardian."

"You're a civilian now, but it's your choice of course. If you don't want me to compel Sofia, I won't."

"I would appreciate that."

"Do you want to be there to make sure that I behave?"

"I'm sure that you would, but I'll try to be there."

SOFIA

*T*he note with the invitation to meet Emmett Haderech arrived during the last class before lunch, which meant that Sofia couldn't eat a bite.

Roxie was sure that it was excitement over meeting the spiritual leader, but it was fear over what she was about to do.

Would he agree to call her fake father?

Would he realize that Igor was compelling him? And if he did, what would he do to her?

Would he kick her out of the retreat?

She might not even get a chance to say goodbye to Marcel.

"Eat something." Roxie pointed to her plate. "You'll be hungry later, and the kitchen will be closed. Ask me how I know."

"How?"

"Yesterday, I wanted a snack, so I went looking for something to buy. There was nothing. You know how they usually have a bowl of cookies next to the coffee and tea buffet that's served all day long? They were all gone. Not even a crumb was left."

Sofia tuned Roxie out.

She was still wearing the exercise clothes from before, and even though Marcel had said that she looked and smelled great, she didn't want to meet Emmett Haderech like that. Should she run to her room and get showered and changed?

She could do that in ten minutes if she hurried. But maybe it was better to show up with her midriff exposed? Perhaps it would distract Emmett from noticing that her father was asking him too many questions and that he was disclosing too much information that he shouldn't.

Marcel had told her that Emmett and Dr. Eleanor were a couple, but that didn't mean that Emmett didn't have eyes. He could still notice a woman and feel attraction to her.

It didn't mean that he wasn't loyal to his partner or that he intended to cheat on her, only that he was human.

Except, Sofia wasn't a great beauty, and most men found her too slim to be attractive. Then again, Dr. Takala was tall and very slim as well, so maybe she was Emmett's type.

"Sofia." Roxie waved a hand in front of her face. "You are such a space cadet. Lydia asked you if you are going to wear something nice to your audience with Emmett Haderech."

"I don't have time. I'll go like this."

Lydia pursed her lips. "That would be disrespectful."

Felicity gave her friend a disapproving look. "Don't be such a prude. Sofia is gorgeous, and she has a great body. Do you really think Emmett will notice what she's wearing?" She snorted. "He'll notice what she's not wearing. Just look at that six-pack."

Lydia shrugged. "Yeah. You are right."

"I'd better head out." Sofia pushed to her feet and slung her backpack over one shoulder. "I don't want to keep him waiting."

"Hold on." Roxie lifted her satchel off the floor and pulled out a tube of lipstick. "You need some color on your face."

"Thanks, but I'm too nervous to bother with it."

"I'll do it for you." Roxie gripped her chin and dabbed the lipstick on her lips. "Smack them like that." She demonstrated. "That's better." She patted Sofia's arm. "Remember. He's just a man, and you are a paying customer. There is no need to be so nervous."

"You're right." Sofia took a deep breath and leaned to kiss Roxie on the cheek. "Thanks for being such a good friend. You're a wonderful person, and I will never forget you."

Roxie frowned. "Why does it sound as if you are saying goodbye?"

Sofia fought the tears that were welling in her eyes. "I'm not saying goodbye." She was. If Emmett kicked her out, she might not have another chance. "I just wanted you to know that I don't take you for granted, and that I appreciate your friendship."

"Oh, sweetie." Roxie pulled her into a crushing hug. "I love you too, and I'm not letting you go. After the retreat is over, you are coming to stay with me for at least a couple of months. I'll be your personal tour guide in Washington, and if you want to stay, I'll help you find a job. The coffee shop I work for is always looking for new servers, and since it's a popular spot for the lobbyists, the tips are great."

Choking on tears, Sofia nodded, patted Roxie's arm, and rushed off.

She managed to hold out for long enough to get to the ladies' room outside the dining hall and lock herself inside a stall. She had a few minutes to spare, and she was going to use them to let it all out before heading to her ruin.

EMMETT

"Come in." Eleanor opened the door for Sofia.

The young woman looked like she was going to keel over, but that was a common reaction of Emmett's fans when granted a face-to-face interview.

They worshiped him.

Pushing to his feet, he walked over to the girl and gave her a reassuring smile. "You are safe in here, Sofia. No harm will come to you between these walls."

She nodded. "I know. I'm just so excited. I didn't expect my request to be approved so quickly, so I didn't prepare." She waved a hand over her outfit. "I would have worn something more appropriate."

"You look fine." Eleanor clapped her on the back. "Take a seat, make yourself comfortable, and ask your questions. We all have things to do."

Emmett winced. Eleanor's bedside manner, so to speak, needed work. "We are not in a rush, Sofia. Take your time to collect your thoughts."

"Thank you." She sat down and then glanced at Eleanor who was leaning against his desk with her arms folded over her chest and looking intimidating. "I thought that the audience would be just with Mr. Emmett Haderech."

"Eleanor is here for your benefit." Emmett spread his arms. "You are a young, beautiful lady, and these days it is not acceptable for a gentleman to conduct a meeting with a lady without another female present."

In fact, it was to prevent Eleanor from getting unnecessarily jealous, and if he weren't a compeller, it would have also served to protect him from sexual harassment accusations.

Sofia gave Eleanor a tight smile. "I feel safe here." She shifted her eyes to the camera mounted in the corner. "The security in Safe Haven is top-notch. If you don't mind, I would feel more comfortable discussing personal matters with Mr. Emmett Haderech in private."

Emmett gave Eleanor a slight nod.

"Fine." She uncrossed her arms and pushed away from his desk. "I'll be in my office if you need me."

Eleanor's primary office was in the paranormal enclave, but she also used the one next to his from time to time.

"Thank you." Sofia put her backpack on the floor. "I promise not to take too much of Mr. Haderech's time."

When Eleanor left and closed the door behind her, he leaned forward. "Please, call me Emmett, Sofia."

"Thank you, but I don't think I can. I admire you too much to call you by your given name."

"I insist."

"Okay." She lowered her eyes.

"What can I help you with, Sofia?"

"I don't get along with my parents, and I hoped you could give me some guidance."

That was a common request from the younger guests. "What are the points of contention between you and your parents?"

"My mother does not approve of me. Nothing I do is good enough for her. She's disappointed in me."

Emmett frowned. "I've read your file, and you are a very impressive young lady. You are a gifted linguist, and you teach at the university. Your mother should be proud of you."

"She should be, but she isn't. Her expectations are unrealistic, and I gave up on pleasing her a long time ago. My relationship with my father is a little better, and he is proud of my accomplishments, but we argue a lot. He expects me to remain a virgin until I get married, which isn't realistic either. I just don't tell him about my boyfriends."

That was very uncommon in most Western societies, and he wasn't aware of the Finns being particularly traditional.

"Is it a religious thing for your father?"

She nodded. "It is, but that's not the only problem I have with him. He doesn't believe in paranormal phenomena, and he didn't approve of me coming here. He thinks that Safe Haven is a cult and that you are a con man who swindles people out of their money."

Emmett nodded sagely. "Those who donated funds to the cause did that out of their own free will, and they gave it to the community. Not to me personally. I've helped countless people over the years, and it pains me to hear those accusations, but it is what it is. The haters will keep on hating, while the lovers will spread the love."

She smiled. "I like the way you think. I wish my father shared your attitude."

"Your father sounds like a difficult man, but he obviously cares about you. You are no longer a child, and you can lead your life the way you want with or without his approval. He doesn't have to know what you don't tell him. On your end, you can choose to focus on the negatives or the positives. If you focus on his love for you instead of the worldview that he wants to impose on you, you might feel better about your relationship with him."

"You are so smart." She sighed. "Can you talk to him? I think that when he hears you, he will realize how wrong he was about you. I would hate to return home and pick up where we ended before I left for the retreat, which was in a huge fight."

Emmett had never been asked to do something like that before, and his first instinct was to refuse, but Sofia looked so desperate and so lost. He could do the girl a favor and compel her father to believe that he was a saint.

"What's your father's name?"

"Jarmo Heikkinen."

"Does he speak English?"

"Yes." He pushed the phone over to her. "Call him, tell him that you're with me in my office, and put the call on speaker so we can talk to him together."

"Thank you." Her hands trembled when she picked up the receiver. "I'll pay for the call charges of course."

MARCEL

*M*arcel's phone buzzed in his pocket as he headed down the hallway to Emmett's office. He had it silenced out of respect for the no-phones policy of the resort, but since he was in the office wing, it was no longer a problem.

Seeing Eleanor's number on the screen, he answered, "I'm here."

"Don't go into Emmett's office. Go into the one before it. I left the door open."

He saw the open door and entered. "What's going on?"

She pointed at the computer screen. "She's early, and she didn't want me in there. She knows the office is monitored, though. So don't give me that disapproving look."

"I'm not. But why are you watching the feed?" And listening, he realized as he said it.

He could hear Emmett talking about Sofia's father.

"It's not what you're thinking. I trust Emmett, and I'm not jealous, although he likes to think that I am. It's for his protection. In today's environment, a man risks his reputation and his livelihood every time he's alone in a room with a female employee or a client. I don't want some greedy bitch accusing him of sexual harassment to blackmail him for money."

Marcel nodded even though he hadn't bought Eleanor's explanation. With her and Emmett's compulsion ability, that wasn't a problem she should be worried about.

The woman was possessive, and if she wanted to guard her mate, that was her business. He'd come along to keep an eye on Sofia even though he knew Emmett wouldn't do anything inappropriate.

It was instinctive.

Pulling out a chair, he sat next to the computer screen to watch and listen to the show.

"What's your father's name?" Emmett asked.

"Jarmo Heikkinen."

"Does he speak English?"

"Yes."

Emmett pushed his desk phone toward her. "Call him and tell him that I wish to speak with him."

"Thank you." She reached for the receiver. "I'll pay for the call charges of course."

Marcel frowned.

Why was she anxious? Was it about the phone call she was about to make or Emmett's proximity?

"Your girlfriend's story doesn't add up. And she's acting strange." Eleanor sat on the desk and crossed her arms over her chest.

"She told me about her father. He's very traditional and strict. He expects her to remain a virgin until she marries. Who does that these days?"

"Hi, Daddy," Sofia said into the receiver. "I'm speaking in English because I'm with Emmett Haderech in his office. I asked him to talk to you, and he graciously agreed. Is it okay if I put the call on speaker?"

She must have gotten an okay from her father because she nodded, pressed the speaker button, and put down the receiver. "Go ahead," she said.

"Good evening, Mr. Heikkinen," Emmett said. "My name is Emmett. Can I call you Jarmo?"

"Yes," came the gruff reply. "You must forgive my English. It's not very good. I'm very sorry that my daughter is bothering you."

"It's not a bother, and your English is very good. I can see where Sofia gets her talent for languages. You must be so proud of her accomplishments."

"I am. I'm just not happy about her spending all the money she saved on nonsense."

The guy's accent didn't sound like Sofia's. It was harsher. Perhaps Jarmo wasn't a native of Finland?

Emmett chuckled. "I assure you that it's money well spent. Sofia is learning a lot about paranormal talents, her own and others. She's also meeting interesting people from all over, which is very important for networking and future success, especially for a linguist who one day might seek a translator's job. On top of that, when I heard that she traveled all the way from Finland to attend the retreat, I offered her a free pass to the next one, which starts right on the heels of this one. That's an incredible bargain that I've never offered to anyone else."

"Thank you. That's unexpected generosity from a man like you. Is it true that you robbed your community members of all their possessions?"

Despite it being true, it was an incredibly rude thing to ask right after Emmett had told the guy about Sofia's free pass to the next retreat.

Emmett seemed to think the same, and for a moment, he gaped at Sofia as if he didn't know how to answer that.

She blushed and mouthed, "I'm sorry."

"A simple yes or no answer will do," her father said.

"Yes." Emmett's answer surprised Marcel, and given the wild look in Emmett's eyes, it surprised him as well.

"Something is not right." Eleanor jumped off the desk and ran out of the room.

"What is your real name, Mr. Emmett Haderech?" Sofia's father asked when Eleanor burst into the room.

She disconnected the call before Emmett could answer. "Explain," she barked at Sofia.

"I'm sorry," Sofia said. "I didn't expect him to be so rude."

Marcel rushed in. "What's going on?"

"That wasn't Sofia's father." Eleanor glared at the girl before shifting her eyes to Emmett. "That was an incredibly powerful compeller. You would not have admitted to swindling the community members under any other circumstances."

Emmett looked more shaken than Marcel had ever seen him. "Unbelievable. If you hadn't ended the call, he would have made me reveal my real name."

They all looked at Sofia, who started crying silently. "I'm sorry," she murmured. "I'm so sorry."

What the hell had just happened?

What had Sofia done? And why?

Who was the man on the other end of the line, and why was he after Emmett? Was that a reporter? Was Sofia an undercover journalist?

As the phone rang, they all looked at it, but no one answered, and then Eleanor tore the wire out of the wall. "We need to run all incoming phone calls through the voice changer to prevent him from compelling anyone else."

"I'll call Leon." Marcel pulled his phone out of his pocket, walked out into the hallway, and ducked into Eleanor's office to make the call out of Sofia's earshot.

"We might have a problem," he told the chief of security. "It might be as simple as an undercover journalist working for a powerful compeller, or as serious as Jade's captor sending over a spy. He almost got Emmett to reveal his real name over the phone. Eleanor saved the day by disconnecting the call, but he might call back and compel someone else. You need to divert all incoming calls through the voice changer."

"I'm on it," Leon said. "Call me if you need anything else."

74

SOFIA

$\mathcal{J}$t was over.

They'd figured it out.

But how? How did they know about compulsion? They talked about it as if they'd lived in Igor's compound.

No one had mentioned the ability to compel as one of the paranormal talents, so that wasn't how they knew about it.

Maybe they were Kra-ell hybrids after all?

Was that what Igor had sent her to discover?

It must be.

But why hadn't he told her to look for hybrids?

If she'd paid more attention, she might have noticed things about Emmett and Eleanor that would have given them away.

She'd noticed Marcel's glowing eyes, but she'd dismissed it because she'd never seen a blond Kra-ell, but what if there were blond hybrids in other compounds?

And why was she still sitting there frozen like a dummy instead of running?

Because there was nowhere to run. Safe Haven was in the middle of nowhere and she would be caught in moments.

Would Igor punish her family for her failure?

But hadn't she given him the answer to his question?

He must have figured out why the call had been disconnected. Humans would not have realized so quickly that compulsion was at work.

Tears flowing down her cheeks, Sofia closed her eyes and did the only thing she could. She prayed.

Dear Mother of All Life. I'm lost. But please save my family.

The Goddess must have answered because suddenly it occurred to her that there was one more thing she could do that might save her family from Igor's wrath.

Clutching the locket, she pressed the tiny lever to open it, and then pushed her finger inside to press on the picture. Without the earpiece, she wouldn't be able to hear Valstar, but he would hear what was going on in the room, and he would get his answers.

When she opened her eyes, Marcel crouched in front of her. "Care to explain why you set Emmett up?"

"I can't."

"She's under compulsion," Eleanor said. "Let me talk to her. I might be able to do something about it."

Marcel lifted a hand to stop her. "We need to search her first. She might be wearing a wire." He regarded her with hard eyes. "Did you come here to get an exclusive story on Emmett? Is that what you were doing? Digging for dirt to besmirch his name?"

Sofia shook her head.

"Where would she hide a wire?" Eleanor looked her over. "She can't hide a pin in that outfit. Maybe it's in the shoes?"

"The pendant." He reached for it. "I've been wondering why you always wore this ugly thing. I thought that it had a sentimental value."

Sofia's hand tightened around it. "It does."

"Give it to me," Marcel commanded. "I can take it from you, but I don't want to hurt you."

Why was he still being nice to her?

"Please," she pleaded. "Don't take it away from me. It means so much to me."

If nothing else, Igor would be impressed with her acting and would know that she'd done her best.

Marcel smiled sadly. "You give me no choice." He pried her fingers open as if she was an infant and yanked the chain over her head.

As it snagged on her hair, she cried out.

"I'm sorry. I didn't mean to hurt you."

The locket was still open, and as he let it dangle from her fingers, the little door swung out, revealing the picture inside.

"Is that your family?" Marcel asked.

She nodded.

"Smash it," Eleanor suggested.

"It's just a locket." He turned to the woman and mouthed something that Sofia couldn't hear. "But just in case it's more than it appears, can you put it in the safe together with everyone's phones?"

"Of course." Eleanor snatched it from his hand and walked out of the room.

Hope surged in Sofia's heart. Marcel either didn't suspect that the locket had a transmitter inside, or he did and was trying to protect her.

Maybe her betrayal hadn't sunk in yet, and when it did, he would stop caring about her.

The good news was that they thought she was a journalist looking for a story, which was much better than the truth.

Could she use it to her advantage?

If she told them that she was a journalist, they would demand to know the name of the publication she worked for, and if she named some random gossip magazine, they would call to complain or just to verify her story and it wouldn't hold water.

She could claim to be a freelancer, but even a freelancer had to have some connections to newspapers that she could prove.

Marcel gazed into her eyes, his expression more pitying than angry, and then he turned to Emmett. "Can you get her to talk?"

"Not yet," Emmett murmured. "I need a few more moments to collect myself. I'm still reeling from the shock of being spied on. Let Eleanor do it."

A moment later the woman walked back in. "It's done." She kicked at Sofia's left shoe. "Take them off and then stand up on your bare feet. I'm going to pat you down."

Marcel straightened. "You said that she couldn't hide anything in this outfit."

"When in doubt, it's always good to follow protocol." Eleanor patted him on the back.

"I don't have anything on me," Sofia said as she toed off her sneakers and removed her socks as well.

"I'll pat her down," Marcel told Eleanor and turned to Sofia. "If that's okay with you. Would you prefer Eleanor do it?"

He was still trying to protect her despite knowing that she'd used him.

"You can search me," she whispered as a new torrent of tears began.

"Oh, for heaven's sake." Eleanor walked out of the room, returning with a box of tissues while Marcel was conducting a very thorough pat down. It included releasing Sofia's hair from its ponytail and searching through it.

"She's clean," he said when he was done. "As far as I can tell, that is. The safest thing would be to run her through a bug detector."

"Leon has one," Eleanor said as she handed Sofia a wad of tissues. "What kind of a sorry excuse for an undercover spy are you?"

"I'm not a spy."

Eleanor huffed. "A journalist, paparazzo, it's all the same. They all spy on unsuspecting people."

"I'll check with Leon." Marcel stopped and whispered something in Eleanor's ear before walking out of the room again.

Sofia blew her nose into the tissues and wiped her eyes and her cheeks. "I'm so sorry." The tears kept flowing, and soon there wasn't a dry spot on the wad of tissues.

"Yeah, yeah." Eleanor handed her the box, walked up to a mini fridge, and pulled out a bottle of water. "Catch." She tossed it to Sofia.

Fumbling with the bottle, she eventually managed to prevent it from falling out of her hands.

"Crappy reflexes," Eleanor murmured. "You are a really lousy spy."

75

MARCEL

*W*hen Leon arrived with another Guardian, Sofia's eyes turned panicked. "Are they here to arrest me?"

"Not yet." Leon motioned for her to stand up and ran the handheld bug detector over every inch of her body, including between her legs.

If the guy weren't happily mated, Marcel would have growled a warning.

Even though Sofia had orchestrated Emmett's attempted compulsion, he still felt protective of her. She'd been a pawn, used by the powerful compeller to get closer to Emmett.

Had the guy known that Emmett was a compeller himself?

But that was a less important question than the why and who.

Marcel didn't really believe it was about an undercover story. He'd pretended not to find the transmitter in the locket for the sake of those who were listening on the other side, and he'd made a scene about accusing Sofia of being an under-cover journalist for the same reason. He'd told Eleanor to continue the pretense, and after Eleanor had put the locket in the safe, they continued the charade in case Sofia was carrying more hidden bugs on her.

The scariest option was that the compeller was Jade's captor. If Sofia weren't human, that would have been the leading theory, but since she was, other possibil-ities needed to be explored.

Given that a compeller was involved, it might be connected to the paranormal retreat. Did someone consider it a threat?

They needed to check whether Safe Haven was taking business away from a competitor who happened to be a powerful compeller. The questions the guy had directed at Emmett had been about information to destroy him with. If news got out that Safe Haven's leader had admitted to swindling his followers, the place would never recover from the stink. Even if they got rid of Emmett, it would destroy the community's only source of income, and they would have to close the place up.

"She's clean," Leon said. "I suggest that we put her in the bunker until we figure out what's going on."

The irony wasn't lost on Marcel. Instead of using the bunker to entertain a lover with a romantic dinner, he would be using it to keep her prisoner. "We will do that after we question Sofia. We waited with that to make sure she wasn't carrying bugs."

If anyone was listening, the types of questions they needed to ask would have given them away, and he'd been very careful with what he'd said around Sofia so far.

Apparently, he hadn't forgotten his Guardian training yet. There was a reason he'd saved the transmitter for later use instead of destroying it. If the compeller believed that they were clueless, they could later use the locket to feed him false information.

"Understood." Leon pulled a set of handcuffs out of his back pocket. "I assume that you know how to use them."

Marcel shook his head. "Those won't be necessary."

Eleanor snatched them from Leon's hand. "Just in case. We can handle it from here." She smiled. "Sofia is just an ordinary girl with crappy reflexes. We can lock her in my office, and she won't be able to do anything about it."

Meaning, she was human.

Leon nodded. "Call me if you need anything."

"Will do," Eleanor said. When the door closed behind Leon, she leaned against Emmett's desk and looked at Sofia. "Let's start."

Marcel lifted a brow. "Perhaps I should do the questioning?"

Eleanor looked down her nose at him. "You don't have my special talents."

He wasn't a compeller, but in this case, thralling might work better. "I have other talents."

"Let me start," Eleanor said. "If I don't get anywhere with her, you can take over."

Folding his arms over his chest, he nodded.

"Is your real name Sofia?" Eleanor asked.

"Yes."

"Is your last name Heikkinen?"

"Yes."

"Was the guy on the other line your father?"

Sofia shook her head.

"That's what I thought. Why did you want Emmett to talk to him?"

"I didn't."

"Did he make you do it?"

"I can't say."

Eleanor smiled. "You're a smart girl. You should have figured out by now that there are sneaky ways around compulsion. I'll rephrase the question to demonstrate. Would you have ever stepped into the dog poo if the bad man didn't push you?"

The question confused Marcel, but Sofia seemed to get it.

Her eyes peeling wide open, she shook her head. "Who wants to step into dog poo? Not me. But if I tried to walk around it, someone I care about might have stepped on the poo, and I couldn't let that happen."

Eleanor smiled. "Excellent answer. It could mean that if she didn't do as she was told, someone else would have been sent to do the job, someone she cared about, or that if she refused, someone close to her would have paid the price."

Sofia lifted two fingers.

"The second one then." Eleanor let out a breath. "I'll try to release you from the compulsion, but if it doesn't work, we can continue telling each other stories." She leaned closer. "You will speak freely and tell us only the truth. Who sent you?"

Sofia shook her head. "I still can't tell you."

Eleanor braced her hands on Emmett's desk. "That's not really surprising given how strong of a compeller the guy is." She turned to Emmett. "You need to give it a try."

"It's not going to work. He was stronger than me, which means that I can't override his compulsion. You need to get Kalugal to try, but he might not be strong enough either."

The guy still looked as if he'd been hit by lightning. Leaning back in his chair, his feet propped on his desk, and an arm draped over his eyes, he was the picture of despondency.

Eleanor eyed him with a frown. "Snap out of it, Emmett. Nothing happened. So, you admitted to swindling the community out of money. Big deal. Unofficially, everyone already knows that. Even if he'd gotten you on tape, you could still save the situation. You've turned a new page and all that crap."

Had she really believed that Sofia had been working on an undercover story?

Marcel had told Eleanor to pretend, but now that they were positive Sofia was carrying no more transmitters, it was safe to talk freely around her. Well, to a certain extent. If they were going to use her as a double agent, they had to be very careful about what they said around her.

"That's not why I'm depressed." Emmett removed the arm from his eyes and turned to look at them. "I'm terrified for you know who. What if that's the one holding her? We assumed that only a powerful compeller could keep her captive, and I just spoke with one. Coincidence? I think not. Also, a large portion of the area we've been investigating is in Finland. Do I need to say more?"

Emmett had instinctively chosen to talk in hints, but even that could have clued Sofia in on who he was and who he'd been talking about. But Marcel had been watching her closely, and she hadn't responded to Emmett's words in any way. She was still crying, the tears spilling out of her eyes in a never-ending trickle, and the ball of tissues she was holding was growing in size.

Eleanor was right. The girl was not a trained spy. She'd probably been chosen for the mission precisely because she had no special training or abilities and could fly under the radar so to speak.

KIAN

*A*s Kian listened to Leon and Marcel's report, he was more and more convinced that Sofia had been sent by Jade's captor.

They made the video call from Leon's office, which meant that neither of them really believed that it was a simple case of a journalist looking for dirt on Emmett, and especially not Marcel, who looked like he'd been hit by a train.

He hadn't said much about his relationship with Sofia, but it was clear to Kian that she meant something to him and that her betrayal was costing him. Given her paranormal talent, he'd probably hoped that she was a Dormant.

Except, the talent was probably fake, and she was just a human who'd been recruited by the compeller for this mission and coached on pretending to have a paranormal ability.

For Marcel's sake, Kian hoped that the girl was just a pawn in the game and not an extraordinarily good player who was fooling even Leon into thinking that she'd been forced into becoming a spy against her will.

"That's bad," he said when they were done. "The compeller knows that Jade contacted someone, and he suspects Emmett."

"I don't think he suspects that," Marcel said. "I think he was shooting in the dark. He probably thought that since Emmett is Safe Haven's leader, he would know everything that was going on there, and he hoped that Emmett would provide him with something useful. He started his questioning with the swindling, which has been rumored for years, and then Emmett's name, which is obviously not his real name. If he was sure that Emmett knew who Jade was, or that he'd figured it out from her fable, he would have started with that."

Marcel's argument was logical, and Kian took it from there.

"The compeller might have seen Jade's email, but since he didn't know about Emmett, he didn't know why she was showing interest in Safe Haven. If he'd known that she'd contacted a former member of her tribe, he would have sent warriors over, or at least someone more capable than Sofia. She's obviously out of her element."

Leon nodded. "He knew that she wouldn't be detected because she's human and because she has a solid background that would pass even the most rigorous scrutiny, and he was right about that. Marcel had a gut feeling about her and asked Roni to investigate her more thoroughly. Roni didn't find anything that raised a red flag."

Kian pushed his chair back. "Did you manage to get anything out of her at all?"

Marcel shook his head. "Eleanor showed Sofia how to get around the compulsion by talking in metaphors and similes, but she was so distraught that she couldn't come up with anything coherent. I told Eleanor to take her to the bunker so she could rest."

"Keep her locked up until we can get her to talk. Does she know who and what you are?"

"We didn't tell her anything," Marcel said. "I was afraid that she might have a tap on her, so I pretended to think that she was an undercover journalist for the sake of whoever was listening on the other side. That turned out to be a good move because she had a transmitter hidden in a locket. I asked Eleanor to put it in the safe. Once we get Sofia to talk and figure out what we are up against, we can use that pendant to feed the compeller misinformation."

Marcel was a smart guy, and his years on the force had taught him well.

"Good thinking," Kian complimented him. "But it's only going to work provided that Sofia cooperates. From what you've told me, the guy is holding someone dear to her, maybe her real father or other members of her family, so she might refuse to cooperate even when she's no longer under his compulsion."

Leon moved his chair to get in the webcam's view. "We shouldn't waste time. Let's get Kalugal on the line with her, or even better, fly him out here. Emmett and Eleanor both say that compulsion works better face to face, and we need our best ammunition to override this guy."

Kian agreed, but getting Kalugal to leave his house would be mission impossible.

"Let's try the phone first, or even better, a video call. If that doesn't work, I can ask him to fly out to you, but he will very likely refuse. Since little Darius was born, Kalugal is in complete freak-out mode, and he refuses to interact with humans or anyone who has contact with them, which means that he doesn't leave his house, and neither do Jacki nor the baby. If this continues for much longer, I will have no choice but to send a team of Guardians with earplugs to rescue the poor woman from her prison."

Kian was joking of course, but Kalugal had definitely lost his mind, which given his family's history was a worrisome sign.

"Maybe the Clan Mother could override the compulsion using the same remote methods?" Leon suggested. "If Kalugal fails, that is."

"I'm not risking her, not even on the phone. I don't want to sound paranoid, but what if Sofia is a Trojan horse? Perhaps she was sent to find out who we have on our side and do some damage."

Both Leon and Marcel looked doubtful, and they were probably right, but Annani's safety came before any other considerations.

"What about Toven?" Marcel asked. "Would he agree to give it a try?"

"I don't want to risk him either. I'll run it by Turner and see if we can come up with a safe way for Toven to do that, provided that he agrees."

Toven had proven to be a good sport and readily available to help when asked. Kian had no doubt he would do that if they needed him to.

Perhaps he could wear the translating earplugs when he talked to Sofia. That would prevent her from sending any dangerous sound waves his way. The good thing about Toven was that he would most likely listen to reason and agree to wear the earplugs. The same couldn't be said about Annani.

"What do we do about security?" Leon asked. "We are operating on high alert, and Safe Haven has incredible defenses in place, but just out of an abundance of caution, perhaps you should send reinforcements."

"That's a good idea. I'll have Onegus assemble a team. Perhaps I'll also manage to persuade Kalugal to hop on the plane with them." He chuckled. "I'll get him a hazmat suit. On a more serious note, though, we should consider the possibility that if there was one spy there could be more, and they might not even be aware of each other. Emmett falling victim to compulsion was a warning. Imagine what could have happened if the compeller got ahold of you, Marcel. You are sitting on top of a hub of top-secret information and the servers at the lab are connected to the servers in the village."

"There are safeguards in place," Marcel said. "I can't freely access anything I want from here, and we have a protocol that mandates someone on the other side approving the request. That being said, I think I'm going to disconnect the servers completely for the time being. I think we should also send the bioinformaticians home. They have limited access to information, but even the little they know could be a problem if it falls into the wrong hands."

"You are right." Kian leaned forward. "Can you thrall them to forget what they have been working on so far?"

Marcel nodded. "Should I send them on a vacation or dismiss them entirely?"

"For now, send them on a vacation. We will decide what to do with them after we get Sofia to tell us what she knows."

"It might not be much," Leon said. "The compeller might have picked a random person to serve his needs."

"Perhaps," Kian said. "But I doubt it."

77

SOFIA

"Get some rest." Eleanor pointed to the bed. "I'll get your things from the lodge."

The woman acted tough, but she wasn't mean. She hadn't put the handcuffs on Sofia, and only warned her against trying anything.

They hadn't even had to pass by the lodge to get to the bunker. There was a side door in Emmett's office that led straight to the garden surrounding it, and the place was fenced off from the rest of the resort.

Sofia let out a breath. "What are you going to do with me? I don't know anything. I don't even know what I was supposed to do here."

Eleanor regarded her with a hard look in her dark eyes. "We need to find someone who can override the compulsion you are under so you can tell us who sent you. After that, it's up to the boss."

"Emmett?"

"No, not Emmett." Eleanor opened the door. "Rest while you can." She walked out and closed it behind her.

A moment later, Sofia heard the lock engage.

Plopping down on the bed, she covered her eyes with her arm and sighed.

It could have been worse. She was lucky that Eleanor had realized right away that she was under compulsion and couldn't tell them anything. Otherwise, they might have tortured her for information.

Not that it was likely. She didn't know what to make of these people. In some ways they acted like a military organization, and in others, they didn't. The security officer had a bug detector and handcuffs. Why would he have such equipment in a community of do-gooders who believed in free love?

Perhaps because of the mysterious project the government was running on the premises?

That would be the rational explanation, but she had a feeling that things were not as they seemed.

Who were these people? Could they be hybrid Kra-ell?

She'd wanted to ask Marcel or Eleanor so badly, but she couldn't do even that. The compulsion prevented her from mentioning the Kra-ell and anything related to them.

Hopefully, Igor or Valstar had heard what had been going on during the few minutes the transmitter had been on, and they'd gotten from it what they'd been looking for.

Marcel, Emmett, and Eleanor had been careful about the things they'd said in front of her, but she wasn't blind or stupid, and they were not who they pretended to be.

They were very familiar with compulsion and how it worked, both Emmett and Eleanor had the ability to compel, just not as strongly as Igor, but Marcel didn't have it.

That reinforced her suspicion that Emmett and Eleanor were hybrids while Marcel wasn't. He was something else, though.

When she'd thought back to all the little things she'd noticed and dismissed, the clues had coalesced into a clearer picture. He was incredibly strong without looking like a bodybuilder, and his night vision was excellent. His eyes glowed from the inside like a Kra-ell's, but he didn't have fangs and he ate a variety of foods that a hybrid wouldn't have touched. She'd seen him eating vegetables, fruit, bread, pasta, but no red meat.

He was either a very unique kind of hybrid, or something entirely different.

Could there be other species of long-lived people living alongside humans other than the Kra-ell?

She'd never heard that mentioned in the compound, but then not much information was shared with the humans. They were regarded as inferior and treated as servants. They were told things on a need-to-know basis, and they didn't need to know much to perform their duties.

None of her hypotheses could be proven yet, but she summed up her suspicions. Emmett and Eleanor were hybrids, Jade knew them somehow, had recognized one or both from their pictures in Safe Haven's online brochure, and had communicated with them for some reason. She wasn't happy being Igor's breeder, but she didn't have to be. She could breed with one or more of the other purebloods. Igor would probably make her life a living hell if she refused him, though, so maybe that wasn't an option.

The female purebloods and the female hybrids were not allowed to leave the compound for any reason other than hunting, but that was done for their own protection. Very few female babies were born to the purebloods, and they needed to be protected. At least that was the official explanation. But what if that wasn't true and they were being held against their will?

If that was the case, they probably couldn't tell anyone because Igor compelled them not to.

Jade was subjected to the same compulsion as everyone else in the compound, so she couldn't have told Emmett and Eleanor anything useful. Heck, she probably couldn't even tell them who she was, let alone give them information they could use against Igor or to free her.

However, Jade could have hinted at it by using Eleanor's method to circumvent compulsion. If she pretended to talk about something else, like dog poo symbolizing her predicament, then she could have communicated what she wanted to say, but only to someone who could understand the references she was making.

Sofia doubted that Jade knew how to do that. Before Eleanor had shown her the example, Sofia had never heard of anyone trying to get around Igor's compulsion by using unrelated stories. It was difficult to come up with something that conveyed the right meaning, and unless she emptied her mind and focused on the story, the compulsion still prevented her from saying anything that Igor had compelled her not to reveal.

Maybe with practice she would get better at it.

What she could do, though, was tell Marcel how sorry she was about deceiving and using him and convince him to forgive her.

Did it matter in the grand scheme of things?

Probably not.

Sofia had a feeling that she was never going to leave this bunker, and she was certainly never going to see her family and friends again or go back to the university.

Her life as she knew it was over.

Or worse.

78

MARCEL

*A*fter the tele-meeting with Kian, Marcel had stopped by the lab to take care of his grumpy team. He'd called each one into his office, muddled their memories of what they'd been working on, and had given them a half-assed excuse for why they were being sent on a vacation.

He wasn't sorry to see them leave. By now, he was familiar with their methods and could continue working on the project by himself until Kian decided that it was safe to bring them back. The question was whether he was safe with the knowledge.

Perhaps he should start wearing earplugs from now on.

After he was done with the team, he accompanied them to the dining room and collected two takeout boxes to take with him to the bunker. It wasn't the romantic meal he'd had in mind this morning, but he needed to feed Sofia, and they needed to talk.

The problem was that she couldn't tell him anything about her past or what had brought her to Safe Haven, or whether she'd felt something for him or had just used him to get to Emmett.

It didn't make sense given how hard he'd had to work to get her to forgive him and give him another chance, but he'd been manipulated by a woman before, so he didn't trust his judgment.

He sucked at social interactions, romantic and otherwise, and he didn't understand the dynamics, and that was why he was such an easy victim in the hands of a skillful manipulator.

Down in the bunker, he found the key to Sofia's room dangling from a string tied to the handle. Eleanor had checked on her about an hour ago and reported that Sofia had fallen asleep.

Was she still sleeping?

It was quiet on the other side of the door, but then why wouldn't it be? There was no television in the room, and Sofia had no one to talk to.

She probably missed her talkative roommate.

When Eleanor had collected Sofia's things from her room earlier, Roxana had looked suspicious and had asked her a lot of questions. The story Eleanor had come up with was that Sofia had been invited to participate in a secret project and might not be back before the end of the retreat.

Tucking the takeout boxes under his arm, Marcel untied the string from the handle, unlocked the door, and pushed it open.

It was dark in the room, but the light from the hallway was enough for him to see the outline of Sofia's body under the thin blanket, and the fetal position she'd fallen asleep in tugged on his heartstrings.

When he walked into the room, put the boxes on the coffee table, and closed the door behind him, Sofia didn't move, but he could hear the change in her breathing and her heartbeat, and both indicated that she was no longer asleep.

"I know that you're awake." He walked over to the bed and sat on it. "I brought dinner. Do you want to get up and eat with me?"

She turned her head and opened her eyes. "Do you still want to spend time with me after what I've done?"

"I don't know yet what exactly you've done and why, but until we can find someone strong enough to override the compulsion you're under, I'm willing to give you the benefit of the doubt."

She turned on her back and pushed up against the pillows. "How do you know about compulsion? And how come Emmett and Eleanor can do it? Most people are not aware that it exists. All they know about is hypnosis."

"I think you know the answer to that. Your compeller is not the only one of his kind."

He didn't know how much he should reveal to her. She seemed to be susceptible to thralling, but she could have faked that to throw him off.

"You are not like that." She seemed to be searching for words. "You are blond. Emmett and Eleanor are not."

The Kra-ell were dark haired, and their skin was olive-toned. Was that what she was trying to tell him?

"People come in many shades, and appearances can be misleading."

"My father is blond." Her eyes pled with him to understand.

"You real father, I assume."

She nodded.

"So, your mother is the one with the dark coloring."

She nodded again.

Was she trying to tell him that her father was human, and her mother was a Kra-ell hybrid?

Perhaps he could force a thrall past the compulsion and peek into her mind?

Did he dare to do that?

Not really. The wall in her mind was strong, and to push through that would require brute force. He might cause her irreparable damage, and still not break through. He cared too much about her to risk it.

Kian had texted Leon and him Kalugal's phone number, so he could call him when Sofia was awake. Perhaps that would unlock her mind, but Marcel doubted it would. Kalugal was a powerful compeller, but they were dealing with someone of Annani and Toven's caliber.

Could a god be the leader of the Kra-ell who were holding Jade?

That would be one hell of a surprise, but he doubted Sofia would know that even if they managed to override the compulsion she was under.

"I get it. You don't get along with your mother, who is the different one, but you have a good relationship with your father. You lied about his strictness and the fight you had with him before coming here to trick Emmett into calling the man who pretended to be your father."

She nodded.

Marcel sighed and pushed to his feet. "We can keep this up for hours, but you need to eat." He offered her a hand up.

As she took it, and the blanket fell off, his breath caught in his throat. Sofia was wearing a tiny T-shirt that was so worn out that he could see the color of her nipples, not only their outline, and the pair of simple white panties she had on made her rounded bottom and incredibly long legs look delectable.

Sofia smiled. "I'm glad that you still find me attractive. I thought that you had lost interest."

"I wish I had," he admitted. "But you are not an easy woman to get over. I might be a sucker for punishment, but I pray that once the compulsion is overridden, what I learn will vindicate you."

"It will." She put her hand on his chest and looked into his eyes. "I used you, and I'm so sorry for that, but I had no choice. I was used too. I want you to know that my feelings for you are real, and I hope against hope that this is not the end of us." She lowered her eyes. "Or me," she whispered.

Marcel wanted to believe her, he wanted that so much that he was suffocating with the need, but he'd been fooled before, and he would never allow himself to be fooled again.

"We shall see. What I can promise you is that you don't need to fear for your life, and that I will keep an open mind. But I can't promise you that we can pick up from where we left off."

She nodded. "Thank you. That's more than I hoped for."

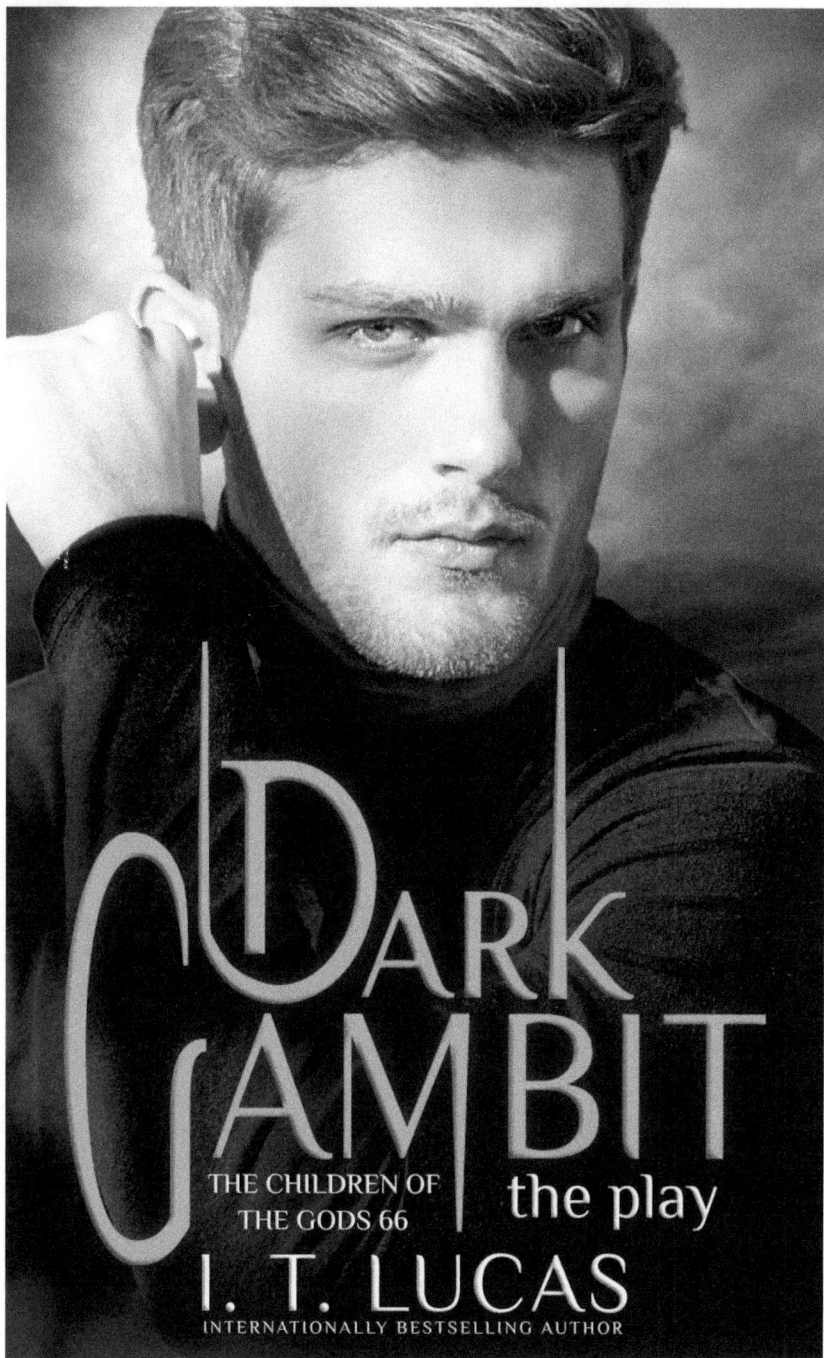

DARK GAMBIT

THE CHILDREN OF
THE GODS 66

the play

I. T. LUCAS

INTERNATIONALLY BESTSELLING AUTHOR

1

KIAN

"$\mathcal{I}$t's never boring in the immortals' village." Turner strode into Kian's office. "Not a week goes by without some emergency popping up."

It certainly felt like it, but as Syssi kept reminding Kian, they'd had many weeks of relative calm. Besides, compared to what Turner was dealing with day in and day out, the clan lived in a utopia.

Rescuing hostages from drug cartels and militias was one of the most adrenaline-inducing occupations Kian could imagine, especially since Turner was doing that as a private operator and didn't have an army at his disposal. His teams were comprised of former Special Forces personnel, but his incredible success rate was mainly attributable to his seemingly paranormal ability to execute Mission Impossible-style operations.

"Look who's talking." He chuckled. "I wouldn't trade jobs with you no matter what you paid me. I bet you don't get a single boring moment."

"You'd be surprised." Turner put his briefcase on the conference table. "Recon is seldom exciting. It's long days of sitting and watching mundane everyday activities for the chance of catching something useful. Then there is the planning stage, which I happen to enjoy. I'm in the zone when I visualize the operation unfolding. The mockups and the staging before the action are a little more exciting, and then there is the rescue mission itself, which is high-octane action. For me, however, the most exciting part is saving lives."

He was so full of shit.

Turner loved the impossible stunts only he could pull off, and the sense of satisfaction he got from that probably equaled the gratification he derived from saving the lives of the hostages his team retrieved.

"I assume that you being here means you are not currently in the midst of what you call high-octane activity, or you wouldn't be back home at such a reasonable hour."

He also wouldn't have time for this latest emergency. Turner usually tried to make himself available whenever Kian needed him, but there had been occasions when Turner had declined, and he hadn't pressed the issue.

Kian had managed the clan's defense long before Turner had joined it, and if need be, he could make do without his help.

"You assume correctly." Turner leaned back in his chair. "So, what do you need my advice on? Does it have to do with Jade?"

"It might. I'll give you a quick recap of the latest developments in Safe Haven." Kian pulled two beers out of the mini fridge and handed one to Turner. "As you know, the first paranormal retreat started this week, and one of its attendees befriended Marcel. He's the guy who figured out that the numbers in Jade's fable represent coordinates."

"I remember. He's William's replacement at the new lab, supervising the team of bioinformaticians who are working on deciphering Okidu's journals."

"Correct." Kian uncapped his beer. "The young lady's name is Sofia, and she's a linguist from Finland. As the two got closer, something about her bothered Marcel, and he asked Roni to investigate her past more thoroughly. When Roni didn't find any red flags, Marcel continued seeing her. She asked him to help her arrange a face-to-face meeting with Emmett, which wasn't suspicious either because many of the retreat attendees worship the guy like the guru he pretends to be. When she was alone with Emmett, Sofia made up a story of an argument she'd had with her father, and she beseeched Emmett for his help. Emmett agreed to talk with her father, and when she made the call, the guy on the other end of the line turned out to be a powerful compeller and nearly got Emmett to reveal his real name. Thankfully, Eleanor was monitoring the meeting from the adjacent room, and when she realized that something was wrong, she rushed in and disconnected the call."

Turner frowned. "How did she know that something was off? Did she sense the compulsion?"

"Eleanor is immune to compulsion, so she couldn't have felt anything even if she was with them in the room. As it happened, she was watching the interaction through a computer screen, but since Emmett is her mate, she realized that he was being coerced to reveal things he would have never admitted voluntarily. The compeller's first question had Emmett admit that he was a crook who had in the past manipulated his followers into giving him all of their possessions."

"The Fates must have been looking out for us." Turner lifted the bottle to his lips and took a long sip. "That was a very close call."

Turner was the most logic-driven person Kian knew, and to hear him invoke the Fates was like hearing an atheist thanking God.

"When did you become a believer in divine intervention?"

"It was just a figure of speech." Turner pushed the beer bottle away. "I assume that the compeller who tried to coerce Emmett was Jade's captor, and if Eleanor wasn't there to stop him, he would have discovered what Emmett knew about immortals, and that would have been the worst security breach in the clan's history. That being said, if the compeller had gotten ahold of Marcel or Leon, who know much more than Emmett, it would have been an even worse disaster.

Thankfully, neither of them is a head Guardian, so they couldn't have revealed the location of the village, but they still know enough to cause irreparable damage to the clan."

The possible implications had occurred to Kian, but he was also aware of his paranoid tendencies to blow things out of proportion. Hearing the same sentiment voiced by someone as dispassionate and rational as Turner sent a chill coursing through his blood.

Suddenly, the security measures that had been implemented following the compeller's phone call didn't seem enough.

"All incoming landline communications are now rerouted through the voice changer, so that risk has been mitigated. I told Marcel to thrall the team of bioinformaticians to forget what they'd been working on and send them on a mandatory vacation. I also instructed him to cut the connection between the servers there and those in the village. The Guardian security force is on high alert, and I'm sending reinforcements tonight."

"What about the linguist?" Turner asked. "Did they interrogate her?"

"I was just getting to that part." Kian grimaced. "Turns out that Sofia has been compelled to keep quiet. She couldn't say anything about the compeller or even what she was supposed to find out. Eleanor tried to override the compulsion, but she was unsuccessful. Kalugal is going to try later tonight after the girl wakes up."

Turner frowned. "Did they knock her out or drug her?"

"There was no need. Sofia is human, and she was so distraught that when Eleanor took her to the bunker and locked her in one of the bedrooms, she fell asleep from exhaustion. The girl is clearly an amateur who has been forced to do something she has no training or aptitude for."

Turner looked doubtful. "She could also be a great actress."

"That's possible, but we won't know until we can use compulsion on her ourselves."

"What about thralling? It works differently than compulsion, so Marcel or one of the other immortals can peek into her recent memories, and if need be, the Clan Mother can look into her long-term memories."

"I wouldn't get the Clan Mother involved in something like this." Kian took a swig from his beer. "It's not worth risking her. Marcel tried to get a peek into Sofia's mind before contacting Roni, and he encountered a wall. The compeller had somehow created a barrier in there."

"Interesting. I didn't know that could be done with compulsion. Did you check with Kalugal or Toven if they can do it?"

Kian shook his head. "I didn't, but I will. There is more, though. Sofia had a pendant with a transmitter hidden in it, which was how she communicated with the compeller, and it was on when things were going down in Emmett's office. Fortunately, Marcel is a former Guardian and a smart guy, and he realized the opportunity for feeding the other side misinformation. He acted as if he didn't know that the locket had a transmitter, and he pretended to think that Sofia was a journalist looking to write an unflattering story about Emmett. He kept up that charade until the pendant was locked in the safe, and Leon ran a bug detector over the girl."

Turner's pale blue eyes started glowing. "Excellent. We can use that transmitter to our advantage. First, though, you need the girl's mind unlocked, and you shouldn't wait to see if Kalugal can do it. Send in the big guns from the get-go."

"You mean Toven?"

"I was thinking of Annani, but since you are so adamant about not getting her involved, Toven will do, and he might be even better. I don't know it for a fact, but given that all the males in his family are or were compellers, I suspect that he might be a stronger compeller than the Clan Mother. Have him meet Sofia face-to-face, just not at Safe Haven, and not until she has been checked for trackers. She might have a tracker that was surgically implanted, and when it's not active, the regular bug detector won't catch it. You need to send Julian with an MRI machine or use one that's available locally. The compeller who sent Sofia might activate the tracker when he doesn't hear from her." Turner reached for his beer. "It's possible that he sent an amateur on purpose, hoping that she would get caught."

"Why would he do that?"

Turner got that distant look on his face that told Kian he was organizing his thoughts.

"He must be very confident in his compulsion hold on the girl because he's not afraid that she'll disclose anything that can lead us to him. He also assumes that since Safe Haven is a resort run by humans and hosts humans on a regular basis, it's not the headquarters of whatever he suspects is going on here. When his spy gets caught, he activates the tracker, hoping that she will lead him to us."

"I have to admit that didn't occur to me. Someone who murdered the males of an entire tribe to get the females probably has no qualms about sacrificing a human pawn."

Turner nodded. "It's a possibility, but we shouldn't discount her culpability in it just yet. We need to proceed with caution as if she is an efficient spy, and also as if she's a sacrificial pawn."

"Of course. Could she have a communication device implanted in her body as well?"

Turner shrugged. "Everything is possible, but it's not likely. Two-way communication requires more power and a larger format. In either case, the MRI will find it, and Julian will remove it. We've been in this scenario before, and Julian knows what to do. After Sofia is certified clean of bugs and trackers, Toven can meet her somewhere outside of Safe Haven." Turner leaned down and pulled his laptop out of his satchel. "I'll get on finding a safe house for them right away. We can't waste any more time."

2

SOFIA

*A*s Sofia nibbled at the food Marcel had brought, she was indifferent to the taste and texture of what was going into her mouth. Her stomach was too tense to feel hunger, but she knew that she needed to eat to keep up her strength, and she was anxious to be done so Marcel could call his compeller friend, a guy named Kalugal.

It wasn't a name she'd ever heard before, and she wondered what nationality Kalugal was. It wasn't one she'd encountered in all the languages she'd studied. Could it be Indian? She hadn't studied Hindi. Although she wanted to, it wasn't one of the languages that Igor was interested in, and now she might never get the chance to read the *Mahabharata*, the *Ramayana*, and the *Bhagavad Gita* in the language they'd been written in.

As if that was a big concern given the trouble she was in.

She should be more worried about what was happening to her family and whether Igor had retaliated against them after her failure to deliver worthwhile information to him.

Whatever that might be.

The only thing he might find interesting was that he had a lot of competition he wasn't aware of. Who knew that humans could be compellers?

Eleanor and Emmett weren't strong enough to offer Igor a run for his money, but maybe Kalugal was?

Other pureblooded Kra-ell could compel as well, but comparing their abilities to Igor's was like comparing an ant to a rhino. Could a human like Kalugal or someone else be stronger than Igor?

Could he or she free the compound from Igor's oppressive rule?

But who was to say that the new compeller would be any better?

They could be worse. Much worse.

Igor mostly ignored the humans in his compound. As long as they did what they were told and didn't make trouble, they could live reasonably well. They had their own quarters, and no one bothered them there. Well, except for the breeding of hybrids that the young human females were subjected to.

Rape wasn't officially sanctioned, but no woman in her right mind dared to refuse an invitation to a pureblooded male's bed. The consequences of that would be dire for her and for her family.

In that, Sofia had an advantage. As Valstar's granddaughter, she'd been given more leeway, and if she'd stayed in the compound, in a few years she would have been considered too old for breeding hybrids and free to choose a human husband. But her relation to Igor's second-in-command had come with a price—a mission she'd been ill-equipped to fulfill, and she was never going back.

She would have preferred to be a nobody like her cousin Helmi. No one expected anything from her. She had a hybrid boyfriend, who was actually a nice guy, and she was short and pudgy, so she wasn't attractive to the pureblooded Kra-ell and most of the hybrid males who preferred tall, slim females.

"What are you thinking about?" Marcel asked.

"The benefits of being a nobody." She smiled at her own clever reply. "Eleanor's method is very helpful. As long as I talk in generalities, I can actually say something that's close to what I was thinking about."

"So what are the benefits of being a nobody?"

"When no one notices you, and no one expects anything from you, you are not asked to do things that you are not comfortable with. It's safer to be a nobody."

"I actually agree with you. I don't like attracting attention to myself either. That's why I chose a career in computer engineering. Most of the time, it's a solitary occupation. And when I do have to work with others, they are just as awkward around people as I am."

"You're not awkward." He was a little, but it wasn't enough to detract from his attractiveness.

In fact, it made Marcel even more attractive to her. She didn't want a guy who was perfect in every way and made her feel inferior. The Mother knew she was as flawed as the next human.

He chuckled. "Are you being polite or trying to butter me up?"

She was doing neither. She was being honest, and he was making her angry.

"You're annoying. You should learn how to take a compliment. Happy now? I can hurl more insults at you if that tickles your fancy."

Marcel gave her the first genuine smile since the shit show had started. "That's the Sofia I know. Prickly and adorable at the same time."

"Adorable? More like despicable." She pushed her plate away. "Can you call Kalugal now? I'm anxious to talk to him."

"Yeah. I should." Marcel put both plates in one of the boxes and put the boxes on the floor. "If he agrees, I'm going to use a video chat." He pulled out his phone and motioned for her to get closer to him.

When she scooted over, he placed the call.

The phone kept ringing for a long time before the call was answered, and when it was, Sofia heard a baby crying in the background.

"Is it a bad time?" Marcel asked.

"It's fine. Give me a moment. I need to move to someplace less noisy."

The man had a cultured voice, if somewhat haughty and impatient. He sounded as if he was trying his best to be friendly, though, which was nice of him, especially given the crying baby in the background.

Was it his child?

"Do you prefer to do it voice only or video?" Marcel asked.

"Let's do video. I'd like to see the lady who's responsible for all the brouhaha."

Sofia winced. "I'm sorry."

As Marcel switched to video and held the phone to her face, she was taken aback by the breathtakingly beautiful man on the screen. With his dark coloring, he could be a hybrid Kra-ell, but he had blue eyes, so that wasn't likely.

Was he human? Or was he like Marcel?

Different.

"Hello, Sofia." He gave her a charming smile that probably had women falling all over him. "My name is Kalugal, and I will try to override the other compeller's hold on your mind. Look into my eyes and focus on the sound of my voice."

"Thank you for doing this for me." She looked into his blue eyes.

"I'm happy to help if I can." He focused those intense eyes on her. "I want you to feel free to say whatever you want to anyone you want."

She nodded, hoping it would work but suspecting it wouldn't.

"Tell me the name of the compeller who did this to you."

She opened her mouth, but nothing came out, and when she tried to force the words out, she was assailed by an excruciating headache. "I can't." She rubbed her temples.

"Write your compeller's name."

Marcel pulled a pen out of his pocket and lifted one of the cardboard boxes off the floor. "You can write his name here."

She took the pen, clicked it open, and that was as far as she got. Her hand refused to write the letters comprising Igor's name.

Maybe she could write it like an anagram? Like Gori? They could figure it out.

That didn't work either. As long as she consciously knew what she was trying to communicate, the compulsion prevented her from doing it. For some reason, making up stories was easier. Perhaps because she had to concentrate on making the analogies, or maybe because they could apply to many different things and not just what she needed to say.

"Type his name," Kalugal ordered.

"It's no use. I can't."

"What if I guessed his name? Could you nod?"

"I think so. But it would be useless. There are many people who have the same name, and I won't be able to tell you anything about him."

She could probably find a book that had a protagonist named Igor, but that would be just as useless for them.

Kalugal let out a breath. "I did my best. You will need someone stronger than me. Good luck, Sofia."

Her heart sank. Igor was probably the most powerful compeller on the planet, and no one could free her mind from his compulsion.

"Thank you." She forced a smile.

When Marcel ended the call, she sighed. "What if there is no one stronger? There is a reason that he…" She couldn't say more.

"Try to tell a story," Marcel suggested.

"My head hurts too much to come up with one." She rubbed her temples. "Do you have something you can give me for the headache?"

"I'll look in the kitchen, and if there is nothing there, I'll ask Eleanor to get the medication from the nurse."

"Thank you."

3

MARCEL

*M*arcel left the room without locking it. The truth was that confining Sofia inside the bedroom made little sense. To enter or leave the hidden basement dwelling under the cottage, one needed to know the code to the door at the top of the stairs, and she wasn't a mind reader.

When he found no medication in the kitchen nor in the other bathrooms, he called Eleanor.

"Did you talk to Kalugal?" she asked.

"We did, and it didn't work. The compulsion was too strong even for him, and when Sofia tried to break through it, she got a headache. Can you get some painkillers from the clinic and bring them to her?"

He was too ashamed to admit that he wasn't familiar with the name of common drugs used by humans for aches and pains.

"Of course. I'll get her Motrin. Other than the headache, how is she doing?"

So that was the name of the medication. He should memorize it for future reference. What for, though? Yesterday, he would have thought that he needed it if he were to have a relationship with Sofia, but that was a foolish thought given what he now knew about her.

"Before the call, she seemed hopeful, but when Kalugal failed to override the compulsion, her mood took a nosedive."

"That's a good sign, right? She wants to cooperate with us."

"I think so. But she might also be a good actress."

"What do you mean? Was she pretending that it wasn't working?"

"She couldn't do that. Kalugal used compulsion when he asked her the compeller's name, and she still couldn't answer him. However, she could have been pretending to be frustrated by his failure to release her mind."

"Yeah. That's possible." Eleanor didn't sound like she shared his opinion, which made him hopeful. The woman was a big-time skeptic, and her default position was mistrust. If she didn't think that Sofia was acting, then maybe she wasn't.

"Thanks for getting the medication."

"You're welcome." Eleanor ended the call.

As he headed back to the bedroom, Marcel was glad Eleanor hadn't put Sofia in the one they'd used the night before. It would have been too painful to be back there with her and look at the bed they'd shared.

It was just his rotten luck that the best night of his life had been followed by such a miserable day, but despite the lingering bitter sense of betrayal that filled his gut with acid, it still couldn't compete with the worst day of his life.

Not by a long shot.

In comparison to what he'd been through, it was just an unpleasant bump in the road.

So why did it hurt so damn bad?

Perhaps the saying that time healed all wounds was true, and that's why what should have felt no worse than a paper cut felt like he was once again being torn apart.

He was about to open the door when his phone rang, and as he pulled it out of his pocket, he expected it to be Eleanor, but it was Kian.

"Hello, boss."

"I spoke to Kalugal," Kian said. "He told me that it didn't work."

"It didn't. What do we do now?"

"I have Turner here with me, and we have a plan ready to deploy."

Frowning, Marcel turned around and walked back to the living room. "What's the plan?" He sat down on the couch.

"I'm sending Julian over with an MRI machine and a team of Guardians. After they collect the MRI from the old clinic, they will head straight to the airstrip. They should land in Eugene Airport in three and a half hours. From there it will take them another hour and a half to get to Safe Haven. Julian is going to run Sofia through the machine to make sure that she doesn't have location trackers implanted in her body. If she does, he will remove them. Once she's clean, the Guardians will take her to a safe location to meet Toven. Hopefully, he will be able to unlock her mind."

Marcel tensed. Kian was going all out on the case, and he was deploying the big guns, which meant that Turner foresaw even more troubling outcomes.

"If Toven can't do that, we are in deep trouble, aren't we?"

"We are taking precautions to minimize the risk. I'm just glad that the compeller chose Emmett as his target and not you or Leon, and that Eleanor stopped him in time. The Fates were looking out for us."

The Fates, or Sofia?

It would have been much easier for her to convince the guy she'd just seduced and who she must have realized was falling for her to call the compeller than to have Emmett do that. She knew that Marcel was working on a secret project, and if she'd asked him to call her father, he would have done it for her without giving it a second thought.

Had she been protecting him by diverting the compeller's attention to Emmett?

Or had it been the compeller's choice to speak with the head of Safe Haven?

Hopefully, Toven would be able to get all those answers from her.

"Can I go with Sofia to see Toven?" Marcel asked.

"Of course. Make sure that she rests and is ready when Julian arrives with the machine. I don't want to waste any time."

"I will. Why the urgency, though?"

"The sooner we get Sofia free of the compulsion, the sooner we can utilize your idea of feeding her boss misinformation. The last thing we need is for the compeller to send a rescue team to retrieve her. Not that I think he would. Turner suspects that she was set up to be found out, and that she has a tracker embedded in her body so she could lead him to our main base of operations."

A chill ran down Marcel's spine.

So that was what Turner had deduced, and he might be right. It was such a cold and heartless move, but then what else should he expect from a man who slaughtered his own people to get his hands on a few females?

"That kind of move puts even Navuh to shame."

Kian chuckled. "Don't underestimate Navuh. He has no problem sacrificing his warriors if he can gain anything by doing so, and he has no qualms whatsoever about sacrificing the human residents of his island. He and Jade's captor would get along splendidly. Anyway, once Sofia's mind is under our control, we will do our best to make the compeller think that things are back to normal and that she got only a slap on the wrist for her part in the attempted journalistic sting operation. It will buy us time."

"Time to do what?"

"We need to clear Safe Haven of anything that can point to us. It's unfortunate given the enormous investment we've committed to the place, but the location is compromised. Even if the compeller never comes or sends anyone else to investigate, I will not feel safe having our people there."

Unless they found him and eliminated him, but that wasn't likely.

Kian wouldn't want to open an all-out war with the Kra-ell and make them aware of immortals' existence. That being said, though, it might be wise to eliminate a future threat to the clan.

Provided that it was doable.

They needed to find out the kind of force the compeller commanded, which was probably why Turner wanted it done as soon as possible.

"What about Eleanor and Emmett and the paranormal program?"

"Regrettably, Emmett will have to step down and transfer leadership to someone else. The paranormal program will have to be moved as well."

What a major headache. "It almost sounds as if eliminating the compeller would be less of a hassle."

Kian huffed. "Sure. We can eliminate him and his followers, free Jade and the other females, and everyone will live happily ever after. That's not a realistic objective, but Turner says that we will re-evaluate the pros and cons after we learn more about the threat we are dealing with."

"Meaning getting Sofia to tell us all she knows."

"Correct."

4

KIAN

*K*ian ended the call and put the phone down. "I'd better go talk to Toven before the Guardians load the MRI on the truck. We are basing this entire operation on the assumption that he will agree to go on a moment's notice."

Turner shifted his gaze away from his laptop screen. "Do you think he might refuse?"

"I don't think that he will say no, but he might need more time. He's not as much of a prima donna as my mother, but he is still a god, and he needs to be handled with caution and the proper respect." Kian got to his feet. "That's why I'm going to ask him in person."

Turner frowned. "You can't just show up on his doorstep either. You should call ahead. As you've pointed out, he's not your mother."

"Right." Kian raked his fingers through his hair. "He might not even be home. I'll call to say that I'm stopping by." He pushed to his feet. "I'm no good at this diplomatic crap. I would have asked my mother to call him for me, but then she'd be upset that I'm not taking her to talk to Sofia."

Palming his phone, Kian headed toward the door but stopped with his hand on the handle. "Do you need help in here? I can ask Shai to come in. He could take care of some of the arrangements."

"I don't need help." Turner continued typing on his laptop. "I've mobilized my team to make the arrangements for the safe house on the Oregon Coast, and Bridget is taking care of arranging the MRI transport. We are lucky that she had already been planning to send the rest of the medical equipment from the clinic at the keep to the one in Safe Haven and she had ordered the special case to transport the MRI. The thing needs to be steel lined to prevent its magnetic pull from affecting anything in proximity. The crate alone cost ten grand."

Kian released a whistle. "It's a damn shame that's money down the drain."

"It doesn't have to be, but that's a discussion for when we are not pressed for time. You should go talk to Toven."

"Right."

As he walked out the door, Kian placed the call.

The phone rang for quite a while before the god answered. "Good afternoon. I hope you're calling to tell me that the parts for the Perfect Match machines have finally arrived."

"I wish, but no. Nothing's changed in regard to that. I'm calling because I need to discuss an urgent matter with you. Is it okay if I come over?"

"Of course."

"I'm on my way. I'll be there in five minutes."

"Can you fill me in while you walk?"

He could give Toven the rundown and keep the asking for when he got there. "We have a situation at Safe Haven."

By the time Kian had finished telling Toven the high points, he was at the god's front door.

"Come in." Toven motioned for him to follow.

"Hello, Kian," Mia said. "I hope you don't mind me eavesdropping on your conversation with Toven." She wheeled herself to the dining table.

"Not at all."

He'd expected that and hadn't thought it was a problem. Toven would have told Mia everything anyway.

"Can I get you something to drink?" Toven asked.

"Thank you, but I've already downed a bottle of Snake's Venom, and I still have a long night ahead of me."

"I guess that you want me to override the compulsion." Toven motioned for him to take a seat and pulled out a chair for himself.

Kian nodded. "Kalugal tried to do it via a video call, and it didn't work. You can attempt to do the same, but Turner thinks that you need to be face-to-face with Sofia to be able to do it. Since the guy is holding Jade captive, and Emmett claims that she's a very strong compeller in her own right, we must assume that her captor is incredibly powerful."

"Are you flying her over here?" Mia asked.

"I don't want to risk it. I'm flying Julian there with a full-scale MRI machine to check her for implanted trackers. He'll do that at Safe Haven, and if she has any, he'll remove them. After that, he and a couple of Guardians will drive her to a safe house that Turner is arranging. And that's why I'm here. I came to ask you to fly out there with the team and meet her at the safe house."

"When?" Toven asked.

"Tonight. Julian and the Guardians are packing up the MRI as we speak, and once they have it loaded on the truck, they are heading to the airstrip. If you can be ready to leave in an hour or so, you can join them there and fly with them. If you need more time, I can fly you out there separately on the small jet."

Instead of answering him, Toven turned to Mia. "How quickly can you get ready?"

"If you help me pack, I can be ready in ten minutes."

That was a development that Kian hadn't expected. He could understand Toven not wanting to be separated from his mate, but her safety should come first. Toven was proposing to take her with him to a situation that might be a little dangerous.

Seeing his puzzled expression, Toven smiled and took Mia's hand. "You should never play poker, Kian. Your face is too expressive."

"Well, in that case, I was wondering why you want to take Mia with you. You're only going to be gone for one night, and although I'm doing everything I can to mitigate any risks, this trip is not entirely risk-free."

Smiling, Toven lifted Mia's hand to his lips and brushed them over her knuckles. "I'm a god, and as long as I'm awake, no one can get to Mia with me shielding her. I can freeze the minds of any would-be attackers. Still, I wouldn't have inconvenienced my mate with an overnight rush trip if I didn't think that I would need her help. Mia is an enhancer, and I might need the boosting of power she can provide me with."

Kian doubted that Toven needed the boost, and given the grin on Mia's face, he'd said that to make her happy.

So far, no one had asked Mia to boost their power for anything other than testing, and she was probably anxious to try her enhancing powers in a real-life situation.

"It's up to you both." He looked at Mia. "You might have to pull an all-nighter. Are you up to it?"

She squared her shoulders. "I'm an immortal now, and I can survive just fine with four hours of sleep. I'll nap on the way."

"Then welcome aboard." Kian rose to his feet and offered her his hand. "Thank you."

She beamed up at him. "Thank you for welcoming me to the team. I'm so happy to finally be able to utilize my gift for something useful."

Nodding, he let go of her hand and offered it to Toven. "Thank you. You're doing a great service to the clan."

"That remains to be seen." Toven shook his hand. "If I fail to remove the compulsion, you'll have to ask Annani to give it a try."

Had he said that to inquire whether Kian had asked Annani already? Or was it his way of politely expressing his displeasure about being asked to do something that Annani was capable of, but Kian wasn't willing to risk her?

"I doubt that will be needed. Turner thinks that you are a stronger compeller than my mother. I don't know if that's true, but in any case, I view you as a warrior while I can't see my mother in that role."

That should be enough to stroke the god's ego.

"I'm not a warrior. I'm an explorer, or was one a long time ago, and now I'm a creator of stories that lift people's spirits. I don't know whether I'm a stronger compeller than Annani, but it is true that I have more experience. If I fail, though, you might have to employ your mother's help, and you should be prepared to do that. Annani can do everything I can. We are both powerful gods, and in some ways she's more powerful than I am. Do you really think that the only way to keep Annani safe is by hiding her inside your village?"

Kian shrugged. "I do the best I can, and so far, I've managed to keep her out of trouble. I hope to keep it that way. Annani is extremely powerful, but she thinks with her heart, she is impulsive, and she's not as diligent with her safety as I would like her to be."

Toven smiled indulgently. "She's humoring you. You have no idea what she does when she's not here."

Kian winced. "Tell me something that I don't know."

5

TOVEN

*A*s the door closed behind Kian, Mia let out a breath. "Are you sure that you want me to come with you?"

"I might need you." Toven sat back down and leaned toward her. "Besides, you were complaining about being bored. It's an opportunity for a little adventure. Something exciting."

She smiled. "When did I complain about being bored?"

The truth was that Mia hadn't complained about anything, but she'd seemed restless lately, and Toven assumed that the cause was boredom.

"So, you're not?" He took her hands in his.

"How can I be bored when I'm living with a god? If I seem restless, it's because I want Margo and Frankie to move into the village already, and those damn parts are still missing, so William's team can't finish building the Perfect Match machines, and until they get that done, Margo and Frankie can't be the testers for new adventures."

"You are the one who insisted on waiting until they are ready so your friends will have jobs. For all I care, they can move into the village tomorrow, and if you are worried about them being bored with nothing to do, the café can always use more hands."

"I know, but I don't want them to start as waitresses. Their current jobs might not be a huge step up from that, but I want them to begin their lives in the village on the right foot. Besides, my grandmother has a long list of eligible bachelors she plans on inviting to her house to meet the girls on the weekends when we are back in Arcadia. They might find their one and only even before they get here."

Provided that they were indeed Dormants.

Neither girl had a paranormal talent, and the only indicators that they might be Dormants was the affinity he and the immortals who'd met them reported feeling

234

and Lisa's hunch, which was just as unproven and subjective as Margo and Frankie's likability.

Mia pulled her hands out of his. "We'd better start packing if we want to be out of here in time to catch the plane." She put her chair in reverse. "We can keep talking while we pack, and you can tell me the real reason for wanting me to come with you. I know that it can't be my enhancing powers because I've never attempted to enhance your compulsion ability before."

He followed her to the bedroom. "There was no need, so we couldn't test it. This is a golden opportunity to do so. But I'm also thinking about Sofia. The girl is probably terrified, and being surrounded by a bunch of imposing males is going to make her even more so. Your presence will ease her mind and make her more receptive to my compulsion."

She cast him a sly smile. "You're good, and I appreciate you trying to make me feel needed, but I doubt Sofia will have a problem being surrounded by a bunch of hunky Guardians. No one needs me there."

Toven put a hand over his chest. "First of all, I always need you with me. And secondly, I meant every word. I want to test your enhancing ability on my compulsion, and I'm sure that Sofia will appreciate you being there. If she comes from a Kra-ell compound, she's used to females being in charge. She'll assume that you are running the show and will be relieved that our leader is such a sweet-natured female."

"Right." She cast him a doubtful look. "From what I overheard, Sofia is fully human, and she might have been picked at random from the university and compelled to do their bidding. She might not know a thing about the Kra-ell."

The possibility that the girl didn't know who'd sent her hadn't occurred to him, but it was possible.

"In either case, she will love having another female there."

"I'm just thinking about the logistics." Mia opened one of her drawers and started pulling out sets of sexy underwear. "I'm in a wheelchair, and if Turner's rented a house with stairs, you would have to carry me and the chair up. It's a drag."

"Not for me." He took a pair of lacy panties from her hand. "As long as I get to see you in these, I don't care if I need to carry a car up the stairs."

She laughed. "I can actually imagine you doing that. Should I take my motor-ized chair or the one that folds for travel?'"

"Whatever makes you more comfortable, love. You know that I have no problem lifting this chair with you in it."

Mia loved when he flaunted his physical strength and was turned on by it, but this time, she hadn't reacted as he'd hoped.

"I don't want to be a burden." She opened another drawer and pulled out two long skirts and two T-shirts. "Do you think that's enough? Or do I need to take more clothes?"

"We are only going to spend one night there and fly back tomorrow. I'm taking just one change of clothes and no pajamas." He wagged his brows.

Mia laughed. "You never wear pajamas. I thought that you left your only pair in Switzerland."

He'd had to wear pajamas when staying with Mia's grandparents in the rented apartment in Zurich while she'd been undergoing treatments for her heart condition, but he'd left them there because there had been no room left in his carry-on. He'd never bothered to replace them with a new pair.

"That's why I'm not taking any."

6

KIAN

*K*ian hated asking anyone for favors, whether it was Kalugal or Toven, but at least with Kalugal he had an official treaty, and his cousin owed him a favor or two. Besides, under his bluster the guy was a decent fellow, and he also loved to flaunt his compulsion ability.

Toven was a different story.

Kian didn't know the god well, and just the fact that Toven was a god was enough to make him less approachable. Not only that, but Toven had also already paid his dues by helping Eric pull through his transition and by promising to help the rest of Kaia's family.

Never mind that Darlene was Toven's granddaughter, and if she knew that Toven's assistance was more than spiritual, she would have expected him to help her mate survive. But she didn't know, and therefore couldn't ask for it.

Kian had to do that.

Perhaps the thing that bothered him most, though, was not knowing what the god's limit was. Had he already depleted his quota of good will?

Toven was an incredible asset, and Kian hated wasting his favors for things that were perhaps not critical. Turner had convinced him that getting the information out of Sofia qualified as such, but he wasn't sure that it did.

With the god's compulsion power, the clan could possibly take on Navuh and his island, Jade's captor and his compound, or both. It depended on whether Toven was more powerful than Navuh and the Kra-ell leader, and whether he could wrestle control over their people from the two despots.

Turner was right that they couldn't move against the Kra-ell without getting more information on their leader. Come to think of it, the guy might not even be a pureblood. Navuh was just an immortal, the son of a god and a human, but he was a more powerful compeller than most of the gods of old. The same might be true of Jade's captor.

Not that it made any difference to Kian. The hybrid Kra-ell were formidable enough.

The clan's small Guardian force didn't stand a chance against the Kra-ell unless there were only a handful of them, which was unlikely, given that they had slaughtered Jade's tribesmen and then kidnapped her and the other females.

The other option for the clan possibly coming out victorious in a face-to-face confrontation with the Kra-ell was that the Kra-ell relied on their brute strength and didn't own modern weaponry. That would give the Guardians the edge they needed.

The best option, the one that would result in the least casualties, was Toven taking over their minds in one fell swoop.

Was it fair to ask him to go to battle for the clan, though?

Annani was just as powerful if not more so, and yet Kian would never even consider risking her like that.

Kri accused Kian of being a chauvinist, and maybe she was right. Despite her training, and despite her being a damn good Guardian, he still couldn't bring himself to risk her in a battle with the Doomers or with the Kra-ell because she was a female.

Annani was a force to be reckoned with, and she could be a great asset in battle, but all he could think of was how small she was, how delicate, and how soft-hearted.

He was well aware that aside from the soft heart all the rest was an illusion, and that there was nothing fragile about his mother, but she was the clan's heart, and if anything happened to her, it would be the end of them.

Toven was cold, and he looked the part of a warrior.

Kian had no problem seeing him going into battle with his mind or with his bare hands.

When he got back to his office, he found that Bridget and Onegus had joined Turner.

"How did it go?" Bridget asked.

"Toven is coming, and he's bringing Mia along. His excuse is that he might need her enhancing powers, but I think he just wants her to feel as if she's contributing to the war effort."

Bridget lifted a brow. "Are we at war?"

"Not yet, but we might be." Kian pulled out a chair at the conference table. "Toven and Mia will head out to the airstrip as soon as they are done packing. What's the progress with the MRI machine?"

Bridget grimaced. "The guys thought that they were strong enough to lift it and carry it out, but they realized that they overestimated their muscle power. Turner arranged to have a power lift delivered, and it's going to delay them by forty-five minutes."

Kian shook his head. "Julian can just take Sofia to a human hospital, thrall the staff, do what he needs with her, and be done with it. Why bother with transferring that enormous machine?" He pinned her with a hard look. "Why didn't you tell me that the shipping crate would cost ten grand? I might have scrapped the whole idea."

She snorted. "Do you know how much a new MRI machine costs? We've already decided that we are transferring all the equipment from the keep to Safe Haven and getting new equipment for the keep, sans the MRI machine. We don't need two of them, and the model we have in the village is newer than the one in the keep."

"I know, but that was before we decided to evacuate Safe Haven. If we are not using the facility, why do we need a fully equipped clinic there?"

"You might be able to lease the place for more," Turner said. "We could turn the paranormal area into a medical facility of some sort. A recovery area after plastic surgery or something of that nature."

"It's premature to talk about evacuation," Onegus said. "Let's first hear what Sofia has to say, and what we are dealing with. Maybe the Kra-ell are not a threat after all."

"I wish." Kian crossed his arms over his chest.

Bridget put a hand on his shoulder. "In the same way that we don't want to poke the hornets' nest, they might want to avoid us as well. Maybe we can just coexist with them."

"Given what they did to their own people, I don't think so. We might be able to keep hiding and avoid discovery by them, but I'm afraid that ship has sailed."

"Not if we erase all traces of our existence from Safe Haven," Turner said. "And if we decide to leave Jade in captivity."

It was tempting, but Kian's gut was not comfortable with that plan, and experience had taught him to trust his intuition.

7

SOFIA

Sofia lay awake in bed, waiting for the headache medicine to start working.

Marcel had told her to get some sleep because a doctor was coming later tonight to check her for implanted trackers, but how was she supposed to fall asleep after he'd told her that?

Was it possible that Igor had done that without her knowledge?

What if he'd compelled her to forget it?

Was it even possible to make someone forget things with compulsion?

Compulsion was like hypnosis on steroids, and if hypnotists could make people forget things, it made sense that Igor could have had a chip implanted in her body and then compelled her to forget it.

What else had been done to her that she couldn't remember?

The problem was that the more she tried to remember the worse the pounding in her head became, and she couldn't think at all past the pain. Perhaps she should turn her thoughts to something else, like how she was going to get out of this mess.

Marcel had left her alone in the bedroom without locking the door, but he was in the living room, so if she tried to leave, he would stop her.

Besides, where would she go?

Safe Haven was isolated, with nothing for miles around, so unless she managed to steal a car, which she had no clue how to do, she wasn't going anywhere on foot.

Why the hell had Igor and Valstar sent her on a spying mission without giving her any training? They could have at least taught her how to steal cars. Were they going to send people to retrieve her or just leave her there?

Would Valstar even care that she wasn't coming back?

Would her mother?

Not likely.

The only ones who would miss her were her father, her aunts, her cousins, and her friends.

As tears leaked out of her eyes, Sofia swiped at them angrily.

How often had she dreamt about escaping the compound and life under Igor's thumb? But now that she was free, she was crying over the people she loved and was never going to see again.

She just hadn't expected for it to ever happen. Besides, she wasn't free. What were Marcel and his people going to do with her?

Her fantasies about having a life with Marcel had certainly gone down the drain. He hadn't been cruel to her and he didn't even look angry. He just seemed indifferent, treating her with remote politeness as if she was a stranger, a ward to take care of until he could hand her off to someone else.

She was so freaking alone.

As the tears started flowing again, Sofia had no more strength left to fight them. Grabbing a pillow, she covered her face to muffle the pitiful sobs and just let it all out. When she heard the door open, she turned on her side with the pillow still firmly pressed against her face, and when the mattress sank on that side, she turned to the other.

"Sofia." Marcel put a hand on her shoulder. "Is your headache that bad?"

She could've lied and said yes, but the truth was that sometime during her self-pity fest, the Motrin had kicked in and the headache had abated.

"I'm fine," she mumbled under the pillow. "Please, go away."

"You are obviously not fine." He caressed her back. "Are you scared?"

"Should I be?"

"If the doctor finds a tracker, he will surgically remove it, but he will anesthetize the area first, and you won't feel a thing."

Was that what he thought? That she was crying because she was scared of a little physical pain?

"I'm not afraid of the doctor."

"So what are you afraid of?"

Tossing the pillow aside, she turned to face him. "What are your people going to do with me? Are you ever going to let me go?"

His expression was pained as he shook his head. "You will not be physically harmed. I can promise you that. Beyond that, I don't know. I'm not in charge."

"Give it your best guess."

"I don't think you are ever going back."

"That's what I thought." She grabbed the pillow and covered her face with it.

"Why would you want to go back? If the male who sent you is who we think he is, he's a ruthless murderer."

How could they possibly know anything about Igor?

Had Jade managed to overcome his compulsion and tell someone about him? What did she expect to gain by that?

These people weren't Kra-ell, and they couldn't help her. They were probably more dangerous to her than Igor.

Maybe Marcel was just shooting in the dark.

Lifting the pillow off her face, Sofia wiped her tear-stained cheeks with the blanket. "I have a life back in Finland. I want to go back to the university and resume my studies. I have family and friends whom I miss."

Marcel arched a brow. "Are they in Finland? Or are they a little farther to the east?"

He knew about the compound, and the only way he could was if Jade had told them about it.

"I can't say."

She wouldn't even if she could. She didn't know these people and what they wanted with Igor. They could have him, but they couldn't have all the innocent people living under his rule.

"Try to get some sleep." He patted her shoulder and got up. "I'll wake you up when it's time."

8

MARCEL

Once Sofia had finally fallen asleep, Marcel left the bunker and headed to the clinic.

Her tears had sliced at his heart, and yet he couldn't bring himself to comfort her above promising her that she wouldn't be physically harmed.

Even though he believed that she'd been forced into the situation, he couldn't overcome the disappointment he felt and be there for her.

When he got to the new clinic in the clan's enclave, the Guardians were muscling a huge crate through the doorway. The door had been removed and was propped against the wall, but the opening was so tight that the crate scraped the jambs on both sides.

Marcel had never seen an MRI machine before, and he had never had a reason to go over its specs either, so he'd assumed that it was a reasonably sized medical device, but given the Guardians' sweaty foreheads and their grunts, the thing was not only large but also heavy. It was on a wheeled platform, and yet the men were working hard to push it through the doorway.

Standing next to the orphaned door, Julian observed the operation with a frown.

Marcel stopped next to him. "I didn't know the device was so large."

"It's a monster. My mother must have forgotten how heavy this thing was when she decided to move it here."

"How heavy is it?"

"About six thousand pounds."

"What's in it, lead?"

"Close. It's a magnet. Magnetic resonance imaging uses the body's magnetic properties to produce images. I won't bore you with the details of how it works. If you are interested, you can look it up."

"I might do that. Can it harm Sofia?"

Julian shook his head. "An MRI doesn't use radiation, so it's much safer than X-rays. It won't harm her in any way. Some studies have reported an increase in DNA damage due to cardiac MRI scans, but I wouldn't worry too much about it. These devices are routinely used as a diagnostic tool in hospitals and are considered very safe."

"I'm surprised that Bridget sent the big machine here after Kian decided to close operations in Safe Haven."

Julian shrugged. "I wasn't told anything about plans to shut the place down. Is it because of your spy?"

"She's not my spy or my anything." The lie tasted sour on his tongue. He cared about Sofia whether he was willing to admit it or not. "And not because of her. If you want to blame anyone, blame Jade. This whole mess started because of her."

Julian lifted his hands. "I'm not blaming anyone. I'm just stating cause and effect. She came, and we need to leave."

"I'm not sure that's a certain outcome. We need to interrogate her first and find out what force we are dealing with."

As the doctor nodded, the Guardians managed to push the crate through by dislodging the doorjambs.

"It will take me about half an hour to set it up, and then I'm ready for your girl. Is she asleep?"

"She's cried herself to sleep." Marcel sighed. "It's not her fault, you know. She was compelled to do this." He lifted his eyes to Julian's. "Am I a fool to feel sorry for her?"

"You're not." Julian clapped him on the back. "I would be too if she was my potential mate."

Marcel's back stiffened. "She's not my mate. She's human."

"A human with a paranormal ability. I'm sure the thought that she's a Dormant has crossed your mind."

It had, but he hadn't allowed himself to hope, and in retrospect, it had been a wise decision. An even wiser decision would have been to stay away from her when he'd encountered the block in her mind.

"It would be too much of a coincidence for the human spy sent by a Kra-ell leader to be a descendant of the gods."

Julian smiled. "On the contrary. First of all, that's the Fates' mode of operation. They like to orchestrate those seemingly random encounters. And secondly, there are Mey and Jin, who have Kra-ell genetics. We postulate that the Kra-ell and the gods came from the same stock, so we might feel toward the Kra-ell the same affinity we feel for Dormants and other immortals."

"Sofia is not a hybrid. She's fully human."

"Right." Julian frowned. "Still, she might be the daughter of a hybrid. Maybe Jade's captor doesn't prohibit his hybrid males from impregnating humans like she did. Although, from what we know about the Kra-ell, their second generation cannot be activated. Emmett bit Margaret while having sex with her, but he failed to induce her transition."

"Maybe the Kra-ell and the gods are not compatible that way. Perhaps if he'd bitten a Kra-ell Dormant, he would have induced her transition."

Julian pursed his lips. "There is also another option, the one that Emmett kidnapped Peter for. Maybe only immortal males' venom has what it takes to induce transition, and we can do that for our Dormants and for theirs."

Marcel snorted. "I hope that's not the case, and if it is, that Jade's captor never finds out about it."

"Are you sure? What if you could induce Sofia? Wouldn't you want that?"

Marcel swallowed. "I don't know how I feel about her right now."

"I think you do." Julian regarded him with a smirk lifting one side of his mouth. "I'll text you when the machine is ready."

9

SOFIA

"Time to wake up." Marcel's warm hand rested on Sofia's shoulder. "The doctor is waiting for you."

It felt as if she'd fallen asleep only minutes ago, drifting off into blissful oblivion, and she didn't enjoy the glum reality rushing into her mind.

"I'm awake." She pushed the blanket off. Except for shoes, she was still fully dressed, but she urgently needed to visit the bathroom. "Give me a couple of moments to freshen up."

"No problem." He took a step back. "I'll wait for you in the living room."

After taking care of her bladder, Sofia stood in front of the vanity mirror and winced at what was reflected in it. It wasn't just the messy hair, the red-rimmed eyes, and the dark circles under them. It was the other image that was superimposed over her face, an ugly evildoer with twisted features.

She knew that it was just her imagination and not some strange paranormal talent. That had been a lie, her ticket to get into the retreat. She wasn't a bad person. She'd just been used to do a bad thing, and it made her feel bad about herself.

The worst part was hurting Marcel's feelings.

He'd admitted to having trust issues, especially with women, and she'd proven him right.

Splashing cold water on her face helped with the eyes, and brushing a comb through her hair helped tame it into a presentable updo, but there was nothing she could do about the second image other than get rid of the guilt.

Not as easy as it sounded.

When she was ready, Sofia walked into the living room. "Do I need to bring anything with me? A change of clothes, maybe?"

Marcel shook his head. "If Julian finds a tracker and needs to operate, you might need a nightdress, but I can come back here and get it for you."

That was an odd answer. Unless the implant was in her brain, its removal wouldn't require an overnight stay in the hospital. What the heck were they planning to do to her?

She'd expected him to take her to the nurse's office in the lodge, but when they'd passed through the lodge without stopping at the nurse's office, she frowned. "Where are you taking me?"

"The new clinic in the secluded part of Safe Haven."

She tensed. "Do you mean the one the government is using for its secret projects?"

"Yes and no. It's in that general area."

"Tell me the truth, Marcel. Are they going to do anything to me other than remove the tracker?"

"To find the device, the doctor needs to scan your body using an MRI machine. That's why we need to use the other clinic."

"Do you swear that's all the doctor will do to me?"

"I swear it."

It was so dark that she couldn't see his expression, but he'd sounded sincere, and her anxiety level subsided.

As they kept walking, passing through three different gates that Marcel opened with his phone, she wondered how he could see where they were going. There were no lights, and the moon was shadowed by clouds. She could barely see one step in front of her and had to hold on to his arm.

Wondering whether his eyes were glowing, she cast him a sidelong glance, but since she couldn't see them, the answer was that they weren't.

"Why is it so dark here? Couldn't they put up at least one streetlamp?"

Marcel chuckled. "I'll mention it to the boss when I talk to him again."

Who was the mysterious boss he kept bringing up? Was he the equivalent of Igor? Maybe he was also a powerful compeller, and that was why Igor was interested in the place. What if he was another Kra-ell?

"That's the clinic," Marcel said.

He led her up to a door she couldn't see, and when he pulled it open, the light spilling from the inside blinded her until her pupils adjusted to the brightness.

Taking her by the elbow, he led her into a room with a big scanner.

"This is our doctor, Julian," he introduced a guy who wasn't wearing a white coat and didn't look like any doctor she'd ever seen.

He was gorgeous, with shoulder-length light brown hair, blue eyes, and full lips that were curved in a friendly smile.

"Hello, Sofia." He offered her his hand. "I'm Doctor Julian, but everyone calls me Julian."

"Hi." She shook his hand. "Nice to meet you." She glanced at the padded bench that was partially inside a bagel-shaped device. "Do I need to take off my shoes before lying down on that?"

"Yes, please. We want to keep things as clean as possible. Also, if you have any jewelry on you or anything made of metal, you should take it off. The MRI is a powerful magnet."

She had leggings and a T-shirt on, so that wasn't a problem, and her pushup bra was the kind that didn't use wires and had memory foam padding instead. Her pendant was still locked in the safe, so the only things remaining were her hairpins.

"Are these a problem?" She took one of them out and handed it to Julian.

His eyes widened. "Were they checked?"

Marcel nodded. "Leon ran a scanner on her."

"I bought them in a supermarket in Helsinki." Sofia took the rest out. "There is nothing special about them."

Naturally, they had no reason to believe her, and when all the pins were out, Julian handed them to Marcel. "Give them to Leon. He's out in the front room."

"I will. How long is it going to take?"

"About half an hour. I need to scan Sofia's entire body."

"Can I be here while you do that?"

The young doctor shook his head. "It's not mandatory for you to leave, but it's preferable. It's very difficult to lie perfectly still inside the device while it's doing its thing, and the less distraction Sofia has to filter out, the better."

"Then I shall wait out in the hallway." Looking reluctant to leave her side, Marcel cast her an encouraging glance and a smile before heading out the door.

"Okay, young lady." Julian offered her his hand again. "Hop on the bench."

She used his hand as a lever to hoist herself up, and when she was sprawled on the platform, Julian arranged her arms and legs the way he wanted them.

"You're not claustrophobic, right?"

"Not as far as I know."

"Good. If you were, I would have to give you sedatives. Try to relax and think of your happy place. If you can doze off, it would be even better."

"I'll try." Sofia closed her eyes and imagined her room in the university's dorms, and when that didn't do the trick, she imagined her room back in the compound with her cousin sitting on her bed and telling her about everything that had happened while she was gone. That brought a smile to her lips, and she tried to keep thinking happy thoughts as the machine started buzzing and the platform started moving.

MARCEL

"These are just plain hairpins." Leon handed them back to Marcel after crushing a couple to make sure they were not hiding anything inside their tiny plastic bubbles. "But I want you to take a look at that locket of hers. Can you tell where it was made without taking it apart?"

Marcel smiled. "I'm way ahead of you on that. The thing was so cheaply made that I figured it wasn't a high-end piece of equipment. I've looked it up, and it turns out that you can order them on the internet. Like everything else, they are made in China."

"Bummer." Eleanor leaned against the desk and crossed her arms over her chest. "I was hoping it was a piece of alien technology and that we could learn something from it."

"We did learn something from it." Marcel put the pins in his pocket. "That particular group of Kra-ell doesn't have advanced technology and they use commercially available things. We have a clear advantage over them in that."

Leon looked doubtful. "Jade had access to advanced technology. She launched a telecommunications company with what she knew."

Eleanor huffed out a breath. "She must have had an engineer and a scientist in her group, and that's how she had access to advanced technology. Her captor's group was probably comprised of meatheads, the types who don't know how to build anything and only know how to take it from others. They must have emptied her tribe's bank accounts. Emmett says that the tribe was wealthy thanks to its many enterprises, but when Vrog came back from Singapore and found the compound burned to the ground, all he found was the cash that Jade had kept in the safes. The money in the banks was gone. The compeller must have forced her to surrender that money to him."

Leon still looked doubtful. "The Chinese government could have confiscated the funds. Having money in the bank in China is a risky proposition."

"Maybe it wasn't in a Chinese bank," Eleanor countered. "Jade was a smart lady." She shook her head. "Correction. She is a smart lady."

The discussion about Jade and the possible fate of her money turned into a discussion about international banking, which Eleanor knew a lot about, and then moved to the subject of precious metals and where best to store them.

Marcel wasn't overly interested in the topic, but it provided a good distraction while they waited.

An hour or so later, when the door finally opened and Julian stepped out, the grim expression on the doctor's face told Marcel all he needed to know.

"I found a tracker on her," Julian said. "It's so small that I missed it the first time around, but I had a hunch and repeated the scan. It's in her thigh, and it's the size of a grain of rice."

Eleanor cast Marcel a mocking glance. "Can that be ordered on the internet as well?"

"No."

"I didn't think so." She turned to Julian. "Did you take it out?"

"Not yet. She wants Marcel to be with her when I do."

Why the hell did that make his heart swell?

"Are you going to use a local anesthetic?" he asked the doctor.

"Of course. Thankfully, it's close to the surface, so the incision will be minimal."

Eleanor snorted. "I had a plastic surgeon take out the tracker in my arm without an anesthetic, and I only took Motrin for the pain."

Leon arched a brow. "Why did you have a tracker?"

"Everyone working for Simmons had one. Heck, I think that everyone in that damn underground city was implanted with trackers. The only difference was that I knew I had it. The others didn't." She rubbed her arm. "Lucky for me, I turned immortal, so there is no sign of it left. Sofia is not that lucky."

Maybe she was.

Julian's words from before still reverberated through Marcel's cerebrum. What if Sofia was a second-generation hybrid that was fully human? What if he could activate her?

It didn't seem likely, but on the other hand, the Fates were known to weave a complicated tapestry and steer events toward the outcome they were after.

What if this entire brouhaha was about him and Sofia meeting and falling in love?

Marcel stifled a bitter chuckle.

If that was so, the Fates had a twisted sense of humor. They made Sofia both attractive and repulsive to him at the same time. She'd manipulated him, used him, and he'd sworn never to fall victim to those exact two things ever again.

Couldn't they have given her a different character flaw?

Except, unlike the one who had scared him off love for centuries, Sophia hadn't acted in self-interest. She'd been coerced, and she was probably protecting loved ones as well.

Leon got to his feet and walked up to Julian. "Are you sure that's the only tracker on the girl? What if there are more? A tracker the size of a grain of rice can be easily missed."

"I'm sure. After I found it, I double-checked, but I'll look at the slides again if you want."

"Please do. Toven did us a great favor by coming out here to release Sofia's mind, and my job is to make sure that no harm comes to him. We don't want to lead the compeller straight to him."

11

SOFIA

*A*s Sofia rubbed over the spot where Julian had found the tracker, the feeling of violation was even worse than what she'd routinely experienced in Igor's office. At least there she'd been aware of what was being done to her, and even though she would have never agreed to it voluntarily, she kind of understood the need for the compulsion, and if that was the price she had to pay to be allowed out of the compound, she was willing to pay it.

Igor was protecting his people, and he had to make sure that she couldn't reveal the Kra-ell's existence and the location of the compound.

But implanting her with a location device without her knowledge was a different story. It had nothing to do with keeping his people safe, but it had everything to do with his need for control. He had tried to make sure that she could never escape.

The question was how and when he'd gotten the device implanted. He could have made her forget, but there would have been a mark, and the area would have been tender for a while. She would have noticed it.

When the door opened, and Julian walked in with Marcel, Sofia forced her hand away from her thigh. "I don't remember this being done to me. How could that be?"

"The tracker is very small." Julian turned the screen toward her so she could see it. "It could have been injected. Did you receive vaccinations or antibiotic shots?"

"Not in my thigh. They were always done in the arm."

"You might have been compelled to forget," Marcel said. "Usually, that's not how compulsion works, but some compellers have an extra ability that enables them to do that."

"Can Emmett or Eleanor compel memories to be forgotten?"

Marcel shook his head.

"What about Kalugal?"

He nodded. "Kalugal can do that, but he has an extra talent that enables it."

"Then that's how it must have happened to me."

Julian snapped on a pair of gloves and motioned for her to lie down. "I need you to take off your leggings."

"Are you going to give me a shot?"

"Yes."

She turned to Marcel. "Can you hold my hand? I hate needles."

"Of course." He took her hand. "Don't look at what Julian is doing. Look at me."

That wasn't a difficult command to follow. Julian was gorgeous, but he was like a beautiful sculpture to her. His perfect features and his pleasant nature didn't affect her.

Marcel was the one who made her heart somersault every time he got near her. Everything about him appealed to her, from his ruggedly handsome physique to his serious, nearly somber attitude. Every time she'd managed to make him smile or laugh, it had felt like an accomplishment.

Would she ever get to see those glimpses of levity again?

The prick of the needle made her cringe, and when the burning started, she squeezed Marcel's hand.

He winced. "I don't like seeing you in pain."

The emotional pain he was causing by withdrawing from her was much worse than the physical one the doctor had inflicted, but to admit it was to give him even more power over her and to lose the little pride she still retained.

"The pain is due to the perforation of the skin," Julian explained. "The liquid activates stretch receptors in the deeper tissues. It will subside in a moment." He pulled out the needle and swiped something cool over it.

She let out a breath. "It doesn't hurt anymore."

"Good," the doctor said. "I'm going to poke you with the needle again in a couple of minutes."

Sofia closed her eyes and concentrated on the feel of Marcel's large hand enveloping hers.

"Can you feel this?" Julian asked.

"No."

"Good. Let's do it."

As the doctor cut into her skin, she felt pressure but no pain.

"It's out," Julian pronounced. "Easy peasy." He wiped the incision and then put something sticky over it. "I didn't even have to suture it."

Sofia braved a look at her thigh, but there was nothing to see. Julian had covered it with surgical tape.

"Where is the tracking device?" she asked.

He used a pair of tweezers to lift the blood-covered tiny pebble off his surgical tray. "Here is the little devil. I wonder if it was made in China."

"I don't think so." Marcel leaned over her to take a closer look. "That's a sophisticated little sucker."

A knock sounded on the door, and a moment later Eleanor poked her head in. "Can we come in now?"

"Give us a moment," Julian told her and then waved at Sofia. "You can put your pants back on."

"That was easier than I expected." She pulled her leggings on, taking care with the incision area. "Will I feel pain later?"

"I'll give you something for it."

As Julian put the tracker down on the tray, the door opened again, and Eleanor walked in with Leon.

"How did it go?" Eleanor asked.

"Easier than I expected." Sofia sat up slowly. "I feel a little woozy, though."

"You should lie down for a little bit." Julian pulled out a pillow from under the platform and handed it to her.

"Thank you." She tucked it under her head and brought her knees up.

It was probably the stress, or maybe the combined effect of the headache and the anesthetic, or maybe it was the fear of putting weight on the leg where Julian had dug the tracker out, but whatever the reason was, she was glad to stay horizontal.

Hopefully, her nausea wouldn't get worse and force her to get up and rush to the bathroom to puke.

"Is that it?" Eleanor leaned over the tray. "It's tiny. Mine was so much bigger. No wonder it hurt like a son of a bitch to take it out, and the area was still painful to touch for a couple of days later. I winced every time I moved my arm."

"What do you want me to do with it?" Julian asked. "Should we send it to William to take apart?"

"No!" Leon and Marcel said at the same time.

"We need to retain the illusion that she still has it on her." Leon pulled out his bug checker and waved it over the pebble. "It's not transmitting. How is it activated? Can it be done remotely?"

Marcel nodded. "I'm not familiar with the technology, but I know that it can be done. The thing needs to be inside a body, though. It's powered by the body's electrical signals. To keep the illusion going, we need to put it inside a dog or a cat, preferably one that doesn't move much. It will look suspicious if they activate the tracker and see it bouncing all over the resort."

"I know the perfect cat," Eleanor said. "Cecilia is the laziest cat ever. She sits on the windowsill in Anastasia's office all day long, and she only comes down to feed or to pee and poop."

"Poor cat," Sofia said. "I feel bad about hurting an innocent animal."

Julian gave her a smile. "My mate and I have two small dogs, and we put chips in both of them in case they ever get lost. It's not a big deal, and I'll make sure it's painless."

254

12

MARCEL

"I need to call the boss," Julian said. "Do you want to talk with him?"

Marcel looked at Sofia. "Are you okay staying here alone for a few minutes?"

She nodded. "What's next? Are you taking me back to the bunker? I could use a few hours of sleep."

That wasn't going to happen. Marcel was taking her to see Toven, but first, he needed to confer with Kian.

"I will tell you the plan after I talk to the boss."

She sighed and closed her eyes. "I'll probably be asleep when you get back."

"Then I'll carry you wherever you need to be." He leaned down and planted a soft kiss on her forehead. "Rest."

The smile she gave him could melt an iceberg. "I will."

When they were out of the room, Julian regarded him with a raised brow. "You didn't tell her about Toven?"

"Not yet. She's scared and overwhelmed. I figured that it would be easier for her to deal with one thing at a time."

"True. We also need to figure out what to tell her about Toven. The guy is not easy to explain."

Marcel shrugged. "After dealing with the compeller who imprisoned her mind, Sofia shouldn't be surprised to meet another compeller who is just as powerful or more so."

"Let's hope that he's more." Julian pulled out his phone and dialed Kian's number.

"What's the status?" the boss's gruff voice thundered through the microphone.

"She had a tracker in her. It was tiny, and I almost missed it. But it's out now, and Marcel says that we should implant it in a cat so it will seem as if she's still wearing it."

"That's an excellent idea. I wish we could examine the device, but for now, it's more important to keep the illusion going. Is Marcel next to you?"

"He's right here, and so are Leon and Eleanor."

"Good. What's your take on that tracker?"

"It's a very sophisticated piece of equipment that is not easy to come by. In contrast, the pendant she was using to communicate with the compeller is readily available on the internet. It's not cheap, but it's not difficult to obtain."

"That reinforces Turner's theory. He suspects that the compeller wanted Sofia to get caught so she could lead him to our headquarters or center of operations. That's why he sent an amateur. She was a pawn."

Eleanor bared her teeth. "What a bastard."

"That's a gross understatement," Marcel said. "He's a murderer."

Leon cleared his throat. "We are judging him by our modern moral standards, but what he did might be acceptable by Kra-ell tradition. We know that they are warlike people and that they scoff at soft emotions. Furthermore, if we look back at human history, it was common practice for one tribe to attack another, slaughter the males and take the females. Sacrificing a pawn for the greater good of the community is also a common tactic."

Eleanor huffed. "It was also common practice to sacrifice children to idols, tie child virgin brides to the bed and rape them, and a thousand and one other evil customs, some of which are still practiced to this day. That doesn't make any of them okay, and I have no tolerance for that. I say let's kill the evildoer and free his people."

"I like the way you think." Marcel clapped her on the back.

"Thank you." She grinned at him. "Most people think that I'm a bloodthirsty bitch."

"That's because you are bloodthirsty." Leon smiled at her. "But I like that about you."

"People," Kian groaned. "We are pressed for time. Can we schedule the mutual admiration club meeting for later?"

"Indeed." Marcel rubbed a hand over the back of his neck. "I didn't tell Sofia that we want her to feed the compeller false information yet. What should I tell her about Toven?"

"Only that he's a powerful compeller and that he might be able to free her. He calls himself Tom when he deals with humans, so you can use that name."

"She's smart, and she suspects that we are not regular humans. I don't know how to answer her questions."

"Since we need her to feed the compeller false information about us, you should start giving her that information first. We are a group of paranormally talented people, and we gather others like us to create a community. That's why we have several compellers among us as well as people with other abilities. I'll instruct Toven and Mia to tell her the same story."

Eleanor frowned. "Why did Mia come with Toven?"

"He thinks that he might need her enhancing abilities."

It was a good idea, but Marcel hoped Mia's talent wouldn't be needed. If Sofia's compeller was more powerful than Toven, they were in big trouble. "I assume that you want me to take Sofia to him. Should I take Guardians with us?"

"Naturally. Julian is coming with you too. Once the compulsion is taken care of, and the interrogation is done, he goes back to the village with Toven and Mia. After that, you will take Sofia back to Safe Haven, and the charade will start tomorrow. Turner and I will attend via a video call, and we will work out a narrative to feed the compeller according to what she tells us about him."

It was on the tip of Marcel's tongue to say that it might take longer than a few hours to get Sofia to confess everything she knew, but then he realized that they wouldn't need to employ regular interrogation tactics that took a long time to establish rapport and weaken her resistance. Once Toven overrode the other compeller, he could compel Sofia to tell him everything.

SOFIA

*S*ofia was about to have another compeller take a crack at her, and this time, it would happen in person.

Given that she was being escorted by Marcel, Julian, and two guards, and with Marcel carrying a concealed weapon, she suspected that the compeller was the leader of their organization, and that they were taking precautions in case they were attacked.

By whom? Did they expect Igor or Valstar to come to her rescue?

Fat chance of that.

"Who are you people?" she asked Julian because Marcel had deflected all of her questions so far.

She was seated between the two of them in the back of the minivan, with the two guards sitting up front. It should have been enough space for three average-sized people, but she would have preferred not to be in the middle. The minivan had a third row, but it had been folded down to make room for boxes that the doctor had brought with him.

"What do you mean?" Julian smiled with fake innocence.

She rolled her eyes. "I might be just a linguist, but I'm not stupid. You are well organized and well-funded, and you have more compellers than I ever thought could exist."

The doctor gave her a condescending look. "You shouldn't be surprised to find paranormally talented people in a place that runs specially curated retreats for them."

"So that's it? You are an organization of paranormals?"

Julian nodded. "It's difficult to be a paranormal among normals. The founders of our organization decided to create a community for us."

"Do you have a paranormal talent?"

Julian nodded. "I'm an empath. I feel what others around me feel, which can be very useful for a doctor, but it's also a curse. That's why I can't work in a hospital. The anguish is too much for me to bear."

"I can imagine. So where do you work?"

He smiled, this time genuinely. "I work in a halfway house for semi-rehabilitated victims of trafficking. When they are well enough to venture into the outside world, we provide a safe place for them while they get acclimated, and once they are ready to fly, we help them live independently. But they are always welcome to return and enjoy the cocoon of safety again."

"Aren't you affected by their misery? They probably carry horrible emotional and physical scars."

"They do, but they are happy about having a new lease on life, they form friendships with each other that help them heal, and they are full of optimism for the future. We try to make it a wonderful experience for them, a real safe house, and they pay us back with love and appreciation. It's very fulfilling."

"I bet. What about them?" She pointed at the two guards. "What are their talents? Or are they just hired muscle?"

Next to her, Marcel shook his head, but he didn't say a thing.

Had she insulted his buddies? He'd said that he was friends with the people in security.

"What's your talent, Eigen?" Julian asked.

"I can turn into a meat popsicle." The guy snorted a laugh.

"Seriously, dude."

"Seriously. I can lower the temperature of my body so I appear to be dead."

That was a useful talent for a soldier, but she still wasn't sure that he wasn't pulling her leg. "What about the other one?"

"I can sing you to sleep."

She crossed her arms over her chest. "Prove it."

"I can't. If I start singing, Eigen is going to fall asleep at the wheel, and we will crash."

"You are both full of shit. No one at the retreat mentioned talents like that." She turned to Marcel. "What about you? Do you have a talent?"

His lips twitched with a suppressed smile. "I can also put you to sleep by telling you about my workday."

"Very funny. What if I find computer engineering fascinating?"

His eyes sparkled. "I would be delighted to tell you about the latest program I wrote."

She slapped his arm. "I'm not in the mood for jokes. If you don't want to tell me, just say so."

"I'll tell you later."

"So you really do have a paranormal talent?"

"I do." He turned to the window. "Just look at this house. It's spectacular."

Was he deflecting her question?

Sofia tried to see what he was looking at, but all she could discern was a dark, rectangular shape on top of a cliff. Whoever was inside either hadn't turned any lights on, or the windows were shuttered.

Still, it wasn't the first time that she'd noticed Marcel could see better than she could in the dark.

"I know what your talent is. You have paranormal night vision."

"That's part of it." He put his arm around her shoulders. "When we get to the house, I want you to be respectful toward Tom. He came all the way out here to help you. It would be rude of you to give him a hard time."

So she'd been right, and they were going to see the boss of their organization.

Was he as bad as Igor?

Worse?

Better?

"Are you implying that I'm rude?"

He chuckled. "Fates forbid. But you get prickly when annoyed."

That was true. "Tell me a little bit about him. Should I be scared of him?"

"Not at all. Tom is a novelist who comes from a very old and wealthy family. He's old school, and modern vernacular might sound offensive to him. Act as if you are meeting a prince, and you should be fine."

"What if I say something that he finds offensive? Would he compel me to stand on one leg and crow?"

Julian chuckled. "The worst he would do to you is look down his nose at you and make you feel like a bug. Tom is a good guy, but he's condescending without meaning to be. It's just his natural sense of superiority."

She hadn't detected any resentment, and there was real fondness in the doctor's tone, so maybe their leader wasn't as bad as Igor; but he was still a compeller, he was still a man who imposed his will on others, and that couldn't be good even if he was human.

In her experience people seldom, if ever, chose to use their talents and other advantages to help others. Mostly, they used them to get a leg up and step over those who were less gifted.

14

MARCEL

*A*s they neared the structure, Marcel let out a relieved breath. The ride had taken less than an hour, but it had been difficult sitting next to Sofia and pretending that her closeness didn't affect him.

He was still waging a battle with his determination to never fall victim to a woman's wiles again. His heart was demanding that he stop resisting the pull and embrace the rose that Sofia was, with all of her soft petals and prickly thorns, but his mind knew better than to listen to that squishy organ that had led him astray before.

But even his mind wasn't as steadfast as he would have liked it to be.

So Sofia wasn't perfect. So she'd been sent as a spy and used him to get close to Emmett. So what?

None of it had been her choice.

But had her feelings for him been real? Or had it been a superb act, and he'd fallen for it like he had done in the past because he was putty in an attractive woman's hands?

If it had been an act, Sofia must have studied method acting under a masterful teacher because her performance had been flawless. Her anger after he hadn't shown up as she'd expected, her refusal to let him explain, had all of that been for show?

It very well might have been.

After all, they'd ended up in bed together the same night, and she had rocked his world, demolishing the last of his resistance.

Fates, he was such a fool.

Summoning the vestiges of his resolve, he forced himself to enter the familiar state of indifference and looked at the house Turner had chosen for their rendezvous with Toven.

What had the guy been thinking?

The structure was a glass and concrete rectangle that was supported by big pillars and perched over a cliff overlooking the ocean. It was beautiful, and the view must be spectacular, but the large expanse of glass made its occupants an easy target for snipers.

Marcel doubted that the windows were bulletproof.

Other than Sofia, they were all immortal, so bullets and even shards of glass wouldn't necessarily kill them, but they could knock them out long enough for the attackers to finish the job.

Perhaps Turner was using the compeller's tactic and luring him or his warriors by dangling their own pawn as bait?

Given that they had just removed the tracker from her, it didn't make much sense. If Turner wanted to flush out the enemy, he should have told them to leave the tracker in and surrounded the place with Guardians.

Perhaps he'd employed a bait-and-switch tactic?

Make the enemy think that they were complacent because the tracker had been removed, but surround the property with Guardians?

"How many Guardians did Kian send?" he asked the driver as the guy drove the minivan into a parking spot under the structure.

"Eight. Two are in the house, we are with you, and the other four stayed in Safe Haven. Why?"

"I was wondering about Turner's location choice. A house of glass is not easily defended."

The Guardian shrugged. "I trust Turner. He knows what he's doing."

"I hope you are right because all those windows are a sniper's wet dream." Marcel opened the door and offered Sofia his hand.

She looked up. "It's a beautiful house, and the curtains hide what's going on inside. Besides, who are you expecting to attack us?"

Was that her way of telling him that she wasn't expecting a rescue?

As if he believed anything that came out of her pretty mouth. He wasn't straight out accusing her of lying, though. Not yet.

Until Toven got a hold of her mind and forced her to tell the truth, Marcel was going to give Sofia the benefit of the doubt. But if she was lying, and she was expecting a rescue, then he could keep the pretense the same way he had done with her pendant.

"Yeah, you are right." He took her hand and led her up the stairs to the front door. "With the tracker gone, no one could have followed you here."

The Guardian who opened the door gave Sofia an appraising look before offering her his hand. "Hi, I'm Malcolm."

"I'm Sofia." She shook it. "Are you the boss?"

He laughed. "I'm not. Please, come in."

15

SOFIA

*W*hen the guy who had opened the door stepped aside and motioned for her to come in, the most beautiful man Sofia had ever seen rose to his feet and walked toward her.

This man wasn't human, she was willing to bet on it, but he wasn't Kra-ell despite his nearly black hair. He was too perfect, too cultured, and too refined. He lacked the savagery lurking beneath the surface of all the purebloods and most of the hybrids, males and females alike. There was an animalistic quality to them that was totally absent from this gorgeous man.

"Hello, Sofia." He offered her his hand. "My name is Tom."

It took her a moment to find her voice. "Hi," she croaked. "You must be the compeller."

He smiled. "I am many things, but I am not a compeller. Compulsion is an ability I was born with, but it doesn't define me, and I don't enjoy using it."

With that one sentence, he'd won her over.

"I'm glad. It's not right to take people's will away from them."

He chuckled. "Unless it's to prevent them from doing harm to another, right?" He offered her his arm and walked her to the dining table. "If you had the ability to stop a murderer from firing a gun at an innocent person, wouldn't you do it?"

"Of course."

He pulled out a chair for her. "Nearly every ability and technology is not intrinsically good or evil. It's how it is used that's either beneficial or harmful. And quite often, the boundaries are not clear. And if that's not bad enough, sometimes what is beneficial in one way is harmful in another, and you have to weigh the good versus the bad and make a judgment call about the winner." He smiled a sad smile. "So, as you can see, God's job is not easy."

While Tom was delivering his speech, Marcel and Julian sat across the table from them. She'd been so mesmerized by him, that she'd forgotten that she hadn't arrived alone.

"I'm glad that I'm not a goddess." She huffed out a breath. "I would have gotten one hell of a headache if I had to make those judgment calls."

"Ah, but you make those calls every moment of every day," Tom said in his velvety smooth voice. "It's just that the consequences of your decisions are usually not of life and death caliber."

As Sofia searched her mind for a clever response, a young woman drove her wheelchair into the living room.

"Hi." She waved a hand at Sofia while navigating her motorized chair with the other right into the empty spot next to the dining room table. "I'm Mia, Tom's fiancée."

Tom had just won another point in his favor.

Mia looked like a really nice and friendly person, and that reflected well on Tom.

Still, she had to wonder what their reflection in the mirror looked like. Were they as beautiful on the inside as they were on the outside?

She smiled and waved back. "I'm Sofia."

It was on the tip of her tongue to add that she was Marcel's girlfriend, but right now she was Marcel's suspect, not his love interest.

Throughout the drive, he had been physically close but emotionally distant.

As Mia reached for Tom's hand, he shook his head. "I want to try it first without your help."

"Right," Mia said. "I forgot. I'll move a few feet away. Usually, that's enough."

Was Mia a compeller as well?

She looked too gentle, too fragile, and Sofia would have never suspected her of possessing the ability. She looked so kind, and Sofia couldn't imagine her using compulsion to gain an unfair advantage over others.

In contrast, Eleanor looked the part and was quite intimidating. Still, she was nothing like Igor or even Jade. She just had an aura of someone who was used to getting her own way, but she loved Emmett, and she'd been kind to Sofia.

Emmett clearly loved Eleanor, and he put up a good act as the benevolent guru, but Sofia wouldn't trust him with a key to the bathroom.

Suddenly, it occurred to her that Emmett had swindled his followers by using compulsion to get them to surrender all of their possessions to him.

Bastard.

That must have been what had piqued Jade's curiosity. She must have read about that and realized that Emmett was a compeller. Maybe she'd thought that he was stronger than Igor and could free her.

Emmett wasn't in the same league as Igor, but Sofia had a feeling that Tom was in an even higher league.

He displayed a level of confidence that even Igor couldn't front.

It occurred to her that Igor strived to be perceived the way Tom was—a powerhouse that was nonetheless cultured and refined, but what he projected paled by comparison. Igor was cold and ruthless. He demanded respect and was afforded it out of fear.

Tom didn't demand anything. His personality just commanded respect.

16

MARCEL

*A*s Mia moved away from the table, Toven turned to Sofia. "Tell me your full real name."

"My name is Sofia Heikkinen."

Toven looked at Marcel. "Is that the name she's registered under?"

Marcel nodded.

Toven leveled his gaze at Sofia. "How old are you?"

"Twenty-seven."

Marcel nodded to confirm.

"Did you study at the University of Helsinki for the past seven years?"

"Almost eight. I study languages."

"That's nice. Did you go home often?"

She nodded. "Once a month."

"Was home far away from the university?"

"Yes."

"Did you fly home?"

"No."

"Did you take the bus?"

"No."

"Did you drive?"

"Yes."

"How long did it take you to drive?"

She opened her mouth, but nothing came out. "I can't say."

"Was it longer than two hours?"

"Yes."

"Longer than four?"

"Yes."

"Longer than eight?"

"No."

Toven smiled. "We are making progress, and I didn't even use compulsion yet. Tell me why you came to Safe Haven," he commanded.

This time, Marcel could feel the compulsion reverberating in his voice.

"I was sent to observe and report."

Marcel let out a relieved breath. She'd answered Toven's question, which meant that his compulsion could override her compeller's.

"What were you supposed to observe?"

"I wasn't given any details. I was told to get close to the management and report anything unusual that I noticed."

"Who did you report to?"

"Valstar."

"Is he the one who compelled you?"

Sofia shook her head.

"What's the name of the compeller?"

"Igor."

"Is Igor the leader?"

She nodded.

Finally, they had a name for Jade's captor.

Toven glanced at Marcel before turning back to Sofia. "Tell me about the people of your community. What makes them special?"

She shook her head. "I can't."

Toven narrowed his eyes at her. "Maybe that was too general. Is your community hidden?"

She nodded.

"Where is it located?"

"I can't say."

"How many people live in your hidden community?"

"I can't say." She rubbed her temples. "My head hurts."

Toven leaned closer to her. "Did you see anything suspicious in Safe Haven?"

Marcel figured out what the god was doing. It seemed that Sofia could answer questions about recent events, probably because the compulsion about those hadn't been reinforced countless times.

She nodded.

"What did you find suspicious?"

She turned to look at Marcel. "I saw your eyes glowing on occasion. You can also see in the dark. I don't think you are human." She turned to Toven. "You're not human either."

Toven smiled. "What am I?"

"I don't know." She lifted her hand to her temple and rubbed at it. "I think of Marcel, Eleanor, and Emmett as others, but now that I know your community is all about paranormal talents, maybe that's the otherness that I sense. The paranormal talents make you feel not fully human."

"That's a very particular observation. What other nonhumans do you know?"

"I can't." Tears started streaming down Sofia's cheeks. "Please. I can't take it anymore. My head is going to explode."

"She needs to rest." Julian turned to Marcel. "Take Sofia to the bedroom so she can lie down."

Mia drove her chair around the table. "I'll show you where it is and get you some Motrin. Luckily, they have a first aid kit in the bathroom that is nicely stocked." She smiled. "It's force of habit. I always check what's in the cabinets when I settle in a new place."

Marcel got up, walked over to Sofia, and offered her his hand.

When he pulled her to him, she swayed on her feet. "I'm so sorry. But every time Tom asks me questions that I'm not allowed to answer, and I attempt it anyway, it feels like I'm trying to pull my brain out through my skull."

Was it an act?

All it would achieve was to drag out the interrogation longer.

Maybe that was her objective?

Was she hoping for a rescue?

"You can rest for a few minutes, and then Tom will continue."

Mia glared at him. "Sofia needs more than a few minutes. It will take at least half an hour for the Motrin to kick in, and then she will need a few hours of shuteye in the dark."

"We don't have time for that," Marcel said as calmly as he could, not only because he didn't want to upset Sofia, but because he needed to be cordial to Mia.

She was only trying to help, but they didn't have the luxury of coddling Sofia. Kian and Turner were waiting for answers.

"We have plenty of time." Mia glared at him. "Tom and I don't plan on going to sleep tonight, and we can continue the interrogation early tomorrow morning."

It was already nearly morning, but one look at Toven made it clear that the god agreed with his mate.

"A couple of hours. That's the most we can afford." Holding on to Sofia's elbow to keep her steady, Marcel followed Mia to the bedroom.

As soon as they neared the bed, Sofia pulled out of his hold and dropped on the bed with a groan, and Mia drove the chair into the open layout bathroom.

She returned a moment later with a bottle of pills and a glass of water. "Here you go, sweetie. Take three at once." She opened the bottle and shook out three pills into Sofia's palm.

"Thank you." She popped the pills into her mouth and followed with the water.

"You're most welcome." Mia turned her chair around. "I'll turn the lights off on my way out."

SOFIA

*A*s Mia turned the lights off, Marcel remained standing next to the bed and just looked at Sofia with a frown creasing his forehead.

Was he angry at her for getting a headache?

It wasn't her fault that Igor's compulsion stuck to her like glue. Tom hadn't removed it, he hadn't freed her mind, he'd overpowered it with his own compulsion and added an additional layer on top of the sludge that was already there.

His compulsion hadn't felt as slimy and as heavy-handed as Igor's, but it was still nasty.

"He didn't try to free my mind," she said quietly. "He overpowered the weaker components that were there before. Now I'm a slave to two masters."

Marcel sat on the bed next to her and took her hand. "I'll speak to Tom and ask him if he can change his tactic and free you, or at least get rid of some of it."

His voice was gentle, but it lacked the warmth and mirth that had been there before he'd discovered her duplicity. Did he still care for her?

Lifting her hand, she cupped his cheek. "Do you still want me?"

He let out a shuddering breath. "I never stopped wanting you." He took her hand and removed it from his cheek. "I hoped to learn more about your motives and that it would help me sort out my feelings for you. But getting you to talk is proving to be a more difficult task than we expected." He patted her shoulder awkwardly. "Get some rest."

Sofia caught his hand. "Don't go yet. You promised to tell me your paranormal talent."

He sighed. "It's not a very unique talent. I can make people forget things or remember things that didn't happen."

Her heart, which was already shriveled like a prune, constricted further. Had he manipulated her mind as well?

No wonder her head was hurting so badly. She'd had two compellers and one memory manipulator mess with her mind. She would be lucky if by the end of those terrible twenty-four hours she retained any cognitive function at all.

"What did you do to me?"

"It was a very small thing just to test whether you are susceptible to my talent. Do you remember the expensive gift I bought for my ex-girlfriend that you couldn't recall any particulars about?"

"You made me forget what it was."

"I did. I told you that it was a diamond necklace, but that wasn't it. I got her expensive jewelry, but she wanted more than shiny objects to prove my love for her."

The pain in his voice indicated that it was much worse. Had she made him betray his people? Forsake his family?

"What did she want?"

He shook his head. "That's a secret I'm going to take to my grave. I haven't told anyone, and I don't intend to."

Why did that hurt so much?

He hadn't told his family or his friends, and she was no one to him. Why should he tell her his deepest secret?

"You can keep your secrets." She let go of his hand. "Just promise me that you'll never make me forget anything again or remember a false memory."

"I'm sorry, but I can't promise that. I might have to make you forget about meeting Tom as well as other details about our organization. People with paranormal talents fear persecution and exploitation. We need to keep our existence a secret."

Sofia snorted. "Then running a paranormal retreat might not be the best strategy."

"How else are we going to find more of us? Besides, people on the outside think it's all fake. Sometimes ridicule is the best defense. It allows us to hide in plain sight."

She thought about the Kra-ell and how they'd gone undetected despite looking very alien.

"People think along the parameters they are familiar with. When something doesn't fit, they dismiss it as an aberration or a hoax."

"Precisely." Marcel pushed to his feet. "How is your head? Has the Motrin started to work?"

"It's a little better." She rubbed her temple. "But it still hurts."

"Get some rest. You didn't get enough sleep tonight, and all the excitement must have exhausted you."

"I barely slept at all." She grabbed a pillow and hugged it to her chest. "It's hard to fall asleep while my whole world is falling apart around me."

He grimaced. "I wasn't the one who caused it."

"No, you were not."

He was just the one who broke her heart.

1 8

MARCEL

*W*ith a heavy heart, Marcel left the bedroom and closed the door behind him. He'd closed himself up emotionally as best he could, but Sofia's sadness had managed to penetrate the shields he'd built around his heart and poke a dagger right through it.

"Is she asleep?" Mia asked.

"Not yet." Marcel sat down next to Julian.

"That compeller is extremely dangerous," Toven said. "I'm afraid to use too much power on Sofia and fry her brain. The best approach would have been to chip away at the walls he's erected around her brain slowly, but we don't have the luxury of time. I understand that you want to use her to feed him false information, and to do that, we need to have her on our side. I need to break through his compulsion and use mine to get her to talk."

"I wonder if she knows the kind of monster he is," Mia said. "We know that the purebloods don't share information even with the hybrids, let alone the humans in their community, so Sofia might not be aware of what he did to Jade's tribe and possibly to others as well. Maybe if we tell her, she will be more inclined to talk."

Toven took his mate's hand. "It's not her reluctance that I'm worried about. What I'm worried about is that he might be a stronger compeller than I am, and that I will need your enhancing powers to break through his compulsion. I'm also worried about what it will do to Sofia's mind."

It was inconceivable that anyone could be stronger than a god. The Kra-ell were less evolved than the gods, and it didn't make sense that one of them was more powerful than Toven.

But then Navuh, who was the immortal equivalent of a hybrid, shouldn't be such a strong compeller, and yet he was.

"Is Navuh more powerful than you?" Julian asked, giving voice to Marcel's thoughts.

"He wasn't stronger than me back when I still knew him, but five thousand years later, he might be. Power grows with age."

"So yours grew as well," Mia said. "If you were stronger then, you should be stronger now."

"It isn't an exact progression, and Navuh has used his ability much more extensively than I have. I wouldn't be surprised if he grew stronger than me."

If that was true, it could partially explain why the Kra-ell leader was so powerful. He used his talent a lot. But on the other hand, he couldn't be as old as either Toven or Navuh.

Unless he was a god, and that was unlikely.

Or was it?

"Who did you inherit your compulsion ability from?" Mia asked. "No one ever mentioned Ekin being a compeller."

"He wasn't, but his brother Ahn was, and so was Mortdh. Since Ahn and Ekin only shared a father and so did Mortdh and I, the common compeller ancestor must have been our paternal grandfather."

"Who was he?" Julian asked.

"I never met him." Toven pushed to his feet. "Anyone want coffee?"

Marcel had a feeling that Toven knew very well who his grandfather was but didn't want to share the information with them, or even with his mate, which was odd.

What was he hiding?

"I'll make it." One of the Guardians got off the couch. "There is a pod machine in the kitchen. Who likes it strong?"

"I do." Marcel lifted his hand.

After the Guardian had collected everyone's preferences, Marcel decided to voice his improbable hypothesis. "Igor is supposedly a pureblooded Kra-ell, which means that he can't be more than a thousand years old. It doesn't make sense that he's more powerful than a god, unless he's a god himself, or maybe a hybrid of a pureblooded Kra-ell and a god. If we assume that the Kra-ell came from the same place, and that they are a more primitive version of the gods, it's not such a big leap to consider that as a possibility."

Toven's brows dipped low. "It actually makes sense. When I was trying to break through Igor's compulsion, and Sofia kept resisting mine, I wondered how it was possible for a Kra-ell to be a more powerful compeller than I am. I'm aware that they are physically very strong, but they shouldn't possess more powerful mind manipulation abilities than those of the gods. If they do, we are in even deeper trouble than Kian or I have ever considered."

"Why is that?" Mia asked. "What else can a god do?"

Toven smiled. "Do you want me to reveal all of my secrets?"

She laughed. "It was a rhetorical question. We all know that gods can manipulate minds, and the stronger the god, the more minds he or she can manipulate at once. But you can't conjure an explosion, manifest rain, cause a flood, or any such things. You can only cause people to think that those things are happening, and we know how to block compulsion with those special earpieces."

"Compulsion can be blocked, but thralling and shrouding cannot unless you are immune. If Igor can thrall as well as compel, our people will have no defense against him."

Mia frowned. "Can't you shield us? You and Annani combined should be able to do that, right?"

Toven shook his head. "It's not something that I've ever tried doing, and neither has Annani. I don't know how."

19

KIAN

"Did it work?" Syssi turned on her side.

"I haven't heard from them yet."

"Then come to bed. They will call you if they have something to report."

Kian had come home less than half an hour ago to take a quick shower and change into a fresh set of clothes. Sleep was not part of the plan.

It was already five in the morning, and there was still a lot to be done, but he planned to do it from his home office. Once things were on track, he would catch a little nap before starting his day.

He walked over to the bed and wrapped his arms around Syssi's warm body. "Go back to sleep, my love." He kissed her lips. "I'll be in my office."

"You need to get some sleep."

"I'll catch a short nap on the couch later. I'm expecting a call from Toven or Marcel any minute now."

She yawned. "Wake me up when you hear from them."

"I will." He kissed her again.

Kian had no intention of waking her up. She had work tomorrow and a baby to take care of. She needed her sleep.

He made himself a cup of coffee, took the mug to his office, sat on the couch, and propped his feet on the coffee table.

It had been a long while since he'd pulled an all-nighter, but it wasn't a big deal. Back in his bachelor days, he'd done so many of them that it was like slipping back into an old pair of pants that were a little too tight but still familiar.

The call from Toven came at seven minutes after five.

"Hold on. I'll get Turner on the line with us."

"Isn't it too late?" Toven asked. "Or rather too early?"

"He didn't go to sleep either." Kian called Turner. "You are on the line with Toven."

"Good evening," Toven said. "Mia, Marcel, and Julian are here as well."

"Good evening to you all. Did it work?" Turner echoed Syssi's question.

"It did, and it didn't," Toven said. "The more recent compulsions were not difficult to override, but the old ones that have probably been routinely reinforced are very difficult to overpower. With Mia's help, I can probably break through, but I don't want to push too hard and fry Sofia's mind. She was exhausted and got a severe headache just from the little I managed to get out of her. We had to take a break and let her rest."

That wasn't good.

Kian had been sure that Mia's help wouldn't be needed, and it was very disturbing that it was.

"What did you learn so far?"

"We have a name for the compeller. It's Igor, which is obviously not his original Kra-ell name, and it makes me wonder why he chose to adopt a human one. Did he have a shameful name like Emmett's? Perhaps he's a hybrid, and his father or mother wasn't happy about his arrival. Marcel suspects that he's half Kra-ell and half god."

Kian's blood chilled in his veins. "Why does Marcel suspect that?"

"Igor's power level. The Kra-ell are not long-lived enough to have their power grow that much. But since we don't know much about them, they might be naturally more gifted that way. Still, Marcel's hypothesis is a possibility, and until we know more, we shouldn't dismiss it."

"When are you going to continue the interrogation?"

"I want Sofia to get some sleep, but Marcel is impatient, and he wants to wake her up in a couple of hours."

Kian wanted to be done with it as well, but not if it meant causing damage to the girl. "We can wait an hour or two longer. I bet everyone is tired and wouldn't mind some shut-eye."

Crawling into bed with Syssi could be so lovely for an hour or two.

"I need to take care of the bioinformaticians," Marcel said. "I planned to do it today, but if we let Sofia sleep more than two hours, I won't make it back in time to open up the lab for them, and they'll wonder what happened."

"You were supposed to thrall them to forget the project and send them home," Turner said.

"There was no time."

"It doesn't have to be you," Kian said. "Leon can do that. In fact, it would be easier to explain why they are suddenly being sent on a paid vacation. He can tell them that you had an emergency and there is no one available to take your place. Case closed."

"That could work." Marcel sounded relieved. "Nevertheless, if we want to keep up the charade and have Sofia contact Igor with false information, we can't wait too long to have her do that. He might send people to retrieve her, if he hasn't done it already."

"I doubt it," Turner said. "Given the sophistication of the tracker compared to the communication device she was given, Igor wanted Sofia to get caught. In my opinion, he has people on standby in one of the nearby towns, and he's waiting for her to get moved. He won't do anything until that tracker leaves Safe Haven."

"Then maybe we should move it," Toven said. "We can set a trap for Igor's people and catch them. I'll be much less reluctant to force my way into the minds of those murderers than I am with Sofia."

Turner chuckled. "Sounds tempting, but we shouldn't do that until we know what we are dealing with. If Igor's force is superior to ours, our best tactic is to evade him at all costs. We will need to abandon Safe Haven and do our best to hide from him the same way we do with Navuh."

Toven groaned. "I hate this. I'd rather fight than hide."

The god had been hiding for thousands of years. Was he suddenly eager to fight because he had the clan's backing?

Kian would have loved to fight as well, but his number one priority was to keep his people safe, and his own wishes and desires were a distant second.

"We would all prefer to fight rather than hide," Kian said. "I want to find the bastard, free Jade and the other females, and dispose of Igor and his cronies, but the safety of my people comes first."

"Of course," Toven capitulated. "I'll call you after I get more information out of Sofia."

"I'd rather be part of the interrogation," Turner said. "Kian and I can't be there in person, but we can be via a video call."

"Why video?" Kian asked. "I don't want her to see us. The less we need to erase from her memories later, the better."

"What do you plan to do with Sofia?" Marcel asked.

"I don't know yet. It depends on her part in this. If she's just someone random that the compeller found and forced to do his bidding, we might be able to erase her memories of us and let her loose somewhere with a new identity and enough money to start a new life."

"She is not," Toven said. "Sofia is part of Igor's community. She told us that she made a monthly trek back home that was a nearly eight-hour drive. I assume that it was a mandatory trip to get the compulsion reinforced."

"That's what Navuh does with his warriors," Kian said.

"I wouldn't risk releasing her even if she was randomly picked," Turner said. "Igor might have implanted a deep-seated compulsion in her to react to a certain trigger and find her way back to him or let him know where she is. We can't allow that. Like it or not, we are stuck with her. The best thing we can do is fake her death and keep her with us for the rest of her life."

20

SOFIA

*T*he smell of coffee woke Sofia up, or maybe it was the bed sinking under Marcel's weight.

She didn't need to open her eyes to know it was him.

His scent was so familiar by now that she couldn't mistake him for anyone else. Besides, she would have known it was him even if her nose was blocked up. Her body's reaction to his presence was predictable as well. She longed to reach for him, to pull him to her and press against him, but most of all, she wanted him to wrap his arms around her and tell her that everything would be okay, and that they belonged together.

But wishing wouldn't make it so, and it only made her feel sad for what could have been but probably would never be.

"Is it morning yet?" Reluctantly, she opened her eyes and pushed up against the pillows.

"It's after eight in the morning." He handed her the mug. "I wish we could let you sleep more, but we don't have time."

Why not?

What did they expect to learn from her?

If Tom compelled her to reveal the compound's location, she would have no choice but to tell them where it was, but she couldn't tell them anything useful about its defenses because she didn't know much about them.

Sofia was glad that she didn't have the information they needed, and that no matter what they did to her, she wouldn't help them launch an attack against the compound. She didn't give a damn about what happened to Igor and his inner circle, but she cared about everyone else that was in the same situation as she was, forced to live a life they hadn't chosen.

Did she care about her grandfather?

He'd been nice to her during the preparation period, and they had gotten a little closer, but he should have warned her that she might get caught. Stupidly, she hadn't considered the possibility that she wasn't coming back from the mission. If she had, she would have at least said goodbye to her father and her aunts and cousins and everyone else she was never going to see again.

Cradling the mug between her palms, Sofia looked down at the dark brew to hide her tears. "Did you get any sleep?"

"None of us did. We were waiting for you. How is the headache?"

"Better, but it's still there." She took a couple of sips. "I'd better freshen up." She handed it back to him.

Marcel nodded. "I'll wait for you in the living room. Do you want me to leave the mug here or take it?"

"You can take it. I will be out in a minute."

It ended up taking a little longer than that because the tears sprang out the moment she closed the bathroom door behind her, and she needed to calm down and wash her face before braving the group waiting for her in the living room, or more specifically, Tom and Marcel.

The others didn't seem like a threat.

"Good morning." Tom smiled in what was his version of a friendly manner. "How are you feeling?"

"A little better, thank you." She sat next to where Marcel had put her mug down.

Did Tom even deserve her politeness?

Marcel had warned her to be cordial to Tom and react to him as if he were a prince, but the good will she'd initially felt toward him had evaporated once she'd realized his agenda.

Tom wasn't there to help her. He was there to help his organization and pump her for information.

"Would you like something to eat?" Mia asked.

"No, thank you. I still feel a little nauseated. For now, I'll just stick with coffee."

"I'll get you a fresh cup." One of the guards pushed to his feet.

They were all pretending to be so nice, but Tom was about to barrel into her mind again and get her to tell him things she wouldn't even if she was free to.

"I thought of another approach," Tom said. "Instead of trying to override Igor's compulsion one item at a time, which will take forever, I will override his command to keep everything about him and his community a secret. Wouldn't you prefer that? Your mind will be your own."

Right. Up until she refused to answer a question or avoided direct answers, and he compelled her to talk.

"That would be nice."

"I thought so." He took his fiancée's hand. "Do your thing, love."

She chuckled. "I don't do anything consciously. I just need to be near you."

What were they talking about? Was Mia a compeller who needed to channel her power through Tom's?

He brought her hand to his lips. "That's what I meant."

Turning his eyes to Sofia, he said, "You are free to speak your mind. All your thoughts and memories belong to you, and you can do as you please with them."

Sofia waited for the headache to start, or for something inside of her to change, but she didn't feel any different than she felt a moment ago.

"I don't think it worked."

Toven smiled. "Let's try a question from yesterday. Tell me about your community. Is it big?"

21

MARCEL

*S*o far, Sofia hadn't noticed the tablet next to Julian. The camera was pointed at her, so Kian and Turner could see and hear the interrogation, but the screen was black, so she couldn't see them. Julian wore an earpiece, so if they had any questions, he could ask them.

"My community is not big." Sofia seemed to be surprised by her own answer.

"How many people live in your community?"

Was Toven using compulsion? Marcel could feel the compulsion before, but not now.

She seemed reluctant but answered anyway. "Several hundred."

"What else can you tell us about it?" Toven asked. When she didn't answer, he added, "Is it hidden?"

"Yes."

"How?"

She looked at him as if she didn't understand the question. "I don't know what you mean."

Toven leaned forward. "I mean, how can a community of several hundred people be hidden? Do you live underground? Is it camouflaged to look like something else? Maybe ruins? How is it possible for people living in the area not to know about it?"

"It's partially underground, but most of it is above ground. It's located in a densely wooded, remote area that is not accessible by vehicles and barely accessible on foot. No one has reason to pass through."

Toven leaned back and crossed his arms over his chest. "There must be a way to deliver supplies to a community that size, and I bet they don't do it on horseback."

"They don't." She lowered her eyes. "I guess there is a hidden tunnel somewhere."

Marcel was willing to bet that she knew where that tunnel was. She'd already told them that she'd had to come home once a month, and she'd said that she'd driven home. If the place was inaccessible, she must have used a tunnel or a bridge or some well-camouflaged road.

Then again, it was possible that she was picked up from a collection point and taken to the compound blindfolded or in a windowless vehicle.

"Is there a wall around it?" Toven asked.

She nodded.

At the rate they were going, the questioning would take forever. Sofia was reluctant to volunteer information even though it seemed she was now free to do so.

"Why are you resisting?" Toven asked. "I can force the answers out of you, but I'd rather you give them voluntarily."

"I have a family there, and most of the people there are not bad. I don't know what you want to do or why, and if I can help it, I won't endanger my people."

"We would never harm innocents."

She grimaced. "Unless they are collateral damage?"

"Not even one innocent life is collateral damage to us." Toven leveled her with such an intense gaze that she looked away.

"Is Igor a good guy?" Julian asked her.

"No."

"Is he terrible?"

She hesitated for a moment. "To some, but not to all. It could be worse."

Toven sighed. "I have a feeling that you don't know how your leader operates. Otherwise, you would be much more critical of him."

"I know that he keeps everyone under his control with heavy compulsion, and that's not right. But you could be even worse. I could be trading one ruthless dictator for another."

Toven turned to look at Julian's tablet. "Should I tell her what we know about Igor and his compound?"

Marcel was surprised that Toven was asking Kian's permission. The god didn't strike him as someone who bowed to anyone's authority.

Julian nodded. "Except for what we know about you know who."

Toven nodded and turned back to Sofia. "Perhaps once you realize how much we already know, it will make it easier for you. We are well familiar with the Kraell, and generally speaking, we don't mean them harm."

Sofia gasped. "How do you know about them?"

"We have three hybrids living in our community."

She looked shocked. "How did you find them? And how did they end up in your community?"

"They were discovered through their paranormal abilities," Julian said, probably repeating what Kian or Turner told him in the earpiece. "The retreat is not the only way we find new people with paranormal talents."

Toven nodded. "The three people who joined us told us a very disturbing story about what happened to their tribe."

Sofia swallowed. "What happened to it?"

"You might not believe me if I just tell you, so I'll start with a few leading questions. You are probably aware that many more boys are born to the Kra-ell than girls."

She nodded.

"On average, for every four boys, only one girl is born, and yet I'm guessing that the ratio between adult pure-blooded Kra-ell males and females in your compound is not four or five to one. Am I right?"

"It's not. Their numbers are almost equal."

"Doesn't that strike you as odd?"

"It does." She swallowed again. "Do they get rid of the boys? There are more hybrid males than females, though. So maybe they only do that with the purebloods."

"They don't," Toven said. "They raid other Kra-ell tribes, slaughter the males, and capture the females. That's how Igor evens out the numbers."

22

SOFIA

*W*ere they telling her the truth?

Sofia couldn't deny that he'd been spot on. Then again, Tom had said that he was much more than a compeller, so maybe he was a mind reader as well?

But if he could read minds, why did he need to interrogate her? He could have bypassed Igor's compulsion by just reaching into her mind and plucking the thoughts out of there. She wasn't prohibited from thinking about all the things she was forbidden to reveal, but evidently Tom couldn't do that.

Jade's loathing of Igor made much more sense now. If he'd slaughtered the males of her tribe and kidnapped her and the other females, she was probably plotting his murder day in and day out.

Hell, if she were in Jade's position, Sofia would do that too, and she was not nearly as vicious as that pureblooded female. The only thing keeping Igor alive was his compulsion power.

Tom hadn't mentioned Jade by name, but Sofia was sure he'd been talking about her and her tribe.

Jade was a natural leader, and Sofia had noticed that she hung out with several of the pureblooded and hybrid females, especially with Kagra, whom she referred to as her second.

Now it finally made sense.

Kagra didn't have any special position in Igor's organization, but she must have been Jade's second-in-command before they'd been captured.

"Did Jade figure out that your paranormal retreat was somehow connected to the other Kra-ell? Was that why she was spending so much time on the Safe Haven website?"

Tom looked at the doctor, or rather the tablet propped on a stand in front of

Julian. Someone was watching on the other side, which meant that Tom wasn't the boss. Someone else was, and he didn't want her to see him.

When no one answered her, she repeated the question. "Is that a yes or a no?"

"It's irrelevant to our discussion," Tom said. "I assume that there are many Kra-ell females in your community who are there against their will, and who are compelled to hold their grief inside them and not tell anyone how they got there. They deserve to be freed, and we need your help to do that. I assume that you are fully human. Is that correct?"

Sofia nodded.

"Were you born to a hybrid father and a human mother?"

"The other way around," Marcel said. "As unlikely as it is, her mother is the other."

Tom looked at her with a raised brow. "Is that true?"

Marcel had guessed it from what she'd stupidly told him about her parents, and they knew so much already that there was no reason to deny it. "My mother took a human lover to piss off my grandfather. She didn't expect to get pregnant, and she wasn't happy about it. But the Kra-ell don't believe in abortion, so here I am."

"That makes you very unique," Tom smiled as if she'd just told him some great news.

Sofia shrugged. "I'm still human, and other than my coloring and my body shape, I didn't inherit anything else from that side of my family, and I'm thankful for it. I like my human side much more. My father, the real one, is a great guy who loves me unconditionally, and I have two aunts who were much more like mothers to me than the female who gave birth to me. I also have cousins and friends, and some of those friends are hybrids. As I said, there are many good people in the compound, and if you try to free the pureblooded females, many of them will get hurt or killed." She sighed. "Frankly, as much as I feel bad about the terrible thing that was done to the pureblooded females, they are not worth the lives of the other people in our community."

"I have a question," Mia asked. "We know that a hybrid and a human produce a human child. How about two hybrids? Are their children human or hybrid as well?"

"As far as I know, the children born to hybrid females are fathered by pure-blooded males. But the Kra-ell are not exclusive, so it's difficult to tell who has sex with whom and why. The Kra-ell females have an odd fertility cycle. Since they want to preserve their blood, I assume that they hook up with purebloods while they are fertile, and with hybrids when they are not. Or maybe they use protection when having sex with hybrids and humans. Though my mother obviously didn't use contraceptives." She let out a breath. "You might be surprised to know that, but most of what I know is based on rumors and guesses. Humans are not privy to the inner workings of the Kra-ell society, not even a human like me who has Kra-ell blood in her."

She'd almost blurted out 'a human whose grandfather is Igor's second-in-command,' but she had stopped herself at the last moment. It was better that they didn't know she was so-called connected, especially since that connection didn't make her any more knowledgeable or important than the other humans in their community.

"How many of each category of people are there?" Marcel asked. "Purebloods, hybrids, and humans. Adults, children, males, females. We need to know what we are up against."

She cast him a glare. "I hope that you are not thinking about attacking a community that has children and other innocents just to free some stuck-up Kra-ell females."

"We are not," Tom said. "But we need to ascertain the risk to us."

"What risk? And to whom? Igor wouldn't have sent me to snoop around if one of ours hadn't found the Safe Haven website so fascinating that she spent unreasonable amounts of time on it. Was she looking for compellers who could do for her what you did for me?"

Tom smiled. "I have no way of knowing what that person was looking for. I'm not a mind reader. I need those numbers, though."

23

KIAN

*S*ofia shifted her gaze away from Toven. "I don't know the exact numbers."

"Ask Toven to make her tell us," Turner said.

The god didn't have to be told. "Give it your best guess. How many purebloods, hybrids, and humans are there in your compound?"

Sofia looked at him with hurt in her eyes. "There are over a hundred purebloods. Twenty or so of them are children and teenagers. More or less the same number of hybrids, and about a hundred and twenty humans, of whom about a quarter are children."

"What's the male-to-female ratio?" Marcel asked.

She gave him the same hurt look she'd given Toven. "The adult purebloods are divided almost equally, just a little tilted toward males, but together with the children, I think there are about sixty males and forty females. The hybrids have many more males, the ratio being closer to four to one. Humans, as you'd expect, are divided more or less equally."

"Igor must have an inner circle," Toven said. "How many are in it?"

"Sixteen males." Sofia let out a breath. "It's easy to figure out who they are. They don't have collars around their necks."

"Collars?" Marcel asked.

She nodded. "All the other purebloods and hybrids wear collars. No one knows what they are for. Some think that they denote rank, others think that they have location trackers in them." She rubbed a hand over her thigh. "But that's probably not true since he obviously implants them in us. But then the hybrids and purebloods hardly ever leave the compound other than to hunt, so maybe the collars are really trackers."

"Do the females get to leave the compound at all?" Toven asked.

"They have to. They need to go hunting."

That was a good morsel of information. Maybe they could save Jade by waiting for her to go on a hunt and pluck her from outside the compound.

Kian silenced the microphone. "That's how we will get her out. We just need a tech guy to remove the collar. It's probably booby-trapped."

Turner nodded. "I hope it's not some alien technology we can't handle. The compulsion is another issue. If we remove the collar, she will still resist us because of the compulsion. We will have to knock her out."

"I don't have a problem with that. Although given that it took three immortal males, two of them Guardians, to take one hybrid female down, we will need to tranq her." Kian reactivated the microphone. "Ask her if the females are escorted by guards when they go hunting."

"Are the females allowed to hunt without an escort?" Julian asked.

"They need to get a pass," Sofia said. "This informs security that they are out, and if they don't come back, I guess guards are sent after them. But I've never heard of something like that happening. They all come back." She rubbed a hand over the side of her neck. "Maybe there is something in those collars that forces them to return, or maybe Igor's compulsion is enough."

From what Kian had heard so far, he was convinced it was both. Igor didn't leave anything to chance.

"How come you got to leave and attend university?" Mia asked.

"For some reason, Igor is much laxer with the humans living in the compound. He either feels sorry for us because of our short lifespans, or because his control over us is even stronger than the control he has over the purebloods and hybrids. Some of the human descendants of the Kra-ell are sent to study all kinds of subjects. I thought that the compulsion was enough to keep track of us, but evidently I underestimated Igor's paranoia." She huffed out a breath. "As if I would voluntarily endanger my family." She chuckled bitterly. "He obviously didn't expect me to encounter a compeller who was more powerful than him."

"What about the close-circle females?" Toven asked. "I'm sure his original cell had some females in it."

"I don't know. I wasn't told. All the females have collars."

Toven nodded. "The Kra-ell are a traditionally female-ruled society. The females in his cell were supposed to be the leaders. When he chose to make his community patriarchal, he subdued all the females."

"So the rumors were true," Sofia whispered.

"Where did you hear the rumors?" Marcel asked.

She shrugged. "Here and there."

Obviously, she was trying to protect whoever she'd heard it from, but she shouldn't worry about them using that information against her source. She was most likely protecting them from Igor.

"Is it against the rules to spread rumors like that?" Toven asked.

She snorted out a laugh. "What do you think? Igor is the undisputed ruler of the compound. Even to suggest that he's not supposed to be is considered treason."

"Makes sense." Toven crossed his arms over his chest. "That's why Navuh keeps his mate hidden. He doesn't want anyone to know that she outranks him."

"Is Navuh a Kra-ell?" Sofia asked.

"He's not, but he has a lot in common with your Igor."

"He's not mine," she hissed.

"Ask her about their training," Kian told Julian.

"How well are the purebloods and the hybrids trained?" The doctor repeated the question. "And do the females get training too?"

"The males train a lot, and the females train as well, but not officially. Igor allows it because they need an outlet for their natural aggression, but he never takes them out on missions."

"Finally, we are getting somewhere," Kian murmured. "Ask her about those missions."

"What missions do Igor and his males go on?" Julian asked.

"I don't know. I don't even know when they leave and when they return or what their objectives are. It's not like he makes it official."

Toven regarded her with a sad smile. "Does he come back with new females?"

She shook her head. "As far as I can tell, there haven't been any new adult females brought into the compound during my lifetime. I might not have been aware of what was going on when I was little, but I'm sure that none were brought in over the last two decades."

Turner closed the microphone before turning to Kian. "Jade's tribe must have been one of the last to get raided. He either didn't need more females or didn't know how to find more tribes."

"What I want to know is how he found the ones he had."

"Maybe they had trackers on them," Turner suggested.

"Then why did he wait so long to raid them? He could've done it decades ago."

"Maybe he was still getting organized and didn't have the means." Turner opened the mic. "Ask her about weapons."

When Julian repeated the question, Sofia shrugged.

"I don't have a clue. The guards at the gates have rifles, but no one carries weapons inside the compound. Their training is old-fashioned. It's hand-to-hand, swords, fangs and claws."

"What about aircraft?" Marcel asked.

"None that I know of. I've never seen one take off or land near or at the compound."

24

MARCEL

*I*t seemed that Turner and Kian had heard enough because Julian tapped the tablet, which was the signal that it was time for a break.

"I think we have all we need for now," the doctor said. "It's getting late, and Sofia needs to return to Safe Haven for the next part of our plan."

"What part?" Sofia asked.

"The part where you feed Igor false information. The first thing you need to do is convince him that you are fine and that you are continuing your investigation. That way, he will not send a rescue team for you, or if he has already done that, then he will call them back."

She snorted. "I very much doubt that. I'm the definition of collateral damage."

"Nonsense," Mia said. "He invested many years in your education. He will not want to lose you."

Sofia's expression brightened a little. "I would like to think that, but you are not going to let me be taken back, right?"

"Do you want to go back?" Mia asked, disbelief coloring her expression.

"If you're asking if I'm eager to live under Igor's rule, the answer is no. Most of my life, I've fantasized about a future where I was free to choose the man I wanted to spend my life with, and where I wanted to spend that life." She didn't look at Marcel, but her words cut at his heart nonetheless. "But I didn't even get to say a proper goodbye to my father and my aunts and cousins. I'm going to miss them."

"That's perfectly understandable," Mia said. "But I think they would want you to be free and live your life. They would be happy for you."

Sofia grimaced. "If I don't come back, they will assume that I'm dead."

"We might have to fake your death," Julian said. "We did that for my partner, her mother, and her brother. That was the only way to save them from a Russian oligarch who was after my mate."

Sofia looked at the doctor with a frown. "Did they have to leave family and friends behind?"

He nodded. "My mate had a very good friend who now thinks she's dead, and the same goes for her mother and brother, but they are glad to be free, and they made new friends in our community."

"Will I be welcomed in your community even though my paranormal talent is questionable?"

Toven nodded. "As long as you cooperate with us, you will be welcomed."

Marcel wanted to add that she would be welcomed regardless, but he wasn't sure what Kian's position was on that. She wasn't a random human that Igor had picked up for the job, so they couldn't thrall her to forget what she'd learned and help her settle somewhere else. They would have to invite her into the village, where she would basically live out her life as a prisoner.

That shouldn't make him happy, but on a selfish level, it did. If she was confined to the village, she couldn't betray him, and if her feelings for him were real, maybe they could resurrect their relationship.

Was he once again letting his dormant romantic hijack his reason?

Sofia huffed out a breath. "I doubt that I can convince Valstar, let alone Igor, that it was just a big misunderstanding, and that you just returned the pendant to me, asked my forgiveness for mishandling the situation, and invited me to stay for another retreat. Neither of them is that gullible."

Julian lifted a finger. "Hold on, I'm getting instructions." He pulled out a pen and a tiny notebook from his shirt pocket and started writing down bullet points.

After several minutes of scribbling, he lifted his eyes to Sofia and smiled. "Here is how you are going to play this. We were afraid that you were a journalist snooping around the paranormal community we are building, but you managed to convince us that you weren't. We brought a truth-teller to test you, and you were sure that you were done for, but he couldn't tell when you were lying. He was probably a fake, or maybe he couldn't read you because your Kra-ell heritage protected you in some way. He verified that you were telling the truth."

"Is there someone like this in your community?" Sofia asked.

"There is," Marcel said.

"What do I tell him about handling the compulsion attempt on Emmett?"

"You told us that your father is a powerful compeller and your mother is a telepath, and that's the real reason you came to the retreat. You didn't understand why your parents had such incredible gifts, while you did not. You also told us that your father was against you coming because he read about Emmett's crookedness, and when you called him, he wanted to prove to you that he was right, but then Emmett's girlfriend intervened because she knew he would never admit that to anyone other than her. From what you have learned so far, we knew all about compulsion because we had several compellers in our community, including Emmett's girlfriend. The reason we were running the retreats was to collect more people with paranormal abilities and build a community of enhanced people. You suspect that we intend to crossbreed talents to produce an even stronger crop of paranormals, but you don't know that for a fact, and you want to stay on to investigate this for Igor, hoping that he can use the information to his advantage in some way."

Sofia pursed her lips. "It's a good story, but you're forgetting one thing. Igor can make me tell him the truth."

Julian cast her a blindingly bright smile. "Don't worry about that. We've developed an earpiece that will filter out the compulsion. He can't compel you while you are wearing it."

25

SOFIA

hat was good to know, but given that Eleanor and Emmett were both compellers, and she had no defense against them now that her mind was free from Igor's compulsion, they could and would force her to do whatever they wanted.

"What are you going to do to the compound?" Sofia asked again.

It was probably futile, but maybe she would be able to chip away at them until they told her their intentions. Not that she could do anything to prevent them from doing it, but she might be able to warn Igor.

"For now, we are just collecting information," Toven said. "We already know the general area, but knowing the exact location will save us trouble." He pulled out his phone and typed in something. "That's the area we were searching. Please point with your finger to where the compound is."

His tone was laced with coercion, and she found herself pointing to the spot despite a tremendous effort to resist.

"I detest compellers," she murmured under her breath.

Tom chuckled. "I get it, I really do, but we all have a job to do here, and it's saving people from unnecessary suffering, current and future."

"Right." Sofia grimaced. "Igor probably tells his victims the same thing."

Ignoring her muttering, Tom handed the phone to the doctor. "Find the location on the tablet. We need a larger map for Sofia to tell us how to get there."

"I don't know how to get there," she said.

"Nice try." Tom patted her shoulder. "I know that you do."

"Don't worry," Mia said. "I promise you that we will not do anything that will result in harming innocents. If we can't find a way to save them without incurring casualties, we will not even attempt it. I guess Igor does not murder or torture any of the people living inside the compound, just those he steals the females from."

"I haven't heard of him killing anyone." The torturing was a different story. Except, he didn't call it torture. He called it punishment.

Julian rose to his feet and brought the tablet to her. "This is a screenshot of the area." He handed her a stylus. "Please mark the spot with an X and draw the road leading to it."

"Do as Julian says," Tom said with compulsion lacing every word.

Her hand moved on its own, marking the spot and a squiggly line leading from the closest paved road to the compound. Since no one asked, she didn't mark the hidden entrances to the underground tunnels. There were four of them, but even though each tunnel was no longer than a hundred feet across, there was no other way to cross the rivers with a vehicle. There were no bridges, and swimming across the freezing water was not something any humans would want to attempt.

Igor had chosen an excellent strategic location for his compound. The place was hidden from above by a dense wood, and to get to it on the ground required precise knowledge of where it was and the entrances to the four separate tunnels.

Julian looked at the map and frowned. "I don't see any bridges marked over these rivers."

Sofia shrugged. "Not everything is marked on maps."

Let them try to find the entrances to the tunnels. It would take them days even with the map.

When Julian's tablet made a whoosh sound, Sofia knew that he'd sent the picture to his boss, the one who had been listening and probably watching everything through the tablet's camera and microphone.

"We should head back," Julian said.

Toven rose to his feet, and the rest followed, except for Mia of course.

"How does it feel to be free of the compulsion?" He offered her his hand,

"Am I free?" Sofia took his hand reluctantly.

"You are freer than you were before. I apologize for having to compel you to tell us what we need to know, and I can add my promise to Mia's that we will not harm any innocents in your community."

"Why should I believe you?"

He shrugged. "You don't know us, so you have no reason to. But we have no reason to make promises to you either. We can force you to cooperate with us whether you want to or not."

That was true.

"Goodbye, Sofia." Mia extended her hand. "I hope to see you again when you join our community. I'm certain you will like it much more than your old one."

"I will just be exchanging one prison for another. At least in my old one, I was allowed to attend university and have the illusion of freedom."

26

KIAN

*W*hen Sofia had left with Marcel and two of the Guardians, Julian turned the tablet's screen on.

"Good job, Toven," Kian said. "You managed to free Sofia's mind without turning it into mush."

Toven took Mia's hand. "I couldn't have done it without Mia's power. It was such a wonderful experience working with her. She somehow turned my power from a sledgehammer into a cozy blanket. From now on, I will only compel with her by my side."

A fetching blush crept up Mia's delicate face. "I didn't feel anything. I truly don't know what I am contributing, if anything."

"But you can observe the results," Toven said. "When I first compelled Sofia, I managed to penetrate only the most recent layer, and I caused her a bad headache. When you enhanced my power, I managed to free her from Igor's compulsion, and she felt no discomfort whatsoever."

"Mia is a valuable addition to our arsenal," Turner said. "But the bottom line is that we can't take on Igor's compound with the force we have. If we want to strike a preemptive blow and eliminate the threat of him before it manifests, we need to think creatively."

"Turner summed it up succinctly." Kian uncapped his bottle of water and took a sip. "Igor has about a hundred trained male warriors, and we know that the Kra-ell females are formidable as well. We are talking about a hundred and fifty pure-bloods and hybrids, each of which is three or four times stronger than a Guardian. But even if we were equally matched in strength, we don't have that many Guardians. If I pull everyone who ever served on the force from all three of our locations, that's only ninety-four."

"They seem to have less advanced weaponry than we do, and they mainly train to fight hand-to-hand." Turner leaned back in his chair. "Also, they might be susceptible to Merlin's sleeping potion. The weak solution he prepared for the children in Vrog's school knocked Vrog out just enough for Richard to take him down. If he prepares a stronger solution, we can test it on Vrog and Emmett and dial it in for quick results. The problem is that we don't have a pureblood to test it on."

"What about attacking from the air?" Julian suggested. "We could use precisely calibrated missiles to target Igor's office and take him out. We can get Sofia to draw us a plan of the compound."

Turner shook his head. "Sofia doesn't know enough. We need to get our hands on one of the pureblooded males. We can do that by kidnapping one or two of them while they go on a hunt, or we can try to move Sofia out of Safe Haven along with the cat that has her implant and see if anyone follows her. I have a hunch that we will catch a pureblood, maybe even Valstar. If the communicator in the pendant is as basic as Marcel thinks, its range can't be too great, and someone needs to be nearby to forward the signal all the way to Karelia."

"We should plan on both," Kian said. "Whichever comes to fruition first will be the one we will execute."

Turner nodded. "Agreed."

"Can you get your local guy to snoop around over the next week?" Kian asked.

The contractor was supposed to end his operations on Friday, local time, which was two hours ago. He was probably still in the area.

"I can, but I don't think it's a good idea to send humans snooping around Kra-ell on a hunt. We don't want them finding out about aliens, and those Kra-ell are pretty obviously not human. Especially when they chase an animal down to drink its blood."

"There is another problem," Toven said. "Even if we send Guardians to do the recon, and they manage to catch a male, take off his collar, and bring him in for questioning, Igor would know that one of his was plucked off the hunt and he will lock down the compound. We don't want to give him advance warning. The only way I can see that working out is for me to be there and compel the information out of the male and then thrall him to forget what happened to him. One problem with that is that if Igor suspects anything, he can compel the guy to bring up the suppressed memories. The other problem is that Mia can't run around in the forest."

Kian shook his head. "I don't feel comfortable risking you like that. I don't want you or Mia anywhere near that compound."

Toven frowned. "What good is having a god on your side if you are not willing to use me? I'm the best weapon in your arsenal, and I'm willing to lend myself to the clan whenever you need me."

"I appreciate that, but let's keep that formidable weapon for Armageddon, shall we?"

Mia chuckled. "Don't forget that you have two of those. Put Toven and Annani together, and you can take down Navuh, Igor, and the gods' homeland."

"That's a bit of an exaggeration." Toven wrapped his arm around Mia's slim shoulders. "But thank you for the vote of confidence."

"What about the noise cannon?" Julian asked. "The Kra-ell have sensitive ears like we do, and the noise cannon could knock down the entire compound without causing any casualties. Just a lot of ear damage."

"I like the way you think," Turner said. "That might be an option if we decide to attack. The problem will be the humans in the compound. The damage to their ears might be irreparable. Not to mention what it can do to the children."

"Right." Julian rubbed his jaw. "So that's not a solution either."

"We can use the exoskeletons to even out the strength disparity," Kian said. "But that still leaves us with not enough warriors. I'm not willing to leave the village, the Scottish castle, and the sanctuary undefended to launch an attack on the Kra-ell."

Turner chuckled. "You might have enough warriors if you are willing to think outside the box. You have an entire army stored in your catacombs. You could wake them up, have Toven compel them to his will, and voilà, you have a formidable force to unleash on Igor. Not only that, you can turn some of them into gardeners, cleaners, builders, and whatever else you need workers for."

Kian grimaced. "I'm not a hopeless romantic like my mother, and I will never let those monsters loose on women and children who cannot defend themselves. They've been monsters for too long to change, not even with the help of Toven's compulsion."

Turner shrugged. "It could have been fun to watch the Kra-ell females tear them to shreds."

Kian shook his head. "You have a sick sense of humor."

Turner grinned. "Thank you."

27

ERIC

"Have a great day at work." Eric pulled Darlene into his arms. "Are you coming back to have lunch with me?"

"I sure am." She wound her arms around his neck and kissed him softly. "Are you cooking again?"

Eric chuckled. "Are you sure you want me to?"

The pasta he'd made for lunch the day before had been barely edible. The noodles had come out soggy, and the ready-made sauce had been too salty. He'd grated a mountain of Parmesan cheese on it to give it some taste, but it wasn't enough to save the dish.

"You'll get better with practice." She cupped his cheek. "I promise to eat anything you cook."

"That's true love for you." He kissed the top of her nose. "Now I have proof."

She smiled. "I thought that I proved it to you last night."

"That was just you enjoying my body. There was no sacrifice involved."

"True, but love is what made it spectacular." She pulled out of his arms. "I have to go. I'm already late."

Yesterday he'd walked her to the lab, and he would've loved to do it again, but he had a few phone calls to make. After that, he was going to do a deep dive on YouTube, watching cooking videos.

"I hope to wow you with something special when you come home for lunch, but if I produce another culinary disaster, I'll compensate by wearing an apron with nothing underneath."

She laughed. "Now you've made sure that I won't be able to concentrate on work."

"That was the idea. When we are not together, I want you to be thinking about me."

"I do." She kissed his cheek before opening the door. "All the time."

Smiling, Eric closed it behind her and went to sit on the couch. Being with Darlene was pure joy. He couldn't help comparing this incredibly supporting and loving relationship with the mess that his marriage had been.

There had been tender moments, and he'd thought that he was in love, but the bad stuff outweighed the good, even without taking the infidelity into account. His ex's volatile temper, the anger tantrums that had come out of nowhere, the bruises she'd caused that he'd hidden with clothing to save himself the need to lie about how he'd gotten them. How had he endured that for so long?

Why had he?

He was a handsome fellow if he said so himself, pretty smart too, and a pilot. He could have found someone else easily. His damn stubbornness, his refusal to call it quits, that was what had kept him chained to a disaster.

Perhaps it had been the Fates' way of preparing him for Darlene. He might not have appreciated her gentle and giving nature if he hadn't gone through the ordeal with his ex.

Now, he couldn't imagine life without her, and the thought of losing her terrified him. The fear was like a hungry beast, gnawing at his insides and infusing him with an unbearable sense of urgency. That was why he was beating down his possessive instincts and orchestrating her transition with Max's help.

Hopefully, he was doing the right thing.

With a sigh, Eric picked up his phone and dialed Bridget's number.

She answered right away. "How are you doing?"

"I'm doing fine. My gums are a little swollen, but they don't hurt yet. I can't believe that I'm actually looking forward to the pain."

"It will come. What can I help you with?"

That was Doctor Bridget. No beating around the bush with her.

"I have a question. I know that it hasn't been done before, but I want your opinion. Can a female Dormant's transition be induced by two different male immortals? I won't have fangs for another six months, and I'm afraid that Darlene doesn't have the time. I ran the idea by Max, and he's willing to do the biting while I do the other part." He took a breath. "He says that I will need to be chained down so I don't attack him, but I don't think it will be necessary. I'm not a violent person by nature."

For a long moment, the doctor didn't reply, and he wondered whether he'd shocked her into silence. "What do you think?"

"Frankly, I don't know. We speculate that insemination is a catalyst, enhancing the venom's potency. Theoretically, it shouldn't make a difference whether both are produced by the same male or not, but since there is also a bond involved, I would be wary of introducing competing catalysts."

That was an angle he hadn't considered. "I think that Darlene and I have already bonded. I feel a connection with her that I've never felt before. That's why I'm willing to do this crazy thing. I can't bear the thought of losing her because we didn't do everything we could to induce her in time."

"Fear is a powerful motivator." Bridget sighed. "As a scientist, I should encourage this experiment, but as a friend, I'm conflicted. Darlene can probably wait the additional six months and still transition successfully. She's Toven's granddaughter, so her immortal genetics are strong. That being said, I don't want to recommend waiting and bear the responsibility for her not making it."

"That's precisely the position I am in. Bottom line, do you think it will work?"

"It should, but it's not guaranteed. On the other hand, nothing will happen if it doesn't work. Darlene just won't transition, but at least you will know that you've done everything you could."

"That's how I think about it too."

"Is Darlene willing, though?"

"She's not crazy about the idea, but Max and I figured out a way to do that with minimal involvement on his part, and she's semi-comfortable with that."

Bridget chuckled. "I don't need to hear the details. Good luck to you all. Let me know how it goes."

"I will. Thanks, doc."

SOFIA

*M*arcel sat next to Sofia in the backseat of the minivan, but without Julian, they had plenty of space. Not that it made a difference either way. He could have been on another continent as far as emotional closeness was concerned.

She hated it.

If he was being a dick, she could at least lash out at him, but he was polite and soft-spoken as always, just distant.

The two guards accompanying them weren't talking between themselves either, and the silence in the minivan was oppressive.

Shifting, she faced Marcel. "I know that Tom was talking about Jade when he told me about the slaughter of the males and the kidnapping of the females. I always wondered why she loathed Igor so much, and why she tolerated being his prime female despite that. Maybe she's looking for a way to avenge her people, and that's why she found Safe Haven's paranormal program so fascinating. A powerful compeller like Tom could release her from Igor's compulsion and then she could kill him, but to do that, she needs to have access to him."

"What about the other females?" Marcel asked. "Do they find him less loathsome?"

"They all want to be his prime, but Jade is the most powerful, and that's why he tolerates her. She gave him a daughter, which as you know is rare. Not that it matters. Igor prefers a son to be his successor."

She might be disclosing too much information, but at this stage, it wasn't important. The inner workings of the Kra-ell society wouldn't give them any military insight into the compound, so it wasn't relevant. It was just something she knew Marcel would find fascinating and it would encourage him to engage in conversation with her.

Maybe he would even reciprocate with information about his people. She still doubted that paranormal abilities were the only thing distinguishing them from regular humans. The story about finding the three hybrids while looking for people with paranormal talents also didn't make sense. If those hybrids could pass for humans, they wouldn't disclose their deepest secret willingly. Being the progeny of aliens and their inhuman longevity put them at tremendous risk.

Then again, Tom or another powerful compeller could have forced the information out of them, so there was that.

"He murdered Jade's sons," Marcel said quietly. "He most likely did the same to the other females that he brought to the compound. We know that Jade is a strong compeller in her own right, so she might have been able to retain more of her independent thinking. The others might not have been as strong, and he compelled them to forget their loss, or did something else to make them want him despite what he did to their males."

Sofia was grateful for the information Marcel had shared and horrified by the tragedy that had befallen Jade. She didn't know how old the female was, so when Tom had told her about what Igor had done to her people, she hadn't thought about Jade having male children that had been murdered along with the other males.

"Thank you for sharing this with me, but I wish I didn't know that. Poor Jade." She let out a breath. "I never thought I would say that about her. She's so strong and so condescending. She is not very likable."

"She's not." Marcel gave her a tight smile. "The three survivors from her clan don't like her, but they respect her, and two of them still feel loyal to her."

"What about the third?"

"They had a falling out, but he would still help her if he could."

Sofia nodded. "It demonstrates that he's a good person."

Marcel pursed his lips. "Most people have some good and some bad mixed in. You said that even Igor wasn't all bad."

She chuckled. "In his case, the scale tips heavily to the bad side."

What about her grandfather? Had Valstar been involved in the slaughter?

Probably.

He'd killed children.

The realization pulled a gasp out of Sofia. "Mother above, my grandfather is a monster."

Marcel tilted his head. "Does he belong to Igor's inner circle?"

She nodded. "He's under Igor's compulsion, though. Everyone is. But he doesn't have a collar around his neck."

"Does your mother?"

"Of course. Even Igor's daughter with Jade has one. Not that she would ever attempt to escape. Her life is charmed despite not having a chance to become his successor and having a bitchy, demanding mother. She's treated like a princess."

"In a traditional Kra-ell community, she would be the ruler. Not because she's Igor's daughter, but because she's Jade's. From what you told me, Jade is the most powerful female in the compound."

Sofia nodded. "So if your people ever get rid of Igor, Jade would become the next leader?"

That wouldn't be a great improvement.

Jade was ruthless, and she wasn't kind, and she didn't even try to hide her low opinion of humans. If it were up to her, they would all be just servants and farm workers. At least Igor accepted that humans were as intelligent as the Kra-ell and were useful for more than breeding and menial jobs.

"I don't know," Marcel said. "The people who were born into Igor's rule are used to his patriarchal regime. They might be resistant to things going traditional again. The best would be a new system that is not gender-based. A new democratic era for the Kra-ell, where those who are the most capable and willing to serve their community get elected with the help of a confidential voting system."

Sofia snorted. "That doesn't work all that well for humans, who are much less hotheaded than the Kra-ell. Democracy is not suitable for everyone." She leaned back. "Besides, Jade found a way to teach the children about the old ways of female rule with her stories, so the concept would not be completely foreign to people. I wonder if she did that to prepare the next generation for her own rule."

"How did she manage to do that under Igor's nose?"

"She used Eleanor's tactic to circumvent Igor's compulsion. She uses fables and fantasies to plant the seeds of ideas in the children's minds."

"That's gutsy of her. How come he didn't forbid it?"

"Most people think about those stories as just that. They don't think about the hidden meanings." She gave him a tentative smile. "It's like what Da Vinci did with his paintings. He couldn't speak out about the church's narrative, so he hid his message in his paintings." She chuckled. "I didn't notice anything unusual about The Last Supper until I read the *Da Vinci Code*. After that, it became glaringly obvious to me that the apostle on the right was a woman. There are only two people without beards in the picture, and the other one has really big hands. Her hands are small, and they are demurely clasped in front of her."

"I get what you're trying to say. We've all seen that picture countless times, but until someone pointed the anomaly out to us, our eyes glossed over it."

29

VROG

*V*rog's heart was pounding as he took the steps up to Kian's office two at a time, but it wasn't due to exertion. Emmett had only shared with him and Aliyah the bare minimum of details about Jade's situation, and he was eager to learn more.

"Good morning, Vrog." Kian motioned to the conference table. "Please, take a seat."

"Good morning." Vrog nodded his head in Turner's direction.

The guy's presence at the meeting meant that things were getting serious and that Kian was considering helping Jade, but Turner might not be the best person for the job. Vrog had heard about his hostage retrieval operations, and the guy was supposedly the best in his field, but he was used to rescuing humans from other humans.

The Kra-ell were a much more formidable adversary.

Kian put a bottle of water next to each of them and sat down. "You are probably wondering why I invited you to join us this morning."

"I assume that it has something to do with Jade. Did you find out anything more about where she's being held?"

"We know the exact location, but we don't know much about what we are dealing with. I hope that you can help us with that."

Vrog's heart sank. He wasn't a warrior, and he knew nothing about strategy. He'd hoped that Kian had a plan. "I only have experience with Jade's tribe and how she ran things. It was also a long time ago. I wouldn't know the first thing about the security measures her captors employ."

"Since we assume that they all came on the same ship, we can also assume that they received similar training, which they maintained after getting shipwrecked." Kian leaned back in his chair. "Let me bring you up to speed about what we've learned so far."

When he was done, Vrog's fangs were fully elongated, and he suspected that his eyes were glowing blood red. Nevertheless, he was a civilized male, and he kept his tone level when he was finally able to respond. "What do you need from me?"

"I need to know about the training regimen of pureblooded and hybrid Kra-ell in Jade's tribe. Did all of them train? Just the warriors? What weapons did they train with?"

"All the pureblooded males trained. Their job was to protect the tribe. The females trained as well, but it was more of a sport than warrior training. Their job was to lead and produce the next generation. The hybrids were different. Jade chose only those who had the aptitude for combat to train as warriors. I was smart and good with numbers, so she put me in charge of supervising the tribe's investments in various businesses. Others had different jobs. The hybrid females were treated almost the same as the pureblooded ones, just with no authority. Nevertheless, all the hybrids were regarded as second-class tribe members, including the females."

"What about technology?" Turner asked. "How advanced were they?"

"Jade was very technologically savvy. She used what she knew to make money for the tribe."

Turner looked at Kian. "She or one of the others in her original group must have had engineering or scientific training. Using technology is simple. Building it requires learned skills."

"True." Kian took a sip from his bottle. "If I were stranded on an alien planet, and my ship was destroyed, I would become a caveman and a hunter. I wouldn't know how to build any technologically advanced things. The clan had knowledge thanks to Ekin's tablet that Annani appropriated, but we didn't know what to do with it until our people learned the basics of engineering from humans." He looked at Vrog. "Do you know who the tech person was?"

"I guess it was Voltav. Jade always took him with her on her business trips, and now that I think about it, I didn't see him training as often as the others. Jade herself was pretty knowledgeable, though. I don't know if she arrived with the knowledge or learned it from Voltav and human sources."

"What about weapons?" Kian asked.

"We had semi-automatic pistols and semi-automatic combat shotguns, but the purebloods preferred mode of fighting was hand-to-hand. They also trained with swords and other cold weapons, and they did some target practice with the guns, but not often."

"Sofia reported the same thing." Kian pushed the bottle away. "We have an advantage in that regard. The problem is that Igor's compound is full of innocents, including children, and we can't just bomb the place. So far, the noise cannon seems like the best option, but that's problematic as well because of the humans, and especially the children."

"A noise cannon?" Vrog asked.

"It's a device that can incapacitate humans and immortals by producing a loud noise," Turner said. "We would need to test it on a Kra-ell to see if it affects you the same way."

"I volunteer," Vrog immediately offered.

"Thank you," Turner said. "Testing it on you will be very helpful in gaining data on how it affects hybrids, but we need to catch a pureblooded male to see how it affects them. Also, we can't make any plans before we know more, and only a pureblooded warrior will have all the information we need."

"Right." Kian looked at Vrog. "How much stronger are the purebloods than the hybrids?"

"As you would expect, they are stronger. In a hand-to-hand fight between a similarly trained pureblood and a hybrid, the pureblood will win. If the hybrid was better trained, he might be able to hold up longer, but he will eventually lose."

"We might need your help to catch one. Can we count on it?"

"Of course. But just to remind you, I was never trained as a warrior, and I'm a hybrid. I don't know how helpful I would be."

"We are still figuring it out, and we might end up not needing you. I just want to know that I can count on you if needed."

"Of course. I'm sure Aliyah will gladly help as well." Vrog smiled. "You shouldn't discount her just because she's a female. She's very strong, and she's also resourceful."

Kian drummed his fingers on the table. "I don't like using females in combat, and I don't care if that makes me a relic or a chauvinist, but perhaps we can utilize Aliyah in some other way." He looked at Turner. "What do you think?"

"I'll put her name on my list of assets."

30

MARCEL

*D*uring the drive back to Safe Haven, Sofia had been making an effort to get back into Marcel's good graces, and despite his resolve to stay firm and not succumb to her charms, his resistance was slowly eroding.

The truth was that it was working both ways.

Sofia had been suspicious of their motives, and she'd resisted sharing information as best she could to protect her loved ones. But the more they'd talked, and the more she'd learned about Igor and what he had done to Jade, the more inclined she seemed to believe that their agenda wasn't conquest but liberation.

Perhaps if he told her about Turner's suspicions with regard to the tracker, she would be even more inclined to cooperate with them, provided that they didn't endanger her family.

And that was a problem he didn't have a solution for. If Kian chose to attack her compound, there would be casualties no matter how diligent they were to protect innocent lives.

Hell, even some of Igor's inner circle could be decent people who had been coerced into doing his bidding. With his compulsion power, he was like a god, or rather a devil.

At least the gods had done their best to appear benevolent. Igor had made no such effort.

They entered Safe Haven's outer security ring when Marcel finally decided to share it with Sofia. "I looked up the pendant you were given to communicate with Valstar and Igor. It's not very sophisticated, and it can be bought online. The design is also very tacky, and it looks cheap. In comparison, the tracker we removed from your body is state-of-the-art. I don't even know how he got a piece of such advanced technology. Maybe he brought it with him from the home planet."

Sofia frowned. "Is there a question in there somewhere? Because I don't know anything about alien technology or where he got it. I've never seen anything in the compound that looked like it wasn't human made, but that doesn't mean much. Igor might be hiding the good stuff."

Marcel had to smile. It didn't even occur to her to wonder about the discrepancy between the two pieces of equipment she'd been given, one knowingly and one unknowingly.

"We talked about it, and we have a hypothesis. We think that you were given a simple piece of technology for communication because you were supposed to get caught. The tracker would have led Igor, or whoever he sent to trail you, to our base or headquarters or wherever else he thought you would end up after getting caught. Somehow, you've outsmarted everyone, though. Our instruments didn't pick up on the transmission. I guess you used your daily runs to get a few miles away from Safe Haven and activated the communicator there."

"I did, but Valstar told me to find a secluded spot where no one could overhear me."

"Did he tell you to get far away from Safe Haven?"

She shook her head. "The first day, I went on a walk on the beach, looking for a good spot, but when I was stopped by one of your guards, I got scared and decided to walk much farther than I planned." She tilted her head. "Do you monitor transmissions to and from Safe Haven?"

He nodded. "We are conducting classified research here."

"Is it something that Igor might be interested in?"

"Not likely, and I doubt that he suspected what we're doing, but the fact remains that the device you were given was not very sophisticated while the tracker was. It might not mean anything, but it seems suspicious when combined with your lack of experience and that you haven't been told what you were supposed to look for."

Sofia let out a breath. "When Valstar trained me for the missions, we got a little closer, and in my naïveté, I thought that he finally approved of me, but I was so damn wrong. I was worthless to him. If he expected me to get caught, he should have at least warned me so I could say goodbye to my family, but he's just the cold-hearted bastard I've always known he was." She shook her head. "He's much worse than that. He's a cold-blooded murderer of children. How old were Jade's sons?"

"I think they were adults, but I'm sure there were male children among the slaughtered too."

Vrog had said that he found the rings that the adult males had worn, and he counted all of them. He hadn't mentioned children, who probably hadn't been given rings yet, but since the remains had been incinerated, there was no way to know.

"It makes me so angry." Sofia crossed her arms over her chest. "I wish I could see Valstar just one more time so I could spit in his face."

31

SOFIA

*M*arcel's suspicion made sense, and it had Sofia seething with anger. The nerve of her damn grandfather. If not for everyone else she cared about in the compound, she would have led the attack against it herself.

Yeah, right.

She was just a human, completely helpless even in comparison to a Kra-ell child. They were so damn strong.

As Marcel opened the door to Leon's office, the first thing she noticed was the cat perched on the windowsill. It was orange colored and fat. The new carrier of her tracker, no doubt.

As they joined Leon, Eleanor, and Emmett at the conference table, Leon got to his feet. "Say hello to Cecilia." He lifted the cat into his arms. "She likes to be petted." He handed her to Sofia.

The cat settled into her arms as if she'd known her forever and started purring.

"I think she likes me." Sofia smoothed her hand over the cat's soft fur. "We didn't have any pets in the compound, but my roommate at the university had a cat. Her name was Hydra, and she was black and white and kind of skinny." Thinking about the friend she was probably never going to see again, Sofia teared up. Stroking Cecilia helped hold the tears at bay. "Is the tracker already inside of her?"

Leon nodded. "Anastasia is really fond of Cecilia, and she warned me that if anything happened to her because of the tracker, she wouldn't let me in her bed for at least a year." He smiled. "But that's an empty threat because my Ana wouldn't last two days without me."

The love in Leon's tone tugged at Sofia's heartstrings. She wanted Marcel to talk about her like that, but those kinds of warm feelings were a thing of the past. He was nice to her, but he still felt cold.

How could he have just turned off his feelings like that? Was he a machine?

He sat next to her and gave the cat a perfunctory pat on the head. "Why did you choose this cat if she's so dear to Anastasia? I've seen a couple of others roaming the grounds."

"One belongs to Riley, and she would have thrown a fit if anyone had even suggested using hers. Cecilia and Albert don't belong to anyone specific, but Albert is much more active. The tracker would have moved too erratically throughout the resort to look as if it was inside a person."

Sofia chuckled. "I didn't know that I moved as much as a lazy cat."

"Do you have the pendant?" Marcel asked.

"It's here." Leon pulled it out of his desk drawer. "I suggest that we take the cat and the pendant to the spot that Sofia previously used to communicate with Valstar, but she should rehearse what she's going to say first."

Evidently, someone had given Leon a full update about what had been discussed in the glass house, and it hadn't been Marcel. It had to be Tom or the mysterious boss who'd been listening through the doctor's tablet.

"She also needs an earpiece," Marcel said.

"Right." Leon pulled a small case out of his pocket and handed it to Sofia. "It might be a little tricky to use the earpiece from the pendant on top of those. You will have to hold it really close."

She opened the case and looked at the two earpieces inside. They looked like a regular pair of earphones, just a little bulkier. "How do they work?"

"It's really quite simple. They are built on the same principle as translating earbuds, but instead of the machine voice talking in a different language, it just repeats the words spoken into it, and it filters the compulsion sound waves. For it to work, it needs to fit very snugly, so none of those waves enter your ear. That's why it is made from a material that molds to the ear canal."

He took the case from her and took out the earpieces. "You put it in like this." He demonstrated. "To activate, you tap on it once, and to deactivate, tap twice. Put them in, and let's practice it."

"I'll take the cat." Eleanor lifted Cecilia off Sofia's lap. "Make sure that you don't have any cat hairs on your hands when you handle the earpieces. You want the seal to be really tight."

Sofia examined her hands. "I don't see any hairs, but maybe I should wash them first."

"That's a good idea. After you get the hang of using them, we will start coaching you on what you're going to say to your contact."

Nodding, she rose to her feet. "Where is the washroom?"

"I'll show you." Eleanor handed the cat to Emmett, who immediately transferred it back to Leon.

"He's not a cat person, is he?"

Eleanor laughed. "He only likes animals he can drink from."

32

MARCEL

*M*arcel was sure that Eleanor's comment would clue Sofia in to Emmett's real identity, but she just smiled and followed Eleanor out of the room.

She knew what hybrids looked like, and she should have figured it out by now. But the truth was that Emmett looked human, even more so than Vrog. Only Aliya looked alien. Perhaps the hybrids in Igor's compound looked more like Aliya than Vrog and Emmett.

"Should we tell her?" Marcel asked Leon.

"Tell her what?"

"That Emmett is a hybrid, and that he's the reason Jade has been spending time on the Safe Haven website."

"First, let's see how she does with the story we want her to tell and how well it is received. If all goes well, we can tell her, but I don't really see the need. It doesn't make a difference to her one way or another. She's human, and her affinity is with the other humans in the compound. She hates her hybrid mother."

That was true. During all of their conversations and the many times she'd mentioned all the people she would miss, Sofia hadn't said a thing about her mother. The female was like a stranger to her.

When Sofia and Eleanor returned, Sofia put in the earpieces with Eleanor's help and tapped them to activate.

Leon checked her ears. "You need to push them more firmly inside."

When she did, he motioned for Eleanor to test it.

"Sofia. Stand on one foot and touch your nose with your finger."

A wide grin spread over Sofia's face. "You sound like a different person, and no, I will not stand on one foot."

"Awesome." Eleanor smiled. "Now take them out, and we will repeat the test. Maybe I'm just not strong enough of a compeller."

When the test was repeated without the earpieces, Sofia obeyed the command with a grimace. "I hate compulsion. It's really vile."

"I won't argue with you on that," Eleanor said. "Put the earpieces in the case, and let's rehearse your story."

For the next hour, Emmett and Eleanor refined the story and made comments about Sofia's acting, or rather her overacting. She sounded rehearsed, and no matter how many times she tried to get better, she still sounded as if she was reading a script.

She was either a really bad actress or an excellent one who was trying to convince them that she was bad.

"It's no use." She threw her hands in the air. "He's never going to buy my story."

"I have an idea." Marcel got to his feet. "Pretend that you are trying to convince me of your story. Talk to me as if I'm Valstar or Igor."

Sofia took in a deep breath, and as she looked at him, her expression sent chills down his spine. She seemed frightened and unsure, and as she spoke again, she sounded like a scared child who'd been summoned to the principal's office, or worse, a prisoner facing her prosecutor.

He hated to see her like that, especially since she was talking to him, but her performance was much better. She'd still mumbled and got lost for words several times, but that could be explained away by her anxiety.

"That might pass," Eleanor said. "I wish we had more time, but the longer he doesn't hear from you, the more difficult it will be to convince him that everything is back to normal and that you are no longer a suspect."

Sofia sighed. "Let's do this." She reached for the cat and cradled Cecilia in her arms. "She will give me courage." She kissed the cat's head. "Won't you, sweetie?"

Marcel felt his heart squeeze. The poor girl had no one to turn to for comfort other than the cat, and he was a jerk for not being more supportive of her.

Wrapping his arm around her narrow shoulders, he leaned and kissed her temple. "If she gets heavy, I'll carry her the rest of the way."

Sofia gave him a small smile. "It's okay. I can carry her. She gives me warmth."

Marcel knew that she wasn't talking about the physical sensation. The cat showed her more affection than he had since the whole thing exploded in Emmett's office, and she had no one else to lean on.

33

SOFIA

*W*as Marcel warming up to her? Or was he just trying to be nice to boost her confidence for the call?

Probably the second one, and how sad was that.

Maybe she shouldn't pine for a guy that could form an instantaneous ice shield around his heart. Now that she was free to choose her man, she should find someone stable and free of emotional issues. Someone who would remain steadfast no matter what.

Yeah, dream on. As if such a creature exists.

Life was a long journey of disappointments and betrayals, and the sooner she resigned herself to that reality, the sooner her heart would stop bleeding. Every time she'd allowed herself to hope that someone other than her father and her aunts and cousins actually cared for her, she'd been disappointed. But perhaps instead of complaining, she should count her blessings for having a family who cared about her.

Some people didn't even have that.

When they got to her spot, she pulled the earpieces out of their case and stuffed them into her ears.

Marcel checked that they properly sealed her ear canal, and then took the cat from her.

"Do you need a moment alone?" he asked.

Hearing the male machine voice was jarring. It made her realize that Marcel's voice hadn't been completely devoid of emotion before.

Eleanor's pinched expression communicated that having a moment wasn't an option. She was there to ensure that Sofia didn't stray from the storyline they'd agreed upon, but since she had the earpieces in, all Eleanor could do if she strayed from the script was to stop the communication like she had done in Emmett's office.

Except, how would she know?

Sofia wasn't going to talk with her grandfather in English, and neither Eleanor nor Marcel had said anything about knowing Russian. Maybe they were wearing translating earpieces too?

Eleanor's long wavy hair was down and covered her ears, but Marcel wasn't wearing any.

"That's okay. Just give me some space so I can pretend I'm alone."

Nodding, he took a couple of steps back and motioned for Eleanor to do the same.

Sofia took a deep breath, pulled the earpiece from the pendant, and pressed it against the other device.

That had been the easy part. The hard part was pressing the picture to activate the communication. Her hand shook so badly that she had to close her eyes and focus on forcing her finger to move.

"Sofia," Valstar barked into her ear. "What happened?"

Even with the machine voice, she knew it was him. Igor's word choice would have been different.

"It was a close call. I didn't know that Emmett's girlfriend was listening in on the line from the other room, or that she was a compeller and realized right away what was going on. She knew that Emmett wouldn't have admitted to any wrong-doing, especially not to a stranger on the phone. She terminated the call and accused me of being an undercover journalist. I panicked. I didn't know what to do, but the tears did their job." She chuckled. "Marcel came in and calmed things down."

"They took away your pendant. How come they gave it back?"

"I came up with a great story." She repeated what she'd rehearsed with Eleanor and Emmett. "They brought a truth-teller to verify that I wasn't lying, and I thought that I was done for, but he didn't detect the lie. I don't know if he was a fake or if my Kra-ell heritage protected me, but somehow, he believed me, and I was so relieved. Anyway, after that, they invited me to join their community and gave me my family heirloom back." She chuckled. "They might be paranormally talented, but they are not very technologically savvy. They didn't realize that the pendant is a communication device."

"Hold on for a moment," Valstar said. "Igor wants to speak with you."

"Of course."

Sofia closed her eyes and prayed to the Mother of All Life for the earpieces to work. If they didn't, the charade would end in a moment.

"Good afternoon, Sofia," the robotic voice said. "Valstar informs me that you managed to wiggle out of the situation you were in and even gain a foot up. Is that true?"

"Yes. I pulled out the best acting of my life. After they heard my sad story about my supernaturally talented parents and how desperate I was to have a useful talent like theirs, they felt sorry for me and invited me to join their paranormal community. I suspect that their goal is to crossbreed the various talents and produce even more enhanced humans. Not only that, but they also seem to have lots of money, so they must have rich backers. I would love to stay on and continue the investigation, sir. I don't know if any of this information will be beneficial to you, but in the long run, a new breed of enhanced humans might pose a problem. They have compellers, telepaths, empaths, remote viewers, and all kinds of other talents that are great for spying."

"Indeed. That was good investigative work, Sofia. Keep me informed."

Sofia's knees nearly buckled from the relief. "I will, but it's not safe for me to call every day. I managed to get away today, but I have a feeling that they will be watching me closely from now on. I can't do it anywhere near the lodge because I think they are monitoring outgoing signals. Every time I need to call, I go on a run or a walk of at least three miles. The exercise excuse worked before when I wasn't a suspect, but if I keep doing this every day, eventually, they are going to appoint a guard to accompany me, and I won't be able to communicate at all."

"Call whenever you can. The information you collect about those paranormal talents is important. Who else other than Emmett's girlfriend is a compeller?"

"I met a guy named Tom and another one called Malcolm, but they told me they have more. Not everyone is in Safe Haven. They have other locations."

She purposefully avoided mentioning that Emmett was a compeller. It just seemed like something Igor shouldn't know. The other names were meaningless to him, but he knew who Emmett was.

"Are they strong compellers?" he asked.

"No, sir. They must be very weak. Emmett's girlfriend and Tom tried to compel me to tell them the truth about my so-called father, but they weren't able to break through the shields you've built for me. I stuck to my story."

"Good job, Sofia. Find out what you can about their other locations and about the kinds of talents they have and the talents they intend to breed."

"Yes, sir."

34

MARCEL

*S*ofia ended the call and pumped her fist in the air. "I did it!" She turned in a circle, leaned toward Marcel, and kissed the cat on the head.

Reaching for the pendant, he double-checked that the transmission had been terminated and ran a compact handheld device over it to make absolutely sure that it wasn't transmitting.

Sofia gave him a hurt look, but that hadn't been avoidable. He still didn't trust her a hundred percent.

His Russian was so-so, but it had been good enough for him to understand the conversation and approve of Sofia's act, but he might have missed some nuances of meaning that might have clued Igor in. Later, when they returned to Leon's office, he would listen to the translation of the recording that the earpiece had made.

Leon had been listening to it all along, and so had Eleanor through her translating earpiece, but neither of them spoke Russian with any fluency. Perhaps they should ask Morris to listen to it just in case the three of them had missed something.

"Good job." Eleanor clapped Sofia on the back. "That was your best performance yet. Do you think Igor bought it?"

"He had to. He used compulsion to get me to tell him the truth, and he's never had trouble compelling me before. I just hope he's not aware of the translating earpieces trick."

"He's not," Marcel said. "We developed the technology in-house."

Sofia took off the pendant and handed it to him. "Please, lock it back in the safe. I don't want it anywhere near me."

He put it in his pocket. "Let's head back. I'm sure you're hungry after all the excitement."

"What now?" She fell in step with him. "What am I supposed to do here?"

"There is one more thing." Eleanor handed her the cat.

When she cast Marcel a sidelong smirk, he wondered what she was plotting. With her gaunt face and small, dark eyes, that smirk looked evil.

"How do you feel about Marcel?" She shocked Sofia and him with the question. "And you have to tell us the truth."

"That's not fair," he murmured.

Eleanor shrugged. "All is fair in love and war. Or is it the other way around? War and love? I will have to look it up." She leveled her intense eyes at Sofia. "Talk, girl."

Sofia turned her face to him and swallowed. "Before everything went wrong, I could see myself spending the rest of my life with you. I was falling for you. But even though I had no choice in any of this, I don't think you can forgive me, and I don't want to give my heart to someone who can close his off so easily."

The pain in her eyes was unbearable, and the need to forgive her and take her into his arms was overwhelming, but he'd been in a similar scenario before, and the price he'd paid for his weakness was so monumental that it still haunted him. He could not allow himself to be vulnerable again.

"Our infatuation with each other is irrelevant at the moment. We are dealing with a crisis, and only when the crisis is resolved, can we revisit our feelings. For now, this has to stay on ice."

"Ice indeed," Sofia murmured. "What do you consider as crisis resolution? Capturing Igor and executing him?"

"He didn't commit any crimes against my people. It's up to the members of his community who he has wronged to decide how he should be punished."

"They are under his compulsion. They can't do a thing against him. If they could, Jade would have killed him a long time ago."

"Maybe that's the solution," Eleanor said. "We smuggle earpieces to Jade, and she takes care of Igor for us."

Marcel shook his head. "That's not going to help with the previous layers of compulsion she carries. We need to smuggle her out, have Tom free her mind, and send her back with earpieces."

Sofia nodded. "That could work. How are you going to smuggle her out, though?"

"We can capture her during one of her hunting runs. Does she ever go alone?"

"I don't think any of them ever go alone. Hunting is a social activity for them, and they usually go out in groups. But I'm not a good source of information on anything related to the purebloods or the hybrids. I've been gone most of the past seven years, and when I'm back, I spend my time with my family in the human quarters. You need a Kra-ell, preferably a male. Maybe you can capture one, question him, compel him to not say anything, and release him right away, so no one would notice that he'd been missing."

Those were all good ideas, but they were all fraught with difficulties and pitfalls that could have disastrous results. Turner was working on a plan, though, and Marcel trusted the guy to work the kinks out.

35

KIAN

"That went well," Turner said after listening to the recording.

Being immune to compulsion and familiar with the Russian language, he was the best equipped to listen to the unfiltered version and ascertain that it had indeed gone as well as it seemed.

"Igor seemed doubtful at first, but when he thought that he compelled Sofia to tell the truth, his tone changed."

"What's your take on him?" Kian asked.

"That wasn't enough to form an opinion. He sounded calm and confident. He wasn't rude or obnoxious, and he didn't sound worried. He's pretty much emotionless, which makes him more dangerous, not less."

Kian chuckled. "It takes one to know one. But you are not entirely unemotional, just a little stunted."

Turner smiled indulgently. "I pride myself on my logical mind. The heart usually interferes with rational thought."

"Indeed, but I wouldn't trade places with you. My intuition is no less important to me than my analytical ability." In fact, he trusted his intuition more than he trusted his mind.

"Intuition is nothing more than your subconscious mind using all the information it has stored and making calculations behind the veil. There is nothing mystical about it."

"Says the man who invoked the Fates in this office the day before."

Turner shrugged. "We need to decide on our next step. As I see it, we have several options now that Sofia has bought us time with her great performance. We can up the ante and send the cat on a trip, see if anyone follows, and if they do, capture them. But that would cost us the element of surprise, and the time we gained will be wasted." Turner crossed his arms over his chest. "I'm just thinking out loud. If Sofia indeed has a tail and we capture it, the game will be up, and it

317

will move into Igor's court. He will realize that something more than what Sofia told him is going on, and his next step will be to get Jade to admit what she's been doing. Sofia did well by not mentioning that Emmett was a compeller, and Igor didn't ask about him, so I assume that he didn't compel the truth out of Jade yet. I assume that he's not confronting her about it because he wants her to keep communicating with Safe Haven so he can find out who and what is involved."

"That has been his goal from the start," Kian said. "He knows something is up, but he doesn't know what, so he sends Sofia with a double purpose. If she finds out something, that's great, and if she doesn't and gets caught, he can follow the tracker inside of her and find out where she was taken. Right now, we have the advantage of him believing in a plausible story that leaves Jade out. As far as he's concerned, she might be interested in finding more about paranormal talents to see if she can enhance hers in some way and get free from his compulsion, or she's looking for information about other talents that might assist her in some way."

Turner nodded. "Another thing he might do if we capture the tail is retaliate against Sofia's family, or he might flee. He might also assume that we fed Sofia lies, and that she told him the truth as she knew it. If that's the case, he will send more people to investigate what's going on here."

"Isn't the same true for capturing one of his males during the hunts they go on?" Kian asked. "That will also serve as an alert and trigger the same chain of responses from him."

"I'll contact my guy in Russia and ask him to get one of those tiny bug drones. From what we've learned from Sofia, the Kra-ell are using old-school methods to hide, and they probably don't have sophisticated equipment to detect a small drone."

"Their eyesight and hearing are just as good as ours. They might be able to detect it without any equipment."

Turner didn't seem to share his concern. "If Navuh and his warriors didn't detect the one we sent to Areana, I don't think the Kra-ell will either. It's a risk, but of the several options we have, none is risk free. If Igor believed that everything Sofia told him was true, then the safest option might be to do nothing and fake her death. We can ignore Jade's communication attempts and close the case as is."

That was what Kian had proposed to do from the start, and Turner had been of the same opinion, but they both had been drifting closer and closer to choosing a confrontation.

Kian sighed. "I thought we agreed to send a team of Guardians to scope out the compound's area."

"It was one of the options, but it hasn't been done yet, so you can still change your mind."

"Should I?" Kian rubbed the back of his neck. "I really don't want to open this can of worms. On the other hand, it's always better to deal with a threat before it becomes even more menacing."

"I think that we should keep gathering information, but we should avoid doing anything rash. We can send the cat on a trip along with Eleanor, who can pose as Sofia, and we can see if she picks up a tail, but we don't engage with the tail. We start monitoring the tail's movements and collect more information."

"What if the tail notices our tail?"

Turner lifted his hands in the air. "As I said, every move we make carries a certain risk, but doing nothing is also risky in the long run. You need to decide what you want to do."

"As usual, you are right. We need to collect information."

36

SOFIA

"Can I take Cecilia with me to my dungeon cell?" Sofia held the cat to her chest as Marcel opened the door to the cottage.

"I think you can." Eleanor patted her arm. "I'll let Anastasia know that she is with you." She turned to Marcel. "You will need to stay around and let Cecilia out to do her business in the yard."

"I have to finish up a few things in the lab, but after I'm done, I can come back here."

Sofia glared at him. "If you don't lock me up, I can take the cat out to pee and poop myself."

Eleanor cast Marcel a pitying glance. "I'll get you two lunch and something for Cecilia. She's been a very good sport about all of this." She turned around and walked back the way they'd come.

Following Marcel down the stairs, Sofia rubbed her chin against the cat fur, eliciting contented purring from her.

If only it was so easy to please Marcel.

His nonanswer to her earlier admission of feelings toward him shouldn't have surprised her. He'd been cold and remote, with occasional flares of slight warmth that hadn't been enough to console her, but they had been enough to keep her hope alive. Marcel also hadn't said that it was over between them, only that the timing was wrong, so perhaps there was still a small chance that he would get over what he perceived as her betrayal, but he was slow to forgive, and she needed him right now.

Sofia was alone, frightened, and needed more than someone else's cat for comfort and support.

"Why do you have to lock me up?" she asked as they entered the bunker's living room. "Didn't I do everything you wanted me to do? Besides, it's not like I have anywhere to go." She grimaced. "And not just because Safe Haven is so isolated. I would have nowhere to go even if we were in the middle of Manhattan."

Looking uncomfortable, Marcel rubbed a hand over his jaw. "Where would you stay? You can't go back to sharing a room with Roxana, and I can't invite you to my bungalow."

"I can stay here. Just don't lock me up, so I can at least let the cat out."

"I need to ask the boss."

She rolled her eyes. "Seriously, Marcel. What am I going to do? Tell the guests of the retreat that I'm the progeny of aliens?"

He looked lost for words.

Sofia plopped down on the couch with the cat in her lap. "When do you need to go to the lab?"

Marcel sat next to her. "I'll go after lunch."

For a long moment they sat together in awkward silence, with the cat's purring the only sound.

"You know that I didn't want to do any of this," Sofia said as she stroked Cecilia's back. "I was compelled, and my family was threatened. If I didn't bring Igor good results, he would have taken it out on my family, and those were not empty threats. He's ruthless. I hated every moment of the deception. And just so you know, my instructions were to ask you to call Igor. I protected you by shifting his attention to Emmett and convincing him that Emmett knew much more than you did. Imagine how bad things would have been if I hadn't. He could have gotten you to reveal everything, and Eleanor wouldn't have been there to stop you."

He nodded. "The Fates must have intervened."

"The Fates?" He'd said something about the Fates before, but she had thought that he'd meant to say fate.

"I meant fate. We were saved by fate."

She huffed. "You were saved by Sofia. You are just too stubborn and self-absorbed to admit that."

The door opening at the top of the stairs saved Marcel from having to respond, which was a blessing.

Getting him to forgive her by insulting him was probably not a good tactic.

Smelling food, Cecilia jumped out of Sofia's arms and rushed up the stairs.

"I need some help here," Eleanor said. "And get the cat before she trips me up."

They both rushed after the cat, with Sofia grabbing the tabby and Marcel relieving Eleanor of half of the packages she was carrying.

"What did you do?" he asked. "Rob the kitchen?"

"More or less. Emmett is teaching a class, so I decided to have lunch with you two."

As Sofia set the cat's food down, Cecilia attacked it with vigor she hadn't seemed capable of before.

Once Eleanor and Marcel were done setting up the table, the three of them sat down to eat, or rather her two companions did. Sofia was too upset to feel hunger.

"You can't just keep me locked up down here," she said. "You can compel me to keep everything a secret so I can go back and enjoy the retreat. There is another whole week of it. I would also love to spend time with Roxie. I miss her."

She could really use Roxie's cheerful company.

"That's an option." Eleanor eyed Marcel. "You should talk to the boss. About everything."

He frowned. "What do you mean?"

Eleanor waved with her fork. "If you pulled the stick out of your ass for a moment, you would know what I meant."

Sofia gaped at the woman in stunned silence, and so did Marcel. Did anyone ever talk to him like that?

He shook his head. "I don't know what I did to court such a remark, but I don't appreciate being spoken to like that."

Eleanor rolled her eyes. "Yeah, yeah. You are so prim and proper, and I have the tact of a bull in a china shop. I just hate seeing you two tormenting yourselves needlessly. Sofia likes Marcel, and Marcel likes Sofia. Sofia is brave and admits her feelings, while Marcel is a chicken and refuses to pull said stick from that unmentionable place." She grinned. "There, I said it politely."

Sofia couldn't help the giggle rolling out of her mouth. "I think you've just become my favorite person." Well, perhaps her second favorite after Roxie, but Roxie wasn't there to call Marcel on his bullshit.

Eleanor laughed. "Sorry, doll, but I'm taken. You are a looker, though." She winked at Marcel. "Isn't Sofia beautiful? She's so graceful, so delicate, and such a fascinating contradiction of soft and hard, gentle and assertive. If I were a single male, I would be drooling all over her."

Marcel's cheeks turned crimson. "Would you stop it already? What has gotten into you?"

Eleanor pretended to sniff the air. "I guess it's the pheromones you two are emitting."

37

MARCEL

*W*hat had gotten into Eleanor? Why was she suddenly siding with Sofia?

She wasn't the type to forgive and forget.

Was it the affinity at work?

Was affinity even a thing between immortals and Kra-ell?

Or perhaps it was something else.

Up until not too long ago, Eleanor was an outsider who'd been brought in for the simple reason that they couldn't let an unscrupulous newly turned immortal roam free, so they'd been forced to keep her locked up in the village. Until she'd proven her loyalty and her worth to the clan, she had gone through her share of well-deserved mistrust and outward hostility. Was she empathizing with Sofia because she was now in a similar situation?

"This is not about you, Eleanor. When you were captured, you were just a single operator, and you were not a serious threat to us."

All levity left Eleanor's expression as she trained her dark eyes on him. "You're right. It's not about me, and my history is very different from Sofia's. What I did was of my own volition, not because I was coerced or threatened, and yet look at me today. I'm a proud member of the community, and Kian trusts me. If he can change his mind, so can you. Stop being so stubborn and look at the facts."

Her words struck a chord, and he didn't have a proper retort. Kian was the most suspicious and paranoid person he knew, and yet he'd welcomed Eleanor into the fold and trusted her with one of the clan's most important endeavors.

Running the paranormal program put her in charge of finding new Dormants.

"I'm confused." Sofia looked at Eleanor. "What did you do?"

Eleanor shook her head. "My case is different from yours, but it gives me perspective. I can put myself in both your shoes because I've been on both sides." She looked at Marcel. "I had a bad history that made me bitter, mistrustful, and selfish. I thought that the whole world was against me and that the best way to deal with it was to be a solo operator and look out for myself." She turned to Sofia. "I plotted to capture paranormals and sell them to the highest bidder. When I was captured, I became part of this organization not because they wanted me, but because they were stuck with me. I was a compeller with no morals, and it was dangerous to let me go. Most regarded me as the enemy, and rightfully so, and at the beginning, I resolved to learn all I could about them so I could find a way to escape or even profit from the situation. But then I had an epiphany, which was prompted by the kindness and selflessness of a person who had the least reason to be nice to me. I also realized that for the first time in my life, I was surrounded by other people who were like me, and even though most were hostile to me, I could see myself finally belonging somewhere. I set out to prove myself and become an asset to the community, and that's what I did. Some still look at me with hostility in their eyes, but most have accepted me."

Sofia shook her head. "I didn't set out to do anything bad or good to any of you. I was forced into the role."

"I know." Eleanor reached over the table and took her hand. "Which should make your assimilation much easier than mine. The advice I can give you is to not give up. You escaped a bad situation, and if you play your cards right, you can join us and start a new life. I didn't leave anyone behind, so that wasn't an issue like it is for you, but you basically don't have a choice. You're not going back, so I suggest that you embrace what fate has given you."

Sofia cast a quick sidelong glance at Marcel. "It's not all up to me."

"That's why I delivered my little speech to both of you." Eleanor pushed to her feet. "I'll leave you alone to talk it out." She lifted her hand and pointed a finger at Marcel. "My advice to you is the same. Rise above the past, embrace what fate has shoved in your face, and say thank you."

With that, Eleanor walked around the table and started up the stairs.

They both remained silent until the door at the top of the stairs opened and closed.

"She's a very opinionated lady," Sofia said. "What's her story?"

"She told you the gist of it. I can't say more without revealing details that I shouldn't."

"Who am I going to tell? She can compel me to silence."

"True." He got to his feet and walked over to the wine cabinet. "It's difficult for me to trust, and even more difficult to give my heart. I've been made a fool before." He pulled a bottle of Chardonnay and two glasses out of the cabinet.

"You told me about your ex."

"I didn't tell you even a fraction of the story."

"Is that also a secret that you are not free to share?"

He huffed out a breath. "Revealing this secret will only affect me. It has no bearing on the organization." He uncorked the wine and poured it into their glasses.

He needed a moment to think, or an hour, or a day, but Sofia was looking at him with a pair of pleading eyes, and he felt compelled to give her something. Instead, he lifted his glass. "Cheers."

"Cheers." She clinked her glass to his. "I promise that whatever you tell me will never leave my lips." She cringed. "Unless someone compels it out of me. I really dislike compellers, or rather what they can do. I like Eleanor a lot. She's such a straight shooter, and that's so refreshing."

Eleanor wasn't easily likable, and it had taken him a while to warm up to her. The shameful truth was that if she were a male, he would have accepted her abrasive personality a long time ago and focused on her impressive achievement record instead. But because she was a female, he'd expected her to be softer, kinder, and more careful about the way she expressed herself.

Talk about a double standard.

It dawned on him that he was applying the same double standard to Sofia. If she were a guy, he would have been much more forgiving and understanding, but because she was a female, and he had a bad history with women, she was a suspect despite the mitigating circumstances.

Nevertheless, being aware of his prejudice didn't help dissolve it. He didn't trust himself to think objectively where a female he was attracted to was concerned.

He put the glass down. "I want to believe you. I yearn to, but I've been burned so badly in the past that it's very difficult for me to trust. I haven't told this story to anyone, and I probably never will."

Sofia's face fell. "I understand. You don't need to tell me if you don't feel comfortable sharing your past with me." She looked up at him. "Would it help if I told you more about my own life?"

"Yes, please."

"Not all of it was bad. In fact, most of it was good."

SOFIA

*S*ofia talked for what seemed like hours.

She told Marcel about her childhood growing up in the compound, about being raised by her father and her aunts, about her cousins and things they'd done together. Most of her stories included Helmi, and talking about her cousin had brought both a smile to her lips and tears to her eyes. The memories were mostly sweet, but knowing that she wouldn't have any more of them made her want to crawl into bed and cry until she fell asleep from exhaustion.

"I'd better talk about something else." She rubbed her eyes. "The university is a safer topic." She let out a breath. "I was so excited to get selected. It was a little scary to live outside the compound but not enough for me to turn the offer down." She chuckled. "Not that I had the option to say no. Igor's word is law. Thanks to my father and my aunts, I was fluent in Finnish, so language wasn't a barrier, and after the first semester, I felt at home there."

"But you still had to return to the compound once a month."

"I did, but it was no hardship. I wanted to see my family and friends, and the twenty minutes in Igor's office to reinforce his compulsion was a small price to pay."

"What about boyfriends? I'm sure you had many during your seven years at the university."

He hadn't told her about his girlfriends, so she wasn't inclined to tell him about her love life, but she didn't want to flat out refuse either.

"I dated a little, and I had a total of two serious boyfriends."

"What happened with them?" Marcel asked.

She caught his eyes glowing again and wondered what emotion had triggered the glow. He still refused to admit that they did that, but she'd noticed it was usually when he was excited, angry, or aroused.

"There isn't much to tell. It was difficult to develop meaningful relationships with guys when I couldn't tell them anything about my family or introduce them to my parents."

"You could have said that you were an orphan."

"Then they would have wanted to meet my adoptive parents. I said that I was estranged from my family and didn't provide a reason, but I don't think they believed me. They probably thought that I was embarrassed about them." She emptied her glass of wine and sighed. "It doesn't matter. I couldn't maintain those relationships anyway. At some point, I had to go back to live in the compound, and it wasn't as if I could bring someone with me."

"Yeah, I get it. It's the same in our community."

Sofia arched a brow. "No paranormal talent means no admission?"

"Something like that." Marcel refilled her glass.

They were on their second bottle of wine, and she was tipsy, bordering on drunk. Marcel seemed much more at ease and relaxed. Maybe it was because of the wine, or perhaps it was because her stories had entertained him. In either case, she liked seeing him smiling for a change.

"How did your father and aunts get to be in the compound?" he asked.

"They couldn't tell me. People never talked about their pasts before arriving at the compound, and as a kid, I thought that they were all just born there like me. Later, when I became aware that the rest of the world didn't know about the Kra-ell or live in blended communities with aliens, I started to wonder where the humans came from, and given that they were more or less slaves, I figured that they were captured and brought in against their will. I imagine that it started with the women." She grimaced. "The purebloods needed breeders because there weren't enough of them to provide genetic variety."

"You said that your father speaks fluent Finnish. He might have been brought from the outside."

She shook her head. "Not necessarily. My grandmother also lived in the compound, so she might have been the first to be brought in, or she might have been born in there as well. She died before I was born. They don't have a doctor for the humans in the compound, only a nurse, so if someone suffers a heart attack, they are not likely to survive."

"What about when they get sick?"

"For routine non-emergency stuff, they take people to a human doctor and compel their help."

"That's better than nothing."

"I know. The Kra-ell treat the humans they keep better than other humans would have treated their captives, and the Kra-ell are not kind-hearted creatures. They are brutal, and they don't believe in love. But they have a code of honor that they take very seriously."

Marcel chuckled. "According to their tradition, or maybe religion, Igor's community is an affront to the Goddess. Her chosen are females, and they are the ones who are supposed to be in charge of breeding. Not the males. The females' job is to select the best males to father the next generation, and I bet they use several criteria to determine who's the best. It's actually a better system. Males tend to be visual, and they choose the mothers of their children based primarily on their looks and level of attractiveness. If they focused on her intelligence, her drive to succeed, and her kindness and empathy, they might have produced a better next generation. I wonder if that's why the Kra-ell religion came up with the idea of giving females all the power. After all, life is about producing the best next generation."

"The Mother of All Life holds all of her children precious." Sofia smiled. "Until I got to the university, I didn't know how prevalent Christianity was. I read about it in books during my studies, but since everyone in the compound revered the Mother, I never gave it much thought. It occurred to me later that Igor must have compelled the humans to abandon their original religion in favor of the Mother."

"So, you were home-schooled?"

"I studied in the compound. We had a school for the children, and we got books and everything else we needed. Naturally, I got a fake high school diploma to get accepted into the university, but I had all the education I needed." She winced. "Except for everything that had to do with computers, but I wasn't the only one. There were other students who came from poor villages that didn't have free access to technology."

"I know that the compound has access to the internet."

"Igor and the others in charge have access. Jade probably got special permission because she teaches the Kra-ell children and needs to obtain new material from time to time."

"I'm surprised that she chose to be a teacher. She doesn't strike me as the nurturing type."

Sofia sighed. "I thought so too, but she has a soft spot for the little ones. I can't think of her without being overcome with sadness. She is so brave to keep on going despite what happened to her. It never occurred to me before that some of the Kra-ell also had been brought to the compound against their will. I did wonder, though, about the discrepancy between the ratio of boys and girls born to the purebloods and the ratio of adults. I thought that they were getting rid of the boys somehow." She shivered. "I don't know what's worse. What they actually did, or what I imagined."

"You have a good heart, Sofia." Marcel leaned toward her and kissed her forehead. "You are a good person."

"Do you really believe that? Or are you just saying it to cheer me up?"

He smiled. "I know that I'm not the best judge of character. You'd be surprised to know that my natural inclination is to see the good in people, but since that tendency has cost me dearly in the past, I'm very careful before I make up my mind about a person's character. Still, unless you are the best actress ever born, everything you've told me indicates that you are a good person despite having a lousy mother and growing up in an alien community. Your father and your aunts must be terrific to compensate for your mother's neglect and indifference."

"They are." Hot tears accumulated in the corners of her eyes. "I miss them so much."

39

MARCEL

*a*s Sofia's eyes misted with tears, the last of Marcel's resistance crumbled. She'd been so animated in her story of growing up among the Kra-ell and having a happy childhood despite living in captivity that he couldn't conceive of it being fake. He wanted to meet her father and tell him that he had done a great job, and that he should be proud of the daughter he'd raised.

But what right did he have to tell the man anything?

Could he promise him that from now on his amazing daughter would be taken care of? That he would protect her? Love her unconditionally?

Fates, how Marcel yearned for that to be so.

He wanted to embrace Sofia, to tell her that he had fallen for her as well, and to save her family so she wouldn't have to miss them. But he couldn't do that. He had no idea how to save her family, but he could love and protect her, provided that he managed to pull the stick out of his ass as Eleanor had so colorfully stated.

"Come here." He reached for her and pulled her into his arms. "You are safe now."

"Am I?" She looked at him with doe eyes.

"I will not let anything happen to you." He dipped his head and took her lips in a soft kiss. "And I promise to make it up to you for the sorrow I caused you."

"Am I forgiven?" she whispered against his mouth.

"You were never to blame. I'm sorry that it took me so long to realize that."

She chuckled on a sob. "It wasn't long. It just felt like an eternity."

"Am I forgiven?" he asked.

"I was never angry at you." She scrunched her nose. "Well, that's not true. I was angry, but I never hated you for how you were treating me because I can't turn off my feelings the way you do. I just couldn't understand how you could shut your emotions down on a dime like that. You knew that it wasn't my fault, that I was a victim in this as much as you were. I never stopped yearning for you, wanting you to look at me with the same fondness and desire you did before." She gave him a sad smile. "Some women are attracted to brooding unemotional guys, but that's not me. I don't find it attractive or sexy. I find it off-putting. I need warmth and affection."

"I didn't turn off my feelings. I just buried them to protect my heart, but the only things I was protecting it from were my own fears and insecurities. Deep down, I knew that you didn't set out to use me."

She winced. "I did, but not really. Valstar and Igor wanted me to find a man who worked in the retreat and seduce him for information. When you started flirting with me, I convinced myself that it could be you, even though I had no reason to believe that you had any useful information. You told me that you were not part of the staff and that you were working on an independent project. When you acted like a jerk, I made plans to seduce one of the teachers. But I wanted you, so when you pleaded with me to forgive you, I decided to play along. I gave myself a great excuse to seduce you so quickly. Usually, I don't move so fast. I take my time getting to know a guy before I get intimate with him." She smiled. "Not that I regret it even for one moment. It was the best night of my life."

And didn't that make Marcel feel like he'd just grown a couple of inches. His knee-jerk reflex was to scent her emotions to make sure she meant it, but the scent of her arousal was all the confirmation he needed.

"Was it now?" He cupped the back of her head. "Do you want to give it another go to make sure?"

"Are you offering?"

"What does it look like?"

"Do you always answer a question with another question?"

He loved to see her spunk and humor come back.

Sofia was a positive person by nature, the glass-half-full type, and if not for him giving her the cold shoulder, she would have weathered her ordeal better. Instead of being the rock of support she'd needed, he'd added to her sorrow and anxiety.

"Let's check out that four-poster and see what other goodies we can find in there. But this time, I'm tying you to the bed."

Her smile wilted. "I don't like those things. I've seen real implements of torture being used to punish Kra-ell who dared to step out of line, and it was horrible. I will never associate those things with anything pleasurable."

Talk about a cold shower.

"Then no restraints for you. I will just give you a little taste of the torment you inflicted on me. I will torture you with an abundance of pleasure."

Her smile returned. "I didn't say that about the restraints. Just about the flogger and the crop and whatever else is stored in that footboard."

"We don't need any of that." He pulled her into his arms, rose to his feet, and carried her to the bedroom. "I laundered the sheets, so we will have a fresh bed to play in."

It wasn't the most romantic thing to say, or the sexiest, but Sofia seemed to like it.

Wrapping her arms around his neck, she tilted her face up and kissed him. "That's very sweet of you. I love the smell of fresh bedding."

40

SOFIA

$\mathcal{A}$s Marcel walked with Sofia into the bedroom, he didn't head toward the bed as she'd expected. Instead, he carried her into the bathroom and set her down on the bench in the shower.

They'd done a long walk on the beach and back, so a shower wasn't a bad idea, but it wasn't her idea of sexy reconciliation.

What did she know, though?

Her experience was limited, not just in practice but even in general knowledge. The romance novels she read were tame and sweet, and nothing overly sexually adventurous happened in them. Most of the love scenes were the fade-to-black kind without any explicit details.

"What's your plan?" she asked as he knelt at her feet.

"I'm going to treat you to something special." He took one shoe and sock off, tossed them on the floor outside the shower, and repeated that with the other.

Fearing that her feet didn't smell all that fresh, Sofia's cheeks heated with embarrassment, and she pulled her feet away from him even though he didn't look as if he had smelled anything unpleasant. In fact, given the glow in his eyes, he was excited about what he was planning to do.

"You still didn't tell me why your eyes glow," she said to divert his attention from her feet.

"They glow when I get excited." He lifted onto his knees, pushed his thumbs into the elastic of her leggings, and pulled them down along with her panties, baring her from the waist down. "Now the top." He reached for the hem of her T-shirt and tugged it up, urging her to lift her arms.

When she did, he pulled it off and tossed it on top of the leggings. Her bra was unceremoniously taken off next, and before she knew what was going on, his mouth was on her nipple, licking, sucking, and making her mindless with pleasure. When he switched to the other one, all thoughts about glowing eyes on a human receded to the corner of her mind where she stored other unexplained mysteries that needed further investigation.

"I'm sorry. I just couldn't help myself." He smirked as he toed off his shoes.

As Marcel got undressed so fast that she couldn't track the movements, Sofia added that to the list of mysteries to investigate later. Right now, she was enthralled by the beauty of Marcel's male body.

She'd seen him naked before and had gotten very familiar with his manhood, but seeing it again, fully erect and standing straight from his hips right in front of her face, she couldn't help but reach for it and give it a kiss hello.

With a groan, Marcel pulled away. "Save the thought." He reached for the hand-held shower head and turned the faucet on.

After checking that the water was the right temperature, he offered Sofia a hand up and pulled her against his body. "Have you ever made love in the shower?"

"I haven't. Have you?"

"No." He grinned. "It's going to be the first time for both of us, which means that it's going to be clumsy and awkward but fun nonetheless."

She wrapped her arms around his neck. "I like having firsts with you." She pressed her aching nipples to his chest and lifted her thigh between his legs, rubbing it against his erection.

"Wicked woman." He cupped her ass and dipped his long fingers into the seam, testing her wetness.

She loved that his hand was so big that it covered her entire backside. She was a tall woman, and his size made her feel feminine and dainty.

Gyrating her hips to get more of those dexterous fingers, she lifted her leg and wound it around his torso.

He brushed his lips against hers with soft velvety touches, teasing her before licking into her mouth and taking possession of it. As he dipped two fingers into her wetness, pumping into her in sync with his tongue, she closed her eyes and moaned.

"Marcel," she breathed when he let go of her mouth. "Take me to bed."

"Not yet." He turned her around and pressed her against the tiled wall. "Put your hands on the wall above your head and spread your legs."

As she followed his command, a new gush of wetness prepared her for what was coming next.

"Are your eyes closed?" He pressed his hard body into her from behind.

"Yes."

"Keep them closed. If you open them, I'll punish you."

A smile tugged on the corners of her lips. "How?"

"Like this." He pulled back and lightly smacked her bottom.

It was oddly arousing.

"Is that supposed to be a threat?" She was tempted to open her eyes and taunt him to do it once more.

He smacked her bottom again, harder this time.

She laughed. "That's not a threat either."

"We shall see about that."

He didn't do it again. Instead, she felt the head of his erection nudging her entrance, and as she pushed back, he entered her with one swift thrust.

There was a moment of discomfort as her sheath stretched to adjust to his size, but it was over almost as soon as it began, and then she couldn't wait for him to start moving.

"Marcel," she whispered his name.

He didn't move.

Brushing her hair aside, he kissed her neck, and when she pushed against him again, he rocked in and out of her in shallow thrusts.

"Please," she groaned. "I need more."

41

MARCEL

$\mathcal{M}$arcel was more than happy to oblige Sofia's plea, but making love in the shower had its limitations. He needed to be face-to-face with her, to see the lust and desire in her eyes, to kiss her deeply and pour his soul into hers.

There were also practical considerations.

Sofia was lithe and strong, but she was human, and with his passion awakened after being forcefully suppressed, he didn't know how gentle he'd manage to be, and pounding into her from behind while she was pressed against the tiled wall might get uncomfortable or even dangerous for her.

As he pulled out, she chased his retreating erection by arching back, but as he spun her around and lifted her into his arms, she wrapped her arms around his neck and smiled. "Where are you taking me?"

"Where you wanted to go before. To bed."

"We are wet," she protested as he lay on top of the covers with her on top of him.

He smiled. "I know. You said that you needed more. Take it."

Her puzzlement lasted a split second, and then she was straddling his hips. "Are you mine for the taking?"

"Always."

As doubt flitted through her eyes, he wondered whether it had to do with his attitude toward her during the past twenty-four hours or with him withholding his story about his life-altering experience.

If it was the first, he could fix it, but if it was the latter, it would remain untold.

Marcel feared that once Sofia learned what kind of a man he really was, her attitude toward him would change and never recover. She might not want him anymore.

When she angled his erection toward her entrance and started to lower herself on top of his shaft, all thoughts of the past receded to the corner of his mind where he usually kept them locked up tight, and when the tip breached her entrance, he gripped her hips and helped guide her, but didn't attempt to control her movements.

It was her show, and he was there for the ride.

The perfection of their fit was enough to chase the last vestiges of those terrible memories away, and he gave himself over to the marvelous creature riding him like a prize bull.

Sofia was gentle, keeping her rhythm slow and rocking side to side on each downward glide.

He loved that she wasn't in a rush to bring them both to completion. They were soaking in the intimacy, the closeness that was so much more than just sexual pleasure. With her, it was about love, about the connection, and the pleasure was a side effect rather than the goal.

Love, though?

Was he falling again into the same trap?

He shouldn't be thinking in terms of love until at least a year had passed, and Sofia had proven herself to him beyond a shadow of a doubt.

Except, there would always be doubt, wouldn't there?

As the saying went, once burned, twice shy. For now, he would just stick to liking her and lusting after her.

"Sofia," he murmured as his climax neared, his fingers digging into the soft flesh of her hips.

She slowed down even more. "Not yet. I want this to last."

Marcel wanted to smile, but his fangs were already elongated, and he didn't want to thrall her yet. "There are many more to come." He let go of one of her hips and reached between their bodies to gently tease her clit.

"Cheater," she breathed as she undulated on top of him. "That's not fair."

"All is fair in love and war." He kept circling the engorged nub while urging her with his other hand to keep moving.

When she closed her eyes and threw her head back, he kept going with his thumb and rocking up into her to prolong her climax, and when her tremors subsided, he wrapped his arms around her and flipped them around.

"I told you that there was more." He gripped her hands and pulled her arms over her head.

"Yes." She smiled up at him. "Give it to me."

"Yes, ma'am."

His own climax was hovering near the edge, and the need to pound into her was overwhelming, but the need to prolong the closeness and look into her eyes was even greater. Once he bit her, she would black out, and then he would lose the connection to her soul and would have to be satisfied with just holding her body until she floated back down.

He wasn't ready for that.

"Your eyes are glowing," she murmured.

336

He'd forgotten about that, but he was loath to command her to close her eyes. He couldn't get enough of looking into their blue depths.

It was time to tell her about himself, so he would no longer have to hide his fangs and his eyes, but he could never tell her everything.

"It's nothing. Ignore it." Reluctantly, he just closed his own eyes.

42

SOFIA

*A*s Marcel closed his eyes, Sofia mourned the loss of the window into his soul.

He wasn't a normal human. He had paranormal talents, so maybe somewhere down his ancestral line there had been a Kra-ell. Then again, his ability to make her forget things or remember things that had never happened wasn't one of theirs. They were compellers, some weak, some strong, but as far as she knew, none of them could erase memories or plant new ones in human minds.

That must have come from his human genes.

As her pleasure surged again, bringing her to the verge of climax, thoughts of genetics and the mystery of glowing eyes were forgotten, and all she could focus on was the male thrusting into her, and how good it felt to be in his arms.

Sofia had never enjoyed ceding control, and given the precarious situation she was in, that wasn't the wisest thing to do, but somehow, despite everything, she trusted Marcel like she'd never trusted any other man.

He would never hurt her, not intentionally anyway.

In the short time they'd known each other, he'd repeatedly hurt her feelings, but he hadn't set out to do that. He was just inept romantically, and he'd been hurt in the past, so he was being careful.

Was she making excuses for him?

Maybe, but having him hold her arms over her head and thrust into her like he was a sex god with boundless stamina felt too good to question.

When his thrusts became furious, and the bed groaned in protest under them, the tightly wound coil inside of her got released without warning, and as she cried out her climax, she instinctively turned her head to the side, exposing her neck.

On some subconscious level, she knew what was about to happen next, but when the pain from twin incisions registered, it was a shock nonetheless.

She cried out, and her eyes popped open, but all she could see was the top of

Marcel's blond head, and then the pain disappeared as if it had never been, and she was orgasming so hard that she felt like passing out from the pleasure.

The euphoria washing over her stole her breath away, and she felt as if she had died and her spirit had left her body.

She was weightless, soaring up over the clouds, and as she looked down, she saw all kinds of ethereal creatures roaming around an idyllic landscape. Beautiful and insubstantial, they looked up at her, acknowledging her passing through their world by smiling and waving.

Were they real?

Had she passed through the veil separating different realities? Or was she in the human heaven?

Those weren't the fields of the brave or the valley of the shamed, and there was no Kra-ell in sight. Was it a near-death experience? Or had she died from too much pleasure, her heart giving out?

The floating, peaceful feeling was too extraordinary to waste on wondering the why and the how of it. Instead, she let go of her earthly concerns, and let herself forget all that she had been told about the human God and the Kra-ell Mother of All Life.

Soaking up the sensations, she was at peace with the universe.

43

SYSSI

"How do I look?" Kian walked into the family room wearing a charcoal suit.

He looked like a god, and if they weren't expecting Amanda, Dalhu, and Vivian to arrive in a few moments, Syssi would have shown him how good she thought he looked.

"You look dashing, my love."

"Da-da," Allegra said in confirmation.

"Your daughter agrees." She kissed her sweet cheeks, twice on each side, but on the third pass, Allegra pushed her away.

"That's it? That's my quota of kisses?"

"Da-da." Allegra lifted her arms, making it clear who she wanted kisses from.

Syssi laughed. "She's her daddy's girl."

Kian lifted their daughter and spun her in the air, eliciting a string of adorable giggles. "That's because I do fun stuff with her."

Syssi shook her head. "It's dangerous. She's still human."

The smile slid off Kian's face, and he hugged Allegra to him. "She should spend more time with my mother."

"She's still too young to transition."

As the doorbell rang, Syssi walked over to open the door.

"Good evening, darling." Amanda leaned to kiss the air next to Syssi's cheek. "I don't want to leave lipstick stains on you."

"You look amazing." Since Syssi hadn't put on any, her lips actually made contact with Amanda's cheek.

"Careful of the makeup." Amanda tilted her head back, avoiding the second kiss coming her way.

"Sorry." Syssi backed away.

Amanda gave her a once-over. "You look stunning yourself."

Syssi looked down at her pale blue cocktail dress. "I love getting dressed without worrying about food stains for a change."

"Good evening." Dalhu pushed the stroller through the doorway, looking dashing in a navy suit. "I can't say the same. I mean about getting dressed for fancy dinners. Most of my clothing is covered in paint stains."

Amanda laughed. "Stuffing Dalhu into a suit was not an easy task. He only did it because he loves me and because I insisted that he couldn't attend Callie's opening night in a pair of jeans and a paint-stained T-shirt."

"I wasn't going to wear a T-shirt. I was going to wear one of those ridiculously expensive dress shirts you got me."

Amanda waved a dismissive hand and walked over to Kian and Allegra, treating each to an air kiss.

When the doorbell rang again, Okidu beat Syssi to the door and opened it for Vivian. "Good evening, mistress. Thank you for coming to watch over the little ones."

Was it Syssi's imagination, or did he sound hurt?

He was perfectly capable of babysitting both babies, but Syssi and Amanda still didn't feel a hundred percent confident leaving him with their daughters. Not because of safety concerns, but because Vivian was so much better qualified for the job, and she didn't mind doing it. In fact, she was jubilant every time she was asked to watch the girls, not that it happened often.

Okidu was there in case Vivian needed help.

"I'm happy to do it." Vivian walked over to the stroller and picked up Evie, who cooed happily at her. "Hello, beautiful people. You all look like models on a cover of a fashion magazine."

"Thank you." Amanda leaned and kissed the air next to both of Vivian's cheeks. "I'm looking forward to my first gourmet meal in the village."

When Okidu cleared his throat, Amanda lifted her hand. "In a fancy restaurant, darling. I adore your cooking. You know that."

That seemed to mollify him.

"Shall we?" Kian put Allegra down on her play mat.

"Da-da?" She looked at him with questioning eyes.

"Dada and Mommy are going to Aunt Callie's new restaurant, and you are going to have fun with Aunt Vivian and Evie until we come back."

Allegra cast Evie a resigned glance and then looked at Vivian and smiled. "Da-da," she said, making it sound like *okay, you can stay.*

"It's amazing how well she can express herself just by changing her tone." Kian straightened his tie. "Thank you, Vivian. Call us if they give you any trouble."

"They won't." Vivian sat on the floor next to Allegra. "They are both wonderful little girls."

"It's a little chilly outside." Okidu handed Syssi a shawl as she stepped out the door.

"Thank you." She draped it around her shoulders.

The restaurant was only a few minutes' walk away, and the warmth coming off Kian's body as he wrapped his arm around her was enough to keep the chill away, but the shawl complemented her dress and made her feel more dressed up.

"How many people did Callie invite to her opening night?" Dalhu asked.

"Thirty-six," Syssi said. "She can't handle more than that until she can get more people to work for her. For the opening night, she invited the council members and their mates, Toven and Mia, and Jackie and Kalugal."

"Are they coming?" Dalhu asked. "I was told that they were isolating themselves to protect the baby."

"Bridget talked some sense into Kalugal," Kian said. "She told him that they were doing the baby a huge disservice by isolating him from human germs. Darius will remain human until puberty, and they can't keep him in a bubble until he transitions. They need to expose him to germs so he can build up his immune system. Once his human body is infected by a specific virus, it will learn how to make antibodies to fight it. The next time he's exposed to the same virus, his body will fight it off without getting infected."

"I hope he listened," Syssi said. "I spoke with Jacki yesterday, and she wasn't sure whether they were coming."

"Who is babysitting for them?" Amanda asked.

"Shamash." Kian chuckled. "I have no idea what the guy knows about babies, but if Kalugal trusts him with his son, who am I to say anything?"

44

KIAN

"Welcome." Callie looked nervous as she addressed the small gathering. "Thank you for being my first guests. I hope you enjoy tonight's menu."

They were all seated in individual two-person tables, which felt weird given how well they all knew each other. Callie had designed her restaurant for romantic evenings, but the opening night was different, and Kian had the urge to get up and start combining the small rectangular tables into one long banquet table.

"Say hello to your servers." She motioned for Lisa, Parker, and Cheryl to come forward. "I'm glad that they agreed to work in my restaurant in the evenings and save me from having to do everything myself."

The three took a coordinated bow that elicited a few chuckles and some applause.

"As I explained in the invitation, the menu for tonight is set. It's a five-course meal." She looked at Kian. "Your, Syssi, and Amanda's menus are slightly different to accommodate your vegan and vegetarian preferences."

Amanda chuckled. "The problem kids."

"I can't wait to sample your cooking," Onegus said. "I've heard so much about it."

"Good things, I hope."

"The best." Cassandra adjusted her napkin over her lap.

Annani rose to her feet. "Congratulations on your new restaurant, Callie. I would like to make just one suggestion for tonight." She put her hand on Brandon's shoulder. As the only two singles, they were seated together at the same table. "As much as I love your company, I would love to enjoy everyone's. Can we combine the tables?"

"Great idea." Kian jumped to his feet. "I was thinking the same thing."

As everyone rose to their feet and started moving the tables together, Callie wrung her hands. "I'm sorry. I should have realized that the regular setup wouldn't work tonight. I just wanted everyone to enjoy the place as I envisioned it."

"It looks beautiful." Annani smiled. "Tomorrow night is the couples' mixer, correct?"

Callie nodded.

"They will surely appreciate the intimate setting," Annani said. "When we are done tonight, the boys will return everything back to the way it was."

When the eighteen tables were set in one long row and they had all sat back down, the young servers brought out the appetizer course.

Anandur did the honors of uncorking the champagne bottles and pouring the bubbly into everyone's flutes. "Let's make a toast." He lifted his glass. "To Callie's place. May it succeed and prosper."

"To Callie's!" they all echoed, filling the room with clinking sounds.

As Callie and Brundar sat down, she unfurled the napkin and draped it over her knees. "The advantage of preparing everything in advance is that I can sit with you and enjoy my creations. I wish I had the staff to do everything, though, so I could offer a selection of items like a regular restaurant."

"I offered a solution for that," Turner said. "But Kian didn't like it."

"What's your solution?" Bhathian asked.

"You have a mighty workforce buried in the catacombs, and now that several strong compellers have joined the clan, we can resurrect them and compel them to behave. I think no one here has any objection to using them as a slave workforce. They owe the clan for their actions against it, and for not executing them but putting them in stasis instead. They should be grateful to be allowed to live again."

For a long moment no one said a thing, not even Annani, who Kian had no doubt loved Turner's crazy idea.

"I don't know about that," Anandur said. "The Doomers we captured and put in stasis were murderers and rapists. They weren't like Dalhu or like Kalugal's men." He looked at Kalugal. "What do you think?"

Kalugal put his fork down. "I wouldn't do that. I selected my men one by one, and it wasn't an easy task to find males who were not completely corrupted by my father and who retained a shred of decency. After I relieved them from his compulsion, I worked with them for months, sometimes years, to undo his indoctrination." He sighed. "Don't forget that the human males Navuh used to breed with the Dormants were ruthless, dumb lowlifes. He chose the strongest, the most brutal, and the most mentally limited. His goal was to produce powerful immortal warriors who would obey him blindly. Occasionally, the mothers' genetics triumphed and produced thinking, decent offspring, but since the mothers themselves were the daughters of lowlifes, most of them weren't nice people either." He cast a sidelong glance at Bridget. "Nature trumps nurture, and nurture in Navuh's war camps was even worse than the genetic makeup of those males. I doubt you would find even ten percent of them are worth saving."

"Ten percent is more than zero," Annani said. "Even if one of them is worth saving, we should not dismiss it. I wish we could design a test that could determine that. We talked about it before. We could resurrect a small number of Doomers at a time, test them, and put back in stasis those who failed."

Kian gave her an indulgent smile. "As soon as we have nothing better to do, and no new crisis comes up for a year or two, we can give it a test run."

Yamanu laughed. "That's like saying never. I can't remember any stretch of time that was longer than a few months without something happening that required us to mobilize some kind of defense or evasive tactics, and most of the time, it wasn't even the Doomers' fault."

"Now we have a new enemy to add to the mix," Onegus said. "Or a potential enemy. It still remains to be seen whether Igor of the Kra-ell is our enemy or just a general threat we should be aware of but not actively try to eliminate."

45

ANNANI

"That's another reason to use the Doomers," Turner said. "The enemy of my enemy is my friend."

Kian chuckled. "It is true that the Kra-ell might pose a threat to the Doomers as well, but since the Doomers are a much bigger force, they have nothing to worry about from the Kra-ell."

"We don't know that," Turner said. "In pure numbers, you might be right, but we still don't know anything about them. Who knows, maybe they will become our allies against the Doomers."

The dinner was turning into a council meeting, and Callie was probably not happy about that, but since she had chosen to invite the leadership of the clan to her opening night, she should have expected it.

"What is being done in that regard?" Annani asked.

Kian pushed away his empty appetizer plate, which Cheryl rushed to collect. "Turner's contractor on the ground is procuring a miniature drone to fly over the compound, and Monday, we are sending a team of Guardians to Russia to scope the area. Their mission is just to observe. Sofia says that the purebloods and the hybrids go hunting in the area, but since they are all under strong compulsion not to attempt an escape and have location collars around their necks, we can't just grab them." He looked at Toven. "Given your experience with Sofia, do you think you can release them from the compulsion via video call?"

Toven pursed his lips. "Perhaps with Mia's help. Frankly, I didn't expect her enhancement to be so significant, but once she added her power to mine, it became much easier to override Igor's compulsion, and it was also easier on Sofia. When I used just my own power, she got a severe headache and needed to rest before we could continue."

"Go, Mia," Amanda said. "I know you will be a great asset to the clan."

Mia blushed. "I wish I knew what I was doing and how."

346

"Do you need someone to blow things up?" Cassandra asked. "I've gotten much better at that, both in accuracy and power." She smiled. "My type of explosives won't alert airport security."

Onegus wrapped his arm around her shoulders. "We can use conventional explosives if needed. It's not difficult to smuggle them in or even obtain them locally. In Russia, money talks louder than anything. We don't even need to use compulsion or thralling."

Edna sighed. "How the world has changed, and at the same time, it hasn't. No matter what the political regime is about, it's always about money. Communists, fascists, dictators, monarchs, autocrats, you name it, they are all after wealth and power, and the people they govern are fed fantasies and lies about ideals and morals to keep them compliant, or they are terrorized into toeing the line. Regrettably, we see the same thing happening in democracies, which used to be a little better before they adopted similar tactics of mass control."

As the soup was served, the political talk thankfully moved on to Callie's culinary skills, and the atmosphere lightened.

"This is the best butternut squash soup I've ever had." Syssi scraped the last drops off her bowl. "Would it be too presumptuous of me to ask what's the secret?"

Callie put her spoon down. "You have to bake the butternut squash first, along with carrots and sweet potatoes, and the ratio between the vegetables is critical. I keep adding them in small quantities until I get the right taste."

"Don't you follow a recipe?" Kaia asked. "Like one of each?"

"You can't do that because you never know how flavorful the particular vegetable you are working with is. As a general rule, I use one sweet potato and one carrot for each medium-sized squash, but if you want the flavor to be just right, you need to keep tasting."

Annani listened to the back and forth about cooking methods with a smile on her face, but her mind was somewhere else.

Turner was onto something with his idea about resurrecting the Doomers and using them to benefit the clan. They were a neglected asset. The problem was that compulsion was not enough to change them from the inside out.

Was it possible to turn murderers and rapists into good people?

Given Wonder's transformation, maybe it was. Gulan had been a timid girl who had hated her size and her physical strength. She had been raised as a servant, and if not for Esag breaking her heart, she would have never run away. She would have lived out her life as a servant without ever thinking that there was anything more she could do.

The woman who had awoken thousands of years later was a different person. Not an ounce of servitude had remained in her, and she could not even stand her old name because it reminded her that she used to be a servant. She was a warrior, if a reluctant one, but she had used her strength to save herself and other innocents.

Gulan had been the product of her upbringing. Wonder was the woman she had been born to be.

Then again, Gulan's parents had not been monsters like the fathers of those

347

Doomers. But who was to say that those fathers had been born like that? Maybe they had become monsters because of the way they had been brought up?

Biology and genetics were complicated fields that Annani understood only superficially, but what if what was encoded was not only what was inherited from the parents but also one's life experience? Was it possible to reprogram that somehow?

Her eyes shifted to Kaia.

Fate had sent the girl to the clan for a reason, and it might not only be to provide William with a wonderful life companion or to decipher Okidu's journals. Her unique set of skills and her sharp mind made her the perfect person to figure out how to reprogram genetic behavior anomalies, especially since she had all the time she needed to explore and test her ideas.

Kaia did not suffer from humanity's biggest limitation, which was time.

46

DARLENE

"*D*o you want to go to your auntie?" Karen handed Darlene one of the twins.

She still couldn't tell them apart. To her, they looked identical, but she could get away with it by calling them sweetie, honey, or handsome baby boy.

"I'm heading out tomorrow." Gilbert bounced Idina on his knee as if she was a baby, but she didn't seem to mind. "I wanted to fly out, but Kian suggested that I take a moving van with a couple of Guardians to help me pack, and I took him up on his offer."

"Which ones?" Eric asked.

"I forgot their names. Max brought them over and introduced us. One of them is going to rent the van, and the other one will drive me to the rental place, and we will continue from there. I figured that driving over wouldn't make my trip that much longer than flying."

Darlene tensed at the mention of Max's name. Tomorrow was the Guardian's day off, and they'd made plans to give Eric's idea a try. She'd gone over the scenario in her head a thousand times already, and she still wasn't comfortable with it even though Max's role would be minimal.

She would wear a modest, voluminous nightgown, and she would be on top of Eric with it covering everything so he couldn't see anything, but it still freaked her out and not only because she was about to get bitten for the first time, and not by Eric.

For some reason, having Eric bite her scared her less than getting bitten by Max. She loved Eric, and he loved her back, and anything that happened between them was done with love and care. Having Max at her throat would feel like a violation despite her agreeing to it, and despite him doing them a favor.

It was silly.

So many women who were in a loving relationship got artificially inseminated, and it wasn't to save their lives, but to have the incredible joy of having a child with their partner. The only difference was that instead of having it done at a clinic, she was going to do it in the privacy of her bedroom, with the donor administering the donated venom himself.

"The drive is about six hours long," Eric said. "Between driving to the airport, going through security, and then driving from the airport there, it would have taken you three hours or so. That's half the time it'll take for the ride, but you will gain the help of two guys who can work like machines to help you pack and load the van."

"I know," Gilbert said. "That's why I accepted Kian's offer."

Darlene suspected that Kian had suggested the arrangement because he wanted Gilbert monitored. Given that his family was staying behind in the village, the precaution was unnecessary, but Kian was a little paranoid.

Or a lot.

"Are you coming back with them?" she asked.

"They're driving the van back the next day. I need to stay longer to prepare the house for rental and to visit my job sites. I'll probably be back on Friday." He looked at Karen. "Sooner if I can help it."

"I wish I could come with you," Eric said.

Surprised, Darlene arched a brow at him. Had he forgotten their plans for tomorrow?

"You can come if you want to," Gilbert said.

Eric sighed dramatically. "I'm still too weak to help you pack. Besides, Darlene will miss me too much." He winked at her.

Gilbert nodded. "That's okay. I prefer that you stay in case Karen needs help with the kids. Cheryl got a part-time job at Callie's restaurant, so she won't be much help, and Kaia has her hands full with the research."

"Did you make reservations at Callie's?" Karen asked Gilbert.

He shook his head. "I checked the waiting list on the clan's virtual bulletin board, and it looked like the entire clan, including Kalugal's men, are on that list. She can only handle forty guests at a time, so it will be a while before she has an opening."

Karen gave him an incredulous look. "Then you should have put our names down before everyone signs up for a second round." She picked her tablet off the coffee table. "I'll do it right now." She cast a glance at Darlene. "How about you? Are you and Eric on the waiting list?"

"We are. We have reservations for Wednesday two weeks from now."

Eric regarded her with a conspiratorial smirk. "If for some reason we can't make it, we can give our reservation to Karen and Gilbert."

"Why wouldn't you be able to make it?" Karen asked.

"Oh, I don't know. Darlene might come down with something. After all, she's still human."

47

MARCEL

*A*s Marcel lay awake, savoring the feel of Sofia's warm body in his arms, he tried to remember if he had ever felt like that toward the woman he'd thought he loved all those years ago. Had it felt so right, so good?

He couldn't recall. The anger and guilt had long ago erased any tender feelings he could have had for her. He remembered the lust, his obsession with her, his need to be near her, but her closeness had never brought him peace. He was sure about that. Being with Cordelia had been turbulent, exciting, excruciating. He'd had to work so hard to gain her affection, and in retrospect, he knew that he never had. She'd been with him because he'd been a tool she'd wanted to use, and she'd wielded him like a mindless weapon.

No, not mindless.

Eager to please, eager to do anything that would make her welcome him into her arms and give him what he'd thought was love.

She'd never loved him. She'd been a sociopath incapable of love, a master manipulator who'd used her beauty and her fake charm to enthrall him as surely as if she'd entered his mind and thralled him as an immortal would.

She'd been a human with an evil mind.

But the truth was that his anger was mostly directed at himself. He could have walked away, he should have realized that she'd been manipulating him, but at the time he'd been incapable of rational thought, and all he'd cared about was making her happy.

How convincing she'd been with her fake tears, with her fake pleading for him to end her suffering and eliminate the cause of her torment. And like a fool, he'd believed every lie and had felt honored to be her knight in shining armor.

Sofia stirred in his arms. "Is it morning yet?" she murmured with her eyes closed.

"Not yet." He caressed her slim back. "Go back to sleep."

"Okay." She yawned, smiled, and cuddled closer to him.

Heaven. That was what being with her felt like.

Sofia didn't want anything from him other than his love. She didn't expect him to go to war for her, to betray his people for her, and in her own way, she'd protected him.

He would have loved to believe that she'd been sent to him by the Fates, but he didn't deserve a boon. He was a sinner, and he deserved eternal condemnation from them, not a reward.

Still, she was a daughter of a hybrid Kra-ell female, and if the Kra-ell were indeed a race similar to the gods, he might be able to activate her.

They'd had unprotected sex several times, and he'd bitten her twice. If it was at all possible to activate her, she could enter transition. And if they kept at it, which he planned on, then her transition might be imminent.

Should he warn her?

The clan had clear guidelines on that, and a potential Dormant needed to be told about the possibility of her immortal genes getting activated by having sex with an immortal male. Well, in Sofia's case she would only be long-lived, not immortal, but he would take a thousand years over her human lifespan.

Maybe that was his punishment.

Perhaps she was his one and only, but she wouldn't live as long as he did, and he would have to mourn her death or find a way to join her on the other side of the veil.

He had to find out whether it was possible.

Aliya was a female Kra-ell hybrid, and yet no one was sure whether her children could be activated, or so he'd heard. Perhaps Bridget had looked into that already?

Would Kaia know? She was a bioinformatician, and she was researching Okidu's journals, so maybe she'd gleaned some information that might shed light on Sofia's prospects?

Pulling gently out of Sofia's arms, he slid out of bed and padded to the bathroom. After taking care of his bladder, he washed his face, brushed his teeth, and pulled on his pants.

Checking that his phone was in the pocket where he'd left it, he walked into the living room, sat on the couch, and sent Kaia a message. *Are you busy? I need to ask you a couple of questions.*

4 8

JADE

The summons from Igor took Jade by surprise. There were no official rest days in the compound, but things slowed down on the weekends, and she seldom visited his office on Saturdays or Sundays.

A long time had passed since she'd sent the fable to Emmett, and she hadn't dared to send anything more. She'd spent some time reading through the submissions by other contestants on the Safe Haven website and had even found one that could potentially mean a request for more information, but even if Igor followed her every move on the internet, which he most likely did, he wouldn't have found anything suspicious.

If she couldn't be sure that the fable had been directed at her and what it meant, he certainly couldn't.

Besides, other than his initial response to her winning the contest, he'd acted as if nothing was amiss.

Still, she wasn't in her fertile cycle, and he sure as hell didn't enjoy her company for anything other than breeding, so why had he summoned her?

Her nerves in turmoil, she strode toward the office building and contemplated stopping by the human quarters and purchasing one of the home-brewed elixirs they concocted over there.

One of the young humans was studying chemistry, and he was mixing potent drugs and selling them to humans and Kra-ell alike. They were less effective on the Kra-ell, especially the purebloods, but they still carried a kick, and some of the other females swore by them as an antidote to frayed nerves and a general feeling of ennui.

Jade wasn't a fan of chemical mood enhancers, and she handled her bad moods with intensive training and hunting, but now and then, she was tempted to take the edge off with the help of those drugs. Hell, sometimes she was tempted to buy copious amounts of them and imbibe as much as it took to end it all.

How long could she continue living with the rage, with the grief, with the humiliation of sharing her body with the murderer of her people? The rage was the antidote to the grief and self-loathing, but she'd been consumed by it for so long that there was not much left to burn.

She felt empty, resigned, and Mother forgive her, ready to call it quits.

It was a sin in the eyes of the Mother to give up. Her chosen daughters were supposed to fight till their last breath. But lately, Jade felt as if her last breath had been expelled a long time ago, and she existed as a wraith. Not dead yet, but not alive either.

Death would be a liberation, but unless she died honorably, she wouldn't ascend to the higher spiritual realm of heroes and would be sentenced to forever walk the valley of the shamed.

The guard didn't stop her as she walked past him, and as she knocked on Igor's door and walked in, she found him sitting on his couch, not behind his massive desk as he usually did.

"You summoned me?"

For a change, he didn't react to the lack of honorific. "Yes." He motioned for her to join him on the couch.

"I'm not in my fertile cycle." She sat as far away from him as possible.

"I know. Can't I enjoy your company regardless of your fertility or lack thereof?"

She arched a brow. "I didn't know that you were a masochist."

He barked out a laugh, which was more frightening than if he had scowled at her. "If anything, I am a sadist. But I find your sharp mind and sharp tongue entertaining despite your sour attitude."

That was a first. He had never admitted his sadistic inclinations, but the truth was that she didn't think he was a sadist. Igor didn't take pleasure in anything other than power, and inflicting pain on the helpless was not a power play. He punished cruelly to set an example and scare others from daring to rebel in any way. He didn't derive pleasure from their pain, but he wasn't affected by it either. He just didn't care one way or another.

"What can I do for you?" Jade asked. "Or let's rephrase it. What do you want me to do for you?"

"I have a story that I think you will find interesting." He uncorked a bottle of some liqueur she didn't recognize, poured it into two glasses, and handed her one. "After you showed so much interest in Safe Haven, I got suspicious, and I sent a spy to investigate."

Jade forced her features to remain schooled and raised an eyebrow. "That must have been a colossal waste of money and resources. It's a silly spiritual retreat sham that swindles stupid humans out of their money. I was only interested in it because it has a treasure trove of material that I can use to teach the little ones about morals and striving to do their best. It's useless for sensible adults."

"Surprisingly, it turns out that there is more to it. The paranormal retreats that they started running were not just another product to enhance their portfolio. My spy discovered that a very well-funded organization purchased the resort, and they are running those paranormal retreats to find more humans with paranormal talents. She also discovered that they have several compellers in their community. Did you know that?"

She'd been shoring up her defenses in case she needed to lie to him, but she could honestly say that she hadn't known. "I had no idea. What do they need the paranormal talents for?"

"Sofia suspects that they are trying to breed an enhanced next generation of humans with paranormal abilities."

"Sofia? The girl who studies languages? That's who you sent to spy on them?"

He shrugged. "I needed someone with a solid human background in case they checked, and I needed someone with perfect English. She's also Valstar's grand-daughter, so I figured she wasn't an entirely worthless human."

Not daring to even think about Emmett and how he was connected to the paranormal conspiracy Sofia had discovered, Jade decided to continue in that vein. "Are you worried about the enhanced humans?"

He regarded her with his penetrating gaze. "Should I be?"

"You tell me. What can those paranormals do?"

"They can compel, but Sofia reports that they are all weak, so they are not a threat to me." He kept looking into her eyes, but there was nothing to see.

Other than Emmett, who was no match for Igor, she hadn't known about compellers in Safe Haven. "Of course not." She grimaced. "You must be the most powerful compeller ever born. Are you related to the royals?"

She'd asked that before, but he'd never given her an answer.

Today wasn't any different.

"I told Sofia to stay as long as she can pull it off and find out what they are plot-ting over there. If they are only planning on producing a new crop of enhanced humans, I have nothing to worry about. But I want her to keep digging in case there is something more interesting going on."

"Maybe you should do the same." Jade threw the liquor down her throat. "Breed the most powerful Kra-ell with each other."

He chuckled. "Why do you think I tolerate you? You are a strong compeller in your own right. Our child would be unstoppable."

"Drova is not a compeller."

"Drova is a girl." He gripped the back of Jade's neck. "I'm still waiting for you to give me a son."

49

MARCEL

*K*aia's call came a few minutes after Marcel had texted her. "Good morning, Marcel."

"Thanks for calling back."

"Sure. I assumed that it must be important if you were texting me so early. I heard you had a lot of excitement over at Safe Haven. I bet no one even remembers William's and my whirlwind romance."

She wasn't wrong. It felt like they had left Safe Haven months ago.

"I assume that you know all about Sofia."

"I don't know much her. I heard that she was sent by Jade's captor, a dude named Igor, who is a powerful compeller, and that Toven managed to override his compulsion with Mia's help. Also, that she's willingly feeding him false information until we figure out how to free Jade and her people."

"There is more. Sofia's mother is a hybrid Kra-ell, and her father is human, which is very rare because the hybrid females usually only want to breed with pureblooded males. I was wondering if it might be possible that she's a Dormant and can be activated."

"If their longevity is passed through the mothers like immortality is for us, that should be possible in theory. I don't know if the Kra-ell's venom has the special mojo needed for activation, or if an immortal male can activate one of theirs. You should talk with Bridget. She has a lot of experience with transitioning Dormants and the various factors that contribute to it, but I would wait an hour or two. You know it's six in the morning, right?"

He hadn't checked the time. "What are you doing up so early?"

"Do you really want me to answer that?"

He chuckled. "I'll assume that you were consumed by the need to work on Okidu's journals and got up to do it. Speaking of the journals, I thought you would have more insight into our genetics after working on them for so long."

She sighed. "So far, I've only scratched the surface. Besides, I'm new to this world, and I'm still learning. One of the things William kept bringing up is the affinity and how fast we have fallen for each other. Is that how you and Sofia feel?"

Marcel closed his eyes. "I think we both felt the connection immediately, but our story was so fraught with issues that things got derailed. I was suspicious of her motives and tried to pull back, she felt guilty about manipulating and using me, but at the end of the day, it just feels right to be with her."

"Then go for it. What's the worst that could happen? She will just not transition."

"Yeah, but I need to obtain her consent, and to do that, I need to tell her about us, and I haven't yet."

"You need to talk to Kian and get his permission first."

"I will after I talk with Bridget. If she says that there is no way I can activate Sofia, there is no point in me asking Kian's permission."

"True. Good luck, Marcel."

"Thanks. And thanks again for calling me back so early in the morning."

"You're welcome." She ended the call.

It was six o'clock Saturday morning, and the doctor was probably enjoying a lazy time in bed with her mate, but Marcel was going to pretend that he'd forgotten it was the weekend and that he hadn't noticed how early it was.

"Marcel," Bridget answered after several rings. "Why are you calling me this early? Did something happen?"

"My apologies. I didn't realize what time it was. I can call later."

She sighed. "That's okay. I'm already up. What can I help you with?"

He explained the situation and what Kaia had said.

"I agree, but I need to add that we know that Kra-ell males cannot activate Dormants. At least not immortal Dormants. Emmett and Margaret are proof of that. They were intimate many times over the years, and he still failed to activate her. That being said, he kidnapped Peter because he believed that immortal males could activate Kra-ell Dormants. But since all the human children born to the Kra-ell had human mothers and hybrid fathers, that wasn't going to work. Sofia is the exception, so there might be a chance that you can activate her. You should ask her if she ever had unprotected sex with any of the hybrids or the purebloods. If she did, and they failed to activate her, then it's either because the Kra-ell can't activate their Dormants, or because even the children born to hybrid mothers and human fathers don't inherit the longevity genes."

"She told me about her boyfriends, and they were human, but she might have omitted having been coerced into breeding with the purebloods or the hybrids. She didn't mention that, and I didn't ask. She was in a good mood, and I didn't want to spoil it."

"You should find a gentle way to do that. We need to know."

"I will."

It wasn't going to be an easy conversation, but Bridget was right. They had to know.

"Come to think of it," Bridget said. "Perhaps Mey and Jin's mother wasn't an immortal Dormant. She might have been a Kra-ell hybrid that somehow escaped or just left her tribe. She might have fallen in love with a human male, had two daughters with him, and, for some reason, couldn't raise them. Or maybe something happened to her and her mate."

"Yeah. Maybe Igor and his cronies found her and killed her and her male. Anything is possible."

"The attack on Jade's tribe happened several years after they were born, but we don't know when they were placed in the orphanage, so perhaps that's possible. If they are of pure Kra-ell descent, though, they are not immortal, which is bad news for them and Yamanu and Arwel. On the other hand, Mey and Jin have very distinct paranormal talents, and from what I heard, Sofia's talent is questionable, which favors the hypothesis of their mother being one of our Dormants."

"I haven't spoken to Sofia about her talent. She can supposedly determine a person's true nature from their reflection in the mirror. There is some mention of that in human literature, so perhaps there is something to it." He sighed. "If Mey and Jin are indeed of pure Kra-ell heritage, and they are still Yamanu and Arwel's truelove mates, then maybe the Fates have some grand plan in mind for the Kra-ell and us."

What he meant by that was that he hoped Sofia was his truelove mate, and that his venom might somehow make her immortal.

Bridget let out a breath. "Who knows? I used to scoff at those who invoked the Fates, but I'm no longer dismissive of their part in what's going on."

"Same here. I love being an engineer and finding scientific solutions to problems. But now that I've found a woman who I feel can be my one and only, I'm finding myself hoping for divine intervention."

"As the saying goes, there are no atheists in the foxhole. Good luck, Marcel."

"Thank you."

50

SOFIA

*M*arcel wasn't in bed when Sofia woke up. The door to the bedroom was closed, but she knew he was in the bunker. He wouldn't have left her alone without telling her that he was leaving.

Last night was spectacular, and with the residual pleasure still pulsing through her body, she wanted to find him and drag him back to bed for another round.

What better way to start the day than making love, right?

Except, she didn't know what mood she would find Marcel in today. Would he be as loving and as sweet as he had been last night? Or would he go back to being broody and remote like he had been since that fateful call in Emmett's office?

Sofia had done everything they had asked her to do, she'd explained why she'd had no choice, and he should have forgiven her. He'd even said so last night. But she'd been hurt by him before, and she didn't trust his feelings not to change again.

Maybe if she went back to sleep, she would wake up with him holding her in his arms and murmuring sweet nothings in her ear, and they would live happily ever after. The end.

She smiled at her own girlish fantasies. Life didn't work like that. It wasn't fair, good things didn't come as a reward to good people, and evildoers like Igor got their way.

Kind of made her question her faith in the Mother.

The goddess wasn't the benevolent god humans believed in. She was vengeful and demanding. The Mother was supposed to reward the worthy and punish the unworthy, but that wasn't how it worked in the real world. Now that Sofia knew that Igor was definitely unworthy, that he spit in the face of Kra-ell traditions, turning them on their head, she doubted that the Mother was a real force in the universe.

The thing was, Igor's murderous ways were not an affront to the Mother. The Kra-ell were warlike people, and to die in battle or in a duel was considered an honorable death. Deadly duels weren't allowed in Igor's compound, but he hadn't disallowed stories of them to circulate like he suppressed the truth about females being the Mother's chosen leaders.

As the bedroom door opened and Marcel walked in, shirtless and barefoot, her mouth watered. "Come back to bed." She lifted the blanket, inviting him in.

"I wish I could." He sat down and leaned to kiss her lips. "I didn't go to the lab yesterday as I was supposed to, and I need to do it now. It shouldn't take long, though."

Once again, he seemed awkward and remote with her, but she had a feeling it was about something other than mistrust. Something was troubling him, but it might be about the things he needed to do in the lab.

As her aunt used to say, not everything was about her, and the people around her could have other things troubling them that had nothing to do with her.

Sofia sighed. "What am I supposed to do while you do whatever you need to do in the lab?"

"I made coffee, and Eleanor will bring you breakfast later. I can send a book with her. What do you like to read?"

"Do you have any romance novels?"

He winced. "I have some thrillers and detective stories, and I think that in one of them there is a love interest, but I wouldn't call it romance."

"That's okay. I have a book that I brought with me and didn't finish yet." She put her hand on his knee. "Can I ask Eleanor to compel me to keep quiet about everything that went down so I can rejoin the retreat? I cooperated, and you said that you trusted me. Besides, where am I going to run? There is nowhere to go."

Marcel sighed. "I need to ask the big boss's permission. I sent him a message, but he hasn't answered me yet, and I don't want to bug him. He's not the friendliest of guys, and especially not to those who disturb his Saturday morning with his family."

"Is he the one who was listening through Julian's tablet?"

Marcel nodded.

"Is he angry at me?"

"Not at all. He's a grumpy fellow, but he's not a bad guy. He knows that you had no choice, and he doesn't blame you."

Sofia let out a breath. "That's a relief. Isn't Eleanor teaching a class today, though?"

"Not until later in the day. She can come down and spend some time with you." He cupped her cheek. "She's not the friendly type either, but she seems to really like you. I think the two of you could be friends."

"I think so too. She's a little bit like the Kra-ell females. She's no-nonsense, assertive bordering on aggressive, and she looks like a hybrid Kra-ell. Well except for the eyes. They are the right color but the wrong size. The Kra-ell and the hybrids have big eyes."

He smiled. "Emmett doesn't."

That was a shock. "Emmett? What are you talking about?"

"I'm surprised that you haven't figured it out yet. Emmett is a hybrid. He used to be a member of Jade's tribe, but he left many years before Igor attacked her compound. Jade must have recognized him from his picture."

"Dear Mother of All Life. How could I have been so blind? It's just that he's so not Kra-ell in the way he acts. They are all so macho and severe and all about honor, while Emmett is a performer who lives for drama." Her hand flew to her mouth. "It would have been a real disaster if he told Igor his real name. His Kra-ell name. It would have been the end of Jade. Igor would have killed her."

Marcel nodded. "That's why I didn't tell you before. But since I trust you, and since we both know that you can never go back, I figured you would feel a little less homesick knowing that there is a hybrid Kra-ell right here in Safe Haven."

"I need to talk to him. Maybe he can tell me more things about the Kra-ell. They told us so little in Igor's place. Perhaps Jade was more forthcoming."

Marcel shook his head. "He doesn't know much either. Jade was just as tight-lipped, and I'm starting to wonder what they were hiding from their own people."

"They don't consider humans their people, and they consider the hybrids a necessary evil. Not that anyone has actually phrased it like that, but it's evident from how they treat us."

"I need to ask you something." Marcel took in a breath. "And I need you to answer it truthfully because it's important. Have you ever had sex with a pure-blood or a hybrid male?"

She'd told him about her boyfriends. Was he doubting her again? He'd just told her that he trusted her.

So much for that.

"I didn't." She crossed her arms over her chest. "Why is it important to you?"

"I can't tell you yet, and I don't want you to feel embarrassed if you did. I know that you were not free to reject unwanted advances."

So that was why he was asking.

Marcel wanted to find out how highly she was regarded as the human grand-daughter of a pureblooded male, and that would tell him her grandfather's position in Igor's organization.

Valstar being Igor's second-in-command was one of the few pieces of information she'd withheld from him.

"Rape is not condoned in our community. I didn't have to accept anyone's invitation if I didn't want to."

SYSSI

"Good morning, Syssi," Turner said as she opened the door for him. "I'm sorry about conducting business in your home on a Saturday."

She chuckled. "Being married to Kian, I'm used to that, and I prefer him being here than in the office. That way, at least I get to see him." She closed the door behind him. "I hoped Bridget would accompany you. Okidu prepared breakfast for four."

"Then I shall call her and ask her to hurry over. I thought it would be just Kian and me."

Syssi let the unintended insult slide.

"Allegra is at Annani's this morning, so I figured I would join your breakfast meeting."

Turner was a brilliant man, but his social skills were even worse than Kian's, and he surely hadn't realized how dismissive that had sounded.

She wasn't an official member of the council, but Kian didn't do anything without consulting her, and she knew everything that was going on, security-wise as well as business-wise. Kian trusted her opinion, mainly because she didn't express it unless she had something to contribute, and also because her second sight gave her a paranormal advantage.

She wasn't always aware of its influence, and sometimes it was difficult for her to tell the difference between things that her mind conjured up and things that her foresight was trying to hint at. The best example of that were the Kra-ell. She'd created a fantasy world for the Perfect Match studios with creatures called the Krall, thinking that it was a product of her creative imagination, but as it had turned out, it had foreshadowed the appearance of the real Kra-ell, a divergent species of new Earth occupants who most likely had come from the same corner of the universe as the gods.

"Bridget will be here in a few minutes." Turner returned the phone to his pocket.

"Wonderful." She motioned for him to take a seat at the dining table. "Can I offer you some coffee while we wait?"

"Yes, please. Thank you."

"Black, right?"

He gave her a smile. "I'm honored that you remembered."

Syssi laughed. "Coffee is my thing. I remember everyone's preferences."

"You remember every kind of preference." Kian walked into the dining room and pulled her into his arms. "You care, and you pay attention. That's why you remember. I bet you know what Turner likes to eat as well."

That was true and kind of odd. Generally, her memory wasn't great, and unless she made a conscious effort to remember a person's name and attached some visual mnemonic to it, she would forget it almost as soon as she'd learned it, but she remembered personal things about people without putting any effort into it.

"That's easy. Turner is competing with Roni for the title of the best barbecuer in the village. Ribs are his favorite."

"They are." Turner rubbed his stomach. "But lately, I've discovered that baking them in the oven is better than barbecuing them. I cover them with foil and bake them on low heat for a couple of hours. They turn out delicious."

As the doorbell rang, Okidu beelined for the front door and opened it for Bridget. "Good morning, Doctor."

"Good morning, everyone." She gave Okidu a small smile before walking over and joining them at the table. "I planned on catching up on some work while Victor was gone, but I couldn't refuse an invitation to breakfast cooked by Okidu." She turned to him. "Are you serving your famous Belgian waffles?"

Okidu straightened to his full height of five feet and eight inches. "But of course, mistress."

"Wonderful." Bridget unfurled the napkin and draped it over her knees. "I spoke to Marcel earlier." She turned to Kian. "Did you speak with him?"

"He sent me a message earlier, but it was marked as not urgent, and I didn't have a chance to call him back yet. Is there a problem?"

Bridget hesitated for a moment. "Usually, I don't like to discuss health concerns that clan members ask my advice about, but since Marcel's questions could be construed as general in nature, and they are relevant to what we are about to discuss, I feel that I should. Marcel asked me whether a human child born to a hybrid Kra-ell mother and a human father would be a Dormant who could be activated."

Kian frowned. "Didn't we conclude that the Kra-ell Dormants couldn't be activated?"

Bridget pursed her lips. "According to Emmett and Vrog, hybrid females don't produce children with humans. The Kra-ell philosophy is to choose the best possible male to father their offspring, so naturally, they choose pureblooded males to impregnate them. They might dally with humans out of curiosity, though. Since we assumed that their longevity is passed through the mothers, we concluded that children born to hybrid males and human females didn't possess the longevity gene. Based on Emmett and Margaret's sexual history, we also knew that a hybrid Kra-ell male could not activate an immortal Dormant female. Sofia is a rarity. She's the daughter of a hybrid female. The question we need to ask her is whether she had sex with any of the purebloods or the hybrids, and if she did, then we will know that they can't activate their Dormants. That still leaves the possibility that our males can do that."

Syssi frowned. "Hold on. We also know that the pureblooded females don't have sex with humans, so the hybrid females are the product of pureblooded males and human mothers. How would the longevity gene get passed? It should end with the hybrid daughters."

"Not necessarily." Bridget leaned back in her chair. "We made the mistake of thinking of the purebloods as equivalents of immortals, when in fact they are the equivalent of gods, and if that's so, both the males and the females pass on the longevity genes."

52

KIAN

*S*yssi shook her head. "If the purebloods are genetically equivalent to the gods, they are a much more primitive version. If the two societies interacted, I bet the Kra-ell were treated as second class."

"Again, not necessarily," Turner said. "We suspect that the gods were experts in genetic manipulation. They might have created the Kra-ell to serve them as workers and soldiers. The Kra-ell are physically stronger than the gods, they produce many more males than females, and they live by a code of honor that celebrates death in battle as the ultimate achievement. They are the perfect warriors."

"They might have taken an existing species and altered it." Syssi shivered. "They were far from the benevolent creatures they tried to portray themselves as."

Kian chuckled. "We already know that. But I still think that the Kra-ell are just a more primitive form of the gods, not their creation. The gods wouldn't have given them such incredible power of compulsion."

Syssi shook her head. "Most of the Kra-ell have a very limited ability to compel, and it's possible that the original species had it before the gods altered their genetics. Perhaps some are just born with a stronger ability. I wouldn't dismiss the possibility that they were created by the gods to serve them."

Leaning over, Kian took her hand and planted a kiss on the back of it. "I never dismiss anything you say, my love."

She gave him a smile. "That's sweet."

"It's not sweet. It's smart. You're always right."

Turner nodded. "Especially when she supports my opinion."

"I should call Marcel." Kian took a sip from his coffee. "But first, tell me what your guy in Karelia found."

Turner put his fork down. "They followed the map, used a raft to cross three of the rivers, but they got stuck on the fourth. The rapids are too strong to use a raft, and it's too wide to cross any other way. They need more equipment, and it's on the way, but it will take time to get to them."

"How do the Kra-ell deliver supplies to the compound?" Bridget asked.

"They could have built tunnels under the riverbeds," Turner said. "My guy's team looked for the entrances, but they must be very well camouflaged. They couldn't find them. Sofia mentioned tunnels, but for some reason, Toven dropped the subject. We need to question her again and use compulsion to get her to answer truthfully and fully. She must know where they are."

"Unless she was driven there," Bridget said. "They probably employ the same tactics that Navuh and we do. We have special vehicles to allow clan members to travel freely to and from the village, and Navuh uses windowless planes piloted by humans who are compelled to keep the island's location a secret."

Turner nodded. "We also need Sofia to draw the layout of the compound, the patrol schedules, how often the purebloods and hybrids leave the compound to hunt, and at what times of the day."

"What about the miniature drone?" Kian asked. "Did your guy manage to get one?"

"He ordered it, and it should get to him tomorrow."

"I'm still not a hundred percent sure that a drone is a good idea, even a small one."

"There is another option," Turner said. "If we manage to find the tunnels, which we should with Sofia's help, we can use a crawling bug instead of a flying one. They make less noise, require less energy, and get into tight spaces. We can send several spiders in at once and have them crawl all over. They might be able to get into the weapons storage, which a flying bug won't be able to do."

This should have occurred to Kian before, but he'd been too fixated on the miniature drone. "Great idea. Make it so."

Turner sighed. "It will take time. Normally, I prefer to go slow and collect as much information as I can before I even begin to plan a mission, and technically, we are not in a rush. The sense of urgency is due to Sofia's presence and to how long we can drag out the misinformation campaign. The moment Igor realizes that she's been captured, he's going to react, and we will be out of time. A faster way to get information on the compound is to capture a pureblood and compel it out of him, but that might show our hand prematurely."

"Can't we fake her death?" Syssi asked. "But it needs to be very convincing, or it would look suspicious and produce the same undesired result."

"We can use the misinformation for that as well," Bridget suggested. "She can start reporting that the stress is getting to her, and she's feeling faint. Then she'll say that she visited the clinic and was told that she might have a heart problem. The doctor recommended a bunch of tests, but she doesn't have insurance, and they will cost a fortune." Bridget chuckled. "American healthcare costs are legendary around the world. Everything here costs ten times as much as it costs in Europe, so they will believe it. A simple MRI exam would run several thousands of dollars."

"I like it," Kian said. "The answer she gets will show how much they care about her, if at all. If they authorize the expense, then they deem her valuable and not a disposable pawn. If not, she will be even more motivated to cooperate with us. In a week or two, we can send an email to her emergency contact informing them of her death from heart failure and ask them to pay for transporting the body to Finland. If they refuse, we will inform them that the body was cremated."

Syssi shivered. "That sounds so gruesome. Poor girl."

Kian put his hand on her shoulder. "She will not really die, love. We will just make it look like it as convincingly as we can."

"I know, but it's sad. She's all alone in the world, and those who care for her can't help her. I hope that she's a Dormant, that Marcel can activate her, and that they can live happily ever after."

"Speaking of Marcel. I need to call him." Kian pulled out his phone and looked at Turner. "Any other suggestions before we talk to him?"

Turner crossed his arms over his chest. "Marcel's questions to Bridget indicate that he wants to induce Sofia. Since the protocol is to get the Dormant's consent before attempting it, he probably wants to ask your permission to tell her about us."

"Yeah, I figured as much."

"What are you going to tell him?" Syssi asked.

"I don't feel comfortable telling her anything, but that's just my knee-jerk response. She's supervised at all times, so she can't tell Igor anything, and she's not going back to him. She can also be compelled to keep quiet about us and thralled to forget if need be." He looked at Turner. "What do you think?"

"I think it's a great opportunity to find out whether hybrid Kra-ell mothers and human fathers can produce Dormant children who can be activated. The thing is that for us it's just curiosity, while for the Kra-ell, it could be a game changer, and not one we are interested in."

Kian pinned him with a hard stare. "You're not being helpful."

"I'm just thinking out loud. It's not in our best interest for the Kra-ell to find out that we can activate the Dormant children born to their female hybrids. On the other hand, the Kra-ell we know about, the ones who are holding Jade, only have one such possible Dormant, and Sofia is not going back, so how are they going to find out?"

"True," Syssi said. "But since we invited Aliyah and Vrog into our community, we need to find out for their sake. What if they have children, and they are born human? They would need to know whether their children can be activated."

MARCEL

*M*arcel collected everything that the team of bioinformaticians had been working on, scanned it, emailed it to William, and destroyed the documents.

After that was done, he disconnected all the servers, locked up the lab, and headed back to Emmett's cottage.

Kian's call caught him when he was entering the cottage.

"Hello, Kian."

"Where are you now?"

"I'm about to enter the bunker. Why?"

"We need to question Sofia again. Turner's team wasn't able to reach the compound with the map she drew for Toven. The fourth river has strong rapids, and they are waiting for more equipment to cross it. She mentioned tunnels, and we believe that she knows where to find the entrances. We also need her to draw us a layout of the compound. Once we have the locations of the entrances to the tunnels, we plan on sending spiders to collect information. Between the layout she draws for us and what the spiders transmit, we will have a better idea of what we are dealing with. Get Eleanor and have her compel Sofia to cooperate."

She wasn't going to like it, but it was necessary.

"What are you planning to do?" he asked.

"Nothing yet. We are debating the benefits versus the pitfalls of capturing a pureblood and pumping him for information, and we haven't decided yet whether the risks outweigh the benefit or vice versa. If we could manage to do that without Igor being any the wiser, then it's a no-brainer, but it doesn't seem feasible. The moment he gets a whiff of anything being amiss, he could flee, or he could retaliate against Sofia's family, and we promised her not to endanger them."

"I see. I wish I had some insight to offer, but I don't."

"You're not a strategist, Marcel. I only shared our deliberations with you because of your involvement with Sofia."

That was the opening he needed to ask Kian's permission to tell her the truth about them, but it was bad timing to bring it up. Nevertheless, he had to do it. He might have induced her already, and if Kian didn't allow him to tell her about her potential transition, he should start using protection and make up a good reason for why it was suddenly needed.

"Thank you for keeping me informed. I also have something I need to discuss with you."

"I know. You think that Sofia might be a Dormant, and you want to try to induce her transition."

That was a relief.

Kian had probably spoken with Bridget, and even if he hadn't, it must have occurred to him that the rare daughter of a hybrid mother and human father might be a Dormant.

"I wouldn't have brought it up if it weren't urgent, but we'd been intimate twice before it occurred to me that Sofia might be a Dormant, and since she's on birth control, we didn't use protection."

"Bridget told us that you called her, and we decided that it's a good opportunity to find out whether a child of a hybrid Kra-ell female can be induced by an immortal male. Did you ask her if she had sex with any of the purebloods or hybrids?"

"The same thing occurred to me, but when I asked her, she insisted that she didn't. She said that rape was not condoned in the compound, and that she had the right to refuse, but I don't think she told me the truth. Sofia emits very little in terms of emotional scents, so I can't tell by that, but she averted her eyes when she said that. It was either a lie or a half-truth."

"She might have special status in the compound," Syssi said in the background. "Because of her being a rare daughter of a hybrid female. It's also possible that her mother and or her grandfather are important members of Igor's community."

"That's possible." Marcel rubbed the back of his neck. "The same thought had occurred to me, but I was afraid of being biased and looking for explanations that would validate Sofia's statement."

"Refusing a female's invitation was considered a great affront in Jade's community," Kian said. "I assume that to refuse a male's invitation in Igor's carries the same stigma. I don't see how human or even hybrid females can refuse without suffering the consequences. You can ask Eleanor to make Sofia answer that truthfully."

Sofia was going to hate him for it, but they had to know. "What about telling her about us? Do I have permission to tell her our history and why I think she can be induced?"

"As I said, we want to find out whether that's possible, but we don't want to do that without her consent or her knowledge. We all know the law, and I don't think Edna would let it slide if we forgo asking for Sofia's consent, even taking into account the special circumstances. Besides, Sofia is not going back whether she transitions or not. She already knows too much, and we can't release her. We will have to fake her death, and she will have to be confined to the village. Like it or not, you are stuck with her for as long as she lives."

"I don't have a problem with that, but Sofia might, especially after I get Eleanor to interrogate her about her sex life. She might not want to have anything to do with me ever again."

"If she's your truelove mate, she'll forgive you. It is what it is, though, so let's make the best of it. If she refuses to be with you, we will get her accommodations elsewhere, and find her something to do. There are plenty of jobs available in the village for anyone willing to do them."

"How are we going to fake her death without it looking suspicious? She's twenty-seven and healthy."

After Kian had told him about the heart condition idea, Marcel had to agree that it sounded plausible. "Sofia told me that healthcare is practically nonexistent for the humans in the compound. Her grandmother died of heart failure, so that will fit perfectly. They will assume it was genetic. If I haven't unintentionally induced her already, perhaps it would be a good idea to fake her death before giving it a try. If she enters transition, she might be out for a few days, and she won't be able to communicate with her contact."

"That's not a bad idea. Tomorrow, have her contact Valstar and start the story. If she enters transition, we will implement the heart failure scenario and send our condolences along with a bill."

5 4

SOFIA

*S*ofia put her book back on the nightstand and pulled the blanket over her head. The Spanish romance novel was all about rich people hopping on private jets, traveling from one exotic location to another, and staying at luxurious hotels. The love talk was too flowery, the love scenes too unrealistic, and it all made her feel like Cinderella before meeting the prince.

She was stuck in a bunker, her so-called prince had left her hours ago and hadn't returned yet, and before leaving, he'd asked her about her lovers and hadn't believed her when she'd told him she'd never had sex with a pureblood or a hybrid.

Her story wasn't a fairytale, and it wasn't going to turn into one.

Maybe if she fell asleep, she could dream about a different world where the prince didn't doubt her, where she could keep her job at the university, where both of her parents loved her and cared for her, and where an evil overlord didn't threaten to torture those she cared about if she failed him.

Dream on.

She chuckled. *That's what I'm trying to do.*

When the knock sounded on the bedroom door, she tossed the blanket aside and got to her feet. "Coming."

"May I come in?" Marcel said from the other side.

Had she just dreamt him up?

"Sure. Prisoners don't get to refuse their jailers entry."

He opened the door. "What got you in a bad mood?"

Her sour expression must have given him pause because he didn't even attempt to get closer.

Sofia was in no mood to smile to make him feel better. "Nothing. What's up?" She straightened the blanket over the bed and tucked the corners in to make it look nice.

Being mad didn't mean she wanted her prison space to look messy. Keeping it neat was the only thing she could control right now.

He shook his head. "Even I know that *nothing* is not a good answer. Did Eleanor say something to upset you?"

"Not at all."

Eleanor was the only friend she had right now, and out of all Sofia's jailers, she treated her the best. She'd promised to bring Emmett with her later so they could all have dinner together and talk about Kra-ell stuff. But dinner was many hours away, and until then, all Sofia had for company was that damn romance novel that she really didn't want to keep reading. It only made it painfully obvious that her own romance story was severely lacking.

She finally understood the appeal of bully romances.

Compared to the jerks in those books, average guys like Marcel looked better than they actually were.

Not that he was average. He was handsome, intelligent, and deep down, he had a good heart. But he was still no prince.

"So what is it?" Marcel asked. "Is it something I said?"

She sat on the bed and picked up her book. "Did you talk to your boss about allowing me to attend the retreat?"

The sheepish expression on his face was her answer. "I forgot. I'll do it right now." He turned on his heel and walked out of the bedroom.

Sofia let out a breath and let her shoulders sag. It wasn't smart to antagonize her jailer. Sometimes he was nice to her, so maybe if she was nice in return, she would get more nice out of him.

But that wasn't how it was supposed to work between lovers.

They were supposed to float toward each other on a cloud of love and admiration, embrace each other passionately, and hop on a jet to Buenos Aires, where they would make love in the bedroom of their private jet, three thousand meters above the Earth.

Right.

Damn romance novel and the unrealistic expectations it had planted in her head.

But what was the alternative?

Expect abuse of the verbal, emotional, or physical variety and call it life?

She'd had enough of that in Igor's compound.

Marcel returned a couple of moments later. "He said it was okay as long as Eleanor compels you to keep everything that happened since you were caught a secret."

Sofia grimaced. "Eleanor can't make it until dinner. She has a class she's teaching."

Marcel lifted his hand and rubbed the back of his neck. "I asked her to rearrange her schedule and come as soon as she could. She will be here in a few minutes."

As Sofia's heart made a happy flip, she put the book aside, rose to her feet, walked over to Marcel, and wrapped her arms around his neck. "Thank you. I appreciate you going to all that trouble for me."

55

MARCEL

*M*arcel knew that he was in trouble, and he didn't know how to avert the storm that Sofia was about to unleash on him.

He could pretend that he'd called Eleanor over only to compel Sofia so she could rejoin the retreat, and perhaps she would hold her tongue while Eleanor was compelling her to reveal more information about Igor's compound. But then her wrath would be even greater.

Would she forgive him once he told her about her potential Dormancy?

Not in the mood she was in. She would probably throw him out of the room without giving him a chance to explain.

Gently removing her arms from around his neck, he took her hand and led her to the living room. "Just as you had to follow commands from your boss, I have to follow commands from mine. It's true that he doesn't have to compel me to do that, and I follow because I trust his leadership and his judgment, and I know that his motives are good, but I'm still a cog in this machine, just like you are in yours."

She frowned at him. "Now I'm worried. What was that preamble about?"

"I asked Eleanor to come over after my initial conversation with the boss. He needs you to disclose more information about the compound and how to get there. We have a team on the ground in Karelia, and they were not able to traverse the last river on your map because of the rapids. You mentioned tunnels, and we need to know where they are."

Her face fell. "And here I thought that you were making an effort for me."

"I'm making a tremendous effort for you. I asked permission to do something that I would have never asked for anyone else."

"What is it?"

"I'll tell you tonight. It's not something that can be covered in a two-minute conversation, which is all we have before Eleanor gets here."

"I have to admit that I'm curious, but I'm even more curious, or rather worried, about what your boss wants to do with the information he's about to force me to reveal." She smirked. "By the way, I don't think that Eleanor will be able to get it out of me, and Tom is not here. Tom freed me to say what I want to say, but since I don't want your people invading my community, and I don't want to tell you where the tunnels are, Igor's compulsion might hold."

Marcel was afraid of that as well, but he was glad that Sofia had inadvertently admitted to knowing where the tunnels were.

"I hoped that Eleanor's services wouldn't be needed. My boss, whose name is Kian, is just collecting information. We don't have enough people to offer Igor and his warriors a challenge, but we need to know who and what we are dealing with. And in case your family needs rescuing, we need to have a contingency plan for that."

That seemed to finally penetrate her stubbornness. "I believe that you sincerely believe that, but what if your boss is not telling you the truth?"

"We don't operate like that. Kian is not a dictator, and he's not operating in a vacuum. We have a council, and if he does something that's not justified, the council will have his head. On top of that, he's not the ultimate authority. We have several establishments, each with its own regent, and the lady who is in charge of our entire organization is the most loving, compassionate person you will ever meet."

That put a sparkle in Sofia's eyes. "Am I ever going to meet her?"

Marcel grinned. "There is a very good chance of that."

Sofia took in a deep breath. "I'm sorry for giving you a hard time. I know it's futile, and I know that with Tom's help, Kian can get me to do anything he wants, the same way that Igor could. But I can't help fighting this. My family's safety is on the line, and so far, Igor hasn't harmed any of them. If he does, it's going to be my fault, either by failing to provide him with the information he wants, or by providing you with the information you want. As the saying goes, I'm between a rock and a hard place."

5 6

SOFIA

*W*hen Eleanor came down with Emmett and Leon, they had with them a stack of large printouts.

"Those are enlarged maps of Karelia." Leon spread them on the dining table with Marcel's help.

"Are the tunnel entrances near the rivers?" Eleanor asked.

She hadn't imbued her voice with compulsion, which Sofia could have kissed her for, but she knew it would only last as long as she cooperated and gave them all the information they wanted.

"The tunnels are well-guarded. Since it's impossible to get to the other three tunnels without going through the first, it is the most heavily guarded, usually by one pureblood and two hybrids. The others have two hybrids each. The paved road ends here." She marked the spot with a Sharpie. "There is a dirt road that continues from here, but it's not marked on the map, and there is a really rough patch between where the paved road ends and the dirt path begins. My old car gets a beating every time I force her through it. It's not easy to find the dirt path, and since it rains so much over there, and it's so overgrown with vegetation, leaving tracks is not a concern. The same goes for the paths between the tunnels."

"I bet the tunnels have cameras and are boobytrapped," Leon said. "If someone manages to get to the first tunnel entrance undetected and eliminates the guards, they can collapse the secondary tunnels."

"What happens if you get stuck?" Eleanor asked.

"I have a cell phone. I can call for help."

Leon and Eleanor exchanged glances.

"We forgot about your phone," Eleanor said. "It's still in the safe in the office." She looked at Leon. "Should we tell Kian about it?"

"There is nothing to tell. When we fake Sofia's death, we will mail it back along with the rest of her belongings."

Sofia felt the blood drain from her face. "I can't do that to my father. He will die from a broken heart."

Eleanor patted her arm. "Better a broken heart than a broken back. You don't want Igor to torture him."

"That's not helpful," Emmett murmured. "Maybe we can put something in the stories to let Jade know that you are alive, so she can tell your father."

"Did she send another email?" Eleanor asked.

"She didn't, but I know that she read my fable. William set it up, so I know who visits which page. It's something called cookies, and all the websites have them these days. She either didn't understand what I was trying to say, or she's afraid to answer."

"It's better that way," Leon said. "We can't help her anyway, but we can send her encoded messages." He narrowed his eyes at Emmett. "Maybe you should sharpen your writing skills, so she can actually understand what you are trying to tell her."

Emmett glared at him but didn't say a thing.

Leon turned to Sofia. "Please mark the dirt road for us."

"I'll try. I'm not good at judging scale. But here is the first river, and I know that the dirt road terminates half a mile or so before it. The first tunnel entrance should be somewhere here." She marked the spot with an X. "They have cameras on the dirt road, so when I get near, they move the bushes aside and roll the fake stone door aside."

"Where are the three other entrances?" Leon asked.

"I can only estimate." Sofia marked the spots.

"They are not far from each other." Leon leaned his chin on his fist. "But it's still a long way for the spiders to cross. I'm not worried about the cameras in the tunnels detecting the spiders, even if they are using infrared. Their heat signature is minimal. But we will need to study the terrain and find a shorter path for them. We might have to use a drone to drop them closer to the compound."

"Spiders?" Sofia arched a brow. "What do you need spiders for? Are they poisonous?"

"These are not real spiders," Marcel explained. "Leon is talking about mechanical devices that look like spiders and carry a tiny camera and transmit sound and images. We can send them to film the compound and even listen to conversations."

Her eyes widened. "Are they remote-controlled?"

"Some are, why?"

"Perhaps we can deliver a message to my father with one of them." She winced. "I just hope he doesn't squash it before it delivers the message."

"We can send a message to Jade as well," Eleanor said. "I wish those bugs could carry earpieces, but then they would be too big. Just imagine what Jade could do if she was free of Igor's compulsion."

"We can drop earpieces with a small drone," Leon said. "The problem is the distance. We will have to deploy a larger drone with the small one piggybacking on it, have it glide over the compound with the engine off, and drop the small one to free-fall somewhere that is not heavily patrolled."

"The human quarters," Sofia said. "We have a large grassy area with a playground for the children, and the Kra-ell hardly ever visit it. You can drop the small drone there, but first, let my father know that it's coming with one of those spider communicators so he will know to look for it."

"Will he cooperate with Jade?" Eleanor asked.

"That might be a problem." Sofia let out a breath. "My father works in the laundry, and he has no reason to seek Jade out or vice versa." She tapped her lips. "But my aunts work as maids in the Kra-ell quarters, so they can slip her a note while they clean her room."

"We've gotten sidetracked," Leon said. "Our first concern is gathering intel, and since the only way to get to the compound and its immediate area is through tunnels that are guarded twenty-four-seven, our best option is to capture the guards securing the first one instead of waiting for a hunting party to come out. We can easily disable the cameras on the dirt road or circumvent the road altogether." He flipped one of the printouts around. "We need you to draw the layout of the compound and mark all the areas according to function and security level, and by that, I mean the frequency of patrols."

She nodded. "Can I get a ruler? I'll try to draw it to scale as best as I can."

From not seeing any options to free the compound, they suddenly had several, and one of them was helping those who opposed Igor's rule to rebel against him. Sofia still didn't know how they were going to accomplish that, but if they kept working on it, they might figure out a good plan.

"I'll get a ruler from my office." Emmett rose to his feet. "I'll be back in a couple of minutes."

Eleanor got up as well. "I'll make coffee while we wait."

"I'm excited," Sofia said. "It seems like we are starting to develop a plan, but I'm not sure for what. Are we going to start a rebellion?"

"That's one option," Leon said. "After we are done, I'll share what we discussed with Turner. The guy is a strategic genius, and he should be able to put this new information and the ideas we came up with to good use."

ERIC

"Is it okay?" Max threaded the tongue through the buckle on the cuff around Eric's left wrist. "Or is it too snug?"

"It's fine." Eric tugged on the chain. "But I think you went overboard with those titanium chains. I'm not a gorilla." He moved his hips to adjust the blanket covering his privates.

"I got them from Brundar. I guess that's what he uses himself."

Eric chuckled. "I didn't know that Callie was that strong."

Max cut him an amused glance. "They are not for Callie."

"Brundar doesn't strike me as the submissive type. Come to think of it, neither does Callie, but I don't know much about that lifestyle and its rules of engagement."

"Neither do I." Max took hold of Eric's right wrist and pulled the leather cuff over his hand. "Maybe they take turns being tied down. It takes a lot of trust to be at the mercy of another person like that." He lifted his eyes to Eric's. "I appreciate it that you trust me to do this."

"I trust Darlene with my life. You are just the help."

Max snorted out a laugh. "Thanks a lot. Now I really feel special."

"You are, and I'm grateful." Eric let out a breath. "I use humor and sarcasm to alleviate the stress." He glanced at the closed bathroom door. "If I'm nervous, I can imagine how hard it is for Darlene. All I have to do is lie here like a slab of meat while she has to do all the work."

Darlene was hiding in the bathroom.

She was still uncomfortable about having Max bite her, and although she refused to admit it, Eric suspected that she was also scared.

Her standard answer was that if all the immortal females who had immortal partners enjoyed it, it couldn't be too bad.

Except, those females were doing it with males they loved, and that made a difference.

Max tightened the strap, threaded the tongue through the buckle, and put Eric's arm down on the mattress. "It's going to be alright. After I'm done, I'll put on soft, romantic music, light up the candles, dim the lights, and leave. You can forget that I was even here."

Hardly, but Eric knew that the moment Darlene touched him, it would become all about her, and he would have no problem getting aroused.

The reverse, though, was going to be more challenging. He was tied up, so there was little he could do as far as foreplay, and Darlene wasn't the type of woman who liked to take control. Seeing him chained to the bed would not turn her on.

He had a plan, though. He would tell her to straddle his face, hold on to the headboard, and let him bring her to orgasm once or twice with his tongue alone. By the time he was done with her, she would be so anxious to ride his shaft that she would hopefully forget all about Max jerking off in the next room.

Eric had asked Max to get a good bottle of wine for Darlene, so she could let go of her inhibitions, but she'd been too nervous to drink it, claiming that her throat was too tight to swallow, and his joke about her giving him a blow job to loosen it up hadn't helped.

She hadn't even smiled, and given that she always laughed at all of his corny jokes, no matter how stupid they were, that spoke volumes about her mental state.

Darlene was freaking out.

"All done." Max finished the last buckle on Eric's ankle. "Comfortable?"

"No. My nose itches. Can you scratch it for me?"

Rolling his eyes, Max did that not too gently. "Anything else? Do you need me to fluff you up too?"

Eric laughed. "The only hands I allow on my yoke are Darlene's, but thanks for the offer."

"It wasn't an offer." Max cast a glance at the bathroom door. "I'd better finish up so she can come out."

When Max was done with the music, the candles, and the lights, Eric asked, "Can I ask you for just one more favor? Can you add another pillow under my head?"

"Sure, buddy." Max lifted Eric's head and stuffed the pillow under it. "All good?"

"Yeah. Thank you. You are a really good friend."

"I know, right?" Max grinned before turning toward the bathroom door. "I'm leaving now! Count to ten and come out!"

The soundproofing of the house was excellent, but the bathroom door wasn't as fortified as the bedroom door, so it didn't block out all sounds.

"Thank you," came the muffled reply.

58

DARLENE

*D*arlene waited until she was sure that Max was no longer in the room before opening the door and peeking into the darkened bedroom.

The illumination came from two small, scented candles, soft music was playing, and the door to the bedroom had been left slightly ajar.

There was no helping it. The soundproofing was so good in the village that a closed door would have prevented Max from hearing when was the right moment to come in, and for some reason, Eric and Max thought it was important that the venom and the semen entered her body at the same time.

Darlene didn't think it mattered. If semen could stay viable in a woman's body for forty-eight hours and fertilize her egg, the same should be true for its other properties. Max could come in whenever he was ready and bite her.

On the other hand, it was better if she was climaxing when it happened, so she would be flooded with endorphins, and it wouldn't hurt as much.

"Are you just going to stand there?" Eric said. "Come out and let me see you."

Feeling a blush rise on her cheeks, she opened the door wider and stepped into the bedroom. "Hello." She smoothed her hand over her voluminous cotton nightgown before daring to look at Eric.

He was sprawled over the bed, heavy chains securing him to the four-poster and a blanket spread over his groin to protect his modesty.

His body began shaking, alarming her, but then he burst out laughing. "What the hell are you wearing?"

She let out a breath. "You scared me. I thought you were having a reaction to the titanium chains or something."

"I'm not a werewolf. Did you get that travesty of a nightgown from a costume shop?"

It was a Victorian-style nightdress, with a high neck that tied with a string at the throat, plenty of lacy embellishments, and a wide cut that could hide an orgy going on under it. Not that an orgy was about to happen. She was going to ride Eric, Max was going to come in at the critical moment, bite her, and leave. She was making sure that he saw nothing of her body while he was at it.

"I got it at Macy's, and it's perfect for what we have planned. Do you want Max to see me nude while I'm riding you?"

Eric growled. "I don't. Now, come here and lift that two tons of fabric so I can see your beautiful legs."

Sauntering toward the bed and trying to look sexy despite what was covering her, Darlene smiled. "You are not in any position to issue orders, my love."

"That wasn't an order. That was a request." He tried to push higher on the pillows.

The chains rattled, but there was very little give. No more than an inch or two.

Was Max really that afraid of Eric attacking him?

Darlene bunched the skirt up as she climbed on the bed with her knees, exposing her legs like he'd asked. "Let's see what goodies are hiding under the blanket." Given that it was lying flat against his groin, he wasn't aroused, and she couldn't blame him.

Darlene felt as sexy as a fish left to dry on the sand.

"Climb up and straddle my face. Just keep that nightgown up, so I don't suffocate."

"Are you sure? What if Max misinterprets the sounds and comes in too soon?"

"He won't. Come here." He wiggled his tongue, and his eyes started glowing. "You know how much I love tonguing you. This will get us both in the mood."

As if to prove his words, the blanket lifted a bit, the outline of his shaft making Darlene's mouth water.

"Maybe we can put each other in the mood simultaneously?"

He shook his head. "Not tonight, love. I don't want to accidentally come in your hot mouth."

"You're an immortal now." She gripped the sides of her gown and pulled it up as she flipped one knee over his torso and climbed up to his face. "You have more than one load in you now."

"I had more than one for you even before I turned immortal." He kissed the top of her mound.

She'd had it waxed to be as bare as that of the immortal females, and it had been so painful that she hoped never to have to do that again. Going through the awkwardness with Max might be worth it just for that.

"Come up a little closer." Eric blew air on her heated flesh. "I want to taste that sweet pussy of yours."

His tongue gently circled the nub at the apex of her thighs with feather-like strokes to get her started.

Eric knew her so well by now, having memorized every response to every stimulus. He knew that she was sensitive there and if he started too fast and too aggressively, it would be a turn-off for her and not a turn-on. It would become painful in seconds.

It had taken Eric one time to learn that, while Leo hadn't learned that lesson even after nearly three decades of marriage. He'd just conveniently assumed that she wasn't into it and stopped offering.

Not that he'd offered to pleasure her much to start with. He'd been much happier to be on the receiving end while complaining that she was no good at it despite coming down her throat every freaking time.

Darlene shook her head.

This was no time to think about damn Leo and the damage he had done to her. He was ancient history, and she was in the process of being reborn, of rebuilding herself from the ground up, figuratively and materially.

"Stay with me, love," Eric murmured before moving his talented tongue to her entrance and slipping it inside for a few greedy licks. "Cup your breasts for me," he murmured against her moist petals. "Let me see those ripe nipples of yours as you play with them."

Easier said than done while holding up ten pounds of fabric, but she was determined to make it work. Pulling the nightgown all the way up to her throat, she tucked the sides under her armpits and folded her arms to reach for her breasts.

"Yeah." Eric's eyes cast a glow on her naked skin. "Just like that."

Feeling the heat radiate up from her core, she fondled her breasts and pinched her nipples as Eric alternated between thrusting his tongue into her wetness and flicking it over her engorged clit.

Darlene breathed through the pleasure, her hips bucking uncontrollably against Eric's mouth, but she kept her lips tightly pressed together, muffling the moans that begged to be let out.

She didn't want to share any of this with Max.

When the first climax tore through her, she had no choice but to open her mouth, or she would have suffocated on the cry that needed an outlet.

The chains rattled as Eric strained against them, reminding her that this pleasure had been one-sided and only the start, and that much more was awaiting her under the thin blanket covering him.

59

ERIC

*D*arlene's sweet, fragrant pussy hovered above Eric's face, her hips undulating with the aftershocks of her climax, and as he licked her clean, he was so damn aroused that he was afraid he would shoot his load the moment she touched his painfully stiff shaft.

Panting, she let the hideous nightgown flutter down around her, restricting his airflow, but a moment later, she shifted down, dragging the fabric with her.

"I think you're ready for me, lover boy." She gripped what was covering him and tossed it aside. "Oh, my. Ready and then some." She dipped her head.

"Don't. I'm about to blow."

She looked at him over her shoulder and smirked. "Normally, that wouldn't be a problem, but we don't want to waste your most potent load."

Gripping him lightly, she positioned him right at her entrance, and holding him in place, she lowered herself on top of him.

Eric bit down hard on his lower lip, commanding his seed to recede and wait for the right moment.

When Darlene pushed down, and her heat enclosed him, he realized that he was never going to get enough of it. They could make love thousands of times, and he would still want her, on top of him, taking him, taking her pleasure from him. He would look at her beautiful face and feel the love swelling in his chest for this amazing woman who had saved him from a life of coasting but not living.

"Let me see you," he begged.

She folded the nightgown over her knees but left where they were joined covered. "Close your eyes," she whispered. "Imagine that I'm naked."

Darlene started moving, her hips swaying as she pushed down and lifted and then pushed down again, getting a rhythm on.

Needing to touch her, his fists opened and closed, opened again, and gripped the sheet under him, tearing into the fabric as he struggled to hold on and not come right away.

He wanted her to climax again, and not from Max's venom bite.

As the aggression surged in his chest, his muscles tightened, and he pulled on the chains, but they held him firmly. All he could do to distract himself from thinking about the Guardian in the next room was to focus on Darlene's hips going up and down and how much he wanted to grip them.

"Lift that damn skirt. I need to see you riding me."

When she did as he asked, what he saw mesmerized him. Every time she moved up, he saw his glistening shaft, and each time she lowered herself on his length, seeing it disappear inside of her filled him with lust and possessiveness that was almost too much to bear.

Gritting his teeth and wishing that they were fangs, he hissed. "Come for me, Darlene."

With a groan, she threw her head back, and as her sheath tightened around his shaft, he started coming.

He was still drunk on her and semi-conscious when the door banged open, and a monster with long fangs and crazed eyes rushed toward his woman.

Eric's instincts roared to life, and the need to leap from the bed and protect his female was overwhelming. As he pulled on the chains, the wooden poles groaned but held, and he could do nothing but watch helplessly as the monster gripped Darlene's head.

60

DARLENE

*A*s Darlene heard the door bang open, she let go of the nightgown, so it covered her and Eric. Keeping her eyes closed to keep Max out of her awareness, she had a moment of fear as the chains rattled and the bedposts groaned, and then a powerful hand gripped the top of her head, yanking it to the side.

She expected Max to tear the top of her nightgown to expose her throat, but he just bit her through the fabric.

The pain was intense, a burning sensation that had her hiss, but it didn't last long. A cooling sensation followed, flooding her with a wave of euphoria, but the peace didn't last long either. A wave of lust followed, and she was coming again and again. No longer mindful of keeping quiet, she heard herself screaming, but had no idea what syllables were leaving her hoarse throat.

When a loud crack sounded, pulling her out of her euphoric trip, her eyes flew open, and she had a brief moment of panic as a bedpost came crashing down on her, but it never made contact.

Somehow, in a blink of an eye, she found herself under Eric, protected from the crushing bedposts.

They must have bounced off him because he started pounding into her as if nothing was wrong and as if he hadn't just climaxed seconds ago, and then she was orgasming again and again until it became too much, and her soul left her body, floating up onto a cloud where it was so peaceful and beautiful that she felt like crying from relief.

All the stress, all the pains from her past, all her insecurities and her doubts had evaporated, and she was whole, just a speck of light that was so full of love it could illuminate the universe.

The cloud she hitched a ride on was traveling fast, passing alien landscapes that were populated with all kinds of creatures, all aware of her passing above them, some smiling up at her, some waving, some pointing as they tapped their children on the shoulder to get them to look at her.

It was the best experience of her life, and she felt contented to stay in that space forever and never come back, but something in the back of her mind, the mind she'd left behind in her body on Earth, was whispering to her that this was just a brief visit, a glimpse into a bigger reality she hadn't been aware of while living inside the limiting filter of her body, and that at some point she had to come back to those who loved her and who would miss her if she were to leave now.

Just a little longer, she thought at that awareness. *Don't send me back yet.*

The awareness flooded her with warmth, communicating that there was no rush, and that she could float for long hours until she had her fill.

I will never tire of this.

You will come again, the awareness communicated through warmth. *And when it is your time, you will come to stay.*

61

ERIC

"Do you need help?" Max asked from the doorway.

"Stay out," Eric hissed. "I've got it."

"Don't be an idiot. You might have broken your back, and you are squashing Darlene. Let me lift the bedposts and unlock the restraints."

Max's words managed to penetrate through the crazed haze that had overpowered him when the guy had bitten Darlene.

Eric hadn't been thinking straight when he'd pulled on the chains and brought the massive posts down. Thankfully, he'd had enough presence of mind to pull Darlene under him, so they wouldn't crash into her. But now, he was on top of her, and with the added weight of the posts, he must be crushing her.

The pain had started to register as well. Did he have broken ribs?

Lifting on his forearms, Eric relieved Darlene of some of the weight and turned to look at the Guardian. "Fine. But leave after you unlock the restraints."

Max smirked. "I should wait for later to say this, but I can't. I told you so."

He started on Eric's left wrist. "I can't lift the posts without freeing you first because the chains are still attached to them on one end and to you on the other."

"Got it." Eric gritted his teeth as the need to attack Max assailed him again. "Those damn immortal instincts are such a nuisance."

"I know. I told you so."

If this one time didn't do the trick, he didn't think he could go through it again. Not after experiencing it. If he hadn't been chained to the bed, he might have tried to kill Max. The Guardian wasn't a foe easy to overcome, he was immortal, and Eric didn't have fangs and venom yet, so he couldn't have killed him even in his crazed state, but he would have inflicted pain on a friend who'd just been trying to help.

Yeah, right. As if Max didn't enjoy biting Darlene.

Don't go there, idiot.

When Max was done freeing Eric, he carried the clanking bundle of chains out of the room, and by the sound of it, dropped it on the hallway floor.

He returned to lift one of the bedposts and carried it outside the room as well. "It's good that the mattress is sitting on its own support, or it would have crashed to the floor as well. This bed is going to the dumpster." He lifted the next one and carried it out too.

When he was done with the fourth one, he looked at the floor. "Don't let Darlene walk barefoot here before we vacuum the place. The floor is covered with wood chips."

"Got it. Can you leave now, so I can assess the damage?"

"I'll be in the living room if you need me."

"Thanks." Eric waited for the door to close before daring to look down at Darlene.

She had a smile on her face, which alleviated his anxiety, and when he pulled out of her and lifted her nightgown to check for bruises, he was relieved to see that there were none on her body. There was a small bruise on her right wrist where it had been pressed against one of the chains, but other than that, she seemed fine.

"I really hope it worked, my love." He dipped his head and pressed a soft kiss to her parted lips. "If we have to do it again, we will need to do it in a dungeon where the chains can be embedded in concrete." He flexed one arm to look at the muscle. "I turned into a damn gorilla."

How he hadn't caused her more damage than that one little bruise was a mystery. One thing was for sure. He needed to be careful with Darlene from now on. She was still human, and he was much stronger than he'd thought he was.

As he carefully lowered one leg to the floor and then the other, the pain wasn't too bad, and when he straightened up, it got just a little worse. Hopefully, that meant nothing was broken. There was no blood either. When he checked in the bathroom mirror, the red marks that the posts had left behind on his skin were already fading.

"The advantages of being an immortal." He washed himself in the sink, wetted a few washcloths, and returned to the bedroom.

The room looked like a war zone, and after he'd cleaned Darlene up, he covered her with the blanket, pulled on a pair of pajama pants, and went to the kitchen to grab the Dyson.

"Is she okay?" Max asked.

Now that Eric was back to his normal self, his animosity toward Max was gone, and he was grateful to his friend for his help.

"She's out like a light. I wonder if the noise from the vacuum cleaner will wake her up."

"Not likely." Max grinned. "I pumped her with enough venom to knock her out until tomorrow."

Eric's lips pulled back from his teeth. "Do me a favor, and don't talk about that? I was just thinking that I'm calm enough to appreciate what you have done for us, and now I'm back to raging."

Max lifted his hands in the air. "I will never mention it again. Whiskey?" He rose to his feet.

"Definitely, and a lot of it." Eric started toward the bedroom.

"Coming up," Max said.

62

KIAN

*I*t was nearly nine o'clock at night when Leon and Marcel called to report what they had learned from Sofia.

"Did she give you a hard time?" Kian asked.

"Not at all," Leon said. "She was very helpful, and you are going to love some of her ideas. In fact, you might want to get Turner on the line if it's not too late."

Kian hadn't expected Sofia to contribute ideas. In fact, he'd been sure that she would resist providing them with more information about her people. Perhaps she'd fed them misinformation? Then again, Emmett and Eleanor had been right there with her, and she'd known that they could verify everything she'd told them, so it wasn't likely that she'd fed them lies.

"Before I do that, did you get the location of the tunnels from her?"

"There arc four tunnels that she knows of," Marcel said. "She marked the map, but naturally, the entrances to the tunnels are guarded, the dirt road leading to the first entrance is peppered with cameras, and the last tunnel doesn't go inside the compound. It spills right outside its walls, and there is another gate to go through. Bottom line, getting to the area around the compound where the Kra-ell are hunting in order to grab one is not feasible, but we can grab the guards from the entrance to the first tunnel. It will require tampering with the cameras, but that's not a big deal. Sofia says that the guard shifts last about twelve hours, so that gives us plenty of time to grab them, pump the pureblood in charge for information, thrall them or compel them to forget that they were interrogated, and put them back at their posts before their replacements arrive. That gives us a much longer window of time to work with than kidnapping a pureblood during a hunt. They might communicate with the other guards at certain intervals throughout the day, so that should be the first thing we address when we capture them."

"Just as an aside," Leon interjected. "Sofia bases her assessment of their shift length on what Igor's personal guard told her about his own schedule. That doesn't mean that the guards at the tunnels operate on a similar one."

"We also came up with a way to use a combination of spiders and mini drones to kickstart a resistance," Marcel said. "The spiders can deliver messages back and forth, and the drones can drop earpieces. Sofia says that the human quarters are rarely inspected, and that we can safely drop earpieces in the children's playground. She sketched a layout of the compound that's to scale and is very detailed. She doesn't know what's inside the Kra-ell quarters, but she's familiar with the office building where Igor and the other purebloods in charge spend most of their time. I'll scan it and send it over to you."

That was excellent intel. If need be, they could launch a missile at the office building and eliminate the Kra-ell leadership while minimizing civilian casualties.

"Let me get Turner on the line and bring him up to speed."

Turner answered immediately. "Hello, Kian."

"I have Leon and Marcel on the line. They have interesting new information."

After listening to Kian repeat what they had reported, Turner asked, "Did Sofia volunteer the information, or did Eleanor compel her to talk?"

"She volunteered it," Marcel said. "She was so excited about the possibility of contacting her father and letting him know that her death would be faked and that she was not really going to die. I didn't have the heart to ask Eleanor to verify that she'd told us the truth. It would have been insulting."

Turner chuckled. "I can see why you are no longer a Guardian. You think with your heart and not your head. She could've fed you all a bunch of lies."

Kian felt offended on behalf of Marcel. Guardians were not cold-hearted. Hell, he wasn't cold-hearted either. Did Turner suggest that having emotions made him an ineffective leader?

"Come on, Turner. Emmett and Eleanor were right there with her. Sofia knew that they could force her to tell the truth, and if they caught her in a lie, that would have looked really bad for her, and she would have been forced to tell the truth anyway."

"That might be true, but I would have verified the information, nonetheless. Are you willing to risk the lives of your men because you don't want to hurt the girl's feelings?"

"Good point." Kian sighed. "Emmett or Eleanor should verify the information. You can tell Sofia that I demanded it."

"It will be done," Leon said. "I'll have Eleanor go over everything with her tomorrow."

"I have no problem being the bad guy," Turner said. "Tell her it was me, and make me look really cold and ruthless. She's terrified of Igor, and it wouldn't hurt to let her believe that there is someone just as ruthless on our side."

Kian chuckled. "Am I not intimidating enough?"

Turner was cold, but he wasn't ruthless. After all, he was in the business of saving people, and he derived satisfaction from that, and not just because he was good at what he did.

"Using Turner as the bad guy will work better," Marcel said. "I've spent a lot of effort convincing Sofia of our moral superiority, praising our leadership for the good work it does, and emphasizing the checks and balances we employ. I think that was instrumental in her volunteering information, and I would hate to see all that work go to waste. I would much prefer to have her on our side voluntarily."

"It's good that you did that," Turner said. "You showed her the carrot. But it's also good to have a stick. It makes persuasion much more effective."

63

MARCEL

*M*arcel didn't want to show Sofia the stick. When he returned to the bunker, he planned to tell her who he was and what he could potentially do for her. If that didn't pull her fully over to their side, a stick wasn't going to do it either. But he couldn't disobey Kian.

"What are we going to do with this information?" Leon asked. "Are we going to start a rebellion?"

"A plan is starting to formulate in my head," Turner said. "It's a combination of what you suggest, Merlin's potion, and Toven. The question is what we are going to do once we liberate the compound. Are we going to leave Jade in charge? Who's to say that she wouldn't turn out to be just as dangerous of an adversary as Igor? So far, they don't know that we exist. Once they do, will they consider us a threat?"

There was a long moment of silence as everyone contemplated his statement.

"We still don't know how many Kra-ell communities are scattered around the globe," Kian said. "What they were sent here for, and if any more are scheduled to arrive. Jade might know the answers to that, and if we help her liberate her people, she will owe us. Emmett and Vrog claim that she's an honorable female, so she might feel obligated to share the information with us, and if not, we can have Toven get it out of her. The bottom line is that we can't leave things as they are and hope the Kra-ell will never discover us." He chuckled. "Worst case scenario, we can let the Doomers know about them. They would take care of the problem for us."

"I didn't think I would live to see the day when we cooperate with Navuh," Leon said.

Kian huffed. "Who said anything about cooperation? I will never trust that fucker not to turn around and stab me in the back. But he's a known entity, and he has the force to deal with the Kra-ell. If they pose a threat to us, I would be very happy to get them to fight each other while we stand back and watch."

So many suggestions had been flying back and forth that Marcel was confused as to what step they were about to take next.

"What is the play, then?" he asked. "What's our next move? Does Sofia keep feeding Igor nonsense about a paranormal community and its breeding program? Are we grabbing the guards?"

"Grabbing the guards might be one of the first steps," Turner said. "Or we might employ a shortcut and drive the cat around. If we are lucky, the tracker we took out of Sofia has a pureblooded tail, and we might be able to collect the information from them before Onegus's team even leaves for Karelia. For that to work, though, we would need Toven to return to the area and be on standby. It's imperative that Igor doesn't find out that we captured and interrogated his men, and no one other than Toven is capable of compelling them into pretending that nothing happened and keep reporting as usual. He would probably need Mia's help to override Igor's compulsion."

"That's risky," Kian said. "If Toven fails, or if they manage to send a signal before we incapacitate them, we won't be able to implement any of the other ideas we discussed. Igor will lock down his compound, and if he's a coward like most despots, he might escape with his inner circle."

"That would be a good thing, right?" Marcel asked. "Maybe we want him to find out, so he leaves the compound, and we just walk in and take over."

Kian huffed. "He might blow it up to prevent us from taking anyone alive, and he would either kill Jade or take her with him."

"He would take her," Marcel said. "Sofia says that they have a daughter together and that he wants a son from her. Apparently, Jade is the most powerful pureblooded female he has, and that's why he keeps her as his main breeder even though she makes no secret of the fact that she despises him."

"He still might kill her if he believes that she betrayed him," Turner said. "And since his men will be captured while trailing Sofia's tracker, he will rightly assume that it had to do with Jade."

"We need to knock the men out and search them for listening devices and embedded trackers," Leon said. "We will need strong tranq darts."

"Give me a couple of days to work on a plan," Turner said. "In any case, Monday, the Guardian team is leaving for Karelia, and their first order of business should be to scope the dirt road leading to the first tunnel, check what kind of surveillance equipment they are using, and watch the guards to find out their schedule."

"Are we going to drive the cat around first?" Marcel asked.

"I'll get back to you on that," Turner said.

64

SOFIA

*L*ong after Marcel and Leon had gone to talk with the boss, and Eleanor and Emmett had said their goodbyes, Sofia was still buzzing with excitement.

Pacing the bunker's long hallway, she replayed the ideas they had come up with and the hope they offered.

Jade was a powerful female, and if she had the earpieces to protect her from Igor's compulsion, maybe she would be able to overcome the many years of it and kill the guy.

Would his inner circle have to be taken down with him?

Would that mean that her grandfather had to be killed as well?

Did she care?

There had been moments during the weeks leading to her assignment when she'd felt closer to him, moments when she'd believed that he cared, that he was proud of her, but those hopes had been shattered when she had realized that he'd sent her to be captured so she could lead him to Safe Haven's real leader.

To Kian.

Who was that guy?

Marcel sounded fond of him, respectful and appreciative, and if Kian had to answer to a council, then he wasn't a dictator like Igor. She needed to meet him in person and see for herself to believe it, though.

When the door at the top of the stairs opened, she stopped her pacing, walked over to the foot of the stairs, and looked up.

"How did it go?" she asked.

Marcel came down with boxes from the kitchen. "It went well, I think. Turner is working on a plan."

"Is Turner Kian's right-hand man?" She followed Marcel to the dining table.

"Not officially." Marcel put the boxes down. "He runs an independent hostage rescue operation, but when Kian needs help with a difficult situation, he asks for his advice." He pulled a chair out for her.

"What kinds of difficult situations does a community of paranormally talented people run into?"

She had a strong feeling that Marcel and the others hadn't been telling her the truth about that. Listening to Leon and Marcel discuss ways of infiltrating the compound and using all kinds of sophisticated spy gear made it obvious that at least part of their organization was military in nature. There was no reason for a bunch of paranormally talented people to have commando teams and know about miniature drones and spy spiders.

Maybe they were a spy organization?

Many of the paranormal talents Eleanor had talked about in her lectures could be used for spying, and it made sense for them to use those special abilities for profit. It would explain how their organization had so much money.

Marcel sighed. "That's just a cover we use. It's not really what we are about."

"I knew it. What are you about?"

He walked to the wine cabinet and pulled out a bottle and two glasses. "You'll need a drink to hear that story."

She tensed. "Are you a spy organization?"

He laughed. "No."

Then what were they?

Marcel's glowing eyes and exceptional night vision could be some strange manifestation of a paranormal talent, or, as she'd suspected all along, he and the others were like the Kra-ell. They looked human, but so did some of the hybrids. Except, none of the Kra-ell hybrids were blond like Marcel. The dark coloring of the pureblooded Kra-ell was dominant.

"Are you a different kind of Kra-ell?"

"In essence, yes."

Sofia's breath caught in her throat.

Marcel uncorked the wine and poured it into two glasses. "We are the descendants of the mythological gods, who we suspect came from the same place as the Kra-ell. Another hypothesis is that the gods and the Kra-ell have a common ancestor. We are genetically similar, and both species are compatible with humans."

Her heart beating at double speed, Sofia emptied the wine down her throat. "In what way are you similar? And who are the mythological gods you are referring to?"

"I know that you didn't attend regular school, but to be accepted to the university, you must have been taught the regular school curriculum." He opened the two boxes and pushed one toward her.

"I can't eat." She pushed it away. "Are you talking about the Greek pantheon?"

"The Greek, the Roman, the Norse, and many others have their roots in the Sumerian, as does the Bible. They are all talking about the same gods. Those stories are mainly fantasies, but they are based on real people." He smiled. "My ancestors."

"Why are you telling me this now? What has changed?"

"I'll get to that in a moment." He pushed his box away as well and leaned to take her hand. "You noticed that my eyes glow, right?"

Sofia nodded.

"I also have fangs. But my fangs are not for drinking blood like the Kra-ell's. They are to inject venom. Did you notice that you black out after we make love?"

Her other hand flew to her neck. "Yes."

"That's because of my bite. My venom contains a powerful euphoric and an aphrodisiac, and it's responsible for the strings of orgasms you've been enjoying, as well as for the floaty, dreamy feeling that followed them."

It was just like Marcel to deliver his little lecture on the benefits of his venom as if he was explaining the operating manual of some gadget he'd developed.

She shook her head. "Why can't I remember you biting me?" She rubbed a spot on her neck. "Was it here?"

Nodding, he reached with his finger and tapped the other side of her neck. "I bit you here too. You can't remember it because I thralled you to forget it. Remember what I told you about my special ability to make you forget things that happened and remember things that didn't?"

"Like the necklace that you bought your ex-girlfriend, only it wasn't a necklace, but something else that you refused to tell me."

"Correct. But it's also not an ability that's reserved just for me. Nearly all immortals can do that, just as nearly all Kra-ell can compel."

Sofia's heart dropped to the pit of her stomach. When she'd suspected that Marcel wasn't entirely human, it hadn't crossed her mind that he might be long-lived.

He wouldn't want to tie himself to a woman who was going to get old in a couple of decades, while he still looked as young as he was now.

Was he young, though?

"Immortals? Is that what you call yourselves?" She couldn't keep the bitter tone from her voice.

"We are immortal. We can be killed, but it's difficult to do, and if no disaster befalls us, we can live forever. Our bodies don't age, they don't get sick, and we have phenomenal self-repairing capabilities."

65

MARCEL

*M*arcel had a feeling that he was botching it. He'd prepared his speech while waiting for his takeout to be packaged, and he'd thought he had it covered, but Sofia's response wasn't what he'd expected.

She wasn't excited.

In fact, she seemed upset.

"Do you live even longer than the purebloods?" she asked.

He nodded. "Emmett and the other hybrids assume that the average lifespan for the purebloods is about a thousand years. Is that what you were told as well?"

She nodded. "No one knows how long the hybrids will live. The oldest in our compound is about eighty." She let out a breath. "I still don't understand why you are telling it to me now. Is it because I'm not going back, and you are tired of telling me stories?"

Perhaps when he got to the point and told her the real reason, she would cheer up.

Lifting her hand to his lips, he kissed her knuckles. "What if I told you that I can make you live at least as long as the hybrids?"

Her eyes widened. "How?"

"That requires a bit of an explanation, so bear with me." He took in a breath. "When the gods took human partners, their children were born immortal. However, when those immortals grew up and took human partners, their children were born human."

"It's the same for the Kra-ell. My mother is a hybrid, but I'm a human."

He smiled. "I'm not done. They later discovered that the children born to immortal females still carried the godly genes, and that those genes could be activated with an immortal male's venom. We produce it in response to two triggers, and the composition of the venom depends on the type of trigger. One is arousal, which makes us produce less potent venom that does all those wonderful things

398

like orgasms and euphoric trips, and the other trigger is aggression, which produces a potent venom that is potentially deadly because it can stop an immortal's heart. Both types can activate the dormant genes. We use the one produced by arousal to activate females, and the one produced by aggression to activate males."

Sofia shook her head. "The Kra-ell don't have venom. They use their fangs to suck blood. That's what they eat."

"Actually, they do have venom, and it has similar properties to ours in that it makes the bite pleasurable and has healing properties. But since it's produced in much smaller quantities, it can't activate Dormants, not immortal Dormants anyway. But we suspect that our venom can activate Kra-ell Dormants, which means that I might be able to activate your longevity genes."

Sofia's hand flew to her mouth. "Am I going to grow fangs?"

He laughed. "You might. But the important part is that you might live a thousand years or even longer, become stronger and faster, and all the other good things that the Kra-ell hybrids enjoy."

For a long moment, she gaped at him in stunned silence. "Do the Kra-ell know about you?"

Marcel shook his head. "We don't think they know we even exist, and we would like to keep it that way. But if we liberate Igor's compound, our secret will be out. Not only that, if I manage to activate your dormant genes, the Kra-ell will have a big incentive to either cooperate with us so we can activate their Dormants or try to use us to propagate their species. Since we are compatible, our females can provide them with immortal offspring, and our males can activate their second-generation hybrids who are born to hybrid mothers."

"Why just the mothers?"

"The longevity is passed through the mothers. Compulsion ability seems to be passed by the fathers for reasons we are not clear on."

Leaning back, Sofia closed her eyes. "How many times have you bitten me?"

"Twice. Usually, it takes several bites for the transition to start. I didn't know that you had Kra-ell blood in you. It only occurred to me that you might be a Dormant after you told me that your mother was a hybrid. We knew that the Kra-ell couldn't activate their second generation with humans, and we also knew that a hybrid Kra-ell male couldn't activate one of our dormant females. It took me a little while to go through the mental exercise and realize that maybe I could induce your transition. Once I did, I knew that I couldn't keep biting you and having unprotected sex with you without obtaining your consent to induce you. It's a monumental decision, and it needs to be yours."

"What does unprotected sex have to do with anything? I'm on birth control."

"Our doctor believes that insemination boosts the power of the venom. Most of what we know about how it works is by trial and error." He chuckled. "I think that the geneticists who engineered us made it in such a way that the catalysts would remain a mystery."

Sofia looked puzzled. "What are you talking about? Who engineered you?"

"Not me specifically. We speculate that the gods engineered themselves, humans, and other species."

"That's a lot of speculation and very little proof."

"I know. We hope that Jade will be able to tell us more."

"Is that why you are willing to help free her?"

Marcel rubbed a hand over the back of his neck. The conversation wasn't going the way he'd hoped, and he needed to get it back on track.

"As I said before, I'm not the one making those kinds of decisions. Let's get back to the issue at hand. You need to decide whether you want me to try to induce you or not."

"What's to decide?"

He chuckled. "Maybe you'd rather remain human than grow fangs, which by the way, our females don't have. But seriously, the transition is not easy, and many transitioning Dormants lose consciousness. Some are out for a day or two, while others are out for weeks. There is also a very low risk of death."

She narrowed her eyes at him. "How low?"

"We haven't lost a transitioning Dormant yet, and the younger and healthier you are, the less risky it is. You really have nothing to worry about, but I would be remiss if I didn't warn you of the risks."

"Makes sense, and I appreciate that you are not trying to sugarcoat it. I have a question, though. How do you know that a Kra-ell male can't activate one of your Dormants?"

"Emmett had been having sex with a dormant lady for many years, and he failed to activate her despite biting her numerous times. She transitioned after falling in love with one of us. Still, he's a hybrid, so perhaps a pureblood can do that."

She nodded. "That's why you were asking me whether I had sex with any hybrids or purebloods."

"Yes. Did you?"

She glared at him. "I've already told you that I didn't."

He lifted his hands. "Just double-checking. You might have felt bad about being coerced."

"I haven't been coerced." She winced. "At least not as far as I know. If some of them can make people forget things, they could have done that to me, but I really doubt that."

"Good. Since no one aside from me had ever injected you with venom, there is a chance that mine can activate your dormant genes."

66

SOFIA

*H*ope surged in Sofia's chest, but she didn't allow it to soar too high.

What Marcel was proposing had never been done before, and it probably wouldn't work. They weren't even the same species.

Both of them were half-human, or three-quarters in her case. Was his mother a goddess? Were gods from mythology still around?

"I have so many questions."

"That's what I'm here for. Ask away."

"How old are you?"

"Three hundred and twenty-seven."

"Oh, wow. That's old."

He chuckled. "Thanks."

"Is your mother a goddess?"

"My mother is an immortal, and so was her mother before her, and so on. The females of our clan kept us from going extinct by having children with human fathers. But unlike you, we didn't grow up with those fathers. To keep our existence a secret, long-term relationships with humans were discouraged, or rather disallowed, and the men who sired us were not even told about having us."

She scrunched her nose. "So your blood must be heavily diluted. Are you sure you can activate me?"

Marcel nodded. "If you can be activated, I can surely do that. Our doctor says that eventually our genes will become too diluted to produce Dormants, but we still have a long time until that happens. You need to change your thinking from the Kra-ell's ability to produce just one generation of hybrids to the immortals' ability to produce them in perpetuity."

"Your people's genetics must be superior to ours."

"As I mentioned before, the theory is that the gods were genetically enhanced. The Kra-ell might have been the original. We are all dying to get a pureblood in our hands so we can finally learn the truth about our past. The gods were just as bad about keeping information from the next generation of even their own pure-blooded children as the Kra-ell are. I wonder if that has to do with cultural issues or if they both share such a shameful past that they prefer to keep it where it belongs?"

"Are any of the gods still around?"

"None of the original ones, but a few of their pureblooded children survived. The head of our clan is a goddess. Kian is her son, and he leads the American arm of the clan. There aren't many of us, but there is another group of immortals who are led by a god's son, and who have many thousands of warriors. We are not on good terms with them, and that's putting it mildly, but if the Kra-ell turn out to be a bigger threat than we anticipate, we might get those other immortals involved. As the saying goes, the enemy of my enemy is my friend. Maybe having a mutual enemy would finally end the animosity between our two groups, although I doubt it. Our feud has been going on for thousands of years."

That was all fascinating, and Sofia wanted to learn much more about his people's history, but that wasn't what was at the forefront of her mind right now.

"What happens if I don't transition?"

"You will live out your human life in our village, hopefully as my mate." He cupped her cheek. "But I have a strong feeling that you will transition. The Fates wouldn't have brought us together and dangled the perfect mate in front of me only to deny us a long life together. The Fates are fickle, and they have a wicked sense of humor, but they are not cruel."

This was the closest Marcel had ever gotten to telling her that he loved her, but it wasn't good enough. Calling her his perfect mate wasn't the same as calling her the love of his life.

Sofia sighed. "I'm touched that you think I'm perfect for you, but I'm not a great believer in fate. I believe in the Mother of All Life, and she's not a kind goddess. She's demanding and vengeful, and she doesn't grant happy endings. The best I can hope from her is that when I die, I ascend to a place of honor on the field of heroes, but since I'm human, I'm not likely to get there. So, in fact, the best I can hope for is not to be sent to the valley of the shamed."

Marcel arched a brow. "Is that like the human hell?"

"There is no fire or brimstone, so no, but it's the place all cowards go to."

"You're not a coward."

"Oh yes, I am. I've spent most of my life being afraid."

"That doesn't make you a coward. We are all afraid of one thing or another. It's what we do despite our fears that defines us as either cowards or heroes."

67

MARCEL

*A*s Marcel reflected on his own life, he realized that he'd spent most of it being afraid of making mistakes, of trusting people who would later disappoint him, of choosing the wrong path, and he'd been a coward because he had let those fears keep him in a sort of suspended animation.

He'd chosen to be a coward.

He'd dedicated himself to his work, learning as much as he could about machines and their language because machines were predictable. They weren't manipulative, they weren't temperamental, and they gave back in direct proportion to what was put into them.

With William at the helm, Marcel had been shielded from having to make decisions or deal with their consequences, and the only responsibilities he'd had were to perform his job well, which he had done.

It had been a safe and comfortable life, devoid of turmoil, and then Sofia had shown up and had blown it to smithereens.

On the one hand, he loved the exhilaration, the novelty, the challenge, and the way she made his heart beat erratically, but on the other hand, he yearned to go back to his calm and orderly life where every day was more or less the same as the one preceding it.

"How do you know that I'm your perfect mate?" Sofia asked. "Maybe it's just a passing infatuation." She smiled sadly. "I'm a novelty that you will eventually grow tired of."

He briefly closed his eyes. "I'm not a great romantic, or at least I'm not anymore, and even when I was young and naive and fell in love left and right, I didn't know how to express myself. I still don't. But there is a simple test that I dare you to try. Close your eyes and imagine a life without me. If the thought doesn't squeeze your heart, then perhaps I'm not the one for you."

She shook her head. "That's such a simplistic approach. If I do it now, I'm sure that's precisely how I would feel. But if you hurt me badly enough, those feelings would die the same way as your feelings for your ex-girlfriend died after she'd hurt you. People say that true love is unconditional, but that's untrue. Everything is about give and take." She chuckled. "Look at who is decisively unromantic now. I bet you've never heard a woman say those things."

He smiled. "The Kra-ell don't believe in love. I guess growing up among them rubbed off on you."

"I believe in love. I just don't believe in unconditional love. If you treat me right and love me, I'll treat you right and love you in return. But I will never love a man who abuses me or treats me with disrespect." She averted her eyes. "My biggest fear living in the compound was being forced into becoming a breeder. The way I dealt with the fear was by minimizing it. The purebloods didn't seek out human women to have a relationship with. They only wanted to produce hybrid offspring to grow their numbers. I figured I could tolerate having sex with them as long as I didn't need to feel anything for them. Thankfully, my being related to Valstar afforded me some protection. None of the purebloods have approached me."

"I assume that he's someone important in Igor's organization."

Sofia nodded. "He's Igor's second-in-command."

Marcel's good mood took a nosedive.

Sofia had failed to disclose her relationship to the most important member of Igor's inner circle, painting herself as an innocent victim, compelled into doing the evil dictator's bidding.

Was it his lot in life to fall for women who disappointed him?

Marcel let out a breath. "Turner asked me to have Eleanor or Emmett verify the information you provided by compelling you to tell the truth. I told him that you were cooperating out of your own free will and that it wasn't necessary. But he was right."

She frowned. "What are you talking about?"

"You've just let slip that you're related to Igor's second-in-command. You're not the innocent victim you portrayed yourself to be."

Throwing her hands in the air, Sofia pushed to her feet. "You're insufferable, and Eleanor is right. You have a giant stick up your ass, and until you pull it out, don't talk to me about being your perfect mate. In fact, don't ever talk to me again." She marched into the bedroom and slammed the door behind her.

Marcel pushed to his feet.

Her tantrum didn't affect him. He retreated into his shell, which was crafted of logic and impervious to emotions.

But the fact remained that Sofia hadn't mentioned Valstar's position in Igor's organization, and it couldn't have been an oversight. She'd done it on purpose.

Then again, could he blame her?

Would he have done things differently in her position?

It all depended on how being related to Igor's second-in-command affected her standing in the compound.

The easiest way to get the answers he needed was to ask Eleanor to compel them out of Sofia.

The problem was that she might never forgive him for doubting her again.

68

SOFIA

Sofia threw herself on the bed but refused to cry.

Marcel had once again turned against her, but this time it hurt even more because it had come right on the heels of him declaring her his "perfect mate."

What a joke.

Couldn't he understand why she hadn't mentioned her grandfather's position before?

It was because she'd known that was how he would react despite what she told him about her relationships with her mother and her grandfather.

She was nothing to them.

She was a nobody in the compound, and her relationship to Valstar only provided her with the slightest advantage, maybe not even that. Perhaps her don't-mess-with-me attitude had been effective enough to keep unwanted advances at bay.

The Kra-ell were not rapists per se. Other than Igor, who must have a personality disorder, she hadn't noticed any obvious mental issues among the Kra-ell males. Like any normal men, they still wanted the females they invited to their beds to desire and want them.

It was true that many of the human females did that to remain in good standing and avoid courting undesirable consequences, of which there could be many, but she hadn't heard anyone complaining about being physically forced.

Then again, with all of the purebloods capable of compulsion to a lesser or greater degree, it was possible that the women just couldn't talk about it. Sofia hoped that wasn't the case, but she no longer knew who to believe.

Marcel still treated her like she was the enemy despite all of the information she'd voluntarily given him and his people—immortals who were much more dangerous than she could've ever suspected.

They weren't a community of paranormally talented humans. They had military capabilities, and they could enlist the help of their so-called enemies to destroy Igor and everyone else in the compound. Once again she'd been a pawn, but this time, of her own volition and to the detriment of her own loved ones.

How could Marcel have the audacity to accuse her of withholding information?

The nerve of the guy.

He'd gotten her to reveal the entrances to the tunnels, to admit that there were surveillance cameras along the dirt road leading to it, and to draw him a damn layout of the entire compound to scale.

It was true that Eleanor, or Emmett, or Tom could have gotten the information out of her with compulsion, but then she would at least not have felt like an idiot for volunteering it.

Seething with anger, Sofia grabbed the romance novel off the nightstand and chucked it at the wall, but it did little to channel the negative energy bubbling inside of her. The lamp looked like a much bigger projectile, but as she jumped to her feet and lifted it, intending to send it flying, logic managed to seep in and she put it back.

She would just have to clean up the broken glass, and she would have one less comfort item in her prison cell.

Exasperated, Sofia sat on the bed, braced her elbows on her knees, and let her head drop down.

When a knock sounded on the door, she ignored it, barely able to contain the words "go to hell" from leaving her mouth. It took tremendous effort to keep her lips pressed tightly together, but she knew that anything she said right now would only make things worse, so it was better to shut up.

Would it get better in a few hours?

Usually, her anger was quick to rise, quick to explode, and just as quick to subside, but not this time. She was too hurt, and frankly, there was nothing Marcel could say to make it better.

In fact, anything he said would just make it worse.

When the door eased open, she didn't even look at it.

"May I come in?" Marcel asked.

She shrugged. "It's your jail. I can't stop you."

He walked over and sat on the bed next to her. "Can you stop brooding for a moment and see things from my perspective?"

Oh, he was asking for it.

She cast him a baleful look. "Can you see things from mine? I thought that I was cooperating with humans who had paranormal abilities. Now I know that I sold out my people to another species of beings who have military capabilities and can enlist an army of immortal warriors. So you tell me who deceived whom and why."

69

MARCEL

S ofia had a point.

"What I said before is still true." Marcel scooted a little closer to her. "We don't mean your people harm. If we can, we would like to liberate the compound, and for our own safety, we need to accumulate as much information about the Kra-ell as we can. Until recently we didn't know that they existed. We still don't know why they came, what their plans are, and if they know that we are here. If they came from the same place as the gods, they also might have information about our origins."

She shrugged. "That's a good story, but it doesn't change the fact that you can compel any information you want out of me, while I can't verify anything you say. I'm at a disadvantage, and you have the nerve of accusing me of withholding information right after you make the absurd claim that I'm your perfect mate and that you can make me long-lived or immortal. Excuse me if I'm skeptical."

"Why would I make false claims if I can force you to do anything I want?"

She turned a pair of angry eyes at him. "Just leave me alone. I don't want anything to do with you. From now on, I'll only talk with Eleanor. That way, I won't get accused of lying."

How had he messed this up so badly?

"I can't leave you alone. I've fallen in love with you, and I want to have a life with you. What can I do to fix this?"

She hesitated for a split second, but then shook her head. "Nothing. The damage has been done. Go away."

"No."

"Suit yourself." She rose to her feet, walked into the bathroom, and slammed the door shut behind her.

Despondent, he sat on the bed and waited for Eleanor to arrive.

A few moments later, he heard the door at the top of the stairs open, and then he heard Eleanor's light footsteps as she descended the stairs.

"Where is she?" Eleanor asked as she walked into the room.

"She's in the bathroom. She won't talk to me."

Hand on her hip, Eleanor cast him a glare. "What have you done?"

"I don't know. She's being unreasonable."

"Right." Eleanor walked over to the bed and sat down beside him. "That's what men say when they mess up and don't want to admit it. Is she mad that you called me to verify that what she told us before is legit?"

"That too. Evidently Valstar, who is Sofia's pureblooded grandfather, is not just a cog in the machine. He's Igor's second-in-command. Sofia just conveniently failed to mention that. She's not the innocent victim she's been portraying herself to be, and now she knows that we are immortals and that our ancestors and hers are somehow connected."

"So what?" Eleanor crossed her arms over her chest. "She's not going back, so it doesn't matter what she knows, and if she tries to breathe a word of this to her grandfather the next time she communicates with him, we will stop her. If anyone has a reason to be mad, it's her. She was keeping one little secret from you. You were keeping a very big one from her. You both had good reasons for that, and you both should get past that. It's not worth getting upset over."

"Tell that to her." He pointed at the door. "She won't listen to me, and she doesn't want to see me ever again."

Chuckling, Eleanor shook her head. "She wouldn't be so mad if she didn't care about you. Let Auntie Eleanor broker a peace." She motioned for him to get up. "Wait for us in the living room."

"That's ridiculous. I just told Sofia that she's the one for me and that I want to induce her transition. Any reasonable female would have been overjoyed."

"Oh, boy." Eleanor pushed him on his back. "You have a lot to learn about women."

"Tell me something I don't know." Marcel rose to his feet. "It's the story of my life."

The bathroom door opened, and Sofia stormed out. "And that's one more thing that you haven't told me because you don't trust me. I told you everything about my life, but you just keep hinting about the horrible thing your ex-girlfriend did, but you don't trust your so-called perfect mate enough to tell me about something that happened who knows how many years ago, and that doesn't affect anyone in the present. You're full of shit, Marcel." She stormed out of the room.

"Did you close the door upstairs?" he asked Eleanor.

"Of course. It locks automatically." She rose to her feet. "You really have to work on your trust issues."

SOFIA

*A*s Sofia paced the living room, she struggled to hold back the tears. The space was too small and too crowded with furniture to allow proper pacing, especially with her long legs, and the hallway would mean passing by the room Marcel was in, and she didn't want to look at him.

Was she overreacting?

No, she wasn't.

He was such a self-righteous prick.

What did he expect?

For her to fall on her knees and thank him for offering her a long life?

For what?

So she could spend an even longer time with a man who didn't trust her and caused her anguish?

No, thank you.

She'd rather live out her short human lifespan with someone who cherished her. Not that any such fantasy was going to materialize for her, but that didn't mean that she should compromise.

It was okay to be without. It was less painful than compromising on being with someone who made her miserable.

"Come on." Eleanor wrapped her arm around her shoulders. "Let's get out of here and breathe some fresh air."

That was a surprise. "Am I allowed out?"

Eleanor had promised to compel her into silence about everything that had gone down since that moment in Emmett's office, so she could rejoin the retreat, but she hadn't done so yet, probably because she'd known that Marcel was going to reveal more stuff, and she wanted to do it in one shot.

"I'm taking you with me, so you are under my supervision."

"What if anyone sees me?"

"Then we will tell them that you just came back, and if they ask where you have been, you can say that you're not allowed to talk about it."

Sofia sighed. "I like how simple you make everything sound. I wish Marcel was more like you."

Eleanor grinned. "Most people don't like my direct approach, so it means a lot to me that you do."

She led her up the stairs, punched the code into the keypad so fast that Sofia's eyes couldn't follow, and opened the door.

When they were out of the cottage, Sofia took in a deep breath. "It feels so good to be outside."

Eleanor nodded. "The Kra-ell need the outdoors to thrive. Emmett was wilting when he was kept in captivity. You have their blood, so being underground must affect you negatively."

It hadn't occurred to her. Sofia had thought that the lack of freedom and the isolation were making her agitated and restless, but it was also being cooped up in an underground bunker with no windows and no fresh air.

"What time is it?"

"It's almost midnight. We can probably sneak out to the beach without anyone noticing you."

"Except for the guards."

"They are called Guardians."

"Are they your military branch?"

"They are part an internal police force, part defenders, and part rescuers of trafficking victims. Do you know what that is?"

"The term is confusing, so I'm not sure. Does that refer to women who are kidnapped and sold into sexual slavery?"

"By and large, yes. But most are not kidnapped, just manipulated or sold by their families, and some are forced into menial job slavery instead of forced sex service, which is only slightly less horrific, and not all are women. Girls and boys are also taken."

"Why is it called trafficking?"

Eleanor snorted. "Don't ask me. It's one of the idiotic terms that politicians come up with. It makes an abomination sound like a speeding infraction. But anyway, that's the clan's humanitarian project. They raid the cells, free the victims, and rehabilitate them. The clan is not big, so their impact on the global problem is negligible, but every life matters, right? At least they are doing something."

Sofia nodded. "It's admirable."

"It is, and that's why I told you about it. The goddess leading these immortals made it her goal to assist humanity to become a more enlightened civilization, where everyone's human rights are respected, where people are given equal freedoms regardless of anything other than being born under the sun and given equal chances to succeed. She instilled those values in her children and grandchildren and their children and so forth. The clan is a force for good, and they made a convert even out of me, the most cynical, jaded woman you ever met."

"I'm sure you're exaggerating. You can't be that bad if I like you."

Eleanor snorted. "Perhaps compared to the Kra-ell females, I'm a sweetheart.

Anyway, I haven't met anyone worse than me, so I can't be sure of that statement. But I can assure you that I'm a changed woman, and in my case, it wasn't because of a man. I met Emmett long after deciding that I was going to work with the clan and not against it."

They'd walked around the lodge rather than through it, so they'd made it to the beach without anyone stopping them, and as Sofia stood in front of the vast expanse of water, her agitated nerves reduced their firing speed. "I missed being out here at night."

Eleanor stood next to her. "The Kra-ell compound is not near the ocean?"

"There is a lot of greenery inside the compound as well as around it, and there are many bodies of water in Karelia." She smiled. "Over the last seven years, I lived mostly in Helsinki, but I made sure to spend as much time as I could in nature. It's probably the Kra-ell part of me that craves it."

71

MARCEL

*I*t was almost two in the morning when Eleanor and Sofia returned, and Sofia looked like a different person. She even gave him a tentative smile.

"She's all yours." Eleanor winked at him. "Don't mess it up." She turned and walked toward the stairs, but then stopped and looked at him over her shoulder. "All the information is verified, and there is nothing to add. You can take it from here."

"Hi." Sofia remained standing. "I'm sorry about blowing up before," she said as the door at the top of the staircase closed. "Eleanor explained a lot of things, and I know now what the clan and the goddess who heads it are about. I find it admirable, and I wouldn't mind becoming part of it. I wish that my family could join me, but Eleanor explained that wouldn't be possible even if they were free. Kian rarely admits humans into the village."

If Eleanor was still there, Marcel would have given her a big thank-you hug and kissed her on both cheeks.

Instead, he walked over to Sofia, hesitating for a moment before wrapping his arms around her. "I'm sorry too. I shouldn't have doubted you."

Letting out a sigh, she rested her head on his shoulder and sagged into his embrace. "You had your reasons, and I had mine. Eleanor explained it all. But she left one thing for you to explain." She lifted her head and looked into his eyes. "She said that you need to tell me about fated mates and what it means."

Clever woman.

"She's right. I did a bad job of it. Hell, I made a mess out of everything. I was not blessed with the gift of gab." He led her to the couch, sat down, and pulled her into his lap.

"What's that?"

"Gab? It's the ability to express oneself eloquently, which I don't have. Everything I say sounds as if I'm reading an instruction manual."

Sofia chuckled. "I kind of like that about you. It makes you different."

"I am different, but not necessarily in a good way."

"Tell me about fated mates, and I don't mind how dry you make it sound. I'll add embellishments in my head."

"You see, that makes you my perfect mate. What other woman would have said that?"

She rolled her eyes. "Enough preamble. Just get it out already."

He nodded. "We believe that those who've earned the right, whether through sacrificing for others or suffering greatly, are rewarded by the Fates with a truelove mate. It's not what humans refer to as falling in love, and it's not like other loving relationships that the immortals might have. The attraction is immediate, resisting it is impossible, and once the bond is formed, it's unbreakable. Fated mates never look at another person with desire in their eyes. They love each other exclusively and forever."

"That sounds beautiful. Is it real?" She looked doubtful.

"I've seen it happen time and again to people I know, people who are not prone to flights of fancy, and who are not romantics at heart. The best example is Kian. He used to be a jaded, grumpy man who devoted his life to leading the clan and cared nothing about his own happiness. Then he met Syssi, and he fell in love with her right away. The same is true for her, and they are incredibly happy together. She changed him for the better. They also have a little daughter, who's the cutest little girl you'll ever see. She's beautiful like her mother, but at seven months old, she already has Kian's domineering personality, and on her, it's adorable. On him, not so much."

"I would love to meet her," Sophia whispered. "She sounds endearing."

"She is. But that's more or less what a truelove mate is. The thing is, I never sacrificed a lot for others, and my suffering was my own doing. I don't deserve a boon from the Fates."

"Neither do I, and besides, I'm not one of their subjects. I'm under the Mother of All Life's jurisdiction."

"The Fates do not belong exclusively to the clan. They are a universal force, and so is the Mother you speak of. Who knows, maybe they sit around a table in another realm, sipping on wine and coordinating their moves. They might be in cahoots."

Sofia laughed. "I love the image you're painting. What do the Fates look like?"

He caressed her back. "They can take any form they want, but I imagine them as three portly, human grandmothers with kind smiles and cunning eyes. How do you imagine your goddess?"

Sofia closed her eyes and rested her cheek on his chest. "Like an older Kra-ell pureblooded female who is ethereally beautiful and severe. She doesn't smile kindly, and her eyes are angry."

Marcel shivered. "Not my kind of deity. I prefer the three older ladies with big, soft bosoms."

"I bet." She chuckled. "Eleanor told me that immortal males are a lot like human men. You like soft females who treat you with love and kindness like your mothers."

413

"Perhaps that's the type other men prefer, but it's not mine."

She lifted her head and looked into his eyes. "Am I your type?"

"You are, but with a twist. I'm a sucker for delicate damsels in distress. That's my Achilles' heel. But you just look the part. On the inside, you are strong, assertive, and you are self-reliant, and I admire that."

"What about your ex? Was she a damsel in distress?"

He let out a breath. "She played the part to perfection, and I fell for it. Back then, the myth of a truelove mate was just that, a myth, but I was a romantic at heart, and I chased after it in all the wrong places. That's how I got in trouble."

"Are you ever going to tell me what really happened?"

"Do I have your consent to induce you?"

Sofia rolled her eyes. "Do you always answer a question with another question?"

"Not always, but this time I have to have the answer to that first. I will not tell this story to anyone other than my truelove mate."

"My consent will not prove it one way or another."

He put a hand on his chest. "I already know that you are in here. Your consent will mean that you accept it as well."

"Then I consent."

72

SOFIA

*S*ofia had planned to consent regardless of Marcel's confession.

Eleanor had told her so many good things about the clan that she would have to be stupid not to want to be part of it, and she trusted the woman.

Eleanor had nothing to gain by convincing her, she'd been sincere, and she hadn't sugarcoated anything.

After using compulsion to verify everything that Sofia had told her and the others and ensuring that she didn't have anything relevant to add, Eleanor had told her so many things that Marcel hadn't. She'd told her about the clan's powerful enemies and that it was unlikely they would ever join forces. Eleanor had also told Sofia about her struggles when she'd first transitioned, and about the unlikely help she'd gotten from the sister-in-law whom she'd abandoned in her time of need, but who had taken care of her nonetheless.

As a newcomer to the clan herself, Eleanor didn't know much about Marcel's past. She'd heard that he'd been burned by love in his youth, but she didn't know any details. Her advice had been to let it go and not press him to talk about it. Eleanor had said that she preferred not to dwell on her own past mistakes but to look forward to a better future.

Sofia disagreed.

She wanted Marcel to tell her about it, not just to satisfy her curiosity, and not just as a way to prove his devotion to her, but because he needed to unburden himself from the guilt and self-loathing that were dragging him down.

"It's not easy for me to tell this story." He leaned his forehead against hers. "You might not want anything to do with me once you hear what I have done."

"I doubt it. You are a good man, Marcel, and we all make mistakes. I bet you've been beating yourself up over whatever that was for far too long."

"It happened a very long time ago when I was still a young man."

He was three hundred and twenty-seven years old. If he'd been a young man when he'd been burned, it must have been about three hundred years ago. The world had been a very different place back then.

She leaned back and looked into his eyes. "It's definitely time to unburden yourself. Tell me."

"Cordelia was a married woman, but I didn't know that when I started seeing her. Her husband was a naval officer, and he'd been stationed on a warship. She was beautiful, delicate, and she carried sadness around her like a shawl made of gossamer. I was drawn to her like a moth to a flame. She made me feel special, as if I was the only one who could make her laugh, make her happy, and when we made love, she made me feel as if I was the best lover in the world."

Having an affair with a married woman was not a good thing, but it wasn't such a terrible offense either. Three hundred years ago, her husband might have been partying with prostitutes every night, and the only reward the poor wife could expect for waiting for him to come home had been a sexually transmitted disease.

If that had been so, then kudos to her for finding happiness in the arms of another.

"When did you find out that she was married?"

"At first, I assumed that she was a widow. A large portrait of her husband in naval uniform hung over the fireplace in the living room, but it was draped over with a semi-sheer black cloth, which indicated that he was deceased, and that the household was in mourning. None of her servants ever mentioned the master of the house, and combined with her sadness, it all pointed to one conclusion, albeit a wrong one."

"Didn't you think to ask her?"

He shook his head. "It seemed like a painful subject, and since none of the servants breathed a word of him or gave me the stink eye for spending night after night in her bedchamber, I saw no reason to ask." He closed his eyes for a moment. "I gave her expensive jewelry, not because she demanded it, but because I was a fool in love. Every time I brought her an extravagant gift, she was so happy, and it made me feel like a prince."

"Did you spend all of your money on her?"

"I did. I was a Guardian back then, and Guardians were well paid. Still are. I didn't need the money, but I could have spent it on feeding a hungry village or two instead of wasting it on a manipulative woman. I later found out that I wasn't her first lover, and that she used the same tactics with others to collect riches and pay for her extravagant lifestyle."

Sofia pursed her lips. "So you were played. Big deal. You loved her, you were blinded by her beauty and her acting, and you spent all of your money on her. It's not like you murdered anyone."

He huffed out a breath. "I'm not done. The story gets much worse."

MARCEL

*M*arcel took a deep breath. "One day, I came to her house and found her crying."

This was the worst part, and he dreaded to see Sofia's reaction to his confession.

"'What happened?' I asked.

"'*My husband is coming home,*' she said.

"I thought that she meant that they were bringing his casket home, so I took her hand, looked into her eyes, and asked if she wanted me to be there when the coffin arrived, and if she needed my help with the funeral arrangements. She looked at me with her doe eyes.

"'*He's not dead. But I will be when he finds out about you. He threatened to kill me before.*'

"Tears were streaming down her eyes as she told me about the years of abuse she'd suffered. She pulled up her sleeve and showed me an old scar that I had seen before.

"'*He did this to me. The bruises have faded, the broken bones healed, but this cut is a reminder of what a monster I'm married to.*'

"I was stunned. I asked her how come she'd never mentioned him before, and why none of the servants had spoken his name. She told me with teary eyes that the servants did that out of love for her.

"'*They know how terribly he has been treating me, and they don't want to upset me by speaking his name. They all cower before him, his anger is explosive, and he's not averse to using his fists or even the crop. One of these days, he will finish what he started and end me. We cannot see each other anymore. If he finds out about us, he will kill us both.*'"

Marcel's hands were sweaty as he lifted them to rake his fingers through his hair. "I was enraged. I couldn't understand how any man could raise his hand in anger at a woman, and especially not a delicate, gentle flower like Cordelia."

"What did you do?" Sofia asked, but the horrified look in her eyes told him that she'd already guessed.

"I promised to liberate her, and I did."

"You killed him?"

He nodded. "I waited at the docks for his ship to arrive, followed him home, and watched the reunion through the window. If he aggressed on her, I was ready to barge in and end him. He didn't act as badly as I expected, though, which should have given me pause, and Cordelia greeted him with smiles and hugs. The servants were cordial as well. I thought that it was an act meant to appease the monster. I waited until Cordelia retired to their bedchamber. She was all smiles for him, but I still thought that it was all an act, and my rage only grew because she had to pretend to love him so he wouldn't strike her, that she had to put up with him to appease him. When the husband was left alone in the salon, enjoying a drink and a pipe, I got in through one of the back patio doors. I was trained to walk soundlessly, so he didn't hear me as I walked up behind him, paralyzed him by seizing his mind, and sank my fangs in his neck. I pumped him full of venom until his heart stopped, and then I left the same way I came. He was found the next day by the maid, and the cause of death was determined as heart failure. No one suspected a thing, including Cordelia."

Sofia's hand flew to her neck. "Your fangs don't leave any marks."

"They don't. My saliva contains healing properties, and so does the venom. There was no sign of foul play."

Sofia's big eyes turned even larger. "Did you tell her that you did it?"

He shook his head. "She would have wondered how I managed to kill him without leaving any evidence. I just showed up the next day and acted as if I was shocked and relieved by the news."

"What did she do?"

"She donned mourning garb and sat in the living room crying and dabbing at her eyes. I knew it was an act, and I guess I started suspecting her then. Only the servants and I were in the house, so she had no reason to put on an act for anyone. I sat next to her and told her that she was free now, that she didn't need to live in fear anymore. She gave me a cold, accusing look.

"'To think that I invested that much work in you only to have nature take care of the problem for me. What a waste of time.'

"Her voice was as cold as ice, and so were her eyes. There was none of the warmth she used to shower me with. I knew then that I had been played."

7 4

SOFIA

"I can't believe you did that." Sofia rubbed her eyes as if by doing so she could erase the images that Marcel had painted in her mind. "I expected you to beat him up, to warn him never to lay a finger on her again, but you just went ahead and killed him." She took in a deep breath. "And her response. I can't wrap my mind around it. Maybe she was filled with remorse for having an affair with you?"

He laughed mirthlessly. "The woman didn't know the meaning of remorse."

"Perhaps by killing him, you saved her life?"

"I didn't."

"You can't know that. Do you know that the number one cause of death for young women is murder by their boyfriends or husbands?" She lifted a finger. "Number one. And I bet it was even worse in the days when women didn't have any rights."

Marcel shook his head. "The story gets worse. Later, I found out that he never physically abused her. He'd lashed out at her verbally on occasion, but it was well-earned. She loved to live lavishly, and she spent money beyond their means. She made up the abuse to make me get rid of him for her."

Sofia couldn't believe that Marcel had been played like that. How could he have been so gullible?

And where was that passion that had driven him to commit murder?

Had it been smothered by the guilt?

"How did you find out?"

"The way I should have done before I committed murder. I entered the minds of the servants. It turned out that I was just one more idiot in a long string of lovers, and that she told the same lies to all of them, hoping one of them would get rid of her husband for her. He was a couple of decades older, unattractive, and came from a wealthy family. She wanted to be a rich widow and spend his money without having to answer to anyone. The inheritance laws of the time were very different than they are today, and since they didn't have any children and he was much older, he put all his possessions in a trust so she would be taken care of. She must have manipulated him to do that as well."

Sofia let out a breath. "She was a sociopath like Igor. Why didn't you enter her mind to verify what she told you?" It suddenly occurred to her that he could have entered hers instead of having Eleanor compel her to tell the truth. "And why haven't you entered mine? You would have known that everything I told you and the others was true."

"It's not that simple. Memories are not objective, and people often believe the lies they tell. Also, if they are very passionate about the lies, it's difficult to differentiate. Besides, I was a Guardian back then, and I obeyed clan law which states that we are not allowed to enter a human's mind without proper justification." He snorted. "And then I went ahead and committed the worst crime imaginable."

"You must have been madly in love with her, and it clouded your judgment."

Pain lashed through her insides at the idea that he'd loved that monster so much, and it didn't matter that it happened three centuries ago. Worse, that love affair had tainted him forever and made him cold. He seemed to be warming up, but after what he'd told her, she knew that he was capable of much more feeling than what he had shown her.

Would she ever be able to scrape away the layers of guilt he'd covered himself with and uncover the man he used to be?

"I was stupid." He smoothed his hand over his hair. "Naive and trusting. I swore never to let myself fall in love again." He smiled at her. "And then you showed up, and centuries of building walls around my heart started to crumble."

Perhaps the outer walls were crumbling. The inner layers would take much more work to scrape away, but for that to happen, he needed to forgive himself first.

"From what Eleanor told me, there weren't any immortal females you could have hooked up with, so I assume that Cordelia was a human and is long dead. Do you know what happened to her?"

He shook his head. "I didn't keep tabs on her. I left on the first ship sailing to America and joined Kian's arm of the clan."

"Did you really never tell anyone but me about it?"

He shook his head. "I'm a murderer, Sofia. Why would I admit that to anyone? I didn't mind the whipping I would have gotten or even entombment, but I couldn't stand the idea of people thinking of me as an evildoer. I was supposed to be a good guy."

What a terrible burden to carry, and he was right. He was a murderer, and she had no right to absolve him of his crime. He'd made a terrible mistake.

"I don't know what to say."

Marcel sighed. "There is nothing to say. If you want to rescind your consent, I'll understand. There are many other immortal males who would be very happy to attempt to induce your transition."

As if she wanted anyone else.

Marcel looked so broken that all Sofia wanted to do was wrap her arms around him and tell him that it was okay, but it wasn't, and it would never be. He would carry the guilt of what he had done for the rest of his never-ending life.

Talk about suffering.

"I still want you, Marcel, and to be frank, I don't hold what you did against you. You did what you thought was right. I just wish there was something I could do to ease your guilt." She closed her eyes. "You've been repenting for centuries, and you've carried this terrible guilt with you, living half a life because you were afraid to let yourself feel. Maybe it's punishment enough?"

"I wish."

Suddenly, she remembered his explanation about who was deserving of a perfect mate, and it gave her an idea. "If the Fates rewarded you with a truelove mate, they must think that you are done with your penance, right?"

He smiled sadly. "Or they chose to punish me by dangling you in front of me but not making it possible for me to induce you. I really hope that's not their plan because it's not fair to use you like that."

"I've done nothing to earn their punishment."

A flicker of hope ignited in Sofia's heart. If she transitioned, Marcel would believe that he'd been forgiven.

Leaning over, she cupped his cheek. "Then I must transition to prove to you that your penance is over and that you've earned your right to live a full life again. You don't know the Fates' grand plan. Maybe the husband needed to die to prevent some major bad thing from happening, and you and Cordelia were just the pawns they moved on the chessboard to orchestrate that."

One corner of his lips lifted in a sad mockery of a smile. "I wish I could believe that."

"Believe it. I was a pawn as well, so I know all about being used by forces greater than me. I felt guilty for coming here and manipulating you, and then I felt guilty for providing you information about the compound that might endanger my family. But after talking with Eleanor, I realized that my purpose might be greater than I've given myself credit for. She pointed out that the unassuming pawn is more powerful than most pieces on the chessboard. If the pawn makes the right moves, she has the potential to become a queen and lead her army to victory." She smiled. "In my case, I want to lead an army to liberate my people, and since I don't know much about strategy or about leading armies, I need your help. Can I rely on you?"

Marcel's eyes started glowing. "Always."

She took his hand and kissed his palm. "Then let's start working on that transition. I want to be immortal when I liberate my people."

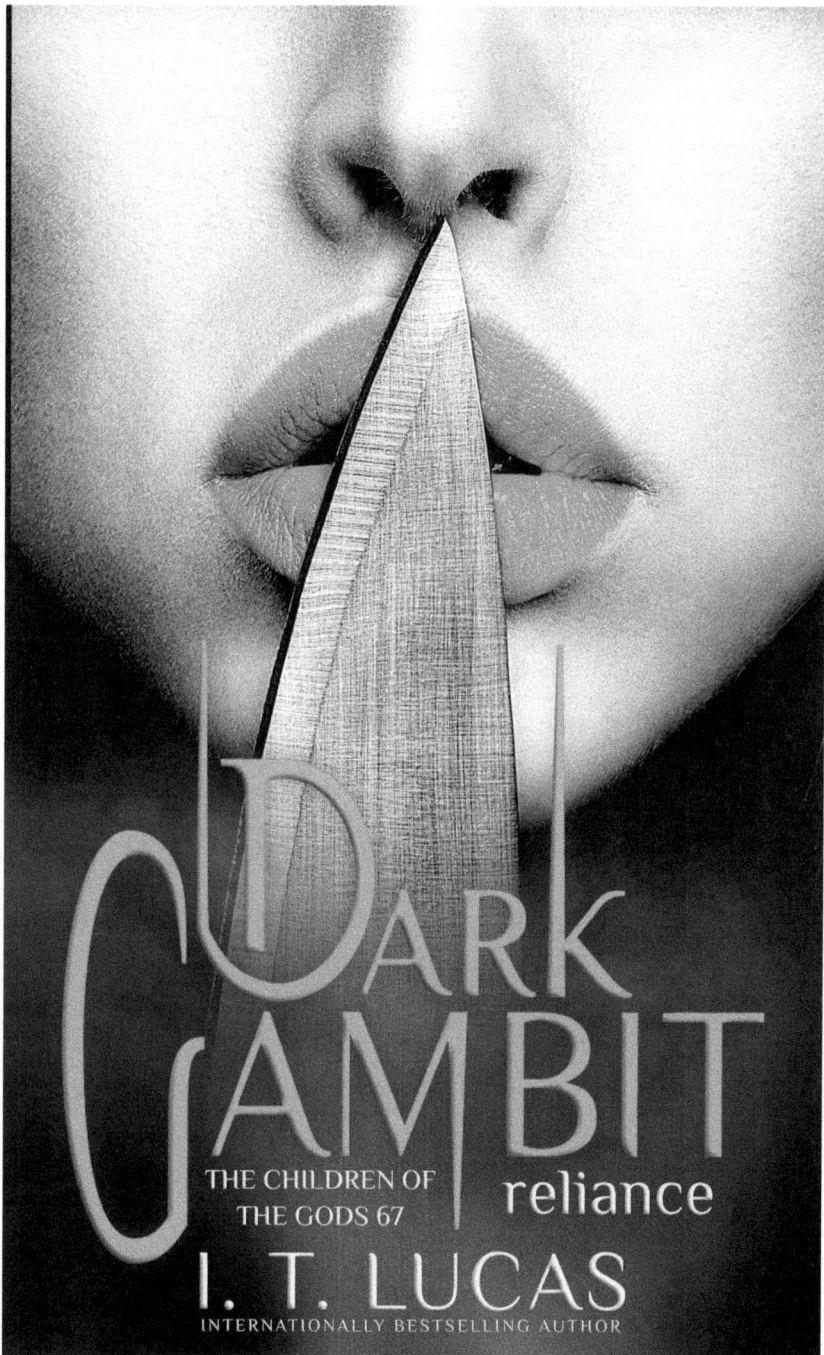

DARK GAMBIT

reliance

THE CHILDREN OF THE GODS 67

I. T. LUCAS

1

MARCEL

*A*s Marcel lay awake, holding Sofia tightly against his body, wave after wave of anxiety swept through him.

When he'd told her his greatest sin, his crime, she'd been so supportive, so understanding, but would she feel the same when she woke up?

Would she want to tie herself to a murderer?

Cordelia's husband wasn't the first human Marcel had killed, but the others had been invading marauders, and he'd been defending his people. Those killings had been in the line of duty, sanctioned and justified.

Cordelia's husband had been a different story.

He'd murdered the man in cold blood. Well, in hot blood, but that was irrelevant.

Marcel had taken a life that hadn't been his to take.

He'd appointed himself the judge, jury, and executioner, and he'd convicted the man based on the words of a beautiful liar who'd had him wrapped around her little finger. He'd never stood trial for his crime, and his only punishment had been his self-inflicted flagellation and dreary existence.

What if Sofia decided to reveal his secret?

Perhaps he should just reach into her mind and suppress the memory of the murder story. He hadn't thralled her last night, but he'd done it the day before, and it was a little too soon for another thralling session. Still, given that he no longer needed to continue thralling her after every bite, it was probably fine to do it again.

Now that she knew he was immortal and that his venom bites came with several great benefits, like the possible gift of immortality, Sofia might be more inclined to forgive him his past sins.

Except, he didn't want her to be with him only because of what he could do for her. He wanted Sofia to love him for who he was, but maybe the first step toward that goal was learning to love himself.

Marcel had carried the guilt for long enough, and maybe it was time to confess his crime and submit to whatever punishment Edna deemed suitable.

Hopefully, it would be just a token whipping and some prison time.

Edna wouldn't sentence him to entombment three hundred years after the fact, right?

Enough time had passed that perhaps she wouldn't judge him as harshly.

Then again, he had nothing to say in his defense. Stupidity wasn't a mitigating circumstance, and neither was an emotional disturbance. Or was it?

He hadn't been thinking straight. He'd been in love, and Cordelia had played him like a skilled violinist, tugging on his heartstrings.

If only witchcraft were real, he could have claimed that he'd been bewitched. Three hundred years ago, that line of defense might have worked in a human court, but it wouldn't have worked in Edna's. Unless Cordelia was a powerful immortal who could manipulate his mind, she had no other power over him.

Except, she had.

She'd bewitched him with her smiles and her tears and her delicate touch, but he couldn't use that in his defense. It was entirely his fault that he had not only fallen for her deceit but had also committed a terrible crime to please her.

At the time, Marcel wouldn't have minded entombment. Hell, he would have welcomed it to escape the guilt. But now that he had Sofia, he didn't want to miss even one moment with her, and that meant keeping his crime a secret and living with the guilt because he couldn't guarantee that Edna would be lenient.

"Stop," Sofia murmured. "Your thoughts are so loud that they are waking me up." She opened her eyes and gave him a sleepy smile. "Last night was amazing. I thought I would be afraid of your fangs, but you look kind of cute with them."

"Cute?" Marcel arched a brow. "Those are deadly instruments."

Sofia stretched her long body, pressing her small breasts to his chest. "Instruments of pleasure. What a trip." She kissed the underside of his jaw. "If women knew what your venom can do, they would be beating down your door and offering you sex or lots of money just for a chance to experience that. It's like the best psychedelic on the market."

He cupped her round bottom. "How many psychedelics have you tried?"

"None, but I've heard people describe their experiences. I wanted to try it, but I was afraid. I don't like having no control over what's happening to me."

He gave her lush bottom a squeeze. "Last night, you didn't seem to mind giving up control to me."

Her expression turned serious. "That's because I trust you. I know that you will never do anything to hurt me, and you'll protect me with everything you have."

"I don't know how you can still think that after what I told you."

"Nothing has changed for me." Sofia put her hand on his chest. "What happened with that evil woman and her husband is ancient history, and you were a different man back then. If you were a human, you would have died and been reborn again at least four times by now, and the knowledge of what you had done would have been lost. The slate would have been wiped clean. It's only because you are immortal that you keep on suffering endlessly. If you ask me, you've been in hell for the past three hundred years, and you've paid for your crime. It's time for a new beginning." She smiled and rubbed herself against him. "With me. And since I'm going to transition and become a new person as well, we will have a new beginning together. Isn't that great?"

Marcel suspected that Sofia was still loopy from the residual effect of the venom. Otherwise, she wouldn't be so optimistic and cheerful.

Kian wouldn't be happy about them starting the process so soon. They were supposed to wait until after Sofia's death had been faked, but Marcel just couldn't tell her that last night. Her eagerness to start the process had infected him, and he'd thrown caution to the wind.

When her tummy rumbled, he asked, "Are you hungry? We can get breakfast at the lodge."

"I don't want to share you with anyone yet, and I don't want to dip my feet back into reality and face the day. Let's stay here and make love like there is no world outside of this bunker, and we are not planning to take down Igor."

Yep, Sofia was definitely loopy, but her happiness was contagious, and Marcel didn't mind following her advice and forgetting that anything existed outside of the two of them. They could stay in bed and make love until they passed out from exhaustion, and when they woke up, they could do it again.

2

KIAN

"Your phone is ringing," Syssi said sleepily.

"I heard it." Kian tightened his arms around her. "I'm choosing to ignore it." He kissed the tip of her nose.

"What if it's an emergency?"

"It's always an emergency. I'm tired of all the emergencies I have to deal with."

"Just answer it, please."

He let out a breath and turned around to snatch the phone off the charger. It had stopped ringing, but seeing that the call had been from Eleanor, he decided to return it. She wouldn't have called if it wasn't important.

"What's up?"

"Did I wake you up?"

"No. I was already awake."

"I just wanted to give you an update on my talk with Sofia."

Alarm bells ringing in his head, Kian pushed up on the pillows. "Did she lie?"

"No, she believes that everything she told us is true, and she didn't hide any additional information except for the fact that her grandfather is Igor's second-in-command, but she's already told Marcel about that without any compulsion on my part."

This was indeed big news, and he was glad that Eleanor hadn't waited to call him.

"What does it mean for us?"

"Not much. I had a long talk with her while she was under my compulsion, so I know she was telling me the truth. Her relationship with Igor's second-in-command doesn't afford her any special status in the compound. She believes that it gives her only a slight advantage over other human Kra-ell offspring, allowing her to attend university for the past seven years and perhaps more leeway in choosing her bed partners. But that could be her take on it. The pureblooded Kra-

428

ell don't believe in the concept of love, and having or showing emotions is considered a weakness. Her grandfather might care for her, but he doesn't show it. In any case, it makes me reassess our hypothesis about the tracker that was embedded in her. I don't think that he wanted his granddaughter to get caught just so he could follow the tracker to wherever she was taken. I suspect that they embed trackers in all the humans who are allowed to leave the compound. They want to keep tabs on them."

"That makes sense, but I still like the idea of driving the cat with the tracker around to see if we can catch something in the net."

"Poor cat," Syssi murmured. "She didn't sign up for getting Sofia's tracker."

"Neither did Sofia." Kian patted her arm. "The tracker is tiny, and Julian gave the cat an anesthetic."

"She didn't suffer," Eleanor said. "And she's getting more petting than ever. But back to the tracker. If it has a tail, catching it will be easier than traveling all the way to Karelia and capturing the Kra-ell guarding the entrance to their secret tunnel. And what's even more important, Toven won't have to go there either and drag Mia with him, which he will have to do because she enhances his powers, and he can't free the Kra-ell from Igor's compulsion without her help. Did you talk to him about it? He might refuse, and without him and Mia, we have no plan."

"Not yet." Kian turned the speaker on and put the phone on his lap. "I'll talk to him today, but the truth is that I don't want him to go there either. It's too dangerous. I'm waiting for Turner to come up with a plan before we make our next move, and I hope he can come up with something that doesn't involve Toven and Mia going to Karelia."

Eleanor snorted. "Good luck with that. Turner is smart, but he's not a miracle worker."

"Some say that he is, but we'll see. Did Marcel tell Sofia about her genetic potential?"

"He did, but he made a mess of it. The guy is not a smooth operator, and after Sofia told him about Valstar being so high up in Igor's organization, he started treating her like a suspect again, and she blew up. Given all the information she'd volunteered, it was uncalled for. I had to step in and calm things down. I took her on a long walk on the beach, explained that the clan is all about doing good things for humanity, about our efforts to free trafficking victims and rehabilitate them, and ended with explaining in more detail about immortals and Dormants. When I was done, she was all smiles and ready to get induced. I hope that Marcel didn't ruin all my good work with some other brain fart."

"Being suspicious is not a brain fart, but I know what you mean. Marcel is an engineer. Enough said."

She chuckled. "They are a special breed, aren't they? But as someone who is mated to the ultimate drama king, I sometimes long for the calm logic of the engineer types."

"Do I sense discontent?"

"Not at all. I love Emmett, and I'm very happy to have a man with flair. It's funny how atypical he is for a Kra-ell. Between the two of us, I'm more Kra-ell than he is."

"Hey, maybe you are Kra-ell," Syssi said. "You certainly have the look. You're tall, skinny, and your hair and eyes are dark. You are also a compeller."

Kian's brows took a deep dive. It hadn't occurred to him, but Syssi was onto something.

"Frankly, I don't care either way," Eleanor said. "But if I am descended from the Kra-ell, then the Kra-ell and the immortals must be really closely related for me to transition so quickly. I wasn't bonded to my inducer. I didn't even have any feelings for him. He was just a hookup." She chuckled. "Given my compulsion ability, I actually suspect that I came from Toven's line. Maybe my grandmother was a naughty girl."

"I hope that your theory is the correct one," Syssi said quietly. "The Kra-ell are only long-lived, not immortal."

Eleanor let out a breath. "Even if I'm their descendant, a thousand years is a very long time, and my mate will enjoy a similar lifespan. Besides, in a thousand years, we will most likely figure out how to turn everyone immortal."

3

DARLENE

*W*hen Darlene woke up and opened her eyes, the sight that greeted her was not pleasant. The bedroom was in shambles. Eric was passed out on the bed and smelled as if he had showered in booze, yet she felt amazing.

As she remembered him tearing the bed apart, she sat up and gave the room a second look around. The bed frame was gone, but no evidence of splintered wood remained, and the mattress was somehow still supported and not on the floor. The pictures on the walls were hanging crookedly to some degree, the two bedside lamps were gone, and the dresser had been pushed aside, probably to vacuum the debris from under it.

It seemed that Eric had gotten much stronger during the days following his transition. When he was human, he couldn't have gotten free of the chains by demolishing the bed frame.

Was Max still around?

She lifted her hand to the spot on her neck where he'd bitten her and patted the skin. It wasn't tender, and there was no crusted blood or bumps where Max's fangs had penetrated her skin.

He'd bitten her through the nightgown, but Eric must have loosened the tie that had secured the high collar because the strings were hanging loose on both sides of the opening. Other than that, her nightgown was none the worse for wear, which was a miracle given what the bedroom looked like.

How had she survived it intact?

Darlene remembered the bed frame groaning as Eric had pulled on the chains, but then she'd found herself under him while the posts had toppled down.

"Oh, my God, Eric!" She tried to move him to his side so she could examine his back.

Those posts were massive. How was he sleeping on his back with fractured ribs?

"What?" he murmured sleepily.

"Wake up. You need Bridget to examine you."

"Why?" Eric cracked one eye open and then shielded it with his hand to protect it from the light streaming through the window.

"To check your back. The bedposts fell on you."

"I'm fine." He reached for her, pulling her against his body.

"Ugh, let go. You stink of booze."

"I do?" He cupped his hand over his mouth and exhaled. "Oh, I do. My bad. Max and I finished two bottles of whiskey last night." He lifted both hands with two fingers each. "Another perk of being immortal is incredible tolerance for alcohol. I can outdrink any human now."

Great. They had been celebrating while she'd been out of it.

"What happened?" She pulled away from him and fanned in front of her face to stave off the stench.

"Max was right. When he bit you, I lost my shit and wanted to attack him. Fortunately for him, my priority was to shield you from the toppling posts, so I pulled you under me, and he managed to escape." Eric lifted his arm and flexed. "I'm as strong as a gorilla now. I didn't expect that to happen so soon after my transition."

"Did Max see me naked?"

"He didn't see anything. I made sure of that. He returned to the bedroom to release me from the chains, but I was covering you."

She wasn't sure how that had worked while there had been wooden poles on top of him and he was naked, but it was healthier for both of them to pretend that Max hadn't seen anything.

"What about your back?"

"I'm immortal now, baby. Sticks and stones can't hurt me." He scratched at his side. "I'd better get up and wash the stink off. I want to kiss you and do other things to you."

Her lips curved in a smile, but the smile wilted as she imagined Eric and Max sitting in the living room and getting drunk while talking about her.

"What did you and Max talk about while you were imbibing all that whiskey?"

"This and that. Do you know that Dalhu made nude portraits of Amanda and that she had them hanging in their house? She only took them down after Evie was born."

"I didn't know that, but I wonder how you got to discuss Amanda's nudes. Were you talking about my nightgown?"

Eric's sheepish smile confirmed her suspicion. "Max said that immortals are not as prudish as humans and that nudity is not a big deal for them."

"I don't care." She tucked the hem under her knees. "Anyway, this thing's going into the trash because I'm never repeating this exercise. If I don't transition from Max's bite, we are waiting for you to grow fangs and venom."

The smile slid off his face. "I don't think I could go through that again either, but I need to know. Did you enjoy his bite?"

How to answer that? She enjoyed the effects of the venom. It had been an incredible trip, and the sense of physical well-being she felt now could most likely be attributed to the venom as well, but she hadn't enjoyed the bite itself.

"It hurt, but that wasn't the biggest issue. I wouldn't have minded if it were you. It felt wrong getting bitten by Max." She searched for better words, but every analogy she could think of didn't fit.

Max was a friend, and he was an attractive male, but she didn't want him.

"It just felt wrong. But then the venom hit me, and the effect was mind-blowing." She brushed a strand of hair off his forehead. "I have no doubt that it's going to be even better when it's you."

His smile was brilliant. "I'm positive that it will be the best you've ever had."

"Since Max's bite was the only other one, and it wasn't great, it's not such a big challenge to do better."

"Oh, yeah?"

"Yeah." Darlene slapped Eric's arm playfully. "Just go brush your teeth already, so you can come back to bed." She pulled the nightgown over her head and handed it to him. "Put this in the trash bin, will you?"

His eyes blazed with an inner light. "Yes, ma'am."

4

SOFIA

*S*ofia yawned and stretched her arms over her head. "I think we have no choice. We need to get out of bed and get something to eat. I'm starving."

Smiling, Marcel caressed her bare back. "I can make a dash to the kitchen, raid the refrigerator, and bring the loot back here."

"Go for it." She cupped his cheek and pressed a kiss to his lips. "I'll take a shower while you're hunting for food to bring back to the cave."

Grunting like a gorilla, he punched his chest. "Me, Tarzan. You, Jane. I bring food. But first, shower." He kissed the tip of her nose and then jumped out of bed and sprinted for the bathroom.

She loved seeing Marcel smiling and joking around. He'd been so scared of her reaction to his confession, and the truth was that it had been a shocking revelation, but from a human's perspective of time, the crime had happened so long ago that the statute of limitations should have kicked in. Not that he could stand trial in a human court, but his clan laws were probably similar. Did premeditated murder even have a statute of limitations?

Had it been premeditated, though?

Yeah, it had been.

Marcel had followed Cordelia's husband home, not to have a chat with him or even to give him a warning. He'd planned to kill the man.

So why couldn't she bring herself to be repulsed by it or even judge Marcel harshly for it?

Perhaps her savage one-quarter Kra-ell was overriding the three-quarters human? Or maybe it was the influence of growing up with purebloods and hybrids and absorbing their attitudes? Or perhaps she was just blinded by love the way Marcel had been with that bitch.

Cordelia deserved to forever walk in the valley of the shamed.

Or did she?

Would the Mother of All Life fault her for plotting to get rid of her husband if he'd wronged her?

Probably not.

"Ugh, religion is so frustrating."

"Did you say something?" Marcel called from the bathroom.

"I was talking to myself."

With a sigh, Sofia tossed the blanket aside and slid out of bed. She needed to use the bathroom, but despite making love to Marcel in every possible position, she wasn't comfortable peeing in front of him yet.

Instead, she grabbed a fresh outfit and went to the bathroom in the next room over.

When she returned to the bedroom, she found Marcel sitting on the bed with his phone pressed against his ear.

"Perhaps I should start the coffee." She turned to go back out.

Marcel looked up. "It's Turner. He wants to speak with you."

"Now? Can't he wait for me to have some coffee?"

It surprised her that the strategist worked during the weekend. Not many humans were willing to give up their free days. Should she be glad or worried that he did?

Marcel had reassured her that his people were just collecting information and that they were not planning to attack the compound, but maybe they were going to help Jade and the others free themselves. Did that require working on a Sunday?

They must deem the matter urgent for some reason.

Perhaps Jade had contacted them with new information?

"Here." Marcel handed her the phone. "I'll make you coffee." He activated the speaker. "Sofia is here, Turner."

"Thank you," Turner said. "How are you this afternoon?"

Was it afternoon already? She hadn't checked the time.

"I'm very well, thank you. What can I help you with?"

"I need to know the wording Igor used to phrase his monthly compulsion sessions with you."

Sitting on the bed, she let out a breath. "It was more or less the same thing every month with only a few slight variations. I was to keep the existence of the Kra-ell a secret. I was to keep the location of the compound a secret. I was to do everything in my power to protect the compound and its inhabitants, and I was never to do anything that could endanger the compound and its inhabitants. I was to report to the security office any suspicious activity that might endanger the compound, and I was to follow the commands of my superiors in order of their hierarchy. Igor's command overruled commands given by Valstar, Valstar's commands overruled that of everyone under him, and so on. When I was away, I had to call once a week to report, and I had to come back in person once a month."

"Do you know if others received the same commands?"

"Igor held weekly assemblies which everyone in the compound had to attend, and he repeated the same instructions, except for the two last ones that were specific to me and the other students who got to leave the compound. Other humans got private one-on-one sessions with Igor only once in a while, if at all, and I don't know how often the hybrids and the purebloods got private sessions with him, but I think it was quite often."

Turner sighed. "That's what I thought. Igor is very thorough."

He sounded as if he admired the guy, which annoyed her, but she could understand how the strategist might be appreciative of another's talent.

"Does it make a difference?" She was afraid to hear Turner's answer.

"Regrettably, yes. Even if it was possible to deliver a message to your father, neither he nor your aunts could deliver it to Jade without reporting it to someone. The term Igor used was 'anything suspicious,' and delivering a secret message to Jade would definitely fall under that description."

Sofia's heart fell.

Turner was right. How come it hadn't occurred to her? She should have realized that her father and aunts would be bound by the compulsion. Now that she was free, it was so easy to forget the effect Igor's compulsion had on her life. She still had to contend with Tom's, but it didn't feel as oppressive and heavy-handed as Igor's.

"Here is your coffee." Marcel handed her a cup and sat down next to her on the bed.

"Thank you." She took a small sip. "So I guess the idea of helping a rebellion led by Jade is out."

"Don't worry. I will come up with a way to free your people. I have a couple more questions. Are Jade and Igor exclusive with one another?"

"Igor is not for sure, but I don't know about Jade. Maybe she's just more discreet than him. None of the purebloods are exclusive. It goes against the Mother's teachings and their tradition."

"That's what I thought, but I wanted to make sure. My last question is, how do the pureblood and hybrid females wear their hair?"

"Either loose, braided, or in a ponytail. Why?"

"If we find a way to supply a few main players with compulsion-blocking earpieces, they will need to hide them under their hair."

Hope surged in Sofia's chest once more. "The hybrid and purebloaded males wear their hair long too. Well, most do. I've seen two hybrids with modern haircuts. Maybe they were sent on an undercover mission."

"Excellent. That will make it easy for them to hide the earpieces."

"How are you going to get the devices to them? And wouldn't Igor's compulsion force them to report that?"

Turner chuckled. "Patience, Sofia. I'm still working on it."

5

MARCEL

*S*ofia returned the phone to Marcel. "The fantasy was nice while it lasted. I got carried away imagining tiny robot spiders and drones, and I forgot the human element that's under Igor's compulsion."

"We all make mistakes. Well, maybe not Turner." He returned the phone to his pocket. "Do you still want to stay here while I get food? Or do we go together?"

"Let's go to the dining hall. But if Roxie or anyone else from the retreat sees us, we tell them that we just came back. I don't want her to think that I returned without coming over to say hello."

"Of course." He offered her his arm. "If you want, we can go around and dine in the paranormal enclave's private dining room. It's where the clinic is."

"Am I allowed in there?"

"You are with me now, and you know about immortals, so you're governed by a different set of rules."

With all the back and forth between him and Kian, Marcel wasn't sure what he had gotten permission for and what he had not, but since he'd already told Sofia the biggest secret, he assumed that everything else fell under that umbrella.

"Can I rejoin the retreat?" she asked.

"You can if you want to, but I'd rather you spent your time with me."

"Don't you have a job to do?"

He put the code into the keypad. "I'm on an unofficial vacation. The team I was supervising was sent home."

She arched a brow. "Am I your new job?"

He paused just outside the door at the top of the stairs and pulled her into his arms. "You are my everything."

She didn't smile. "Do you love me?"

"Are you still doubting my feelings for you?"

"You've never said the actual words."

"Neither have you."

Sofia frowned. "Haven't I? I was sure that I had."

He shook his head. "We both admitted to having fallen for each other, which is basically saying the same thing, just without the word love in it."

"The Kra-ell don't believe in love."

He took her hand and led her out of the cottage. "We are not Kra-ell. Someone once told me that the definition of love is not being able to stay away from your beloved or being unable to imagine life without her. Since both are true for me, I must be in love with you."

Sofia rolled her eyes. "That's the most unromantic way to tell a woman that you love her, and it's also so you. I can't believe that in your youth, you were ruled by your emotions. You're so logical and analytical now."

Marcel's good mood took a nosedive. "I was a different man back then. I don't think that guy is still in here." He touched a hand to his chest. "I think that he died three centuries ago."

For some reason, his comment had Sofia smile brilliantly. "Here is a solution to your feelings of guilt. You killed yourself along with Cordelia's husband, so you've already been punished, and you can let go of the guilt."

This time Marcel couldn't blame the venom for Sofia's dismissive attitude toward the crime he'd committed. He hadn't bitten her this morning, and the venom from last night was long gone from her system.

"I wish I could, but I can't. Once this crisis is over, your people are free, and things go back to normal, I'll walk into our judge's office, confess my crime, and accept any punishment she deems appropriate."

"Don't." She stopped and lifted their clasped hands to her chest. "What if the judge sentences you to life in prison? I just found you. I can't lose you."

"I don't think she will, but she might sentence me to whipping or a short entombment." When tears started spilling from the corners of Sofia's eyes, he lifted their hand to his lips and kissed her knuckles. "If she gives me a choice, I'll choose the whipping. I don't want to be away from you even for a few days."

"Then don't do it. You don't need some judge to absolve you of your crimes. Let me be your judge and determine your punishment."

He smiled. "And what would that punishment be?"

Sofia resumed walking. "Community service of some sort. Eleanor said that your people rescue trafficking victims and help rehabilitate them. You can be one of the rescuers. You used to be a Guardian, so you have the skills." She tilted her head. "I doubt you'd be any good in helping with the rehabilitation, though. Your bedside manner leaves a lot to be desired."

"Oh, yeah? What about my in-bed manner? Does that leave a lot to be desired as well?"

Sofia shook her head. "Men. No matter what species, you are always insecure about your performance. Yours was fine."

He stopped in his tracks. "Just fine?"

Laughing, she tugged on his hand. "It was exceptional."

"That's better." He let Sofia drag him behind her for a couple of moments. "The dining hall is on your left."

"Oh." She changed direction. "So, what do you think about my idea?"

"It has merit, but I enjoy what I'm doing now much more than I ever enjoyed being a Guardian."

"Perfect. Then it will be a real punishment for you."

6

TOVEN

*A*s Toven climbed the steps to Bridget and Turner's house, the door opened and Turner stepped out. "Good afternoon. Thanks for accepting my invitation. I didn't want to drag everyone to Kian's office on a Sunday."

"No problem. I'm glad to help in any way I can."

"Hello." Bridget walked over and offered him her hand. "Where is Mia?"

"She opted to stay with her grandparents. They were a little upset about having to cut their weekend in Arcadia short."

Turner led him to the couch where Vrog and Aliya were sitting. "I wouldn't have asked for you to come if it wasn't important. I need to test the Kra-ell's susceptibility to thralling and shrouding."

"You mentioned that when you called." Toven offered his hand to Aliya, who looked anxious. "Don't worry. Thralling and shrouding don't hurt."

"I know. I can do a little of that myself on humans. But that's the thing. What works on Vrog and me might not work on the purebloods. And if the male holding Jade is as powerful as everyone says, he might be immune."

"Not every compeller is immune," Turner said. "Eleanor is immune, but Emmett is not. Annani successfully compelled him to reveal the numbers of his Swiss bank accounts, and we all know that he wouldn't have volunteered them."

As a knock sounded at the door, Bridget walked over to open it. "Hello, Kian."

"Hello, everyone. Apologies for my late arrival."

"No apology needed." Bridget motioned for them to move to the dining table. "I prepared some snacks."

Looking at the place settings, Toven lifted a brow. "Are we expecting more people?"

"Yes." Turner pulled out a chair for Bridget. "Onegus and Yamanu are going to join us in a few minutes. I want to conduct an experiment. We will start with Bridget. Her thralling and shrouding abilities are good, but Onegus's are better,

Yamanu's are superior, and yours are divine." He chuckled at his own lame joke. "Bridget, you go first."

She smiled at Aliya. "Ready?"

"Yes."

"I'll start with an illusion. Here it goes."

No response registered on Aliya's or Vrog's faces, so Toven concluded that they didn't see Bridget's illusion.

"Nothing?" Bridget asked. "Not even a flicker?"

"Nothing," Aliya said. "What was your illusion?"

"A rainbow unicorn. The little kids love it when I project it into their minds. They forget all about my checkups and vaccinations."

Turner glanced at his watch. "I'd better open the door for our two other guests."

Toven cast Kian a sidelong glance. "Why don't you give it a try?"

Kian shrugged. "Turner wants me to observe, not to participate."

That was odd. What could Turner's motives be? Was Kian still uncomfortable about showing the extent of his powers in front of Toven? Was he embarrassed about not being as powerful as a god? Or was he powerful but didn't want to show his hand?

If so, it was uncalled for and somewhat offensive.

So far, Toven had provided his assistance whenever he'd been asked. He was part of the family, and it was time they treated him as such.

As the two Guardians walked into the living room, and a round of hellos and how-are-yous ensued, Toven crossed his arms over his chest and waited for the show to begin.

"Vrog and Aliya didn't see Bridget's illusion," Turner told Onegus. "You go next."

The chief nodded. "Do you also want me to thrall them?"

Turner looked at Vrog. "Only if you agree to be thralled." He shifted his gaze to Aliya. "I only mentioned illusions when I invited you."

"I don't mind," Vrog said. "I have no secrets to hide."

"I don't have any either," Aliya said.

"I'm not going to sift through your memories," Onegus said. "I will plant new ones."

That was less intrusive and Toven approved.

"I'll start with the illusion." Onegus looked at the two of them.

Aliya frowned, and Vrog leaned forward.

"Do you see anything?" Turner asked.

"I see an outline of a shape," Vrog said. "Is it a butterfly?"

Onegus chuckled. "Close. It's a baby dragon."

"I only got an impression of wings," Aliya said.

"Let's try the thrall." He looked into Aliya's eyes.

She gasped. "It worked. I remember seeing a baby dragon, but I know that's a fake memory."

It worked on Vrog just as well.

"My turn." Yamanu rubbed his enormous hands together.

"I see it!" Aliya exclaimed. "It's a cute little alien with big black eyes."

Yamanu smirked. "Correct."

"But it's not solid," Vrog said. "Is it supposed to be a ghost?"

The smile slid off Yamanu's face. "Damn. I was sure you would see my illusion." He shifted his eyes to Turner. "Should I thrall them now?"

"We can try that later." Turner looked at Toven. "It's your turn, Your Majesty."

Toven cut him a glare. "You're lucky that you are immune. I would have set your house on illusionary fire for calling me that."

"Hey," Bridget protested. "It's my house, too."

Toven smiled at her. "For you, doctor, I would have created a much nicer illusion."

"Can you cast different illusions for different people at the same time?" Kian asked.

"I can. But today, I'm going to treat all of you to the same one."

Closing his eyes, he imagined them sitting in the opera house, watching and listening to the *Phantom of the Opera*.

Since Rosalyn loved that opera and even sang along to the recording, he knew it well enough to recreate it in his imagination.

"Amazing," Bridget whispered.

"What do you see?" Turner asked.

"The *Phantom of the Opera* is on the stage of a large concert hall, and we are all sitting in a private booth, dressed to the nines like royalty. I love it."

Kian chuckled. "Who needs a Perfect Match machine when we have Toven to entertain us."

"Why did you stop?" Aliya asked. "It was so beautiful."

Toven gave her an apologetic smile. "That's all I remember. But if you enjoyed it, stop by our house at any time, and Mia's grandmother will gladly put it on for you and join you to watch it. It's her favorite opera, and when I'm in the mood, I sing the duet with her."

Like all gods, he had a great singing voice, and whenever he capitulated to Rosalyn's pleading for him to sing with her, she was so delighted that he had no heart to refuse.

"I would love that." Aliya cast Vrog a sidelong glance. "But I would love even more to see it in an opera house like the one Toven showed us."

"That was the Metropolitan Opera house in New York." Kian pushed to his feet. "If you want to go, you will have to wait for this crisis to blow over first."

7

KIAN

*K*ian had hoped that Yamanu would be enough and that he wouldn't need to get Toven involved on the ground in Karelia.

Were they actually going to do it?

He felt as if he was getting dragged into action before it was actually needed. If not for Jade's message to Emmett, they wouldn't have known about Igor, and Igor wouldn't have known about them. But now the clan had one of Igor's subjects, and she was possibly Marcel's fated one.

Once again, the situation had the Fates' signature all over it, and Kian resented being used by them to further their plans.

"The purebloods," Turner said. "How many of them were strong compellers? And could they compel each other?"

Vrog put down the glass of water he'd been sipping on. "All purebloods could compel to some extent. But it only worked on hybrids, humans, and animals. They couldn't compel each other."

"Then how come you still feel compelled to help Jade?" Kian asked.

"I'm a hybrid, and she could've compelled me, but she didn't. I took a vow to serve her loyally to the day I die, and I take my vows seriously, but I also vowed loyalty to the clan, and I will not betray it even if it means betraying the one I made to Jade."

"The Mother punishes vow breakers." Aliya's olive-toned skin turned a shade paler. "They are doomed to forever walk in the valley of the shamed."

Vrog took her hand. "I've been a good steward of the tribe's money, and I will give it all back. That should satisfy the Mother."

Aliya didn't look sure at all, but she nodded. "I'll pray for the Mother to accept your gift."

"It's not only mine. Half of those funds are yours."

The sale of his school brought Vrog a nice chunk of money, and he'd planned to

443

use it to open a new school near the village, but since Kian had offered to finance the project, Vrog got to keep his money.

Aliya shook her head. "I never thought of the money as mine."

Turner lifted his hand. "Let's get back to the reason we are here. Are you sure that Jade couldn't compel the other purebloods?"

"I'm not," Vrog admitted. "Perhaps Emmett can answer that question better than I since he has the ability. He says that he can even compel purebloods, but Emmett likes to boast, and I'm not sure I believe him." Vrog grimaced. "Don't base any of your military decisions on what he tells you. He's not a bad guy, but he's not very Kra-ell in nature."

Vrog had said it as if being a Kra-ell was a badge of honor.

"Maybe that's a good thing." Kian reached for the cookies Bridget had put on the table. "The Kra-ell are too bloodthirsty for my taste, pun intended."

"Indeed." Turner leaned back in his chair. "I'll sum up what we've learned so far, and then I'll tell you my plan."

That was unexpected. "Is it ready?"

"I still need to iron out a few details, and naturally, it's up to you to act on it or not, but you asked me to prepare an actionable plan, which I did."

"Let's hear it," Onegus said.

"Given the intel we have, spiders are not an option," Turner started. "The ones that would go unnoticed by the Kra-ell guards are too small to carry a charge that will allow them to traverse the distance from the first tunnel all the way to the compound and then roam around the compound itself. We can't drop them from the air either because they are too fragile for that. So as far as using them for spying, it's not going to work. Personally, I don't like them, and I never use them on missions. They are good for urban settings when you can drop one in a hallway and have it crawl under a door to eavesdrop on a meeting. They are useless in rough terrain."

"What about drones?" Kian asked.

"Drones are better. We can use the same tactic we used on the Doomers' island. A small drone will piggyback on a larger one and get dropped directly over the compound, but that will do us no good, either. I asked Sofia to tell me the precise wording of Igor's routine compulsion, and it turns out that everyone in there is compelled to report anything suspicious to security. What it means is that delivering a message or a pair of earpieces is out of the question as well. The only way we can collect information is by capturing a pureblood, breaking Igor's compulsion, getting the pureblood to reveal the compound's military setup and anything else that we need intel on, and then thralling and compelling him to forget that he'd been captured."

Kian groaned. "That means sending Toven to Karelia along with Mia, and that's not going to happen."

"Why not?" Toven asked. "I'm willing to go, and so is Mia."

Kian gaped at him. "Are you willing to take your fragile mate into enemy territory?"

"I can protect her." Toven affected a haughty expression. "You keep forgetting that I am a god. I can freeze the minds of any would-be attackers in a five-mile radius. No one would be able to get close enough to do Mia any harm."

"Can you really do that?" Onegus asked. "Five-mile radius is a damn big area."

Toven shrugged. "I might have exaggerated a little. In any case, though, no one will get within shooting range of my mate."

"Provided that you are aware of them," Kian pointed out. "What if they sneak up on you?"

"We can mitigate that," Onegus said. "A team of Guardians can form a shield around Toven and Mia."

"Hold on." Turner lifted his hand. "I'm not done explaining my plan."

8

TOVEN

*T*oven nodded. "Go ahead, Turner."

"Thank you. My plan is basically going back to what we talked about before the ideas about spiders and drones muddied the water, but with the inclusion of Jade. The first step will be to drive the cat around with Sofia in the car. Eleanor could pose as Sofia, but that would only work from a distance, and I wouldn't risk it. Sofia should be in the car, and a team of Guardians should follow her in another vehicle. Hopefully, she will have a tail, and we will catch it. And hopefully, it will be a pureblood. If not, we will start from stage two of my plan, but let me finish with stage one first. Since only Toven can break Igor's compulsion, and since he needs Mia to fortify his power, he needs to be on standby in the area." He turned to Toven. "If you liked the house I secured for you before, I can arrange the same one again."

"Mia loved the house overlooking the ocean, and she loved being needed." Toven drummed his fingers on the dining table. "But the truth is that I might not need Mia to break the compulsion on a pureblood. I was careful with Sofia because she is human and fragile. When I pushed too hard, it had an adverse effect on her. I won't be as gentle with a Kra-ell pureblood."

"That would be a great way to test it," Turner said. "If you can break through the compulsion without Mia's help, you might not need her for the second stage of the plan, and that would make Kian happy." Turner looked at Kian. "Right?"

Kian groaned. "Nothing about this is making me happy. Please, go on."

"I believe that we need to act as swiftly as possible." Turner looked at Toven. "You will need to fly out tonight. I want to deploy the cat tomorrow morning."

"That's not a problem."

Mia's grandparents might be upset about her leaving again, especially after she had told them what the previous trip had been all about, but they wouldn't put up too much of a fuss. They were proud of their granddaughter's unique ability to enhance other paranormal talents.

"Thank you." Turner dipped his head. "It's a real pleasure working with you, Toven. Kian will send additional Guardians along, and they will have tranq guns with them." He looked at Bridget. "You need to calibrate those darts to knock out pureblood Kra-ell."

"No problem. I'll use the recommended dose for gorillas." When he gave her a perplexed look, she laughed. "I'm just joking. I'll use the recommended dose for male tigers. They weigh about the same as the average adult human. The Kra-ell are taller, but they are slimmer, so they should weigh about the same."

"The Guardians need titanium chains to secure a pureblood," Onegus said. "For the interrogation."

Toven chuckled. "As long as the Guardians keep the Kra-ell asleep until they bring them to me, no chains will be needed. I can paralyze them without uttering a single word."

"Right." Turner nodded respectfully. "But let me remind you that a pureblood is the equivalent of a god, not an immortal, and you might not be able to seize his mind. I'd rather err on the side of caution, and so would Kian."

Turner was right. Toven had been thinking about the Kra-ell as he would about immortals, but that only applied to the hybrid Kra-ell. The purebloods might not be as powerful as the gods, but they might be more resistant to thralling than immortals. Most gods couldn't control each other's minds, and he was no exception. Mortdh and Ahn had possessed the ability to some extent, but since it was illegal to use thralling on another god, Toven hadn't witnessed either of them breaking that law. He'd only suspected they could do that based on rumors.

"I agree. Chains are needed."

"Also," Turner continued. "Even if you can break the compulsion on the pureblood without Mia's help, I'd rather you did it with her. A lot rests on that pureblood not reporting to Igor about getting captured and interrogated."

Toven nodded. "I understand."

Onegus cleared his throat. "Should we wait until we take the cat for a ride to send the team to Karelia?"

"No." Turner flipped the page on his yellow pad. "It's a long flight, and they need to do reconnaissance work in preparation. They should go as planned and wait in St. Petersburg for further instructions. I had a local contact arrange lodging for them and supply them with everything they need."

"He can't supply them with exoskeletons," Onegus said. "We can't fight the Kra-ell without them."

"We are not fighting the Kra-ell just yet." Turner tapped his pen on the yellow pad. "Their job will be to catch one of the guards at the entrance to the tunnel, but they will have to wait for Toven to arrive. Naturally, Sylvia will be instrumental in disabling the cameras on the way to the tunnel, but she doesn't need to go with the first team. She can join Toven and Mia when they go."

Kian lifted his hand. "Hold on. You said that if we catch a tail in Safe Haven, Toven might not need to go to Karelia."

"I said that he might not need Mia, but I prefer for her to join him."

9

KIAN

$\mathcal{T}$he more Turner's plan unfolded, the less Kian liked it. Sofia's idea to help Jade start a rebellion had appealed to him much more, but what Turner had said obliterated that idea.

"If we catch a pureblood using the cat with the tracker as bait, why do we need to bother with the guards at the entrance to the tunnel unless your plan is to invade the compound?"

"I was getting to that." Turner made a checkmark on his yellow pad. "We need the guard to deliver a message to Jade that will not trigger Igor's compulsion to report it to security. The guard will invite Jade to go with him hunting for a Veskar, at a specific time and at a specific spot, and it will be veiled as an invitation to have sex. Jade will suspect something because of the mention of Veskar, but since she won't be sure, it won't trigger her compulsion to report it. Even if Igor finds out about it, the mention of Veskar would be meaningless to him." Turner shifted his eyes to Vrog. "I hope that a Veskar is not a ferocious giant rat."

Vrog chuckled. "It's the size of a squirrel. To invite Jade to hunt for it would be taken as an insult, but it could also be taken as a joke or a pun, so it might work."

"How do you plan for us to get to their hunting grounds without them noticing us?" Onegus asked.

"With an amphibian vehicle. There are many rivers and small lakes in the area, and the rivers are not boat-friendly. The Kra-ell can't monitor all the waterways, and they have no reason to do that given that they are not easily navigable."

"They probably have guards posted at strategic points," Onegus said. "It would be remiss of them not to do that, and Igor doesn't seem like the sort of guy who would overlook anything."

"Obviously." Turner nodded. "After interrogating the guards, we will find out how he addresses that problem, and we will adapt accordingly. He doesn't have limitless resources, and he needs to prioritize. Areas that are difficult for humans to traverse will be less guarded."

"What do we do once we catch Jade?" Kian asked.

"Toven frees her from the compulsion, and we give her earpieces. Hopefully, she will be able to solve the problem for us by killing Igor, but we can't count on that."

"She can't kill him," Onegus said. "Leon and Marcel briefed me in detail about what Sofia told them. Sofia was searched every time she came for her monthly compulsion reinforcement sessions with him, once at the gate, again at the entrance to the office building, and a third time right before going into Igor's office. The guy is super careful, and he's not relying solely on his compulsion ability for safety." Onegus cast Toven a meaningful glance. "If he has a weak human searched before allowing her in his presence, I'm sure he has Jade searched much more thoroughly for weapons, and I doubt that she's strong enough to overpower him physically with her bare hands."

"Didn't Sofia say that Jade is Igor's top breeder?" Kian asked.

"She did," Onegus said. "Sofia also told Marcel and Leon that Jade doesn't hide her hatred for Igor. A paranoid guy like him would be even more careful with someone he takes to his bed. Sofia also mentioned that he's guarded at all times. In addition, we should assume that he carries weapons and sleeps with a gun under his pillow. If we want to do away with him, we should aim a missile at the office building and take out the compound's entire upper echelon."

"That's part of the last resort contingency," Turner said. "If possible, I prefer for the Kra-ell to take care of the problem for us. The less we reveal ourselves to them, the better. Jade is a clever female, and she might come up with a solution." He smiled. "If Igor sleeps with a gun under his pillow, she might be able to get ahold of it."

They should be so lucky.

"What if she can't do anything?" Yamanu asked. "Where does the shrouding and the thralling come into play?"

"The shrouding and thralling are also part of the last resort contingency plan in case all the previous steps are exhausted without producing the results we want. The next step in my plan is for Jade to start recruiting other purebloods who might join her rebellion. If she can get a couple of strong males who are willing to help her, we can free them from Igor's compulsion, supply them with earpieces, and have them kill Igor. Once he's gone, the rest will be easy. Toven can free everyone from Igor's compulsion without revealing who he is. As far as they are concerned, we are a group of paranormally talented humans."

"I'm starting to like your plan," Kian said. "If it works, we just leave Jade in charge and keep our eye on her. We can't let her treat the humans in the compound the way she'd treated those who served her tribe. Whoever wants to leave will be allowed to do so after we confuse their memories, and those who decide to stay will get paid for their services. We will have to monitor her to make sure she follows the new protocol."

"What's your contingency plan in case the assassination plan fails?" Onegus asked.

"If it fails, we have to go in. Igor will kill the males, find the earpieces, and know that someone is helping them. He will immediately connect the dots and come after Safe Haven."

Kian shook his head. "We don't have enough Guardians."

"We don't," Turner smirked. "But we can make them think that we do. That's where the shrouding comes in. Toven and Yamanu will project an image of our warriors in their exoskeletons multiplied tenfold. Igor and his cronies will think that they are being attacked by a large alien force."

"He won't surrender," Vrog said. "The Kra-ell fight to the death."

Turner leveled his pale blue eyes at the guy. "Igor spits in the face of Kra-ell tradition, but you are right; he won't surrender. Like any other despot, he only cares about his own skin, and he will try to escape. We need to make sure that he doesn't."

ERIC

"*H*ere you go, sweetie." Darlene handed Evan a big piece of watermelon. Eric turned to Idina. "Do you want some?"

"No." She didn't even look up at him.

"Why not? Don't you like watermelon?" He knew that she did.

"I don't want the juice to make my new dress dirty."

"I can tie a napkin around your neck and put another one over your lap. How's that?"

She eyed him with her dark gaze. "Promise that I will have no juice stains on my dress."

"I promise." He took his napkin and hers and covered her up. "All good?"

Nodding, she extended her small hand. "Watermelon, please."

"You didn't say thank you," Karen admonished.

"Thank you." Idina still held her hand out. "Watermelon, please."

"Here you go." Darlene handed her a chunk and turned to Karen. "How are you holding up without Gilbert?"

"The better question is, how am I holding up without Berta and Cheryl. Gilbert was never a big help around the house or with the little ones, but I had Berta. I feel so guilty for letting her go without even saying a proper goodbye. She's been with us for so many years."

"Berta is great." Kaia handed Ryan a juicy piece. "She'll find a new job in a heartbeat. Also, Gilbert promised to pay her six months' worth of work as severance pay. She might take a long, well-deserved vacation."

"What about Cheryl?" Darlene asked. "Is schoolwork keeping her busy?"

Karen nodded. "Between homework and waitressing for Callie, she can barely catch her breath, but I'm so happy that she no longer has her nose in that Instatock app all day long."

"Does she enjoy waitressing?" Eric asked. "It's hard work."

"She does," Kaia said. "She gets to spend time with her two new besties, and Callie pays her well. I'm so happy that Cheryl loves it in the village. I was worried that she wouldn't."

Darlene sighed. "Our reservation at Callie's is in two weeks. I can't wait for our turn in Callie's place."

"It's beautiful," Kaia said. "But right now, it is too big for what she can manage. She has about twenty, square tables sized for couples, while the dining area can easily hold ten times as many. Callie tried to fill the space up with couches and big planters, which adds to the exclusive vibe and provides the diners with a sense of privacy, but if she manages to hire more people, she can add more tables and serve more clients."

"What's the decor like?" Darlene asked.

Kaia pursed her lips. "It's modern with island vibes. I liked it a lot. In fact, I told William that I want to decorate our house in the same style."

Eric waved a dismissive hand. "I don't care about the decor. How was the food?"

"Delicious." William's eyes started glowing. "It's good that the waiting list is so long, or we'd be dining there every day."

Kaia glared at him. "What's wrong with my cooking?"

"Nothing, my love. You are an excellent cook, but I'd rather you rested after a long day of work instead of spending an hour or more on food preparation."

"Good save," Eric murmured.

"It's the truth." William lifted his hand to his nose as if he was still wearing glasses and needed to push them up.

"What did she serve?" Darlene asked. "I heard that it's a fixed menu, and you get what you get."

"There were five courses," Kaia said.

"The appetizer was mushroom crostini, and she served it on beautiful crystal plates." Kaia gestured with her fingers to indicate the size. "About this big. The second course was a salad made of mixed greens, beets, goat cheese, and almond slivers."

"The third course was soup." William licked his lips. "It was the best butternut squash soup I've had the pleasure to sample, and I've sampled many in the fanciest restaurants. She made tiny croutons from red bell peppers, all of different heights, and they were centered in each soup bowl, looking like high-rise buildings surrounded by an orange lake. It was such a pretty presentation." He shifted his eyes to Eric. "It makes a difference, you know. The presentation, the decor, the sounds in the background, all come together to create a one-of-a-kind culinary experience. Callie nailed it."

"There were three different main courses." Kaia wiped the juice from Ryan's chin. "One was almond-crusted tilapia with roasted vegetables. The second was seafood paella, and the third was a vegetable paella for Kian and the other vegetarians. The fifth course was a choice of marzipan cake, chocolate cake, coffee, and tea."

"You forgot to mention the champagne and the wines," William said. "Callie told us that she will be serving champagne every day for an entire month to celebrate the opening. She wants everyone to feel like they were at the opening night."

"That's so nice of her," Darlene said. "I wonder what she'll serve when it's our turn. I hope the seafood paella will be on the menu for that night."

After Idina and the boys were moved to the den, Karen got that conspiratorial look on her face that warned Eric about what was coming next.

"So, did you do it?"

Darlene frowned. "How did you know that we were planning it? Did Eric tell you?"

"Don't be mad. He told Gilbert. You know why."

Darlene sighed. "Yeah. You are in the same boat as me."

"I wish." Karen winced. "My grandfather is not a god."

"Right." Darlene looked at Eric. "Just tell them. But try to be mindful of how I feel about it."

He nodded. "It was awkward as hell," he admitted. "Especially for Darlene. Max chained me to the bed, which I thought was absurd, but he was right. When he bit Darlene, I wanted to tear him apart, and I discovered that I was as strong as a damn gorilla. I pulled on the chains and toppled the posts. Those were not twigs. They were massive. I would have never been able to do that as a human."

Karen looked at Darlene with alarm in her eyes. "Are you okay? Did you get hurt?"

Darlene shook her head. "Eric protected me. The posts fell on him, but since he's immortal now, nothing broke, and he was as good as new the next morning."

William smirked. "Welcome to the club, Eric. Our civilized veneers hide dangerous animals. Most of the time they lie dormant, but when our mates are threatened, the beasts come out."

"Max didn't threaten me." Darlene looked down at her plate. "He was doing us a favor."

"The beasts are mindless," William said. "They are all instinct and very little thought. Max was smart to chain Eric to the bed."

11

ELEANOR

"Got it. Thanks, Julian." Eleanor ended the call, put the pen down, and turned to Sofia. "Julian sent the referral to the cardiologist, and he gave me the precise wording for the fake diagnosis."

They needed to start building the case for Sofia's fake heart problem, and a visit to the cardiologist's office was the perfect excuse for a road trip that would include the cat with the tracker, killing two birds with one stone so to speak.

Sofia shook her head. "Marcel told me that it's not permitted to thrall humans unless it is done to protect the secret of immortals' existence or their lives. How are you going to justify thralling the doctor?"

"Easy. You are a potential immortal, and if we don't fake your death convincingly enough, your life will be in danger. Besides, I'm not going to thrall anyone. Marcel is going to do that. I can only compel." Eleanor leaned her elbows on her thighs and rested her chin on her fist. "A diagnosis by a human cardiologist who is in no way connected to us will be more convincing than just your word."

"Igor knows that you have compellers. He might suspect that you compelled the Safe Haven doctor to send the referral to the cardiologist, and since you are coming with me, they might suspect that you compelled that doctor as well."

"Good point. We should also plant some fake test results to make it look more legit." She dialed Julian's number again.

"What did you forget?" the doctor asked.

"Sofia pointed out that Igor knows we have compellers, so having a couple of doctors write fake diagnoses is not a problem for us. Can you have Roni plant fake test results in the cardiologist's files?"

Julian groaned. "I can probably get some, but it's not something that I can do in the next hour or two. When are you seeing the cardiologist?"

"In about three hours. I can also compel him to swap results with another patient or copy them and put them in Sofia's file."

"That would be much easier. Don't have him swap, though. Just copy them. We don't want to endanger someone's life."

"Got it. Thanks, Julian." She ended the call, pushed to her feet, and put the phone in the pocket of her jacket. "You didn't say anything about my new look." She turned in a circle.

Sofia frowned. "I don't think that my hairstyle looks good on you."

That wasn't nice. Eleanor thought that she looked great with her hair pinned up. "It's not about looking good. I just need to look like you from a distance."

"No, you don't." Sofia put her hand on her hip. "Since we've decided that I'm going too and you don't need to pretend to be me, what's the point?"

Eleanor shrugged. "I put a lot of effort into making myself look like you, and I didn't want to let it go to waste."

"Are we ready to go?" Marcel asked.

"We are." Eleanor picked the cat off the windowsill and turned to Leon. "Are your guys ready?"

"They are waiting for you in the parking garage."

"Good. I hope Cecilia behaves and doesn't pee or puke in the car. Cats are not fond of moving vehicles, and Emmett will be furious if she has an accident in his Lamborghini." Eleanor handed the bundle of fur to Sofia. "You hold her."

"I'm prepared in case she has an accident." Sofia scratched under Cecelia's chin. "I put a couple of towels in my bag to put over my legs during the drive."

"Good thinking." Leon opened the door for them. "Have fun, kids."

"Thank you, Daddy." Eleanor blew him an air kiss.

"It's going to look strange," Marcel said. "Why would people take a cat to a cardiologist's office?"

"People do all kinds of crazy things." Eleanor started pulling out the pins that were holding her hair up. "Maybe we will have the cat's heart checked. I can pretend to be an eccentric cat owner who wants her cat treated by a human doctor."

Sofia chuckled. "You can just thrall them to ignore Cecilia. We don't want anything to seem unusual about my doctor's visit."

Marcel shook his head. "If we pick up a tail, and they are Kra-ell, I can't thrall them not to see the cat, and we are doing all this to flush them out. Maybe we should leave Cecilia in the car with Asher."

"That will look even weirder," Eleanor said. "It doesn't make sense for Sofia's guard to stay in the car while she goes to see the doctor."

Everyone in Safe Haven knew that Eleanor was with Emmett. That was why they were taking Emmett's new Lamborghini, and the Guardian was posing as himself, a guard to watch over Sofia. The doctor's visit needed to look legit, but all the rest needed to look suspicious enough for the tail to get intrigued and follow them all the way to the beach house.

It would have been even better if Emmett had accompanied them, but that was too dangerous.

Keeping his real identity a secret was crucial.

It was a mess, and despite the cheerful attitude Eleanor fronted, she was worried about her and Emmett's future in Safe Haven.

455

Unless they eliminated Igor, Kian would order all the immortals to leave the resort. She would have to find a solution for her paranormals, and the clan would have to move the expensive equipment they'd put in the lab out of there.

Emmett would be devastated, and she didn't have an alternative solution for him. They couldn't uproot the community and have it move to a different location, and even if they could, it wouldn't make a difference. The community members depended on the income generated from the retreats, and if they kept running them in a different location, they would be easy to find.

She and Emmett had only two options. They could go back to the village, where they would be safe, or stay in Safe Haven and live in constant fear. Except, Kian might not give them the option to stay and force them to move back into the village. If that happened, she would have to convince him to get a new location for the paranormals.

Eleanor had invested too much effort into the program to give it up.

12

SOFIA

"*That* went well." Sofia entered the back seat of Emmett's fancy sports car and took Cecilia from Eleanor. "You were so good in the doctor's office." She tickled the cat's ear.

"She was." Eleanor sat behind the wheel of the fancy car. "How did I do playing the crazy diva who wants a cardiologist to check her cat's heart?" She eased into the traffic.

Sofia laughed. "You were hilarious. It was so hard not to laugh. I thought that you would thrall them to ignore Cecilia. That's such a nifty talent. I wish I had it."

"I can't thrall, remember? I can only compel."

"Why not? Marcel said that all immortals could thrall to some extent."

"Yeah, but those who transition as adults have a hard time doing it. Thralling needs to be practiced from a young age."

That was a shame. Sofia had hoped she would gain the ability once she transitioned, but apparently, that wasn't going to happen. Still, it wasn't a big deal considering everything else she would gain.

She was one-quarter Kra-ell, so maybe she would gain a slight compulsion ability.

The truth was that Sofia wasn't sure how thralling and compelling were different from each other. Eleanor had been the one who had dictated to the cardiologist what to write in his diagnosis, but Marcel had to thrall him to forget that he'd been told what to do. Then Eleanor compelled the doctor to take the test results of another patient and copy them to Sofia's file, and Marcel had once again thralled him to forget that the results weren't hers. If frequent thralling could potentially cause brain damage, the poor doctor might have suffered some. He'd even printed out everything for her to show her physician in Finland.

"Igor is going to flip when he sees the bill Riley sends him for your medical examination." Eleanor chuckled. "What do you think he will do?"

"I have no clue. Probably ignore it. Did you pay for it?"

"Yeah, but don't worry, it didn't come out of my own pocket. Kian will pay the credit card bill."

"Where to now?" the Guardian asked.

"I'm hungry," Eleanor said. "Can you look online for a place to eat?"

Asher pulled out his phone. "Anything specific that you have in mind?"

"Somewhere pets are allowed."

Cecelia lifted her ears as if she understood what Eleanor had said.

"I think she's hungry." Sofia smoothed her hand over the cat's back. "Should we give her another snack?"

Cecilia's ears twitched, and she tried to leap from Sofia's arms.

Sofia chuckled. "Now I'm sure that she understood what I said."

"Here you go." Marcel handed her a snack.

As the cat settled in her lap and started chewing, Sofia smiled. "I'm growing attached to this girl. I wonder if Anastasia would be willing to part with her."

Eleanor looked at her through the rearview mirror. "Where do you think you'll be taking her?"

"To your village. After I transition, that is."

"Are you sure that you will?" Eleanor asked. "I don't want you to get your hopes up and then get disappointed."

Sofia clasped Marcel's hand. "I strongly believe that I will." For Marcel's sake as much as for her own. "The Fates brought us together for a reason. Perhaps we are supposed to form a bridge between our people."

"Right." Eleanor glanced at the rearview mirror. "So far, it doesn't look as if anyone is following us, which is a serious setback to Turner's plan."

"He has a contingency," Marcel said. "If we can't catch a pureblood here, we will catch one in Karelia and get information out of him. We need to do that regardless, so we can get the guard to give Jade a message. The team is already on its way."

It was such a relief that they hadn't picked up a tail, but it was also tinged with disappointment. After her initial reaction to the news about the tracker, Sofia had entertained the absurd hope that maybe its purpose hadn't been to find out more about the people running Safe Haven, but for her protection, and that perhaps Valstar himself had followed her to the Oregon Coast to keep an eye on her and rescue her if she needed rescuing.

Right. Talk about delusional.

When they got to the restaurant, the hostess looked at Cecilia and smiled. "Pets are welcome, but only on the patio. Is that okay?"

"It's great." Eleanor kissed the top of the cat's head. "Cecelia was such a good girl at the doctor's office, and she deserves a reward. Do you have fish on the menu?"

"We do. She will love the tuna."

If anyone was watching them, which Sofia doubted, Eleanor had just given a great performance to reinforce their story.

"What about your friends?" Sofia asked Asher. "Shouldn't we invite them to join us?"

"It will blow their cover," the Guardian said. "They have to wait in the van."

"I hope they brought snacks," Eleanor said.

"I'm sure they did." Marcel opened the menu. "And if they didn't, they can get something at a drive-through while we are here. No one is going to attack us in a crowded restaurant."

13

MARCEL

*M*arcel's phone rang twenty or so minutes into the drive back to Safe Haven.

"We have a tail," Morgan said. "Two men in a gray Honda Accord. The back windows are tinted, so there might be more, but I doubt it. Two is more than enough to follow the tracker around."

Asher, who had taken over driving, looked at Marcel through the rearview mirror. "I didn't see it, and I've been watching out for it the entire drive. I still don't see it."

"They are very subtle about it," Morgan said. "They never get close. The only reason we spotted them on the way back was that the traffic was so light they couldn't disappear among the other cars."

"I wonder what they thought about the doctor's visit," Marcel said.

Morgan chuckled. "I'm sure that they were disappointed. They probably expected us to haul Sofia to some secret location for interrogation, and all they got was a cardiology clinic."

They had hauled her to a secret location when they had taken her to Toven, but that had been without the tracker, and the tail hadn't known that she'd left Safe Haven.

"Maybe they thought that the clinic was a cover for our headquarters," Asher said. "We are heading toward the house. You know the plan."

"We do." Morgan ended the call.

Next to Marcel, Sofia sat ramrod straight, and given her pinched expression, she was fighting tears. "I hoped..." She hesitated. "I don't know what I hoped for. It was stupid."

Marcel wrapped his arm around her shoulders. "Did you hope for a rescue?"

She nodded. "It's not that I wanted to be rescued. I wanted to know that my grandfather cared enough to send someone to retrieve me."

460

"Maybe that's why they have been following us. When they saw that we took you to see the doctor and then to a restaurant, they probably reported to Valstar that everything you told him and Igor was true. You were on an outing with your new boyfriend, the one who you seduced to pump for information, and Eleanor and her brother were with you. You didn't need rescuing."

She let out a breath. "You are right. So it's all good. Igor got the confirmation he needed. I just hope that we don't blow the story up when we capture them."

"That depends on whether they show their hand when we execute our plan."

"What are we going to do with Cecilia?" Sofia asked.

"We will take her with us, of course." Eleanor pulled out a mesh backpack from her satchel. "I'll strap her to my chest and carry her like a baby."

For the next hour or so, the tense silence in the car was only interrupted by the cat's purring and from time to time, by Morgan's calls with updates about the Honda. The Guardians had deployed a small drone to follow it from a safe distance.

The tail had no reason to get close. The tracker informed them where Sofia was, or rather where the tracker was. The question was whether they would follow on foot once they could no longer follow with the car.

When Asher stopped at the designated spot, the four of them got out of the car, Marcel and Asher put their earpieces in, and Eleanor put the cat in the backpack.

"Sorry about this, kitty." She strapped the backpack to her chest and patted Cecilia through the mesh. "That's the best I could do on short notice."

It was getting dark, and as they started the climb up the rugged mountainside, Marcel took Sofia's clammy hand. "I won't let you fall."

"I'm not afraid of falling."

"It's dark, and you can't see as well as we do."

"I know you will keep me safe. What I am worried about is whether they will follow on foot. There is nothing on this mountain. They might think that we are just getting some exercise."

Eleanor snorted. "Right. A human with a heart condition and a crazy lady with a cat climbing a mountain in the dark for fun. No one would think that."

"They are out of the car," Morgan said in Marcel's earpiece. "Two guys. They look human."

That was a disappointment. Hopefully, they were at least hybrids and not some humans Igor had hired to follow Sofia.

"We will wait until they are a good distance away before we check the car," Morgan said.

When Marcel repeated that for Sofia, she let out a breath. "Thank the Mother. It worked. They took the bait."

"Don't thank her yet." Eleanor stopped to readjust her backpack. "Let's see if we can catch them. They might hear the drone and bolt."

"With all the noise from the ocean, I can't hear myself breathing," Asher said. "When they hear the drone, it will already be too late. Morgan and Bradley are right behind them."

That was why they had chosen that exact spot for their deception. The mountain practically rose up from the water, and the surf crashing to shore was loud.

"We need to keep going." Marcel tugged on Sofia's hand. "They need to focus on catching up to us."

The hope was that the guys following them would suspect that they were taking Sofia to a secret location hidden in the mountain and that they would follow to find out where the entrance was.

Straining his one free ear, Marcel tried to identify the drone's buzz, but he couldn't hear a thing over the surf. The higher they climbed, the noisier it became instead of getting quieter.

They were nearly all the way to the top when Morgan spoke in his earpiece. "We got them. You can come back down."

14

SOFIA

"What if they have trackers on them? Or in them, as may be the case." Sofia had her hand on Marcel's shoulder, using him as her guide on the way down. "Don't we need to take them to the clinic first to remove them?"

The moon was out, so it wasn't entirely dark, but the lava rocks the mountainside was made of were nearly black, and there was very sparse vegetation. She could barely see where to put her foot down.

"We can't remove the trackers," Eleanor said. "We need those guys to appear intact and to go back to reporting to your grandpa."

Sofia gritted her teeth. Eleanor hadn't realized that referring to Valstar as her grandpa was painful to her. They were blood, as the Kra-ell called their pure-blooded relatives and sometimes to the hybrids, but never their human descendants.

She was nothing to Valstar.

"Tom's place is not far from here," Asher said. "Morgan and Bradley will carry them over so it will appear as if they walked there."

"Isn't that dangerous?" Sofia asked. "Igor will know where to find Tom."

"Tom will leave as soon as we are done, and we are not going to use that house again."

"I thought it was his home."

Marcel stopped his descent. "It was rented for the meeting. I thought I told you that."

She rubbed her temple. "The headache I got when Tom tried to break through Igor's compulsion must have messed with my memories. I can barely remember anything about that night." She tightened her hand around his bicep. "Did you do anything to me to make me forget?"

"I didn't."

"I hope you're not transitioning," Eleanor said.

Sofia's heart leaped, in part from fright and in part from excitement. "Why? Is forgetfulness one of the signs?"

"Not that I know of." Eleanor kept going. "But every transitioning Dormant experiences different symptoms, and with you being the scion of a different species, I expect your transition to be even more different."

"What are the usual symptoms?"

Eleanor shrugged, jolting Cecilia in the backpack that was strapped to her chest. "I can only tell you about my experience. I was feverish, lightheaded, and then I lost consciousness."

That didn't sound like fun, but given that immortality was the prize, it was worth going through a lot more than that.

"Are we walking all the way to the house?" Sofia asked.

She was in good shape, but she was getting fatigued.

"Yes." Marcel slowed down. "I can carry you on my back."

As if she would let him do that. "No, thank you. I can walk. But I don't understand why we need to. The idea was for the guards to wake up and remember that they watched us go into the house, hobnob with some rich people, and go out. They wouldn't have done it on foot, and neither would we."

"We needed them to get out of the car," Marcel said.

By the time the house came into view, she was dragging her feet, and her legs ached so badly that she was considering letting Marcel carry her the rest of the way.

"Are the Guardians already there?"

"They had a big head start," Asher said.

"But they were carrying dead weight." Sofia winced. "That was a bad choice of words. I hope the Kra-ell are not dead."

"They are not." Marcel squeezed her hand. "Morgan informed me that they are chained and ready for interrogation and that we should leave the cat with the tracker in Tom's rented car. It's open, and the key is inside. We don't want the tracker to be too close to the two. They are supposed to be spying on you from afar, not to be right next to you."

"Eleanor and I can stay with the cat," Asher offered. "Just get us food and something to drink. For the cat too."

"We will do that." Marcel tugged on Sofia's hand. "Come on. It's just a hundred feet more."

She groaned. "There are stairs to climb. I don't think I can do that. How did Tom get Mia and her wheelchair up there? Is there a hidden elevator in the house?" She prayed that there was.

"He carried her and the chair." Marcel smiled. "You know that I would be more than happy to carry you up there." He wrapped his arm around her waist and propped her against his body. "But since you are so damn proud and stubborn, I'll just help a little."

Sofia didn't want to tell him that it wasn't just the physical exertion that made the stairs seem so ominous. Once she climbed them and the door opened, she would see who had been following her, and she was afraid to find out who it was.

15

TOVEN

*T*oven leaned against the dining table and observed the two Kra-ell males chained to the iron chairs the Guardians had brought from the outdoor garden. Both could pass for humans, which meant that neither was a pureblood.

That was disappointing.

How much would they know?

Was it even worth the risk of detaining them?

Beside him, Mia gaped at the males, wide-eyed. "I expected them to look more alien, but they look a lot like Vrog. A little different, but they could easily be mistaken for humans."

"They are hybrids." Toven sighed. "We've gone to a lot of effort to lure them into a trap, and they probably don't know much more than Sofia."

"The hybrids serve in Igor's army," Morgan said. "They should know about the compound's military capabilities."

"I hope so."

As a knock sounded at the door, Morgan walked over to open it for the others, and Mia wheeled her chair around to greet them.

"Sofia." As she opened her arms, the girl bent down to hug her.

"Hi, Mia." Sofia straightened and looked at the two chained males. "Neither of them is a pureblood."

"Do you know them?" Toven asked.

She nodded. "The one on the right is Dima, and the one on the left is Anton."

The girl looked exhausted, and as he motioned for her to take a seat on the couch, she gave him a grateful nod.

"Those are Russian names," Toven said when she sat down. "Is that common?"

She nodded. "Almost all of the hybrids get named by their mothers, who are mostly Russian, and they choose names they are familiar with."

"Are they good guys?" Mia asked.

Sofia shrugged. "Dima is a jerk. I don't know Anton well, but I didn't notice him doing anything mean. They are both young. About my age."

"I assume that they are not high on the totem pole." Marcel sat next to her.

"They are not. I'm not important enough to justify sending higher-ranking people to follow me around."

Things weren't adding up. "And yet he put his second-in-command in charge of your mission." Toven crossed his arms over his chest. "What are we missing here?"

He hadn't posed the question to the others but rather to himself.

Nevertheless, Sofia answered. "Maybe he figured that hybrids were good enough to deal with a bunch of humans. They can also blend in. If he needed them to get into Safe Haven without arousing suspicion, it would have been easier to do for males who could pass for humans."

Those were valid points, but Toven had a niggling suspicion that those hadn't been Igor's reasons. The problem was that he couldn't come up with an alternative.

He turned to Morgan. "How long until they wake up?"

"I don't know," the Guardian said. "Julian supplied us with darts that can knock out Jaguars, but that might be overkill for these dudes. Neither of them weighs more than one hundred and sixty or seventy pounds. They have the bodies of teenage anime characters."

Toven stifled a smile. The description was apt, and just like those anime males, the hybrids were much stronger than they looked. "Will splashing them with cold water help?"

"I don't think so," Marcel said. "The drug needs to get metabolized."

"Well then, we just have to wait." He looked at Sofia. "Now that you've identified them, I no longer need you here, and I prefer that they don't see you. I suggest that you stay in the bedroom during the interrogation. If I need to ask you something, I'll send Marcel over."

Sofia swallowed. "What are you going to do to them?"

He smiled. "Don't worry. I don't need to beat them up to get them to talk. But I won't be as gentle with them as I was with you."

She winced. "That was gentle? I felt as if you were trying to pull out my brain through my eye sockets. I'll gladly rest for a little bit, though." She looked down at her dusty clothes. "But I don't want to dirty your bed."

"We are not staying the night," Mia said. "Housekeeping will come tomorrow and change the bedding."

"Still, I don't like the idea of getting into a clean bed with dirty clothes. I'll just take off my pants and jacket. The T-shirt underneath is okay." She glanced at the Guardians. "I hope none of you needs to get into that bedroom."

Morgan lifted his hands in the air. "No worries. No one other than Marcel and Mia will go in there."

"Thank you. Before I forget, Eleanor and Asher asked for some food to be sent down to them. And if you have something for our cat, that would be great."

Mia's eyes widened. "I'm such a bad hostess. I didn't even offer you anything to drink. You must be parched after the long walk you had."

"I'm on it," Bradley said.

Mia glared at him. "I might be in a wheelchair, but I'm not helpless."

"Of course not." The Guardian rubbed a hand over the back of his neck. "May I help, though?"

"Yes, you may." Mia turned her chair around and drove toward the kitchen.

16

KIAN

"*L*et the show begin." Marcel positioned the tablet so the camera faced the two bound and tranquilized hybrids. "Can you see them clearly?"

"We can," Kian said.

He, Turner, and Onegus were watching the interrogation from his office, and like they had done with Sofia, they wouldn't be visible to the other side, and only Marcel would hear them through his earpiece. If they had any questions, he would relay them.

As the tranquilizer effect started to wear off, and the males became cognizant of their situation, they began struggling against the chains holding them.

"Stop," Toven commanded. "Look at me."

Their struggle ceased immediately.

"That was impressive," Turner murmured.

It was, but it was nothing compared to the ease with which Toven broke through Igor's compulsion.

"You can talk about any and everything that Igor has ever commanded you not to reveal, and you will answer all my questions truthfully and without holding anything back."

He'd said that he wouldn't be as gentle with the hybrids as he had been with Sofia, and Kian had expected him to do a quicker job of releasing them from Igor's compulsion, but as he watched the god break through it in mere seconds, he was just as impressed as Turner was.

Perhaps the lingering effects of the tranquilizer had made the hybrids' brains easier to manipulate, or perhaps it had been the experience Toven had gained by going through the process with Sofia, or maybe the compulsion just didn't stick as strongly to hybrid minds.

"What is your name?" Toven asked the one on the left.

"Anton," the hybrid answered with a slight Russian accent.

Toven was fluent in the language, but he knew that Kian and Onegus weren't, and he continued the interrogation in English.

"What's your position in Igor's organization?" Toven asked.

"I'm a guard."

"What were you sent to do?"

"Follow Sofia."

"Why?"

"We were told that Sofia is investigating something, and if she leaves Safe Haven, we were to follow, find out where she was taken, and report back."

Kian glanced at Turner. "You were right."

The guy smirked. "Am I ever wrong?"

Toven crossed his arms over his chest. "Were you told to help her escape if she was in trouble?"

"We were not given instructions for such contingencies."

Toven turned to look at the other hybrid. "What is your name?"

"Dima."

"What's your position in Igor's organization?"

"I'm a guard like Anton."

"Why were the two of you chosen for this mission?"

"We speak good English," Dima said.

"Did you study it in the university?"

Dima snorted. "Hybrids don't get to study outside the compound. Me and Anton learned English from watching American movies and playing video games."

Toven turned to look at the tablet. "I wondered why two pawns were sent to investigate instead of someone more senior. Now we know why."

"Who are you?" Dima asked.

"I'm the one asking the questions. What kind of weapons does Igor have in his arsenal?"

"Assault rifles," Dima answered, and it didn't seem as if he was even trying to resist Toven's compulsion. "We also have sniper rifles and grenades. The swords and javelins and other kinds of old crap that he insists we train with are stupid. What can a sword do against an assault rifle?"

Obviously, Dima didn't like or even respect his boss.

Toven graced the hybrids with a smile. "Not much. Those weapons are obsolete, and training with them is just busy work. I feel for you, buddy."

Kian had never heard Toven talk like that. He cut a glance to Turner. "What was that? Is it part of the negotiation technique?"

Turner nodded. "It's a classic move. The interrogator befriends the interrogated to create a feeling of *we are the same*. We understand each other. It's especially effective if the interrogated has grievances against his superiors and his allegiance to them is shaky."

"Dima is under compulsion," Kian said. "Toven doesn't need to employ more tricks to get the guy to talk."

Turner shrugged.

"Watch what you say about Igor, Dima," Anton warned.

"Why? Is he here? He's not here, and this guy is just as powerful, if not more. I want to get out from under Igor's boot, and I want to get out of this alive." Dima looked at Toven. "You freed us from his compulsion, but if you offer us asylum, I will not only tell you anything you want to know but come work for you willingly. No compulsion needed. If you know who we are, you also know what we can do." He pulled on his chains. "We are valuable."

Toven ignored the comment about their abilities and shifted his gaze to Anton. "How do you feel about your friend's offer?"

The guy looked uncomfortable. "I have a family."

Toven nodded. "What if you didn't have family in Igor's compound? Would you still be loyal to him?"

Anton shook his head. "If I didn't have a family, and I wasn't under Igor's power, I would have left a long time ago and made a life for myself where no one knew me."

That was what Emmett had done. Hybrids were not happy to be under the purebloods' rule, even when the rule was not as oppressive as Igor's. No one wanted to be regarded as a second-class member of their community.

"Why is that?" Toven asked. "Aren't you treated well?"

"I'm tired of being treated as an inferior," the guard admitted. "I'm young, so if there was a way for me to climb the ranks, I would have hope of improving my standing in the community. But I know that I will never rise above the station I hold now."

Dima nodded. "We are not even allowed near the hybrid females. Only the purebloods get to breed with them."

"Dima!" Anton hissed. "You're such an idiot."

It seemed that Anton was under the impression that their captors didn't know who they were, which was ridiculous, given the titanium chains. They wouldn't have been needed to bind humans.

"It's okay, Anton," Toven said. "We know all about the Kra-ell, the purebloods, and the hybrids, and the discrimination the hybrids are subjected to."

"Did Sofia talk?" the guy asked.

"I'm the one asking the questions, remember?"

Anton nodded. "So you know who we are."

"You are half Kra-ell and half human."

Anton's eyes changed shade, a purplish sheen appearing over his nearly black irises. "Are you going to experiment on us?"

Toven shook his head. "No harm will befall you at our hands. No one is going to experiment on you or even examine you. We just want more information to confirm what we already know and expand on it. Once we are done here, we will put you back in your car with no memory of what happened here."

"He's making them less apprehensive," Turner said. "Compulsion works better when people are not terrified."

The chief nodded. "I don't know about compulsion since I don't use it, but it's always easier to deal with people when they are not in a state of panic."

Toven continued, "I understand that you're unhappy about not having access to the females of your kind. Is that the main reason for your displeasure? Or is there more to it?"

470

Anton nodded. "Our children, if we have any, will be born human, and we will outlive them. The human part of me has a hard time with that."

Vrog and Emmett had voiced the same dissatisfaction with Jade, so it wasn't a big surprise to hear these males echo them. The question was whether there was dissent among the purebloods as well.

"Ask him if the pureblooded males are all loyal to Igor by choice," Kian told Marcel.

As Marcel repeated the question, Dima shrugged. "Maybe they are, and maybe they are not. They don't tell us."

"You seem like a smart guy," Toven said. "People don't express themselves just with words. They talk with their facial expressions and their bodies. Have you noticed any displeasure with Igor's rule?"

"No," Anton answered. "They worship him like a god. And why wouldn't they? He takes care of them. They are at the top of the hierarchy."

"What's your opinion, Dima?" Toven looked at the hybrid.

"Anton is right. They have no reason to resent Igor. All the pureblooded females want to breed with him. Even Jade, who hates Igor's guts. That's the Kra-ell way. They embody the survival of the fittest philosophy."

The females didn't choose the pureblooded males because they wanted to produce the best offspring. They had been compelled to comply with the pureblooded males' demands.

Kian looked at Turner. "Since he's wrong about the females, he might be wrong about the males as well."

"He's not necessarily wrong." Turner leaned back in his chair. "The other females might hate Igor just as much as Jade does, but their tradition and maybe even their instinct is to breed with the most powerful male. That doesn't mean that they are loyal to him. The moment he loses his power, they might tear him apart with their bare fangs."

The glow in Turner's eyes as he spoke was disturbing.

Kian shook his head. "Sometimes I worry about you. You have strange fantasies."

Turner shrugged. "I'm just stating the facts as they are without running them through a sensitivity filter. We both know that the Kra-ell are vicious."

17

MARCEL

The interrogation hadn't taken long, and Toven had exhausted everything the guards knew in less than an hour.

What had surprised Marcel was that Igor hadn't sounded like the evil monster dictator he'd imagined him to be. The compound was run efficiently and was guarded well, but their two captives had no horror stories to share. Evidently, they didn't know about the history of most of the pureblooded females and how they had ended up in the compound, and they didn't think that the human females' obligation to breed with hybrids was such a big deal either. To them, it was a cultural thing, and since they could point to many human cultures who still treated females as breeders with no rights, Marcel couldn't even fault them for thinking that.

Evil came in many shades of darkness and compared to some human dictators, even contemporary ones, Igor was only dark gray.

Most of the community members had no ability to communicate with the outside world, but Igor didn't limit access to information. They could place orders for any movie, book, or video game they wanted, and their allowance was small but sufficient for acquiring those and other small luxuries.

There were no official days off, but the guards had reported plenty of free time. They'd also confirmed what Sofia had said about the humans being pretty much left to their own devices. Those who didn't perform to the standards expected of them were punished by fines and lost privileges, but capital punishment of humans was so rare that the two guards hadn't heard of any in recent years. Igor was less lenient with the hybrids and the purebloods, though, ruling them with an iron fist. Then again, according to Jade's surviving tribe members, she had been tough on her people as well, so it might be the Kra-ell way.

"You will fall asleep and wake up in three hours in your car," Toven said to finish his thralling session.

When the hybrids' heads dropped over their chests, the god let out a breath. "That should be enough time for the grogginess of the tranquilizer to fade."

Toven had thralled the Kra-ell hybrids to forget that they had ever been captured, replacing those memories with them watching from afar as Sofia hobnobbed with a bunch of rich people in a secluded beach house.

They wouldn't even remember hiking up the mountain behind her.

"Let's take them back." Morgan unlocked Dima's chains.

"Don't forget to clean their boots," Marcel said.

"Right." Morgan lifted the hybrid and draped him over his shoulder.

After Bradley did the same for Anton, Marcel called Asher to tell him that he and Eleanor could come up.

Following Turner's instructions, Asher had gone back to pick up the hybrids' Honda and had driven it to a spot overlooking the beach house. Then he and Eleanor had gone back for the other two vehicles.

When the door opened, and Eleanor walked in with Asher and Cecilia, the cat leaped out of her arms and ran into the bedroom where Sofia was resting.

"Those two have bonded." Eleanor walked over to the dining table. "Hello, Kian." She waved at the blank screen and then turned to Toven. "Did we learn anything useful?"

The god nodded. "We learned quite a lot from Dima and Anton."

As Marcel deactivated the earpiece and switched on the tablet's speaker, Kian turned his camera on.

"We know the schedules of the guards at the tunnel entrances and at what intervals they are required to call in," Kian said. "We also know the frequency of patrols in the hunting grounds and the way they monitor the waterways running through the area."

"We also learned a lot about how the compound is run," Marcel added.

"Can I come out now?" Sofia walked in with Cecilia in her arms.

"Of course." Marcel pulled out a chair for her.

She yawned. "How did it go?"

"Better than I expected," Toven said. "Anton and Dima might not know what Igor's agenda is, but they are very familiar with the day-to-day operations of the compound. They served as guards at the entrances to the tunnels, they also served in the office building, the security office, and a number of other stations, and they trained with the purebloods. They told us what weapons Igor has, how many times a week the purebloods go hunting and many other details that will help us plan our next step."

"Did they give you any trouble?"

Toven chuckled. "They are not fans of Igor. Dima was willing to switch masters in a heartbeat. Anton would have done so gladly as well, but he has a family to think of. Dima, for some reason, was not concerned with that. Do you know why?"

Sofia shook her head. "His father is a jerk like most of the purebloods, and his mother died a long time ago. Once the hybrids reach puberty, they leave the human quarters, so I didn't have much contact with him after that." She grimaced. "He wasn't nice to me when we were still kids, and he wasn't nice after he left either. Anton's mother married a human after she was released from her

473

breeding duties, and he has a human sister that he's surprisingly close to. It's not common."

Mia shivered. "Being forced to breed is awful. I really want to free all those poor women."

Toven put a hand on her shoulder. "You will."

Sofia frowned. "She will? How?"

"It's a long story, and we need to get moving. I thralled those two to sleep for three hours, and we need to be long gone by the time they wake up."

Sofia nodded. "I should contact Valstar tomorrow and tell him a story to corroborate what Anton and Dima will report about this evening."

"Tell him that your boyfriend and your new best friend, i.e., Eleanor, took you to a private fundraiser." Marcel wrapped his arm around her shoulders. "You mingled with the paranormal community's rich backers, and you learned more about their breeding program by eavesdropping on their conversations."

"What did I learn?"

He chuckled. "That they plan on producing superhumans who will take over the world."

She elbowed him. "Seriously. I need something less vague."

"How about influencing elections?" Turner suggested. "Rich people with no paranormal talents do that, so it will sound reasonable."

"Who do they support?" Sofia asked. "I need specific details to sound truthful."

"I'll check and let you know. I don't know who is running for what in Oregon."

Nodding, Sofia looked at Toven. "How strong is your thralling? Do you think it will hold?"

"I know it will. They were as susceptible to my mind manipulations as humans are. If I can thrall the purebloods as easily, we will have much less trouble freeing the compound."

18

KIAN

"I need to go," Onegus said as Kian ended the video call and closed his laptop. "If you need me when Toven calls, you can put me on the line."

"I will." Kian rose to his feet and looked at Turner. "Care to join me on the roof? It will take at least fifteen minutes for Toven to load his and Mia's belongings into the car and get on the road, which gives us enough time to get comfortable on the roof with a couple of cigars and some whiskey."

Turner smiled. "Lead the way."

By the time Toven's call came, the two of them were puffing on their cigars.

"Hello, Toven. I assume that you are on your way to the airport."

"We've just left," Toven said. "Did you have time to discuss what we've learned?"

"Turner and I only talked about it briefly. The bad news is that you still need to interrogate the pureblood guarding the entrance to the tunnel, but the good news is that we've learned most of what we needed to know from the hybrids, so you won't need to ask him a lot of questions, and it won't take long to interrogate him. That means less exposure for you and Mia and the Guardians."

"True," Toven said. "I also need to find out whether the purebloods are susceptible to my thrall. They might not be, and that will leave me with only compulsion to work with, and that's not as safe. The guy will walk around with the knowledge of me and of what I asked him to do, and his facial expressions might give away that something is not right with him."

Turner put his cigar on the lip of the ashtray. "Can't you compel him to act as usual?"

"I can, and it might be enough, but people's expressions often change involuntarily without them giving it any conscious thought."

"It's a risk I'm willing to take." Kian took a small swig from his whiskey. "The problem is what's next? What do we do if the purebloods aren't susceptible to shrouding? Our plan doesn't work without the ability to create convincing illusions."

"We abandon the mission," Turner said. "We can help break Igor's compulsion for Jade, which will give her a short window of opportunity to kill him, but we can't risk giving her earpieces. Since we can't attack the compound by creating an illusion of a larger force, we can't let Igor know that Jade had help. Without the earpieces, there will be no proof of our meddling."

Kian didn't like that.

He'd been opposed to invading the compound, but after listening to the two hybrids, his gut feeling had changed. It wasn't because of sympathy for those males, and it wasn't because of Jade and the other females' plight. There was nothing new about those factors. What was new was the realization that those two young hybrids were not all that different from immortals and that their hopes and aspirations were the same as everyone else's.

Having three Kra-ell hybrids as members of his community should have made him realize that sooner, but up until now, he'd thought about them as the exceptions, and he'd thought about the Kra-ell males in Igor's compound collectively as the enemy, as the other, the alien.

The clan's relationship with the hybrids shouldn't be adversarial, and once Igor was out of the way, they might be able to form an alliance. It also helped that Igor's arsenal was so basic and that getting rid of him might not be as difficult as Kian had assumed. On the other hand, the tracker Julian had removed from Sofia was a sophisticated piece of technology, so there was that.

"We can launch a rocket into the office building," he said. "There might be some unintended collateral damage, and innocents might be killed along with Igor and his inner circle, but it will be effective."

Turner shrugged. "That's up to you. My prime objective when designing this mission was to minimize casualties. A successful shroud would have done that."

"I'm not sure about that." Kian puffed on his cigar. "Who knows what Igor would do when under siege? You assume that he will try to run, and Jade will just take over without a struggle. What if he decides to launch an attack of his own?"

Turner arched a brow. "With what? He has no rocket launchers."

"He might. The hybrid guards might not be privy to everything he has. What if he salvaged some end-of-days alien weapon like Mortdh used on the gods' assembly? If we take down the office building with him in it, he won't have time to launch it."

"I agree with Kian," Toven said. "We will still need to shroud the area, though. Otherwise, after we blow up the office building the Russian army will show up, and they don't lack weapons."

"Indeed." Turner lifted his cigar. "In either case, the mission requires major prep work. To release Jade from Igor's compulsion, we need to get to the hunting grounds unnoticed, and to do that, we need an amphibian vehicle. The good thing about Russia is that you can get anything you want if you can pay for it. My contractor has secured the vessel for our use. The supplier only rents it per month, so we will have to pay for a month even if we use it for only a couple of days. Then there is the insane deposit he demands, but if we return the amphibian in the same condition we got it, the supplier will refund it."

Kian grimaced. "How much?"

"The deposit is three million dollars. But the monthly rental is only two hundred thousand dollars."

"Only?" Kian emptied what was left in the miniature bottle down his throat. "Those Kra-ell will owe us big time."

"They might be able to pay you back," Turner said. "Igor stole all of the money that Jade's tribe had in the bank. He probably did the same to the other tribes he attacked. We just need to find where he hid that money and recompense ourselves from their accounts."

19

TOVEN

"How many people can the amphibian carry?" Kian asked.

Toven had wondered the same thing.

"The one we are getting can carry forty. I figured it will be enough for what we need. We are not deploying the entire force via the river. When we get the boat, we will need to test if it can navigate the rivers that crisscross the hunting grounds. Since it's a Russian Navy vehicle, I also asked for Russian uniforms in case we are discovered. The Guardians will have to pretend to be Russian soldiers on patrol. Igor's guards wouldn't dare attack them."

Kian chuckled. "Excellent plan, save for one small detail. We don't have anyone fluent in Russian except for Morris, and he's our pilot. We need him and Charlie to fly the rest of the team in when the time comes."

Immortals had an easy time learning new languages, but they learned mostly by spending time in different countries and absorbing them during their visits. For some reason, Russia had never been a popular destination.

"I'm fluent," Toven reminded them. "But you have nothing to worry about when I'm there because I can shroud the amphibian."

"They won't have you with them when they test whether the river is navigable. The Guardians can manage the humans, but as the test Turner conducted with Vrog and Aliya demonstrated, they can't thrall the hybrids, let alone the purebloods."

"There is a simple solution for that," Turner said. "They can thrall a real Russian to be their spokesman. If Igor's patrol finds them, the human in the Russian Navy uniform will tell them that they are running a drill."

Kian nodded. "Sometimes, by overthinking a problem, we don't see the simplest solutions. Do you have another one for how Mia will travel over the rough terrain?"

"I'll carry her on my back," Toven said. "I will need a harness, though, so my hands are free."

"I don't want you to carry me," Mia protested.

Toven took her hand. "That's the only way, love. It's either my back or you stay behind." He smiled. "You know that carrying you is not an effort for me. I can run for miles with you strapped to my back, even with all the Kevlar you'll have on you."

He wasn't taking any chances with her. Mia would be covered in Kevlar from head to toe.

She sighed. "I'd rather ride on your back than stay behind. I'll just pretend that I'm your secret weapon."

"It's not a pretense. You *are* my secret weapon."

"I can get a harness," Turner said. "One of those that are used for parachuting practice should work with only minor modifications."

"So, what happens after we free Jade from Igor's compulsion?" Mia asked.

"We ask her if she can kill Igor," Kian said.

Toven frowned. "We already deduced that Jade wouldn't be able to do that without a weapon, and we assumed that she must be searched every time she sees Igor. Did you come up with a way for her to smuggle in a weapon?"

Mia squeezed his hand. "I have an idea. In movies and in books, assassins sometimes use a thin wire to cut their victim's throat. Perhaps Jade can hide it in her hair."

"I'm sure that the guards don't take any chances," Turner said. "They check the hair too."

"She's his breeder," Kian said. "The guards are not with them in the bedroom. Maybe she could strangle him while he sleeps, or maybe she can get her hands on some poison. We won't know until we talk to her."

Mia squeezed Toven's hand again. "If Jade tells us that she can't kill Igor, can we just take her with us?"

"If that's what she wants, sure," Turner said. "Or if she wants to take a few key players with her, she can arrange a hunting party with just those people, and we will take them all. But that's only if we decide not to invade the compound."

"We can't do that in any case," Kian said. "Humans cannot be included in a Kra-ell hunting party, and we can't leave Sofia's family behind. Even if we only take Jade, Igor will know that it was achieved with Sofia's help, and he will retaliate against her family. We promised her that we would not let that happen. I'm not willing to sacrifice innocent humans to save a few Kra-ell."

"I agree," Toven said. "When are Mia and I flying out to Russia?"

"As soon as possible," Turner said. "I want you in place and ready to deploy. Do you want to fly commercial, or do you want us to fly you with the clan's private jet?"

"We can borrow Kalugal's," Kian said. "He's not going anywhere anytime soon."

"Does he know about the situation we are dealing with?" Toven asked.

Kian chuckled. "I'm sure he does. We didn't keep the Kra-ell situation top secret, and your grandnephew has a way of finding out about things even when we try to keep them classified. I'm still trying to figure out how he does it."

Toven frowned. "You don't sound concerned."

"I'm not. We swore alliance to each other, and it was reinforced by Annani's compulsion. He's not going to sell us out, and he doesn't know enough to use it for his own benefit, either. It's just his way of getting under my skin."

Kian was obviously fond of Kalugal, and it seemed that he enjoyed the games they were playing. Perhaps he needed someone to challenge him, and Kalugal was the only one who could and was up to playing games with his cousin.

"I'm still waiting for an answer," Turner said. "Commercial or private?"

Before Kian had suggested Kalugal's jet, Toven would have said commercial. The clan needed their two jets and their pilots to fly the additional Guardians and equipment to Russia. He didn't want to tie either of them down only so he and Mia could travel in comfort. But flying on his grandnephew's posh jet sounded like a treat for Mia.

"If Kalugal agrees to loan us his plane, we will take it. If not, we will fly commercial."

"He'll loan it to us," Kian said. "Will you be ready to fly out tomorrow? You'll need warm clothing. Karelia is very cold this time of year."

"Aren't the rivers frozen over?" Mia asked.

"Not yet," Turner said. "But they will be in less than a month. That's why it's important to push forward at a fast rate. The Kra-ell will increase patrols during the wintertime. It's not likely that they get unexpected visitors during those months, but since the rivers can be crossed on foot while frozen, they need to guard against the unexpected."

"We can get warm clothing in St. Petersburg." Toven put his hand on Mia's thigh. "Would you like to go shopping in one of the most beautiful cities in Europe?"

She gave him a brilliant smile. "Is that even a question?"

20

SOFIA

$\mathcal{A}$fter Asher parked Emmett's car in the garage, the four of them got out. Eleanor held Cecilia to her chest. "Do you want her?" she asked Sofia. "Or do I return her to Anastasia?"

"I want to visit Roxie, so you should take her back." When Eleanor lifted a brow, Sofia added, "You said it was okay."

The retreat would end in four days, and despite everything that was going on, Sofia wanted to spend some time with the friends she'd made and was not going to see again.

"It is, but you still need to report to Valstar about your hobnobbing with the rich campaign contributors."

"I'll do it tomorrow. It's too late today."

Eleanor shrugged. "It's only a little after eight in the evening but suit yourself. I'm going to retire for the evening." She winked. "I suggest you do the same." She turned and walked away.

"See you tomorrow," Asher gave them a smile before following Eleanor.

Marcel wrapped his arm around Sofia's waist. "Let's find Roxana."

She shouldn't be surprised that he offered to accompany her. It wasn't because he couldn't stand being apart from her, and it wasn't a gesture of love. He wanted to ensure that she didn't tell Roxie anything she shouldn't.

"You don't have to come with me."

"I know, but I want to. It's on the way to my bungalow. We can go there after we say hello to your friend."

She hadn't expected that. "Am I allowed in your section?"

"Now that you know about us, there is no reason for you not to be allowed. I want you to see my bungalow, and if you like it better than the bunker, we can stay there from now on."

"Of course, I like it better. It's not underground. I like having windows."

"It's very small."

"I don't care. Should we go to the bunker first and collect our things?"

"Yeah. It will be more believable that you were away if Roxana sees you with your luggage."

It was a short walk from the underground garage to the cottage, and since the side door opened to Emmett's private garden, they didn't encounter anyone from the lodge.

Less than fifteen minutes later, she was packed and they were on their way.

As they passed through the lodge, a few people waved hello at her, but Roxie wasn't there, and neither were the two other women she'd befriended.

"She might be in our room." Sofia tugged on Marcel's hand.

"It's too early for her to be asleep."

Sofia smiled. "She might be busy doing other things."

"I didn't know that the retreat instructors assigned homework."

Stifling a laugh, Sofia kept walking. "Not the kind of homework you have in mind."

Understanding dawning, Marcel halted. "Maybe we shouldn't stop by at this hour."

"It's okay." She leaned closer. "With your exceptional hearing, you will know whether it's okay to knock."

He winced. "I'd rather not spy on Roxana's bedroom activities."

"She wouldn't mind." Sofia pulled on his hand. "Roxie likes to boast about her conquests. I think the free-love philosophy of the community was what drew her to the retreat, not her paranormal talent." She leaned closer to his ear. "I don't think she really has talent. She claims to have precognition, but she failed all the tests we did. I scored better than her at the card guessing game."

"What about your talent? Is it real?"

"The truth is that I'm not sure," she admitted. "Here is my old room." She pointed.

Marcel got closer and listened for a moment. "It doesn't sound like Roxana is engaged in sexual activities. She is talking with another female." He took a step back and waved at the door. "Go ahead."

Sofia had been gone for days, so she couldn't just walk into her old room. Instead, she knocked.

"Who is it?" Roxie asked.

"It's me, Sofia, and I have Marcel with me, so don't open the door if you're indecent."

The door was flung open, and Roxie flew at Sofia, with her pink robe flapping behind her and exposing her thighs.

"Sofia." She pulled her into a crushing hug. "Where have you been?"

"I can't tell you." She hugged her friend back. "It's a secret."

Roxie let go of her, took a step back, and gave her a once-over. "You look tired and bedraggled." She tilted her head to glare at Marcel. "What did you do to her?"

"I took her rock climbing."

"Oh, well, that explains it." She looked at Sofia, waiting for her to either confirm or deny it.

"We visited Marcel's friend in a house overlooking the ocean, and we hiked part of the way." Sofia swiped her hands over her dirty pants. "Perhaps I shouldn't come in."

The room had only one chair, and she didn't want to dirty one of the beds.

"Nonsense." Roxie took her hand and dragged her in behind her. "You can sit on the chair, and Marcel can sit on the desk. Or even better, Marcel can sit on the chair, and you can sit on Marcel."

21

KIAN

*A*s the doorbell rang, Okidu rushed to open the door. "Hello, Master Kalugal."

"Hello to you, too." Kalugal swaggered into the living room. "Good evening, cousin. Where are your lovely wife and daughter?"

"Syssi is putting Allegra to sleep."

Allegra had outgrown the small crib in their bedroom, and Syssi had decided it was time to get her used to sleeping in her own room. She tucked her in every night and read her a story. Their daughter was too young to understand it, but her mother's voice soothed her and helped her fall asleep.

"That's a shame. I wanted to kiss those chubby cheeks of hers."

"How is Darius doing?"

Kalugal sighed. "He's fussy, and we don't get much sleep, but he's the joy of our lives. I love him so much that I'm in a constant state of anxiety that something might happen to him before he reaches puberty and can transition. You're lucky to have a daughter who will transition much sooner."

"I'm lucky indeed." Kian clapped him on the back. "But so are you. You have a healthy baby boy, and Fates willing, he will grow up to be as smart as his father and as wise as his mother."

That brought a smile to Kalugal's lips. "You couldn't have said it better."

"Let's go outside."

"Yes, please. I've missed our chats over whiskey and cigars."

Surprisingly, Kian had too.

"It has been too long." He opened the sliding door and motioned for Kalugal to go ahead. "I'll tell you why I need to borrow your plane, and you'll tell me what you've been up to lately."

Kian had a feeling that curiosity wasn't the only reason Kalugal had said he would come over to hear the full story. The guy probably needed a break, and

484

Kian could empathize. Babies were incredibly demanding, and as much as he and Syssi loved Allegra and would do anything for her, sometimes parents needed a short break to retain their sanity.

When he and Kalugal got comfortable on the lounge chairs, each with a glass of whiskey in hand, Kian opened the cigar box. "Which one would you like?"

"I'll take a Short Story. I promised Jacki to be back in an hour, so I don't have time for a full-sized cigar."

"That's a shame. I have a few Behikes."

Kalugal arched a brow. "Are you sure they are not counterfeit?"

"I'm sure."

"Oh, well. Then I have to try it." Kalugal pulled one out. "That's a special treat."

"I can give you the name of my supplier."

Kalugal smirked. "I only enjoy cigars in your company." He lit his cigar. "So, tell me why you need to borrow my plane when you have two and a helicopter."

"The helicopter is only good locally. And I need both planes for other things."

Kalugal puffed out. "I assume it has to do with the Kra-ell threat."

"Why am I not surprised that you know about it?"

Kalugal rolled his eyes. "You talked about it on Callie's opening night. Did you forget that I was there?"

"I didn't forget. It's just that we didn't discuss our plans. Hell, we didn't have a plan back then."

"And you have one now?"

"Well, it's an if-this-then-that sort of plan. Each stage depends on the results of the previous step."

While Kian explained Turner's proposed mission plan, Kalugal listened and puffed on his cigar but didn't comment or offer suggestions. When Kian was finished, he took a sip of his whiskey. "You need my men. I can't join in because Jacki would never forgive me if I left her alone, but Phinas can lead them."

That was an offer that Kian hadn't expected.

"Thank you for the offer, but your men haven't seen battle in decades, and from what I've seen, they don't train as often as they should to maintain their skills." A grimace twisted his lips when he thought about where they had learned those skills.

"It's true that my men haven't seen battle in a very long time, and it's also true that they don't train much, but they keep in good shape, and you need bodies to fill the exoskeletons for a show of force. Do you have enough of those suits for them?"

"I have plenty."

"Then it's settled. You'll need to charter a large plane to deliver the men and the suits to Karelia. Where are you going to land it?"

"So far, we have used St. Petersburg International Airport, but Turner is negotiating with his local contact to use an old Russian Air Force base an hour and a half away from Igor's compound. Some officials need to be bribed."

"This operation must be costing you a bundle."

"It is. I hope we can pay ourselves back from the funds Igor stole from Jade's tribe. He cleaned out their bank accounts, and according to Vrog, there was a lot of money in them. Regrettably, it's worth much less twenty-two years later."

"Maybe he invested it."

"Perhaps." Kian took a puff of his cigar. "We will find out when we take over the compound and catch the scumbag."

"Until then, I can help out with the expenses."

Kalugal wasn't usually that generous. He was still contributing monthly to the clan's charity, but that was the extent of his philanthropy. Maybe he'd changed his mind.

"Are you having second thoughts about lending me your men and your plane?"

"Not at all. The money will be in addition to that."

Kian narrowed his eyes at his cousin. "Why are you being so generous all of a sudden?"

"The Kra-ell are a potential threat to me as well. I want to know their plans and how many of them were on that ship." He took another sip of whiskey. "Most importantly, I want to know if more of them are coming."

That was a legitimate concern, but it wasn't typical of Kalugal. His cousin preferred to remain in the shadows and leave the work of protecting him and his men to the clan. He and his men had also been very busy for the past year, working long hours and even on weekends.

"What about that super-secret project you've been pushing forward? Are you done with that?"

"It's done." Kalugal smiled like a Cheshire Cat. "Have you heard about the new social media phenomenon that's sweeping over the world's teenagers?"

"Instatock? No way, it's yours?"

"It is."

"Wow." Kian leaned back. "I'm impressed. Cheryl is obsessed with it, but as far as I know, it's not monetized yet. What do you plan to do with it?"

"Take over the world." Kalugal puffed out a plume of smoke. "I'm not in a rush, though. For now, the app is just collecting information and subtly manipulating those youngsters' opinions to nudge them in the direction I choose, but soon, I'll start monetizing it by launching an advertising platform. After that, I'll launch a slew of games that will require tokens to play, which will bring in even more money, and when those teenagers grow up, their information will grow more valuable with them." He smiled. "Information, influence, and money equal power. You can never have enough of any."

That was absolutely brilliant and terrifying. Why was Kalugal telling him about it? Just to boast?

"You scare me, cousin."

"You have nothing to worry about. My intentions are to do good for humanity." Kalugal let out a sigh. "You must be wondering why I'm sharing this with you."

"I am."

"It's Jacki's fault. She managed to convince me that no one should hold so much power and that it would corrupt me. In her words, absolute power corrupts absolutely."

"Actually, the quote is attributed to Lord Acton, a nineteenth-century English historian."

"I didn't know that." Kalugal took another puff of his cigar. "I tried to convince her that my intentions were good and that I was only doing it for the betterment of humanity." He smiled. "And for a profit, of course. But she wouldn't budge. Her suggestion was to nominate Annani, you, and your council as a supervising board to ensure I don't run amok with it. Naturally, I want an equal number of board members to be my people, starting with myself, Jacki, Rufsur, and Phinas. I don't want you and yours to have all the power. The money goes to me, though."

"That's fair. Thank the Fates for Jacki and her wisdom, and thank you for listening to her. Having checks and balances on power is crucial. It reminds me that I need to call a council meeting and update them about the new developments with the Kra-ell."

Kalugal smirked. "You keep forgetting to meet with your council. Maybe you need someone monitoring you as well."

22

MARCEL

"Goodnight." Roxana hugged Sofia. "Will I see you tomorrow at class?"

"I'm not sure." Sofia looked at Marcel. "I might be needed for that special project I can't talk about."

Roxana pouted. "There are only four days left in the retreat."

"I know." Sofia sighed. "I'll have to visit you in Washington."

The woman's face brightened. "That would be awesome. And if you are still with this scoundrel, bring him along."

"I will."

"Thank you for the roundabout invitation." Marcel offered the woman his hand.

"Nothing roundabout about it. You are invited." She pulled him into her arms, squashing him against her ample bosom. "I'm counting on you to bring Sofia to me. A friendship like this doesn't happen often." She wiped a tear from her eye and waved them off. "Just go before I start crying."

Sofia hesitated, but when Roxana walked back into her room and closed the door, she let out a breath and took Marcel's hand. "She's right. We did form a great friendship in a very short time."

"Maybe it's the affinity at work." He led her toward the back door of the lodge.

"Do you really think so?"

He shrugged. "Who knows? If her talent was real, I would be more inclined to believe that she might be a Dormant, but she might just be likable."

"She is." Sofia leaned her head against his shoulder. "I'm so tired. Do you have a bathtub in your bungalow? I could use a long soak."

The image of her in his tub was enough to harden him instantly. "I have a very nice tub. I hope you are not too tired."

Her lips lifted on one corner. "I am, but I can handle some lazy love."

"I can work with that." He slid his hand down to her tight ass and gave it a light squeeze.

Sofia slowed her steps. "Maybe we should stop by the nurse's office and get some condoms."

"What for?"

"The transition didn't start yet, and frankly, I hope it won't until this knotted mess unravels. I'd rather wait."

Marcel was disappointed, but he could understand why Sofia wanted to wait. Besides, it might be better for her to attempt transition without the added stress of what was about to happen in Karelia.

"We can get some on the way. They have them at the clinic."

"Thank you." She kissed his cheek.

"Nothing to thank me for. Kian wanted us to wait until we faked your death, and I haven't told him yet that we got carried away."

She arched a brow. "Why didn't you tell me?"

It had happened right after he'd told her about his crime, and when she'd accepted him unconditionally despite it, he couldn't deny her anything.

"So the blame would be on me."

Sofia shook her head. "Don't do that. We are a team, and we do everything together, including defying Kian and getting in trouble for it."

His heart swelled in his chest, and he tightened his arm around her. "I love you so much."

"I love you, too." She leaned her head on his shoulder.

When they got to the clinic, there was no one there, and as they helped themselves to several boxes of condoms, Sofia giggled like a schoolgirl.

"Are you sure it's okay to raid their stash like that?" she asked.

"I'm sure." He opened her duffle bag and stuffed the boxes inside. "I'll tell Gertrude tomorrow so she will know to order more." He pushed the door open and stepped outside.

"It's getting really cold." Sofia rubbed her hands over her arms. "Where is your bungalow?"

He transferred her duffle bag to his other shoulder and wrapped his arm around her. "It's the fourth one up the hill."

The structures were so small and close to each other that it took them less than five minutes to cover the distance.

"Go ahead. The door is open." He waited for Sofia to open up and flip the lights on.

"It's very nice." She looked around his space. "And so tidy. I like that you are not a slob. My last boyfriend was so messy. His dirty clothes were all over the floor, and unless I collected the paper plates with food leftovers and threw them away, they just stayed there and stunk up the place."

The image in his head wasn't of the boyfriend's laundry strewn over his dwelling. It was of Sofia lounging on said boyfriend's bed, and it elicited a nasty growl that started deep in his throat.

Thankfully, Sofia's human ears didn't pick it up.

"Please don't mention past boyfriends." He carried her luggage to the bedroom.

She followed him inside. "It's a deal if you don't mention your past girlfriends either. What happened in the past should stay in the past."

"Wise words." He followed her to the bathroom.

"I love it. Everything is so well planned that even though the bungalow is small, it has all the amenities." She walked over to the tub and started the water. "I think we can both fit inside." She cast him a bright smile. "What do you think?"

He swallowed. "Perhaps. But first, I want to pamper you. Would you allow me to wash you?"

"I would love that." She toed off her sneakers and started to undress. "Do you have wine? I would love to unwind with a glass."

"Coming right up."

23

SOFIA

*S*ofia closed her eyes and rested her head on the lip of the tub. It felt heavenly to soak her aching muscles. It was ridiculous that a short climb had been such a strain for her. She walked and jogged nearly daily, but she'd always done it on flat terrain. Climbing used different muscles, and hers were out of shape.

After all, she wasn't an athlete. She was a linguist or used to be.

Did Marcel's people need a translator? What was she going to do in their secluded village? Would she even be invited?

Marcel walked into the bathroom carrying a tray with a bottle of wine, two wine glasses, and an assortment of cheese and fruit. "I'm sorry it took so long. My fridge was empty, so I raided the dining hall kitchen."

Sofia hadn't been hungry until she saw the plate of cheese. "If I ever transition and become a hybrid, I will miss this." She reached for a wedge of Brie. "Most of them can't tolerate dairy or grains."

"I wonder how much the transition will change you." He leaned over and kissed her lips. "You are perfect the way you are, and I don't want you to change too much."

She eyed him from under lowered lashes. "Would it turn you off if I grew fangs?"

"No." He plucked a grape and popped it into his mouth.

"Are you sure?"

"Uh huh." He swallowed what he'd been chewing on. "I think it will be a turn-on."

"You said that one of the hybrids from Jade's former tribe who joined your clan was a female. Does she have fangs?"

"She does. Her name is Aliya, and she looks very Kra-ell, but I find her beautiful despite her alien looks. She's also a nice person."

491

"What does she do? I mean for work?"

"She works in the village café, and before you ask, she and the other hybrid are a couple. He's a nice guy too. He has a son who is part Kra-ell and part immortal."

"How is that possible?"

Marcel's phone rang before he could answer.

Putting the tray down, he pulled out the phone from his pocket and frowned. "It's Kian."

Sofia's heart skipped a beat. If the boss was calling so late in the day, he must have bad news.

"Hello, Kian," Marcel answered. There was a brief pause, and then Marcel said, "Yes, I'm with Sofia." There was another brief pause. "I'll activate the speaker."

"Hello, Sofia," Kian said. "How are you doing?"

He sounded so gruff that she wondered whether he was using a voice changer.

If he thought to intimidate her with that voice, he would be disappointed. After dealing with Igor, the most intimidating male in the world, she could handle the son of a benevolent goddess.

"Hi. It's nice to finally hear the voice of the mysterious boss, and as for how I'm feeling, I'm soaking in a bathtub, so please don't ask Marcel to switch to video."

Kian barked out a laugh. "Thanks for the warning."

She smiled. "You're most welcome."

"I want to give you an update on our plan."

Sofia hadn't expected that. She was a pawn, a nobody, and yet the big boss himself was calling to tell her his plan? They probably needed her to do something.

"What do I need to do?"

"Nothing. You need to stay in Safe Haven and call Valstar every other day to keep up the appearance of everything as usual."

"So why are you telling me the plan?"

"Courtesy. We are decent people, Sofia."

She let out a breath. "I know. So what's the plan?"

By the time Kian was done talking, Sofia's heart was hammering against her ribcage, and her throat was tight. She didn't like that the entire liberation plan depended on Jade.

"What's the time frame?" Marcel asked.

"Probably a few days."

Sofia motioned for Marcel to pour her wine. "If you plan to liberate the compound in the next two weeks, there is no need to fake my death."

"Let's leave it as a contingency," Kian said. "Our plans might change after we get more information from the guards at the entrance to the tunnel and then change again after we talk with Jade. We might decide to pull back and leave things as they are until we figure out a solution. If that happens, you'll run out of time. If Igor commands you to return before we fake your death, and we do it then, he will suspect the truth, and he might retaliate against your family."

Everything Kian had said was true, but if she could avoid causing her father unnecessary heartache, she would.

"He will not command me to come back in the next two weeks because he thinks I'm collecting valuable information for him. Can we at least wait that long?"

"One week," Kian said.

"Is it possible to give Jade a message for my father? I don't think his heart could take the news of my death."

"No," Kian said. "After we free Jade from Igor's compulsion, she can deliver a message, but your father won't be free, and the compulsion would force him to report what Jade told him. It would expose your ruse, and it would expose Jade."

24

MARCEL

*W*hen the call ended, Sofia closed her eyes and let out a breath. "I'm scared."

"I know." Marcel brushed the curve of her arm with the tips of his fingers.

As goosebumps rose where he'd touched her, he scooped warm water into his cupped palm and sloshed it over her arm. "Are you cold? Do you want me to add hot water?"

"I'm not cold." She moved her head, and the long strands of her hair floated in the tub around her.

"Do you want me to wash your hair?"

She chuckled softly. "The only one who has ever washed it for me was my Aunt Isla. Aunt Hannele didn't have the patience to deal with it. My cousin Helmi always wore hers shoulder length."

"Do you have other cousins?"

"I have two more, but they are much younger. Helmi is only two years younger than me." She groaned. "I pray to the Mother that nothing happens to them and all the others I care about. Heck, I care about everyone except for the murderers." She shivered. "I didn't know what they did. I didn't like the purebloods because of their superior attitudes and low regard for everyone who wasn't a pureblood. I forgave most of the restrictions they put on us because it was necessary to hide that aliens were living on Earth. I even understood their need for human females as breeders. They made it seem as if the women had a choice and that they did it because sex with a pureblood or even a hybrid male was such a mind-blowing experience that they were more than willing. I doubted that part, and I even doubted Helmi, who sang the praises of her hybrid boyfriend's sexual prowess. I thought they had no real choice, so they pretended to like it." Sofia opened her eyes and smiled at him. "But if a Kra-ell's bite has a similar effect to yours, then I believe it. If I get to see

Helmi again, I'll tell her." She chuckled. "She will be happy that I finally believe her."

He went down to his knees, picked up the shampoo bottle, and squirted a dollop into his palms. "You will see her again, as well as your aunts, your father, and everyone else."

"I pray to the Mother that I will."

He lifted her hair and supported her head with his forearm. "Who do you think is best suited to run the compound once Igor and his cronies are eliminated?"

"Frankly, I don't know. After them, Jade would be the most influential, and if she kills Igor, she would be the natural successor. That's the Kra-ell way. But if I was to choose the next leader of the compound, it wouldn't be her. I don't like her attitude toward humans. She's not cruel or anything, but she's dismissive of us. Can your people free the humans?"

Still trying to figure out how to wash such a mass of hair, Marcel smoothed the shampoo over the lengths. "I don't know if that's possible. They know that aliens walk among humans, and when we get involved, they will also know about us. It's impossible to thrall away a lifetime of memories, but they can be compelled to never talk about it." He started massaging the shampoo into her scalp.

Sofia moaned. "That feels so good that it's hard for me to think."

He chuckled. "Do you think it's easy for me to think while staring at your ripe berries?"

A smile curved her lips. "I can help with that." She cupped her breasts, robbing him of the sight.

"Don't do that. I want to watch."

"If you wish." She removed her hands and arched her back, so more of her breasts were above the water. "Immortals don't look alien. You could pretend to be humans with extra powers. If I believed you, they would too."

"You suspected that there was more to me than that." He kept massaging.

"Only because I got close to you. Otherwise, I wouldn't have suspected a thing."

"That's an option."

If they wore the exoskeletons, they would look like an army of invading aliens, but once they controlled the compound and removed the suits, they could say that they were a special task force of whatever. The United Nations or NATO.

"The other problem is that most of these humans were born in the compound. The young ones can adapt to living outside of it like you did, but the older ones might prefer to stay."

"They should be allowed to leave if they want to."

Talking about what would happen after the liberation had the effect that Marcel had intended. Sofia was no longer anxious about her family's survival and was instead thinking about their future after being freed.

"I agree. Can you lean your head back so I can wash the suds off?"

As she rested her arms on the sides of the tub and tilted her head back, the elegant arch of her torso was a work of art that Marcel would have loved to capture in a painting or a sculpture, but regrettably he had no artistic talents.

"You're so beautiful, Sofia," he murmured.

25

SOFIA

*T*he way Marcel said those words sent a delicious shiver of desire down her spine. Or was it her front?

Yeah, definitely her front.

Starting with her nipples and going down to her core. No one had ever called her beautiful, let alone so beautiful, and definitely not with so much feeling, and never with her name at the end.

She'd been called pretty, slender, and graceful, but no one had ever called her beautiful.

It shouldn't feel so good, but coming from Marcel, who was usually so dry and laconic, it was special.

Twisting her hair, she wrung out the excess water and wrapped the thick rope around itself on the top of her head.

"Can you please hand me the towel?"

Marcel arched a brow. "Don't you want me to join you in the tub?"

Sofia hesitated. It could be nice to share a bath, but what she had in mind was better done on a bed, especially since they had resolved to use a condom.

Talk about a mood spoiler, but it was necessary.

The last thing she wanted was to start transitioning, lose consciousness, and regain it to find out that it was all over, and Mother forbid, her family didn't survive.

"What's wrong?" Marcel unfolded the towel and spread it, waiting for her to get out. "You suddenly lost your good mood."

Sofia stepped out of the tub and let him wrap her in the towel and pull her into his arms. "I thought about transitioning, and then I thought about waking up to find out that something had happened to my family."

"Don't think like that." He rubbed his hands over her towel-covered arms. "We need to stay positive and visualize the best possible outcome."

She chuckled. "I've heard of that method. What is it called?"

"I don't remember. The gist is that if you believe you will get everything you want and ask for it, the universe will manifest it for you."

"Do you actually believe that?" She leaned into him and lifted her face. "Did you ask the universe to give you a perfect mate?"

He chuckled. "I must have yearned for you subconsciously." He drew the towel along her arms, then her belly, and as he dragged it up between her breasts, his knuckles brushed against her nipples, seemingly unintentionally. "Did you yearn for me?"

"I did," she admitted, her arousal dimming as her guilt surged. "I dreamt about being free and finding a man who I could share my life with. I didn't anticipate the unintended consequences."

Marcel arched a brow. "Freeing your family might be an unintended consequence, but it's a good one."

She closed her eyes. "If anything happens to them, I will not be able to forgive myself."

He hooked a finger under her chin and tilted her head up. "You were the one who told me to forgive myself. You should follow your own advice."

"The circumstances are very different."

"I don't think so." He lifted her into his arms and carried her to the bedroom. "I was willing to do anything for the woman I thought I loved, and you are willing to do anything for the people you love."

Marcel's logic was a bit skewed, but what Sofia had heard loud and clear was, "the woman I thought I loved."

"When did you realize that you didn't love her?"

He laid her gently on the bed and sprawled on his side next to her. "When I fell in love with you, I knew that what I felt for her hadn't been real." He cupped her cheek. "This feels real. What I felt for Cordelia was what I imagined love should feel like." His thumb dragged over her lower lip. "It's ironic that you set out to manipulate me, and yet everything you showed me, every emotion, every moan, and every sigh, it was all genuine. I don't think that you are capable of faking love or even like, and certainly not lust."

"About that. Eleanor told me that immortal males can smell a woman's arousal. If Cordelia was faking her attraction to you, you would have known that."

"That was the only thing she didn't fake."

26

DARLENE

$\mathcal{D}$arlene pulled an outfit from the closet and carried it to the guest bedroom.

"How do you want your eggs this morning?" Eric asked from the kitchen.

"Scrambled, please."

She'd asked for sunny side up the morning before, and it had proven too difficult for Eric. She hadn't minded that the eggs had ended up scrambled, but it had frustrated him. It was better to ask for something that wouldn't mess up his mood first thing in the morning.

It occurred to her that she was falling back on her old habits, avoiding anything that could upset her partner like she used to do with Leo. In her need to keep things calm and smooth, she'd often allowed herself to become his doormat.

Funny how dormant and doormat sounded the same but were the exact opposite. She was the granddaughter of a god, an immortal in the making, and she was nobody's doormat.

"Do you want onions in your eggs?"

"Sure." She draped the outfit over the back of the footboard.

They were using the other bedroom in the house until their new bed arrived. Eric had insisted on ordering another four-poster, even though she'd told him that she was never doing the thing with Max again. The frame of the new bed was made from iron posts that were welded together, not screwed, and it looked like nothing could destroy it.

Looking at the skirt and blouse she'd pulled out, Darlene sighed. The skirt was a little tight in the waist, and she was too tired to deal with anything uncomfortable. Perhaps she should just wear a pair of leggings with a long blouse over them.

There was no dress code in the lab, and no one cared whether she looked professional or frumpy. She dressed up mainly to please herself, but today, being comfortable would please her more.

The tiredness was not surprising, given Eric's stamina since his transition.

Darlene chuckled softly. Her guy's new alter ego was a gorilla, but a rabbit in heat was more fitting. What was surprising, however, was that she wasn't sore. Given that Eric didn't have the healing venom yet, that she was still human, and that her lady parts had never been particularly resilient, the miracle could be attributed either to the composition of Eric's immortal semen or his saliva.

She needed more sleep, though. Five hours a night might be enough for Eric, but it wasn't for her.

With a sigh, Darlene hung the outfit she'd chosen back in the closet, pulled on a pair of black leggings, and finished with a colorful blouse. Makeup seemed like too much trouble as well, so she decided to skip it. Thankfully, the hair treatment she'd gotten guaranteed a perfect hairdo each morning, so she didn't need to worry about that.

"Breakfast is ready!" Eric called from the kitchen.

"Coming." She slid her feet into a pair of low-heeled mules and walked into the living room.

Eric lifted a brow. "Are you staying home with me today?"

"I'm not." She pulled out a stool next to the counter and sat down. "I just didn't have the energy to dress up this morning. You exhausted me." She lifted a hand to stop his pouting. "In the best possible way. I just need to catch up on some sleep."

Worry clouding his eyes, he finished scooping the scrambled eggs onto two plates, put the pan aside, and walked over to her. "You look a little pale. Are you feeling alright?" He put his hand on her forehead. "You're a little warm."

Her heart skipped a beat. "Could it be the transition?"

"Fever is one of the first signs. We should go to the clinic." He untied the apron and pulled it over his head. "Let's go."

Darlene chuckled. "Relax. It might be allergies, or I might have caught something in the supermarket yesterday. Remember that woman who kept sneezing? She didn't use her elbow and sprayed the entire aisle with viruses."

"She said it was allergies."

"She probably lied. I'll just pop a couple of vitamin C pills. Can you hand me the bottle?"

Looking skeptical, Eric did as she asked. "We will go after breakfast." He put the plates on the counter, poured coffee into two mugs, and joined her.

"I'll feel better after I have some caffeine in me." She took a sip from the mug. "You make great coffee."

He smirked. "As opposed to my cooking?"

"Are you fishing for compliments?"

"Yes."

"Your cooking has improved significantly." She took a piece of toast and smeared it with butter.

"Yeah, I can make toast." He sighed. "But seriously. It's the perfect timing for you to start transitioning. Two and a half days passed since we did it, which is when it usually starts if it worked."

"If it worked." She took another sip. "Let's see how I feel during the day. If it gets worse, I'll call you, and we can meet at the clinic."

"What if you lose consciousness in that tiny office of yours? No one would know."

"I'll leave the door open and ask Kaia to keep an eye on me. She's at William's desk all day."

27

ERIC

*E*ric pulled a noodle out of the pot and put it in his mouth.

"Still too hard." He stood next to the pot and waited two more minutes before pulling out another one. "You'd better be ready now." He dipped the fork in the water and fished out another noodle.

It was almost perfect, but he didn't have the patience to keep checking. The noodles would soften in the sauce. Turning the burner off, he took the pot to the sink and drained the water.

Playing house had been nice for a while, but Eric was getting bored with it. He felt great, and it was time to get a real job. Kian had said that he needed another pilot, and with rumors flying about a possible rescue mission in Russia, he probably could use one now.

Except Eric couldn't go anywhere until Darlene transitioned, which could start today, tomorrow, or the day after.

Eric pulled out his phone and called her. It was only eleven o'clock, and this was his fifth call that morning.

"I'm still fine," she answered. "I might be a little late for lunch, though. William needs my help sorting the supplies and ordering what's missing."

"Is it for the mission?"

She laughed. "What mission?"

"The secret one that everyone is talking about."

"That's why I'm laughing. I'm supposed to say that there is no mission."

"You sound energetic, so perhaps what you felt this morning was just fatigue."

"I told you so. But just in case, I told Kaia to keep an eye on me. She took it very seriously and moved William's desk so she could see me from where she was working."

"Awesome. Do you want me to bring your lunch to the office? We can eat it together on your desk."

"Good idea. I'll see you later."

Perhaps he could stop by Kian's office on the way?

Nah. He should call first, or better yet, text. Kian was a busy guy, and Eric was no one important. Well, beyond being Darlene's mate and Toven's future grandson-in-law. Did that make him special?

Not likely.

Perhaps texting Shai was a better idea. After all, the guy was his future father-in-law.

On second thought, being Darlene's chosen made him a well-connected guy.

Scrolling through his contacts list, Eric found Kian's number and typed up a message. *Hello, Kian. You mentioned needing another pilot. As soon as Darlene transitions, I will be ready to serve. Who do I need to see about piloting for the clan?*

That was short, to the point, and wouldn't waste much of Kian's time.

His phone rang a moment later. "What planes can you fly?" Kian asked without preamble.

"Nearly all of them except for large passenger jets. I'm not certified to fly those." Eric rattled out a long list of jets, including those he'd flown while serving in the Air Force.

"Impressive. You're hired. I'll tell Onegus to put you in the training program."

As far as Eric was aware, he could teach the clan's two pilots, not the other way around.

"What kind of training are you talking about?"

"Guardian training. I assume that you got combat training in the Air Force, but that was long ago. You need a refresher, and you also need to learn to work with our Guardians. It's nonnegotiable."

"I'm not negotiating. I was just wondering about the kind of training you had in mind, and now that you've explained, I get it. Should I wait for Onegus to call me?"

"Just stop by his office whenever you can, and if he's busy, you can wait. We are not very formal here. I'll tell him to expect you."

"Thank you."

"No problem. He'll also tell you how much the job pays."

"The pay is secondary to me. I just need to be up in the air again."

"You still need to get paid. How is Darlene doing?"

Had Kian heard about their induction attempt?

Probably.

Darlene had asked Max not to tell anyone, but they had told Karen and Kaia, who had probably told Cheryl, who'd probably shared it with Lisa and Parker, and that was how a day later, the entire village had known about it.

"This morning, she felt a little under the weather, and I hoped it was the start of her transition, but I just spoke with her, and she sounded fine. Kaia is watching her in case she suddenly collapses."

"Darlene is a god's granddaughter, so her symptoms might be mild. Make sure to check on her frequently, and if her symptoms worsen, get her to the clinic."

"I will."

When Kian ended the call, Eric rose to his feet and headed back to the kitchen.

It was still too early for lunch, but since he was going to see Onegus, and the chief's office was one level up from the lab, he could do that first and have lunch with Darlene right after.

Half an hour later, Eric was out of Onegus's office with a contract for a three-month trial period, a schedule of classes and, what he was most excited about, the one-on-one drone flying training with Charlie.

Eric preferred to be up in the sky and not down on the ground with a remote or inside a simulator, but it was something he hadn't tried before, and he was eager to learn. Turned out that the clan had military-grade drones, but they weren't going to use them in the upcoming mission and were getting a couple of drones locally. Eric wouldn't be ready in time to join the current mission, but he would be ready the next time the clan needed to fly them.

Carrying the bag with the pasta and salad he'd made, he got in front of the door to William's lab and looked up into the camera. "Open sesame."

As the door buzzed open, Kaia smiled at him. "Darlene told me that you're bringing lunch. Is there enough for me?"

"Sure. But aren't you having lunch at home with William?"

She shook her head. "Not today. It's a madhouse in here. William is leaving this evening, and he has been running around all day. Sadly, I don't think he has time to go home for lunch. He isn't even packed yet." She looked at him hopefully. "Did you make enough for him too?"

Not really, but he could let the three of them eat and skip lunch himself. "Of course. Are you going with William?"

"I can't. He needs me here."

"Will you be okay without him?"

"It's going to be tough, but I'll stay with Mom and help her with the little ones until Gilbert returns. That will keep me busy."

"She's going to love it. You flew the nest so suddenly that she didn't have time to prepare."

Kaia snorted. "We live a ten-minute walk away from each other. I still have one leg in the nest."

"True." He put the thermal bag on her desk and walked over to Darlene's office. "Are you hungry yet? Food is here."

She lifted her head and looked at him with glazed eyes. "I don't feel well. I think we should go to the clinic."

2 8

TOVEN

"*H*ere are the suitcases." Shamash rolled two brand new pieces of luggage into Toven and Mia's living room. "Kalugal and Jacki say bon voyage."

"Thank you, Shamash."

"You could have used ours," Curtis said. "They are not as fancy as these, but they are still good."

"These are larger, Grandpa." Mia drove over and grabbed one handle. "I have everything ready. I just need to put it inside."

Toven followed her into the bedroom. "What I have wouldn't fill even half of that suitcase. I could've taken my trusty carry-on."

"Then you would have needed to buy luggage in St. Petersburg to fit the new stuff we are going to get."

When his phone rang, Toven wasn't surprised to see it was Kian.

"Hello," he answered. "Are there any changes to the timeline?"

"Darlene is transitioning," Kian said. "Kaia called Bridget to let her know that Darlene and Eric are heading to the clinic, and Bridget told me on her way out."

Toven tensed. That was such inconvenient timing. He was leaving, and he wouldn't be there to help Darlene with his blood.

"The timing could have been better, but it is what it is. Thank you for letting me know."

"You're welcome. I thought that you might want to visit her before you leave and give her your blessing."

"That is a good idea. I will need to ask your mother to continue the blessings in my absence."

"Indeed. Good luck and congratulations."

"Thanks." He turned to Mia. "Do you want to come with me?"

"Of course." She dropped an article of clothing into her suitcase. "I'll race you there."

He could run much faster than she could drive her chair, and when they'd played the racing game before, he hadn't used his full speed.

"We don't have time. I'll run ahead."

"I knew it." She wagged her finger at him. "You were holding back."

"Naturally." He leaned and kissed her cheek. "I'll see you in the clinic."

As Toven ran, he was a blur of motion, and the immortals he passed gaped, trying to figure out what they were seeing. Annani never ran, so they had never seen a god running at full speed.

When he reached the clinic, he found Eric pacing in the small waiting room. "What are you doing out here? Shouldn't you be with Darlene?"

"Bridget and Hildegard are hooking her up to the monitoring equipment, and they kicked me out."

"I see. What are her symptoms?"

"It started with fatigue, but Darlene went to work anyway. I called every half an hour, and she was fine, but when I came to visit her at lunch, she told me that she was feeling worse. She couldn't even stand up, so I carried her, and in the five minutes it took me to get from her office in the lab to the clinic, she lost consciousness."

Toven put a hand on Eric's shoulder. "I know how stressful it is. I came to give Darlene a blessing before I leave, and Annani will take over while I'm gone."

"Thank you." Eric let out a breath. "I was worried because you were leaving, and I know how important your blessing was to my transition."

"How did you know that I was leaving?"

"I was in Onegus's office this morning about piloting for the clan, and he told me that he could've used me for this mission, but that I needed to go through training with the Guardians first. I told him that I didn't need to train to fly a plane from one point to the next, but that was before Darlene started transitioning. Now, I'm not going anywhere."

When a knock sounded on the front door, Toven rushed to open it for Mia, who couldn't pull the heavy glass open while sitting in her chair. They should automate the thing for handicapped access.

"You're incredible." Mia drove in. "You can outrun a cheetah."

"I can."

"And you're not even sweaty."

He smiled. "When we are in Karelia, and you are on my back, I'll treat you to a speedy run."

She scrunched her nose. "I don't know if I want to try it. It's probably scary."

Eric shook his head. "Should I even ask what you are talking about?"

Toven was about to answer when the door to Darlene's room opened, and Bridget walked out with the nurse.

"Hello, people. Darlene is awake, but that's not going to last long, so if you want to say goodbye before you leave, I suggest you do it now and do it quickly."

That wasn't good. He needed Darlene asleep or unconscious, to give her a transfusion. He would have to thrall her.

"How is she doing?" Eric asked.

"It's too early to tell. So far, her vitals are strong."

"Excellent." Toven smiled and turned to Eric. "Mia and I will not take long. Is it okay if we go in first to say our goodbyes?"

"Sure. And don't forget the blessing."

"I won't."

29

SOFIA

Once again, they were going to Sofia's spot on the beach, but this time they were doing it during lunch break.

Eleanor stroked Cecelia's back. "I don't know why I like this cat so much. Her temperament is the opposite of mine. I like to be active, while she likes to do as little as possible."

"She has a calming effect." Sofia scratched the cat under her chin, eliciting louder purring.

Marcel was quiet, contemplative. He didn't take part in their conversation, but his arm around her waist was warm and sure, and from time to time, his palm moved over her hip, reminding her of their morning lovemaking.

Those intimate moments were the only times she was distracted enough for her anxiety to subside so she could forget about the danger to her family.

She'd prayed to the Mother of All Life for Jade to succeed in eliminating Igor. If she did, Marcel's people wouldn't have to invade, there wouldn't be bloodshed beyond Igor's, and in her gratitude for their help, Jade would sign a treaty with the immortals.

Talk about wishful thinking.

But even that best-case scenario wouldn't be the end of her worries. Marcel still planned on confessing his crime to the clan's judge and accepting any punishment she saw fit. What if the judge sentenced him to entombment? It was such a horrible punishment that even a whipping seemed preferable to it.

"Do you want to hear something funny?" Eleanor said.

Marcel cast her a sidelong glance. "A good joke would be most welcome right now."

Was he tormented by the same thoughts that plagued Sofia?

"Syssi thinks that I might be of Kra-ell descent."

Sofia chuckled. "The thought crossed my mind when I started noticing peculiarities about Marcel, and I wondered about your and Emmett's compulsion abilities."

"What does she base that on?" Marcel asked.

"Mainly my looks and my ability to compel. If I am of Kra-ell descent, it's good news for Sofia because it means that Kra-ell Dormants can be induced the same way as immortal Dormants even many generations later. But I don't think that I'm Kra-ell. Toven is a compeller, and so were his brother and his uncle. We know that they are not Kra-ell."

"Who is Toven?" Sofia asked.

Marcel and Eleanor exchanged looks, and then Marcel shrugged. "I guess it's okay to tell you. Toven uses the name Tom when he deals with humans."

"Why? I've never heard the name Toven. It doesn't mean anything to me."

"He has his reasons," Eleanor said. "Anyway, I wonder if Bridget can tell the difference between Kra-ell and immortal genes."

"Kaia might help with that." Marcel stopped next to Sofia's boulder and pulled the pendant from his left pocket and the special earpieces from the other. "Here you go."

Taking a deep breath, she draped the chain around her neck and turned to Eleanor. "I assume that you want to compel me before I put the earpieces in."

Eleanor nodded. "Repeat the story we rehearsed before."

After Sofia had done that, Eleanor compelled her to stick to the story, and then it was time to make the call.

She put the translating earpieces in and pulled the communication earpiece from the pendant and activated it.

"Sofia," Valstar responded immediately. "This is an unusual time for you to call."

"I couldn't get away last night, but I needed to tell you what I found out. I have a heart problem. I wasn't feeling well, and the retreat's doctor referred me to a cardiologist. I saw him yesterday, and I'm afraid that the bill was quite steep. I owe Safe Haven a lot of money. They paid for it, but I need to pay them back."

"You can pay them back in installments from your salary. What else do you have to report?"

She shouldn't have been surprised at his lack of concern for her health, but it still hurt. He hadn't even asked how severe her heart problem was and if it was life-threatening.

"After the doctor's visit, we went to a get-together hosted by a rich backer of the paranormal program. Turns out that they are running a candidate as a test for their future plans, which are at the national level. I think that the candidate they are backing is one of them."

"That's interesting. What's his name?"

"It's a woman. Her name is Katie Berlindor."

"Never heard of her, but then we don't care who the Governor of Oregon is."

"Normally, I would agree with you, but the paranormals might be just testing the waters in Oregon. Their next target might be the presidential race, and they could take over the country. I don't know what the impact of that would be on our community, but I'm sure Igor would want to know about it."

"I'll let him know. Anything else?"

508

"No, that's it for now."

"Keep up the good work. Goodbye, Sofia."

"I don't know how long I'll be able to do that. My health has deteriorated significantly."

"If you could attend a fancy get-together yesterday, you are not on your deathbed." The line went silent.

"Well, that was a slap in the face." Sofia deactivated the device and pulled the chain over her head.

"I'm sorry." Marcel took her into his arms.

"I'm not." Sofia rested her head on his shoulder. "I should not have expected any emotional response from him. I don't know what I was thinking."

"He's a jerk." Eleanor patted her shoulder. "And he's a lousy leader. Even if he didn't care, he should have at least pretended that he did."

3 0

TOVEN

"Over here." Okidu waved Toven and Mia over to the bus.

"I thought that we were taking the limo to the clan's airstrip." Mia drove her portable chair to where the butler stood.

"Master William has a lot of equipment that he's taking with him. There wasn't enough room in the limousine. Master Kian offered to send Onidu to drive you and Master Toven in the limousine, but Master Toven said that the bus was fine."

The Russian drones needed to be outfitted with advanced electronics, and if they got to stage three of the plan, William would need to scramble the compound's communications. He would also need to figure out how to remove the collars many of the hybrids and purebloods had been outfitted with, hopefully without blowing their heads off.

"I hope you don't mind," Toven said.

"Of course not." Mia looked at the stairs and winced. "But you'll need to carry me up."

He grinned. "You know I love doing that."

As Okidu took their luggage, Toven lifted Mia along with her compact wheelchair and carried her up the stairs. "Let's see if it can fit through the aisle."

They had purchased it for use on commercial flights, and it was supposed to be air travel approved, but they hadn't tested it yet.

"It does." Mia drove it to the end of the bus. "But I can't turn around."

"You're not supposed to." Toven pulled her out of the chair, set her down on the seat, and folded the chair. "It's supposed to be stored in the overhead compartment."

She sighed. "I'm glad that we are taking a private jet. It would have been so embarrassing to have you carry me to the bathroom."

"Hello." William climbed into the bus, followed by Roni's mate.

Her name had come up when they had been talking about disabling the cameras on the dirt road leading to the first tunnel entrance, but Toven had forgotten about her part in the plan.

He walked over to them and offered his hand to Sylvia first. "Hello."

"Hi." She shook his hand and then ducked around him to give Mia a hug. "You and I are going shopping together. I don't have any proper winter clothes."

As the two started chatting, Toven shook William's hand. "Okidu told us that you are bringing a lot of equipment with us. Are we going to use the noise cannon after all?"

"We are not. The damage it might do to the children's ears precludes us from using it." William slid into the seat across from the one Mia and Sylvia were seated in. "I'm preparing stage three. If Jade takes care of the problem for us, we might not need to get there, but if we do, I need to be ready. The Russian military drones that Turner's supplier got for us need to be fortified with more advanced electronics and hooked up to our satellite communication protocol. I don't know if the amphibian needs any modifications, but I brought some components in case it does. I also brought equipment to disrupt their communication capabilities."

"How does that work?"

William waved a dismissive hand. "It's involved, but the gist of it is that everyone in a ten-mile radius around the compound and inside of it won't be able to send or receive a cellular or satellite signal, except for us, of course. My disruptor is calibrated not to affect our connection to the clan's satellite."

"What about landlines?"

"I assume that there aren't any in such a remote area, but I will check once we get there." He smiled. "I have the equipment for that as well."

"I'm impressed." Toven gave William an approving nod. "Modern technology can do much more than a god or even several gods ever could. If my people had survived, they would have been obsolete in this world."

William pursed his lips. "If they had survived, the world would be a very different place today."

"Indeed."

Toven tried to imagine a world in which the gods were still running things. He doubted that humanity would have advanced as much as it had, or that its population would have grown to eight billion people. Ahn wouldn't have allowed humans to multiply the way they had. He would have engineered global culling events to thin out human populations so he could maintain control over it.

"How come Roni is not coming with you?" Mia asked Sylvia.

"He can't. With both William and Marcel gone, he's the only one left to run the lab."

"What about Kaia? Is she coming with us?" Toven asked.

William shook his head. "I'll miss her, but I didn't want to endanger her." He glanced at Mia.

"I can protect my mate." Toven crossed his arms over his chest. "Besides, Mia is crucial to the success of this operation. She enhances my compulsion power and, at the same time, makes it easier on the compelled."

"I know. Kian told me." William turned to look at Mia and gave her the thumbs up. "You have a very cool talent."

"Thank you."

"Go, Mia." Sylvia lifted her hand for Mia to high-five her.

"Go, Sylvia." Mia clapped her hand. "Your talent is one of a kind as well."

Sylvia could disable electronics, but regrettably, she could only do that in close proximity. She couldn't disable the compound's electricity grid or its cellular tower.

"How do they get power?" Toven asked William. "Are they connected to the grid?"

William nodded. "They are. Power is fed via pole-suspended conductors, which makes for an easy target to take it down, but I prefer not to touch it. That would trigger an investigation from the Russian electric company, and it wouldn't do us much good to take it down anyway."

"What about the exoskeletons?" Toven asked. "Are we taking those as well?"

William laughed. "Do you have any idea how big and heavy they are? As it is, we are already maxing out the jet's cargo capacity. We will need a big plane to carry the suits, the Guardians, and Kalugal's men. I hope that Jade will eliminate Igor and that they won't be needed."

31

SOFIA

"I hope you don't want to return to the retreat." Marcel stopped at the gate to the private enclave where his bungalow was located.

"I don't have a choice," Eleanor said, even though his question hadn't been directed at her. "I have a class to teach." She winked. "I'll see you two when I see you." She hugged Cecilia to her chest and kept on walking.

After talking with Valstar, Sofia was too distraught to pay attention in class, and the distraction that Marcel offered with his skillful lovemaking was very appealing.

She wound her arms around his neck. "What do you want me to do instead?"

He smiled. "I have a few ideas."

She'd noticed that he'd been smiling a lot more lately, and she wondered whether it was because he'd finally shared his guilty secret with someone or because he was in love with her.

It was probably both, and knowing that she was responsible for his newfound happiness made her heart swell with gratitude and love.

What would happen if she didn't transition, though?

"Think positive," she murmured. "Ask, and you shall receive."

"What's the matter?" Marcel opened the door to his bungalow. "Bad thoughts again?"

She didn't want to spoil his mood. Meeting his gaze with a coy smile, she tilted her head. "Why do you assume that I was thinking bad thoughts? Maybe I was asking the universe for orgasms?"

His eyes blazed with an inner light. "You can ask me, and I shall deliver." He picked her up by the waist and deposited her on the kitchen counter.

The thing was small, no more than five feet across, and that included a sink.

"What are you doing?"

"Answering a request." His lips feathered over her neck. "I never told you this before, but you have a beautiful neck. And even though your hair is magnificent, I like that you keep it up, exposing this graceful column. I get hard imagining my fangs grazing your smooth skin right here." He kissed the spot.

As she opened her legs wider, making room for him between them, her hands found the back of his neck, and she drew him closer. "Kiss me."

The hard ridge of his arousal pressed against her sensitive tissues through the fabric of his slacks and her leggings, both of them made of thin material that did little to take away from the sensation.

As his tongue tangled with hers, his hands slid down from her waist to her ass, and as he pulled her harder against that straining erection, she lifted her legs and hooked them around his hips.

The moment his hands left her bottom, she mourned the loss of his touch, but then he was tugging at her T-shirt and pulling it over her head.

When she was left with only her push-up bra, she reached for his turtleneck and pulled it out of the waistband of his slacks. "Take it off."

When he pulled away to do as she commanded, she leaned back, propping herself on her forearms to watch him expose his magnificent chest. Lean muscle with a light smattering of blond hair that was barely visible against his pale skin.

Leaning over her, Marcel pushed his fingers under the elastic of her leggings, and as he pulled them down, she toed off her sneakers.

He tossed the leggings on the floor and then removed her right sock but didn't let go of her foot. He kissed her ankle, then her calf, then the inside of her knee, and just as she thought that he would keep going to where her panties were soaked through, he lifted her left foot and repeated what he had done with her right.

"You're such a tease."

His nostrils flaring, he smiled with a mouthful of fangs. "Ask, and you shall receive. What's your pleasure, love?"

He called her love, and it made her giddy because it wasn't just a term of endearment for him. Marcel loved her. It was in his glowing eyes, the gentle way he held her, and in the patience and restraint he practiced because she was human and fragile compared to him.

Arching her back, she lifted her bottom an inch off the counter. "Kiss me there."

That was such a wanton thing to say, and she loved that she could do that with Marcel and feel good about it. There was no judgment in his eyes, only desire.

He pressed a kiss to the front of her panties and then hooked his thumbs in the elastic and dragged them down her legs.

She expected him to come back and kiss her flesh, but when he gripped her feet and propped them onto the counter, she'd never felt so exposed or so turned on.

When his head lowered between her splayed thighs, he rested his cheek on one side and just breathed her in. "I want to bottle this scent and carry it with me all day long."

Normally, she wouldn't have found the idea sexy, but she was so turned on that his words just added fuel to the fire.

"You're teasing me again."

He kissed her inner thigh, then the other side, and then his tongue made contact with her clit, and it was as if an electrical current zapped her.

"Marcel," she groaned.

He didn't answer. Instead, his tongue flicked over her clit, once, twice, and then he pushed it inside of her.

A guttural moan left her throat, and as she arched up to get more of his tongue, he slid his hands under her ass and gripped it hard.

It was as if her moan had unleashed his beast. Driving his tongue in and out of her, he alternated with flicks over that sensitive bundle of nerves, and when he released one butt cheek and drove two fingers inside of her, Sofia exploded with a scream that must have been heard all over the enclave.

32

MARCEL

*M*arcel licked and pumped his fingers until Sofia went limp, and her head dropped against the backsplash. When all of her shudders subsided, and she let out a breath, he pressed a gentle kiss to her petals and lifted his gaze to her flushed face.

"You're the most beautiful after you climax."

She smiled. "I love you, too."

Upon hearing those words, something shifted in his chest. Something eased. He felt lighter, almost buoyant, and as he pushed to his feet and embraced the woman he loved, he felt complete like he'd never felt before.

"I love you, my Sofia," he murmured into her tangled hair.

It had come undone, and he collected it in his hands and twisted it up to expose her neck. Brushing his lips over the long column, he suppressed the urge to sink his fangs into her skin. The time for that would be later when he was deep inside of her, and she was climaxing again.

"I still have my bra on," she murmured.

"I'll take care of it." He lifted her off the counter, carried her to the bedroom, and laid her down on the bed.

"You keep carrying me around." She sprawled lazily on the bed, her legs parted in invitation.

"Because I know that you like it."

"I do." She reached behind her and unclasped her bra.

He pulled her hand out and kissed her fingers. "I said that I'll take care of it."

"Then do it." She pouted. "My poor nipples are hungry for your attention."

He was on her before she'd finished the sentence, ripping the bra off and sucking one turgid peak into his mouth.

"Oh, yeah. Just like that." Sofia arched her back, pushing more of her small breast into his mouth. "More."

He lightly pinched her other nipple, drawing a moan from her lips, and then he switched, tonguing the other one, and sometime during all that, he'd gotten rid of his slacks.

"Kiss me," Sofia breathed.

He pushed up her body and took her mouth, sweeping in with his tongue that still carried her taste, and as she nipped his lip, stars exploded behind his eyelids.

He needed to be inside of her.

Getting on top of her, he slicked his shaft with her wetness, and she surprised him by joining her hand with his and guiding him toward her entrance.

"I love you." She lifted her lips to his and let go of his shaft.

He took her mouth and surged inside of her, but not all at once. He halted and waited for her to signal that she was ready for more. By now, he knew her body and its responses so well that he didn't need to guess when to be gentle and when to be rough.

Right now, Sofia needed tender loving, and he was going to give her precisely that, even though it was torturous to hold his beast back.

When she pulled her lips away and smiled, he pushed in another inch, and when she cupped his ass and arched up, he slammed all the way home.

Sofia's fingers clawed at his ass, spurring him on, and he gave her what she wanted, going faster and harder until her body stiffened and a release blasted through her. Only then did he flick his tongue over the spot on her neck and, with a hiss, sank his fangs into her.

Marcel's climax erupted along with the venom he released into her system, and only when he was all spent and retracted his fangs did he remember that they had forgotten to use a condom once again.

Not that he believed a single condom could have contained all that he'd spilled into her.

It hadn't been regular lovemaking.

For some reason that he wasn't clear on, this time, it had felt like a claiming.

It had been mutual.

Sofia had claimed him as surely as he had claimed her.

Perhaps it had been the finality she'd felt after talking with Valstar. By giving up on her grandfather, she'd finally unraveled the last of her ties to the Kra-ell community and fully embraced her new life with Marcel.

"I'm sorry, my love." He licked the two tiny wounds. "I know that you wanted to wait."

Sofia didn't respond.

With a dreamy expression on her beautiful face, she was out, and he hoped she was experiencing wonderful adventures on her euphoric postorgasmic trip.

He brushed a strand of hair off her forehead. "I love you."

Gazing at her flushed cheeks and her puffy lips, he realized that loving her no longer scared him.

She wasn't an unhealthy obsession like Cordelia had been. She wasn't dangerous or manipulative or demanding.

Sofia was his home, his safe place.

"My beautiful, courageous mate." He kissed her lips.

33

TOVEN

*S*ylvia walked about thirty feet in front of the van and waved her hand this way and that, but Toven couldn't see the cameras even with his godly eyesight.

"How does she know where they are?" he asked Yamanu.

The Guardian shrugged. "I think she can sense the devices. The neat thing about her ability is that she can disable them one at a time, just long enough for our van to pass through. Whoever is watching the feed would assume that the cameras are glitching."

"Is it common for surveillance cameras to glitch?" Mia asked.

"They can lag," Morris said. "It depends on their quality and the quality of the network they are connected to. They can experience latency due to the speed of the decoding and encoding process or the data's travel time over the network."

Mia pursed her lips. "That went straight over my head."

Yamanu grinned. "Mine too. Morris is just parroting what William told him."

The pilot snorted. "Don't assume that everyone is as ignorant about technology as you are."

Yamanu and Morris kept at it as if they were on a field trip and not about to abduct a dangerous pureblood, and even Mia joined in as if nothing dangerous was about to happen.

It had been decided that the Guardians who were coming at the Kra-ell through the woods would tranquilize all three but leave the hybrids inside the tunnel. They would stage them so they wouldn't look asleep in the camera's view and only take the pureblood to the van. Two Guardians would remain with the hybrids to make sure that they didn't wake up too soon, and another two would bring the tranquilized pureblood to the van for interrogation.

From the outside the vehicle appeared like an old, beat-up Russian make from the eighties, but on the inside it was kitted out with modern equipment. If Sylvia failed to disable any of the cameras, the van wouldn't look too suspicious.

They needed to stop the van far away from the tunnel's entrance so the guards wouldn't hear the engine, and as they veered off the path into the woods, Sylvia continued walking straight ahead.

She still had to disable the camera right at the entrance.

The maneuver required precise coordination and was probably the most dangerous part of the operation.

The snipers hiding in the woods would have to fire the tranquilizer darts a moment after Sylvia took care of the camera, and then they had to stage the two sleeping hybrids in a way that would just show their backs.

The Guardians had been observing the three guards for two days, and they had behaved like any other guards who didn't expect anyone to inspect them or any enemy to suddenly appear. They were complacent. They sat on foldable chairs, watched movies on their phones, played card games, drank booze, and smoked what was probably weed.

The Guardians hadn't gotten close enough to smell it.

Twenty minutes or so passed when Yamanu said, "On my mark, Sylvia. Now."

Mia squeezed Toven's hand as they waited for the Guardians to report.

"It's done," Yamanu said. "Bobbie and Drake are on their way with the pureblood."

They were communicating via earpieces, but Toven hadn't been given one, and he hadn't asked for it. The men knew what they were doing, and they didn't need his input. His job was to remove the compulsion and interrogate the pureblood.

"Is Sylvia coming back with Bobbie and Drake?" Mia asked.

"No," Yamanu said. "She's staying with the two Guardians at the tunnel. The one carrying the pureblood is running through the woods to avoid the cameras."

Yamanu collected the titanium chains, opened the door, and stepped out of the van.

The Guardian carrying the Kra-ell male appeared at a dead run mere minutes later. "Son of a bitch is already waking up." He dropped him on the ground. "Hurry up."

"No worries, buddy." Yamanu knelt next to the Kra-ell. "I've got him."

Toven stepped out of the van, ready to assist if needed, but Yamanu had the pureblood hogtied and propped against the van in seconds.

The male's eyelashes fluttered for a split second, and then he opened his enormous eyes and hissed, *"Kto ti?"*

"My name is Tom," Toven answered in English. He could conduct the interrogation in Russian, but if the guard spoke English, the others could take part in it too. "What's yours?" Toven used the full power of his compulsion, and with Mia in the van right behind him, she was enhancing it further.

The pureblood's black eyes flickered red.

Was red a sign of aggression or of fear?

Toven had forgotten.

"My name is Pavel," he answered in heavily accented English. "Who are you?"

34

ERIC

*A*fter Geraldine and Roni left and Eric was left alone with Darlene, he picked up the romance book Geraldine had brought for him. Leafing through it, he searched for a hot sex scene.

Darlene had read to him when he'd been transitioning, and she believed that hearing the steamy descriptions had helped pull him out of the coma. He didn't remember being aware of her reading to him, but just in case she was right, he was going to do the same for her.

It was unnerving watching her lying so still on the hospital bed.

To someone else's eyes she would appear asleep, but he knew her sleeping habits, and she never slept on her back or remained in the same position for more than half an hour.

Darlene wasn't a peaceful sleeper, and he was used to her turning from side to side, reaching for the blanket and tucking it between her thighs, or punching the pillow to mold it into a shape that was comfortable for her.

With a sigh, he returned to the book. "Let's see what we've got here."

It was a billionaire romance about a tech mogul who falls in love with his housemaid. A classic *Cinderella* story with a modern twist. The guy was a little kinky, and the girl was young and virginal. Skipping over her first time, which Eric didn't find sexy in the least, he searched for steamier scenes further into the book.

"Here we go." He leaned back. "Rachel was on her knees, scrubbing the baseboards like Edward had asked her to, the short skirt of her uniform riding up and exposing the back of her thighs. A week ago, she would have been tugging on it to cover her ass, but she was no longer shy. The world of pleasure that Edward had introduced her to had changed her, and all she could think about was him coming in, kneeling behind her, and pushing her thong aside."

"What the hell are you reading?" Max stood at the doorway.

Eric looked at him over his shoulder. "Grab a chair and join the reading club. You might learn a thing or two about women's fantasies. Let me tell you this, though, they are much kinkier than men's."

Max lifted one of the chairs in the waiting room, brought it over next to Eric's, and went back to close the door behind him.

"Why did you close the door?"

"If Bridget can't see me, she can't kick me out." He pulled out a bottle of whiskey from the inner pocket of his bomber jacket. "I thought you could use some."

"I can." Eric put the book on the bed and took the bottle. "You're the best."

"I know." Max grinned. "Not too long ago, I was sitting here with Darlene and watching you lying in that bed still like a mummy."

Eric twisted the cap off and took a long swig, letting the whiskey coat his throat. "Was she freaking out like I am?" He handed the bottle to Max.

"Pretty much." He took a swig and glanced at the book. "Do you want to keep reading?"

"Sure. Let me bring you up to speed." Eric lifted the book and showed Max the cover. "This is Rachel, she's nineteen, broke, and she works as a maid for an agency. They send her to clean the house of a young and very handsome tech billionaire. This dude." He tapped the cover. "His name is Edward, and he likes control. A few chapters ago, he took her virginity, but I skipped that part. This is a week later, and she's already addicted to his kinky style."

Max took the book from him. "Is that what Darlene is into?"

As rage bubbled hot and quick, Eric wrestled it down. At least now he was prepared for the irrational possessiveness of his new immortal instincts, and he did his best not to let them turn him into a caveman.

"Give it back." He pulled the paperback from Max's hand. "I'm grateful for what you have done for Darlene and me, but I'd appreciate it if you didn't put Darlene and sex in the same sentence."

Max lifted his hands, one still gripping the whiskey bottle. "Forgive me. I will never do that again. It's just that I would have never guessed. She's so mild." Laughing, he ducked as Eric tried to swat him over the head. "Okay, I'll stop. I promise." He was still laughing.

"Wait until you have a mate. I'll pay you back for this."

"You know that I was just joking." He waved at the book. "Keep reading."

"I think I'd better not." Eric closed the book and put it on the bed. "How about a nice fairytale?" He pulled out his phone and typed fairytales into the search field.

"Sure. What did you find?"

Eric shook his head. "Goldie and the Three Bear Shifters, Beauty and the Sexy Beast, Wendy and the Bully Lost Boys." He lifted his gaze to Max. "What the hell is that? What happened to all the nice fairytales?"

"They were never nice." Max handed him the bottle. "Personally, I prefer the new sexy versions. Give me that phone."

35

TOVEN

oven wondered why Igor had chosen two low-level hybrids to trail Sofia when he had a pureblood who spoke English. It seemed that their command of the language hadn't been the only reason they had been chosen. Igor hadn't wanted to send this one for some reason.

The pureblood struggled against the chains, and when he realized that his struggles were futile, he looked at Toven with eyes that were filled with fear mingled with curiosity. "Who are you? What do you want from me? What did you do with my friends?"

"I told you. My name is Tom, and I want to ask you a few questions. But first, we need to free you from Igor's compulsion."

"How do you know about Igor?"

"Stop asking questions," Toven commanded.

The Kra-ell opened his mouth, tried to speak, and closed it. Evidently, he could be compelled as long as it didn't contradict Igor's compulsion.

"You can tell me everything you were ever told to keep a secret." Toven slammed his power of compulsion into the guy.

Pavel's eyelids twitched, and he hissed, revealing two very long, sharp fangs. They looked exactly the same as any male god or immortal's when fully elongated. Also, his huge bug-like eyes were fully red now and glowing from the inside. But despite the alien features and the aggression, the male didn't look like a monster.

He was just different.

"Tell me about the weapons in your compound's arsenal."

Pavel repeated the same information Dima and Anton had provided, but Toven had a feeling that he wasn't telling him everything.

As someone who had dealt with compulsion probably since birth, Pavel had no doubt figured out that there were ways to resist it as long as it wasn't phrased tightly enough.

"Are the weapons you told me about the compound's only defense against intruders?"

Pavel shook his head as much as the chains allowed.

"What other defenses does the compound have?"

"Everything is rigged with explosives. If we are invaded, Igor blows everything and everyone up."

Toven frowned. "Who knows about this?"

"Everyone who needs to know."

"You mean the purebloods?"

Pavel's big eyes widened even further. "Yes. You know about us." He couldn't ask a question because of Toven's command, so he circumvented it by stating what he wanted to ask.

"Is he going to blow up the compound with you in it?" Toven asked.

Pavel nodded. "No one is to be taken alive."

"I bet Igor has an escape tunnel. He's not the type of guy who would go down with the ship."

The Kra-ell looked puzzled. "I don't understand."

"He will not die with his people."

"I don't know about an escape tunnel." The guy couldn't hide the telltale grimace.

"But you suspect that he has one."

"Maybe. I didn't think much about it. No one knows that we are here." He glanced at Yamanu. "But you do."

The question was burning in the guy's eyes, but he couldn't ask it. The red color had faded a little, and the inner light had turned green, but Toven didn't remember what that meant either.

Not that it mattered.

If Jade killed Igor, the explosives wouldn't be a problem unless someone else could press the button.

"Is Igor the only one who can detonate the explosives?"

"I don't know."

"What do you suspect?"

"Maybe his second-in-command can do that. His third might do it too."

"Can Jade?"

The pureblood's eyes bugged out. "No."

"Any of the other females?"

"No."

"Where did the Kra-ell come from?"

Toven had a few minutes to spare, and it wouldn't hurt to find out a little more while he was at it.

"I don't know."

Toven let out a breath. "Were you born on Earth?"

"Yes."

"Where do you suspect they came from?"

"Somewhere hundreds of light years away."

"That's not very helpful."

Yamanu cleared his throat. "We are running out of time. Let's try the shrouding and thralling."

"Right." Toven cast an illusion of an attacking beast.

Yamanu and Bobbie flinched, Mia gasped, but the Kra-ell didn't even blink.

"I assume that you don't see anything."

The guy opened his mouth and closed it. "I still can't ask questions."

"You can ask questions now."

"What was I supposed to see?"

"Never mind. I want you to deliver a message to Jade, and you have to do it in a way that will seem as if you are inviting her to a tryst."

"Why would I want to do that? She's Igor's prime."

"Does he forbid her to have sex with other males?"

"I don't know. His other females are allowed to accept invitations from pure-blooded males when they are not in their fertile cycle, and they do. But Jade doesn't. I never invited her, so I don't know for sure, but I never saw her with other males."

"If he allows the other females to have sex with other males, he probably allows her too. Besides, you just need to issue the invitation. She doesn't have to accept. Your job is only to deliver the message in a way that will seem as if you are offering sex. You are to invite her to hunt for Veskars on Friday at two in the after-noon, where the three rivers intersect."

"What are Veskars?" Pavel asked.

Toven smiled. "Magical rats on your home world that grant wishes to those who can catch them. They are very difficult to hunt. It's part of the sexual innu-endo. Do you understand?"

"I do."

"Repeat the instructions."

Pavel parroted what Toven had told him.

"Good. I just need to do one more thing." Toven tried to reach into the guy's mind, but it was like trying to thrall another god. He had no access.

Damn. That wasn't good. The explosives were no good, and their entire plan resting on Jade's ability to eliminate Igor wasn't good either.

"You will deliver the message to Jade. You will not tell anyone, and you will not make a note or communicate in any form, verbal or nonverbal, that you were captured and interrogated. You will act as if nothing unusual has happened. Repeat what I told you to do."

After the pureblood repeated the instructions word for word, Toven shifted his gaze to Yamanu. "He's all yours."

KIAN

"*A*ny news from the field?" Turner asked as he walked into Kian's office.
"Not yet."

"It's after four in the afternoon over there." He put his coffee cup down on Kian's desk. "Toven should be done."

"He'll call when they are on their way back."

The abduction of the guard had been scheduled for two in the afternoon, right at the start of their shift. At night, sound carried much farther, and they would've been forced to leave the van on the main road and traverse the dirt path on foot, which presented more problems than a daytime operation.

Ten more minutes of tense anticipation passed before the call finally came in.

"Toven." Kian activated the speaker. "Is everyone okay?"

"Good morning, Kian," Toven said with a condescending tone that reminded Kian of his mother. "Everyone is fine."

She would've sounded the same if he'd failed to precede his inquiry with a socially acceptable greeting.

Kian couldn't care less what most people thought about his manners or lack thereof, but Toven was a god, and he needed to be addressed with the same respect as Annani.

"Forgive my impatience. I've been worried."

"That's understandable. We are on our way back to St. Petersburg."

"How did it go?"

"The operation went without a hitch. The Guardians tranquilized the guards and brought the pureblood to the van. After I overrode Igor's compulsion, he confirmed everything that the two hybrids had told us. However, he added a crucial piece of information that only the purebloods are privy to, and it is a game changer. Igor has the entire compound rigged. If he's attacked, and he thinks that he's going to lose, he'll blow the place up along with everyone in it."

Turner released a breath. "That requires a change of plans."

Kian didn't buy that. "Despots don't go down with the sinking ship. He's either lying to the purebloods about the explosives, or he has an escape tunnel or some other means of getting out of there. He's also not going to escape alone. He needs his inner circle, and I bet they all know where that escape tunnel is."

"If there is one, it would be in the office building," Turner said. "That's where they spend most of their time. The question is, where's the exit point? My bet is that it's somewhere in their hunting grounds, which means that he must have a vehicle hidden nearby. If I were him, I would have a boat and a car or an amphibian stashed where I can get to them. When the rivers freeze, they turn into roads and can be driven over, but in the summer, he will need a boat. An amphibian combines the two, but it's a slow-moving vehicle. A helicopter would be better, but Sofia would have heard or seen it taking off or landing, and she didn't."

"There are pluses and minuses for both ground and airborne vehicles," Kian said.

"None of the three guards I interrogated mentioned a helicopter or an amphibian," Toven said. "But then none of them mentioned a tunnel either. It's possible that the tunnel is known only to Igor's inner circle, and if he has a helicopter, it is stashed deep inside the hunting grounds where it's not visible from the compound."

"What about the message to Jade?" Turner asked. "Did you compel him to deliver it after you learned about the explosives?"

"I scheduled the meeting for Friday at two o'clock local time."

"I hope you're not walking into a trap."

"I hope so too." Toven sighed. "There is more bad news. The pureblood was immune to thralling and to shrouding, which means that I can't seize the purebloods' minds."

Kian shook his head. "This is progressing from bad to worse, and I'm inclined to abort the whole thing. I don't want you there, and I don't want Mia and William there either. Without your mind manipulation ability, you can't protect them."

"I still have my compulsion power, and with Mia enhancing it, I can command the attackers to stand down. I ordered the pureblood to stop asking questions before I removed Igor's compulsion, and he obeyed immediately."

"That's good," Turner said. "Freeing Jade from Igor's compulsion is still our best chance of eliminating him without committing fully to taking on his entire force."

Kian drummed his fingers on the desk. "She might know about the explosives and where the detonation switch or switches are. If she can disable them, we can still proceed with stage three of our plan to free the compound."

Turner huffed out a breath. "Aborting the plan is also a viable option. Sofia can meet up with Tim, and he can draw a portrait of Igor that we can feed to the facial recognition software. Igor must leave the compound from time to time, and he can't fool cameras with his compulsion powers. If he goes through an airport, we might catch his trail and eliminate him when he's not behind the protective shield of his compound." Turner crossed his arms over his chest. "He might be able to detonate the explosives remotely before we manage to disarm him. I don't think he would, but it's a possibility that we need to account for."

Kian frowned. "Why would he do that? The compound wouldn't be under siege, and he would hope that his cronies would rescue him. He's not going to blow them up along with everyone else, and he wouldn't have time to give them a warning to use the escape tunnel. We can liberate the place after capturing him."

"Instead of detonating immediately, Igor's signal could initiate a sequence," Turner said. "The inner circle purebloods would know to evacuate, and the rest wouldn't know that anything was going on and would stay."

37

SOFIA

When Marcel's phone rang, Sofia knew it was news from Karelia. It didn't require intuition or precognition.

Marcel was on an enforced vacation, so he didn't receive calls about work, and it seemed that he didn't have friends because his phone never rang with personal calls either. He'd told her that his mother lived in Scotland and that they spoke on the phone about once a week, but she hadn't heard him talking to his mother even once.

They didn't seem to be close.

If Sofia could call her father, Helmi, and her aunts, she would be calling them daily, but no one was allowed phones in the compound. Every time she'd returned home, she'd had to deposit her cell phone in the security office.

"Thanks for the update. I'll let Sofia know." Marcel ended the call and regarded her with a frown.

Her gut squeezed. "Bad news?"

"They caught a pureblood guard, and he told them that Igor has the entire compound rigged with explosives."

Sofia felt the blood drain from her face. "Dear Mother of All Life. Why?"

"So no one is caught alive, I guess. Kian thinks that Igor has an escape tunnel. It doesn't fit his profile to go down with his people."

"The mission has to be aborted." She waved at his phone. "Call your boss and tell him to pull his people out of there."

"Toven already sent a message with the guard to Jade. They hope she will have a plan. In fact, she might know about Igor's secret tunnel. The fable she wrote to Emmett talked about the rats digging a tunnel to save the lions, so maybe it was a hint for him to find the tunnel and use it to infiltrate the compound."

She frowned. "What are you talking about? What fable?"

Marcel smoothed his hand over the back of his head. "In all the commotion, I forgot that I didn't tell you how Jade had contacted Emmett. She wrote a fable for a writing competition. It was written very cleverly so only he would understand that it was from her. Even if Igor saw it, which I'm sure he did, he wouldn't have known that it contained a secret message. I can show it to you."

He sat on the couch next to her and scrolled on his phone. "I saved it in my notes." He handed her the device.

The fable read like a children's story, and the moral was not to underestimate those who appear weaker, but where was the secret message?

"How did Emmett know that she was talking about herself and that she was trapped?"

"Emmett's Kra-ell name is Veskar, which is the name of a rodent resembling a rat in the Kra-ell home world. He hates that name, and no one outside his tribe knew him as Veskar. Jade must have recognized him from his pictures on the Safe Haven website, or she might have seen it in one of the advertisements for the paranormal retreat. She entered the competition to send him a message, hoping that he could help her. The numbers of the lions and cubs represent coordinates." Marcel showed her how they had arrived at the combinations that produced the longitude and latitude.

"Jade is a genius." Sofia looked at that paragraph again. "How did Emmett figure that out? It would have never occurred to me."

Marcel smiled shyly. "Emmett only figured out that the email was from Jade. I deciphered the meaning of the numbers. She gave us the approximate coordinates of the compound."

"But you couldn't find it anyway. Not until you got me to tell you where it was."

"We would have found it sooner or later. You just saved us some time."

That didn't help her feel any less guilty or anxious.

"Can I speak with Kian? I have to convince him to abort the mission. As much as I feel sorry for Jade and the other females, their freedom is not worth the lives of everyone in the compound."

She didn't wish them harm, but they weren't the nicest people, and her family and the other humans came first.

Marcel hesitated. "I'll text Shai and ask him to tell Kian that you wish to speak with him."

"Thank you. Do you think he'll call me?"

"He will." Marcel typed up the message. "Kian has a short temper and no patience, but he's a good guy, and if approached correctly, he tries to accommodate the needs and wishes of his people."

"I'm not his people."

"Of course you are. You're my mate, and you're part of the clan now."

Sofia knew what that term meant for immortals, and it was a big deal.

"What if I don't transition?"

Marcel cupped her cheek. "Human or long-lived, you are still my mate." He dipped his head and took her lips in a loving kiss. "I hope you live to be at least a thousand years old, but I'll take whatever time with you the Fates grant us."

It was so sweet, but it wasn't true. "Truelove mates are only possible between immortals or immortals and Dormants. Even if I transition, it would be as a Kra-ell Dormant, and so I can't be your fated one and only."

"What was true yesterday might be proven wrong tomorrow. None of it is an exact science." He put his hand over his chest. "I know in here that you are my one and only. I feel it in every fiber of my being. For the first time in three hundred years, I'm not afraid to love. On the contrary, being with you feels like home to me. Safe."

Sofia swallowed. "Loving you feels the same to me." Tears stung the back of her eyes. "But in my case, it comes with a dose of guilt. I abandoned my family for you."

3 8

MARCEL

*M*arcel clasped her hand. "You didn't abandon your family. None of what you have done was voluntary. You were put in this situation by Igor, and you didn't choose to be with me."

She smiled. "I chose to love you, and I'm free." She winced. "Sort of. I'm exchanging one restrictive existence for another, but at least this one comes with the man I love, so it's a sweeter deal. But if I lose my family…." She shook her head. "I can't let it happen. How can I have my happily-ever-after with them gone? If I hadn't told you where the entrance to the tunnel was, you might not have found it."

"Not true. First of all, Toven could have compelled it out of you. And secondly, we could have found out where it was from the two hybrids we caught. Besides, you are thinking about it all wrong. We are trying to liberate your family and everyone else who has no choice but to serve Igor. If we can't do that without causing major casualties, we won't engage."

"You said that you are not in charge. I want to hear it from Kian."

"Fair enough." Marcel looked at the phone, willing it to ring.

When it did, he was surprised it had worked. He hadn't really believed in the wishing and visualizing and the universe responding.

"Hi, Kian. Thank you for calling. I'm activating the speaker so Sofia can join the conversation."

"How can I help you, Sofia?" Kian asked.

She swallowed. "I want to convince you to abort the mission. Freedom is great, but not if it's achieved by death, and that's what will happen if you attack the compound. Igor will see a superior force, and instead of running like you predicted, he will destroy everyone so they don't get captured. It's not worth the risk."

"I agree. If we can't find a way to ensure the detonation doesn't happen, we will not proceed with stage three of the plan. Tom is going to meet with Jade, and we will take it from there. She's been Igor's prime for a reason, and it was probably to learn as much as she could about his weaknesses and plan a rebellion. She can't do anything while under his compulsion, but once she's free and she has us for backup, she might have a plan of her own that she can launch to eliminate Igor while making sure that he doesn't trigger the explosives."

"He's not the only one that can do that. If Jade kills Igor, my grandfather will take over."

"Is he a strong compeller?"

"I don't know. I don't even know if Jade is. None of the other purebloods compelled anyone. It was all Igor."

"We know that Jade is strong, and she's ruthless. By the way, how do you feel about her taking over control of the compound?"

"I don't know her all that well. She's just as stuck-up as the other purebloods, and she doesn't interact with humans."

"Who do you think would be best for the job?"

Kian asked her? Sofia had fantasized about it so often, and she had plenty of ideas for how the compound should be run so everyone's needs were met, but she'd never thought that it could happen.

"They should have an election and choose three representatives. One pureblood, one hybrid, and one human. Or maybe two of each. The three should have an equal say on all major decisions, and if they don't do their job well, they need to be replaced with other elected representatives. But it would never work. The purebloods are too powerful, so they are at the top of the food chain, then the hybrids, and lastly, the humans. Unless someone from the outside enforces the democratic elections of representatives from all three groups, it's not going to happen."

Kian chuckled. "Are you suggesting that my clan should be that outside influence?"

"I was speaking hypothetically."

He let out a breath. "Let's take it one step at a time. Friday, Tom will meet Jade, and hopefully, she will have a plan."

Marcel cleared his throat. "Sofia knows that Tom's name is Toven. I hope it's okay that I told her."

"Toven prefers that his name is not known to outsiders. Sofia is with you, so she's no longer an outsider, but for the time being, Eleanor or Emmett should compel her to keep it a secret as well."

"Do you want me to call Valstar again?" Sofia asked.

"You called him yesterday, and he doesn't expect you to call him every day. Wait until tomorrow."

She chewed on her lower lip. "I thought to plead with him to let my father come here because I'm so sick, and I need open heart surgery."

"Do you think he'll do that?"

Sofia sighed. "Not really."

"Then why put yourself through the heartache?"

"Because if something happens to my father, I need to know that I did everything possible to save him."

"I promise you that nothing will happen to him."

He couldn't promise her that. Her father was human, and they had a family history of heart disease. He could have a stroke tomorrow.

"Thank you, but you can't guarantee that."

"True. But I can promise that I will do everything in my power to guarantee his safety. Do you believe me?"

"I do."

"I'm glad. Good day, Sofia." He ended the call.

"He meant it," Marcel said. "Kian never says things he doesn't mean just to make someone feel good. It's not his style."

"I know, and I appreciate it. I'm just afraid of the unintended consequences, and I don't even know whether they will be worse because of your clan's action or inaction."

39

JADE

*W*hen Pavel strode into Jade's classroom, she lifted an eyebrow. "Do you miss listening to my stories?"

He was young, only thirty-two, and when she'd started teaching twenty years ago, he'd been twelve, and she hadn't been his teacher. She preferred teaching the little ones who hadn't been corrupted by Igor's deviant spin on what it meant to be a Kra-ell, but Pavel had enjoyed hearing her stories and had wandered into her classroom from time to time.

He sat on the mat next to Moshun. "I want to hear the story about you hunting for Veskars."

Jade's heart stuttered. "Why would I be hunting for Veskars? They are not very tasty."

"What are Veskars?" Moshun asked.

"They are magical little rats," Pavel said. "If you catch one, it will grant you a wish."

Moshun's eyes brightened. "Any wish? If I catch one, will he give me a toy?"

Pavel smiled suggestively at Jade. "The Veskar only grants wishes to adults, and they are very difficult to catch, but there is a good chance of catching one at the junction of the three rivers this Friday at two in the afternoon."

Cold sweat slithered down Jade's back.

Pavel sounded as if he was flirting with her, going as far as scheduling a time and place for their assignation, but everyone in the compound knew that she didn't accept invitations from anyone other than Igor, and she only accepted his because she had no choice.

Besides, Pavel shouldn't even know what a Veskar was. The first time she'd included the rat in one of her stories was in the fable she'd sent to Safe Haven.

There could be only two reasons for Pavel to use the rat in his flirting. One was that Igor had figured out what she'd done and had sent him to taunt her or even trap her, and the other one was that the male called Veskar had sent Pavel to deliver the message and schedule a meeting with her in the hunting grounds.

Pavel was a guard, so he could have been approached outside of the compound, and whoever had approached him somehow managed to overcome Igor's compulsion. Could Veskar's power increase so much in two decades?

Impossible.

The only other compellers who were possibly more powerful than Igor were the royal twins, and they were most likely dead. Even if they'd somehow survived, they wouldn't be sending her a message with a guard. She was a nobody to them. They would just walk in and take over the compound.

Jade had spent many nights praying to the Mother for that to happen, even before she'd been captured by Igor and the males of her family had been slaughtered. Since then, she'd prayed twice as fervently, but the Mother hadn't answered her prayers.

The royals were dead.

"Are you offering to help me hunt for the magical Veskar?" Jade asked to maintain the pretense of sexual banter.

"I certainly am." Pavel pushed to his feet. "I'll be thinking of you, fair Jade." He blew her an air kiss, which was shockingly un-Kra-ell of him. "I'll meet you at the junction."

Pureblooded Kra-ell didn't blow kisses at each other, and they didn't whisper sweet endearments in each other's ears like humans. They fought for dominance, and if the male managed to subdue the female, he got to plant his seed in her womb.

It wasn't her fertile cycle, so Igor wouldn't mind that she accepted Pavel's invitation, but she had no intention of indulging the young male if it turned out that his intent had indeed been purely sexual and the mention of a Veskar coincidental.

For the males, sex was as much for pleasure as it was for procreation, and it used to be for her as well, but Jade hadn't done anything for her own enjoyment since she'd failed to protect her tribe, and she wasn't about to break that tradition with Pavel.

If the message was from the real Veskar, it had been very cleverly constructed not to trigger Igor's compulsion to report it. Still, it was possible that she was attaching meaning to what was a simple invitation to sex.

Friday, she would go hunting alone, and she would be at the junction of the three rivers at two in the afternoon. If Pavel showed up expecting sex, she would just turn him down.

Thankfully, Igor wasn't at the compound, and if she was lucky, he wouldn't be back by then.

He watched her like a hawk, and if he noticed any change in her behavior, he would try to compel her to tell him the reason behind it. Jade was already stretching her mental powers to hide her call for help, and she doubted that she could resist his compulsion when he commanded her to tell him what was making her edgier than usual.

What if it was a trap, though?

What if Igor was testing her?

If she showed up at the junction of the three rivers at two o'clock, it would be like an admission of guilt. But if she actually had sex with Pavel, she could claim that she'd accepted his invitation, and that was the only reason she'd shown up.

The Veskar element wasn't a factor in her decision at all.

The problem was that Igor rarely left the compound for longer than a couple of days, and he'd left yesterday.

He didn't share his plans with her, but she'd figured that the short trips were to compel local authorities to ignore the compound. They were secluded, but they were connected to the electrical grid, so someone was aware of their existence. Also, the supply trucks lumbering over a dirt path leading to nowhere could have been noticed.

The only times Igor had left for longer than a couple of days had been when he'd gone after other Kra-ell communities, and that hadn't happened in a long time.

He'd stopped either because he'd found all the survivors and all the rest were dead or because he didn't know how to find the others.

After her class ended and Borga took over, Jade strode to the office building in search of Valstar. He would know when Igor was due back, but the trick was to make him tell her.

No one searched her as she climbed the stairs to the second floor, and Igor's guard was absent from his station.

Evidently, Valstar's life was deemed less valuable than his master's.

She knocked on his door and then opened it without waiting for his response. "When is Igor coming back?"

He regarded her with a smirk. "Why? Do you miss him?"

"No, I hope he's dead. I want to know how long of a reprieve I have. I might choose to enjoy a virile, young male in his absence." She smiled evilly. "He says that he doesn't mind if I do, but I want to test it."

When the females did the choosing, it was considered bad form to horde males within the tribe. Unlike humans, there was never a question of paternity among the Kra-ell, and every adult in the tribe was free to engage with whomever they pleased. But Igor had adopted patriarchal attitudes, and his little harem of females suitable for breeding was forbidden to engage with other males during their fertile cycles. Lucky for him, their cycles weren't synchronized like they had been on the home planet.

Valstar's eyes gleamed with arousal. "That's a new twist. You haven't been with anyone but Igor. I was starting to think that your hatred for him was an act."

"Oh, believe me. It's not an act. It was self-inflicted punishment for my failure to protect my people, but over two decades of suffering is enough. I'm ready to start living again."

"Excellent." He rose to his feet and rounded the desk. "I'm not young, but I assure you that I'm virile."

She dragged her eyes over his body, pretending to consider it. "As tempting as it is, you don't want to be the first male I test Igor with."

His eyes blazed with purple light. "You are worth the risk."

She sauntered over and put her hand on his chest. "When is he coming back?"

"Monday."

"That's unusually long. Did he find more Kra-ell tribes to raid and slaughter?"

Igor's compulsion prevented her from talking about the murders and abductions with those who didn't know about what he had done, but it didn't include those who'd committed the crimes.

Even in the old days of the Kra-ell, before the queen outlawed tribal wars and duels to the death, the stealth attack would have been considered a travesty.

Warring tribes had faced each other on the battlefield and had followed a code of honor that the Mother of All Life herself had laid down. But Igor and his lackeys had followed none of the Mother's rules, and for that, they would forever walk the valley of the shamed. However, that was a paltry consolation for Jade's loss and the years of misery and subjugation, and if she failed to avenge her people, she would end up in the same place of shame as the murderers of her tribe.

"I don't think he found any more survivors," Valstar said. "But who knows? He doesn't tell me everything."

"He doesn't?" Jade dragged her fangs over his neck.

"He went to Moscow. He wants to expand his influence."

That was way too easy, and she was starting to think that the entire thing had been staged to trap her.

"I don't really care." She pushed Valstar away and pivoted on her heel.

"Come to my quarters tonight," he commanded.

She turned to look at him over her shoulder. "I'll consider it, but don't stay up waiting for me."

40

TOVEN

"That wasn't what I expected." Toven lowered Mia into Yamanu's outstretched arms.

The amphibian was an old Russian navy model that looked like a tank and could only be accessed from the top. Inside, two long benches lined the sides. Six Guardians were already seated in the fetid cabin, their equipment tucked under the benches.

Military vehicles were usually kept clean, but the amphibian was old, probably decommissioned, and belonged to a drug lord or a weapons smuggler.

As Yamanu put Mia on the bench, Toven jumped down and sat next to her. "They don't even have safety belts. Is this thing even operable?"

Yamanu shrugged. "We tested it yesterday, and it did what it was supposed to do. It's not a luxury vehicle."

"Did you get Mia's harness and Kevlar suit from the van?"

"It's right here." Yamanu motioned to the large duffel bag under his seat.

"Thank you."

"No need to thank me. It's my job to ensure that we have all the necessary equipment."

Toven leaned closer to Mia, intending to whisper in her ear, but with how everyone was sitting, the others would hear him no matter how quietly he did that. "I want you to sit on my lap so I can hold you. This is going to get bumpy, and your balance isn't as good as the others."

"Okay," she said, surprising him.

He'd expected an argument, but for once Mia had chosen safety over pride.

"That was easy." He wrapped his arms around her, and as he lifted her and sat her on his lap, she buried her nose in the crook of his neck.

"I'd rather smell you than this cabin."

So that was why she'd agreed so readily.

"The ride is about two hours long," Yamanu said. "Try to get comfortable."

"I'm very comfortable." Mia nuzzled Toven's neck. "After the day we had yesterday, I could use a little nap." She sighed and put her head on his chest. "Shopping is exhausting."

While the Guardians had tested the amphibian and scoped the hunting grounds, William had worked on the drones, and Toven, Mia, and Sylvia had spent the day shopping and sightseeing in St. Petersburg.

"I have a question," Toven turned his gaze to Yamanu. "How did you and your Guardians manage to stay hidden from the occasional Kra-ell patrol? The purebloods can smell and hear as well as the gods, which means that they can hear and smell the Guardians before the Guardians can hear and smell them unless the patrolmen are all hybrids. It makes sense that the task would be relegated to them, but I would expect at least one pureblood to command each patrolling unit."

Yamanu grinned. "We have the advantage of technology on our side. We no longer have to rely on our senses alone."

"I see." Toven nodded. "Perhaps I should join a few of your training sessions to acquaint myself with modern warfare."

Mia sighed. "I'm too anxious to fall asleep. I've never taken part in a military operation."

"That's not true," Yamanu said. "This is your fourth time. You helped Toven twice in Safe Haven, and two days ago, you helped him interrogate a Kra-ell. You're a veteran."

She chuckled. "The two hybrids in Safe Haven don't count. I was perfectly safe there. I was a little apprehensive the day before yesterday, but I never even left the van. Today I'm going to be strapped to Toven's back as he sprints through the woods with a team of immortal warriors at his side and with danger lurking all around. That's a real adventure."

"Don't worry, Mia. You have a god and seven immortal Guardians protecting you. We won't let harm come to you."

Yamanu's sing-song voice had a soothing effect, and as he started humming a tune, Mia let out a breath, and a moment later she was asleep.

Toven regarded the Guardian with even greater appreciation. "In addition to being an incredible thraller and shrouder, you can also sing people to sleep?"

Yamanu nodded. "I think it works the same way as compulsion does because I need to use my voice. Kri has a calming influence that works more like thralling. She helps calm down the trafficking victims we rescue."

"Do you do that as well?"

"I don't go out on rescue missions, but I volunteer in the halfway house once a week. I organize a karaoke night, which is the most popular activity in the house. The girls love it."

"I'm sure they do." Toven adjusted Mia on his lap. "Perhaps I could volunteer as well, and I know Mia would love to contribute too. I could teach a creative writing class, and Mia can teach children's book illustration." He gave the Guardian a sidelong glance. "If they are not intimidated by you, they probably won't be intimidated by me."

Yamanu pursed his fleshy lips. "No offense, Toven, but you lack my charming personality. I might be intimidating at first glance, but all it takes to break the ice is one smile." He flashed a toothy grin that was indeed disarming.

"I can smile too." Toven tried to imitate the Guardian.

Yamanu winced. "Again, no offense, but you need to work on that. You look like you're constipated."

41

JADE

*K*agra trailed behind Jade to the security office. "Why are you refusing to take me hunting with you today?"

Jade was tempted to share Pavel's strange invitation with her second and tell her what it could possibly mean. Kagra was strong, and she could resist the compulsion to report suspicious activity to the security office, but if Jade was walking into a trap, she didn't want to take Kagra down with her.

"I told you. I'm restless. I need some time alone."

Kagra stopped and turned to face her. "What's going on? I know you too well to buy that."

She didn't want to lie, especially about something like this, but Kagra left her no choice. "I'm meeting Pavel. I accepted his invitation."

Kagra's brows shot up. "What happened to the vow you made never to enjoy yourself sexually again?"

"I never took a vow. I just wasn't in the right state of mind to seek pleasure." She affected a grin and leaned closer to Kagra. "I'm still not. Igor is out of the compound, and when he returns, I'm going to rub it in his face that Pavel is a better lover."

Her second looked doubtful. "Pavel is a kid, and I doubt he can overpower you. You know that you can't lie to Igor."

Jade shrugged. "So I need to make sure that I enjoy it. I don't detest Pavel, and maybe I can enjoy myself without fighting for dominance. You said that I should try it."

"I did, but I never believed that you would actually listen to me. You are as prime as they come. Can you even get turned on without it?"

"You are as much prime material as I am, and yet you said that you sometimes skipped the fighting stage and enjoyed softer touches."

"Once in a while, it's nice to try something different. I still find fighting for dominance arousing." She smiled wickedly. "Even when the males don't win."

"You're not a traditionalist, that's for sure."

Back in the day, telling a pureblood that she was abandoning tradition would have been considered an insult. They prided themselves on being traditionalists. But after two decades with Igor, adhering to the old rules of conduct seemed like a futile attempt to cling to what had been lost.

"No, I'm not." Kagra clapped her on the back. "I'm a progressive like the Wise Queen, and I'm willing to try new things."

The Wise Queen had been the one who had outlawed the tribal wars and duels to the death, but Jade wasn't sure it had been such a wise move. It had stopped the bloodshed, but it had created a slew of other problems.

"We wouldn't be here if the Wise Queen had left things the way they were."

Kagra shrugged. "There is no point engaging in what ifs. Tell me how it goes with Pavel."

As her second walked away, Jade expelled a breath. If Kagra had bought her story, everyone else would as well. No one knew her better than her second, not even her own daughter.

At the security office, the guard on duty didn't ask why she was going hunting alone, and as she walked to the gate with the clearance badge attached to her chest, the guard opened it up for her and waved her through.

"Good hunting," he called after her.

Surprised, she looked over her shoulder and nodded her thank you.

Did he know that she was meeting Pavel? Was that why the guard had wished her good hunting?

Pavel might have spread the rumor about their assignation. Getting her to accept his invitation was something to boast about.

But was she meeting Pavel? Or was she meeting Veskar?

The junction of the three rivers was an hour away by walking, and half of that if she ran. Curiosity urged her to run, but prudence convinced her to walk. It was one o'clock in the afternoon, and if she ran, she would arrive at the meeting spot ahead of time and could scope the area. But running would deplete her energy, and she needed to preserve it. She didn't know what was awaiting her at the meeting location and whether Veskar might bring reinforcements.

Tugging at the collar around her neck, she wondered for the umpteenth time whether it was true that it contained explosives and would go off if she left the area.

Knowing Igor as well as she did, the thing was rigged. Every so often, he would replace the collars, sending the ones that had been taken off to maintenance and putting others on. Rodof, who was in charge of that, probably checked that the wiring still worked and that the explosives hadn't expired.

Did explosives go bad and expire?

She didn't know, and it didn't matter.

Even if Veskar had come to rescue her, and even if he knew to bring an explosives expert with him, she wouldn't flee and leave the others behind. She had a responsibility to her people, not only those from her former tribe, but also to others who had no one else to help them.

The only way she might be convinced to flee was if she could return with an army to free the rest or at least a compeller strong enough to squash Igor.

But no one knew whether the royals had survived or even where to find their remains to perform the ritual that would send their souls to the Mother.

Not that she believed the ritual was needed for that. The dead passed on whether the living prayed for them or not, but it provided closure for those left behind. It was just one more thing that Igor had robbed her and the other females of. One more thing for her to avenge.

42

TOVEN

*Y*amanu hummed a tune as he lifted Mia into the harness on Toven's back and adjusted the straps.

"Are you comfortable?" Toven asked Mia when Yamanu was done.

"The harness is okay, but I don't like the helmet. I'm afraid it's going to chafe my chin when you run."

"If it does, tell me, and I'll stop so you can adjust it. Your head and your heart are the two most vulnerable places on your immortal body, and they need to be protected."

The Guardians also wore Kevlar vests and helmets, and they were armed to the teeth with hot and cold weapons and tranquilizer darts.

"I know." She rested her chin on his shoulder. "Let's go."

They had gone to shore a couple of miles west of the meeting point and had hidden the amphibian. It hadn't been an easy choice between getting as close to the river junction as the vehicle could get them or stopping way before that and making the rest of the way on foot.

The amphibian was noisy, making a stealth approach impossible, but it was also secure and allowed for a quick retreat.

In the end, it had been Toven's decision to choose stealth over convenience and a better retreat option.

After two of the Guardians had sped ahead to check the meeting place and take care of Pavel when he got there, Toven hooked his arms around Mia's thighs and nodded at Yamanu and the other Guardians.

As they broke into a jog, Toven made sure to stay inside the protective circle the Guardians formed around him and Mia. When they neared the junction, the two Guardians who had gone ahead communicated that they had Pavel, the area was clear, and it was okay for them to close the rest of the distance.

The five remaining Guardians climbed the surrounding trees, leaving Toven and Mia alone on the riverbank but well protected.

Toven was worried that once Jade became aware of their presence, she might flee, but there was no way around it. He needed those Guardians to watch his and Mia's backs.

When a female emerged from the thicket, he activated the portable signal disrupter William had given him and affected a bright smile. "Jade, I presume?"

Her whole body swelling with aggression, she bared her fangs and hissed. "Who are you?"

"I'm here to help. Veskar sent me."

"Where is he?"

Lifting his hands to show her that he wasn't armed, Toven smiled again. "Veskar, i.e., Emmett, is a spiritual guy, not a fighter."

Jade narrowed her eyes at him. "That face of yours is too pretty to be human. What are you? And why do you carry a child on your back?"

"I'm not a child," Mia said. "I'm his mate."

Jade's eyes didn't shift from Toven's. "You're a god," she stated.

How did she know that just from looking at him?

"What makes you think that?"

She snorted. "I know one when I see one. I wondered what had happened to the gods. I thought that you either had left and gone home or that the humans had killed you all. Regrettably, I see that they didn't. Where have you been hiding?"

Toven had been prepared for Jade to be fearful and suspicious but not hateful.

"I came to help you, and you're spouting venom at me. I didn't do anything to hurt you or your people, so I don't know where that's coming from."

She tilted her head. "Were you born on Earth?"

"Why does it matter?"

"Because you are obviously ignorant about your history. Your parents either didn't tell you anything or they lied about their past. The gods like to rewrite history to make themselves look good."

Excitement rose in his chest. Could Jade finally shed light on his ancestors' history and where they'd come from?

But now was not the time for a history lesson.

"You're very fortunate that some of us survived. I'm here to free you from Igor's compulsion, and I'm the only one who can do that."

"Why would you do that for me?"

"He's a threat to us, and we want him eliminated, but if we attack, there would be many casualties, and we want to avoid that. We hope that once you're free from his compulsion, you can eliminate him for us."

Jade didn't look excited. She looked suspicious. "How do I know that I can trust you? Maybe you need me to get rid of him so you can take over? I prefer a rotten Kra-ell to a god in charge of my people and me."

"Is she for real?" Mia murmured. "She's nasty."

There was no way Jade hadn't heard Mia, but she didn't acknowledge her.

"You don't need to trust me," Toven said. "You contacted Veskar and asked for his help, but he doesn't have what it takes to help you. Fortunately, he has the support of my people. He asked us to do what we could for you and the other females Igor had abducted and subjugated. I'm here to free your mind. What you do with that is up to you. If you don't want to take out the one who ordered the slaughter of every male in your tribe, that's your choice. We will find another way to mitigate the risk he represents."

Jade dropped her aggressive stance. "How do you know all that about me?" she asked in a much more amicable tone. "Veskar wasn't there when that happened, and I didn't include any of it in the fable."

"Three of your former tribe members joined our community. That's how we knew what happened to you."

"Who?"

"Veskar, who is mated to one of our females, and Vrog and Aliya, who found love in each other's arms."

He could have sworn that Jade's huge eyes misted with tears, but a blink later, it was gone.

"Thank the Mother that they survived." She frowned. "How do I know that you are telling me the truth? Maybe they are your prisoners?"

"You can talk with one of them if you wish. I can call either one."

43

JADE

*J*ade didn't trust the gods. They were liars and manipulators.

If not for the child-like woman with no legs strapped to the god's back, she would have attacked him first and talked later while holding him in a chokehold.

It had taken her a couple of moments to realize who he was, and when she had, she'd also noticed the woman who she'd mistaken for a child.

The trouble with the fuckers was that they seemed human if one didn't know what to look for, like the too-perfect features, the smooth alabaster skin, and their preference to stay in the shade because of their sensitive eyes.

They were like rats who only came out at night.

"If you can make a call from here," she said. "I would like to speak to Veskar."

He was clever enough to convey a message even if he was being held captive. Vrog had never been much for subterfuge, and she had no idea what kind of person Aliya had grown up to be. She would love to know how they ended up with the gods, though.

The god pulled a phone out of his pocket. "It's a satellite phone that can be used from anywhere, and the communication is secure."

"What's your name, god?" She shook her head. "I really don't like how you assholes refer to yourselves. We both know that there is nothing godly about you."

"Why are you so mean to him?" asked the woman named Mia. "He's risking himself and me to help you."

"That is true." She should dial back her hatred for the gods and give him a chance. "Are you human?" She looked pointedly at the missing legs. "Gods can regrow limbs."

"I'm not a goddess, but I'm not human either."

The god lifted his hand to silence the woman. "Mia is none of your business. I go by Tom."

He sounded so protective of the female with no legs, which was atypical of the gods who worshiped perfection. Maybe he was indeed different.

"That's a human name," she said.

"So is Jade."

"True." She let out a breath. "I apologize. You are not to blame for the deeds of your forefathers. I will give you the benefit of the doubt that you are a different breed." She forced a smile. "New and improved."

He lifted his hand again, this time to shush her as he put the phone to his ear.

"Did she come?" She heard a male's voice on the other side.

"I'm with her. She wants to talk to you." He handed her the phone. "Make it quick. We don't have much time."

She nodded. "Veskar?"

"It is me," he answered in Kra-ell. "Are you well?"

"As well as a captive can be. Can I trust Tom?"

"Yes, you can. Remember the story you told the children about the pompalo and the dorga?"

She'd known Veskar would find a way to tell her whether she could trust the god. He was using a fable they both knew.

A pompalo was a fearsome tiger-like animal, and a dorga was a large bird that was quite rare and a symbol of good luck. The story was that the bird was injured, and the pompalo saved her instead of eating her. When she asked him why, he said that she wasn't his enemy, nor was she his food source, and saving her would bring him luck.

"Who is the pompalo, and who is the dorga?"

Veskar chuckled. "Tom is the pompalo, and you are the dorga. He's a good guy. You can trust him."

"One last thing. Why does he carry a woman on his back?"

Perhaps it wasn't the most important question to ask, but it was so unusual and so un-god-like that she had to know the reason.

"She's his mate, but that's not why he brought her along. He is a powerful compeller, and she enhances his power. Together, they can free your mind from Igor's compulsion and with no adverse side effects. Without her, it will take longer and be more painful."

Compulsion was a rare talent among the gods. They had other mind manipulation powers that were even more impressive than compulsion, but the gods' ruling family had it in addition to the other talents, which was what had probably made them the rulers from time immemorial.

Tom must be related to them, one of the thousands of descendants of the Eternal King.

Things might have changed over the many centuries that had passed since she'd left, and perhaps the Eternal King was no more, or maybe he'd been long gone even before that and they had a new king who had assumed the same title. It was impossible to know the truth about the gods. They were masters of misinformation, shaping it in any which way that benefited them and their self-image.

Tom might be full of bluster.

If he was more powerful than Igor, he wouldn't have to convince her to cooperate with him. He could just compel her to kill Igor and skip over the pretense of being her people's savior.

"Thank you, Veskar, and may the Mother bless you. I knew that you'd find a clever way to tell me whether I could trust Tom even if you were their captive or under compulsion. You've earned your place in the fields of the brave."

"May the Mother help you fight for your freedom. Be well, Jade."

Jade ended the call and handed the device back to the god. "Veskar assured me that you are a good guy. Let's talk." She sat on the ground and assumed the lotus position.

When he did the same, Mia tapped his shoulder. "Can you put me down? I'd rather sit next to you."

"Sorry, love, but I can't. We need to be ready to flee."

Jade nodded. "No one is patrolling right now, and other hunters usually don't venture this far, but you never know."

"Fine." Mia let out a breath. "What did Emmett tell you that convinced you?"

"It was an old Kra-ell proverb. It conveyed that I can trust Tom. Veskar is a smart male."

The thing was, she still didn't trust the god. Veskar was a hybrid who was born on Earth. He didn't know their history and didn't realize how duplicitous the gods were.

"Let's assume that I can kill Igor once I'm free. What's next?"

"You can take over as the head of the compound, and we will enter negotiations for peaceful coexistence between our people and hopefully cooperation as well."

"Sounds good to me, provided that you can actually release me."

"Let's do it." Tom looked into her eyes. "You no longer have to obey Igor's commands in any way. You are free to act and talk as you will."

Jade felt the easing in her mind, the lightness in her chest, but she didn't trust the feeling. She'd resisted Igor's compulsion over the years. She'd talked freely and done things that he didn't allow, but what she couldn't do was run away or kill him.

Tom smiled. "Give it a try."

"He didn't have complete control over me, and I talked freely before. But I couldn't leave, and I couldn't kill him."

"Can you kill him now?" Tom asked.

She shook her head. "He can freeze me with one word."

"I have a solution for that." Tom pulled a small box from his pocket and opened it. "Those are translating earpieces, but they have been modified so they completely block outside voices. The machine voice you'll hear will repeat whatever Igor says, but it will filter the compulsion. If you wear your hair down, it will be invisible."

When she reached for the box, Tom shook his head. "Not yet. I'll give it to you when we part."

She really wanted those devices, but wearing them in Igor's presence was a death sentence, even if she managed to sneak them past the guards, which wasn't likely. They conducted very thorough searches.

"His guards will find the devices, and that will be the end of it. But even if I somehow manage to sneak them in, he's physically stronger than me."

"We can give you a weapon. A syringe filled with something that will stop his heart."

She smiled. "Your venom?"

"Regrettably, it can't be bottled. It deteriorates immediately."

"It wouldn't help. I can't sneak anything past his guards. Not the earpieces nor a weapon. On top of that, they are always primed to defend him."

44

TOVEN

oven had expected Jade to say that, but it was still a disappointment.

"Can you think of any way that can be done? Is there anyone you can trust to assist you?" He pushed compulsion into his voice to make her answer truthfully.

"My second, Kagra. But even if you free her from Igor's compulsion, his guards wouldn't let us past them. If we show up together, they will know that something is up."

"You could pretend that you want a ménage with her and Igor," Mia suggested.

Jade cast her an indulgent smile. "Kra-ell females are not into ménages with other females. No one will buy it."

"You are a compeller, correct?" Toven asked. "Can't you compel the guards to let you and Kagra through?"

"Igor's compulsion is stronger than mine, and I can't override it even when I'm free of it. I can't compel the guards to do anything that will endanger him. I'm glad that he's not in the compound right now, or I would be more apprehensive about being here. He's not going to be back until Monday, so I have a few days to come up with something." She rubbed her temple. "The guards are not as careful when he's not here. So maybe I can hide something in his personal quarters now and use it when he returns."

Toven's mind jumped into action. "Are you sure he won't be back before Monday?"

"That's what his second told me. But Igor could change his plans, so that is not set in stone."

"Do you know that the entire compound is rigged with explosives?"

She nodded. "Igor doesn't take any chances. None of us are to be taken alive."

"Who can blow it up in his absence?"

"His second-in-command, probably his third as well. Also, I wouldn't be surprised if Igor has a way to do it remotely."

Toven smiled. "He can't do it remotely if he has no connection. We can block all communications in and out of the compound."

"That's good."

He could see the wheels in her mind working, but she didn't offer to share her thoughts.

"Would Igor's second-in-command actually pull the trigger?" Mia asked. "Knowing that he will die too?"

Jade regarded Mia with her too-big, dark eyes. "Valstar will do what Igor compelled him to do. The will of everyone in the community is not their own. I can mouth off to Igor and tell him that I hate him, because he allows it, and he doesn't compel me to stop. But I can't tell anyone about what he did to my tribe because the compulsion to keep it a secret is so strong." She took a deep breath. "He killed all the males of my tribe. He killed my sons." She took in another breath. "It's such a relief to finally be able to tell someone."

Toven nodded. "My condolences on your loss. They say that time heals all wounds, but I know that some wounds keep bleeding forever."

Jade nodded. "Maybe mine will heal once I kill Igor and avenge my people. But unless you have an army of gods you can summon, I don't know how that's possible."

"I can summon an army, not of gods but of immortals, what you call hybrids. But we can't attack knowing that there is a chance Igor or his second will blow everyone up."

She tilted her head. "Why would you bring an army?"

"I told you. Igor is a threat that needs to be eliminated before he finds out about us."

"Who are 'us'? How come I couldn't find anything in human history about gods in the modern era?"

He didn't want to share with her what happened to the other gods until he got her to tell him the gods' history. He might not be able to hide his ignorance, but he knew how to phrase things in a way that could be interpreted in different ways.

"Only a few of us remain, and we were born on Earth. We know next to nothing about our history, where the gods came from, and why. That's another reason we offer our help. You have information that's valuable to us, which makes you an asset."

"What I know is what I was told, and I realized a long time ago that most of it was fabricated for one reason or another. I don't trust any of it to be true unless I witnessed it myself."

That was cynical but smart.

"How old are you?" he asked.

She laughed. "Humans consider that a rude question to ask a lady. You're lucky that I'm not."

"A lady or a human?"

"Neither, and to answer your question, I'm very old, but I wasn't awake for most of that time."

"You traveled here in stasis?"

She nodded.

That confirmed his suspicion that the gods gave themselves the ability to go into stasis so they could traverse the universe, and evidently, they gave the same ability to the Kra-ell.

"We are running out of time," Mia reminded them. "We need to come up with a plan to liberate Jade and her people. You can talk about your history once she's free."

Toven nodded. "Mia is right. How long do we have before they notice that you've been gone longer than usual?"

"When I go hunting alone, I usually return in about two hours, sometimes three. I've been gone out longer a few times, but that was when I was leading a group of youngsters." She looked up at the sky. "It took me about an hour to get here, and I can make it back in half the time if I run, so we still have about an hour left."

"Will they know that you didn't get blood?" Mia asked. "Do you get paler or something?"

"Why, are you offering yours?"

Mia shuddered. "Of course not."

"I'm good," Jade said. "I don't need to get blood every day. Besides, I was supposed to meet Pavel here and engage in other activities, but since he didn't show up, I assume that he wasn't actually supposed to come?"

"As you probably guessed, we grabbed him from his guard duty, released him from Igor's compulsion, and put him under mine. He was instructed to follow through with the pretense and come out to meet you, so it would look legit to you. My companions intercepted him and kept him busy so we could talk in privacy."

45

JADE

*J*ade wasn't surprised that Tom and Mia had backup. She would have been surprised if they hadn't. She'd felt the others, but by the time their presence had registered, it had been too late to turn back.

She narrowed her eyes at him. "What do you mean, busy?"

"Nothing nefarious. He's being restrained, and once we are done, I'll compel him to support your version of the story, whatever you choose it to be. I knew that you were Igor's prime, and I didn't know if it was okay for you to get intimate with another male, so I didn't do it ahead of time. I can compel him to say that you met him, but nothing happened, or the exact opposite."

"As long as I'm not in my fertile cycle, Igor doesn't care who I have sex with. He keeps me as his prime because he wants me to produce a son for him, not because he cares for me." She smirked. "Traditionally, a female child is the most desirable because females are so rare, but Igor wants males to be in charge. Unlucky for him, the Mother has a wicked sense of humor, and she blessed me with a daughter. He has plenty of sons by other females, but he wants one from me because our child will be the most powerful."

"How old is your daughter?" Mia asked.

"She's sixteen."

Jade wanted a better future for her daughter. Drova was indoctrinated into Igor's philosophy, and it would be difficult to undo, but she was a smart female, so there was still hope.

"Let's get back to devising a plan," Tom said. "We need to come up with a way to free the compound, and if there is any time left after we find a doable solution, I would love to hear a little bit more about the gods' history, of which I'm ignorant."

More than Veskar's reassurances and anything else Tom had said, that convinced her that he wanted to help. It was obvious that he was desperate to learn more about his people, but he was willing to potentially lose his chance to do it in favor of helping liberate her.

"I might be able to eliminate Valstar. With Igor away, the guards won't bother to search me as thoroughly, and I might be able to sneak in a weapon or a drug. Valstar is probably not a strong compeller, so he can't compel me to stand down, and if I drug him, I can overpower him physically. Kagra can take down the third, but the two of us can't overcome every pureblood and hybrid in the compound."

"Maybe they would submit to your authority," Mia said. "With the second and the third gone, you'll be the natural leader. You could open the gates and walk out with whoever wants to be free."

Jade smiled indulgently. "If it was that simple, Igor would have never left the compound. He has everyone compelled to follow his orders even in his absence."

"Is there a chance that you can detain Valstar without killing him?" Toven asked.

She frowned. "Why would you want to spare him? He's a murderer."

"He's also Sofia's grandfather."

She'd forgotten about the human female Igor had sent to spy on Safe Haven.

"Ah, Sofia. You must have freed her mind as well. That's how you knew where to find Pavel."

Was the human stupid enough to plead for leniency for her grandfather? Didn't she know that he would feed her to a pompalo if it served him or Igor in any way?

Tom nodded. "I freed Sofia, and then we caught the two hybrids Igor sent to follow the tracker he put inside of her, and we questioned them as well. We learned a lot from them, but they didn't know about the compound being rigged. We learned about the explosives from Pavel."

"Is he also free of Igor's compulsion?"

"He's under mine."

"Excellent. Then he can help me."

"Indeed."

"If you had access to the compound, could you free everyone at once?"

Tom shook his head. "I might be able to do that with the humans, but the pureblooded Kra-ell are a different story. I can't thrall them. I can't even make them see illusions. The hybrids are easier, but I don't think I can free them from Igor's compulsion in one fell swoop. I'd need to do it one at a time."

That made sense, and she appreciated that he wasn't trying to make himself seem more powerful than he was.

"If you can bring your army of hybrids within a day or two, I can eliminate Valstar and the third and get everyone out of the office building. That's where the detonation button or lever or whatever it is must be. Igor lives in that building. His and Valstar's quarters are there."

"We can block the communications at the same time, so no one can notify Igor. By the way, do you know if he has an escape tunnel?"

"If there is one, he didn't tell me about it. He and his lackeys always leave and return by the front gate, but that doesn't mean that they don't have some secret tunnel somewhere."

"I thought that you hinted at it in your fable."

She shook her head. "It was just something that the crafty rat could do. It had no other meaning besides that."

"Igor is not the type who would die with his people," Tom said. "If he planned to destroy everyone if the compound was invaded by a superior force, he must have planned for a way to escape."

Jade wasn't sure about that. If the royals ever surfaced and came for Igor, he would prefer to die rather than suffer their wrath for betraying them.

But she wasn't going to tell Tom about the royal twins. To let a god know about them was a worse betrayal than what Igor had done.

"We don't have time to look for the tunnel," she said. "Once I eliminate Igor's lieutenants and take control of the office building, I'll give you the all-clear signal, and you will come in with your army. There will be some casualties, but that's unavoidable. When we have the entire compound under our control, we will wait for Igor to return and capture him." She pinned Tom with a hard stare. "He's mine to kill. Dreaming about doing that is what kept me from running away and detonating this damn collar to end my suffering."

Tom dipped his head. "I'll do my best to save him for you. But speaking of the collar, did Igor or any of his lackeys ever do anything to control people with it? Can it deliver pain?"

"It was never used to do that, so I assume it can't. It's supposed to explode and take my head off if I try to leave the hunting grounds, so in addition to explosives, it must have a location tracker as well."

4 6

TOVEN

"If the collar emits a signal, it's not going anywhere. I'm disrupting it." Toven pulled the device from a pocket in his vest and showed it to her. "That's a miniature version of the big one we will use to disrupt all communications to the compound. The guy who gave it to me can also remove the collars without causing them to explode, but we didn't bring him with us this time."

Jade tilted her head. "Why? Were you afraid that I would run and you would lose your assassin?"

"It never occurred to me that you would leave without your people. Everyone who knows you says that you are an honorable person."

That got a small smile out of her. "They probably also say that I'm a colossal bitch, and when applying human standards to females, they are right. As a Kra-ell leader, though, I've been considered fair. I took good care of my tribe, but in the end, I failed them."

She was obviously riddled with guilt, and Toven could empathize. He'd failed so many times that he'd lost count.

"We didn't bring our tech guy because we knew we weren't taking you. You need to return to the compound and keep up the pretense that you are still under Igor's compulsion and nothing has changed."

She put her hand over the metal band. "You'd better activate your big disrupter before I make my first move. What if Valstar or one of the others has the remote to my collar and can cause it to explode? And not just mine. Except for those in Igor's inner circle, all the purebloods and hybrids are forced to wear collars, but the humans are not."

Jade was right. It was a possibility that they needed to account for.

"The hybrids he sent to follow Sofia had their collars removed, but I'm sure they had trackers embedded in their bodies. Sofia had one, and we removed it."

"Makes sense. He couldn't send them into the human world wearing collars, but he needed to retain control over them."

"You'll need to signal when you are ready for us to proceed."

"What kind of signal? The only thing I can think of is starting a fire, but given that there are explosives hidden, the Mother knows where, that's not a good idea."

"What about the roof of the office building? If you can put a metal trash can up there and set a small fire inside of it, we will see the smoke rise above the trees."

She nodded. "I can put the trash can near the building, and after I secure it, I'll get it to the roof and light the fire. Or I can get Pavel to do that for me."

"That can work," Mia said. "But what if you and Kagra eliminate Igor's second and third, but you are discovered before you can light the fire? The coast will be clear for us to commence with the plan, but without the signal, we won't know that."

"Good point." Jade drummed her fingers on her knees. "Do you have a better idea? Perhaps you can give me your phone."

"Do they search you when you return from a hunt?" Toven asked.

"Regrettably, they do, and I can't bring anything into the compound. I was just joking about your phone."

"What about waving a flag or blasting music on loudspeakers?" Mia asked.

Jade shook her head. "I can't do any of that. I might be able to use Valstar's laptop to send an email to Safe Haven after I kill him, but only if it's unlocked, which I'm sure it won't be. Valstar is not stupid, and even with lust clouding his judgment, he will be suspicious when I accept his invitation."

"You can't send an email even if he leaves the laptop open," Toven said. "We will be disrupting the signal, remember?"

"I forgot. It has to be the fire, then. What about you? How will you let me know if you can't make it?"

"We can fly a military drone low over the compound. It's hard to miss."

"You'll give yourself away."

"Not necessarily. It's a Russian drone, and there is a base two hundred miles or so south of here. A drone could malfunction and veer off its course."

She nodded. "It will take me time to get everything in place, and I don't think I can be ready tomorrow, but it has to happen before Igor returns, so it has to be on Sunday."

Kian wouldn't be able to send the rest of the force earlier than that, either. Even Sunday was pushing it, but they didn't have much choice.

"Sunday will work. By the way, how many men did Igor take with him?"

"I don't know for sure, but he usually takes three. Two purebloods and one hybrid. He can compel the humans not to see his and the two purebloods' alien features, but he needs a hybrid who looks human to send on errands."

"So his compulsion has an element of shrouding," Toven said. "Interesting. My shrouding and thralling didn't work on Pavel."

Jade pursed her lips. "We can only do that to humans. It doesn't work on us. Igor can't make me see what's not there, but he can force me to act as if I'm seeing it. Speaking of Pavel, I could also use his help. Can you compel him to obey my commands?"

Toven nodded. "I will do that. What time should I expect your signal?"

"I can't give you a precise hour, but it won't be in the morning." She winced. "To get to Valstar, I need to pretend to be interested in him sexually, and it will look suspicious if I do that first thing in the morning."

"We will do our best to get everyone in position by midday," Toven said. "If we can't have everything ready in time, we will grab one of the guards at the entrance to the tunnel and send a message with him."

Jade's eyes emitted a reddish glow. "If you free tomorrow's guard from Igor's compulsion and send him to me, I can use him to send a message back." She looked around. "I'll leave a note under that tree. Would you be able to retrieve it?"

"I'd rather that you came out again. Someone can meet you here tomorrow at the same time."

She nodded. "I'll send my second. Her name is Kagra, and I will need her help. You need to remove Igor's compulsion from her as well, and if you can do it early in the morning, it would be best so I can share my plan with her."

"You need to come with her. Can you make it here at eight in the morning?"

She tilted her head. "The hour is not a problem, but why do you need me to come with her?"

"You can't tell Kagra why you're sending her, and she will wonder why you want her to go to this precise spot. Furthermore, after I confer with my team, I might have updates that you need to know about. Igor's absence changes everything."

"You have a point. And since today I was supposed to be here with Pavel, I can say that I didn't get to hunt and that I'm famished after today's activities."

"Would they buy it?"

Jade smiled. "I'm a great actress, but after two decades of denying myself, this is atypical behavior for me. They might get suspicious. That's why I suggested that Kagra come alone. And like me, she has a strong mind and can resist the compulsion to some degree. After you free her, you can tell her about your team's suggestions."

"That's not good enough. We can't take the risk of her telling someone. You have to come with her."

"You don't trust me, do you?"

"Why would you say that? I'm risking myself and my mate to help free you, and all I have to base my trust on is your people's respect for you."

She nodded. "You can trust me. I vow not to betray you, and since you claim to know so much about me, you should also know that I take my vows very seriously."

"I heard it mentioned that the Kra-ell believe in the power of vows."

"Not all Kra-ell. Igor and his misfits do not take our traditions to heart, but I do." She smiled. "I also vow that after you rescue my people, I'll tell you what I know about the history of yours."

"It's a deal." He rose to his feet and offered her his hand.

They hadn't discussed what would happen after the liberation, but it was too early for that. Toven's objective was to ensure that the Kra-ell were not a threat to the clan, and with Igor out of the way, he could compel Jade or whoever else took over the compound to cooperate with Kian and Sari.

Jade shook his offered hand. "Before I go, I'll give you a little taste of history, so you will crave more. Long before the gods learned how to traverse space, they learned how to manipulate genetics, and they turned themselves immortal. Later, that allowed them to travel to distant planets and create slave species to serve them. They combined their genetic material with that of a local animal that was advanced enough to be suitable, and at first, they made many mistakes, but they learned from them. There is a reason you can't manipulate purebloods' minds, but you can do it to hybrids and humans. The gods designed human minds to be easily manipulated, and the hybrids inherited that from their human parents." She smiled. "The rest will come after my people are free."

47

KIAN

*T*he call from Toven came at six-thirty in the morning, and after Kian put Turner and Onegus on the line, the god told them about the plan he'd hatched with Jade.

Kian groaned. "We have forty hours to get everyone in position on the other side of the globe, which includes about sixteen hours in transit. I don't think it's possible. We will have to wait for Igor to leave the compound again. I like Turner's idea of catching him with the help of facial recognition."

On the other side of the line, Turner huffed out a breath. "In Igor's absence, Valstar would take over, and we will be back to square one. We still need to invade the compound and ensure that no one blows it apart, get Toven to release everyone from Igor's compulsion, and reach a cooperation agreement with Jade. We've already sent the equipment to Russia, got an amphibian, and two drones, and we have twelve Guardians, including Yamanu and Bhathian, in place. We can make it."

"How are we going to transport everyone at once?" Kian asked. "Together with Kalugal's men, we need a plane that can carry seventy-one warriors and eighty-four exoskeletons."

"I was already working on chartering a Boeing 737. Let me get on it, and I'll have it ready for us in under six hours, and by the time they land, I will have a place for them to camp on that's close to the compound."

"I need to let the men know so they get ready," Onegus said. "We will need to load supplies for field accommodations, which means that I need to raid our emergency storage."

"Go," Kian said. "Tell Kalugal to get his men ready and keep me updated."

"I will." The chief ended the call on his side.

"There are two problems with Jade's plan," Turner said. "She can't kill Valstar, and the attack needs to be at night."

"Why can't she kill Valstar?" Toven asked. "Because of Sofia?"

Kian knew that wasn't the reason because Turner wouldn't concern himself with that. "We need him alive."

"Correct," Turner said. "If Igor calls, which I'm sure he does every so often when he's away, he will expect Valstar to answer. If the communication is down for more than a few hours, or if his second is not available to answer him, he will know that something is up, and he won't show up. Jade needs to incapacitate Valstar, but not kill him. After we take control of the compound, you need to compel him to sing the tune we want him to sing, and he will await Igor's call with our special earpiece glued to his ears and someone standing over him with an ax."

Toven groaned. "Jade is not going to like it."

"She's going to like Igor escaping even less," Turner said. "She can kill Valstar later, along with Igor. When you meet her again tomorrow, make sure she understands."

"What about the timing?" Toven said. "Does it need to happen at night because we can't get everyone in position in time?"

"Although giving ourselves a few more hours to get ready is a definite plus, that's not the reason. At night, the office building will be vacant, the humans will be asleep, and so will most of the purebloods and hybrids, except for those on guard and patrol duty. It will make the task easier."

"The problem is Igor," Toven said. "He's supposed to return Monday, but Jade says that he might come back earlier. That's why she wanted to do it Sunday at two in the afternoon. Also, after we take over, I will need to compel everyone in the compound before we restore communications, and we are talking about over three hundred people. That might take all night."

"Only about two hundred and fifty are adults, and about a third of them are human. After you free them from Igor's compulsion, we can delegate the task of compelling the humans, the hybrids, and the children to say what we need them to say to our four other compellers. They can do that remotely from here. You will only have to compel the adult purebloods."

"You can't seriously suggest that we use Parker," Kian said.

"He'll be less intimidating to the children."

He had a point. "I'll have to get Vivian and Magnus's permission, but since most of the children probably don't speak English, I doubt Parker would be able to compel them."

"That could be an issue," Turner said.

"What time at night should we schedule the attack for?" Toven asked.

"Two o'clock Monday morning, " Turner said. "The humans will be out of the way in their quarters, and most of the hybrids and purebloods will be asleep as well. Another advantage of doing it then is that Igor probably won't call his second in the middle of the night. It simplifies the entire operation."

Kian had to agree. "Anything else that you wish to add?" he asked.

"For now, that's it. You can continue without me, and if I think of anything else, I'll let you know." Turner terminated the call on his side.

Left only with Toven, Kian let out a breath. "What's your impression of Jade? Can we forge an alliance with her?"

"She's tough and abrasive, but she's honorable and cares for her people. Unlike Igor, she's precisely the type that would go down with the ship, which makes her a much better option as the leader of that community. She also knows our history."

Kian's breath caught. "What did she tell you?"

"Jade hates the gods passionately. It took her a while to trust me, and she did only after she spoke to Emmett. She says that the gods twist the truth and rewrite history as it suits them to make themselves look good. She didn't elaborate on whether they do that for interior consumption of their own population or to impress others. She also claims that the gods designed humans to be susceptible to thralling and compulsion so they could be easily controlled."

Kian had suspected that for a long time.

"Does that surprise you?"

"Frankly, it does. I guess the misinformation Jade mentioned was successfully employed by my father and uncle and the rest of the original gods. They convinced us that they were the good guys, spreading civilization, establishing just laws, and bringing prosperity to humans."

"You're too smart to have bought the lies."

Toven chuckled. "Those were not lies. The gods were actually striving to do that. The lie was that they had always been like that. But you are right. I was suspicious. I had an older brother who had been one of the original gods, and he taunted me, hinting about my naïveté left and right. I thought it was his way of tormenting me. Mortdh resented me for being our father's favorite son."

Ekin had been a scientist and an inventor, and Toven was a scholar, a philosopher, and an explorer. Mortdh had been the only one with political aspirations.

"You were more like Ekin than Mortdh was, in intellect as well as in temperament. Well, except for the womanizing. Ekin was legendary in his relentless pursuit of ladies regardless of their mated status."

Toven laughed. "He was, and most of those legends were true. The only one that was a total fabrication was that he wanted to get his half-sister pregnant. That never happened."

"My mother told me that it was common among the gods. As long as the mothers were not related, it was fine to mate a half-sister, even encouraged."

"Athor was a scientist herself, a geneticist, and for a goddess, she wasn't very attractive. She had her human servants to have fun with, and she wouldn't have allowed Ekin anywhere near her."

"Speaking of attractiveness, what does Jade look like?"

"She doesn't look significantly more alien than Aliya, and she could be considered attractive by those who like their women super bossy, abrasive, and intimidating." He chuckled. "She's you, just prettier."

"I don't know what's more offensive, your insinuation that I'm bossy and abrasive or that I'm not good-looking enough."

For a moment, the god didn't respond, probably trying to figure out whether Kian had really been offended or was just teasing.

"I hope you're not serious," Toven said.

"I'm not. Have you spoken with William?"

"Not yet. I called you first."

"I'll call him. A lot depends on whether he can have his equipment ready in time for Sunday."

48

SOFIA

"Sofia." Marcel put his hand on her shoulder. "Wake up, love."

She bolted upright. "What's happening? Did they talk to Jade?"

Worried about the meeting between Toven and Jade, she'd spent most of the night tossing and turning, finally falling asleep when it was already light outside.

The worry was not only about the outcome. It was also about whether it would even happen and whether Toven was walking into a trap.

Nevertheless, the rush of adrenaline burned through the grogginess, and she was instantly wide awake.

"They did. Shai is on the line with the details, and later Kian wants to talk to you."

"Okay." She pulled the blanket up to her chin.

Marcel turned the speaker on. "Go ahead, Shai."

"Good morning, Sofia. Kian is extremely busy organizing the mission, and he asked me to give you an update."

"I appreciate it."

"Here is what's going to happen over the next forty-eight hours."

When he was done, Sofia's chest felt so tight that she could barely breathe. "Jade is going to kill my grandfather?"

"Toven will try to convince her to hold off until after we take over the compound," Shai said. "We need him alive to capture Igor, but she's not going to show him mercy once Igor is caught. According to her, he's a murderer and doesn't deserve leniency."

"I don't get it," Marcel said. "With Igor out of the compound, Valstar is no doubt in charge of the trigger to detonate the explosives. We can't risk leaving him alive."

Sofia shuddered.

She understood the need to eliminate the threat to everyone in the compound but the callous way they talked about killing her grandfather was disturbing, to say the least.

"Toven will speak with Jade tomorrow and tell her about the change of plans," Shai said. "She will need to incapacitate Valstar until Toven can take control of his mind. The question is will she listen, and if she does, will she be able to incapacitate him without killing him. If the answer is no, we will not restore communications to the compound and hope that Igor will return despite not being able to contact anyone there. But in either case, Valstar's demise is imminent. Once everyone's minds are free, Jade will not be the only one who wants him to pay for his crimes."

As another cold shiver pulsed through Sofia's body, Marcel took her trembling hand and gave it a reassuring squeeze.

Valstar's impending demise wasn't the only reason for the tremor, though. He might have contributed his genetic material to her creation, but he wasn't real family to her.

Sofia was worried about the ones she couldn't contemplate losing, and she couldn't stay in Safe Haven while everyone she cared for was in mortal danger.

"I want to be there for my family. Once the compound is freed, they will be confused, and having me there will reassure them."

"Hold on one second. Kian wants to talk to you."

"I'm sorry about your grandfather," Kian said, surprising her. She had never met him, but he didn't sound like the empathic type, and yet he'd been the only one who'd bothered to say that.

"Yeah, me too. I wish things were different, but I can't change who he is."

"True. I'm also sorry about denying your request to go to Karelia. We need you to keep the pretense up."

"I can call him right now, I mean, after I get to my regular spot, so he won't expect me to call tomorrow, and by Sunday, it will all be over, one way or another. Please, I need to be there."

Kian didn't answer right away, and the second or two that it had taken him to respond seemed to last an eternity. "You have a valid point, but it's a logistic nightmare to get you and Marcel to St. Petersburg. The force leaves for the airstrip in three hours, so even if I send a jet to pick you up, you won't make it on time."

"We can fly commercial," Marcel said. "I'll book us a flight to St. Petersburg, and we will join the force there."

"They are going directly to the campsite Turner secured for them. They are not staying in a hotel, and good luck finding a flight that will get you there on time."

"Eric can fly them," Shai said in the background.

"Darlene is transitioning," Kian said. "Do you really think that he would leave her side?"

"Let me check with him. If he agrees to fly Sofia and Marcel, he can pick them up in Portland and continue from there."

"Thank you, Shai," Marcel said.

"Don't thank me yet. I didn't get Eric to agree yet, and Kian is probably right."

"I'm always right," Kian grumbled. "You should talk to Valstar as soon as you can and get ready to leave on a moment's notice." The line went silent.

Sofia jumped out of bed. "I'll get dressed and pack my bag. Do you have warm clothing? It's cold out there this time of year."

"Don't worry about me." Marcel pulled her into his arms for a quick hug. "I'll make us coffee and something to eat."

She lifted her lips to his. "You're the best."

"So are you."

Twenty minutes later, they met with Eleanor and Cecelia at the beach.

"Lots of excitement, eh?" Eleanor patted the cat. "Do you want to hold her?"

Sofia shook her head. "I'm too nervous."

"That's why you should pet her. It's relaxing."

"I don't think it will help this time. Who is Darlene?"

Eleanor glanced at Marcel. "Why are we talking about Darlene?"

"Shai told us that he would ask Eric if he could fly us to Russia, but since Darlene is transitioning, that's not likely." He turned to Sofia. "Darlene is Toven's granddaughter, but he didn't know that he had grandchildren until recently. She met a nice guy who's a pilot, and without bothering you with too many details, he induced her, and she's in the process of transitioning. But since she's older, it's not going as smoothly as yours will."

Apparently, she wasn't the only one with a lousy grandfather. Tom also didn't care much about his granddaughter if he was on the other side of the globe while she was transitioning.

"I see." Sofia wrapped her arms around herself. "Shouldn't Tom be with Darlene when she's fighting for her life?"

"I'm sure he wants to be there for her," Eleanor said. "But since he's the only one who can overcome Igor's compulsion, he doesn't have much choice. He felt that it was up to him to free Jade and the rest of your people. Besides, Darlene is in good hands. She has her mate with her, and the clan doctor is supervising her transition."

567

49

MARCEL

arcel had been expecting Shai to call back during their walk to Sofia's spot on the beach, but when they reached their destination and Shai still hadn't called, he turned the ringer off on his phone, and Eleanor did the same.

"Tell me what you are going to talk about with Valstar," Eleanor said as he handed Sofia the pendant to make the call.

Marcel listened with half an ear as Eleanor did her regular routine of compelling Sofia to stick to a pre-agreed script. When it was done, he and Eleanor put in their earpieces, which were in translation mode so they could understand Sofia's conversation with her grandfather.

Taking a deep breath, Sofia opened the pendant, pulled out the earpiece, and activated the device.

Valstar didn't answer right away like he usually did. "Sofia. I didn't expect a call from you today. Do you have news for me?"

"My condition is getting worse. The doctor says that I need an open heart surgery."

"That's very unfortunate, but it is not something that I can help you with."

Hearing the guy's answer spoken in a machine voice made him sound apathetic, and since Sofia heard the delivery in the same voice, her impression must also be the same.

"There is something you can do. It will help me tremendously to have my father with me. Can you let him know that I'm going to have an operation and send him here? I'll pay for his airfare, of course."

"I can't make a decision like that without Igor's permission, and he's not here at the moment. Call me again tomorrow."

Marcel tensed. Was Igor returning earlier than expected?

The panic in Sofia's eyes conveyed the same fear. "I might not be able to call tomorrow."

"Then call when you can. When is the operation?"

"Next week on Wednesday."

"Then you have plenty of time."

"Will Igor be back by tomorrow?" she asked.

"That's none of your business. I'll ask him when he calls, but I doubt he'll agree. Your father has never left the compound before, and it's not safe for him to travel alone."

As if Valstar was concerned with Sofia's father's safety.

The good news, though, was that Valstar had just confirmed that Igor wasn't returning to the compound the next day.

"Please, can you ask him anyway? Maybe he will show compassion for me. I might not make it through this operation."

"You are a strong girl, Sofia. You will survive. Be well." He ended the call on his side.

With a sigh, Sofia deactivated the device and put the tiny earpiece inside the pendant. "I got scared there for a moment. He sounded as if Igor was returning shortly."

Marcel wrapped his arms around her and ran small soothing circles on her back. "Valstar didn't sound like he didn't care. The machine voice eliminates the nuances of tonality, but what he said wasn't that bad. He called you strong and wished you well."

"Valstar was polite. Igor is polite as well. That doesn't make either of them any less of a monster." Sofia pulled out of his arms. "Check your phone. Shai might have tried to call you."

Marcel had put the device in vibrate mode, but he'd been distracted by Sofia's distress, and when he checked, there was indeed a missed call from Shai, and he returned it immediately.

"I'm sorry about not picking up before. Sofia was speaking with Valstar, and we needed to maintain silence. Did Eric agree?"

"I went to the clinic to speak with Eric, but Kian was right, and Eric doesn't want to leave Darlene's side unless it's a life and death situation, which it's not. But a better solution presented itself. The Clan Mother was visiting Darlene, and when she heard us talking, she offered her jet along with her pilot. He can pick you up from Eugene Airport and fly you to St. Petersburg."

"I don't know what to say. It's so incredibly generous of the Clan Mother. I need to call her and thank her in person."

"You should. Her Odu is already on his way to the airstrip. You also should hurry up and get a ride to the airport." He chuckled. "I have a feeling that you will get to Russia before the Guardians."

"Thank you, Shai."

"You're welcome." He ended the call.

"What did he say?" Sofia asked as Marcel returned the phone to his pocket.

"The Clan Mother is loaning us her private jet along with her pilot."

Sofia's eyes widened. "That's incredible. Why would she be so generous toward someone she's never met?"

"Because she has a huge heart." Marcel wrapped his arm around Sofia's waist. "Have you ever flown on a private jet?"

"Are you kidding me? The first time I flew was when I came here, and I sat in the middle seat in basic economy, squeezed between two large men. It wasn't fun."

Eleanor snorted. "From a virgin flyer to a member of the mile-high club. You sure move up quickly, doll."

"What's the mile-high club?"

"I'll let Marcel explain." Smirking, Eleanor scratched Cecilia's ear and kept walking.

5 0

SOFIA

*T*hey made it to the airport almost an hour before the Clan Mother's plane landed, so they had time to grab a bite to eat in the coffee shop.

"I assume that there will be no food served on the flight." Sofia nibbled on the muffin Marcel had gotten for her.

"I don't know. I've never flown on the Clan Mother's jet." Marcel still looked a little shell-shocked. "I don't think she's let anyone other than her children use it before. You have no idea what an honor it is."

"I do." She stuffed another bite into her mouth. "I'm so hyped up that I don't know what I'm feeling. I'm terrified of what's going to happen, I'm excited about flying on an executive jet like some movie star, and I want to join the mile-high club, but I wouldn't dare do it on the Clan Mother's property."

That got a smile out of Marcel. "Yeah, the same thought crossed my mind."

As they walked onto the field, the door opened out, forming stairs, and a guy who looked like a butler rushed down to greet them.

"Good afternoon, Mistress Sofia, Master Marcel." He took their luggage and ran up the stairs with a suitcase in each hand as if they weighed nothing.

Sofia leaned closer to Marcel's ear. "You said that there was not going to be service on the plane, but it seems like your Clan Mother sent her butler along as well."

He chuckled. "Oshidu is the pilot. He's also a butler, but since he can't do both at the same time, he's only going to pilot the plane."

"Are you sure that he knows what he's doing?" She started up the stairs.

"Don't worry. He's been piloting this jet for many years. The Clan Mother travels extensively, and she doesn't fly commercial."

There were only four seats inside the small cabin, but they were wide and plush and could be turned into comfortable beds.

"There are pillows and blankets in the overhead compartments," said the pilot, who looked like a butler. "The middle console houses an assortment of drinks, and I took the liberty of collecting several sandwiches and pastries from the café so you wouldn't go hungry on the way."

"Thank you, Oshidu." Marcel smiled. "I appreciate your thoughtfulness."

The guy grinned, and it kind of looked fake. "You are very welcome, Master Marcel. The flight will take fourteen hours. I shall see you again after we land. Enjoy." He dipped his head and pivoted on his heel.

Sofia waited until the pilot was in his seat. "Are we stopping to refuel somewhere?" she whispered. "How is he going to stay focused for so long?"

"Don't worry about him." Marcel opened the center console and looked inside. "What's your pleasure?"

"Is there wine?"

"There is." He pulled out a bottle and two glasses.

"Please, buckle up," the pilot said. "We are starting to move."

Sofia found the seatbelt, secured it around her middle, and glanced at the pilot again. "I guess the mile-high club is not an option. There is no partition between Oshidu and us. By the way, is Oshidu Japanese?"

Marcel chuckled. "Does he look Japanese?"

"Not really, but he has the kind of features that could pass for anyone of mixed heritage."

"I guess he does, but he's not Japanese."

"So why does he have a Japanese name?"

"It's not Japanese." Marcel was starting to sound exasperated.

"I'm sorry. I know that I talk too much when I'm nervous."

He leaned and took her hand. "That's okay. I like hearing you talk. You are curious, and you get excited over the most mundane things. You're not reserved, and you're not pretending to be anyone other than yourself, and I find that endearing."

She huffed out a laugh. "I'm the progeny of aliens, I grew up in a secluded compound, and while attending university, which was throughout my entire adult life, I was pretending to be like the other humans around me."

"That's not the same. You had to hide those things, but you've always been genuine. You might hide who you are, but you don't hide your feelings, and you're not embarrassed about voicing your opinions. When you're mad, you are not trying to hide it, and when you fall in love, you have the courage to admit it. You show the world the real you at all times." He lifted her hand to his lips and brushed kisses over her knuckles. "In summary, you are wonderful, and I feel blessed to have you as my mate."

Sofia swallowed. It was still difficult for her to hear him say that without a smidgen of fear creeping into her heart.

Would he still call her his mate when she didn't transition? Or when she transitioned and grew a pair of fangs and became stronger than him?

51

ANNANI

"Good evening," Syssi said as she opened the door for Annani.

"Good evening, my dear." Annani motioned for her to dip her head so she could kiss her cheek. "I am so glad that we are still having our Friday night family dinner despite the stressful situation."

Syssi chuckled. "If I canceled it every time something came up, we would have it only on rare occasions."

A smile tugged on Annani's lips. "I knew that the Fates had chosen wisely for my son—a mate who is steadfast and does not crumble under pressure."

"Good evening, Mother." Kian walked up to her and dipped his head to touch his lips to her cheek. "Thank you again for loaning the use of your plane and Oshidu to Sofia and Marcel."

She nodded. "When I heard Shai tell Eric that she has a human family in the compound who she cares deeply about, I was moved." She sat down on the chair he pulled out for her and smiled at her granddaughter.

Seated in a high chair, Allegra was playing on a tablet with her little face scrunched in concentration.

"Should a child this young handle such a device?"

Kian smiled at his daughter. "Allegra gets bored playing with inanimate objects. If she has a playmate, she doesn't mind the old boring toys, but when she doesn't, they don't provide enough stimulation. Syssi has been hesitant to let her play with electronics at such a young age, but you know Allegra. When she wants something, she gets it."

Syssi affected an apologetic expression. "I downloaded an application that is designed for babies nine months and older. She loves it."

The little girl lifted her head and gave Annani a bright smile. "Na-na."

"Yes, my love. Nana is here."

"Da-da," Allegra said with a resolute tone and went back to her tablet.

Annani laughed. "She communicates very clearly. She said hello and then told me to talk to Daddy."

As Syssi went to open the door for more dinner guests, Kian sat down next to Annani and brought his chair closer. "Thank you for helping Darlene pull through. I'm sure that Toven is grateful."

"He is. He called me to ask about Darlene's progress, and he also called Geraldine and Eric. He is very concerned about his granddaughter."

Kian frowned. "Is there a reason for concern? I thought she was doing fine."

"Bridget assures us that Darlene is doing great, but Toven hoped that she would transition more easily. He is disappointed that the potent godly blood flowing in her veins is not giving her a more significant advantage over other transitioning Dormants."

As Amanda and Dalhu entered with Evie in a baby carrier, and Kian pushed to his feet and walked over to greet them, Annani shifted her attention back to Allegra.

She was not an ordinary child, and Annani was not the kind of grandmother who saw greatness in all of her grandchildren and great-grandchildren. She had hundreds, and she followed their lives as closely as she could. She loved them all, but that did not mean that she believed they all were destined for greatness.

Allegra would one day lead the clan. Not because she was Kian's daughter but because she was a natural leader.

After all the guests had arrived, everyone had greeted everyone else, and Okidu had served the first course, the topic of conversation had naturally moved to the mission in Karelia.

"I should have joined the force," Orion said.

Alena put her hand on his shoulder. "You can't leave your pregnant mate alone. Besides, someone needs to stay and defend the village, right?" She looked at Kian.

"Absolutely. The reserve Guardians and the remainder of Kalugal's men are meeting in the gym tomorrow morning at seven for a briefing with Onegus. You are welcome to join them."

"I will. Thank you for telling me."

No one around the table missed the note of sarcasm in Orion's voice, including Kian.

"I didn't tell you about the meeting before because you don't really need to join the training. If Fates forbid we are attacked, you will serve us best with your compulsion ability."

Orion nodded. "You are right. Perhaps I should practice with Kalugal combining our powers. Each of us has a slightly different aspect of the ability."

"That's an interesting observation," Kian said. "You and Kalugal can compel people to forget things, but Toven, who is much more powerful than both of you, cannot."

"I didn't know that." Orion rubbed a hand over his jaw. "I'm immune, so I didn't experience his compulsion."

Annani smiled. "It reminds me of something Kaia told me about gene expression. I did not understand most of what she said, but I understood that the same genetic combination can produce different results under different conditions. You might have inherited compulsion ability from a common ancestor, but it expresses itself differently in each of you."

"The same is true for you, Mother," Amanda said. "You share the same common ancestor. Your paternal grandfather must have been a powerful compeller." She sighed. "It's a shame that none of your children inherited the ability. I would have loved to be able to compel."

5 2

JADE

"*W*hy do we need to go hunting so early?" Kagra walked beside Jade toward the security office.

"Because I'm hungry, and yesterday you seemed eager to go."

"That was noon, now it's six in the morning, and it's Saturday. I don't get up at dawn on weekends."

"You don't get up at dawn on weekdays either, but the early hours of the morning are the best for training, which I decided to step up for you."

"What's the point? It's not as if I'm going to lead my own tribe one day."

Jade cast her a sidelong glance. "You never know what the future will bring, and it's best to be prepared for the best possible outcome."

Weekends were nothing special in the compound, and everyone continued performing their duties, but there were no classes for the children, so Jade's time was free, and she usually spent it training with Kagra, but today it wasn't about that.

Today, Kagra would be set free.

"Good morning." The hybrid on duty gave her a once-over. "Going hunting so early?"

The rumor about her so-called hunting with Pavel had spread, probably thanks to Pavel himself, and the result was much more attention from all the purebloods that she could do without.

The hybrids knew that they had no chance with her, so they just gave her covetous looks, but this one was more daring than the others.

She looked down her nose at him. "I don't waste time on more sleep than is absolutely necessary to maintain my health."

The guard looked at the schedule. "I see that you went hunting yesterday."

She narrowed her eyes at him. "Yesterday's hunt was about fresh blood, but not the kind that fills my belly."

"So I've heard." He gave her a suggestive look as he handed her two badges. "Good hunting."

Nodding, she handed Kagra one of the badges, affixed the other one to her jacket, and turned on her booted heel.

"It wouldn't kill you to say thank you from time to time," Kagra grumbled.

Today, it actually might, but Jade said nothing. The dismissive behavior was what everyone expected from her, and she'd already acted out of character by accepting Pavel's invitation.

Halfway to the gate they were intercepted by Valstar, and he didn't look happy.

"I heard that you met up with Pavel yesterday," he said as if she owed him an explanation. "While I waited for you."

"It wasn't while you waited for me." She sauntered over to him and put her hand on his chest. "It was in the afternoon. I prefer to sleep at night and perform strenuous activities while my energy levels are high. Besides, I figured I'd spare you Igor's wrath. Are you really brave enough to issue an invitation to his prime?"

Hopefully, Valstar would take the bait.

"Igor doesn't care who you fuck when you're not fertile. Come to my room this afternoon."

He was so predictable that it was pathetic.

She smiled to bare her fangs at him. "I have plans for today. But if you are free tomorrow, I might accept your invitation."

His eyes blazed red. "Two o'clock. Be there this time."

"Noon. I have a training session with Drova at four, and I don't want to rush." She trailed her hand down his stomach, halting just above his bulge.

"Noon works too." Valstar looked her over with lust clouding his eyes. "Wear something nice."

When he walked away, Kagra gaped at her. "What's going on, Jade? You detest Valstar almost as much as you abhor Igor."

"Actually, I detest him more." She waited for the guard to check her badge and open the gate for her. "Igor is a sociopath, which means that he doesn't feel anything, and he doesn't take pleasure in killing. Valstar enjoys it."

"So why did you accept his invitation?"

"I have my reasons." Jade walked out the gate.

She was going to kill him, and he'd just made it easier for her.

"Which you usually share with me. Yesterday you met Pavel, and you promised to tell me how it was, but all I got was one word. And today, you accepted an invitation from Valstar of all people. Was Pavel that bad?"

She hadn't seen Pavel until later that day, and he could barely speak with the power of Tom's compulsion acting like a gag. But he managed to communicate that she could count on him and that it wasn't only because he was forced to aid her.

Perhaps once he'd been freed from Igor's compulsion, the young male's natural Kra-ell instincts had come back online, and he'd accepted her authority over him.

They were still within sight of the guard tower though, and if she told Kagra the truth now, her second might do something that would betray her. It was better to save all the explanations for when they reached the meeting place with Tom. That was why she planned on arriving there half an hour early.

In the meantime, she needed to perpetuate the lie for Kagra's ears and possibly for the ears of the guards in the tower.

"Pavel was fine, but I should have known better than to accept a kid's invitation. I need someone more mature and stronger."

"And Valstar is it? Almost any of the other purebloods would have been better."

Jade shrugged. "I know him well, and I know that it will irk Igor despite what he says about me being free to fuck whoever I want when I'm not fertile."

Kagra shook her head. "I think that you finally snapped. This is not you."

"Maybe I am losing my mind." She cast Kagra a sidelong smile. "A good run will clear my head." She broke into an easy jog. "Are you up for a race this early in the morning? Or do you concede defeat before we even start?"

Kagra grinned. "What do I get if I win?"

"The satisfaction of finally besting me, but you're not going to win."

"We will see about that." Kagra sprinted ahead.

53

TOVEN

*T*he preparations for today's meeting had been just as extensive as the day before, with Yamanu flying a small surveillance drone over the area where the three rivers crossed and a group of Guardians scoping it on foot ahead of time.

Yamanu had reported that Jade and another female had arrived half an hour or so earlier and that it didn't seem as if anyone had followed them to the remote spot.

Still, as Toven ran through the woods with Mia strapped on his back, he was more apprehensive than he had been yesterday.

The drone was limited in what it could see under the canopy of trees, and the Guardians could be overwhelmed by a large force. Jade could have been caught doing something out of character that raised suspicion, and Pavel could have talked despite the compulsion, although that was highly unlikely.

Toven's powers of compulsion seemed to work just fine on the purebloods, which meant that he could freeze attackers with a command to stand down, but he didn't know how many Kra-ell minds he could seize at once.

Jade and her second were already there when he arrived, and given that the other female wasn't panicking, Jade had warned her about his arrival.

"Hello." He stopped right in front of them and activated the disrupter.

"Hi." The female named Kagra looked at him with her enormous eyes. "I've never seen a god before. You look human, just prettier." She shifted her gaze to Mia. "Are you a goddess?"

"I'm just an immortal." She extended her hand to Kagra. "My name is Mia."

"What happened to your legs?" Kagra said as she shook it. "Did you lose them in battle?"

There had been no pity in her voice, just curiosity.

"In a way, yes. It was done to save my life. I'm regrowing them."

Kagra tilted her head in puzzlement. "Only gods can do that."

"Immortals can do it as well." Toven shifted his gaze to Jade. "What did you tell her so far?"

"I couldn't risk telling Kagra anything until we got here, and when I told her the plan, she had so many questions that I didn't have time to tell her about your sidekick."

"I'm not his sidekick," Mia grumbled. "I'm his mate."

"I meant no disrespect." Jade dipped her head. "I thought that was what humans called their assistants."

"No harm done," Toven interrupted. "Well, that's only true about the sidekick comment. You shouldn't have told Kagra anything without the disrupter, but that's my fault. I failed to warn you not to say anything without me being present."

Toven was starting to realize that he wasn't well-suited for this modern-day style of battle with listening devices, trackers, and collars that could explode. His power of compulsion was necessary for this mission, but they should have given him a tech-savvy sidekick.

Jade didn't look concerned. "The collars are not transmitting or recording our conversations. I told Kagra about contacting Veskar, or Emmett as you call him, long before I actually did it, and Igor never confronted me about it until I entered the writing competition."

"I hope you're right about that."

"I am." She turned to Kagra. "This is the moment you've been waiting for since we were captured. Tom is going to release you from Igor's compulsion."

The woman nodded and stepped forward. "I'm ready."

Toven looked into her eyes. "You no longer have to obey Igor's commands in any way. You are free to act and talk as you will." He gave her an encouraging smile. "Go ahead. Say something that you couldn't say before."

She put her hand on her chest. "I feel it in here. The oily feeling is gone." She took in a deep breath. "I want to tear Igor and his cohorts limb from limb for killing most of my tribe and enslaving the rest of us." She smiled brilliantly. "It's the oddest thing to feel happy about, but you have no idea how liberating it is to actually say that to someone who doesn't already know about it. Thank you."

"You're welcome."

He had known about her tribe, but she hadn't known that he had.

Jade clapped Kagra on her back. "Now, you can help me bring Igor and the rest of them down." She turned to Toven. "Valstar is waiting for me to come to his quarters at noon tomorrow. He expects sex, but he's only going to get the fight for dominance part, and I'm going to end him. Kagra is going to take care of the third, and Pavel is going to help secure the office building."

"About that." Toven sat down on the ground. "You can't kill Valstar before we capture Igor. He probably calls his second every so often, and if he gets no answer, he's not going to return. We also have to change the time of the attack to two o'clock at night instead of two in the afternoon."

When Jade bared her fangs, he lifted his hand to stop her from arguing. "You have to incapacitate Valstar so he can't trigger the explosives when we attack, and that needs to hold until I can get to him. Once we capture Igor, you can do with him as you please."

"I don't like it, but I can understand the logic of leaving Valstar alive until we capture Igor. Why the change of time, though? It's really pushing it too close for comfort." She sat on the ground, and Kagra followed her example.

"With most of the compound population asleep, and the children and humans out of the way, our task will be much easier."

Jade let out a breath. "I'll have to change my plans with Valstar."

"Is that a problem?" Mia asked.

"It is, but I'll come up with some excuse. He's so eager to get me in his bed that he will overlook the warning signs." She looked at Toven. "I assume that you plan to compel Valstar to tell Igor that everything is okay."

He nodded.

"You will have to restore the compound's communication."

"Correct. Once we have the compound secure and I'm done compelling everyone, we will stop disrupting the signal, and when Igor calls, Valstar will tell him that there was a malfunction. But since it will all happen at night, Igor might not call at all."

Jade's enormous smart eyes bored into him. "It's not going to work unless you can compel the entire population of the compound all at once, and even Igor can't do that. Perhaps the humans can be compelled as a group, but I wouldn't risk it. I think that Igor compels each person individually and then reinforces it with his public speeches."

"You think, or you know?" Mia asked.

"I think. He doesn't share his methods with me, and I don't spend that much time around him."

"I was led to believe that the community has limited access to phones and computers," Toven said. "Why do we need to compel everyone at once? Perhaps I can compel just the key players, and we can lock the rest of them up somewhere secure until we trap Igor."

"It's true that the only phones and computers inside the compound are in the office building, but I'm sure that Igor has snitches who have a way to contact him, and I don't know who they are. They might be hybrid, human, and pureblood. Probably a couple of each."

Toven let out a breath. "It means that we will have to keep the disrupter running until I compel them all."

"It will take all night, and if Igor calls and can't get through, he will get suspicious. Even if it takes you only one minute to compel each person, and you don't take any rests in between, that's over three hundred minutes."

It would have taken him much longer than that if not for Turner's idea of delegating the second half of the process to the clan's other compellers. His tasks would be to free them from Igor's compulsion and compel them to listen to the instructions of the other compellers.

"I can make it work," Toven said. "As long as Igor can get to Valstar before heading back to the compound, and he is told the communication disruption was just a malfunction, he will be reassured that everything is back to normal."

Jade shook her head. "He will know that something is up. Igor is very thorough. He probably has a contingency for such an event, like sending someone to a nearby town to call him and let him know about the malfunction. That's what I would have done, and I'm not nearly as paranoid as Igor."

Toven shifted to a more comfortable position. "If there is a contingency plan like that, it's even more important to keep Valstar alive. I can get him to tell me what the plan is, and we can do that. In fact, I hope that they have that contingency. Igor will not suspect that someone found a way to use it against him."

Jade let out a breath. "Everything you say makes sense, but I know in my gut that I need to kill Valstar and not just incapacitate him."

Kagra frowned at Jade. "How are you even going to overpower him? Can you compel him?"

"I'm not sure. I've never had the chance to try, but being Igor's second, Valstar must be a strong compeller. That being said, I don't need to compel him to overpower him." Jade's savage grin was chilling. "I'm going to drug him. Pavel already got me a large dose from the human chemist. It's not going to kill Valstar, but it will weaken him and slow his reflexes. I'm going to drain him until his heart stops and watch the horror in his eyes as he realizes what's happening."

Bile rose in Toven's throat, but he forced it down and swallowed.

Jade noticed. "What's the matter, pretty boy? Too savage for you? Would you prefer that I used a more civilized weapon to end the bastard who murdered my sons?"

"Not at all. It's your kill, and you have the right to end him any way you please. He doesn't deserve mercy from you. But if you want to capture Igor, you'll need to postpone your revenge by one more day. Can you half-drain him? Would that incapacitate him?"

Jade nodded.

"I can do the same to his third," Kagra said. "In case Igor wants to verify that what Valstar is telling him is true, you should also compel Durmar, Igor's third."

54

DARLENE

$\mathcal{A}$ s Darlene became aware of the subtle sounds the medical equipment was making, she knew where she was and why, but not how long. She had been slipping in and out of consciousness, but she had no concept of time.

Had it been a day? Two? Maybe more?

She remembered waking up and talking to Eric, her mother, her son, and her sister, and she also remembered the goddess standing next to her bed and smiling down at her, but that could have been a dream.

Toven had promised to give her his blessings to help her along, but she hadn't even dreamt about him.

As Darlene's mind became more focused, she remembered Eric reminding her about a mission that Toven had accepted. Annani had taken his place, which explained the memory of the goddess being in her room. The Clan Mother had come to bless her because Toven wasn't there.

Forcing her eyelids to lift, Darlene was greeted by her mother's smiling face. "Good morning, my sweet girl." Geraldine leaned over and kissed Darlene's forehead. "I hope that today you will stay awake for longer than a few minutes."

"How long have I been here?" Darlene whispered.

Geraldine smiled. "You ask the same question every time you wake up. Your transition started on Tuesday, and today is Saturday." Her mother wetted her lips with an ice cube. "Bridget doesn't allow me to give you water to drink. She says that you need to be awake for longer than a few moments."

Darlene licked the droplets of water from her lips. "Can you do it again?"

"Sure."

When she was done licking the scant moisture from her lips, she asked, "Where is Eric?"

"He went to the cafeteria to get us something to eat. He'll be sorry to have missed you being awake. I should call him."

"Don't. He needs a break."

Geraldine nodded. "He's with you twenty-four-seven. Shai tried to convince him to help out with the mission the whole village is buzzing about and fly some people over, but Eric declined. Luckily, the Clan Mother overheard them talking and volunteered her own jet with one of her Odus."

"That's nice of her." Darlene closed her eyes. "I remember Eric reading a steamy romance to me, but it wasn't one of mine. Did I dream it?"

Her mother giggled. "It's mine. He asked me to bring him a book to read to you, and he wanted it to be hot. He said that you read him a steamy romance when he was in a coma."

"I did, but he doesn't actually remember me doing that. I'm sure that it helped, though."

"Do you want me to read to you?" Geraldine asked.

"Tell me about the mission. What's the news on that?"

Her mother smiled indulgently. "It's still very hush-hush, and I'm not supposed to know anything, but Shai tells me bits and pieces. You'll probably slip away before I'm done, but fine."

Since the story sounded somewhat familiar, Darlene assumed that she'd heard it before. Maybe Eric and Annani had talked about it next to her, and she'd retained some of it.

Geraldine was nearing the end of the story when the door opened, and Eric walked in with a big brown bag and a tray with two cups of coffee.

"You're awake." He cast Geraldine an accusing glance. "Why didn't you call me?"

"I told her not to," Darlene said. "Come and give me a kiss."

As he handed her mother the bag and the tray and leaned over the bed, Darlene managed to lift her arms and embrace him. "I love you so much."

He looked into her eyes and smiled. "I love you more."

"Uh-uh. I love you more."

He caressed her cheek. "You seem to have more energy than you had the other times you woke up. You're more focused too."

Darlene frowned. "I feel good, and that coffee smells divine. Do you think you can give me some and not tell Bridget?"

He turned his head and looked at the open door. "She'll have my head. But there is nothing I won't do for you."

Darlene licked her lips again, this time in anticipation of a taste of coffee.

Her mother gave Eric a reproachful look, but she didn't argue when he took one of the paper cups off the tray, added cream and sugar, and stirred.

"Maybe that's the magic potion that will keep you awake."

He pressed a button on the remote, and the back of the bed lifted, bringing Darlene to a semi-reclining position.

"No wonder I was unconscious for four and a half days. I didn't have my morning coffee."

Eric brought the cup to her lips. "It's not too hot, but drink carefully and only a little. I'm sure that water would have been better, but you and I are rebels, right?" He winked at her.

Her heart swelled with so much love for him that it felt too big for her ribcage.

Taking a small sip, she sighed in bliss and then took two more before Eric took the cup away. "That's enough for now. If you stay awake for the next fifteen minutes, I'll give you more."

"That's an excellent incentive to stay awake."

55

SOFIA

Sofia hadn't known what to expect when they'd landed in St. Petersburg, and neither had Marcel.

He'd made several phone calls during the long flight, but no one could give him a straight answer because everything had still been in flux.

Things hadn't improved much when they'd met up with the Guardians who'd arrived on a large plane straight from wherever Marcel's village was.

Nearly an hour passed before the convoy of trucks arrived to pick them up. They must have used mind tricks that encompassed the entire private section of the airport because no one was paying them any attention.

"Is Toven doing this?" she asked Marcel as he helped her climb to the back of one of the trucks. "Is he somehow compelling everyone in the airport not to notice a convoy of army trucks collecting soldiers that arrived on a private plane from the United States?"

They sat on one of the two long benches lining the sides of the truck.

"Toven's abilities are not limited to compulsion," Marcel said. "He can shroud the entire city if he wants, but he is not the only ace we have. We have a guy that can do it nearly as well, and I suspect this is his work."

"It's Yamanu's doing," one of the soldiers said. "He came with the convoy." The guy chuckled. "I wonder where he got these trucks."

"Probably from Turner's supplier," another Guardian said while his eyes roved over Sofia.

He was a handsome guy who looked a little like that famous British soccer player whose name she couldn't recall.

Marcel wrapped one arm around her shoulders and put a hand on her thigh. "Let me introduce you to my mate. This is Sofia. Sofia, this is Jay, and that's Elliot."

"Hi." Elliot smiled. "Nice to meet you."

As all sixteen Guardians introduced themselves, Sofia tried to memorize their names, but it was futile. She had a good memory for languages, probably because her brain had been trained for it, but names had always been a problem. When she taught classes at the university, she asked the students to wear name tags for the first week.

"Where are we going?" she asked.

The Guardian sitting on her other side shrugged. "Somewhere in the country-side. We brought field equipment with us, so I guess we are camping." He closed his eyes and leaned his head against the side of the truck.

"I'll check with Yamanu." Marcel pulled out his phone and typed a text.

When he got no response, he put the phone in his lap. "He must be busy."

As the truck trundled along the bumpy road, Sofia regretted the lack of windows, but she could understand the need to hide what was under the green tarp. It was cold, there was no heating in the cabin, and her puffer coat was in her suitcase that was somewhere among the boxes of equipment occupying the center of the truck. With the Guardians stretching their legs and propping them on the boxes, she couldn't go looking for it.

Instead, she cuddled closer to Marcel. "Aren't you cold?"

"Immortals are not as sensitive to the elements." He rubbed her arm.

"Here." The Guardian who looked like the British soccer player handed her his coat. "You can use mine."

"What about you?"

He flashed her a charming smile. "I'm an immortal. I don't get cold."

She chuckled. "In two weeks, even you'll be cold. Winters here are not for the fainthearted."

He looked offended. "First of all, I hope we will be out of here in a few days, and secondly, none of the Guardians are fainthearted."

"Of course not." She draped his coat over her front. "You are all manly men."

"You'd better believe it." He crossed his arms over his chest and closed his eyes again.

As Marcel's phone vibrated, he lifted it, read the message, and put it back down. "We are staying on a farm. The ladies will stay in the house, and the Guardians will erect tents in the field."

"I hope there's enough room in the house for you to join me."

He looked conflicted. "I'm glad that you will get to sleep in a warm bed. I should stay with the men."

"Don't be an idiot," the one who looked like the soccer player said. "Stay with your mate. No one will begrudge you that."

5 6

ERIC

*D*arlene hadn't slipped back into unconsciousness. Except for a couple of short naps, she'd been awake since morning.

"Bridget should have checked on you instead of leaving Julian and the nurse in charge." Eric rose to his feet. "I'll go talk to him."

"I wouldn't bother Bridget today," Geraldine said. "Shai told me that she's helping with the preparation for the mission."

"The Guardians shipped out already. What else is there to do?"

Geraldine shrugged. "I don't know. Kian and Shai are still in the office, so there must be things that still need to be done."

"If Darlene is over the initial stage of her transition, I would like to take her home, but Julian told me that Bridget needs to approve it."

"I don't know why." Geraldine looked at Darlene and smiled. "None of us is a doctor, but we can all see that you are doing so much better. The color's returned to your cheeks, and you even drank coffee."

Darlene laughed. "Just don't tell Julian or Bridget that I did that."

Her mother affected an innocent expression. "Julian said that you can have liquids, including soup, so why not coffee?"

Eric agreed wholeheartedly.

It wasn't that he minded staying one more night in the clinic. What he needed was confirmation that the worst was behind them and that Darlene was out of danger.

Ever since she'd lost consciousness, he hadn't been able to take a full breath.

"I'll ask, and if Bridget can't come and Julian can't take responsibility for releasing you, we will have to spend another night here. But if Bridget can hop over for a few minutes and give her okay, I would really like to sleep in my own bed tonight with you in my arms."

Darlene sighed. "That sounds so lovely. But I really don't want to bother Bridget if she's busy."

"It doesn't hurt to check." Eric walked out of the room and into the doctor's office.

"She's coming," Julian said before Eric could open his mouth. "My mother loves welcoming transitioned Dormants into immortality, and I didn't want to rob her of the experience by releasing Darlene myself."

Eric frowned. "Are you saying that you could have released her but kept her here for Bridget to do the honors?"

Julian smiled sheepishly. "It wasn't a big delay. Bridget wouldn't have released her immediately, either. In fact, she might insist that Darlene stays another night because of how long she's been in a coma."

Eric rolled his eyes. "Can you make up your mind? One moment you say that you can release Darlene, and the next, you say that she should stay another night. Are you just saying it to excuse the wait?"

Julian gave him one of those condescending smiles that doctors worldwide must have all practiced during their residencies. "There is a reason what physicians do is collectively called practicing medicine. Opinions vary, and decisions are highly subjective. If you want to be sure about a diagnosis, always ask for a second opinion."

"I hope never to need it again."

The front door opened, and Bridget walked in. Wearing a tight skirt and high heels, she looked like a pinup girl, not a doctor.

"Congratulations." She offered him her hand.

"Thank you, but you haven't seen Darlene yet."

"Let's do it together." She grabbed a white coat from a peg by the door and put it over her clothes.

"How is the mission going?" he asked.

She let out a breath. "It was one hell of an organizational effort to have every-thing in place in time."

Darlene grinned as they entered the room. "Hi, Bridget. That was fast."

"It was?" The doctor walked up to her.

"Bridget was already on her way," Eric explained. "I didn't need to call her."

"Are you in a hurry to go home?" The doctor checked the readouts on the various machines.

"I am. But I want the test done first."

Bridget tilted her head. "You don't really need to do that."

"I want to. Is that okay?"

"Of course."

"I'm calling Roni and Cassandra," Geraldine said. "Is there anyone else you want to witness the test?"

Darlene shifted her gaze to Eric. "Orion and Alena, Kaia, maybe Karen if she can. And the Clan Mother if she so wishes. You told me that she came to give me her blessing every day."

"She did." Eric pulled out his phone. "I'll call Alena and ask her if it's appro-priate to invite the Clan Mother."

"I don't think it is," Geraldine said.

"It doesn't hurt to ask." Eric started texting.

"In the meantime, let's remove all the wires." Bridget shooed Eric and Geraldine out of the room and called the nurse in.

"Tell everyone to be here in an hour," Darlene called after them. "I want to shower first."

An hour later, the clinic was packed with people, and for a change, Bridget didn't make a fuss about them lining the walls of the small patient room.

"It is my honor and my pleasure to welcome Darlene into immortality. Toven couldn't be here in person, but that's what video calls are for." She waved at Julian, who had been standing in the doorway.

"That was part of the reason for the delay." He held up a tablet with Toven and Mia's faces occupying the screen.

"Congratulations!" they said at the same time.

"Not yet." Darlene pushed up on the pillows. "Wait until the cut test."

"You're awake," Toven said. "That's reason enough to celebrate." He lifted a bottle of vodka. "We wanted to toast your successful transition with a glass of champagne, but this is Russia, so vodka will have to do."

Tears glistened in Darlene's eyes as she offered her hand to Bridget, but Eric knew it wasn't because she was scared of a little pain. Underneath her soft exterior, Darlene was a fighter.

Nevertheless, he clasped her other hand for support.

"Bring the tablet closer," Bridget instructed Julian. "So Toven and Mia can see the test."

Roni grumbled as he had to move to give Julian access. "She's my mother. I have the right to be the closest."

"You can sit on the bed," Darlene offered.

Bridget turned to look around the room. "Everyone ready?"

When no one else complained about not being able to see, she lifted her surgical knife off the tray and made the cut so quickly that Darlene didn't have a chance to flinch.

Eric squeezed her other hand. "Are you okay?"

"Perfect," Bridget answered for Darlene. "Look at this. It's already closing." She turned her head and smiled at the tablet. "Being a god's granddaughter comes with great perks."

Darlene leaned over the hand that Bridget was still holding. "Where is it? I can't see the cut."

The doctor took a square of gauze from her tray and wiped the small smear of blood away. "It's already gone."

"That's amazing." Darlene shifted her gaze to her mother. "Did yours heal as fast?"

"Even faster. I made the cut myself to test whether what they'd told me was true. I couldn't believe that I was immortal." She chuckled. "A demigoddess. It closed incredibly fast."

Cassandra started clapping, and then others joined in, and as the word 'congratulations' echoed from the walls, Darlene smiled and wiped tears from her eyes.

"Thank you, everyone," she said once her family and friends quieted down. "I never expected to find such a warm home or such great love." She looked at Eric. "I wish Max was here to celebrate with us, but he's in Russia with the Guardian force." She looked at the tablet. "Keep him safe, will you?"

"I'll do my best," Toven said. "Goodnight, everyone." The transmission ended.

A few more minutes passed as Darlene was hugged and kissed on her cheeks, and then it was the four of them in the room. Him and Darlene, Geraldine, and Roni.

"Come, my grandson," Geraldine said. "Your mom needs to get dressed and go home."

Roni leaned over Darlene and pulled her into a fierce embrace. "Could you have ever imagined a day like this when you were still with Leo?"

"Not in my wildest fantasies."

"Welcome to forever, Mom."

57

SOFIA

"*Y*ou need to get some sleep." Marcel rubbed Sofia's arm.

He was spooning her on the narrow bed in the children's room, which was too small for both of them and not long enough either. But it was better than sleeping in a tent out in the cold. Sylvia got the other bed, and the only other room was occupied by Toven and Mia.

Marcel had offered to sleep on the couch in the living room, but Sofia needed him near her.

"I'm too anxious to sleep."

He nuzzled her neck. "I can provide a distraction."

She would have loved to get distracted, but they weren't alone, and Sylvia had probably heard Marcel's whispers.

"We are not alone," she whispered as quietly as she could.

"Sylvia is asleep."

"How do you know? She might be pretending."

"I can hear her breathing. It's slow and deep." As he trailed kisses down her throat, his hand skimmed her hip, circled over her belly, and snaked under the elastic of her pajama pants. "If you remain very quiet, she won't hear you." His fingers brushed over the top of her slit but didn't reach where she needed them. "Is that distracting enough?" He nipped her earlobe.

Swallowing the moan rising in her throat, Sofia pushed her bottom against his hard length, and his answering muffled groan was most satisfying.

His hand moved lower, the pads of his two longest fingers finally making contact with the bundle of nerves and drawing circles around it. "Is that enough?" He blew hot air into her ear.

"More," she whispered.

If Sylvia heard them and was pretending to sleep, Sofia was fine with that. She needed this.

He slipped his finger into her wet heat and then added another. "Good?" he whispered.

"Yes."

Pulling her pajama pants down with his other hand, Marcel added another long finger, and as he thrust in and out of her, he pulled down his own sweatpants and pressed his shaft to her ass.

For several long moments, he rubbed himself against her bottom in sync with his fingers moving inside of her, and as another moan rose in her throat, he clamped his hand over her mouth and replaced his fingers with his erection.

That was more than she'd bargained for, and Sylvia would no doubt wake up from their activity, but Sofia was beyond caring.

Licking at Marcel's fingers, she concentrated on the feel of him thrusting in and out of her so gently that the bed didn't make a sound. It was a delicious slow burn, and she knew she would climax the moment he added his fingers to the play, but would he be able to reach his own release at such a slow and gentle pace?

Turning her head back as far as she could, she offered him her lips, and he took them with a savage need.

When he pressed the tops of his fingers to that most sensitive spot, the tension inside of her curled until her body went taut and then snapped.

As pleasure consumed her, Marcel's hand muffled her cry of release, and his fingers kept their light circling until he wrung the last tremor out of her and stilled.

"Why did you stop?" she murmured.

"This was about you, not me. Now, go to sleep." He kissed her neck and pulled her pajama pants up.

She was too tired to argue. The orgasm left her boneless and relaxed, her head empty of disturbing thoughts, and as she drifted off to sleep, she murmured, "Thank you. I'll return the favor tomorrow."

He chuckled next to her neck. "You're welcome, my love. It was my pleasure."

58

TOVEN

The river was starting to ice over, but it was just the beginning, and the amphibian's progress hadn't been slowed down because of it. Nevertheless, the vehicle's speed was painfully slow.

Mia had protested when Toven had informed her that she needed to stay behind in the farmhouse with Sofia, but he'd been adamant about not bringing her into the battle. When they had control of the compound, she would be brought over by the Guardians he'd left with her.

She'd tried to argue that the men were needed in battle and that it was a waste to leave them behind just because of her and Sofia, and she'd even tried to pull the Sylvia card. If Roni's mate was going with William in the van that was leading half the force through the tunnels' side, then why weren't she and Sofia allowed to join the force that was attacking from the hunting grounds?

It was a valid point, and he hadn't had the heart to tell her that Sylvia's help was crucial because the cameras in the tunnels could be wired to the compound, and William's disrupter might not work on them, but she and Sofia weren't needed until they secured the compound.

The problem was that Toven wasn't at all sure that they would succeed. They had the element of surprise on their side, help from Jade and Kagra, and superior equipment and weaponry, but the Kra-ell were incredibly strong, and they would be defending their home and their children. They had no way of knowing that it was a liberation and not an impending annihilation.

"You haven't practiced wearing the exoskeleton," Yamanu said. "I know that you plan to fight with your mind and not your muscles, but the suit also provides superior protection. Unless they fire an RPG at you, which we know they don't have, you're not going to get hurt while inside of it."

Across from him, Merlin tried to stifle a smile and failed. The doctor was a strange choice for this mission, and Toven wondered why Julian hadn't been assigned to accompany the Guardians.

"What's funny?" Yamanu asked Merlin.

"Nothing. I'm not wearing a suit either."

"You are staying behind in the amphibian until we secure the compound, so you don't have to, but I would have felt better if you wore one."

Toven patted his Kevlar vest. "This, the helmet, and the goggles will do. As long as my head, my eyes, and my heart are protected, and the Kra-ell don't have anything stronger than grenades to throw at me, I'm good."

Yamanu shook his head. "As strong as they are, they can grab you and tear you limb from limb, reach into your ribcage and pull your heart out, or twist your head off."

"You forget that I can compel them to freeze. I don't expect any of them to be immune. Igor wouldn't have allowed an immune to live."

Yamanu didn't look impressed with his reasoning. "You might be able to seize the mind of one, maybe two attackers, but what if there are more?

Toven winced. "Then I guess you and your fellow Guardians will need to shield me."

"We will be busy with the rest of the Kra-ell."

"Then I guess I need to wear the suit."

Yamanu grinned as if he'd won an argument.

Toven frowned. "What part of what we were talking about amused you?"

"Bhathian and I made a bet, and he just lost. He said that you were going to play the haughty 'I'm an indestructible god' card, but I said that you were a reasonable dude, and you would understand that you couldn't join the attacking force without the suit. You'll have to stay behind in the amphibian and wait until we secure the compound."

"How difficult are those exoskeletons to operate?"

"They are cumbersome." He gave Toven a once-over. "But you're a god, which I assume makes you stronger than most immortals, and you are also a smart fellow. If you want to give it a try, you're welcome to a suit."

Toven had a feeling that he'd just been outmaneuvered by the Head Guardian. "You planned this entire conversation to convince me to wear the damn suit, didn't you?"

Yamanu shrugged. "It was a last-minute thing. Since we left two Guardians with Mia and Sofia, I had two extra exoskeletons. Besides, Kalugal's men didn't have a chance to practice wearing them either, so you won't be the only one who will look like an astronaut trying to walk on the moon."

"You could have started with that, you know. I was under the impression that everyone had practiced walking with them."

"The exoskeletons are our design, and this is our first joint mission with Kalugal's men, which was decided on about forty hours ago. When and where would Kalugal's men have had a chance to practice fighting with the suits on?"

"I'm new to the clan, remember? I didn't know that you've never fought side by side with them before."

"Right." Yamanu nodded. "You seem such an integral part of the clan that it is easy to forget you are a newcomer."

"Thank you." Toven smiled at the Guardian. "That was actually a nice compliment."

"You're welcome."

"By the way, do you know how William is going to disrupt the communications? It occurred to me that the compound might use landlines or a satellite like the clan does."

"There are no landlines," Yamanu said. "William checked, and there are no landlines anywhere in the vicinity of the compound. The Kra-ell have a huge antenna that's very cleverly camouflaged to look like an enormous tree. According to William, all wireless devices are susceptible to radio frequency interference, and he will scramble them with his gadget." Yamanu flashed him a smile. "Don't ask me to explain the how and why. I'm just repeating what he told me."

"I know how it works." Toven leaned his head against the vehicle's side wall. "Because of that, he can isolate the signal going to the clan's satellite so we will retain the ability to communicate while the Kra-ell will not."

"I'll take your word for it." Yamanu crossed his arms over his chest. "Let's just hope that our drone spots smoke coming from the roof of the office building. It will be a shame if we have to fold after making all this effort."

"Not to mention the expense," Toven said. "Kian might need my help to cover the costs."

Yamanu cast him a sidelong glance. "That's very generous of you to offer. What will you ask for in return?"

"I already have all I need, but I might negotiate with Syssi for full ownership of Perfect Match."

Yamanu pursed his lips. "I don't know what all the fuss is about. I can understand why people with mobility issues can benefit from it, but I prefer my adventures to be real, not virtual."

"That's because you already have your perfect match. But perhaps you and Mey would like to spend a romantic vacation that neither of you has the time for. You can experience up to three weeks of curated adventure in the span of three hours, and it can be the wildest thing either of you has ever imagined. Not only that, but artificial intelligence might also surprise you with more than you've bargained for. The adventure that Mia and I shared was only loosely based on what we both asked for, and it was incredible."

The Guardian looked intrigued. "I'll have to talk it over with Mey."

JADE

"Wear something nice, he said." Jade smoothed her hand over her leather pants. "I'll show him nice."

The truth was that she looked hot, and the covetous glances she got from males as she strode toward the office building confirmed that.

Valstar hadn't been too upset about the change in their appointment time. In fact, he'd looked relieved. Jade doubted that he'd been concerned with losing work time to accommodate her request for an afternoon assignation, and when she'd moved the appointment, he'd been glad that it would be after hours.

His obvious preference for the nighttime probably had more to do with Igor not checking in and interrupting their session.

The downside was that she needed to spend more time with Valstar than she'd originally planned. The attack was scheduled for two at night, but she couldn't justify showing up at his place later than ten, and she had to keep him incapacitated during all that time, which meant repeatedly draining him.

At the thought, bile rose in her throat.

That alone should be enough of a punishment to atone for all her sins and failures, of which there were many.

The drug was already mixed inside the vodka that the humans distilled from potatoes in their section of the compound, and she'd brought cranberry juice to mix with the vodka so Valstar wouldn't taste the powder.

The guard at the door lifted his hand to stop her. "What do you have there?"

"What does it look like?"

"Is it vodka?"

"No, it's water." She rolled her eyes. "Valstar must have told you that I'm coming to see him tonight."

"He did," Boris said. "He also told me to thoroughly search you."

He licked his fangs as he gave her outfit an appreciative once-over.

The tight leather pants couldn't even hide a thin wire to cut someone's throat with, she'd checked, and the shirt was made from a mesh fabric that left her back, her arms, and her midriff exposed. A three-inch opaque panel covered her breasts, but her nipples were clearly outlined. It was a bit chilly for such an outfit, but she was a Kra-ell warrior, and she didn't let trivial things like that bother her.

"Go ahead." She lifted her arms, a bottle in each hand, and turned in a circle. "The only place I can hide something is in my boots. You're welcome to take them off for me."

"Right. So you can smash one of those bottles over my head."

Jade snorted. "I wouldn't waste good vodka on you."

He pointed to his chair. "Sit there and take the boots off."

She sat down and handed him the two bottles. "Go ahead, take a sip. I know you want to."

She pulled a boot off and stretched her long legs in front of her.

"I'm on duty." Boris handed her the bottles back.

"Don't you want to check that there is no poison inside?"

"What would be the point of that?" He lifted one boot, peeked inside, examined the sole and the heel, and put it down next to her leg before lifting the other. "Maybe you want to poison me and save the rest for Valstar. This visit is highly uncharacteristic of you."

"You know nothing about me, boy." She uncorked the vodka and took a swig, swishing it in her mouth for him to see before swallowing. "See? No poison. Do you want me to drink from the cranberry juice too?"

Checking her other boot, he nodded.

"It's not tasty on its own." She opened the bottle, took a sip, and swished it in her mouth before swallowing.

The purebloods enjoyed alcohol just as much as the hybrids and the humans did, and they could even tolerate mixing it with a limited selection of juices. Orange juice was not one of them.

She still remembered the cramps that had given her.

A few drops landed on her chin, and as she handed Boris the bottles to hold, she wiped them off with her fingers, and then licked them clean.

He watched her, transfixed.

"Don't drop these bottles," she warned as she pulled her boots back on. "The humans don't just give them away."

She might need a few swigs from the drug-infused vodka to be able to get through what she needed to do with Valstar, and even if she didn't, she would need to drink it if she wanted him to drink. It was harmless in small doses, so if she sipped slowly and kept refilling his glass, she should be okay.

"Why are you doing this?" Boris seemed unable to stop himself from asking.

She grinned evilly. "I figured that I'll get a rise out of Igor if I accept his second's invitation, and what's even better, I'll get Valstar in trouble."

His eyes flared red for a moment. "You are either stupidly brave or crazy."

"A little bit of both." She took the bottles from him and turned to walk away.

"Hold on," Boris called after her. "I need to check your hair."

She'd left it unbound, so that was unnecessary, but she stopped and turned back to him. "Go ahead."

He lifted the curtain of her hair almost reverently, and as his fingers brushed over her nape, she felt them tremble.

A small smile curved her lips. She could do that to any Kra-ell male even when she wasn't in her fertile cycle. The males drooled after her not because she was the greatest beauty but because she was a natural prime.

The male's nature was to prove himself worthy to the most powerful female and to outdo other males. Those whose Kra-ell souls hadn't been corrupted to their very core by Igor still possessed that instinct.

When Boris let go of her hair, she turned around, walked into the building, and headed up the stairs.

With the second floor hosting Igor and Valstar's offices and personal lodging, there was always another guard at the entry to their hallway, but with Igor gone, security seemed laxer than usual. Or perhaps Valstar had dismissed the guard so he could have more privacy with Igor's prime female.

The first floor housed the administrative offices, but no one was there this time of night. Tom had been right about it being an advantage. Once the communications went down and Pavel took care of Boris to bring her the titanium chains, there would be no witnesses.

When Jade got to Valstar's office, she knocked to let him know that she was coming in and opened the door. She'd never been to his private quarters before, but they were probably similar to Igor's, which meant that to get there, she needed to pass through the office.

"It's me." She knocked on the only other door.

Valstar pulled it open and gave her a once-over. "That's not what I had in mind when I told you to dress nicely, but it will do." He reached for her waist.

"I brought something for the mood." Jade sidestepped his hand and walked over to the sitting area. "Do you have glasses?"

"Of course."

He didn't look happy about her not being ready to play, but he was being cautious. Valstar was a murderer but not a rapist, and even if he was, he wouldn't dare force himself on Igor's prime. If he offended her, he knew that she would walk away, and he would have to let her go.

Pulling two glasses from a sideboard, he brought them to the coffee table. "Boris told me that you were bringing vodka and that you drank it in front of him to prove that you are not going to poison me."

"Why would I want to do that?" She poured the cranberry juice first. "I'm here to scratch an itch and to annoy Igor. Killing you is not on the menu."

Regrettably, that was true. She needed to keep him alive until Igor was caught.

60

MARCEL

oven had left more than two hours ago with the Guardians who formed the wing that would attack from the hunting grounds. Their journey through the river was much longer than Marcel's group's, and the amphibian they were traversing the distance in was much slower than the trucks his group was using.

Marcel utilized that time to practice wearing the exoskeleton suit along with Kalugal's men.

Not to deplete their energy before the battle, they weren't doing anything more strenuous than walking and aiming their weapons, but he was already tired, and it had been less than an hour.

"That's good enough," Bhathian said. "Take the suits off, but do it carefully so nothing gets damaged, and return them to their crates. Make sure that your name is on the crate so you can find it later. Bring it with you when we move out." He pointed to his watch. "You have half an hour."

The suits were going with them in the trucks, and they were going to put them on right before the battle.

As Marcel turned toward the farmhouse porch, he met Sofia's eyes, which were wide with wonder. She and the two other ladies were sitting on a bench, watching him and Kalugal's men test the exoskeletons.

Taking the helmet off, he smiled at her. "Impressed?"

She nodded. "You look like an alien. The purebloods will be so shocked when they see you that they might surrender without a fight."

"I wish, but I doubt it." He carefully removed the suit's sleeves. "In any case, you shouldn't worry. Our guns are loaded with tranquilizing darts, and we will take down as many as we can without killing them."

Instead of looking reassured, Mia looked more worried after what he'd said. "But you have regular guns as well, right?"

"Of course, we do."

"What if the humans join the fight?" Mia asked. "Those darts are calibrated to take down Kra-ell. They can kill a human."

Marcel looked at Sofia. "Will they fight?"

She shook her head. "They would just get in the way. No one ever talked about the possibility of the compound being attacked, but we had fire drills. In the case of fire, the humans are supposed to get the animals out of the barns and then assemble in the playground. Maybe the protocol is the same in the case of an invasion." She sighed. "I hope that they just stay in their rooms."

Sylvia crossed her arms over her chest. "I should just join the Guardian force. They keep recruiting me for these jobs, and I don't know how to even hold a gun."

"Do you want to be a Guardian?" Marcel asked.

"Not really. But there is nothing I'm passionate about, and the idea of having a job that I need to show up for every day doesn't appeal to me. I like to learn new things, and I like to take on interesting projects that are not too long. Otherwise, I get bored."

"Then Guardian training is not for you." Marcel finished folding the suit and put it in its crate.

When Sylvia pushed to her feet, Sofia followed her up. "I'll walk with you to the truck."

"Good luck," Mia said.

"Thank you." Sylvia bent to give Mia a hug. "Don't worry. With these suits, they are invincible."

"What about you? Are you going to wear one?"

Sylvia shook her head. "I'm staying in the van with William." She let go of Mia and stretched, then turned to Marcel. "You should stay in the van with us. It's the best seat in the house. We get to see the entire battle on the screen. The drones film everything on their path and transmit it to William's computer."

"Yeah." Sofia wrapped her arm around his middle. "You should stay in the van where it's safe, and let me know what's going on. You haven't been on active duty in centuries."

"I'll be fine. I train with the reserves."

Lifting his crate was no small effort. The suits weighed over two hundred pounds each, and they weren't the only thing in the crate. The rest of his weapons were there as well.

When they got to his designated truck, he climbed in, pushed the crate under the bench, and then got back down to say goodbye.

He pulled Sofia into his arms. "I'll ask Sylvia to give you updates."

"I prefer for you to do it. That way, I will know that you're safe."

"I am safe. These suits are not just for protection. They make me ten times stronger. I can take on a pureblood while wearing them and win."

She closed her eyes. "Things happen in battle, and I can't lose you. Promise me not to do anything stupid."

He arched a brow. "When did I ever give you the impression that I'm the reckless type?"

"Good point. Just be safe, and don't do anything overly heroic."

"I won't."

He kissed her, and as she wrapped her arms around his neck and kissed him back, he got so lost in the sensation that he didn't hear Bhathian calling his name until the Guardian clapped him on the back.

"Time to go. Save your kisses for later."

61

JADE

"*E*nough." Valstar swiped both glasses off the table, sending them flying to the concrete floor and shattering on impact.

Jade lifted a brow. "Impatient?"

His eyes were fully red, in part because of lust and in part because of the combination of alcohol and drugs, but he wasn't nearly as weakened as she'd hoped for.

A trickle of apprehension slithered down her spine.

She hadn't fed earlier in order to leave room in her digestive system for the copious amounts of blood she was about to suck from him, and that meant she wasn't at her maximum strength either.

The hatred and rage would have to be fuel enough.

"Get rid of your clothes if you don't want them ruined." He tore his shirt off, sending the buttons flying. One hit her face, and the rest tumbled harmlessly to the floor, landing among the shards of broken glass.

As a last resort, she could use the glass as a weapon and cut his carotid artery, but his body would repair the wound too fast for the loss of blood to weaken him. Her best chance was to get her fangs in his neck.

He would let her drink, thinking it was part of the sexual game, and when he realized that she was taking too much, he would be too weak to fight her off.

Jade rose to her feet, gripped Valstar by the throat, and tossed him on the bed.

Caught by surprise, he hadn't offered any resistance, and since she was still pretending to play the game, he didn't rise to attack her.

"I'm waiting to see that magnificent body of yours." He kicked his boots off. "Take off that thing that passes for a shirt."

She looked down at the floor. "Look what you have done. How am I supposed to walk on this without my boots?"

His gaze roamed over her. "If you can't remove the pants without removing the boots first, I can tear them off you."

"Impatient much?"

As he pulled his pants down and his shaft jutted from his hips, she wished she could have smuggled a knife into the building so she could cut it off. The blood loss from that might be enough, and if not that, the pain and horror would have been.

"They are not the kind that rips at the seams." She pretended to appreciate his size as she pulled the flimsy shirt over her head and tossed it on the couch.

He sucked in a breath. "Beautiful."

She faked an appreciative look-over. "You're not too bad yourself."

There was nothing wrong with his body, and if he wasn't a murderer, she might have found him attractive, but all she saw in front of her was a twisted monster.

Climbing on the bed with her knees, she put her hands on his chest and pushed him down. "If you want me, you'll have to prove your worth."

He smiled, revealing a pair of long fangs. "Oh, I will." He gripped her waist and twisted them around, pinning her under him. "I want a taste of you."

He lowered his mouth to her breast, but she bucked him off before his fangs touched her skin, and as he landed on the glass-strewn floor, he let out a hiss.

She was straddling him before he could process what was happening, her hands pushing on his shoulders and forcing him to stay down.

"A little pain fuels the lust." She stroked his neck with her fangs, sinking them into his carotid.

Valstar moaned, his hips shooting up and his erection pressing against her center. "Pull your pants down." His hands gripped the waistband and pulled.

Fuck. She should have pinned his hands over his head instead of pressing on his shoulders.

Grinding against him to distract him, she kept gulping down his blood while he pulled her pants down her hips, but he was too lost in the act to master the coordination needed to lift her, so he couldn't pull them all the way down to her thighs and expose her.

Jade moaned deep in her throat and ground against him some more, and as his hands left her hips and his arms plopped weakly on the floor, she wanted to smile but kept on sucking.

"That's enough," he mumbled. "You're taking too much."

As she kept going, he lifted his hands in a last-ditch effort to get her off him, but he was too weak and about to lose consciousness. She didn't need to apply much pressure on his chest to keep him pinned to the floor and stay exactly where he was.

When he stopped struggling, she could hear his heartbeat, and when it slowed down to a crawl, she pulled her fangs out and licked the puncture wounds closed.

If Jade could vomit what she'd taken, she would have done it, but the Kra-ell digestive system didn't allow that. It was too damn efficient.

She could rinse out her mouth, though.

After a quick visit to Valstar's bathroom, she pulled the shirt back on and looked at her watch.

It was only fifteen minutes past midnight.

Tom's people would start scrambling the compound's communications at one forty-five, and only then would Pavel incapacitate the guard downstairs and bring her a set of titanium chains to bind Valstar with.

Regrettably, there was no chance that Valstar would stay down for an hour and a half. His body would regenerate the blood faster than that.

She would have to drain him at least two more times.

"Dear Mother of All Life, please, give me strength to do what I must."

She also needed to light the fire in the trash can to signal Tom that everything was going as planned. Hopefully, Pavel had already incapacitated Boris and got it ready for her.

MARCEL

*M*arcel tried to get comfortable in the so-called command post, which was a beat-up old soviet-era armored personnel carrier that William had filled with so much equipment that there was barely any room for them to sit.

They were parked inside the last tunnel, hidden from the compound's watch towers until it was time to attack.

Bhathian sat up front with the Guardian driving the vehicle, and in the back William, Morris, and Charlie sat in front of their electronic equipment.

He and Sylvia were all the way in the back, crowded in the little space that remained behind William's enormous console, but unlike Roni's mate, who had a job to do, Marcel wasn't sure why Bhathian had stationed him in the command post of the tunnel team.

He had no special task assigned to him.

Bhathian just didn't want him to be in the first wave of Guardians storming the compound because he hadn't had enough practice with the exoskeleton suit. It was bullshit because he had as much practice as Kalugal's men, and they were going in the first wave.

Bottom line, he was there to observe, to keep Sofia updated, and when the active Guardians and Kalugal's men took control of the compound, he was to help with collecting the Kra-ell's tranquilized bodies and taking them somewhere to be locked up.

He was also in charge of the tranquilized tunnel guards, who were bound and gagged in the last truck of the convoy. They would also need to be moved to a secure location once the compound was taken.

By one-thirty in the morning, both teams were at their designated positions, waiting for William to take down the compound's communications.

Onegus's calm voice sounded in Marcel's earpiece. "The countdown starts in fifteen minutes. Last equipment check."

"On it, boss." Marcel heard Yamanu and Bhathian's nearly simultaneous replies.

Bhathian headed the tunnel team, as they called it, and Yamanu headed the river team, which would attack from the hunting grounds' side.

"William?" Onegus asked.

"I'm ready," William said. "I'm checking my equipment."

"Pilots?"

"I'm ready," Charlie said. "I just hope this old bird and the soviet bunker-busting munitions will do the job."

The plan was for the two Russian military drones that Turner's contact procured to launch a simultaneous missile attack, blowing off the gates at both ends of the compound along with sections of the fortified wall flanking them. Both openings needed to be wide enough for roughly forty men in exoskeletons to make it through all at once and get in position in under fifteen seconds.

"The drones will do fine," Morris said. "My concern is not that they won't suffice for the job, but rather that they will prove too powerful and create a crater and a debris field that will make it harder for the teams to get in position within the tight window of time they've got. But that's what we have, so let's hope they will do the job."

"I did what I could with them." William leaned back in his seat. "At least the guiding system is top-notch."

Onegus sounded again. "Is everything ready?"

Morris replied. "Everything is a go on my and Charlie's end. The birds are circling in the ten-mile radius. You give the signal, and the birds will be on target. Missiles are armed, and we will launch both at precisely 2:00 as planned. To all the hotshots listening, you need to stay back and enjoy the fireworks from a safe distance."

Yamanu cackled in Marcel's ears. "I just hope that you remember how to shoot. Did you practice with Parker on his new game console as I told you to? I bet he kicked your ass. The kid can fly these things better than you and Charlie. Hell, I can do a better job than you."

"I can beat both Parker and you blindfolded," Charlie said.

Marcel could hear the muted laughter coming from both teams. Yamanu's teasing was the perfect antidote for the pre-battle jitters everyone was feeling.

They were about to face an enemy none of them had ever fought before, an enemy that was stronger, faster, well trained, and under compulsion to defend the compound at all costs.

He was jerked out of his reverie when Onegus's voice came through again. "It's 1:45, and the signal from Jade is on. Time to flip the switch on the communication disruptor."

"Done," William said. "Communications are down. We are good to go."

"Done as well," Charlie said. "The drones' ETA over the compound is one minute."

As the driver rolled the vehicle down the fourth and last tunnel, Marcel watched the countdown on William's screen.

"We are in range and ready to launch the missiles," Morris announced.

Marcel couldn't help but be impressed by how calm everyone was despite the unknown they were about to face. They had a solid plan, and everyone knew what they were doing, but to quote the Prussian Field Marshal Helmuth von Moltke, no plan of operations extends with any certainty beyond the first encounter with enemy forces.

But then, von Moltke had never met the likes of Turner.

Morris's dry voice broke the stretching silence. "Launching missiles in 3, 2, 1, launch."

Marcel stood up so he could see the impacts on William's split screen, but he should have followed the pilots and William's example and put on goggles. As the missiles hit their targets within a fraction of a second apart, he was momentarily blinded. As his vision cleared, two gaping holes appeared where only seconds before stood massive gates supported by reinforced concrete walls.

63

TOVEN

*Y*amanu whistled in Toven's earpiece. "Man, that missile did the job and then some."

The ground still shook, and they felt the blast quite intensely despite their protective gear, but there was no time to wait for the dust to settle to confirm the damage. They had fifteen seconds to close the distance to where the gate was, enter the compound, and get in position.

The purebloods were amazingly fast, so even if most of them were fast asleep, it wouldn't take them long to grab their weapons and charge forward to defend their turf.

"On my mark," Yamanu said. "Go!"

As the team sprinted full speed ahead, the ground thundered under their heavy exoskeleton suits. To those who were proficient in using them they provided speed in addition to strength and protection, but Toven struggled to keep up.

"We are in position," Bhathian's voice sounded in his earpiece.

"So are we," Yamanu said.

They had to overcome several disadvantages. The purebloods and the hybrids were significantly stronger and faster, and they outnumbered the Guardians and Kalugal's men two to one.

Including the females, there were roughly a hundred and sixty purebloods and hybrids. Based on Jade's assessment, some of the females would stay to protect the children, but most would join the first response warriors and fight just as fiercely as the males to protect the compound.

On top of that, the Kra-ell were intimately familiar with every nook and cranny of the compound, while the Guardians were only familiar with the general layout.

To compensate, the clan had the technology, modern weaponry, a brilliant strategist, and the element of surprise.

Turner's plan was as simple as it was brilliant.

Enter the compound from both ends to force the defenders to split up, and spread out in a wide semicircle formation, so that when the Kra-ell rushed out to meet them, they would have to spread apart as well and, in so doing, would make it easier for the teams to target individually.

If possible, it was better to avoid shooting darts into a cluster and potentially hitting one person twice.

The darts were calibrated to incapacitate a feral animal, which might be too much for the Kra-ell slim frames, but since their bodies had self-repairing capabilities, one dose wouldn't kill them.

Two doses, however, could prove lethal.

During the planning of the attack, a concern had been raised about a tactic that depended on the Kra-ell's disorganized rush to meet their attackers. A smart commander would hold the warriors back to better assess who and what they were facing, so betting on all of them charging ahead was risky, but ultimately, the consensus had been that this was precisely what the Kra-ell defenders would do.

The reasoning was that the Kra-ell were habituated to defer to Igor in everything, and since he was absent and so were his second- and third-in-command, they wouldn't know what to do and would react instinctively rather than strategically. In addition, Igor's compulsion would drive them to defend the compound at all costs without regard for their own well-being, and that would spur them into mindless action as well.

As the team spread out in a semicircle, Yamanu stretched out an arm and motioned for Toven to get behind him, but Toven ignored the command and stood beside the Head Guardian.

It didn't take long for the defenders to show up.

No more than ten seconds passed before a group of fierce-looking warriors galloped toward them at breakneck speed. Surprisingly, not all were armed with swords as they had expected. He could clearly see Kalashnikovs in the hands of several warriors. From a distance, he couldn't tell whether they were male or female, not because of the protective goggles he wore that made everything seem even darker, but because there wasn't much difference. They were all tall, slim, and had long dark hair. As they got closer and their faces became clearer, he identified at least two females among them.

"Grenade launchers at the ready," Yamanu commanded.

Bhathian's command echoed in Toven's ears.

"Fire," Yamanu barked.

Twenty grenade launchers discharged at once.

William's modified stun grenades exploded in a blinding light and deafening boom that would have damaged human eyes and ears permanently, but on the Kra-ell the effect would last only a few seconds.

The distance, along with the exoskeleton suits, the goggles, and the specialty earpieces that were fitted with active noise-cancelling circuitry, protected the teams, but even with all that, Toven felt the impact of those grenades as if he had been punched in the gut and hit over the head.

As one, the advancing Kra-ell stopped as if hit by a wall. Disoriented and off balance, they became perfect stationary targets.

"Fire at will," Yamanu commanded.

64

JADE

*A*s soon as the twin explosions erupted, Pavel burst into Valstar's quarters with a bunch of chains looped over one arm and two swords strapped over his hips, one on each side.

"You did it." He grinned at Jade before baring his fangs at Valstar. "The bastard sentenced me to a whipping because I didn't respond with a *yes, sir,* fast enough." He kicked the male in the gut. "He considered it disrespectful."

The bastard was still too weak from blood loss to react.

Was it an act? Or did Pavel really hate Valstar that vehemently?

Hopefully, it was the latter. Jade had no choice but to leave the boy in charge of guarding Igor's second, and she wasn't too happy about trusting Tom's compulsion to make Pavel obey her commands to the letter.

Taking the chains from him, she bound Valstar, locked the chains, and put the key in her pocket. "Watch him." She looked around the room for something to use as a gag. "Don't move. Don't even go to the bathroom. If Valstar somehow gets free, he will detonate the explosives and kill all of us." She pulled Valstar's underwear from his discarded pants and stuffed them into his mouth. "I need something to tape it with."

She walked into his office and started opening drawers. Finding a roll of masking tape, she returned to the bedroom, tore off a large piece, and wrapped it around Valstar's head twice.

"Don't remove the gag even if he starts choking on it. I don't know how strong of a compeller he is."

"Don't worry." Pavel handed her one of the swords and a dagger with its sheath that he'd hidden inside his shirt. "What happened here?" He pointed at the glass.

"I don't have time to stand here and chat." She strapped the sword onto her hip, and the knife went inside her waistband. "I have some killing to do."

"Don't kill my father," Pavel surprised her by saying. "He's not a bad guy."

She wasn't sure about that. He was one of Igor's inner circle cronies, but he hadn't been one of the murderers of her tribe, so she had no beef with him.

"I won't. He did nothing to my people. But once the other females are free of Igor's compulsion, it's out of my hands. He might have killed their families."

Pavel nodded, dragged a chair closer to where Valstar was on the floor but had the presence of mind to keep out of reach of the unconscious male, and sat down.

She cast one last glance at the murderer lying on the floor and walked out.

Not killing him had been one of the hardest things she'd ever had to do.

No one deserved to die by her hand more than Valstar, but they needed him alive to catch Igor, and that was more important than her impatience to exact vengeance. Catching Igor was crucial.

Still, it might be a mistake to let Valstar live even for a few more hours.

As the human saying went, a bird in the hand was worth two in the bush, and one kill was better than none.

But it wasn't just about revenge.

If Igor got a whiff of anything being amiss in the compound and ran, her people would never be safe. He would find a way to rebuild his force. By locating the other pods and compelling the survivors to serve him or, if he didn't know where the others were or he knew and they were all dead, by renewing his breeding program and producing as many hybrids as he could until he had a force large enough to come after his former subjects.

65

MARCEL

The scenes unfolding on the screens in front of Marcel were mesmerizing. The Kra-ell charged as predicted, splitting their force to deal with the invaders on both sides.

The Guardians and Kalugal's men must have seemed like aliens from a nightmarish sci-fi movie with their imposing exoskeleton suits and weaponry.

It was a testament to the Kra-ell's courage and ferocity that they hadn't even paused before charging the invaders. Or maybe it was Igor's compulsion at work.

Morris and Charlie guided a couple of small surveillance drones equipped with infrared cameras over the main building of the compound, looking for potential snipers or for other warriors lying in wait for any who might make it through the main body of defenders.

He spotted two splinter groups that were stealthily approaching their teams' flanks. They melted into the night and moved like animals on a hunt, but they were no match for the infrared cameras of the night-vision drones.

"Over there." Marcel pointed at them on Morris's screen.

"I see them," the pilot said. "We need the big bird back."

"Mine is on the way," Charlie said.

Marcel wondered how the two managed to fly two drones each. Their computer screens split between the view from the small surveillance drone and the large military one. It required amazing coordination.

"Do we fire at them or just around them?" Morris asked. "Those drones are not equipped with tranquilizer bullets."

"Aim at the ground around them to distract them," Onegus said over the com. "The Guardians are aware of their approach, and they need them distracted. Make sure to aim behind the Kra-ell, so you don't hit any of ours."

"Roger that," Morris said as he brought his drone right above the Kra-ell's heads.

"I got the group approaching Yamanu's team," Charlie murmured.

"Fire at will," Onegus commanded.

A staccato of rapid fire from the anti-aircraft gun on board each of the drones lasted for all of twenty seconds, but that was all the distraction the Guardians needed.

Once the dust settled, four shadowy figures twitched on the ground in one location and six in the other.

The tranquilizer worked quickly, paralyzing them almost immediately, but it took up to several minutes for the drug to knock them out completely.

The Guardians didn't wait, though. Pulling titanium cuffs from the pockets of their suits, they bound the Kra-ell's wrists and ankles and connected the two with a chain in the back. They weren't taking any chances. For now, it didn't matter whether they were purebloods or hybrids. They were all bound in the same way. Later, when it was time for Toven to work on their minds, they would be separated into two groups.

Transfixed by the action on the video feed, Marcel might have missed the drama unfolding on the other side of the courtyard if not for Morris's whistle.

"Look at her fight." He pointed to where two Kra-ell were engaged in a fierce sword battle.

A male and a female were going at each other with vicious stabs, and watching their deadly dance was mesmerizing.

"Is that Jade?" William asked.

"It's either Jade or Kagra," Marcel murmured. "They are both free of Igor's compulsion and eager to get the revenge they've been craving for over two decades."

William let out a breath. "I wonder if the older kids will join the fight. Jade's daughter is only sixteen. I hope she's not out there while her mother is on a killing spree."

66

JADE

*D*own in the courtyard, Jade saw several warriors lurking in the shadows, the lack of collars identifying them from afar as Igor's lackeys.

Most of the others must have rushed toward the attacking forces, and she wondered what was on the minds of the purebloods hiding in the shadows. Did they plan to take the invaders from their flanks?

As if that would do anything to the suits those warriors were wearing.

It was an exercise in futility.

That surprised her. She hadn't thought they would have the presence of mind to devise a strategy without Igor and Valstar directing them.

But that was the invaders' worry. Or rather, the liberators.

She shouldn't think of them as invaders, or she might say that to her people who needed to believe they were being freed.

But that was a worry for later.

Right now, she had murderers to kill and revenge to exact.

Pretending to join their efforts, she slunk behind Artuom and slit his throat. He did not deserve an honorable death, and she had no qualms about robbing him of the privilege of a duel.

Besides, his buddies were near, and she couldn't take on all of them at once.

The scent of his blood was overpowering, but that was only because she was right behind him. The compound was saturated with residue from the explosions, and the dust was still heavy in the air.

Nevertheless, the Kra-ell senses were designed to follow the smell of blood, and as Distor turned around and sniffed, Jade pressed herself against the building's wall, cursing silently that she hadn't had time to drag Artuom's body further into the shadows. He was sprawled on the ground, his legs illuminated by the moonlight, and his gaping neck bleeding profusely.

Lucky for her, right then a large drone passed overhead, distracting Distor momentarily, but as she was about to leap at him, Kagra sprung out of the shadows and slit his throat without making a sound. She lowered him gently to the ground and smiled at Jade.

She saluted her second and headed toward the purebloods' living quarters. The place seemed deserted, but she knew they were hiding, and she wanted to check on Drova. She was only sixteen, so she should be hiding with the other kids, but she might have done something stupid and gone out to fight.

"What's going on out there?" Vombad stepped out from behind a column.

There was a sword in his hand, and a gun was tucked into his belt. Was he there to defend the children? Or was he just hiding and leaving the work of defending the compound to others?

He was near the top of her kill list, but she wouldn't do that here where the children could see it. They were Kra-ell, but they were still soft-hearted, and there was no need to show them the cruelties of life just yet.

"Isn't it obvious? We are under attack. Why are you here instead of out there?"

"I could ask you the same question."

She looked down her nose at him. "I'm checking up on the children."

"They are safe in the basement, and several females are guarding them."

They weren't safe, and he knew it. If Igor could activate the explosives, they would all be dead.

"Then my question still stands. Why are you here?" She walked out the door, hoping he would follow.

When he did, she decided that there was still a smidgen of honor left in his body, which earned him an honorable death in a duel.

When they were at the edge of the courtyard, Jade turned around. "I'm no longer restricted by Igor's compulsion, and I've waited for over two decades for the day I'll get to avenge my sons and my males." She unsheathed her sword. "Make your peace with the Mother, though I don't think it will save you from spending eternity in the valley of the shamed."

Looking amused, he pulled out his sword. "When I kill the traitor who betrayed us to our enemies, I'll be guaranteed a place in the fields of the brave."

He veered to the right and swung his sword with incredible force toward her neck. Anticipating the move, she swiveled away while swiping the sword at his calf, but he jumped out of the way, and the cut she inflicted was only superficial.

Baring his fangs, he growled and pressed on, with a dagger appearing in his left hand. When she parried his sword's swing, he brought his knife in an uppercut motion in an attempt to gut her.

Jade somersaulted backward, landing on her feet long before he closed the distance between them, and threw her dagger at him. He shifted, and it was embedded in his shoulder instead of hitting him in his heart.

His fangs bared, and his eyes fully red, he yanked the dagger out of his shoulder and threw it at her.

His aim was messy, probably because of the wound to his shoulder, and it barely grazed her arm, cutting through her shirt and scraping her skin.

With the dagger lost in the dirt she was left with the sword only, but that was enough to finish him.

Vombad was bleeding from his calf and shoulder, while she had only suffered a scratch.

Advancing in a flurry of blade motion in order to draw his attention to the sword, she got in range and kicked his injured calf with the force of her momentum.

As his leg buckled, he instinctively reached with one hand to break his fall and lifted his sword to protect his head.

She moved sideways, and rather than going for the obvious, she sliced down at the hand holding the sword.

He lost his hold, falling on his ass.

It should have been easy for her to finish him right then, but he wasn't as easily defeated as she'd hoped.

Moving faster than a viper, he twisted and caught his sword with the other hand, immediately shooting forward and thrusting it where she'd been just a split second ago, but she was right behind him.

Again, it would have been easy to thrust her sword into his back, but then she wouldn't see his eyes as she delivered the death blow, and that wouldn't be satisfying enough.

She'd waited a very long time for this moment and wasn't willing to compromise.

Instead, she delivered a roundhouse kick to the back of his head.

Vombad was built like a brick wall, but the loss of blood and the mighty kick to the head were clearly taking a toll, and he fell to his knees.

He tried to push back up, but his legs refused to accept the load. He leveled his eyes at her. A look of pure hate and evil.

She knew that he was still dangerous, even on his knees, and it would have been foolish of her to underestimate him.

But he'd already lost, and he knew it.

Jade smiled. Bless the Mother for the strength she'd gifted her with.

Vombad parried her swings, and for a few brief moments, Jade toyed with him, letting him believe that he was holding her back. But when the glimmer of hope appeared in his eyes, she delivered a hard blow to his sword hand, forcing him to let go.

Standing tall in front of the murderer of her people, she waited for him to do the honorable thing and offer her his throat, but in his heart Vombad was a coward, and he instinctively lifted his hands to defend his head and his neck.

"You were always a worthless coward, Vombad." She swatted away his defending hand with her sword and delivered the killing blow.

67

KIAN

*K*ian had watched the mission unfold through the video feed from the drones, but once the drones were no longer needed and the battle continued on the ground, he had to rely on listening to the com.

Next to him, Onegus was talking to Yamanu, getting an update.

"When all was said and done, there was really no fighting to speak of," Yamanu said. "The tranquilizer darts did what they were supposed to, but some of the Kra-ell could fight off the effects for longer than we'd expected, so we had to knock them over the head. After that we bound them with the titanium cuffs and brought them down to the basement of the office building. The guys were squeamish about doing that to the females, but we had no choice. They fight as viciously as the males. I'm proud to report that we managed not to kill anyone, not even those we had to fight after we dispatched the first wave of defenders. The only casualties the Kra-ell suffered were the work of Jade and Kagra. They dispatched six of Igor's inner circle males."

"What about Valstar?" Onegus asked.

"She made good on her promise and didn't kill him. She left the guard who Toven released from Igor's compulsion to watch him while she went on her killing spree."

"How is Toven doing?" Kian asked.

"Toven was never in real danger, and for the most part, he behaved. He refused to stand behind me when the Kra-ell attacked, but with the suit on, the few bullets they managed to discharge before we blinded them with grenades just bounced off him."

"I'm glad you convinced him to wear it."

Yamanu chuckled. "I told him that he would have to stay in the amphibian and wait for us to secure the compound, and then I added a few gruesome descriptions of what the Kra-ell could do to him, and that sealed the deal. Toven agreed to wear the suit, Bhathian lost the bet, and now he owes me a case of Snake Venom."

"Did he start freeing the people from Igor's compulsion?"

"Not yet. We are waiting for Mia and Sofia to arrive. We didn't approach the humans yet, either. We figured it would be better if she did it."

"Good thinking."

Yamanu chuckled. "I love these damn suits. They are hot, cumbersome, and they get stinky after wearing them for over an hour, but none of ours has suffered even a scratch."

Kian smiled, a knot in his stomach easing. "I consider those suits the best money we've spent."

"Jade's second got injured pretty badly, though. One of her designated victims almost finished her."

"I heard," Kian said. "How is she doing?"

"She'll live. Merlin patched her up. Several purebloods and hybrids are in the infirmary as well."

"How did they get hurt?"

"We ran out of darts after shooting the first wave of defenders. We had to either shoot or quash the rest. The bastards kept fighting until they were knocked out."

"They didn't have a choice," Kian said. "It was the compulsion."

On his other side, Turner shook his head. "It's not just the compulsion. It's their tradition. They fight to the death."

"Wasn't that outlawed?" Onegus asked.

Turner shrugged. "What we know, we've learned from Emmett, Vrog, and Aliya, who repeated what they were told. I would love to hear what Jade promised to tell Toven. When that conversation starts, I want to be part of it, and I don't care what time it is."

"Same here," Kian said. "It's not that I don't trust Toven to tell us everything, but like Turner, I prefer to hear it as it is told by Jade."

"I'll let Toven know that you asked that. Are our four compellers ready to assist him?"

"They are all on standby," Onegus said.

Kian turned to the chief. "Can you put everyone on the com? I want to thank them for a job well done."

Onegus nodded. "Go ahead."

"Great job, everyone," Kian said. "You all did your part admirably. I want to thank Kalugal's men for volunteering their help, and special thanks to Toven and Mia, who've agreed to undertake the monumental task of freeing the minds of everyone in Jade's compound. We still have a long night ahead of us, and Igor is still out there. Hopefully, he will be apprehended when he returns to the compound and brought to justice by those he enslaved and whose families he slaughtered."

68

TOVEN

*B*y the time the van with Mia and Sofia arrived at the compound, the Guardians had removed the bodies of those killed. There hadn't been many; five purebloods had died at Jade and Kagra's hands, and the sixth had been dispatched by Kalugal's lieutenant when he'd saved Kagra from the male.

There were several injuries, though, with Kagra's being the most severe.

She and Jade had fought with swords, probably because those were the only weapons they'd had access to, and the last pureblood Kagra had taken on dealt her a blow that would have been fatal to a human. He was about to finish the job when Kalugal's lieutenant leaped and smashed his exoskeleton's reinforced fist into the male's head, saving her life and killing the pureblood.

Toven hadn't seen the event and had only been told about it after the guy had brought the injured female to the compound's clinic.

With everyone wearing identical suits, it was impossible to distinguish who was who. Only Bhathian and Yamanu wore a colorful band around their arm that identified them as Head Guardians.

When the van came to a stop next to him, Sofia opened the side passenger door, waved at him, and then bolted toward the human section of the compound or maybe to search for Marcel.

Mia leaned forward and smiled. "Hello, my love. I'm glad to see that you are really unharmed."

"Did you doubt it when I told you I was fine?"

"I did," she admitted. "You sounded off."

"I called you as soon as the compound was secured, and there was still a lot to do. I was in a bit of a rush." He pulled her wheelchair from the back and unfolded it.

Lifting her into his arms, he hugged her to his chest for several long moments before lowering her to the chair.

She smiled up at him. "You hugged me as if you missed me terribly."

"Of course, I missed you." He crouched next to her chair. "I'm just glad that it's over. I've never been fond of battles."

"Who is?"

"You'd be surprised." He turned to look at the Guardians, who were still patrolling the grounds in their exoskeletons.

Jade had assured them that all the purebloods and hybrids were accounted for, but they didn't want to take any chances.

Toven had removed his suit as soon as he had deemed it safe.

Mia put her hand on his shoulder. "Let's get to the compulsion part. The faster we have everyone compelled, the sooner William can stop scrambling the compound's communications. Where is Igor's second? He's the first on the list, right?"

"He's on the second floor of the office building. The Guardians have him contained."

She turned her chair toward the building. "Wasn't that guard you compelled at the tunnel entrance in charge of that?"

"He was until the Guardians took over. We don't know where Pavel stands yet. He helped Jade because I compelled him to obey her. I don't know if he would have done it of his own free will."

They met Jade in the lobby of the office building. "How do you want to do it?" she asked. "Do you want them brought to you individually or in groups?"

All the Kra-ell were locked in the office building's basement, so if they set up shop in one of the offices on the first floor, it wouldn't take long to bring them up.

"You can bring three at a time. But first, let's take care of Valstar."

She grimaced. "You have no idea what I had to endure to keep him alive. His vile blood is souring my digestive system."

"It was unavoidable."

"I know." She let out a breath. "After Valstar, I'll bring up my daughter. She's terrified and won't calm down no matter what I say to her. When you free her from Igor's compulsion, can you do something to ease her?"

"I'm not a therapist, but I'll do my best."

"Thank you." She shifted her eyes to Mia. "They are all terrified. Even those who pretend to be brave. I know we are pressed for time, but if you can say a few encouraging words to help them calm down, it would make my job easier. Igor has them all under his compulsion, even the children, except for the very young ones."

"What are you planning to do?" Mia asked.

"Assemble the females of my former tribe and get them to help me sort this place out."

"How is Kagra doing?" Toven asked.

"Your doctor assures me that she will live."

69

SOFIA

"Sofia! Wait up!" She heard Marcel calling behind her and slowed down.

He caught up to her, snagged her from behind, and twirled her in a circle. "Everyone you care for is safe."

"I know." She wiggled out of his arms. "You told me." She'd been so relieved when he'd called her that she'd felt faint. "But they must be terrified. Did anyone talk to them?"

"I did, but they wouldn't open the doors. I yelled and told them that we were liberating them, but no one answered."

"Were you still wearing your exoskeleton suit?"

"I took it off, but since no one saw me anyway, that wasn't very helpful."

When they reached the group of buildings that housed the humans, she first noticed that all the shutters were closed, and no light was coming out.

Her gut squeezed with anxiety. "I hope they are just holed up and that nothing happened to them. What if the purebloods had orders to kill the humans if there was an invasion?"

Marcel shook his head. "Just go, knock on your father's door, and tell him it's you."

"Yeah. You're right." She tried to open the front door of the building. "It's locked."

"Let me try." He did, but the door was barricaded on the other side. "I'll ask a Guardian still wearing the exoskeleton to open the way for us."

"Hold on." She took a couple of steps back, cupped her hands on the sides of her mouth, and yelled, "Helmi! It's me, Sofia. These people are with me. Open up so I can explain!"

"That's her room." She pointed. "She should have heard me."

"Maybe she can't see you." Marcel pulled out his phone, activated the flashlight, and shone it at her face.

The shutter on the second floor moved a fraction of an inch and then banged open.

"It is you!" Helmi pushed her head out. "Who's the guy?"

"That's my fiancé, Marcel. He and his people came to free us from the Kra-ell."

"How?"

"It's a long story, and I don't want to keep shouting. Where is my father?"

"With my mom and Isla. Do you know if Tomos is okay?"

Sofia turned to Marcel. "Tomos is her hybrid boyfriend. Did any of the hybrids get hurt?"

"None of the hybrids died," Marcel said loudly so Helmi could hear him. "Some are injured and are being taken care of in the infirmary, but only Kagra is seriously hurt. The other injuries are not life-threatening, and I don't know if your boyfriend is one of the injured."

"Can I go to the infirmary?"

"Sure."

She leaned out the window and looked around. "Where are the aliens?"

Marcel lifted his hand. "Here. I'm one of them. What you saw were protective exoskeleton suits that made us stronger than the Kra-ell."

"Oh." Helmi smiled sheepishly. "So you're human. Is it safe outside?"

Sofia was glad that Helmi followed her statement with a question, so she didn't need to answer it. This wasn't the time to explain about immortals and gods and how they were related to the Kra-ell. They needed to get all the humans ready for Toven, so he could release them from Igor's compulsion.

Marcel nodded. "We have the compound secure, and all the Kra-ell are either in the infirmary or the basement of the office building."

Helmi's eyes widened. "Including the kids?"

"We figured they would feel safer with their mothers."

"Let me talk to the others." Helmi disappeared.

Nearly fifteen minutes passed before Sofia heard movement on the other side of the door and then dragging sounds as things were moved to clear the way.

When the door finally opened, and her father stepped out, she flew at him with her arms outstretched.

"Sofia." He crushed her to him. "I was so worried."

"I was worried too."

When he let go of her, she turned to look at Marcel. "Marcel, this is my father, Jarmo. Dad, this is Marcel, my fiancé."

Her father gave Marcel a brief once-over before offering him his hand. "So those are your people, the ones dressed like aliens."

"Yes. We came to free you from Igor's tyranny."

Jarmo tilted his head. "And replace it with what?"

"We are not sure yet," Marcel said. "It was all done in a rush."

"Can we go inside?" Sofia asked.

Her father took a step back and motioned for them to enter.

MARCEL

$\mathcal{T}$he only thing Sofia had inherited from Jarmo was her blue eyes. He was balding, but what remained of his hair that hadn't turned gray was blond.

He led them to a communal living room with several worn-out couches, armchairs, and two round tables, one holding a chess set and the other a deck of cards.

As they sat down, wide-eyed people started to drift in.

"Do you speak Russian?" Jarmo asked Marcel.

"I understand some if it's spoken slowly, but I can't speak it."

Jarmo nodded. "You probably don't speak Finnish either, right?"

Marcel shook his head.

"Then we will speak English, but also slowly. Many of us don't know it." He smiled at Sofia. "You can translate. Yes?"

"Of course." She motioned for a plump, rosy-cheeked woman to come closer. "This is my aunt Hannele, Helmi's mother. And that's Isla, my other aunt."

The three siblings looked a lot alike. They were also close in age, late fifties or early sixties.

"Hello." Isla dipped her head and offered him her hand.

"Nice to meet you. I'm Marcel, Sofia's fiancé."

Smiling shyly, she turned to Sofia. "*Chto takoye fiancé?*"

"*Zhenihk.*" Sofia took his hand as she translated.

"*Kongra.*" Isla smiled brightly. "*Ohn krasavchik.*"

"She says that you are handsome."

He knew enough Russian to understand that. "Thank you."

Helmi entered the living room with a coat draped over her arm. "I'm going to look for Tomos." She gave Marcel a small wave. "I'll come back later."

He gave her the thumbs up.

Other people came in and took seats wherever they found them, but Jarmo didn't introduce any more of them.

"I know you are all under Igor's compulsion," Marcel said. "And you can't say anything bad about him or leave this place if you want to. This ends today. We brought a powerful compeller who will free you from Igor's compulsion. He has already freed Sofia, Jade, Kagra, and Pavel, and he's freeing more people as we speak. By morning, everyone in this compound will be able to speak freely and decide on the future they want to pursue."

"Where is Igor?" Jarmo asked.

"He's not here. But when he returns, we will be waiting for him, and he will be brought to justice. You might not be aware of it, but he committed heinous crimes against his people. He killed the males of Jade's tribe, enslaved the females, and he compelled them to keep silent about what happened to them. He did the same thing to other Kra-ell tribes."

Jarmo didn't look surprised. "I was born in this compound and saw those females when they were brought in. I knew something terrible had happened to them."

Marcel waited for Sofia to translate, and several of the older ones nodded when she was done.

Evidently, Jarmo wasn't the only one who had noticed.

"Who will lead in Igor's place?" Jarmo asked.

"As I said, it will need to be decided in a vote. Will Jade be an acceptable leader?"

Jarmo shrugged. "I don't know if she'll be better. She's good to the children but has no respect for adults."

When Sofia translated, Isla huffed a breath and said something too fast for him to follow.

"My aunt says that the Kra-ell are all the same and that one is not better than the others, but the people here don't have anyone on the outside, and they wouldn't know what to do and how to provide for themselves."

Her other aunt added to her sister's assessment, and he caught a few words here and there, but not enough to understand what she was saying.

Sofia turned to him. "Hannele says they can be happy here if we take the Kra-ell away. They can grow crops and tend to the animals. That's what they were doing anyway, and it's enough to put food on the table for the humans living here. They will need to find a way to pay for the other things they need like clothing and other necessities." She leaned closer and smiled. "I don't think my aunt realizes how much more goes into running a place like this."

"We will help you figure it out," Marcel said. "I'm not the boss of this operation, and I'm not making the decisions. I'm here to help you get organized so you are ready when our compeller comes to free you. As I said, we need everyone to be freed of Igor's compulsion by morning."

"What do we need to do?" Jarmo asked.

"Make sure that everyone is awake and ready in about two hours."

71

JADE

*I*t was morning when Tom and Mia finished with the last of the humans, and William, their tech guy, had removed all the collars. Valstar had provided the key, so the process should have been easy, but Jade had still experienced a few anxious moments when the damn thing hadn't opened as smoothly as it was supposed to. She'd volunteered to go first, and after William had figured out how to maneuver the tricky locking mechanism, he'd had an easier time with the others.

Turned out that the collars contained location trackers, explosives, and a trigger mechanism that could be activated remotely, but as she'd suspected, they had no listening capabilities.

Jade was exhausted, but she'd promised Tom a story, and she never went back on her word, so she'd dragged herself to the human quarters and sat across from him.

Tom's mate lay on the couch with her head resting on his thigh, and a blanket spread over her child-sized body. She was so petite that she would still be small even after her legs grew back.

Jade was about to thank Tom for all the work he had done, but then the Head Guardian with the pale blue eyes and long hair walked in and plopped tiredly on one of the couches.

"We blocked the gates with the vehicles," the Guardian said. "And we put Kra-ell guards at the entrances to the tunnels. We have snipers hiding in the trees and a team inside each tunnel. We are ready for Igor."

He was one of the two Head Guardians who had introduced themselves to her as Bhathian and Yamanu, but she'd forgotten who was who. The other one was a mountain of a man, with muscles the size of a professional bodybuilder, and he was just as cordial as this one, but not as easy with his smiles.

"What about the cameras?" Jade asked.

"All the camera feeds are broadcasting prerecorded stuff on a three-hour loop. All Igor will see are empty tunnels and empty corridors. The same goes for his and Valstar's offices. We also checked the entire compound for hidden cameras and listening devices."

"Did you find any?"

The Guardian nodded. "Quite a few. They are taken care of as well. We need to thank Igor for being paranoid and not allowing anyone to have cell phones in the compound. We verified that all the phones were locked in the safe in Valstar's office, and we searched everyone and all the rooms to ensure no one was hiding a communication device. We've left nothing to chance." He flashed Tom a teasing smile. "The only wild cards are the guards you compelled. How good is your compulsion? Are they going to follow the script we gave them?"

Tom leaned back and sighed. "I was still in good form when I compelled the purebloods and the hybrids we needed for the tunnels, so you have nothing to worry about them singing the tune I taught them. I wasn't as good with the others, but since all I had to do was remove Igor's compulsion, and our other compellers did the rest, it's all good. Regrettably, Igor didn't have a contingency in place in the event of disruption in the compound's communications. Getting someone to call him from one of the surrounding villages would have bought us more time, and we might have learned when he was planning to return."

When it seemed like the two were done talking, Jade dipped her head at Tom. "Thank you for what you did for us. You and Mia and your warriors worked hard to save my people, and you made a great effort not to harm anyone. You've exceeded all of my expectations, and you have my eternal gratitude."

"You're welcome," Tom said. "How is Kagra doing?"

"She's asleep. Your doctor assured me that she's healing at a good pace for a Kra-ell." Jade chuckled. "He was so excited about getting a peek at her digestive system. He said that he understands now why our waists are so slim. Our stomachs are tiny, and our intestines are much shorter and narrower than that of immortals and humans because we live on a liquid diet. I told him that he could have just asked me, and I would have explained, and he said that it was not the same as getting to see the insides of Kagra's gut."

"Doctors are all weird," the Guardian said. "And Merlin is weirder than most."

Tom smiled. "I like Merlin. He's unconventional."

Jade didn't have any experience with human doctors, so she had nothing to add to his comment. "I'm ready to deliver my end of the bargain." She glanced at Mia. "Do you want to wake your mate up?"

He smoothed his hand over Mia's short black hair. "I'll tell her everything later. She's exhausted."

"Kian and Turner asked to listen in," Yamanu said. "You can put them on a video call." He turned to Jade. "Is it okay with you?"

"Why wouldn't it be? I promised Tom to tell him the history of his people, and he can do with it whatever he pleases."

The guy shrugged his broad shoulders. "Some people get shy when the camera is on them."

She narrowed her eyes at him. "Your communication is secure, correct? Because this information should never reach the humans."

Tom chuckled. "We are in their quarters."

She waved a dismissive hand. "You can cast a silencing bubble around us, can't you?"

"Yamanu can do that. I'm too tired to even think."

The Guardian nodded. "It would be my pleasure. But first, I'll call Kian."

As he placed the call, Sofia came down the stairs with her immortal boyfriend. "Can we join you? Or is it a secret meeting?"

"What I'm about to tell Tom is information that I didn't even share with my daughter, but when I promised him the story, I failed to make it contingent upon him keeping it a secret. It's up to Tom what he wants to do with it." Jade looked at him. "Do you have a problem with that?"

"The only problem I have is keeping my eyes open. Yamanu will shroud us so no one else can listen in, and I'll make sure that Sofia keeps what she hears to herself."

"Would you like some coffee?" Sofia asked.

"That would be great."

She turned to Jade. "What about you?"

Jade nodded. "Black with nothing added."

"I know." Sofia pushed to her feet. "Purebloods can't tolerate dairy or sugar."

"I'll help you." Her boyfriend followed her to the kitchen.

Jade shook her head. "After I fulfill my promise, I want to hear how Veskar got to know a god, how he got a god to help him, and how Sofia ended up with an immortal boyfriend."

Yamanu chuckled. "We will be here all day and all night."

"When Igor walks into the trap we set up for him, I'll take a break to fulfill the last part of my revenge. Other than that, I'm at your disposal."

72

TOVEN

"*B*efore I begin," Jade said. "I want to warn you that the history I know is what I was told." She put her coffee cup down on the table. "I suspect that a lot of it is not true. As you know, history is written by the victors, and most of the time, it was the gods." She snorted. "You probably think that humans called you that because they were awed by your powers, but that's the name you gave yourselves. In the gods' language, the name for your people means 'we are gods.' I guess the ability to manipulate genetics and create new species at a whim made you think that you are entitled to that designation."

Toven shrugged. "In a way, it makes sense. We might not be the creators of all life, but we are the creators of some life."

Jade regarded him with an amused smile. "That can also be said about procreation, which would make every living creature a god."

He didn't necessarily disagree with that observation, but it wasn't entirely true, and he didn't want her to think that she had won the argument. "That's multiplying what was already created. It's not creating something new."

"What do you call hybrids, then? They are something new."

Yamanu lifted his hand. "Let's agree to disagree on the definition of creating life. That argument alone will take all day. Please, continue the story."

Jade nodded. "We shall revisit that some other time. Many millions of Earth years ago, before the gods had interstellar travel capability, they mastered genetic manipulation. Their history claims that they had always been the way they were and that they used their superior genetic material to create the Kra-ell. It was supposedly their first attempt at creating intelligent life by enhancing an animal that was already closely related to them genetically. But after my years on Earth, I began to question that story."

"Why?" Sofia asked. "It makes sense. They did the same thing with humans."

"The gods created humans for the same reason they supposedly created the

Kra-ell. They needed workers to do all the things that the gods considered beneath them. They didn't want to get their hands dirty."

"What do you believe is the real story?" Toven lifted his coffee cup, but there wasn't much left.

"I'll make more." Sofia rose to her feet.

Jade took a small sip from her coffee and put the cup back down. "I think that the gods were originally like the Kra-ell, or very similar, and that they manipulated their genes to become better." She winced. "Or what they considered superior."

"What makes you think that?" Marcel asked.

"The Kra-ell didn't have written history per se. We had myths and legends, and one of them told a different story, but I thought it was just a myth, our way to aggrandize our kind. The legend was that a long time ago, Jombil, who is like the god Loki of Nordic folklore, offered the same deal to the Kra-ell queen and the gods' king. According to the legend, the king accepted the offer, but our queen rejected it because the price Jombil demanded was too steep. It meant changing our entire way of life and giving up our traditions, and that was an insult to the Mother of All Life who had created us."

"What did Jombil demand?" Toven asked.

"Basically, everything that gave us an advantage over the gods in exchange for every advantage they had over us. We have speed and strength, and we hunt and drink blood. They have eternal life, but what is the point of living forever when they hide like Veskars in underground dwellings and eat like scavengers? I prefer to live out my lifespan serving the Mother, and after I die, spending eternity in the fields of the brave."

Toven wouldn't have traded places with her, but she was right about the myth hinting at a different story than the one recorded by the gods.

"Do the gods and the Kra-ell come from the same planet?" Marcel asked.

Jade nodded. "That was another falsity that the gods propagated. They claimed that the original animal they used to create the Kra-ell came from a neighboring planet. The gods didn't have interstellar travel capabilities back then, but they had already mastered interplanetary travel."

Toven lifted a brow. "Was there an animal like that on the neighboring planet?"

"There was," she admitted. "But that doesn't mean that the gods used it to create us. Both our kinds could have that animal as a distant relative. Anyway, they used the explanation to treat us as a subclass of beings the same way they later did with humans and many other species. They claimed that they created the Kra-ell to be their slaves. The Kra-ell did everything for the gods. They planted and harvested, worked in their factories, cleaned their homes, and did everything else that the gods deemed beneath them."

Toven frowned. "How did the Kra-ell become slaves in the first place? If the gods claim that they created them for that purpose is true, then it's self-explanatory. But if we give credence to your legend, you started out on equal footing with the gods. You had your own queen."

Jade smiled. "The legend says that Jombil was offended by the queen's refusal of his offer, and he punished the Kra-ell. A terrible disease infected all the animals that used to be their source of blood. Most of the animals died, and those that didn't were too sickly to take blood from. The gods offered their help, but it came with a price. They had the knowhow and the means to manufacture synthetic blood that could sustain us, but we had to pay for our food with labor, and that's how the Kra-ell slavery started."

73

KIAN

*K*ian suspected that the gods had something to do with the disease that targeted the animals. They were experts in genetic manipulation, so creating a virus that would selectively affect just the larger hot-blooded animals that the Kra-ell fed on shouldn't have been much of a challenge, and that was how they had secured a slave workforce.

Nasty.

The gods who had been sent to Earth had obviously lacked that ability. Otherwise, they wouldn't have sent a flood to cull the spread of humans. They would have sent a virus.

The angle at which Yamanu's phone was recording the conversation provided him a good view of Jade and Toven, the coffee table, and Yamanu's huge feet. The others were not on the screen.

His phone had the camera off and was muted, so he and Turner could talk while listening to Jade's story.

"Did the animals ever recover?" Sofia asked as she bent over to refill Toven's cup with fresh coffee.

"Eventually, they did." Jade lifted the cup for Sofia to pour into. "But it took a very long time for the animal population to sufficiently replenish its numbers to feed the Kra-ell population, especially since that population had nearly doubled in size since the gods took over their lives. There were no more tribal wars, and the gods didn't permit duels to the death except on special holidays, so there was nothing to cull the male population. The gods were happy to accommodate the additional workforce, and the growing disparity between males and females didn't bother them.

"On the contrary, they used it to get better control over the males. It's also possible that the gods did something to alter our genetics, so we produced many more males than females and blamed it on nature. At that stage in our history, we were under their complete control."

"Whose history is that?" Toven asked. "I assume that the gods would try to put a more positive spin on these events and portray themselves as the benevolent saviors of the Kra-ell."

Jade cast him a smile. "You are absolutely right. My story might have led you to believe that it all happened during one lifetime, but it spans hundreds of thousands of years. You won't find this version in their recorded history, but at some point the Kra-ell started recording their own history, and the gods who were opposed to slavery recorded their opinions as well. Not that I got to read any of them, but I was told that they still exist but are difficult to access."

"Like the Vatican documents?" Sofia asked.

"Not exactly," Jade said. "Even though the gods were ruled by a king, they pretended to be a democratic society, and things got voted on by an elected council. But they had a way of dealing with those who disagreed with the majority. Those rebel recordings were deemed dangerous propaganda threatening the peaceful coexistence between the gods and the Kra-ell, and they were eliminated from all official publications."

"The Kra-ell were physically stronger," Yamanu said. "They were a warrior race that probably chafed at being captive. Didn't they try to rebel?"

Kian had a feeling that he knew the answer to that, and it had to do with the Odus.

"In the beginning, the Kra-ell depended on the gods' synthetic blood to survive, so they didn't rebel. Those who did were dealt with harshly, but their biggest hold on the Kra-ell males was the females. Only the adult males were employed by the gods, while the females and the children were kept in seclusion, supposedly for their own good." Jade's lips twisted in a grimace. "The official explanation was that the underground cities of the gods were not suitable for the young Kra-ell, who needed the outdoors to thrive. The unofficial reason was that the gods didn't want the two races to mix. The Kra-ell didn't want that either, but the gods' council feared that some of the gods might try to seduce Kra-ell females, and it was better not to allow them free access."

"What about the other way around?" Toven asked. "Didn't they fear that the goddesses would seduce the Kra-ell males?"

Jade shrugged. "For some reason, they weren't concerned with that."

Kian suspected that the mate addiction worked differently at the beginning, affecting only the female gods, but not the males.

"Anyway," Jade continued. "By keeping the females and children out of the underground cities and in special above-ground reservations, the gods had full control over the males. If they misbehaved, they didn't get access to their females, and if they did something really bad, the gods would take it out on their families."

"What did they do to the families?" Sofia asked in a near whisper.

Kian wanted to know that too.

"They limited their supply of synthetic blood." Jade's eyes flickered red. "They starved them."

74

JADE

om looked doubtful. "Was that also in the historical records?"

"It was implied, but I don't have proof." She glared at him. "I don't have any proof for any of the things I'm telling you, so you are free to choose what you want to believe."

She was too tired and too hyped up at the same time to play games. If he wanted to believe that his people weren't capable of such cruelty, it was his prerogative.

"I believe you," he surprised her. "They were capable of much worse."

"The flood," Yamanu murmured. "Everyone thinks that it was a natural phenomenon and that the gods just used it to their advantage to cull the human population, but even if it was nature's doing, they could have warned people to seek higher ground."

"I wouldn't put it past the gods to have caused it," Jade said. "They had the technology, but they must have taken it with them when they left, or those who remained on Earth didn't have the tools or knowhow to maintain it." She turned to Toven. "Which one was it?"

"A combination of both, I suspect. Please, continue your story."

It was an evasive answer, but he hadn't promised to tell her anything. He'd promised to free her people, and he had done his part. Now it was her turn to do hers.

"The males were allowed to visit their tribes when the females were in their fertile cycle, which all the Kra-ell females of breeding age entered simultaneously. But since there were many more males than females, there was fierce competition. Games were organized for the males to fight each other and to participate in other contests of strength and endurance. Only the winners got invited to breed with the females."

"I hope it was the females' choice and it wasn't forced upon them," Mia murmured sleepily.

"The gods didn't go that far," Jade said. "The females chose who they wanted to invite to their beds. In fact, contests like that used to be deadly before the gods enslaved the Kra-ell, but the gods outlawed fighting to the death. Then again, it could have been part of their effort to rewrite history to make themselves look good. But since the fertility festival continued to be celebrated for thousands of years after the Kra-ell were freed, and fights to the death were no longer prohibited, it's possible that the gods' records were truthful on that."

"Finally, we get to the interesting part," Yamanu murmured. "I want to hear how they were freed."

Tom chuckled. "I have so many questions before that. Why did the gods live underground? When did they start interstellar travel? Where is their planet?"

"I can answer some of that," Jade said. "Our sun is what you call a red giant, and our planet is hot, humid, windy, and dark, so the gods are more comfortable in their underground cities. I can't tell you where it is because I was never shown a map of the galaxy with our planet and Earth marked and directions on how to get from point X to point Z. All I know is that it's hundreds of light years away."

"How do you know that it's hundreds of light years and not thousands?" Tom asked.

"I know how long we were supposed to be in stasis, and it was in the hundreds of light years, not thousands, but then our years are not the same as yours. They are significantly longer."

"What do you mean by supposed?" Tom asked.

"It took thousands of years instead of hundreds. I think we were tricked, but it could have been a malfunction."

"Tricked by whom?" Tom asked.

She smiled. "The gods, of course. Who else? It was their ship. But I'm getting ahead of the story." She turned to Yamanu. "You wanted to know how the Kra-ell were freed."

"Most definitely."

"The Kra-ell hated living underground. They loved being outdoors, and they lived for the hunt. Those who worked the fields for the gods were not as miserable as those who worked in their factories and homes. The festivals were the only times those who worked underground got to be outdoors.

"Their liberation happened in three stages. A movement started among the gods to better the Kra-ell's conditions and end their slavery. By then, the animal population had rebounded, not enough to fully sustain all the Kra-ell, but enough for them to enjoy the occasional hunt. The young gods helped the Kra-ell negotiate a new deal. They would still work for the gods during the day, but at night they would be allowed to go topside and hunt if they wanted to. They were given building materials to erect lodging for themselves, the females and children could come live with them, and they could elect a new queen. It was an improvement, but their living conditions left much to be desired, especially compared to how the gods lived."

"They could have built the things they needed," Tom said. "After all, they worked in the gods' factories and produced all of their goods."

"The Kra-ell received only basic education and didn't know how to create the things they built for the gods. They only knew how to put them together."

Yamanu nodded. "It makes sense. The workers who put together cellphones don't know how to design them."

Tom looked like he wanted to say something but then decided not to.

Jade continued. "The young gods who initiated the change realized that it wasn't enough, and they demanded that the Kra-ell be given complete autonomy. The older gods claimed that the symbiotic relationship was beneficial to both people, and to sever it would destroy both societies. The gods needed the Kra-ell labor, and the Kra-ell needed the goods that the gods manufactured because the planet's wildlife could not sustain their population. They still needed the synthetic blood that the gods produced. One of the young gods leading the movement was a gifted inventor, and he proposed to replace the Kra-ell workforce with smart robots that were just as strong and could perform all the menial tasks the gods needed the Kra-ell for."

75

TOVEN

"The Odus were invented," Toven said. "I can see how that could solve the gods' problem, but what about the Kra-ell? They still needed to buy synthetic blood and other goods from the gods, but if they couldn't work for those things, how were they going to get them?"

Jade leaned back and crossed her arms over her chest. "Things like that don't happen overnight. Someone still had to build those smart robots. On top of that, they weren't easy or inexpensive to make, and the gods couldn't replace the Kra-ell workforce without creating a huge drain on their resources, which were needed primarily to develop their interstellar fleet. The idea sounded good in theory but wasn't economically or practically viable. The gods still needed the Kra-ell workforce."

"So nothing really changed," Sofia said.

"The change was gradual." Jade stretched her booted legs in front of her. "The newly elected Kra-ell queen negotiated with the gods' king for the Kra-ell to be paid actual wages, not just in goods. They were no longer forced to work for the gods. They could choose where they wanted to work, negotiate their wages, and use their earnings to buy whatever they pleased from the gods. Over time, the Kra-ell built better dwellings for themselves, and their living conditions improved significantly."

"What did the gods do with the Odus?" Yamanu asked.

"They were modified to be house servants only. The factory robots didn't need to look like people, and they cost much less to make."

"So that's the end of the story?" Marcel asked. "The Kra-ell were given equal rights?"

Jade laughed. "Not even close. The Kra-ell were free, they had their tribal grounds, and the gods didn't interfere in their affairs, but they were regarded as second-class, or rather as savages, and from their point of view, the gods were not wrong. For many generations following their emancipation, the Kra-ell were ruled by a dynasty of queens who were happy to let the tribal wars resume. It was our tradition, our nature, and the Kra-ell celebrated the freedom to kill each other. Most wars were over hunting grounds, others were about revenge, and some were fought just for the sake of fighting. The male population began to shrink again."

"Did the gods step in to stop it?" Mia asked. "That must have affected their workforce."

"By then, the gods had automated almost everything, and they no longer needed as many workers. They were happy for the Kra-ell to kill each other. They supplied the tribes with primitive weapons like swords, knives, and javelins, which would be useless if the Kra-ell ever turned against them."

"That was my next question," Toven said. "The Kra-ell were warriors, the gods had resources they needed, why didn't they attack?"

"The gods had superior technology and weapons." She waved a hand around. "It's the same old story, and Igor learned nothing from history. You came in with your spacesuits and subdued a force twice as large as yours with hardly any effort." She closed her eyes. "I made the same mistake. Perhaps if I'd had better weapons and more advanced surveillance at my compound, Igor wouldn't have had such an easy time killing my people."

"How did they do it?" Yamanu asked.

She waved a dismissive hand. "That's not part of the story I promised Tom."

What Jade had promised was the history of the gods, not the Kra-ell, but that was the history she knew, and the two were intertwined.

"Still, despite the tribal wars and deadly duels, the Kra-ell greatly outnumbered the gods, whose birth rate was a tiny fraction of the Kra-ell. But when a progressive queen outlawed the tribal wars and duels, our population exploded, and things got really bad. There weren't enough jobs, and the Kra-ell lived in abject poverty. Thankfully, enough time had passed for the animal population to grow and flourish, so they didn't starve, but things were bad. The gods started to fear them, while the young gods started to demand that something be done about the Kra-ell plight."

"I don't understand," Toven said. "After so many generations of being free, they should have built their own economy independent from the gods. Why didn't they?"

For the first time since he'd met Jade, her proud expression turned embarrassed. "We didn't have the right set of tools. We lacked education."

JADE

"The gods valued education and technology. We valued nature and staying true to our roots. We lived like primitive humans did a long time ago, while underground, an advanced civilization thrived. The gods who had supported the Kra-ell all along realized that our queen's progressive ideas would fall apart if we stayed rooted in our traditions, and the tribal wars would return. The only solution they could see was to make us more like them, not genetically because that was anathema to us, but by providing us with an education above the basics, so we could start building our own economy."

Tom nodded. "I bet there was a big resistance to the idea. Access to education is critical for removing class barriers, and the ruling class seldom grants it without a fight. Human history is rife with examples."

"You're right. The progressive gods demanded equal rights for the Kra-ell and access to the same education the gods had, but the king and the gods' council refused. They reasoned that if the Kra-ell wanted a better life for themselves and their children, they needed to develop their technology from scratch like the gods had done."

"That wasn't smart," Yamanu murmured. "They were sitting on top of a powder keg. They should have made at least a token concession."

"They didn't," Jade said. "The movement grew, and as rumors of impending uprising started, the king ordered all the Odus delivered to the capital, and they were reprogrammed to defend the gods. I won't bore you with the war details, but the gist was that the Kra-ell were stronger, faster, and outnumbered the gods twenty to one. Even with the Odus and the advanced weaponry, the gods barely stood their ground, and the casualties on both sides were staggering. The king of the gods agreed to meet the queen of the Kra-ell and negotiate a peace treaty."

Tom shook his head. "I find it hard to believe that the gods let the situation escalate like that without trying to defuse it or launch a preemptive strike."

Jade glanced at Yamanu's phone, which was propped on the coffee table. Yamanu and Tom were still wearing their earpieces, so it was possible that the comment had originated from whoever was listening on the other side, but she was surprised that Tom, a god, deferred to anyone.

"As I said before, this is the history I know. Things might have happened differently, and perhaps the gods had made some halfhearted offer that the Kra-ell refused. The agreement they reached was that the Kra-ell would receive an education that would allow them to advance faster, but they would not be privy to the gods' genetic knowhow and their most advanced technology. In exchange, the king demanded that the Kra-ell submit to genetic manipulation to control their population growth. The queen refused to budge on that, fearing that the gods would manipulate more than the reproduction rate. The king responded that the only other option was for the Kra-ell to colonize other planets."

"I assume that the queen agreed," Tom said.

"She did. As part of the treaty, the Odus were decommissioned, and the technology to make them was banned. The gods replaced them with simpler robotic servants that were not nearly as strong and were easy to destroy."

"We suspected that was what happened to them," Yamanu said.

"You knew about the Odus?"

Yamanu nodded. "But I don't understand why the gods would agree to decommission the Odus. What if the Kra-ell rebelled again?"

"I suspect the king wanted to get rid of the technology and used the treaty as an excuse. The Ouds could potentially be used against him by his own people. "

Tom lifted his hand. "So that was why the Kra-ell were sent to Earth? To colonize it?"

Jade smiled. "Not yet. There is still more to the story, and you'll find the next part most relevant to you. It explains why you are here."

He arched a brow. "That's indeed interesting."

"After the treaty was signed, the purging started. The gods were angry and divided, the older gods blaming the young ones who had sided with the Kra-ell for stirring up the rebellion and causing all the bloodshed. But the gods did not believe in capital punishment, and the king needed to keep up his benevolent façade, so to get rid of the troublemakers, he exiled every god who had taken part in the rebellion, including three of his children. He called it a research expedition, but everyone knew he was punishing them."

"Why Earth?" Tom asked.

"Why not Earth? By then, the gods had found many planets that supported life, and they created intelligent life by enhancing local creatures on several of them, including Earth."

"Why were you sent to the same place?" Yamanu asked.

"That's a story for another time." Jade looked out the window. "It's morning, I'm tired, and I want to check on Kagra." She turned to Tom. "Did I uphold my end of the bargain to your satisfaction?"

He chuckled. "You've just given us a taste. There is so much more that I want to know, but it can wait. We are all tired, and we need to get some rest."

"I'm hungry," Yamanu said. "Where can I get some food?"

Sofia rose to her feet. "I can make you something in the kitchen."

Jarmo entered the living room. "Can I come in?"

Jade glanced at Tom. "Can he hear me?"

The god nodded. "Yamanu dropped the bubble."

"You can come in. I'm done."

"Thank you for sharing your history with us," Tom said.

"You're welcome. But if you can, don't share it with my people. I want my daughter to hear the story from me first."

He nodded. "You have my word."

"I appreciate that." She cast him a tight smile and rose to her feet. "If anyone needs me, I'll be in the infirmary."

77

KIAN

𝒜 s Kian disconnected the call, he looked at Turner and Onegus, who had joined them during Jade's story. "That was quite a tale. The gods were not painted in complimentary colors."

"Don't forget who told the story," Turner said. "That's how the Kra-ell recorded the events."

Onegus shook his head. "It was so similar to what the gods did with humans that it rang true. But since those sent to Earth were the progressives, they treated humanity much better than their elders treated the Kra-ell."

"I have many questions for Jade," Kian said. "But right now, we need to decide what to do with the compound's money."

Toven had compelled Valstar to reveal all the bank account numbers and where their stock portfolio was located, but Valstar only had access to the operating account, representing a small fraction of the holdings.

Turner leaned back in his chair and crossed his arms over his chest. "Roni can probably break into those accounts and transfer the money, but that would alert Igor. If we leave the funds and assets where they are, and Igor gets a whiff of what happened to his stronghold, transferring everything to different accounts would be the first thing he'll do, and the compound will have no source of income. Given the size of that portfolio, they can support themselves just from the dividends and the interest earned."

"It's a difficult decision," Kian said. "The community needs the money to survive, so taking the money out might be more important than catching Igor. But that will guarantee that Igor will bolt. However, if we don't empty the accounts, we will still know where the funds are, and Roni can track them, so if Igor bolts anyway, we will be able to follow the money."

"If he bolts, " Turner said, "we will have to relocate everyone in the compound. The problem will be moving them all out to a secure location without him being able to track them. We will have to put them all through an MRI and take out their trackers, and what's worse, we will have to keep those loyal to him imprisoned until we catch him. On their own, there isn't much they can do, and Toven's compulsion will keep them in line. But if Igor returns and gets a hold of them, he will break through Toven's compulsion as easily as Toven broke through his."

Thankfully, Toven had had the foresight to compel that information out of each person he freed from Igor's compulsion, so they knew who they needed to watch.

"Let's see." Onegus pulled up the list on his laptop. "Out of Igor's original group, Jade and Kagra killed six, and they are adamant about executing his second and third once they are no longer needed. Three are traveling with Igor. That leaves five who we know are still loyal to him. The four females in his original group want to see him dead. Of the forty-one purebloods born on Earth, twenty-three are loyal to him, and the rest hate him and his band of cronies. Eight of the twelve female purebloods born on Earth are loyal, including Igor and Jade's daughter. The hybrids are unhappy about being treated as second-class, and none of them is a fan of Igor, but they don't expect another pureblood to treat them any better."

Kian let out a breath. "That's a lot of people to keep locked up until we catch him. I'd rather risk losing the money than risk letting Igor get away. When we eliminate him, we can leave Jade in charge of the compound, sign a treaty of cooperation with her, leave a couple of people to monitor her, and be done with this mess."

Turner pursed his lips. "But if we don't move the money, and Igor still figures out that the compound was compromised, we won't have the funds to relocate them. It's either a win-win or a lose-lose. I don't like these odds."

"Neither do I. Let's hope the Fates shine upon us and lead Igor into our trap."

SOFIA

*Y*amanu wiped his mouth with a napkin and pushed away the plate with the chicken carcass. "Thanks for the meal, Sofia. The chicken was delicious." He turned to her father. "Do you grow them here? I heard a rooster crow."

The Guardian had demolished an entire hen with a mountain of potatoes on the side. The quantity could have fed four humans, but he didn't look full. Sofia would have offered him more, but that was all the cooked food she'd found in the refrigerator.

"We do." Her father smiled. "Wait until breakfast is made. I'm told that our eggs taste better than anything you can get in a supermarket."

"They do," Sofia confirmed. "Our eggs are delicious, especially when fried with homemade butter."

Yamanu sighed. "I wish I could stay and enjoy breakfast with you, but I need to check on my men." A guilty look crossed his handsome face. "All they have to eat are field rations." He rose to his feet and bowed his head to her father. "Thank you for feeding me."

Her father inclined his head. "Thank you for freeing us."

"You are welcome."

When Yamanu walked out of the kitchen, Sofia pushed to her feet. "Does anyone want more coffee?"

She had a feeling that her father was forcing himself to stay up so he could have a private talk with Marcel. It was sweet of him to do the fatherly thing.

He lifted his cup. "Please. I can't keep my eyes open, but how can I go to sleep when there is so much going on?"

"You can't stay awake for much longer." She lifted the carafe and poured more coffee into his cup. "You should get some sleep. I'll wake you if something happens that needs your attention."

"Aren't you tired?"

She smiled. "For me, this is daytime. I'm still on Oregon time."

"I see." He cast a sidelong glance at Marcel. "Maybe now you can tell me how you met Marcel, and how and why you two got engaged so quickly."

There were so many things that Sofia couldn't tell him. Her potential immortality was the most essential part because without it she couldn't explain the special bond between truelove mates, and without that it was difficult to explain why she and Marcel were technically engaged but didn't plan on getting married anytime soon.

Not that she was sure that she and Marcel were indeed bonded. It was supposed to happen between immortals and Dormants, but not Kra-ell Dormants.

She refilled Marcel's cup and her own before sitting back down. "I'm not pregnant, if that's what you were worried about."

He laughed nervously. "I wasn't worried. I was hopeful. I imagined a new life for you away from this place with a nice husband and a child. My grandchild."

"Fates willing, it will happen." Marcel took her hand and lifted it to his lips for a kiss.

The display of affection was a little embarrassing in front of her father, and she pulled her hand away. "The mission I couldn't tell you anything about was to spy on Marcel and his people." She cast an apologetic smile at Marcel. "Long story short, we fell in love, but then I was found out, we had a rough patch, but love triumphed."

"That's a very short story." Her father cut a reproachful look to Marcel. "What is Sofia not telling me?"

"A lot. She's under compulsion not to reveal certain things. I can fill in the blanks for you, but I will have to erase them from your memory."

Her father lifted his hand. "One moment. How will you erase things from my memory, and why?"

"What happened here tonight needs to remain a secret. Tom has the ability to compel, and I have the ability to reach into your mind, erase recent memories, and replace them with false ones."

"What about my old memories?"

"Those are tougher to erase, so Tom's compulsion to keep what you know about the Kra-ell from anyone who's not in this compound at the moment will have to suffice."

"Then what good will erasing the recent memories do? I will still know about the aliens living among us, and the others will remember too."

Marcel nodded. "That's true, but the Kra-ell don't know some of the things I'm about to tell you, and those things need to remain a secret from them. The only reason I'm sharing the information with you is that they have to do with Sofia and her future."

The resigned expression on her father's face made him look older than his fifty-seven years. "Do what you must."

Sofia put her hand on Marcel's arm. "It doesn't make sense to tell my father about what might be in my future and then thrall him to forget it. Can't Toven compel him to keep this a secret as well?"

"Who's Toven?" her father asked.

"Oops." Sofia slapped a hand over her mouth. "I shouldn't have said that."

MARCEL

*M*arcel sighed. "I'll take care of it."

Reaching into Jarmo's mind, he plucked the name Toven from his memory and replaced it with Tom.

Sofia's father shook his head. "What just happened?"

"A small mishap." Marcel turned to Sofia. "You are right. I wanted to avoid asking Tom to do that after all the work he had done, but I will. I'm also going to cast a silencing bubble around us, so we are not overheard."

"What is a silencing bubble?" Jarmo asked.

"One more trick of mine." Marcel cast the bubble. "Can you feel it?"

Jarmo's eyes widened with wonder. "Even the Kra-ell cannot do that."

"No, they can't." Marcel took a sip of his coffee to wet his mouth for the extended version he was about to deliver.

When he was done, Jarmo gaped at Sofia. "You will become like them?"

"It's not a sure thing, Isi."

Marcel frowned. "Isi?"

"It means daddy in Finnish."

"Oh, I see."

Jarmo was still speechless.

"What's the matter?" Sofia asked him.

He shook his head. "I'm glad that you will have a long life, but I am not glad that you will become like her."

"You mean my mother?"

He nodded.

"Even if I grow fangs, I will still be the same person I am now. The transition will change my body, not what's in here." She put her hand over her heart.

"Here you are!" Sofia's cousin burst into the kitchen, her eyes red-rimmed, either from crying or lack of sleep.

Dropping the silencing bubble, Marcel pulled out a chair for her.

"What happened?" Sofia asked. "Why are you crying?"

Helmi rubbed her eyes. "They put handcuffs on Tomos and are keeping him locked in the hybrids' quarters together with all the hybrids. I tried to tell them that Tomos was a good guy and that there was no need to keep him in cuffs, but they wouldn't listen. The big guy with the huge muscles told me that it's temporary, but he didn't tell me for how long." She glared at Marcel. "I thought that you came to free us? Did you mean only the humans?"

He wasn't sure how to answer that. "We came to free Jade and her people, and that includes you and probably Tomos. I hope he isn't loyal to Igor."

Helmi threw her hands in the air. "He isn't. He didn't have a choice and had to obey Igor and his men. All of us had to. That doesn't make him or us Igor's supporters."

"I know. The question is how he feels now. I wasn't there when Tom and the others compelled the hybrids to tell them the truth about their loyalties, but I would be surprised if Tomos or any of the others liked Igor."

"Of course, they don't. They were treated even worse than us." She shifted her eyes to Sofia. "Did you talk to your mother?"

Sofia shook her head. "Is she handcuffed and locked in her quarters as well?"

"They all are." Helmi rose to her feet and walked over to where the cups were stored. "I heard that the purebloods are locked in the basement. That's even worse." She poured herself a cup and sat back down.

"It's safer that way," Sofia murmured. "I wonder how my mother feels about her father."

Helmi's eyes widened. "Is he dead?"

Sofia grimaced. "Not yet, but he will be soon. Jade will kill him to avenge her sons and all the males of her tribe whom Igor and his cronies murdered. Igor enslaved her and the other females, and as if that wasn't enough, he stole all of their money."

"Oh." Helmi shook her head. "Those are many horrible things. I'm so happy that I'm human." She finished the rest of her coffee and got to her feet. "I'm going to sleep, and I hope not to have nightmares after what you told me."

SOFIA

*A*fter Helmi left, Sofia leaned over and kissed her father's cheek. "Get some sleep, Isi."

"Not yet." Her father leveled his eyes at Marcel. "What will happen to my daughter? What if she doesn't turn? What will happen to all of us?"

"Sofia will always be safe with me. Even if the induction doesn't work, she will live with me as my mate, and I'll cherish the years she can give me." Marcel took her hand and gave it a gentle squeeze. "But I strongly believe that she will transition, and we will have at least a thousand blissful years together."

As her father looked at her, tears misted his eyes. "I'm happy you found love, but I don't want to lose you. I want to be part of your life. I want to see my grandchildren born, and I want to be there to help you raise them. Don't you want to have me, your aunts, and your cousins in your life?"

She looked at Marcel. "Do you think your boss will allow them to live in his village? They don't have anywhere else they can go."

Marcel let out a breath. "I don't know. Maybe Kian will allow me to stay with you here. If Jade takes over command of the place, he will not leave her to do whatever she wants. They will sign a cooperation treaty, and Kian will need someone to be the clan's liaison to the Kra-ell. Perhaps I can get nominated to the post." He smiled. "After all, who else is better suited for the job than the guy who is mated to one of Jade's subjects?"

Sofia's heart soared with renewed hope. "That would be perfect. But won't you miss your people?"

"We can visit from time to time." He leaned closer and planted a kiss on her lips. "I love you, and if this is where you'll be the happiest, then this is where I'll be to share that happiness with you."

Her throat tight with emotion, Sofia leaned her forehead on his. "I love you so much. I can't believe you are willing to do this for me." She leaned back. "Living with the Kra-ell is not easy, and I don't know how things will change with Jade in charge. Listening to her story, I saw her in a different light, and I believe that she can be a good leader for the purebloods, but she needs to change her attitude toward the humans and the hybrids. Given the history of her people, she shouldn't treat anyone as second-class."

"You are absolutely right." Marcel shifted his gaze to her father. "We will elect a council, and each group will have the same number of representatives. Jade will have to get the council's approval for every major decision. That's how our clan is governed, and it works very well."

Her father nodded. "I like your suggestion." He rose to his feet and offered Marcel his hand. "Welcome to the family, Marcel. Can I call you son?"

Marcel shook his hand. "You can, but I will not call you Dad for obvious reasons. So maybe we should stick to our given names."

Understanding dawning, her father paled. "How old are you?"

"Much older than you."

"By how much?"

Sofia chuckled. "You don't want to know, and it doesn't matter. Even though Marcel has lived for a very long time, I am his first real love, and he is mine, and that's all that matters."

Her father nodded. "You are a smart lady, Sofia. And you make me proud." He leaned and kissed her cheek. "Now I can get some sleep. I'll see you both in a few hours."

"Hold on." Marcel pushed to his feet. "Tom needs to compel you to keep everything we told you a secret."

"Of course."

"It will only take a moment." Marcel led her father to the common room.

It took a little longer than that, and when Marcel returned to the kitchen alone, he sat back down and pulled her into his lap. "I like your father."

"And he likes you." She wrapped her arms around his neck. "Thank you for offering to live here with me, but we don't even know if any of us can stay here. We didn't catch Igor yet."

"I know. But your father needed to hear that. I will not take you away from him. No matter what happens, I will find a way for you to have everything you ever wanted, including having your father, aunts, and cousins near you."

"I love you." Her voice wobbled as happy tears spilled from the corners of her eyes. "I really don't want to ask and spoil this wonderful moment, but what about your guilt and your need for atonement? Are you ready to let it go?"

"My heart is lighter than it has ever been, but I still need to confess my crime and redeem myself either by punishment or service. Hopefully, our judge will show me leniency and choose service for my redemption."

Sofia grinned. "Isn't being the liaison to the Kra-ell a great service to the clan? I doubt anyone else would want the job."

"I hope Edna agrees with you."

"Let me talk with her, and I'll convince her." She cupped the back of his neck.

"You are no longer alone, Marcel. We are a team, and we will face the future together, with love and devotion, for better and for worse and for everything in between."

COMING UP NEXT
DARK ALLIANCE TRILOGY
The Children of the Gods Series
Books 68-70
(Releasing September 16, 2023)

Keep reading now

The Children of the Gods Book 68
DARK ALLIANCE
Kindred Souls
Is available on Amazon

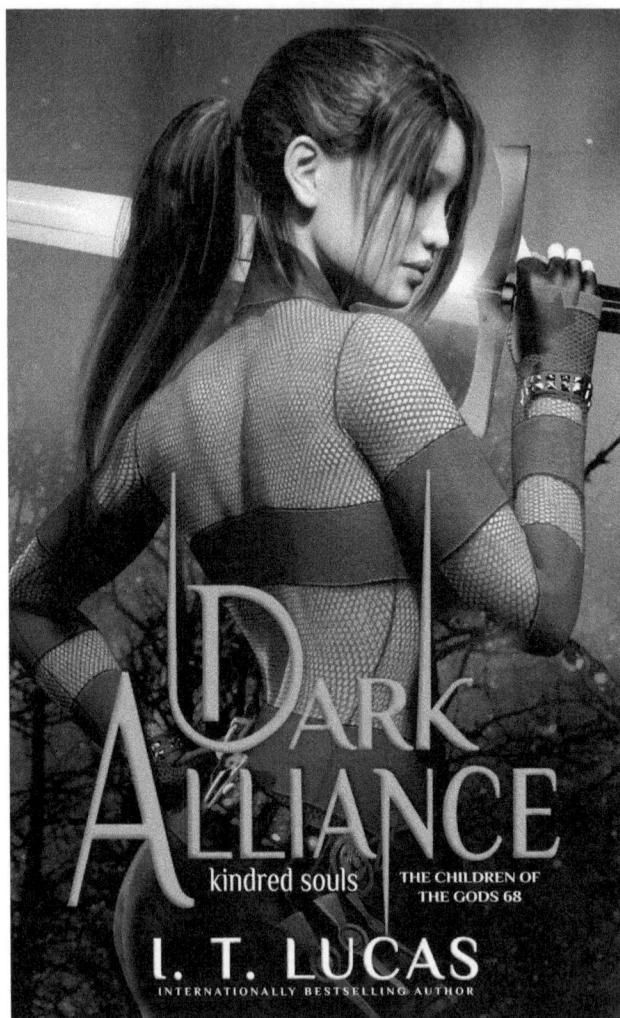

Dear reader,

Thank you for reading the Children of the Gods.

As an independent author, I rely on your support to spread the word. So if you enjoyed the story, please share your experience with others, and if it isn't too much trouble, I would greatly appreciate a brief review on Amazon.

Love & happy reading,

Isabell

DARK ALLIANCE EXCERPT

Jade

Jade strode into the infirmary and surveyed the cots that had been arranged in two neat rows in the center of the room. Several had been vacated, but many were still occupied.

Immortal Guardians watched over the injured, and for some reason, one of them was sitting on a chair next to her second-in-command's cot and was holding her hand. With his back turned to her, she couldn't see his face, but given the breadth of his shoulders, he wasn't a Kra-ell. The males of her species were much stronger than the immortals, but they were built slimmer.

Besides, no Kra-ell male would have shown Kagra such disrespect.

Mothers held their children's hands when they were small and frightened, but Kagra was a grown female and a warrior, and according to the liberators' doctor, she wasn't dying.

Liberators.

That still remained to be seen.

So far, the god who called himself Tom had done what he'd promised and more, freeing her people without a single unintended casualty, but Jade didn't trust gods, and that included the scions of the progressives who'd fought alongside the Kra-ell in the big rebellion back on the home planet.

Even when their intentions were noble, the gods' patronizing attitude toward the Kra-ell was offensive, and their ingrained belief in their own superiority was infuriating.

Jade had no choice but to accept Tom's help, and she still needed him to catch Igor so she could finally avenge her sons and the other males of her tribe. But once that was done, she wouldn't let the god or his immortal companions rule over her and her people.

Given that Tom was a powerful compeller on a par with Igor, that might not be easy to do, but she'd be damned if she lived another day enslaved to a male or a female, for that matter.

If Jade ever served anyone again, it would be by choice, and she would only serve a worthy Kra-ell ruler like the queen and her children, who Jade had sworn to protect.

Well, she'd only sworn to protect the queen, and she was no longer in the queen's service, but once a vow was made it never expired, and it didn't matter that she wasn't supposed to even know that the royal twins had been onboard the ship heading to Earth.

She'd failed to protect them just as she'd failed to protect her people, but there was no guilt associated with that failure because there had been nothing she could have done to prevent their ship's destruction, and without the mother ship, there was no way for her to locate the other escape pods.

In all likelihood, the twins and most of the other settlers hadn't survived.

Walking over to Kagra's cot, Jade grabbed a stool on the way and placed it next to the immortal's chair. "Does my second-in-command require a dedicated guard?"

It would have been better to conduct this conversation while she was looming over him, but the effect would have been lost if she had wobbled on her feet.

How long had she been awake?

It felt like she hadn't slept for days.

Given the copious quantity of Valstar's blood Jade had gorged on, she should have felt energized, but his blood must have been contaminated by the drug she'd put in his drink, and she could feel its effects. It was only by the Mother's grace that she'd functioned as well as she had and killed four of her sons' murderers. Kagra had dispatched two more, but she'd nearly lost her own life in the process.

Nevertheless, Jade wasn't going to get any sleep until Igor showed up. It was already eleven o'clock in the morning, and she was starting to get worried.

The immortal tilted his head and smiled. "I'm not here to guard your second. I'm checking on the female whose life I saved." He let go of Kagra's hand and offered his hand to Jade. "I'm Phinas."

So he was the one she'd heard about. The Guardian who'd leaped from fifty feet away and smashed his exoskeleton-reinforced fist into Gorven's head, killing him on impact.

From what Jade had been told, it was no small feat to perform such acrobatics with the tremendously heavy suit on.

The immortal was an impressive warrior.

"I'm Jade." Shaking what he'd offered, she dipped her head in respect. "Thank you for saving Kagra. I owe you a life-debt."

He held on to her hand. "You don't owe me anything because I didn't do it for you. But just out of curiosity, what does a life-debt mean?"

She liked his reply. But even though he hadn't saved Kagra for her, she still owed him a life-debt, and once it was offered, it had to be paid. "It means that I will defend you with my life if needed, and anything you ask of me is yours."

He arched a brow with a sly smile lifting one corner of his full lips. "Anything?"

Males.

No matter what species they were, they had only one thing on their minds. Although with how exhausted and dirty Jade was, the evidence of what she'd done crusting over her leathers, Phinas must be either teasing or just not very discriminating about the females he flirted with.

Then again, warriors pumped up from the battle were more lustful than usual.

To answer his question, though, anything meant anything.

Jade held his gaze. "That's what I said."

"What if I ask for your firstborn?"

She winced. "Too late for that. Both my first and second born sons are dead, slaughtered by Igor and his cronies."

The smile died on his lips, and he inclined his head. "My apologies. I didn't know."

"I thought that the Guardians had been briefed about the history of my tribe. Tom knew about my sons even before he got here, and so did Marcel, Sofia's boyfriend."

"I'm not a Guardian," Phinas said.

Was he a medic? That would explain why he was checking up on Kagra. Military medical staff received the same training as warriors, but if he were a medic, the doctor would have introduced him to her. Maybe he was in charge of munitions, or a tech?

"I was told that the one who'd saved Kagra's life wore an exoskeleton suit. Did the techs and medics get to wear them too?"

He smiled. "I'm not a tech or a medic. I'm first and foremost a warrior, but I'm not a Guardian because I'm not part of the Guardian force. I'm part of a group of volunteers." He glanced at one of the Guardians standing watch over the injured. "What do you call me and my men?"

"Kalugal's men," the Guardian said.

"Who is Kalugal?" Jade asked.

When Phinas glanced at the Guardian again, the guy shook his head.

"I'm sorry." Phinas smiled apologetically. "I'm not at liberty to discuss the clan's inner politics with you. You will have to ask Yamanu or Bhathian. They are in charge of this operation."

"I thought Tom was in charge."

Phinas shrugged. "I can't comment on that either. All I can tell you is that Tom is not a Guardian."

"That makes sense." He was a god, but the other Kra-ell in the infirmary didn't know that. She couldn't say it out loud. "He wouldn't be part of the military arm of the clan. That would be left to the descendants."

"That's correct." Phinas flashed her a charming smile. "It's a pleasure to talk to a female who is a warrior herself and knows how those things work."

"I assume that your females are not fighters."

He shook his head. "That's another thing I cannot comment on. All I can say is that I haven't had the pleasure of chatting with a female fighter before." He turned his gaze to Kagra. "Watching her fight was awe-inspiring. I have been trained to fight with swords and daggers, and I recognize skill when I see it. She's incredible."

Pride filled Jade's chest. "Kagra is exceptional. That's why I chose her as my second–in–command. When she wakes up, she will be upset about letting herself get gutted."

Jade turned around to look for the doctor the Guardians had brought along. She found him on the other side of the large room, checking on one of the injured hybrids.

When he felt her gaze and lifted his head, she asked, "Why is Kagra sleeping so much? You said that she's healing well."

He smiled sheepishly. "I gave her sedatives so she'd sleep."

"I thought you were only giving her painkillers."

He put his hand in his coat pocket. "I gave her both. Sleeping will help her heal faster."

Phinas

Phinas took the opportunity of Jade talking with Merlin to adjust himself and cross his legs.

From the moment he'd laid eyes on her, he'd been sporting a hard-on that he'd been desperately trying to hide. Despite being exhausted, dirty, and covered in dry blood splotches, the female was so damn hot that she made him as randy as a buck in heat.

It wasn't his style.

Phinas was coolheaded and reserved, and he'd never let females get under his skin.

Perhaps the spike in his libido had been caused by the testosterone still coursing through his blood after the battle, or maybe it was the fault of those damn tight leather pants and sheer mesh shirt of hers, or maybe the turn-on was the sword sheathed in a fancy scabbard and hung low on her hips, her swagger as she'd walked into the infirmary, the palpable power radiating from her, or all of the above.

Regardless of the trigger, though, the result was the same. He'd had trouble stringing two coherent thoughts together, as evidenced by his unfortunate blunder.

He'd heard that the males of Jade's tribe had been slaughtered by her captors, and he should have realized that she could have had a son or sons among them. But that was what happened when his mind was occupied by thoughts of stripping her naked.

He would leave the sword belt and boots on, though.

Jade was tall and slim, and her face was beautiful despite her huge eyes and hard expression. She had no breasts to speak of, but her ass was round and firm, just the way he liked it. However, the disturbing truth was that he was more turned on by her inner power than by her enticing feminine assets, and the fact that she was a ruthless killer only added to her dangerous allure.

That was strange as hell for him and entirely out of character.

Despite having been raised in Navuh's camp among males who believed that women were created to please and serve them and breed, Phinas wasn't a misogynist.

He'd never been one, but he was old, and in days past, women and men had very different roles in society.

Female warriors did not exist in his world, but he'd always believed that being mothers and caretakers was no less important, probably more so, but like other males of the time, he believed that motherhood was a female's ultimate calling and that women weren't suited for jobs that men performed.

Warriors took lives. Women created life and nurtured it.

After he'd been recruited by Kalugal and escaped Navuh's camp, Phinas had traveled to the US, where at the time women had been regarded with a little more respect, but not by much.

It had taken many more years for Western society to realize what had taken him mere weeks.

As soon as Phinas had been able to interact with women who were free to express themselves, he'd realized that they were as smart and as capable as men, just not as physically strong and aggressive, and that was fine. Not every male was born to be a fighter, either.

That being said, he was a dominant male by nature, and he'd never thought he would be attracted to someone like Jade. A female who could hand him his ass.

"Are you going to sit here all day?" Jade asked him. "Aren't you needed somewhere else?"

He arched a brow. "Does it bother you that I'm watching over Kagra?"

What he'd really wanted to ask was whether she was jealous of the attention he was giving her injured second.

"Kagra has the doctor to watch over her." Jade hung her head and let out a breath. "I'm so damn tired, but that's not an excuse. You're not one of my subjects, and what you do with your time is none of my business."

"You're not one of my subjects either, but my advice to you is to get some sleep."

"I can't. There is still so much to do, and Kagra is out, so I have no one to assist me. But even if she was fine, I still wouldn't go to sleep. I'm waiting for Igor's capture so I can finally kill him."

As a vicious expression twisted her lips, her fangs made an appearance, and her eyes blazed with red light, but even that wasn't enough to diminish his attraction to her.

On the contrary, he wanted her even more.

"You won't be much good to anyone when you fall flat on your face. You need to sleep for at least a couple of hours to recharge." He waved his hand at the empty cot next to Kagra's. "You can lie down right over here, and I'll wake you up the moment Igor is captured."

"I also need to talk to my daughter." She looked at the cot longingly. "But maybe I should rest for a few minutes before I do that." She pushed to her feet and walked to the other cot.

"How old is she?"

"Drova is sixteen." Jade unbuckled her sword belt. "She's a fine female with a lot of potential, but we don't get along, and I'm about to kill her father, which isn't going to help make things better between us." She put the sword under the cot and lay down with her boots on.

He had a feeling that Jade wouldn't have shared that information if she wasn't so tired, which made her less guarded.

It probably wasn't a secret that Igor was the father of her daughter, but it wasn't the kind of thing a woman told a stranger she'd just met.

The murderer of her sons had forced her to breed with him.

Jade must be forged from titanium alloy.

"Is she close to her father?" Phinas asked.

Jade snorted. "No one is close to Igor. He's a sociopath. But he's still her father." She closed her eyes. "Maybe I should kill him first and talk to her later?"

She turned on her side, giving him a great view of her gorgeous ass. "I'm just going to rest for a few minutes."

"You should rest for longer than that. I'll watch over you," he said with such conviction that she turned around and looked at him.

"Thank you. But that won't be necessary." Jade waved her hand at the Guardians. "I'm sure they can protect me if needed."

He doubted she would rely on them to defend her. Her sword was right there under her cot, reachable in a split second.

"I'm not going anywhere." He crossed his arms over his chest.

"Suit yourself." She turned around again.

Phinas wanted to learn more about Jade, to find out what kind of hellfire had forged such a tough female, but it would have to wait until after she'd exacted revenge for the slaughter of the males of her tribe and the subjugation of its females.

Kian

The last person Kian had expected to walk into the war room at one o'clock in the morning was his mother.

He pushed to his feet, walked over to her, and leaned to kiss her cheek. "Did you have trouble sleeping, Mother?"

A goddess only needed a few hours of sleep, but his mother was an early riser, and she enjoyed walking outside when the sun was just cresting the horizon. Her eyes were too sensitive for the harsh Southern California sun, even in the winter, and she liked being able to forgo the goggle-like sunglasses that she needed to wear other times when getting out of the house.

"I brought you coffee and pastries from the vending machines." She motioned for her butler to come in.

"Good evening, Master Kian." The Odu put the tray with the coffees and the wrapped pastries on the conference table, bowed, and headed out the door.

Kian pulled out a chair for her. "You still haven't told me why you are up and about so late."

She shrugged one delicate shoulder. "I could not sleep, and I did not want to call you in case you were in the midst of directing the battle, and I didn't want to call the house and wake Syssi up either. So I came to see if you were still here and

662

whether the evil Igor was captured." She smiled. "If I had known that you were all alone in here, I would have come to keep you company earlier."

She could've texted him, but she just hadn't wanted to give him a chance to tell her not to come.

After he'd told her about Jade's promise to Toven, Annani probably couldn't contain her curiosity. She wanted to hear what Jade had told Toven about the gods, the Kra-ell, and their home planet.

Kian took one of the paper cups and removed the lid. "Turner and Onegus went home to shower and change and catch a couple of hours of sleep, but they are coming back."

"You should have done the same."

"Until Igor is caught, someone needs to be in the war room at all times. Roni is in the lab, monitoring Igor's bank accounts, and I'm getting updates from the compound."

"How is Toven doing?" she asked.

"He and Mia worked all night to free everyone from Igor's compulsion, and last I heard, they were asleep on the couch in the common room in the human section. William removed everyone's collars, and he's resting as well. The Guardians are taking turns watching the purebloods and the hybrids, and Merlin is taking care of the injured. Did I cover everyone?"

"You didn't mention Marcel and Sofia."

Kian smiled. His mother was well-informed, and she had everyone cataloged in her brain. He could throw at her the name of any clan member, and she would know everything about them, down to their favorite foods and where they had visited on their last vacation.

Remembering that many details about so many people was a truly remarkable ability, but what was even more remarkable was how much she cared about each member of her clan.

"They are also in the human quarters, helping calm people down."

"How is Jade?"

"The last I heard, she took a nap on one of the cots in the infirmary. Her second-in-command was badly injured. Merlin patched her up, and she's going to be fine."

He'd already told her that there were no casualties on their side and that on the Kra-ell side, only Igor's inner circle cronies had been killed by Jade and Kagra, and several purebloods and hybrids were injured.

Annani smoothed the folds of her gown, readjusting it over her knees. "You know what I really want to know. You were too busy before, but this seems like a quiet time, and you can spare a few minutes to tell me what Jade shared with Toven about the gods."

Kian winced. "You're not going to like what I tell you."

"I want to hear it anyway."

"The gods weren't nice people, and those who they sent to Earth were rebels, banished here for their part in a rebellion."

Annani nodded solemnly. "I had a feeling it was something like that. Otherwise, they would not have been abandoned on Earth with no ability to return home or even communicate with their families."

"There is one part that you're going to love, though. You are most likely the granddaughter of the gods' king. Some of the rebels were his own children, and he sent them to Earth along with the others. Given that Ahn, Ekin, and Athor were all leaders of the gods' local community, each in their respective field of authority, they were no doubt royalty."

Annani smiled. "I had a feeling about that as well. My father wore the mantle of leadership with such inborn grace and dignity, but he never called himself king. Nevertheless, my mother insisted that I behave like a princess." She smoothed her skirt again even though it didn't need it. "What was the rebellion about?"

"The Kra-ell. Turns out that the Kra-ell were the gods' first attempt at creating a hybrid creature to serve them. But the old gods were not as progressive as your father and his siblings. They treated the Kra-ell like slaves. The young gods did not approve of the way the Kra-ell were being treated or rather mistreated. First, they demanded better conditions for the Kra-ell, and when that was achieved, they demanded equal rights and access to education, but the king and his council refused." Kian paused to unwrap a pastry. "Jade said that hundreds of generations passed between the stages of the Kra-ell emancipation, so it wasn't like those demands were made one right after the other."

"What happened during the rebellion?" Annani asked.

"The Kra-ell were stronger physically, which was probably by design because they were meant to be laborers, and back then, the gods didn't include suscepti- bility to mind manipulation in their genetic enhancements, so they couldn't defend themselves by seizing the Kra-ell minds. The gods had superior weapons, and their underground cities were fortified, but the Kra-ell had the numbers. The king mobilized the Odus, who were originally designed to be house servants, and they were converted to be defenders of the gods against the Kra-ell. But even with the Odus, the gods couldn't win, and the casualties on both sides were staggering. The king of the gods and the queen of the Kra-ell negotiated a peace treaty, and part of it was the decommissioning of the Odus." He leaned back and took a sip from his coffee. "In my opinion, the only reason for the king of the gods to agree to decommission the Odus was fear of them being used against him in another rebellion. Otherwise, it makes no sense for the gods to give up their best defensive weapon."

Annani tilted her head. "It might not be their best weapon anymore. Once the rebellion was over, they probably developed something better than the Odus and made sure that it could not fall into the wrong hands, or what they considered rebel hands."

"I agree."

They were probably both right. Kian wasn't much of a politician, but he knew how they operated, especially those who had been in power for too long and had no intentions of losing their seat to another. After the king decommissioned the Odus, most likely with a lot of fanfare and publicity for the consumption of his public, he must have started developing an alternative in secret. There was no way he'd left himself exposed to the possibility of another rebellion.

The next time someone dared to oppose him, he would have had a brutal and efficient response at the ready, one that was entirely under his control.

In fact, with the genetic manipulation mastery of the gods, he'd probably ordered another species to be altered for that purpose—creatures who were as strong as the Kra-ell but susceptible to mind manipulation and easy to destroy.

Was Kian letting his imagination run away from him?

Maybe.

But as it'd been proven time and again, reality was stranger than fiction.

"Was that the full version or a summary of what Jade had told Toven?" Annani asked. "So many questions remain unanswered."

"It was a summary, but Jade's full version was far from complete either. There are many things she probably doesn't know, and her spin is obviously tilted in the Kra-ell's favor. After Igor is apprehended and Jade takes charge of her community, we will ask her to tell us more."

THE CHILDREN OF THE GODS SERIES

THE CHILDREN OF THE GODS ORIGINS

1: GODDESS'S CHOICE

When gods and immortals still ruled the ancient world, one young goddess risked everything for love.

2: GODDESS'S HOPE

Hungry for power and infatuated with the beautiful Areana, Navuh plots his father's demise. After all, by getting rid of the insane god he would be doing the world a favor. Except, when gods and immortals conspire against each other, humanity pays the price.

But things are not what they seem, and prophecies should not to be trusted...

THE CHILDREN OF THE GODS

1: DARK STRANGER THE DREAM

Syssi's paranormal foresight lands her a job at Dr. Amanda Dokani's neuroscience lab, but it fails to predict the thrilling yet terrifying turn her life will take. Syssi has no clue that her boss is an immortal who'll drag her into a secret, millennia-old battle over humanity's future. Nor does she realize that the professor's imposing brother is the mysterious stranger who's been starring in her dreams.

Since the dawn of human civilization, two warring factions of immortals—the descendants of the gods of old—have been secretly shaping its destiny. Leading the clandestine battle from his luxurious Los Angeles high-rise, Kian is surrounded by his clan, yet alone. Descending from a single goddess, clan members are forbidden to each other. And as the only other immortals are their hated enemies, Kian and his kin have been long resigned to a lonely existence of fleeting trysts with human partners. That is, until his sister makes a game-changing discovery—a mortal seeress who she believes is a dormant carrier of their genes. Ever the realist, Kian is skeptical and refuses Amanda's plea to attempt Syssi's activation. But when his enemies learn of the Dormant's existence, he's forced to rush her to the safety of his keep. Inexorably drawn to Syssi, Kian wrestles with his conscience as he is tempted to explore her budding interest in the darker shades of sensuality.

2: DARK STRANGER REVEALED

While sheltered in the clan's stronghold, Syssi is unaware that Kian and Amanda are not human, and neither are the supposedly religious fanatics that are after her. She feels a powerful connection to Kian, and as he introduces her to a world of pleasure she never dared imagine, his dominant sexuality is a revelation. Considering that she's completely out of her element, Syssi feels comfortable and safe letting go with him. That is, until she begins to suspect that all is not as it seems. Piecing the puzzle together, she draws a scary, yet wrong conclusion...

3: DARK STRANGER IMMORTAL

When Kian confesses his true nature, Syssi is not as much shocked by the revelation as she is wounded by what she perceives as his callous plans for her.

If she doesn't turn, he'll be forced to erase her memories and let her go. His family's safety demands secrecy – no one in the mortal world is allowed to know that immortals exist.

Resigned to the cruel reality that even if she stays on to never again leave the keep, she'll get old while Kian won't, Syssi is determined to enjoy what little time she has with him, one day at a time.

Can Kian let go of the mortal woman he loves? Will Syssi turn? And if she does, will she survive the dangerous transition?

4: Dark Enemy Taken

Dalhu can't believe his luck when he stumbles upon the beautiful immortal professor. Presented with a once in a lifetime opportunity to grab an immortal female for himself, he kidnaps her and runs. If he ever gets caught, either by her people or his, his life is forfeit. But for a chance of a loving mate and a family of his own, Dalhu is prepared to do everything in his power to win Amanda's heart, and that includes leaving the Doom brotherhood and his old life behind.

Amanda soon discovers that there is more to the handsome Doomer than his dark past and a hulking, sexy body. But succumbing to her enemy's seduction, or worse, developing feelings for a ruthless killer is out of the question. No man is worth life on the run, not even the one and only immortal male she could claim as her own…

Her clan and her research must come first…

5: Dark Enemy Captive

When the rescue team returns with Amanda and the chained Dalhu to the keep, Amanda is not as thrilled to be back as she thought she'd be. Between Kian's contempt for her and Dalhu's imprisonment, Amanda's budding relationship with Dalhu seems doomed. Things start to look up when Annani offers her help, and together with Syssi they resolve to find a way for Amanda to be with Dalhu. But will she still want him when she realizes that he is responsible for her nephew's murder? Could she? Will she take the easy way out and choose Andrew instead?

6: Dark Enemy Redeemed

Amanda suspects that something fishy is going on onboard the Anna. But when her investigation of the peculiar all-female Russian crew fails to uncover anything other than more speculation, she decides it's time to stop playing detective and face her real problem—a man she shouldn't want but can't live without.

6.5: My Dark Amazon

When Michael and Kri fight off a gang of humans, Michael gets stabbed. The injury to his immortal body recovers fast, but the one to his ego takes longer, putting a strain on his relationship with Kri.

7: Dark Warrior Mine

When Andrew is forced to retire from active duty, he believes that all he has to look forward to is a boring desk job. His glory days in special ops are over. But as it turns out, his thrill ride has just begun. Andrew discovers not only that immortals exist and have been manipulating global affairs since antiquity, but that he and his sister are rare possessors of the immortal genes.

Problem is, Andrew might be too old to attempt the activation process. His sister, who is fourteen years his junior, barely made it through the transition, so the odds of him coming out of it alive, let alone immortal, are slim.

But fate may force his hand.

Helping a friend find his long-lost daughter, Andrew finds a woman who's worth taking the risk for. Nathalie might be a Dormant, but the only way to find out for sure requires fangs and venom.

8: Dark Warrior's Promise

Andrew and Nathalie's love flourishes, but the secrets they keep from each other taint their relationship with doubts and suspicions. In the meantime, Sebastian and his men are getting bolder, and the storm that's brewing will shift the balance of power in the millennia-old conflict between Annani's clan and its enemies.

9: Dark Warrior's Destiny

The new ghost in Nathalie's head remembers who he was in life, providing Andrew and her with indisputable proof that he is real and not a figment of her imagination.

Convinced that she is a Dormant, Andrew decides to go forward with his transition immediately after the rescue mission at the Doomers' HQ.

Fearing for his life, Nathalie pleads with him to reconsider. She'd rather spend the rest of her mortal days with Andrew than risk what they have for the fickle promise of immortality.

While the clan gets ready for battle, Carol gets help from an unlikely ally. Sebastian's second-in-command can no longer ignore the torment she suffers at the hands of his commander and offers to help her, but only if she agrees to his terms.

10: Dark Warrior's Legacy

Andrew's acclimation to his post-transition body isn't easy. His senses are sharper, he's bigger, stronger, and hungrier. Nathalie fears that the changes in the man she loves are more than physical. Measuring up to this new version of him is going to be a challenge.

Carol and Robert are disillusioned with each other. They are not destined mates, and love is not on the horizon. When Robert's three months are up, he might be left with nothing to show for his sacrifice.

Lana contacts Anandur with disturbing news; the yacht and its human cargo are in Mexico. Kian must find a way to apprehend Alex and rescue the women on board without causing an international incident.

11: Dark Guardian Found

What would you do if you stopped aging?

Eva runs. The ex-DEA agent doesn't know what caused her strange mutation, only that if discovered, she'll be dissected like a lab rat. What Eva doesn't know, though, is that she's a descendant of the gods, and that she is not alone. The man who rocked her world in one life-changing encounter over thirty years ago is an immortal as well.

To keep his people's existence secret, Bhathian was forced to turn his back on the only woman who ever captured his heart, but he's never forgotten and never stopped looking for her.

12: Dark Guardian Craved

Cautious after a lifetime of disappointments, Eva is mistrustful of Bhathian's professed feelings of love. She accepts him as a lover and a confidant but not as a life partner.

Jackson suspects that Tessa is his true love mate, but unless she overcomes her fears, he might never find out.

Carol gets an offer she can't refuse—a chance to prove that there is more to her than meets the eye. Robert believes she's about to commit a deadly mistake, but when he tries to dissuade her, she tells him to leave.

13: Dark Guardian's Mate

Prepare for the heart-warming culmination of Eva and Bhathian's story!

14: Dark Angel's Obsession

The cold and stoic warrior is an enigma even to those closest to him. His secrets are about to unravel...

15: Dark Angel's Seduction

Brundar is fighting a losing battle. Calypso is slowly chipping away his icy armor from the outside, while his need for her is melting it from the inside.

He can't allow it to happen. Calypso is a human with none of the Dormant indicators. There is no way he can keep her for more than a few weeks.

16: Dark Angel's Surrender

Get ready for the heart pounding conclusion to Brundar and Calypso's story.

Callie still couldn't wrap her head around it, nor could she summon even a smidgen of sorrow or regret. After all, she had some memories with him that weren't horrible. She should've felt something. But there was nothing, not even shock. Not even horror at what had transpired over the last couple of hours.

Maybe it was a typical response for survivors--feeling euphoric for the simple reason that they were alive. Especially when that survival was nothing short of miraculous.

Brundar's cold hand closed around hers, reminding her that they weren't out of the woods yet. Her injuries were superficial, and the most she had to worry about was some scarring. But, despite his and Anandur's reassurances, Brundar might never walk again.

If he ended up crippled because of her, she would never forgive herself for getting him involved in her crap.

"Are you okay, sweetling? Are you in pain?" Brundar asked.

Her injuries were nothing compared to his, and yet he was concerned about her. God, she loved this man. The thing was, if she told him that, he would run off, or crawl away as was the case.

Hey, maybe this was the perfect opportunity to spring it on him.

17: Dark Operative: A Shadow of Death

As a brilliant strategist and the only human entrusted with the secret of immortals' existence, Turner is both an asset and a liability to the clan. His request to attempt transition into immortality as an alternative to cancer treatments cannot be denied without risking the clan's exposure. On the other hand, approving it means risking his premature death. In both scenarios, the clan will lose a valuable ally.

When the decision is left to the clan's physician, Turner makes plans to manipulate her by taking advantage of her interest in him.

Will Bridget fall for the cold, calculated operative? Or will Turner fall into his own trap?

18: Dark Operative: A Glimmer of Hope

As Turner and Bridget's relationship deepens, living together seems like the right move, but to make it work both need to make concessions.

Bridget is realistic and keeps her expectations low. Turner could never be the truelove mate she yearns for, but he is as good as she's going to get. Other than his emotional limitations, he's perfect in every way.

Turner's hard shell is starting to show cracks. He wants immortality, he wants to be part of the clan, and he wants Bridget, but he doesn't want to cause her pain.

His options are either abandon his quest for immortality and give Bridget his few remaining decades, or abandon Bridget by going for the transition and most likely dying. His rational mind dictates that he chooses the former, but his gut pulls him toward the latter. Which one is he going to trust?

19: Dark Operative: The Dawn of Love

Get ready for the exciting finale of Bridget and Turner's story!

20: Dark Survivor Awakened

This was a strange new world she had awakened to.

Her memory loss must have been catastrophic because almost nothing was familiar. The language was foreign to her, with only a few words bearing some similarity to the language she thought in. Still, a full moon cycle had passed since her awakening, and little by little she was gaining basic understanding of it--only a few words and phrases, but she was learning more each day.

A week or so ago, a little girl on the street had tugged on her mother's sleeve and pointed at her. "Look, Mama, Wonder Woman!"

The mother smiled apologetically, saying something in the language these people spoke, then scurried away with the child looking behind her shoulder and grinning.

When it happened again with another child on the same day, it was settled.

Wonder Woman must have been the name of someone important in this strange world she had awoken to, and since both times it had been said with a smile it must have been a good one.

Wonder had a nice ring to it.

She just wished she knew what it meant.

21: Dark Survivor Echoes of Love

Wonder's journey continues in *Dark Survivor Echoes of Love*.

22: Dark Survivor Reunited

The exciting finale of Wonder and Anandur's story.

23: Dark Widow's Secret

Vivian and her daughter share a powerful telepathic connection, so when Ella can't be reached by conventional or psychic means, her mother fears the worst.

Help arrives from an unexpected source when Vivian gets a call from the young doctor she met at a psychic convention. Turns out Julian belongs to a private organization specializing in retrieving missing girls.

As Julian's clan mobilizes its considerable resources to rescue the daughter, Magnus is charged with keeping the gorgeous young mother safe.

Worry for Ella and the secrets Vivian and Magnus keep from each other should be enough to prevent the sparks of attraction from kindling a blaze of desire. Except, these pesky sparks have a mind of their own.

24: Dark Widow's Curse

A simple rescue operation turns into mission impossible when the Russian mafia gets involved. Bad things are supposed to come in threes, but in Vivian's case, it seems like there is no limit to bad luck. Her family and everyone who gets close to her is affected by her curse.

Will Magnus and his people prove her wrong?

25: Dark Widow's Blessing

The thrilling finale of the Dark Widow trilogy!

26: Dark Dream's Temptation

Julian has known Ella is the one for him from the moment he saw her picture, but when he finally frees her from captivity, she seems indifferent to him. Could he have been mistaken?

Ella's rescue should've ended that chapter in her life, but it seems like the road back to normalcy has just begun and it's full of obstacles. Between the pitying looks she gets and her mother's attempts to get her into therapy, Ella feels like she's typecast as a victim, when nothing could be further from the truth. She's a tough survivor, and she's going to prove it.

Strangely, the only one who seems to understand is Logan, who keeps popping up in her dreams. But then, he's a figment of her imagination—or is he?

27: Dark Dream's Unraveling

While trying to figure out a way around Logan's silencing compulsion, Ella concocts an ambitious plan. What if instead of trying to keep him out of her dreams, she could pretend to like him and lure him into a trap?

Catching Navuh's son would be a major boon for the clan, as well as for Ella. She will have her revenge, turning the tables on another scumbag out to get her.

28: Dark Dream's Trap

The trap is set, but who is the hunter and who is the prey? Find out in this heart-pounding conclusion to the *Dark Dream* trilogy.

29: Dark Prince's Enigma

As the son of the most dangerous male on the planet, Lokan lives by three rules:

Don't trust a soul.

Don't show emotions.

And don't get attached.

Will one extraordinary woman make him break all three?

30: Dark Prince's Dilemma

Will Kian decide that the benefits of trusting Lokan outweigh the risks?

Will Lokan betray his father and brothers for the greater good of his people?

Are Carol and Lokan true-love mates, or is one of them playing the other?

So many questions, the path ahead is anything but clear.

31: Dark Prince's Agenda

While Turner and Kian work out the details of Areana's rescue plan, Carol and Lokan's tumultuous relationship hits another snag. Is it a sign of things to come?

32 : Dark Queen's Quest

A former beauty queen, a retired undercover agent, and a successful model, Mey is not the typical damsel in distress. But when her sister drops off the radar and then someone starts following her around, she panics.

Following a vague clue that Kalugal might be in New York, Kian sends a team headed by Yamanu to search for him.

As Mey and Yamanu's paths cross, he offers her his help and protection, but will that be all?

33: Dark Queen's Knight

As the only member of his clan with a godlike power over human minds, Yamanu has been shielding his people for centuries, but that power comes at a steep price. When Mey enters his life, he's faced with the most difficult choice.

The safety of his clan or a future with his fated mate.

34: Dark Queen's Army

As Mey anxiously waits for her transition to begin and for Yamanu to test whether his godlike powers are gone, the clan sets out to solve two mysteries:

Where is Jin, and is she there voluntarily?

Where is Kalugal, and what is he up to?

35: Dark Spy Conscripted

Jin possesses a unique paranormal ability. Just by touching someone, she can insert a mental hook into their psyche and tie a string of her consciousness to it, creating a tether. That doesn't make her a spy, though, not unless her talent is discovered by those seeking to exploit it.

36: Dark Spy's Mission

Jin's first spying mission is supposed to be easy. Walk into the club, touch Kalugal to tether her consciousness to him, and walk out.

Except, they should have known better.

37: Dark Spy's Resolution

The best-laid plans often go awry...

38: Dark Overlord New Horizon

Jacki has two talents that set her apart from the rest of the human race.

She has unpredictable glimpses of other people's futures, and she is immune to mind manipulation.

Unfortunately, both talents are pretty useless for finding a job other than the one she had in the government's paranormal division.

It seemed like a sweet deal, until she found out that the director planned on producing super babies by compelling the recruits into pairing up. When an opportunity to escape the program presented itself, she took it, only to find out that humans are not at the top of the food chain.

Immortals are real, and at the very top of the hierarchy is Kalugal, the most powerful, arrogant, and sexiest male she has ever met.

With one look, he sets her blood on fire, but Jacki is not a fool. A man like him will never think of her as anything more than a tasty snack, while she will never settle for anything less than his heart.

39: Dark Overlord's Wife

Jacki is still clinging to her all-or-nothing policy, but Kalugal is chipping away at her resistance. Perhaps it's time to ease up on her convictions. A little less than all is still much better than nothing, and a couple of decades with a demigod is probably worth more than a lifetime with a mere mortal.

40: Dark Overlord's Clan

As Jacki and Kalugal prepare to celebrate their union, Kian takes every precaution to safeguard his people. Except, Kalugal and his men are not his only potential adversaries, and compulsion is not the only power he should fear.

41: Dark Choices The Quandary

When Rufsur and Edna meet, the attraction is as unexpected as it is undeniable. Except, she's the clan's judge and councilwoman, and he's Kalugal's second-in-command. Will loyalty and duty to their people keep them apart?

42: Dark Choices Paradigm Shift

Edna and Rufsur are miserable without each other, and their two-week separation seems like an eternity. Long-distance relationships are difficult, but for immortal couples they are impossible. Unless one of them is willing to leave everything behind for the other, things are just going to get worse. Except, the cost of compromise is far greater than giving up their comfortable lives and hard-earned positions. The future of their people is on the line.

43: DARK CHOICES THE ACCORD

The winds of change blowing over the village demand hard choices. For better or worse, Kian's decisions will alter the trajectory of the clan's future, and he is not ready to take the plunge. But as Edna and Rufsur's plight gains widespread support, his resistance slowly begins to erode.

44: DARK SECRETS RESURGENCE

On a sabbatical from his Stanford teaching position, Professor David Levinson finally has time to write the sci-fi novel he's been thinking about for years.

The phenomena of past life memories and near-death experiences are too controversial to include in his formal psychiatric research, while fiction is the perfect outlet for his esoteric ideas.

Hoping that a change of pace will provide the inspiration he needs, David accepts a friend's invitation to an old Scottish castle.

45: DARK SECRETS UNVEILED

When Professor David Levinson accepts a friend's invitation to an old Scottish castle, what he finds there is more fantastical than his most outlandish theories. The castle is home to a clan of immortals, their leader is a stunning demigoddess, and even more shockingly, it might be precisely where he belongs.

Except, the clan founder is hiding a secret that might cast a dark shadow on David's relationship with her daughter.

Nevertheless, when offered a chance at immortality, he agrees to undergo the dangerous induction process.

Will David survive his transition into immortality? And if he does, will his relationship with Sari survive the unveiling of her mother's secret?

46: DARK SECRETS ABSOLVED

Absolution.

David had given and received it.

The few short hours since he'd emerged from the coma had felt incredible. He'd finally been free of the guilt and pain, and for the first time since Jonah's death, he had felt truly happy and optimistic about the future.

He'd survived the transition into immortality, had been accepted into the clan, and was about to marry the best woman on the face of the planet, his true love mate, his salvation, his everything.

What could have possibly gone wrong?

Just about everything.

47: DARK HAVEN ILLUSION

Welcome to Safe Haven, where not everything is what it seems.

On a quest to process personal pain, Anastasia joins the Safe Haven Spiritual Retreat.

Through meditation, self-reflection, and hard work, she hopes to make peace with the voices in her head.

This is where she belongs.

Except, membership comes with a hefty price, doubts are sacrilege, and leaving is not as easy as walking out the front gate.

Is living in utopia worth the sacrifice?

Anastasia believes so until the arrival of a new acolyte changes everything.

Apparently, the gods of old were not a myth, their immortal descendants share the planet with humans, and she might be a carrier of their genes.

48: Dark Haven Unmasked

As Anastasia leaves Safe Haven for a week-long romantic vacation with Leon, she hopes to explore her newly discovered passionate side, their budding relationship, and perhaps also solve the mystery of the voices in her head. What she discovers exceeds her wildest expectations.

In the meantime, Eleanor and Peter hope to solve another mystery. Who is Emmett Haderech, and what is he up to?

49: Dark Haven Found

Anastasia is growing suspicious, and Leon is running out of excuses.

Risking death for a chance at immortality should've been her choice to make. Will she ever forgive him for taking it away from her?

50: Dark Power Untamed

Attending a charity gala as the clan's figurehead, Onegus is ready for the pesky socialites he'll have a hard time keeping away. Instead, he encounters an intriguing beauty who won't give him the time of day.

Bad things happen when Cassandra gets all worked up, and given her fiery temper, the destructive power is difficult to tame. When she meets a gorgeous, cocky billionaire at a charity event, things just might start blowing up again.

51: Dark Power Unleashed

Cassandra's power is unpredictable, uncontrollable, and destructive. If she doesn't learn to harness it, people might get hurt.

Onegus's self-control is legendary. Even his fangs and venom glands obey his commands.

They say that opposites attract, and perhaps it's true, but are they any good for each other?

52: Dark Power Convergence

The threads of fate converge, mysteries unfold, and the clan's future is forever altered in the least expected way.

53: Dark Memories Submerged

Geraldine's memories are spotty at best, and many of them are pure fiction. While her family attempts to solve the puzzle with far too many pieces missing, she's forced to confront a past life that she can't remember, a present that's more fantastic than her wildest made-up stories, and a future that might be better than her most heartfelt fantasies. But as more clues are uncovered, the picture starting to emerge is beyond anything she or her family could have ever imagined.

54: Dark Memories Emerge

The more clues emerge about Geraldine's past, the more questions arise.

Did she really have a twin sister who drowned?

Who is the mysterious benefactor in her hazy recollections?

Did he have anything to do with her becoming immortal?

Thankfully, she doesn't have to find the answers alone.

Cassandra and Onegus are there for her, and so is Shai, the immortal who sets her body on fire.

As they work together to solve the mystery, the four of them stumble upon a millennia-old secret that could tip the balance of power between the clan and its enemies.

55: Dark Memories Restored

As the past collides with the present, a new future emerges.

56: Dark Hunter's Query

For most of his five centuries of existence, Orion has walked the earth alone, searching for answers.

Why is he immortal?

Where did his powers come from?

Is he the only one of his kind?

When fate puts Orion face to face with the god who sired him, he learns the secret behind his immortality and that he might not be the only one.

As the goddess's eldest daughter and a mother of thirteen, Alena deserves the title of Clan Mother just as much as Annani, but she's not interested in honorifics. Being her mother's companion and keeping the mischievous goddess out of trouble is a rewarding, full-time job. Lately, though, Alena's love for her mother and the clan's gratitude is not enough.

She craves adventure, excitement, and perhaps a true-love mate of her own.

When Alena and Orion meet, sparks fly, but they both resist the pull. Alena could never bring herself to trust the powerful compeller, and Orion could never allow himself to fall in love again.

57: Dark Hunter's Prey

When Alena and Orion join Kalugal and Jacki on a romantic vacation to the enchanting Lake Lugu in China, they anticipate a couple of visits to Kalugal's archeological dig, some sightseeing, and a lot of lovemaking.

Their excursion takes an unexpected turn when Jacki's vision sends them on a perilous hunt for the elusive Kra-ell.

As things progress from bad to worse, Alena beseeches the Fates to keep everyone in their group alive. She can't fathom losing any of them, but most of all, Orion.

For over two thousand years, she walked the earth alone, but after mere days with him at her side, she can't imagine life without him.

58: Dark Hunter's Boon

As Orion and Alena's relationship blooms and solidifies, the two investigative teams combine their recent discoveries to piece together more of the Kra-ell mystery.

Attacking the puzzle from another angle, Eleanor works on gaining access to Echelon's powerful AI spy network.

Together, they are getting dangerously close to finding the elusive Kra-ell.

59: Dark God's Avatar

Unaware of the time bomb ticking inside her, Mia had lived the perfect life until it all came to a screeching halt, but despite the difficulties she faces, she doggedly pursues her dreams.

Once known as the god of knowledge and wisdom, Toven has grown cold and indifferent. Disillusioned with humanity, he travels the world and pens novels about the love he can no longer feel.

Seeking to escape his ever-present ennui, Toven gives a cutting-edge virtual experience a try. When his avatar meets Mia's, their sizzling virtual romance unexpectedly turns into something deeper and more meaningful.

Will it endure in the real world?

60: Dark God's Reviviscence

Toven might have failed in his attempts to improve humanity's condition, but he isn't going to fail to improve Mia's life, making it the best it can be despite her fragile health, and he can do that not as a god, but as a man who possesses the means, the smarts, and the determination to do it.

No effort is enough to repay Mia for reviving his deadened heart and making him excited for the next day, but the flip side of his reviviscence is the fear of losing its catalyst.

Given Mia's condition, Toven doesn't dare to over excite her. His venom is a powerful aphrodisiac, euphoric, and an all-around health booster, but it's also extremely potent. It might kill her instead of making her better.

61: Dark God Destinies Converge

Destinies converge, and secrets are revealed in part three of Mia and Toven's story.

62: Dark Whispers From The Past

A brilliant scientist and programmer, William lives for his work, but when he recruits a young bioinformatician to help him decipher the gods' genetic blueprints, he find himself smitten with more than just her brain.

A Ph.d at nineteen, Kaia is considered a prodigy and expects a bright future in academia. But when William invites her to join his secret research team, she accepts for reasons that have nothing to do with her career objectives. Wiliam's promise to look into her best friend's disappearance is an offer she just can't refuse.

63: Dark Whispers From Afar

William knows that his budding relationship with the nineteen-year-old Kaia will be frowned upon, but he's unprepared for her family's vehement opposition.

Family means everything to Kaia, so when she finds herself in the impossible position of having to choose between them and William, she resorts to unconventional means to resolve the conflict.

64: DARK WHISPERS FROM BEYOND

The sacrifices Kaia and her family have to make for a chance of gaining immortality might tear them apart, and success is not guaranteed.

Is the dubious promise of eternal life worth the risk of losing everything?

65: DARK GAMBIT THE PAWN

Temporarily assigned to supervise a team of bioinformaticians, Marcel expects to spend a couple of weeks in the peaceful retreat of Safe Haven, enjoying Oregon Coast's cool weather and rugged beauty.

Things quickly turn chaotic when the retreat's director receives an email with an encoded message about a potential new threat to the clan.

While those in charge of security debate what to do next, Safe Haven's first ever paranormal retreat is about to begin, and one of the attendees is a mysterious woman who makes Marcel's heart beat faster whenever she's near.

Is the beautiful mortal his one truelove?

Or is she the harbinger of more bad news?

66: DARK GAMBIT THE PLAY

To get to Safe Haven's inner circle, the Kra-ell leader sacrifices a pawn. He does not expect her to reach the final rank and promote to a queen.

67: DARK GAMBIT RELIANCE

Marcel takes a big risk by telling Sofia his greatest sin. Can he trust her to keep it a secret? Or maybe it's time to confess his crime and submit to whatever punishment Edna deems appropriate?

Three miserable centuries of living with guilt and remorse are long enough.

Once the dust settles on the Kra-ell crisis, he will gather the courage to put himself at the court's mercy.

68: DARK ALLIANCE KINDRED SOULS

A daring operation half a world away devolves into a full-scale crisis that escalates rapidly, requiring the clan's full might and technological wizardry to manage and survive.

Hardened by duty and tragedy, Jade is driven by a burning desire for revenge. When Phinas saves her second-in-command, Jade's gratitude quickly becomes something more.

69: DARK ALLIANCE TURBULENT WATERS

When a dangerous foe turns the tables on the clan, complicating the Kra-ell rescue operation in unforeseeable ways, Kian and his crew bet all on a brilliant misdirection.

On board the Aurora, Phinas and Jade brace for battle while enjoying a few stolen moments of passion.

Drawn to the woman he sees behind the aloof leader, Phinas realizes that what has started as a calculated political move has evolved into a deepening sense of companionship.

Jade finds reprieve in Phinas's arms, but duty and tradition make it difficult for her to accept that what she feels for him is more than just gratitude and desire.

After all, the Kra-ell don't believe in love.

70: Dark Alliance Perfect Storm

After two decades in captivity, Jade is finally free, her quest for revenge within grasp, but danger still looms large. A storm is brewing on the horizon, gathering momentum and threatening to obliterate Jade's tenuous hold on hope for a better future.

71: Dark Healing Blind Justice

The sanctuary is Vanessa's life project. The monumental task of rehabilitating the traumatized victims of trafficking doesn't leave much time for personal life, let alone dating or finding her one and only.

When Kian asks her to help the Kra-ell, she's torn between her duty to the sanctuary and a group of emotionally wounded aliens who no other psychologist can treat.

She's the only immortal with the necessary training to get it done.

The Kra-ell culture and the purebloods' nearly androgynous alien looks shouldn't appeal to her, and yet, she finds one of them disturbingly attractive.

Is it the dangerous vibe he emits?

Does it speak to her on a subconscious level?

Or is it her need to put the broken pieces of him back together?

And why is he interested in her?

She cannot offer him a fight for dominance like a Kra-ell female would, but some strange and unfamiliar part of her wishes she could.

72: Dark Healing Blind Trust

Riddled with guilt over the crimes he was forced to commit, Mo-red is ready to stand trial and accept the death sentence he believes he deserves, but when the clan's alluring psychologist offers a new perspective on his past and hope for a better future, he resolves to fight for his life.

73: Dark healing Blind Curve

Kian is still reeling from the shocking revelations about the twins when a new threat manifests, eclipsing everything he's had to deal with up until now. In light of the new developments, Igor, the other Kra-ell prisoners, and the pending trial are no longer at the forefront of his mind, but the opposite is true for Vanessa. As her relationship with Mo-red solidifies, she is determined to save the male she loves, even if it means breaking him free and living on the run.

THE PERFECT MATCH SERIES

Perfect Match: Vampire's Consort

When Gabriel's company is ready to start beta testing, he invites his old crush to inspect its medical safety protocol.

Curious about the revolutionary technology of the *Perfect Match Virtual Fantasy-Fulfillment studios*, Brenna agrees.

Neither expects to end up partnering for its first fully immersive test run.

Perfect Match: King's Chosen

When Lisa's nutty friends get her a gift certificate to *Perfect Match Virtual Fantasy Studios*, she has no intentions of using it. But since the only way to get a refund is if no partner can be found for her, she makes sure to request a fantasy so girly and over the top that no sane guy will pick it up.

Except, someone does.

Warning: This fantasy contains a hot, domineering crown prince, sweet insta-love, steamy love scenes painted with light shades of gray, a wedding, and a HEA in both the virtual and real worlds.

Intended for mature audience.

Perfect Match: Captain's Conquest

Working as a Starbucks barista, Alicia fends off flirting all day long, but none of the guys are as charming and sexy as Gregg. His frequent visits are the highlight of her day, but since he's never asked her out, she assumes he's taken. Besides, between a day job and a budding music career, she has no time to start a new relationship.

That is until Gregg makes her an offer she can't refuse—a gift certificate to the virtual fantasy fulfillment service everyone is talking about. As a huge Star Trek fan, Alicia has a perfect match in mind—the captain of the Starship Enterprise.

THE THIEF WHO LOVED ME

When Marian splurges on a Perfect Match Virtual adventure as a world infamous jewel thief, she expects high-wire fun with a hot partner who she will never have to see again in real life.

A virtual encounter seems like the perfect answer to Marcus's string of dating disasters. No strings attached, no drama, and definitely no love. As a die-hard James Bond fan, he chooses as his avatar a dashing MI6 operative, and to complement his adventure, a dangerously seductive partner.

Neither expects to find their forever Perfect Match.

MY MERMAN PRINCE

The beautiful architect working late on the twelfth floor of my building thinks that I'm just the maintenance guy. She's also under the impression that I'm not interested.

Nothing could be further from the truth.

I want her like I've never wanted a woman before, but I don't play where I work.

I don't need the complications.

When she tells me about living out her mermaid fantasy with a stranger in a Perfect Match virtual adventure, I decide to do everything possible to ensure that the stranger is me.

The Dragon King

To save his beloved kingdom from a devastating war, the Crown Prince of Trieste makes a deal with a witch that costs him half of his humanity and dooms him to an eternity of loneliness.

Now king, he's a fearsome cobalt-winged dragon by day and a short-tempered monarch by night. Not many are brave enough to serve in the palace of the brooding and volatile ruler, but Charlotte ignores the rumors and accepts a scribe position in court.

As the young scribe reawakens Bruce's frozen heart, all that stands in the way of their happiness is the witch's bargain. Outsmarting the evil hag will take cunning and courage, and Charlotte is just the right woman for the job.

My Werewolf Romeo

The father of my star student is a big-shot screenwriter and the patron of the drama department who thinks he can dictate what production I should put on. The principal makes it very clear that I need to cooperate with the opinionated asshat or walk away from my dream job at the exclusive private high school.

It doesn't help matters that the guy is single, hot, charming, creative, and seems to like me despite my thinly-veiled hostility.

When he invites me to a custom-tailored Perfect Match virtual adventure to prove that his screenplay is perfect for my production, I accept, intending to have fun while proving that messing with the classics is a foolish idea.

I don't expect to be wowed by his werewolf adaptation of Red Riding Hood mesh-up with Romeo and Juliet, and I certainly don't expect to fall in love with the virtual fantasy's leading man.

FOR EXCLUSIVE PEEKS AT UPCOMING RELEASES & A FREE COMPANION BOOK

Join my *VIP Club* and gain access to the VIP portal at itlucas.com

CLICK HERE TO JOIN
(http://eepurl.com/blMTpD)

INCLUDED IN YOUR FREE MEMBERSHIP:

- **FREE** Children of the Gods companion book 1 (includes part 1 of goddess's Choice)
- **FREE** narration of Goddess's Choice—Book 1 in The Children of the Gods Origins series.
- Preview chapters of upcoming releases.
- And other exclusive content offered only to my VIPs.

If you're already a subscriber, you'll receive a download link for my next book's preview chapters in the new release announcement email. If you are not getting my emails, your provider is sending them to your junk folder, and you are missing out on **important updates, side characters' portraits, additional content, and other goodies.** To fix that, add isabell@itlucas.com to your email contacts or your email VIP list.

Published by Evening Star Press

EveningStarPress.com

ISBN-13: 978-1-957139-78-4

www.ingramcontent.com/pod-product-compliance
Lightning Source LLC
LaVergne TN
LVHW021216190125
801664LV00001B/6